Willis Judson Beecher, Auburn Theological Seminar

General Catalogue of the Auburn Theological Seminary

including the trustees, treasurers, professors, and alumni. 1883

Willis Judson Beecher, Auburn Theological Seminar

General Catalogue of the Auburn Theological Seminary
including the trustees, treasurers, professors, and alumni. 1883

ISBN/EAN: 9783337369521

Printed in Europe, USA, Canada, Australia, Japan

Cover: Foto ©Andreas Hilbeck / pixelio.de

More available books at **www.hansebooks.com**

OF THE

AUBURN THEOLOGICAL SEMINARY,

INCLUDING THE

TRUSTEES, TREASURERS, PROFESSORS,

AND

ALUMNI.

1883.

— ·◄◆►· ——

AUBURN, N. Y.
DAILY ADVERTISER AND WEEKLY JOURNAL PRINTING HOUSE,
1883.

TABLE OF CONTENTS.

EXPLANATORY STATEMENTS.

Please read before consulting the Catalogue.

It is a distinctive feature of this Catalogue that it separates the notices of the deceased from those of the living, arranging the former by themselves in the order in which the deaths occurred. This plan has its disadvantages as well as its advantages. That it renders possible the stereotyping of the Necrological list, in some future edition, when it shall have been made as complete, up to date, as it is ever likely to be, seemed to the compiler a decisive consideration. As long as a man is living, his record is subject to change, and is therefore not ready to stereotype. Under this view of the case, the names of the deceased, in the few instances where the date of death has not been at least approximately ascertained, have been placed in the Class lists and not in the Necrology.

With some variations, each full notice consists of two or three parts, viz: first, statistics of personal history; second, statistics of professional services; third, special statistics. In the professional statistics, the name of a place is that of a field of labor, and presumably, a field in which the man is a pastor or acting pastor. Wherever the case is known to be otherwise, the design has been to indicate it.

The design has been to insert the names of all persons who, at any known date, have been trustees, treasurers, professors or students of Auburn ; and to insert each name in all the lists to which it belongs. But the *full notice* of each person appears in only one list. A reference to this is given in the other places where the name occurs.

The full notice of men who deceased at a known date appears, in all instances, in the Necrological list. In the other lists, simply the name is given, with the date of death, the latter serving as a reference to the place of the full notice. .

The full notice of living men who have been students, appears in the list of Alumni. In the cases in which any of these have also been trustees, professors, or post graduates, only their names are given in these other lists, with a reference to the class to which they belonged.

In the case of men who belonged to different classes in the Seminary, the full notice is given in the list of the class with which they graduated; but if they did not graduate here, usually in that of the class with which they were first connected.

Those who pursued selected studies only are catalogued with the class with which they principally studied.

As the fullest notice includes all the briefer ones, the latter are omitted in the references in the alphabetical index.

Each class is catalogued in two alphabetical lists, the second of which contains the names of men of whom it is known that they did not graduate with the class, though they were at some time connected with it. In a few special instances, men who substantially completed the course have been listed as graduates, although they were not so, technically.

In the Necrological list, the age at death is given by the *nearest* birthday, which is sometimes the *last* birthday, and sometimes not.

When several successive fields of labor or places of residence are in the same State, the mention of the State is ordinarily omitted, except in the first of the successive items. The same method is adopted with names of religious denominations, and of modes of service.

The Catalogue shows some lack of uniformity in the spelling of names of places. In most instances this is due to their being variously spelled by intelligent correspondents. There is also a great lack of uniformity in the matter of abbreviations, but this is the less important since no abbreviations are used except such as are self explaining.

It is probable that some of the ordinations reported as by Congregational Associations were actually either by Consociation, or by Council called within the limits of the Association named.

The compiler has deemed it no part of his duty to publish a record of cases of discipline, either by the Seminary authorities or by the various ecclesiastical bodies to which the Auburn men have belonged. He has tried, however, so to adjust the record that it shall not appear to hold any ecclesiastical body responsible for men whom it has disfellowshiped.

The compiler has taken especial pleasure in the record of those Alumni who did not enter the ministry, or who soon left it for other pursuits. As good citizens and effective Christian workers, the larger number of these men need not blush to compare themselves with their clerical brethren. They are a standing and sufficient proof that a Theological education is not lost, even if its recipient turns out to have no call to the ministry.

As to "published works," the original idea was to include only volumes in this Catalogue. The mention of pamphlets, articles, and other lesser works has been unsystematically and therefore unequally made. The compiler greatly regrets his lack of uniformity of plan in this matter.

He also regrets that the necessary limitations of his work prevent the specific commemoration in it of certain large classes of the friends of the Seminary, or of certain important phases of the work which the Seminary has accomplished. As it now stands, it does not mention the founders of the Seminary, as such, nor its long roll of commissioners from the Presbyteries, nor the generous men and women who have contributed to its endowment. Such of these men as were also trustees or treasurers or professors or students of Auburn, are, indeed, mentioned in those characters, but, with a few exceptions, their gifts and special services, either to Auburn or to other institutions, are not here recorded.

The compiler has kept in mind that this Catalogue is strictly a book of statistics He has carefully filed every scrap of information which has come into his possession, that it might be available for use in case any one should feel called upon to write a volume of *memorabilia ;* but he has refused to admit non-statistical material into the Catalogue. Had it been practicable, however, he would gladly have added the following to the lists herein printed :

First, a list of the founders and commissioners of the Seminary, in the order of their first terms of service. This should have included the persons who were present at the preliminary meetings, before the Board of Commissioners was organized, or who otherwise prominently participated in the founding of the Seminary, together with all the commissioners who have actually attended any meeting of the Board, a notice of all the years in which he attended being attached to the name of each one. If a commissioner has at any time been a student of the Seminary, or a trustee or professor or treasurer, it should have been noted, with date, in this list. If not, and if his relations to the Seminary were somewhat permanent, the list should have included statistics of him. Attached to this should have been the roll of the presidents, clerks, and stated clerks of the Commissioners, with their dates of service.

Secondly, a list of the financial benefactors of the Seminary. This should have been, in form, less strictly statistical than the other parts of the Catalogue. It should have included some account of the various attempts to raise money, from the first, with the names of the financial agents, salaried and unsalaried, who have been employed. To this should have been added the names of the principal donors, in the order of their first noted gifts. If the name of a donor occurs in the previous lists of the Catalogue, there should have been a reference to it, and if not, a brief statistical sketch. In this list it would have been possible to do that which could not be done in the other lists, namely, to make grateful and decorous acknowledgment of the beneficence of the men and women who have endowed the Seminary. It might have been completed by adding the history of the names of professorships, buildings, and halls in the old building, with other memorial names.

Thirdly, there should have been a series of generalizations from the preceding lists ; for example, a complete list of works published by members of the Seminary ; a roll of foreign missionaries, and one of pioneer missionaries ; a roll of pastorates exceeding 25 years ; a roll of College and Seminary presidents and professors, and tables representing the sources whence the Seminary has drawn its supply of students, and the fields whither it has distributed its graduates.

These additions would have been of genuine statistical value. Nevertheless, in view of the current estimates of the worth of such work, the compiler is more afraid of being censured for having devoted too much time to it than too little.

For accuracy and completeness, it is believed that this Catalogue will compare favorably with other works of the kind. But of course it is far from perfect. *If, when you discover an error or a deficiency, you will at once call the attention of the compiler thereto,* you will contribute to the greater accuracy of the next Catalogue.

To the Rev. Henry A. Hazen, statistician of the Congregational Churches, to the librarians or others in charge of statistics in the Congregational House and in Williams, Amherst, Hamilton, Yale, Union, Dartmouth, Middlebury and other Colleges and Universities, to Bros. Page, Day, Robinson and Close of the subscription Committee, to a large number of long-suffering clerks of Presbyteries, Associations, Sessions, Consistories, Churches, and of pastors of Churches of various names, to very many of our Alumni, and of other men and women who love Auburn, and not least, to the patient, painstaking printers of the *Advertiser* office, the thanks of the compiler are due for help rendered him in his task.

WILLIS J. BEECHER.

AUBURN, Jan., 1883.

GENERAL LISTS.

TRUSTEES.

NOTE. When the date of the death of a Trustee is given, the full notice of him will be found in the Necrological list, under that date. When only the Seminary class to which he belonged is given, the notice will be found in its proper place in the list of that class.

As the names of the men who have been elected Trustees, but have not served, have been published in previous Catalogues, it has been thought proper to retain them, but without statistics.

1820-21, *JOHN LINCKLAEN, died Feb. 9, 1822.

1820-22, *GLEN CUYLER, died Sept. 1, 1832.

1820-34, *HENRY DAVIS, D. D., died March 8, 1852.

1820-24, *DAVID HYDE, ESQ., died April 12, 1824.

1820-32, *THADDEUS EDWARDS, died April, 1832.

1820-21, and 1822-31, *GEN. HENRY McNIEL, died May 16, 1844.

1820-64, *REV. LEVI PARSONS, died Nov. 20, 1864.

1820-22, *REV. BENJAMIN BREARLY STOCKTON, died Jan. 10, 1861.

1820-30 and 1835-57, *DIRCK CORNELIUS LANSING, D. D., died Mar. 19, 1857.

1820-34 and 1846-63, *WILLIAM WISNER, D. D., died Jan. 7, 1871.

1820-29, *HENRY AXTELL, D. D., died Feb. 11, 1829.

1820-27, *EBENEZER FITCH, D. D., died Mar. 21, 1833.

1820-28, *REV. DAVID HIGGINS, died June 18, 1842.

1820-49, *REV. SETH SMITH, died Jan. 30, 1849.

1820-35, *WILLIAM BROWN, ESQ., died March 11, 1854.

1821,   *BRADLEY TUTTLE.   Resigned after a few weeks.

1821-29, *COL. SAMUEL BELLAMY, died March 20, 1829.

1821-29, *HON. NATHANIEL WOODHULL HOWELL, LL. D., died Oct. 15, 1851.

1822-36, *HON. JOHN HARVEY BEACH, died Aug. 8, 1839.

1824-50, *ELEAZAR HILLS, died Sept. 25, 1856.

1827–55, *REV. HENRY DWIGHT, died Sept. 7, 1857.

1828–40, *HORACE HILLS, died Sept. 18, 1873.

1829–35, *REV. HENRY PIERCE STRONG, died Aug. 28, 1835.

1829–45, *JAMES SKINNER SEYMOUR, died Dec. 3, 1875.

1829–45, *HON. HIRAM FOOTE MATHER, died July 11, 1868.

1830–32, I. T. MARSHALL. Of Oswego. Removed to Texas. No information concerning him.

1831–46, *JOSIAH HOPKINS, D. D., died June 21, 1862.

1832–38 *HON. SAMUEL MILES HOPKINS, LL. D., died Mar. 9, 1837.

1832-34, *REV. JOHN KEEP, died Feb. 12, 1870.

1834–37, *SERENO EDWARDS DWIGHT, D. D., died Nov. 30, 1850.

1834–74, *HON. JOHN PORTER, died Feb. 3, 1874.

1834–37, *HON. GERRIT SMITH, LL. D., died Dec. 2, 1874.

1835–74, ABIJAH FITCH.
Born in Cooperstown, N. Y., Jan. 6, 1799; united with the Second Presbyterian Church in Auburn, Apr. 6, 1831; married to Miss ELEANOR NELSON, of Auburn, Feb. 22, 1821.
Engaged in Mercantile business and Manufacturing, Auburn, 1817–34; City Real Estate business from 1834.

1836, *REV. MEDAD POMEROY. Declined to serve. Preferred being commissioner.

1836–42, *REV. WASHINGTON THACHER, died June 29, 1850.

1837–43 and 1846–53, *LEONARD ELIJAH LATHROP, D. D., died Aug. 17, 1857.

1838–45, *MILES POWELL SQUIER, D. D., died June 22, 1866.

1838, *JABEZ GOODELL. Never served.

1838–39, *NATHAN MUNRO, died July 5, 1839.

1839, *SALEM TOWN. Never served.

1840– RICHARD STEEL.
Born in Granville, N. Y., Nov. 3, 1795; united with the First Presbyterian Church in Troy, N. Y., May, 1815; served as druggist's apprentice with Dr. Gurdon Corning, of Troy; married to Miss ALTIE HYDE, of Auburn, Feb. 19, 1823; married to Miss SARAH MARKOE KNOWLES, of Darby, Pa., June 1, 1831; married to Miss MARY CALDWELL KNOWLES, of Philadelphia, June 23, 1834.
Treasurer of Seminary, 1823–38, 1847–55; secretary of Trustees, 1844–46; auditor from 1855.
Merchant and druggist in Auburn, 1817–72; still resident in Auburn.

1840-49, SIMEON NORTH, D. D., LL. D.
Born in Berlin, Conn., Sept. 7, 1802 ; united with the First Con-
gregational Church in Middletown, Conn., 1818 ; graduated from
Yale College in 1825 ; studied Theology at Yale Divinity
School ; LL. D. from Western Reserve College, in 1842 ; S.
T. D. from Wesleyan University, in 1849; married to Miss
FRANCES H. HUBBARD, of New Haven, Apr. 21, 1835.
Ordained at Winfield, N. Y., by Oneida Association, May 25,
1842 ; professor of Greek and Latin, Hamilton College, 1829-
39 ; president of Hamilton College, 1839-57 ; since resident in
Clinton.

1841, *AZARIAH SMITH. Never served.

1841-68, *SIMEON BENJAMIN, died Sept. 1, 1868.

1842-48, *ARISTARCHUS CHAMPION, died Sept. 18, 1871.

1843, *HON. ASHLEY SAMPSON. Never served.

1845, *BENJAMIN P. JOHNSON. Never served.

1845, *HON. JOHN J. KNOX. Never served.

1846- SYLVESTER WILLARD.
Born in Saybrook, Conn., (now Chester), Dec. 24, 1798 ; united
with the Congregational Church in Wilton, Conn., 1816 ; studied
at the Academy in New Canaan, Conn. ; College of Physicians
and Surgeons, New York, 1820-3 ; married to Miss JANE FRAN-
CES CASE, of Canton, Conn., Sept , 1830.
Practiced Medicine in Brutus, (now Sennett), N. Y., 1823-34 ; in
Bristol, Conn., 1834-40 ; in Chicago, Ill., 1840-3 ; resident in
Auburn since 1843 ; president of the Oswego Starch Factory
from its organization in 1848 ; first president of Auburn Water
Works Co.; president of Auburn Savings Bank, 1859-79.
Secretary of Trustees of Seminary, from 1846.

1846-52, *HON. ABNER HOLLISTER, died Mar. 13, 1852.

1848-54, *HON. ELIJAH RHOADES, died Feb. 9, 1858.

1848-55, *HIRAM HICKOK SEELYE, died Jan. 1, 1855.

1849-51, *WILLIAM HENRY SPENCER, D. D., class of 1841-44, died
Feb. 16, 1861.

1849- SAMUEL HART GRIDLEY, D. D., class of 1826-29.

1851-76, *PHILEMON HALSTEAD FOWLER, D. D., died Dec. 19, 1879.

1851- TIMOTHY STILLMAN, D. D., class of 1827-30.

1852-58, *ROBERT WOODRUFF CONDIT, D. D., died Feb. 11, 1871.

1854-57, *HON. ALFRED COBB, died Dec. 17, 1860.

1855–   ALBERT TRACY CHESTER, D. D.
Born in Norwich, Ct., June 16, 1812; united with the Congrega-
tional Church in 1829; graduated from Union College in 1833;
studied Theology with Dr. Nott, of Schenectady; D. D. from
Union College in 1847; married to ELIZABETH STANLEY, of
Mount Morris, N. Y., Aug. 3, 1836; married to Mrs. L. P.
HARVEY, of Wisconsin, Nov. 29, 1876.
Ordained and installed at Ballston Spa, N. Y., by Albany Presby-
tery, Oct. 26, 1836; Ballston Spa, 1836–39; Saratoga Springs,
1839–49; Buffalo, North Presbyterian Church, 1849–60; principal Buffalo Female Academy, 1860.
President of Trustees since 1870.

1855–58, HENRY KENDALL, D. D., class of 1840–43.

1855–69, *HON. FREDERICK STARR, died Nov. 27, 1869.

1857–63, *NICOLL HAVENS DERING, M. D., died Dec. 19, 1867.

1858–   JAMES BOYLAN SHAW, D. D., class of 1829–32.

1858–61, AUGUSTUS WOODRUFF COWLES, D. D.
Born in Reading, N. Y., July 12, 1819; united with the First Presbyterian Church in Geneva, N. Y., August, 1835; graduated
from Union College in 1841; studied Theology at Union Theological Seminary, N. Y.; D. D. in 1857; married to Miss FRAN-
CES CAROLINE GOOLD, of Brockport, N. Y., June 15, 1847.
Ordained and installed at Brockport, by Presbytery of Rochester,
February, 1847; Brockport, 1846–56; President of Elmira Female College from 1856.

1860–71, *SAMUEL WARE FISHER, D. D., died Jan. 18, 1874.

1863–70, *HON. JOHN FISHER, died March 28, 1882.

1863–76, *WILLIAM CARPENTER WISNER, D. D., died July 14, 1880.

1865–   LEVI PARSONS, D. D., class of 1851–4.

1869–   HON. ISRAEL SELDON SPENCER.
Born in Camden, N. Y., Sept. 13, 1813; united with the First
Presbyterian Church in Syracuse, Fall of 1852; studied Law in
the office of the Hon. Ichabod S. Spencer; married to Miss
MARY JANE ROBERTS, of Lenox, N. Y.; married to Miss
CLARISSA JANE BENHAM, of Bridgewater, N. Y.
Began the practice of Law in Syracuse, 1845; elected Judge in
1850.
Published several important papers on legal subjects.

1869–73, JOSIAH BUTLER WILLIAMS.
Born in Middletown, Conn., Dec. 16, 1810; united with the Fourth
Presbyterian Church in Albany, N. Y., 1830; studied at Acad-
emy at Middletown; married to Miss MARY HUGGEFORD HARDY,
of Ithaca, N. Y., 1842.
Merchant and banker; resident of Albany, N Y., 1829–38; of
Ithaca, since 1838.

1870-81, *HON. EDWIN BARBER MORGAN, died Oct. 13, 1881.

1872– SAMUEL GILMAN BROWN, D. D., LL. D.
Born in North Yarmouth, (now Yarmouth,) Me., Jan. 4, 1813;
united with the Congregational Church in Hanover, N. H.,
1827; graduated from Dartmouth College in 1831; Andover
Seminary, graduated 1837; D D. from Columbia College in
1852, and LL. D. from Dartmouth in 1868; married to Mrs.
SARAH VAN VECHTEN SAVAGE, of Schenectady, N. Y., Feb.
10, 1846.
Ordained at Woodstock, Vt., by Council, Oct., 1852; professor of
Oratory and Belles Lettres, Dartmouth, 1840–63; professor of
Intellectual Philosophy and Political Economy, 1863–67; president of Hamilton College, 1867–81.
Published " Life of Rufus Choate," 1862, and Inaugural addresses,
eulogies, Historical addresses, &c.

1873– EDWARD C. SELOVER.
Born in Auburn. Sept. 6, 1837; united with the First Presbyterian
Church in Auburn, June, 1866; studied at Hobart College;
married to Miss MARY PERKINS CAMPFIELD, of Newark, N. J.,
June 18, 1867.
In business in Auburn.

1874– HON. CHARLES CHAUNCEY DWIGHT, LL. D.
Born in Richmond, Mass., Sept. 15, 1830; united with the Central Presbyterian Church in Auburn, 1866; graduated from
Williams College in 1850; LL. D. from Williams College in
1874; married to Miss EMMA MUNRO, of Camillus, N. Y., July
29, 1868.
Admitted to practice Law at Albany, 1853; settled at Auburn,
1854–55; elected County Judge of Cayuga County, 1859; enlisted for the war, 1861; mustered out as Colonel of Volunteers,
1865; member of Constitutional Convention of New York,
1867–68; appointed Justice Supreme Court of N. Y., 1868;
re-elected, 1869, 1877.

1874– ROBERT ARMSTRONG NELSON.
Born in Lansingburgh, N. Y., 1821; united with the First Presbyte-
rian Church in Auburn, Feb. 26, 1838; studied at Lansingburgh
Academy; married to Miss CATHARINE KING, of Lansingburgh,
May 27, 1841; married to Mrs. MARGARET CAMPBELL MC-
LAREN EAGER, of Auburn, Feb. 10, 1875.
Lumber merchant in Auburn.

1876– CHARLES HAWLEY, D. D.
Born in Catskill, N. Y., Aug. 19, 1819; united with the Presbyterian
Church in Catskill, N. Y., 1831; graduated from Williams Col-
lege, in 1840; from Union Theological Seminary, 1844; D. D.
from Hamilton College, 1861; married to Miss MARY HUB-
BELL, of Lyons, N. Y., Sept. 10, 1850.

Ordained pastor at New Rochelle, N. Y., by Second Presbytery of New York, December, 1844; New Rochelle, 1844-48; Lyons, N. Y., 1848-57; Auburn, First Presbyterian Church, from 1857.

Published "Jesuit Missions," 1876; "Early Chapters of Cayuga History," 1879; and many important pamphlets and addresses.

1876–   JOHN JERMAIN PORTER, D. D.

Born in Ovid, N. Y., March 20, 1821; united with the Church in Warsaw, N. Y., 1833; graduated from Union College in 1843; studied Theology at Princeton; D. D. from Hamilton College in 1868; married to Miss MARY HALL, of Geneva, N. Y., Sept. 30, 1847.

Ordained pastor, Kingston, Pa., by Presbytery of Luzerne, September, 1847; Kingston, 1847-50; Westminster Church, Buffalo, N. Y., 1850-57; Union Church, St. Louis, Mo., 1857-64; First Church, Watertown, N. Y., 1864-81; Phelps, 1881.

1882–   HENRY AUGUSTUS MORGAN.

Born in Aurora, N. Y., March 14, 1834; united with the Presbyterian Church in Aurora, 1858; graduated from Cayuga Lake Academy, of Aurora; married to Miss MARGARET MAGDALENE BOGART, of Aurora, May 12, 1864.

Merchant and produce dealer in Aurora; farmer in Lansing, Mich.; in the Produce and Warehouse business in Aurora.

TREASURERS.

1820-23, *DAVID HYDE. He was a Trustee. Died April 12, 1824.

1823-38 and 1847-55, RICHARD STEEL. A Trustee.

1838-45, HENRY IVISON.

Born in Glasgow, Scotland, Dec. 25, 1808; united with the First Presbyterian Church in Auburn, 1832; married to Miss SARAH B. BRINKERHOFF, of Auburn, Sept. 19, 1832; married to HARRIET E. SEYMOUR, of Auburndale, Mass., May 31, 1864.

In the Book business with William Williams, of Utica, 1820-30; in the same business in Auburn, 1830-46; in New York, of the firm now known as Ivison, Blakeman, Taylor & Co., 1846-82.

Stated Clerk of Commissioners of Auburn Seminary, 1832-46.

1846-47, *JOSEPH BELL HYDE, died April 10, 1847.

1856–   JAMES SEYMOUR, JR.

Born in Brockport, N. Y., July 5, 1827; united with the First Presbyterian Church in Auburn, April, 1866; married to Miss

MARY OSBURN LODEWICK, of New York City, May 22, 1861.
Book business, Auburn, 1845-50 and 1854-57; Bank of Auburn,
1850-54 and since 1857; cashier of Bank of Auburn, from 1876.
Stated Clerk of Commissioners of Seminary, from 1855.

PROFESSORS.

NOTE. The statistics of Professors who have died are given in the
Necrological list, and those of Professors who are still living, and are
Alumni of this Seminary, in that of the class to which they belong.
To these other lists the dates given in the present list serve as
references.

BIBLICAL CRITICISM.

1821-54, and Emeritus till death, *HENRY MILLS, D. D., died June
10, 1867.

1854-   EZRA ABEL HUNTINGTON, D. D.
Born in Columbus, N. Y., June 12, 1813; united with the Congregational Church in South Hadley, Mass., 1831; graduated
from Union College in 1833; studied Theology at Schenectady; D. D. from Columbia College in 1847; married to Miss
ANNA MASON VAN VECHTEN, of Schenectady, July 30, 1839;
married to Miss KATHARINE VAN VECHTEN of Albany, April
16, 1868.
Ordained pastor of Third Presbyterian Church, Albany, by Presbytery, Feb. 9, 1837; Third Church, Albany, 1836-54; professor in Auburn, from 1854.
Published sermons, addresses and articles; " Notes on Epistle to
the Hebrews," printed (not published) 1866.

ECCLESIASTICAL HISTORY AND CHURCH POLITY.

1821-36, *MATTHEW LARUE PERRINE, D. D., died Feb. 11, 1836.

1837-44, *LUTHER HALSEY, D. D., LL. D., died Oct. 29, 1880.

1847-   SAMUEL MILES HOPKINS, D. D., class of 1834-37.

SACRED RHETORIC AND PASTORAL THEOLOGY.

1821-26, *DIRCK CORNELIUS LANSING, D. D., died March 19, 1857.

1835-37, *SAMUEL HANSON COX, D. D., LL. D., died Oct. 2, 1880.

1839–47, *BAXTER DICKINSON, D. D., died Dec. 7, 1875.

1848–51, JOSEPH FEWSMITH, D. D.
  Born in Philadelphia, Pa., Jan. 7, 1816; united with the Evangelical Lutheran Church of St. John, Philadelphia, about 1833; graduated from Yale College in 1840; studied Theology at Western Reserve College; D. D. from Columbia College, N. Y., in 1855; married to Miss EMMA C. LIVINGSTON, of New York City, Oct. 31, 1843.
  Ordained pastor, Rhinebeck, N. Y., by Evangelical Lutheran Synod, 1843; Evangelical Lutheran Church, Valatie, 1842–43; Winchester, Va., 1843–48; professor at Auburn, 1848–51; Second Presbyterian Church, Newark, N. J., from 1851.
  Published sermons, articles and tracts.

1852–54, WILLIAM GREENOUGH THAYER SHEDD, D. D., LL. D.
  Born in Acton, Mass., June 21, 1820; united with the Brainerd Presbyterian Church in New York, February, 1840; graduated from the University of Vermont in 1839; Theology at Andover, 1840–43; D. D. from the University of Vermont in 1857; married to LUCY ANN MYERS, of Whitehall, N. Y., Oct. 7, 1845.
  Ordained pastor Congregational Church, Brandon, Vt., by Council, December, 1843; Brandon, 1843–45; professor of English Literature in University of Vermont, 1845–52; Auburn, 1852–54; professor of Ecclesiastical History, Andover, 1854–62; associate pastor, Brick Presbyterian Church, New York, 1862 63; professor of Biblical Criticism, Union Theological Seminary, 1863–74; professor of Systematic Theology, same, from 1874.
  Published Translation of Theremin's Rhetoric, 1848; Translation of Guericke's Church History, 1858; "History of Christian Doctrine," 2 vols., 1864; "Homiletics and Pastoral Theology," 1866; "Sermons to the Natural Man," 1868; "Theological Essays," 1876; "Literary Essays," 1878; Commentary on Romans, 1879.

1854–73, and Emeritus till death, *JONATHAN BAILEY CONDIT, D. D. died Jan. 1, 1876.

1874–80, HERRICK JOHNSON, D. D., class of 1857–60.

1880–   ANSON JUDD UPSON, D. D., LL. D.
  Born in Philadelphia, Pa., Nov. 7, 1823; united with the Presbyterian Church in Clinton, N. Y., Nov. 4, 1856; graduated from Hamilton College in 1843; studied Theology at Clinton with Dr. W. S. Curtis; D. D. from Hamilton in 1870; LL. D., Union College, 1880; married to Miss LYDIA WESTON FARLIN, of Sandy Hill, N. Y., Aug. 22, 1860.
  Ordained at Rome, N. Y., by Presbytery of Utica, Jan. 10, 1868; tutor, Hamilton College, 1845–49; professor of Logic, Rhetoric and Elocution, Hamilton College, 1849–70, and of Moral Philosophy, 1849–53; pastor of Second Presbyterian Church, Albany, 1870–80; Auburn, 1880.

CHRISTIAN THEOLOGY.

1823-43, JAMES RICHARDS, D. D., died Aug. 2, 1843.

1844-52, LAURENS PERSEUS HICKOK, D. D., LL. D.
Born in Bethel, Conn., Dec. 29, 1799; united with the Congregational Church in Bethel, May, 1820; graduated from Union College, 1820; studied Theology with Rev. Wm. Andrews and Rev. Bennet Tyler, 1821-23; D. D. from Hamilton College in 1843; LL. D. from Amherst, 1866; married to Miss ELIZABETH TAYLOR, of Bethel, Oct. 8, 1822.
Ordained pastor, Kent, Conn., by Litchfield North Association, Dec. 10, 1824; installed Litchfield, Conn., July 3, 1829; professor of Theology, Western Reserve College, 1836-44; Auburn, 1844-52; professor of Mental and Moral Science, and vice-president, Union College, 1852-66; president of Union College, 1866-68; resident Amherst, Mass.
Published "Rational Psychology," 1849; "Moral Philosophy," 1853; "Empirical Psychology," 1854; "Rational Cosmology," 1858; "Creator and Creation," 1872; "Humanity Immortal," 1872; "Logic of Reason," 1875; Revised "Empirical Psychology," 1882.
Moderator of General Assembly, 1856.

1852-54, CLEMENT LONG, D. D., died Oct. 14, 1861.

1854-76, and Emeritus till death, *EDWIN HALL, D. D., died Sept. 8, 1877.

1876- RANSOM BETHUNE WELCH, D. D., LL. D., class of 1849-52.

HEBREW LANGUAGE AND LITERATURE.

1867-70, *REV. JAMES EDWARD PIERCE, class of 1862-65. died July 13, 1870.

1871- WILLIS JUDSON BEECHER, D. D., class of 1861-64.

ALUMNI.

Note.—When the date of the death of an Alumnus is given, the full notice of him will be found in the Necrological list, under that date.

1821-4.

*Josiah Bacon, died April 14, 1875.

*Jacob Catlin, died Aug. 31, 1855.

George Washington Elliott.
> Born in Thornton, N. H., Sept. 18, 1796; united with the Congregational Church in Campton, N. H., at 19 years of age; studied at Phillips Academy and Dartmouth College; married to Miss Nancy Fitch, of Auburn, May 17, 1826; married to Mrs. Susan Caroline Bates Cowen, of Palmyra, N. Y.
> Ordained and installed, Lenox, N. Y., by Council, Spring of 1826; Second Church, Lenox, 1826–30; Bergen; Mt. Morris, 1832–4; Churchville; Newark, 1836; Lowell and Washington, Ill., 1838–51; secretary of Home Missions, and afterward of Bible Society, for Wis., from 1851, five or six years; since resident in Milwaukee.

Horatio Foote, D. D.
> Born in Bernardston, Mass., 1796; united with the Congregational Church in Burlington, N. Y., 1820; graduated from Union College in 1820; received the degree of D. D. from Chadwick College in 1846; married to Abigail Kirkland, of Bridgewater, N. Y., Feb. 15, 1826.
> Ordained and installed at Kingston, U. Canada, Union Presbyterian Church, by Presbytery of Cayuga, Sept. 1, 1825; Kingston 1825–28; Champlain, N. Y., 1830; Montreal, Canada; Burlington, Vt.; Fourth Church, Hartford, Ct.; Buffalo, N. Y.; Galesburg, Ill., 1839–40; Quincy, Ill., First Congregational Church, 1840–7; Chaplain U. S. Hospital, 1862–5; Quincy, Ill., Centre Congregational Church, 1847–77; resident in Quincy.

William Johnson.
> Born in Fairfield, N. Y., 1797; graduated from Hamilton College in 1821.
> Ordained at Millville, N. Y., by Presbytery of Niagara, June 29, 1825; Barre, 1828; Lexington, 1829–32; Sharon, O., 1835–50 and 1856–8; since when no trace of him.

*Solomon Stevens, died June 7, 1861.

*WILLIAM TODD, died Aug. 11, 1874.

---

*ASA K. BUEL, died June 29, 1837.

*AMBROSE EGGLESTON, died Jan. 23, 1865.

*SAMUEL MANNING, died April 16, 1843.

*CHARLES YALE, died Nov. 28, 1864.

1822-5.

*STEPHEN PEET, died Mar. 21, 1855.

*FRANKLIN PUTNAM, died Oct. 11, 1859.

*GEORGE SEYMOUR, died June 15, 1825.

*NATHANIEL SHEFFIELD SMITH, died Jan. 10, 1881.

*GEORGE TAYLOR, died June 30, 1842.

SIDNEY WELLER.
> Graduated from Union College in 1820; Senior year at Auburn. Reported in Minutes of Assembly, W. C., Halifax, N. C., 1831, Brenkleyville, 1832-40; reported in Seminary Catalogues, Halifax, 1836, '39, '50, '53, and dec'd in Catalogue of 1858.

---

*ZENAS CLAPP, died Jan. 29, 1837.

*JAMES FITCH COGGSWELL, died May, 1862.

*SAMUEL NICHOLAS SHEPARD, died Sept. 30, 1856.

1823-6.

*JOHN WATSON ADAMS, D. D., died April 4, 1850.

JOHN TREAT BALDWIN.
> Born in New Milford, Ct., September 11, 1796; united with the Congregational Church in New Milford, June 17, 1816; graduated from Princeton College in 1823; some months with Dr. Taylor in New Haven; Middle and Senior years in Auburn; married to Mrs. MARIA SCOVILLE SMITH, of New York, Oct. 9, 1831.
> Ordained at Springfield, N. Y., by Presbytery of Buffalo, Sept. 6, 1827; Holley, 1826; Hamburg and Aurora, Erie Co., about three years; then resident for more than 37 years at Franklinville, preaching there and in other places, and laboring for Bible Societies in Pa., Ohio and Mich.; in Missouri part of one year;

in Oregon, 1872–3; in California, doing active pioneer work, from 1873; Yreka, Cal.

*MORRIS BARTON, died Feb. 13, 1857.

*ELISHA COWLES, died May 17, 1826.

*JOHN BERRIEN FISH, died Dec. 22, 1869.

*ROBERT WILLIAM HILL, died Jan. 16, 1856.

*EDWIN HOLT, died June 26, 1854.

*HIRAM HUNTINGTON KELLOGG, D. D., died Jan. 1, 1881.

*OLIVER PLATT, died Sept., 1824.

*GEORGE ROBERT RUDD, died Feb. 1, 1881.

HIRAM SMITH.
  Born in Westfield, Mass., Sept. 21, 1800; united with the Congregational Church in Ellington, Ct., Jan., 1817; graduated from Amherst College in 1823; at Auburn, Middle and Senior years; married to Miss ADELINE FELLOWS, of Montville, Conn., 1836; married to Miss RACHEL C. KELLOGG, of Colchester, Conn., 1838.
  Ordained at Shelburne, Mass., by Franklin Association, Nov. 10, 1830; Marcellus, N. Y., 1827–34; Margaretta, O., 1834–8; Almont, Mich., 1838–42; then resident in Margaretta, preaching 18 years, and teaching for 3 years more; since resident in Hillsdale, Mich., preaching occasionally.

*WILLIAM BEARDSLEY, also 1827–30, died Dec. 13, 1866.

*GARDNER K. CLARK, died Mar. 19, 1870.

*HENRY HOTCHKISS, died Oct. 23, 1831.

*HERMAN NORTON, died Nov. 20, 1850.

*JOSEPH AYER PEPOON, died Dec. 31, 1874.

JOSIAH B. WILKINSON.
  United with the Presbyterian Church in New Providence, N. J., July 1, 1813; Princeton Seminary, 1822–3; entered Senior, Auburn, Dec., 1825; also catalogued in Middle year, with class of 1824–7.
  Licentiate of Presbytery of Elizabethtown, until 1829.

1824-7.

*LEMUEL BROOKS, died Sept. 21, 1881.

*JOEL CAMPBELL, died May 15, 1872.

ROBERT BOND CAMPFIELD.

Born in Newark, N. J., June, 1802; united with the First Presbyterian Church in Newark, May, 1817; graduated from Princeton
College in 1824; course, and one post graduate year at Auburn;
married to Miss HARRIETTE SEYMOUR PERKINS, of Amherst,
Mass., June, 1829.

Ordained and installed at New Preston,Conn., by Litchfield South
Association, Nov. 16, 1831; assistant pastor, Caldwell, N. J.,
1828-9; assist. sec. of Bd. of Dom. Miss. of Gen. Assembly, 16
months; New Preston, Conn., 3½ years; dist. sec. of Am. S. S.
Un., New York, 28 years: Synodical sec. of S. S., 4 years; work
of Am. and For. Ch. Un., 10 years; resident in Newark, N. J.

*ABNER P. CLARKE, died Feb. 6, 1835.

*TERTIUS STRONG CLARKE, D. D., died April 14, 1875.

CHRISTOPHER CORY.

Born in Westfield, N. J., June 13, 1800; united with the First Presbyterian Church in Westfield, 1819; studied at Bloomfield
Academy; studied with Rev. John Ford, 1823-5; Middle and
Senior years in Auburn; married to Miss MARY HEDGES BAKER,
of Westfield, Aug., 1827.

Ordained at Bloomfield, N. J., by Presbytery of Newark, Dec. 25,
1827; West Town, N. Y., 1828-32; Elkhart, Ind., 1834; Lima,
Ind., 1836-49, and resident there since.

HENRY DEAN.

Born in Stamford, Conn., 1792; Senior year in Auburn; Pound-
ridge, N. Y., 1829; Streetsborough, O., 1834-5, residing there
1836-8; New York, teaching, 1839; Brooklyn, teaching, 1846-54.

*ELIAS RIGGS FAIRCHILD, died April 22, 1878.

*LEWIS DUNHAM HOWELL, died Sept. 25, 1847.

*ISAAC JONES, died Jan. 27, 1876.

*BEAUFORT LADD, died March 19, 1879.

ALVAH LILLY.

Born in Ashfield, Mass., Dec. 19, 1799; united with the Congregational Church in Hawley, Mass., 1816; graduated from Williams College in 1824; married to Miss CATHERINE HEADLEY,
of Walton, N. Y., April 14, 1828; married to RUTH OWEN, of
Lisle, N. Y., Aug. 31, 1841.

Ordained at Franklin, N. Y., by Presbytery, July 15, 1829; County
missionary for Delaware Co., 1 year; Columbus, 1 year; Hamilton, 1831-3: Newfield, 1834-9; Gorham, 1839-44; Pewaukee,
Lisbon and Hartland, Wis., 1844-53; Varney, N. Y., 1853-4;
Gorham, 1854-63; Pewaukee, Wis., 2 years; resides in Whitewater, Wis.

*EBENEZER MEAD, died Dec. 28, 1848.

*ADAM MILLER, died Dec. 1, 1881.

*Bennett Fairchild Northrop, died March 4, 1875.

*Frye Bailey Reed, died Aug. 24, 1877.

*Ebenezer Seymour, died June 21, 1879.

*Joseph Steele, died April 25, 1872.

*Timothy Stowe, died Oct. 13, 1860.

*Henry Philip Tappan, D. D., LL. D., died Nov. 15, 1881.

*Daniel Van Valkenburgh, died Nov. 24, 1864.

---

*James Adams, graduated with Class of 1826–9, died Feb. 7, 1857.

*Edwards Abbott Beach, died May 23, 1881.

*Jairus Burt, died Jan. 15, 1857.

*Alanson Baldwin Chittenden, died April 11, 1853.

*Ralph Clapp, died Jan. 19, 1882.

*John Conway, Jr.
  Remained six months in the Seminary, then returned to the farm
  to take care of his parents; married, and died in 1851; beyond
  this, no clue to localities or dates.

*Aaron Garrison, died Dec. 11, 1839.

*George Hornell, graduated in Class of 1825–8, died Sept. 9, 1855.

*Leverett Hull, died Sept. 3, 1852.

*Warren Isham, died May 18, 1863.

*William Weed Marvin, died Oct. 28, 1868.

*John McDonald, died Aug. 15, 1866.

*Erastus Noble Nichols, died Feb. 17, 1882.

*Joel Parker, D. D., died May 2, 1873.

*Ethan Pratt, died Nov., 1850.

George Spaulding.
  Born in Plainfield, N. Y., 1798; united with the Congregational
  Church in Groton, N. Y., January 5, 1817; graduated from
  Hamilton College in 1824; in Auburn to middle of Senior year;
  married to Miss Olive Selover, of Auburn, Feb. 13, 1828.
  Ordained and installed at Madison, N. Y., by Council, Jan. 9,
  1828; Madison, 1827–9; Gilbertsville, 1831–2; Bainbridge,
  1833; Southport, 1837; Varna, 1846–52; Jasper, 1853; Canisteo, 1854–60; Weston, 1861–3; Tyrone, 1864; Newfield, 1865;
  Waverly, 1867; Brooklyn, Pa., 1868–75; Ev. at Canasarega, N. Y.,
  since 1876.

Josiah B. Wilkinson. See 1823–6.

1825-8.

*Isaac Foote Adams, died Nov. 23, 1876.

William Brobston.
Born in Philadelphia, Pa., 1804; united with the Locust Street Presbyterian Church in Philadelphia as early as 1818; graduated from Union College in 1825; married to Miss Hannah Ann Cromartie, of South River, N. C., 1830.
Ordained in Cumberland Co., N. C., by Presbytery, Dec. 18, 1830; went as home missionary to Elizabethtown, Brown Marsh, South River and Big Swamp, N. C.; labored in N. C. till 1848; then in Wisconsin for some years; then for a short time near Shelbyville, Tenn.; then city missionary in Nashville, Tenn., till about 1860; then in Wisconsin again; now for some years resident in Chicago.
Published papers on Temperance, &c.

Robert Brown.
Born in Stockbridge, Mass., March 21, 1803; united with the First Presbyterian Church in Auburn, 1826; graduated from Williams College in 1825; entered Auburn Middle class; married to Miss Eliza Headley, of Walton, N. Y., summer of 1828.
Ordained 1832; Mexicoville, N. Y.; Rose Valley; DeRuyter; according to the Annals of Williams College, he was living in Dayton, Ohio, 1870.

*Isaac Crabb, died Mar. 29, 1866.

*Luke DeWitt, died Oct. 31, 1877.

*Charles Edwin Furman, D. D., died June 10, 1880.

Ransom Hawley.
Born in Bridgeport, Conn., April 24, 1802; united with the Congregational Church in Bridgeport, March 4, 1821; studied with Rev. Elijah Waterman; married to Sarah M. Hall, of Bridgeport, June 14, 1830.
Ordained, Washington, Ind., by Presbytery of Wabash, Nov. 21, 1829; Washington, 1828–34; Bloomington, 1834–41; Putnamville, 1841–65; resident there till 1879, and since then in Terre Haute.
Published several addresses.

*Asa Hixon, died Nov. 16, 1862.

*George Hornell, died Sept. 9, 1855.

*Cyrus Hudson, died Dec. 11, 1875.

*Josiah James Kirkpatrick, died early in 1831.

Ulrie Maynard.
Born in Hartford, N. Y., Nov. 13, 1798; united with the Congre-

gational Church in Adams, March, 1819; graduated from Hamilton College in 1825; married to OLIVE BRANCH, Aug. 26, 1828.

Ordained at Litchfield, N. Y., by Oneida Presbytery, August 6, 1828; home missionary in Union and Fayette Cos., Ind., 1828–32; pastor in Darien, Ct., in 1835; most of his life doing service as a revival evangelist, or an agent; resident in Castleton, Vt.

HIRAM LINDSLEY MILLER.

Born in New Vernon, N. J., Jan. 28, 1804; united with the Presbyterian Church in Morristown, N. J., Aug. 8, 1822; studied at Academies at Basking Ridge and Morristown, N. J.; married to Miss ADELINE LITTLE, June 1, 1830.

Ordained, Sparta, N. Y., by Presbytery of Genesee, Aug. 24, 1831; Buffalo, N. Y., 1828; Lockport, 1828–9; Avon, 1829–30; Brighton, 1831–2; Trumansburgh to 1836; Saginaw City, Mich., a year or two from 1836; since resident there, elder of First Presbyterian Church, engaged in business.

*BENJAMIN COLEMAN SMITH, died Oct. 17, 1861.

*JOEL TALCOTT, died Dec. 25, 1871.

SAMUEL UTLEY.

Born in Dalton, Mass., Feb. 19, 1798; united with the Church in Chesterfield, Mass., 1824; graduated from Union College in 1826; married to MARY J. EASTMAN, of Concord, N. H., April 14, 1834.

Ordained at North Rochester, Mass., by Old Colony Assoc., Nov. 3, 1832; New Bedford, Mass., 1828–30; North Rochester, 1830–5; Eping, N. H., 1835–7; Southfield, Mass., 1837–46; Austerlitz, N. Y., 1846–57; resident in Hudson 1858–60, in Concord, N. H, 1869–74, and since in Chatham, N. Y.

GEORGE WASHINGTON WARNER.

Born in Hardwick, Vt, Aug. 14, 1800; united with the Presbyterian Church in Athens, O., April, 1819; graduated from Ohio University in 1825; married to Miss SUSAN ELIZA WYCKOFF, of Auburn, June 28, 1828.

Ordained pastor, Wooster, O., by Presbytery of Richland, Nov., 1833; Coshocton and Keene, O., 1828–31; Cortland, N. Y., and Jordan, N. Y., 1831–2; Wooster, O., 1832–6; Massillon, 1836–43; agt. Am. Bib. Soc., 1844–6; farmer and evangelist, Cayuga Co., N. Y., 1847–50; Weedsport Presbyterian Church, 1850–62; pioneer work in Colorado, 1862–3; missionary and Bible work in Central New York, 1864–8; Canaan Centre and Canaan Four Corners, N. Y., from 1868.

ASHBEL SHIPLEY WELLS.

Born in Jericho, Vt., Dec. 3, 1798; united with the Congregational Church in Jackson, Me., July, 1816; graduated from Hamilton College in 1824; entered Middle class, Nov. 16, 1826, and studied a year and a half; married to Miss Sophia Hastings, of Clinton, N. Y., Mar. 24, 1828.

Ordained at Utica, N. Y., by Presbytery of Utica, Jan. 23, 1828; New Albany, Ind., 1828–32; Tecumseh, Mich., 1832–6; Troy, Mich., 1836–40; Mt. Clemens, Mich., 1840–4; then 6 years in the service of the A. B. C. F. M.; afterward 18 years of Home Missionary work in Ill. and Iowa; now resident at Fairfield, Iowa.

Published tracts on Fermented Wine, Tobacco, and "The King's Highway."

---

*Silas Clark Brown, died June 14, 1876.

*Ward Childs, died Dec. 27, 1855.

*John Reid Moser, died Apr. 18, 1877.

*George Pierson, died Feb. 2, 1880.

James Remington.

Born in Schenectady, N. Y., Aug. 28, 1799; united with the First Presbyterian Church in Buffalo, Oct. 17, 1817; graduated from Williams College in 1826; Auburn to close of Middle year; married to Miss Charlotte Evans, of Darien, N. Y., Jan. 30, 1830.

Ordained at Cayuga Creek, N. Y., by Presbytery of Buffalo, Sept. 2, 1829; Lancaster, 15 years, from 1827; Alden, 22 years, to 1867; resident at Lancaster, supplying churches as opportunity offered, 1868–79; resident South Saginaw, Mich., 1880–2; E. Saginaw, 1882.

Published some sermons.

*Preston Richardson, died Dec., 1835.

*Seymour Thompson. See 1829–32.

James Bishop Wilcox.

Born in Farmington, Conn., Oct. 11, 1796; united with the Congregational Church in Farmington; graduated from Middlebury College in 1825; Prin. of Academy in Simsbury, Conn., 1825–6; meanwhile studied Theology with Rev. John Maclean; Auburn nearly two years; married to Miss Hannah Hopkins Hodge, of Hadley, Mass., Oct, 1828.

Ordained at Avon, Conn., by Hartford North Association, 1828; Bethany Centre, N. Y., till 1831; Mount Morris from 1831; Gainsville, 1834; agt. for Livingston Co. Bible Soc.; agt. N. Y. Anti-Slavery Soc.; agt. N. Y. State Temp. Soc.; from 1860, for several years, proprietor of Darien Center Seminary; resident at Shortsville.

1826-9.

*JAMES ADAMS, entered class of 1824-7, died Feb. 7, 1857.

DWIGHT BALDWIN, M. D.
> Born in Durham, Conn., Sept. 29, 1798; united with the Con-
> gregational Church in Durham, N. Y., Sept. 3, 1826; graduated
> from Yale College in 1821; taught, and studied medicine;
> received the degree of M. D. from Dartmouth College in 1859;
> married to Miss CHARLOTTE FOWLER, of New York, Dec. 3
> 1830.
> Ordained at Utica, N. Y., by Presbytery of Utica, Oct. 6, 1830;
> preached, Windham, N. Y., and other places, 1829-30; Honolulu,
> 1831; Waimea, 1832-5; Lahaina, 1835-68; afterward teacher
> of Church History and Bible History in the Theological School
> at Honolulu, where he still resides.

*EBENEZER C. BEACH, died April 26, 1868.

*OBADIAH COTTGRAVE BEARDSLEY, died Aug. 23, 1874.

ELIJAH BUCK.
> Born in Great Bend, Pa., March 1, 1799; united with the Presby-
> terian Church in Great Bend, 1815; studied three years at
> Hamilton College; married to MARY A. BUTLER, of Utica,
> N. Y., 1831.
> Ordained at Harford, Pa., by Presbytery of Susquehanna, June
> 28, 1830; Pike, 1830; Massillon, Ohio, 1832; Onondaga Valley,
> N. Y., 1834; Havana, 1836; Jonesville, Mich., 1839; resident
> at Jonesville, 1846-62; Edgewood, Ill., 1863-5; Kinmundy,
> 1866; resident at Centralia, Ill., from 1867.

*HUGH CARLISLE, died June 22, 1871.

*JAMES AIKMAN CARNAHAN, died Jan. 19, 1879.

*CHARLES GRANDISON CLARK, died Oct. 2, 1871.

REUBEN HOLMES CLOSE.
> Born in Genoa, N. Y., Jan. 26, 1800; united with the Church in
> Genoa, Nov., 1817; graduated from Yale College in 1826; Au-
> burn, 1827-9; married to Miss LYDIA MARTHA EASTMAN, of
> Gainsborough, Sept. 12, 1842; married to Miss AMY JANE
> FITCH, Jan. 26, 1847.
> Ordained and installed at St. Catherines, Canada, by Presbytery,
> Jan. 3, 1837; teacher, Sharon, Conn., 1829-34; St. Catherines
> and elsewhere in Canada, 12 years; Middleport, N. Y., 1849;
> resident, Genoa, 1850; tea. and S. S., Groton, 1851-3; tea. Elmi-
> ra, 1854; S. S., Elmira, 1855; agt., Elmira, 1856-65, and resident
> there since.

*BENJAMIN COTHEN CRESSY, died July 10, 1834.

*CHARLES DANFORTH, died April 29, 1867.

*SAMUEL DUNTON, died Oct. 29, 1866.

*MARSHALL LOOK FARNSWORTH, died Nov. 27, 1838.

*NATHANIEL WILCOX FISHER, died Aug. 1 1849,.

ERASTUS JUDD GILLETT, M. D., D. D.
Born in Cazenovia, N. Y., May 15, 1800 ; united with the Church
in Middlebury, N. Y., Dec. 1820 ; A. M. from Hamilton College
in 1842 ; M. D. from the College of Physicians and Surgeons,
Keokuk, Iowa ; D. D. from University of Rochester in 1858 ;
married to AMANDA SMITH, of Munson, Mass., May 9, 1833.
Ordained at Perry Centre, N. Y., by Presbytery of Genesee, May
26, 1829 ; Gowanda, 1829–30 ; Jamestown 1830–7 and 1839–48 ;
Batavia, 1837–9 ; Cazenovia, 1848–9 ; agent A. and F. Chris.
Un. 1849–55 ; president Yellow Springs College, Iowa, 1855–
61 ; First Presbyterian Church, Keokuk, 1862–4 ; professor of
Chemistry, Medical College of Keokuk, 1864, and afterward
president of Faculty ; president of Parsons College, 1879.

*JOHN GRAY, died Jan. 31, 1877.

SAMUEL HART GRIDLEY, D. D.
Born in Kirkland, N. Y., Dec. 28, 1802 ; united with the Church
in Clinton, N. Y., 1820 ; studied at Hamilton College ; D. D.
from Hamilton College in 1855 ; married to Miss MARY ANN
HART, of New Hartford, N. Y., April 20, 1829.
Ordained at Madison, N. Y., by Oneida Association, Sept. 1829 ;
Springville, N. Y., 1829–30 ; Perry, 1830–6 ; Waterloo from
1836 ; emeritus pastor since 1873.
Published sermons and articles ; trustee of Auburn from 1849 ;
vice-president of Trustees from 1870.

BLOOMER KENT.
Resident at Franklin, N. Y., when in the Seminary. The General
Catalogues place him at Hamden, N. Y., 1836 and 1839, Lower
Sandusky, Ohio, 1850 and 1853, and dead, 1858.

ELIPHALET KENT.
Born in Dorset, Vt., March 17, 1800 ; united with the Congregational Church in Greenfield, N. Y., 1818 ; graduated from
Williams College in 1826 ; married to Miss FRANCES CAPRON,
of Tinmouth,Vt., Aug., 1829 ; married to Mrs. FANNIE MORRIS,
Sept. 14, 1844.
Ordained at Pittsford, Vt., by Rutland Association, Aug. 26, 1829 ;
home missionary in Shelby and Bartholomew counties, Ind.,
five years ; pastor of Greenwood Presbyterian Church, Ind., 5
or 6 years ; in charge of Shelby County Seminary till 1844 ;
afterward preaching and teaching ; resident at Shelbyville, Ind.

*MILTON KIMBALL, died Oct. 10, 1865.

*TERTIUS DUNNING SOUTHWORTH, died Aug. 2, 1874.

JOHN TAINTER.
Entered, Junior, June, 1827 ; catalogued as from Boston, 1827–8, and from Coxsackie, 1828–9 ; not in the General Catalogues till 1858, and then starred ; one letter says he went to Ohio.

*SAMUEL WOODBURY, died Nov. 17, 1876.

---

*DAVID R. BARNES.
Junior, 1826–7 ; Middler, 1827–8 and 1828–9 ; catalogued residence, Austerlitz, and Ch. membership, Chatham ; according to General Catalogues, Herkimer County, 1836 and 1839 ; North Wrentham, Mass., 1850 and 1853, and dead, 1858.

*HARPER BOIES, died March 7, 1867.

*DAVID CUSHING, died June 1, 1849.

*ENOCH KINGSBURY, died Oct. 26, 1868.

*JOHN REID MOSER, entered class of 25–8, died April 18, 1877.

*TERTIUS REYNOLDS, died June 25, 1863.

DEXTER WITTER.
Born in Hinsdale, Mass., July 15, 1803 ; united with the Congregational Church in Aurora, Ohio, 1819 ; graduated from Yale College in 1824 ; Auburn, Jun. and Mid. years ; married to Miss EMILY MOSS, of Augusta, N. Y., June 1829 ; married to Miss MARY DEFOREST, of Cincinnati, O., March 31, 1859.
Ordained and installed at Burton, Ohio, by Presbytery of Grand River, March 25, 1829 ; pastor at Burton, and supplying other Churches till about 1849 ; since resident in Burton, supplying Churches ; supply in Burton, 1857–67.

1827-30.

JOSEPH BLOOMFIELD BALDWIN.
Born in Newark, N. J., Nov. 24, 1804 ; united with the First Presbyterian Church in Newark, July, 1817 ; graduated from Yale College, 1827 ; married to Miss SARAH ANN TENNEY, of Brandon, Vt., May 26, 1834 ; married to Miss ROSINA P. WHITMAN, of Windsor, Mass., April 22, 1854.
Ordained in New York, N. Y., by Third Presbytery of N. Y., Aug., 1831 ; missionary New York City ; Essex, N. Y., 2 years ; Ticonderoga, 2 years ; Canaan, 1834–40 ; West Cummington, Mass., 1841– ; Weathersfield Centre, Vt. ; retired from active service, having preached 50 years ; resident West Cummington.

LINUS WILLIAMS BILLINGTON.
Born in Orange, N. J., Jan. 1, 1802 ; united with the Presbyterian

Church in Ludlowville, N. Y., May, 1820; studied at Ithaca Academy and privately; entered Auburn on examination; married to Miss Sophia Gardner, of Bennington, Vt., March 16, 1830.

Ordained Cohocton, N. Y., by Presbytery of Bath, Feb., 1830; Cohocton, 1829-30; Starkey, 1831-3; Dresden, 1834; Richmond, 1835-41 and 49-53; Scottsville, 1841-8; Fairport, Congregational Church, 1848-9; East Mendon, 1853-6; North Bergen, 1856-61 and 1868-9; Barre Centre, 1862-8; resident at Bergen, supplying churches, 1870-1; Allegany, 1871-7; resident at Scottsville since 1877.

Published Review of Andrew Jackson Davis' Revelations, 1848; and addresses and newspaper articles.

*Ansel Bridgman, died Sept., 1838.

*Sheldon Dibble, died Jan. 22, 1845.

*Joel Goodell, died Nov. 24, 1877.

*John Loomis Howard, died June 2, 1830.

*Benjamin Franklin Hoxsey, died Sep. 10, 1835.

Asa Johnson.
Born in South Deerfield, Mass., Feb. 13, 1802; united with the Congregational Church in So. Deerfield, Sept., 1828; graduated from Union College, in 1827; married to Miss Julia Warner Sadd, of Austinburgh, Ohio, July 14, 1830; married to Miss Mary Sophia Sill, of Moreau, N. Y., Sept. 27, 1854.

Ordained at Henrietta, N. Y., by Genesee Consoc., June 2, 1830; home miss. in Southern Mo., and in Hamilton County, Ohio, till 1832; Richmond, N. Y., 1 year; Nunda, N. Y., 4 years; then Peru, Ind., till 1851; Goshen, Ind., 1851-3; missionary of Synod of Albany, N. Y., 1853-5; teaching at Peru, Ind., 1855-7; Adel, Iowa, preaching also in other places, 1857-75; since then living with his son, Rev. E. P. Johnson, of the class of 1872-5, now pastor in Marshall, Mich.

*William Lewis, died April 4, 1838.

Cyrus Nichols.
Born in Reading, Mass., Oct. 31, 1799; united with the Congregational Church in Newburyport, Mass., 1822; graduated from Williams College in 1827; married to Miss Dolly Diana Hurlbut, of Hoosick Falls, N. Y., July 25, 1830.

Ordained Henrietta, N. Y., by Genesee Consoc., June 2, 1830; Palmyra, Mo., 1830- ; collecting funds for Marion College; Racine, Wis., 1836; preached at Racine, Grafton, Decatur; agt. for A. H. M. S., and for the Pres. Board of Home Miss.; resident at Racine.

*John Bower Preston, died Oct. 17, 1877.

*Joseph Merrill Sadd, died Sept. 12, 1872.

LUTHER SHAW.
Born in Rutland, Vt., July 4, 1800; united with the Congregational Church in Rutland, Aug., 1817; graduated from Middlebury College in 1826; married to Miss JULIA CHAMBERLIN, of Romeo, Mich., Aug. 8, 1831; married to Miss LUCY ANN WRIGHT, of Tallmadge, Ohio, 1835.
Ordained at Henrietta, N. Y., by Genesee Consociation, June 2, 1830; Washtenaw Co., Mich., 1830; Romeo and Rochester, 1831–6; Almont, 5 years from 1836; Armada, 5 years; Algonac and Newport, 5 years; New Haven and Ray, 4 years; Armada again, 4 years; in 1863, moved to Tallmadge, Ohio, where he still lives; here he supplied vacant churches for 2 years, and was for 9 years agent of A. B. S. in Summit and Portage Cos.

TIMOTHY STILLMAN, D. D.
Born in Wethersfield, Conn., March 21, 1802; united with the Yale College Church, April, 1820; graduated from Yale College in 1822; received the degree of D. D. from Yellow Springs College in 1856; married to Miss MARY ANN EDWARDS ABELL, Aug. 7, 1832.
Ordained at Sheridan, N. Y., by Buffalo Presbytery, May 12, 1830; resident in Dunkirk from 1830, pastor there 8 years, and agent of Am. Bethel Soc. 30 years; stated clerk of Presbytery from 1834, for 47 years; trustee of Auburn from 1837.
Published History of Buffalo Presbytery, 1867.

*REUBEN TINKER, died Oct. 26, 1854.

*WM. TOBEY, died Sept. 10, 1849.

*ALFRED WHITE, died Oct. 19, 1867.

*JAMES BLAKE WILSON, died April 25, 1879.

*GEORGE CLINTON WOOD, died Jan. 5, 1879.

*ALFRED WRIGHT, died Nov. 18, 1865.

---

*DAVID R. BARNES. See 1826–9.

*WILLIAM BEARDSLEY, entered class of 1823–6; died Dec. 13, 1866.

*BARUCH BUTLER BECKWITH, died July 4, 1870.

*MOSES ASHLEY CURTIS, D. D., died April 10, 1872.

*BLACKLEACH BURRITT GRAY, died Feb. 18, 1870.

*DAVID DOWNS GREGORY, died Sept. 16, 1874.

*WILLIAM A. GREGORY.
From Sand Lake, N. Y.; in Auburn a few months from March, 1828; had poor health, and left the Seminary for secular pursuits; probably died in 1831.

*COMFORT HAMILTON, M. D., died Oct. 9, 1878.

*JOHN KELLEY, M. D., died Jan. 16, 1872.

*LEWIS REMA LOCKWOOD, died Spring of 1880.

*BARNABAS PHINNEY, died Nov. 14, 1848.

1828-31.

*ISAAC BLISS, died Aug. 9, 1851.

EDWIN BRONSON.
    Born in Delhi, N. Y., July 1, 1799; united with the Congregational
    Church in Washington, Conn., July 1, 1820; graduated from
    Union College in 1828; married to MARY HITCHCOCK, of
    Homer, N. Y., March 28, 1832.
    Ordained, Parma, N. Y., by Genesee Consoc., June 8, 1831;
    Springwater, N. Y., 1834; Guilford, 1836; Wysox, Pa., 1838-9;
    Windsor, N. Y., 1840-3; Scottsville, 1844-6; Rome, Pa., 1847;
    agent at Mehoopany; Mehoopany, 1856-61; Laporte, 1862-4;
    resident at Monroeton, from 1865.

CHARLES CHAPMAN.
    Born in Saybrook, Conn., March 4, 1804; united with the Presby-
    terian Church in Catskill, N. Y., 1820; graduated from Hamilton
    College in 1826; married to Miss ELIZABETH HANFORD PORTER,
    of Hamden, N. Y., Jan. 25, 1832.
    Ordained, Franklin, by Delaware Presbytery, 1832; Walton
    Second Church, 1832-7; Jeffers, 1837-40; Colchester, 1840-3;
    Walton Second Church again, 1843-7; Meredith, 1848-56;
    Monterey, 1856-76; resident in Rock Stream, preaching oc-
    casionally, from 1877.

ELIAS CHILD.
    Born in Exeter, N. Y., Sept. 3, 1806; united with the Congrega-
    tional Church in Exeter, May 14, 1820; graduated from Union
    College in 1828; married to Miss MELISSA HOLLISTER, of
    Ballston, N. Y., Aug. 29, 1831; married to Miss SYLVINA
    THORP, of Butternuts, N. Y., May 11, 1833; married to Miss
    SUSAN PARKER CLEAVELAND, of Billerica, Mass., Oct. 16, 1867.
    Ordained Franklin, N. Y., by Delaware Presbytery, 1832; 2 years
    home missionary; 3 years in Smyrna, N. Y.; 2 years in Cass-
    ville; 7 years in Albion, and Clinton, Mich., then left the active
    exercise of the ministry, by reason of ill health; connected with
    Eleemosynary institutions, and in mercantile busines; resident
    in Utica, N. Y.

SYLVESTER COWLES, D. D.
    Born in Otisco, N. Y., Jan. 28, 1805; united with the Church
    in Otisco, Oct., 1824; graduated from Hamilton College in
    1828; received the degree of D. D. from Hamilton College in

1873; married to Miss Mary Hays, of Clinton, Aug., 1831; married to Miss Frances W. Wood, of New Haven, Conn., Sep., 1846; married to Miss Sophia M. Philips, of Milford, N. H., Aug., 1878.

Ordained by Onondaga Presbytery, Sept. 5, 1831; Napoli, 1831; Ellicottville, 1836; Fredonia, 1839; Lodi, 1843; Ellicottville, 1846-50; Olean, 1850-61; Randolph, 1862-6; Gowanda, 1867-74; preached and organized churches in Cat. Co.; Evangelist, residing at Randolph from 1875.

Published sermons and addresses.

*RICHARD MONTGOMERY DAVIS, died June 13, 1842.

*DAVID ROBERTSON DOWNER, died Nov. 28, 1841.

*LEVI GRISWOLD.

Entered Auburn from Choconut, Pa.; graduated from Hamilton College in 1828; Vienna, N.Y., 1832; Marcellus, 1834; Otisco, 1837-9; Brutus, 1840; Ludlowville, 1842-9; resident, Skaneateles, 1849-52; Victory, 1853-4; Genoa, 1855-6; resident, Clinton, Conn., 1858-60; starred in Gen. Catalogue of 1861.

*HENRY REXFORD HITCHCOCK, died Aug. 29, 1855.

*HENRY RICHARD HOISINGTON, died May 16, 1858.

LORENZO LYONS.

Born in Colerain, Mass., April 18, 1807; united with the Congregational Church in Montrose, Pa., April 6, 1823; graduated from Union College in 1827; married to Betsey Custis, of Elbridge, N. Y., Sept. 4, 1831; married to Miss Lucia G. Smith, missionary on Maui, July 14, 1838.

Ordained at Auburn by Presbytery of Cayuga, Sept. 20, 1831; missionary and pastor at Waimea, Hawaii, from 1832.

Published, all in Hawaiian, Articles on the Sabbath, 1834-5; Children's Hymn Book, 1836-7; Scripture Lesson Book for Children; Children's Hymn Book, enlarged, with tunes; Bible Lessons; Lessons on Pentateuch; "Children's Lyre," 1863; "Hawaiian Hymns," three successive revisions and enlargements; Hawaiian Hymn Book, 1870; "Flag of Glory," 1871; "Sacred Songs," 1873; "Golden Robin," 1874; "Royal Diadem," 1878; Exposition of the Seven Apocalyptic Seals, 1878-9; Weekly S. S. Lessons from 1873; besides editorial work on three papers and numerous contributions in prose and verse.

*EDWARDS MARSH, died Nov. 5, 1877.

*WILLIAM A. RICHARDS, died May 2, 1835.

EBENEZER HARRISON STRATTON.

Born in Williamstown, Mass., Oct. 29, 1806; united with the Cong. Church in Williamstown, Sept., 1826; graduated from Williams College in 1828; Auburn till Feb., 1831, completing the course with Dr. Griffin, of Williamstown; married to Miss MINERVA OLIVIA BENNETT, of Auburn, Mar. 10, 1833; married to Miss CHARLOTTE LEWIS, of Orangeville, N. Y., Dec. 10, 1854; married to Miss FRANCES BUSH, of Branchport, N. Y., Dec. 10, 1874.

Ordained at Gaines, N. Y., by Niagara Presb'y, Jan., 1832; Fort Niagara and Youngstown, 1831-2; Mayville, 1832-4; Oakfield, 1834-7; Covington, 1837-8; Fowlerville, 1838-42; Moscow, 1842-5; Somerset, 1845-52; Oakfield, 1852; poor health for two years; Orangeville, 1854-60; Johnsonburgh, 1861-5; Canoga, 1866-72; Branchport, 1872-5, and still resident there.

CONWAY PHELPS WING, D. D.

Born in Marietta, O., Feb. 12, 1809; united with the Presbyterian Church in Oaks Corners, N. Y., May 10, 1822; graduated from Hamilton College in 1828; received the degree of D. D. from Dickinson College in 1857; married to PRUDENCE M. YOUNG, of Marion, N. Y., Jan. 10, 1833.

Ordained and installed at Sodus, N. Y., by Geneva Presbytery, Sept. 27, 1832; Sodus, 1831-6; Ogden, N. Y., 1836-8; Monroe, Mich., 1838-41; Columbia, Tenn., 1841-3; Huntsville, Ala., 1843-8; First Presbyterian Church, Carlisle, Pa., 1848-75; yet resident at Carlisle.

Published many sermons and reviews, and the following works: with Prof. Blumenthal, Translation of Hase's "Manual of Ecclesiastical History," 1856; Translation of Kling on 2d Corinthians, for Lange's Commentary, 1868; "History of the Presbyteries of Donegal and Carlisle," 1876; "A History of the First Presbyterian Church of Carlisle, Pa.," 1877; "History of Cumberland Co., Pa.," 1879.

FORDYCE HARRINGTON.

Born in South Brookfield, Mass., Aug. 31, 1801; united with the Congregational Church in Oakham, 1821; graduated from Amherst College in 1829; Middle and part of Senior years at Auburn; married to Miss CYNTHIA BOUTELLE, of Leominster, Mass., Aug. 14, 1832.

Ordained at Pepperill, Mass., by Middlesex Association, Nov. 1, 1831; home missionary, 3 years; Stanford, N. Y., 9 years; Oneonta, 2 years; Buel, 8 years; Big Flats, 10 years; Campbell, 4 years; residing in Orange, Schuyler Co., N. Y., from 1878.

WILLIAM F. HURD.

Graduated from Union College in 1828; Junior year in Auburn; entered from Canaan, N. Y.; married while in the Seminary; said to have been for many years a minister in the M. E. Church.

JOHN JACKSON.

Admitted Jan. 20, 1830; named (with star) in Gen. Catalogue of 1858, as having been 4 months in the Seminary.

JOHN H. RUSS.
> Born in Hinsdale, Mass., 1797; graduated from Union College in 1825; part of Junior year in Auburn.
> Ordained at Plainfield, Mass., by Mountain Assoc., May 3, 1829; Sandusky, O., 1829; Greenfield and New Haven, 1830–31; Wayne, 1833–4; Braceville, 1832–3; York, 1834–7; Bluffton, Iowa, 1842-5; Ewington, Ill., 1851–6.

SETH SMALLEY.
> Born in New Canaan, N. Y., Feb. 10, 1799; united with the Pres. Church in Sauquoit, 1820; studied at Madison Univ.; Auburn four months from April, 1830, having previously studied Theology in the University; married to MARIA PHILENA PAYNE, of Hamilton, N. Y., Nov. 1, 1826.
> Ordained at Amsterdam, N. Y., by Baptist Council; Bapt. Ch., New York City; agt. Am. Tr. Soc.; Bapt. Ch., Amsterdam; Bapt. Ch., Watertown; Pres. Ch., Scipio, 1830–2; Lafayette, 3 years; Fulton; Huron, O.; Amazon, Ill., 1846; Chemung, to 1853; Concord, Mich., 1854–6; Schoolcraft, 1857; home miss., Augusta, 1858–68; resident Battle Creek; Montana, Kan., 1870–1; resident Saranac, Mich., 1872–3, and since at Albion, N. Y

WATERS WARREN.
> Born in Ludlow, Vt., Oct. 8, 1801; united with the Church in Ludlow, about 1821; graduated from Union College in 1828; Junior and Middle years in Auburn; afterward at New Haven; married to Miss CAVOTINE CLARISSA PARSONS, of Sandisfield, Mass., Mar. 4, 1833.
> Ordained at Guilford, Conn., (Cong.) March 22, 1831; Springfield, Mass., 1833; Fly Creek, N. Y., 1834; Seneca Falls, 1835; Gilbertsville, 1836; Comonsville, 1837; Honesdale, 1838; Trumbull, Conn., 1839; agt. of Anti-Slavery Soc., 1840–2; Ludlow, Vt., 1842–4; Brunswick, N. Y., 1850–2; East Berkshire, Vt., 1854–8; Three Oaks, Mich., 1859–61, and still resident there.

*JEREMIAH WOODRUFF, died July 25, 1868.

1829-32.

*ABSALOM K. BARR, died June 5, 1859.

*WILLIAM URIAH BENEDICT, died Oct. 18, 1875.

*NATHANIEL CATLIN CLARK, died Dec. 3, 1872.

*THOMAS COCHRAN, died Feb., 1849.

*ASHLEY M. GILBERT, died Sept. 9, 1837.

*FREDERICK WILLIAM GRAVES, died Dec. 8, 1864.

*OREN JOHNSON, died Sept. 20, 1866.

STEPHEN JOHNSON.
> Born in Griswold, Conn., Apr. 15, 1803 ; united with the Cong.
> Church in Griswold, June, 1820 ; graduated from Amherst Col-
> lege in 1827 ; after leaving Auburn, studied Medicine ; married
> to Miss HANNAH MARIA PRESTON, of Rupert, Vt., May 26, 1833 ;
> married to Miss MARY FOWLER, of Oxbow, N. Y., Nov. 1, 1840 ;
> married to Miss CAROLINE MARIA SELMER, of Stockholm, Swe-
> den, in Ningpo, China, Sept. 17, 1849.
> Ordained at Griswold, Conn., by New London Mo. Consoc., Feb.
> 21, 1833 ; miss. of A. B. C. F. M. among the Chinese in Siam,
> 1833–46 ; miss , Foo Chow, Bhina, 1846–53 ; in this country,
> preaching as his health permitted, 1853–62 ; gardening, Gouv-
> erneur, N. Y., from 1862.
> Published Missionary Letters and Reports.

*RICHARD KAY, died Jan. 2, 1877.

*CHARLES JENKINS KNOWLES, died Oct. 27, 1850.

*ROYAL MANN, died Aug 10, 1875.

*JEREMIAH POMEROY. died Jan. 5, 1881.

*CHARLES ROBINSON, died March 3, 1847.

JAMES BOYLAN SHAW, D. D.
> Born in New York City, Aug. 25, 1808 ; united with the Brick
> Church in New York, 1828 ; A. M. from Western Reserve
> College in 1840 ; D. D. from Univ. of Rochester in 1852 ;
> married to Miss EMILY E. CHASE, of Auburn, Aug. 15, 1832 ;
> married to Miss LAURA J. RUMSEY, of Silver Creek, May 24,
> 1845.
> Ordained and installed at Attica Village, N. Y., by Presb'y of
> Geneva, July 2, 1835 ; Pompey, N. Y. ; Attica to 1839 ;
> Dunkirk, 1840 ; Brick Church, Rochester, from 1840.
> Moderator of General Assembly, 1865 ; trustee of Auburn Seminary
> from 1858.

LOWELL SMITH, D. D.
> Born in Heath, Mass.. Nov. 27, 1802 ; united with the Cong.'
> Church in Heath, Dec. 1, 1822 ; graduated from Williams
> College in 1829 ; D. D. from Williams College in 1864 ; married
> to Miss ABBA WILLIS TENNEY, of Brandon, Vt., Oct. 2, 1832.
> Ordained at Heath, Mass., by Franklin Assoc., Sept. 26, 1832 ;
> from that time missionary in the Sandwich Islands, at Kaluaha,
> Ewa and Honolulu, where he now resides.

*VINAL SMITH, died Sept. 28, 1867.

NOAH THOMAS.
> Born in Cummington, Mass., Aug. 13, 1802 ; united with the Cong.
> Church, 1819 ; studied at Amherst College, 1822–26 ; never
> married.
> Ordained by Genesee Consoc. ; resident in Maryland, N. Y.

*ELAM HAVILLA WALKER, died Jan. 11, 1849.

*ERASMUS DARWIN WILLIS, died Nov. 12, 1880.

SAMUEL HUBBELL.
At entering, he was a resident of Fairfield, Conn., and member of the Church at Greenwich, Conn.; graduated from Princeton College in 1828; in Auburn 6 months of Junior year; licentiate of Baltimore Presbytery, 1832–4; starred in Gen. Catalogue of 1858.

NEWTON REED.
Born in Amenia, N. Y., 1805; united with the South Presbyterian Church in Amenia, Jan. 16, 1824; graduated from Kinderhook Academy in 1829; Auburn, half of 1829–30, and part of the Middle year in class of 1831–4; married to Miss ANN VAN DYCK of Kinderhook, N. Y., June 9, 1836. He was prevented by ill health from entering the ministry; taught in Canaan, Conn., 1833; farmer in Amenia, N. Y., since 1834.
Published " Early History of Amenia, N. Y.," 1875.

*MARVIN ROOT, died June 6, 1881.

*SEYMOUR THOMPSON.
Born in Augusta, N. Y.; catalogued as Junior, 1825–6; entered Middle class, 1830, and catalogued again as Middler, from " North America," 1831–2.
Ordained at Rodman, N. Y., by Black River Association, May 8, 1832; Evans, N. Y., to 1836; Sparta, Second Church, from 1837; resident Thornton, Ill., from 1846; reported as deceased, of Presbytery of Chicago, in Gen. Ass. Minutes of 1858.

*RICHARD WOODRUFF, died March 9, 1863.

1830-3.

HON. JARED REID AVERY.
Born in Groton, Conn., Sept. 17, 1804; united with the Church in Columbus, N. Y., 1826; graduated from Williams College in 1830; married to Mrs. SARAH ANN SKIDMORE AGNEW, of Lexington, Ky., July 23, 1835.
Ordained at Auburn, by Cayuga Presbytery, Aug. 19, 1833; agt. Am. Tract Soc. in Ky., Tenn., Ala., and New England, 1833–8; Groton, Conn., 1839–51; Franklin, Conn., 1851–60; resident in Groton, from 1860; member of legislature in 1863 and 1866.

WILLIAM BRADLEY.
Born in Lee, Mass., Dec. 7, 1803; united with the Cong. Church in Lee, Jan., 1822; graduated from Williams College in 1827; Senior year at Auburn; married to Miss ELIZABETH A. SMITH, of Williamstown, Mass., Aug., 1828.

Ordained and installed at Fredonia, N. Y., by Presb'y of Buffalo, Jan., 1834; in New York City from 1837, pastor of Allen St. Pres. Ch.; Newark, N. J., from 1842, past. of Central Pres. Ch.; teacher, Newark, 1848–59; teacher, Orange, 1860–70; resident at Clifton Station, Va., from 1870.

*ARTHUR BURTIS, D. D., died Mar. 23, 1867.

*CHARLES CHURCHILL, died Mar. 21, 1862.

CHAPIN RUFUS CLARK.
Born in Columbia, Herkimer Co., N. Y, Nov. 12, 1803; united with the Cong. Church in Winfield, about 1817; graduated from Williams College in 1829; married to Miss MARY BASSETT, of Walton, N. Y., Sept. 10, 1833.
Ordained at Auburn, by Presb'y of Cayuga, Aug. 19, 1833; Norwalk, O., 1833–4; Brownhelm, 3 years; Charleston, 3 years; West Bloomfield, N. Y., 4 years; Lockport, Ill., 1845–6; Granville, 1846–54; South Ottawa, 1854–6; Maine, Ill., farming, 1857; Home Mission work, 1858–64; resident in Le Roy, N. Y., sometimes supplying churches, from 1864.

TITUS COAN, D. D.
Born in Killingworth, Conn., Feb. 1, 1801; united with the Pres. Church in Riga, N. Y., March 2, 1828; studied privately; received the degree of D. D. from Dartmouth College in 1871; married to Miss FIDELIA CHURCH, of Churchville, N. Y., Nov. 3, 1834; married to Miss LYDIA BINGHAM, of Hawaii, Oct. 13, 1873.
Ordained at Park St. Ch., Boston, July 28, 1833; exploring in Patagonia, 1833–4; missionary in Hilo, Hawaii, from 1835.
Published "Adventures in Patagonia," 1880; "Life in Hawaii," 1882; also essays, tracts, &c.

*MOODY HARRINGTON, died Aug. 5, 1865.

SILAS H. HODGES.
Entered Seminary from Rutland, Vt.; member of Church there; graduated from Middlebury College in 1821; studied Law, and was admitted to practice; Senior year in Auburn; married before coming to Auburn.
Chester, Vt., 1837–8; Perkinsville, 1838; said to have returned to the Legal profession; resident Washington, D. C., 1871–5.

*JOHN CHASE LORD, D. D., died Jan. 21, 1877.

*GEORGE GREATHOUSE McAFFEE, died early in 1841.

JAMES McDOUGALL.
Born in Newark, N. J., March 16, 1805; united with the Third Church in Newark, April 3, 1825; graduated from Princeton College in 1830; married to JULIA KITCHEL, Sept. 4, 1833; Ordained by Redstone Presby., June 18, 1835; Morgantown, Va., 1834–6; Huntington, L. I., 1836–55; Freeport, L. I., 1856–62; residing in Huntington.

ENOCH MEAD.

Born in Greenwich, Conn., Sept. 2, 1809; united with the Yale College Church in 1828; graduated from Yale College in 1830; married to Miss MARY EMMA JAMES, of Weybridge, Jan. 29, 1835.

Ordained pastor at New Haven, Vt., by Addison Association, Jan. 7, 1834; New Haven, 1833–7; Rockingham, Wis., 1838–43; Davenport, Iowa, 1844–6; home missionary, Iowa; resident Davenport, from 1851.

*LORENZO WARRINER PEASE, died Aug. 28, 1839.

JOHN STOUT REASONER.

Born near Maysville, Ky., Apr. 23, 1799; united with the Second Church in Pittsburg, Pa., 1820; studied at Washington College, Pa., and Danville, Ky.; Auburn course from June, 1831; married to Miss TRYPHENA NORTHWAY, of Painted Post, N. Y., Dec. 29, 1833.

Ordained at Greenville, Ill., by Presbytery of Kaskaskia, 1837; Hornby Hill and Mead's Creek, N. Y., 1833–4; Barrington, 1835; Kaskaskia, Ill., 1836; Jourdan's Prairie, 1837–40; Newton, 1840–2; Shelby Co., 1842; Poplar Springs and other places, Ind.; Lebanon, Iowa, 1844; Bainbridge, 1845; went to Oregon in 1851; resident Corvallis, Or., since 1874.

ARCHIBALD ROBERTSON.

Entered Seminary from Cambridge, Ky.; member of Church in Fairfield, N. Y.; graduated from Union College in 1830. His record in the Gen. Catalogues is: Constantia, N. Y., 1836; Western, 1839; *1858.

*BENJAMIN SHAW.

Entered from Danville, Ky.; member of the Church there; graduated from Centre College in 1829.

Ordained at Auburn, by Presbytery of Cayuga, Aug. 19, 1833; labored South for Am. Tr. Soc.; Woodville, Miss., from 1837; Grand Lake, Ark., 1842–4, and from 1846; Columbia, Ark., 1845; reported as dead in the Minutes of Ass. of 1854.

LAWRENCE HENRY VAN DYCK.

Born in Kinderhook, N. Y., Oct. 5, 1807; united with the Reformed Church in Summer of 1823; graduated from Amherst College in 1830; married to Miss CHRISTINA HOES, of Kinderhook, Aug. 27, 1823; married to Miss MARY DESIA HOLDRIDGE, of Great Barrington, Mass., Oct. 5, 1852.

Ordained at Auburn, by Presbytery of Cayuga, Aug. 19, 1833; service of Am. Tr. Soc. in Kentucky, 1833–5; Cairo, N. Y., Presbyterian Church, 1835–9; Spencertown, 1839–43; Gilboa, Reformed Church, 1843–52; Guilderland, 1852–6; Blooming Grove, 1856–61; Stone Arabia, 1861–7; Unionville, 1871–6; rector of Hertzog Hall, New Brunswick, N. J., 1876–80; resident Brooklyn, N. Y.

Published a sermon, reports and articles.

*Henry Cowles Williams, died Sept. 1, 1831.

Sylvester Woodbridge, D. D.
Born in Sharon, Conn., June 15, 1813 ; united with the Church in Greenville, N. Y., Aug., 1830; graduated from Union College in 1830 ; Auburn, 1830–3 ; Princeton, 1833–34 ; D. D. from Lafayette College in 1859; married to Mary Foster, of Quogue, L. I., May 8, 1836.
Ordained and installed at Westhampton, L. I., by Long Island Presbytery, April, 1836 ; Hampstead, Nov. 1., 1837 ; Benicia, Cal., Mar. 9, 1849 ; Howard St. Church, San Francisco, April 1, 1870 ; Woodbridge Church, San Francisco, Apr. 16, 1876.

---

*Abraham D. Brinkerhoff, died Mar. 2, 1860.

*Richard D. Forrest, died Nov. 20, 1877.

*Sidney Holman, died Dec. 31, 1874.

*Francis Janes, died Jan. 20, 1855.

*Calvin Morrill, died May 14, 1875.

*Orson Parker, died Mar. 14, 1876.

*Francis Rutherford.
Entered Sem. from Alexandria, D. C.; graduated from Jefferson College in 1830 ; Auburn, Junior and Middle years ; Tuscahoma, Miss., 1836 ; Livingston, 1837 ; reported in Gen. Cat. of Jefferson Col. as having died in 1840.

*Seymour Thompson. See 1829–32.

*Charles B. Woodburn. See 1831–4.

1831-4.

Hiram Worthington Bulkeley.
Born in Williamstown, Mass., March 30, 1807 ; united with the Cong. Church in Williamstown, 1822; studied at Williams College in class of 1831 ; Prin. of Acad. of North Granville, 1830–1 ; A. M. from Williams in 1842; married to Miss Mary Jane Oliphant, of North Granville, N. Y., Dec. 10, 1834.
Never ordained ; preached, North Adams, 1834–5 ; teacher, Greenbush, 1835–9 ; teacher, Ballston Spa., from 1839.
Published "A Word to Parents," 1858 ; and educational tracts and papers.

Daniel Toll Conde, D. D.
Born in Charlton, N. Y., Feb. 7, 1807 ; united with the Pres. Church in Charlton, at about 19 years of age ; graduated from Union College in 1831 ; D. D. from Union College in 1869; married to Miss Andilicia Lee, of Jericho, Vt., Sept. 13, 1836 ; married to Mrs. Hannah Williams, of Cuyahoga Falls, O.

Ordained at Fredonia, N. Y., by Presby. of Buffalo, Sept. 7, 1836; miss. in Sandwich Islands from 1836, Eastern Maui, 11 years, Wailuku, 9 years; resident Saratoga Springs, 1858–68, and Beloit, Wis., from 1868.

*ALANSON C. HALL, died April 13, 1840.

*THOMAS REED RAWSON, died May 20, 1877.

*JOHN H. REDINGTON, died Sept. 15, 1841.

*JOHN HERVEY RICE, died June 20, 1858.

*HENRY ROOT, died April 5, 1860.

*GEORGE RANDALL HOWE SHUMWAY, died Jan. 28, 1874.

NELSON SLATER.

Born in Champlain, N. Y., Sept. 25, 1805; united with the Presbyterian Church in Champlain about 1821; graduated from Union College in 1831; married to EMILY KITCHELL, of Rockaway, N. J., Apr. 29, 1835.

Ordained in Ohio, by Grand River Presbytery, 1836; Berkshire Valley, N. Y., 1834–5; Bainbridge, O., 1835–6; Painesville, O., teaching, 3 years; McHenry Co., Ill., preaching and teaching, 7 years; Racine, Wis., teaching, 2 years; Henando Co., Miss., teaching, 2 years; in California from 1851, preaching, teaching, etc.; resident of Sacramento, Cal.

Published "The Fruits of Mormonism," 1851; jointly with Dr. Platt, "The Traveler's Guide," 1852; and many articles.

*CHARLES B. WOODBURN, died Mar, 14, 1834.

---

*NATHAN BENJAMIN, died Jan., 1855.

JOHN COVERT.

Born in Coeymans, N. Y., Feb. 24, 1804; united with the Reformed Church in Coxsackie, in 1821; graduated from Union College in 1831; Auburn, 1831–2, and 1833; married to Miss LORINDA SALISBURY, of Adams, N. Y., May 18, 1832; married to Mrs. MIRANDA HUGHITT, of Bloomington, Ill., Sept. 3, 1866.

Ordained pastor, by Black River Association, 1834; Jordan, N. Y., 1832–3; Smithville and North Adams, 3 years; established Jefferson Co. Inst., Watertown, N. Y., 1836; Columbus Ac. and Col. Inst., O., 1840; Ohio Female College, near Cincinnati; Glendale Female College, O.; Terre Haute Female College, Ind.; Lyons Female College, Iowa; Mich. Female College, Kalamazoo; the Soldier's College, Fulton, Ill.; resident in Chicago from 1865, preaching occasionally.

*JOHN EASTMAN, died May 19, 1880.

*JARED LEIGH ELLIOTT, D. D., died Apr. 16, 1881.

OVID MINER.
> Born in Rutland Co., Vt., July 7, 1803; united with the Congregational Church in Middlebury, Spring of 1830; educated as practical printer and editor; Auburn, Junior and Middle years; received the degree of A. M. from Middlebury College in 1835; married to Miss ELIZA M. MOORE, of Champlain, N. Y., Feb. 13, 1834.
>
> Ordained at Plattsburgh, by Presbytery of Champlain, 1836; home missionary in Clinton and Essex counties; Penn Yan, 1837-44; Syracuse, 7 years; Hoyleton, Ill., 1859-64; Bellville, 1865; Syracuse, Ilion, Greenbush, N. Y., 1866-9; East Poultney, Vt., 1870-3; resident Syracuse N. Y., supplying churches, from 1874.
>
> Published many tracts, pamphlets and articles.

NEWTON REED. See 1829-32.

*ALFRED ROBERTSON, died March 2, 1846.

*COLUMBUS SHUMWAY.
> Born in Belchertown, Mass., Mar. 22, 1805; graduated from Union College in 1830; Junior and Middle years in Auburn; married to Miss CATHERINE FOWLER, of Montgomery, Mass., Sept. 10, 1833; died at Worcester, Mass. His wife and 2 children survived him.
>
> Ordained at Smithville, N. Y., by Black River Association, Feb., 4, 1834; Townsend, Mass., 1836-7; Petersham, 1837; in Mass., according to Gen. Catalogues; starred in 1858.

*JONATHAN ALDEN WOODRUFF, died Sept. 29, 1876.

1832-5.

JOHN McKNIGHT BALLOU.
> Born in Washington, Mass., Jan. 17, 1806; united with the Congregational Church in St. Lawrence Co., N. Y., 1830; graduated from St. Lawrence Co. Academy in 1832; married to JANE BISSELL, of Madrid, Aug., 1836.
>
> Ordained and installed at Gainesville, N. Y., by Presbytery of Genesee, 1837; Gainesville, 20 years; Clarence, N. Y., 20 years; Byron, N. Y., 3 years; resides at Clarence.

*ORLO BARTHOLOMEW, died May 7, 1864.

*FREDERICK H. BROWN, died July 31, 1861.

*CALVIN CLARK, died June 4, 1877.

*RUSSELL SALMON COOK, died Sept. 4, 1864.

ETHAN BARROWS CRANE.

Born in West Troy, N. Y., July 15, 1811; united with the First Pres. Church in Schenectady, Summer of 1827; graduated from Union College in 1832; Auburn the course, and post graduate 1835–6; married to Miss DEBORAH ELIZABETH PRATT, of Saybrook, Conn., Oct. 8, 1839.

Ordained and installed at Saybrook, by Middlesex Consoc., June 28, 1838; Saybrook till 1851; resided in Brooklyn, N. Y., 20 years, and "labored somewhat in the ministry"; acting pastor at South Meriden, Ct., 1874–9; resident Brooklyn, N. Y., 1881.

*JONATHAN CRANE, died Dec. 25, 1877.

*DAVID ANDREWS FRAME, died Sept. 24, 1879

CHARLES FREDERICK HALSEY.

Born in Plattsburgh, N. Y., Nov. 16, 1803; united with the First Presbyterian Church in Plattsburgh, 1829; studied at Plattsburgh Academy and privately; married to Miss SYLVIA ANN MORSE, of Chateaugay, N. Y., Jan. 4, 1837.

Ordained at Champlain, by Presby. of Champlain, Jan., 1836; Russelltown, Canada, 1835–8; Stockholm, N. Y., 2 years; Carthage, 3 years; Waddington, 5 years; Huntingdon, Canada; Underhill, Vt., 2 years; Richmond, 6 years; Warsaw, Wis., 1858–63; Collinsville, 1863–6; Tamaroa, 1867–8; Brownstown, 1869–73; Marine, 1873–81; Fosterburgh, Ill., 1881.

*WILLIAM HEMPHILL, died May 15, 1833.

*NORMAN KELLOGG, died Jan. 12, 1879.

*MERIT SIDNEY PLATT, died Dec. 3, 1880.

ALBERT RHAMANTHUS RAYMOND.

Born in Sherburne, N. Y., Nov. 5, 1804; united with the Pres. Church in Malta, at 16 years of age; graduated from Union College in 1831; Princeton, 1831–2; Auburn, 1832–5, and post grad., 1835–6; married to Miss MARY LUCY WRIGHT, of Salem, Pa., Sept. 28, 1847.

Ordained by Presby. of Chenango, Sept., 1837; prin. of Classical School, Cazenovia, N. Y., and supply of Pres. Ch., Nelson, 1836–7; Greene, 1837–8; Conklin, N. Y., and Liberty, Pa., 1838–9; Liberty and Franklin, 1839–43; Salem and Sterling, 1844–68; ev., resident at Hamlinton, Pa.

WILLIAM MASON RICHARDS.

Born in Hartford, Ct., July 11, 1805; united with the First Pres. Church in Troy, N. Y., 1826; graduated from Williams College in 1832; married to Miss CAROLINE DOUGHERTY, of Belchertown, N. Y., Dec. 9, 1835.

Ordained and installed at Deerfield, Mass., by Franklin Assoc., Nov. 25, 1835; Deerfield 1835–43; Norwich, N. Y., 1844–5; Oxford, 1845–6; Hamilton, 1847–50; Morrisville, 1850; Waukegan, Ill., 1852; Berlin, Wis., 1857; Princeton, 1868; resident at Princeton.

ABISHAI SCOFIELD.

Born in Greenville, N. Y., Oct. 27, 1805; united with the Congregational Church in Greenville, Spring of 1822; graduated from Union College in 1832; Auburn the course, and post grad., 1835; married to Miss ELIZABETH MARVIN, of Colchester, Conn., 1836; married to Miss CELESTIA S. NORTON, of Peterboro, N. Y., Aug., 1842; married to JANETTE MARVIN, of Colchester, Conn., 1844.

Ordained pastor, Peterboro, N. Y., by Presbytery of Onondaga, Autumn of 1836; Rochester, 1835–6; Peterboro, 1836–43; various Churches, 1843–5; Hamilton, "Free Church," 1845–8; ordained there, 1846; Free Church, Georgetown, 1848–61; miss. of Am. Miss. Assoc., Camp Nelson, Ky., 1864–67; evang. in Central N. Y., 1867–70; sup't and chap., Bethel Home, Wis., 1871–2; Hartford, Wis., 1872–80; resident Cos Cob, Conn., since 1880

Published his "Trial and Defence," 1845; and other pamphlets and addresses.

*CALEB PERKINS SEYMOUR, died Sept. 20, 1875.

*CHARLES WILEY, D. D., died Dec. 21, 1878.

HUET HILLS BRONSON.

Born in Vernon Centre, N. Y., June 25, 1812; united with the Congregational Church in Vernon Centre, 1826; graduated from Hamilton College in class of 1832; Auburn, 1832–3; married to Miss HARRIET ELEANOR BREWSTER, of Mexico, N. Y., Feb. 2, 1836; never ordained; was at one time a merchant, but most of his life a farmer; resident Hannibal, N. Y.

*BENJAMIN HAYES CADWELL. See 1835–8.

L. J. CLARK.

This name appears, starred. in the General Catalogue of 1850, which says that Mr. C. was one year in the Seminary. It is probably a careless repetition of the next name.

*LUCIUS J. CLOSE, died June, 1834.

*ERASTUS CRAFTS.

Resident, Hartwick; member of Church in Cooperstown; graduated from Union College in 1832; Auburn Junior and Middle years; died in shipwreck, going from N. Y. to Charleston, 1838.

*JOHN DUNBAR, died in 1857.

OBADIAH EASTMAN.
Junior year from Beekmantown; Middle year from Haverhill, N.
H.; said to have gone South for his health; agt. of Am. Bib.
Soc. in New Orleans; starred in Gen. Catalogue of 1839.

GEORGE C. HYDE.
Entered Seminary from New York City; graduated from
Middlebury College in 1831; Middle year in Auburn.
Ordained pastor, Readfield, Me.. (Cong.) July 14, 1836; Blooms-
burg, N. J., 1838; tea., Ovid, N. Y., 1842; Castleton, N. Y.,
1843; teacher, Elmira, 1846; domestic miss., Presby. of
Mohawk, 1852–4; Williamsport, La., 1855; Simmsport, 1856–9;
Baton Rouge, 1860; Atchafalaya, 1861; Lake Charles, 1872.

ELIHU PARSONS INGERSOLL.
Born in Lee, Mass., Sept. 20, 1804; united with the Cong. Church
in Lee, 1820; graduated from Yale College in 1832; Auburn,
Junior year, and finished course in Yale Divinity School;
married to Miss FANNY LOUISA PERRY, of Stockbridge, Mass.,
April 29, 1835; married to Miss CATHARINE GILLETT, of Rome,
N. Y., Aug. 16, 1838.
Ordained and installed, Woonsocket Falls, R. I., by Council, Dec.
24, 1834; Woonsocket, 1834–5; professor of Greek and Sacred
Music, Oberlin College, 1835–40; served churches in Mich.,
1840–53; Bloomington, Ill., 1853–7; preaching in Kansas,
1857–62; Illinois; Malden, Ill., 1867; in Kansas from 1868,
preaching occasionally; resident Rosevale, Kan.

CHARLES JONES.
Born in Canada, Aug. 1, 1809; united with the Presbyterian Church
in Brockville, Canada, about 1823; graduated from Union Col-
lege in 1832; one year at Auburn and one at Yale; married to
Miss ELVIRA HOLMES, of Richland, N. Y., June, 1835; married
to Miss CALSINA PATIENCE GARDNER, of Fayetteville, N. Y.,
Apr., 1840.
Ordained at Pelham, Upper Canada, by Presbytery of Niagara,
Jan., 1835; missionary work, Canada, 1835–40; Rome, Oswego,
Brasher Falls, Holland Patent, N. Y., 1840–55; Cambridgeport,
Mass., Battle Creek, Mich., Mannsville, and Lafayette and other
fields, 1855–70; Saxonville, Mass., 1870–9; Tolland, Mass.,
1879–81; resident in Syracuse, N. Y., 1882.

THEODORE JOHN KEEP.
Born in Blandford, Mass., July 31, 1809; united with the Congre-
gational Church in Homer, N. Y., 1831; studied at Yale and
Williams Colleges; Auburn, 1832–4; afterwards Oberlin Theol.
Sem.; A. M. from Yale College in 1879; married to Miss MARY
ANN THOMPSON, of Oberlin, O., Jan. 28, 1841.
Ordained pastor, Oberlin, O., by Gen. Assoc. of Western Reserve,
Oct. 10, 1836; instructor in Oberlin College, and pastor of dif-
ferent churches in O., 1836–61; resident in Oberlin.

ROBERT FOWLER LAWRENCE.
Born in Moira, N. Y., Aug. 10, 1810; united with the Cong. Church in Middlebury, Vt., Sept., 1831; graduated from Middlebury College in 1832; Auburn, 1832-3; studied Theology with Dr. Ashbel Parmelee; married to Miss MARY LUCY CLARK, of Malone, N. Y., Feb. 18, 1834.
Ordained by Presby. of Champlain, at Plattsburgh, N. Y., Jan. 16, 1835; Westport, 1835-6; Gouverneur, 1836-8; agt. Am. Tr. Soc., Fair Haven, Vt, 1839; Claremont, N. H., 1839-63; agt. Freedmen's Relief Assoc., 1863; city miss., New London, Conn., 1864-5; resident, Malden, Mass.
Published, "Lectures to Youth," 1848; "The New Hampshire Churches," 1858.

*SAMUEL LEE, died Jan. 28, 1866.

*JARED FORDHAM OSTRANDER, died Nov. 19, 1874.

*SIMEON SHURTLEFF, M. D., died, 1865.

LEWIS HALSEY TERRILL.
Entered the Auburn Senior class from the Seminary of New Brunswick, Oct., 1834, and remained till March, 1835. The Gen. Catalogue of 1872 says that he was grad. of Univ. of Vt., 1832, and that he was miss. to Boatmen in N. J., and to Freedmen in Va.

1833-6.

ISAAC BRAYTON, D. D.
Born in Western, N. Y., June 26, 1812; united with the Church in Western, 1826; graduated from Union College in 1833; Princeton, 1833-5; Auburn, 1835-6; D. D. from Hamilton College in 1857; married to ELISABETH SCOTT BOYD, of Albany, 1845.
Ordained pastor, Watertown First Church, by Presby. of Watertown, Aug. 31, 1837; Watertown, 1837-64; resident Albany, 1864-73, and Poughkeepsie, from 1874.

HENRY CHERRY.
Born in New York, 1812; united with the First Pres. Church in Auburn, March 21, 1831; Lane Seminary, 1833-4; Auburn. 1834-6.
Ordained, Rochester, N. Y., by Presby., Aug. 31, 1836; miss. to India, 1836-51; resident in Rochester, N. Y., 1851-3; in Boston, Thomasville, Ocklocknee, Ga., 1854-7; Jackson, Dowagiac, St. Joseph, Owasso, Mich., 1858-64; chaplain, Knoxville, Tenn., 1865; Maryville, 1866; went to West Va. about 1867.

EDWARD COPE.
> Graduated from Centre College in 1833; entered Aub., Senior, on dism. from Western Theological Sem.; miss. at Batticotta, Ceylon, 1836–51; East Guilford, N. Y., 1852–3; Gilbertsville from 1854.

*NATHANIEL MARCUS CRANE, died Sept. 21, 1859.

*LUMAN COGGSWELL GILBERT, died June 4, 1878.

*JONATHAN PARSONS HOVEY, D. D., died Dec. 16, 1863.

CHARLES NASH MATTOON, D. D.
> Born in Lenox, Mass., 1812; united with the Cong. Church in Lenox, 1828; graduated from Middlebury College in 1832; D. D. from Farmers' College in 1859; married to Miss ANGELINE T. MARTINDALE, of Wallingford, Vt., 1833.
> Ordained and installed at Canoga, N. Y., by Presby. of Geneva, July 6, 1837; Aurora, from 1841; LeRoy, from 1850; president of Farmers' College, O., from 1857; Rockford, Ill., 1861–2; Monroe, Mich., 1863–77, and still resident there.

*JONATHAN BANCROFT PARLIN, died April 29, 1876.

*JAMES RICHARDS, Jr., D. D., LL. D., died July 30, 1875.

*GEORGE WASHINGTON THOMPSON, died Feb. 6, 1872.

BENJAMIN VAN ZANDT, D. D.
> Born in Gilderland, N. Y., Feb. 18, 1809; united with the First Pres. Church in Schenectady, about 1828; graduated from Union College in 1833; D. D. from Union College in 1866; married to Miss JANE SWART EDDY, of Stillwater, N. Y., July 24, 1836.
> Ordained and installed at Greenwich, N. Y., by Classis of Washington, Sept. 23, 1836; Greenwich, 1836–42; Kinderhook, 1842–52; Nyack, 1852–8; Freeport, Wis., 1858–60; Portage, 1860–2; Canajoharie, N. Y., 1862–9; Leeds, 1869–78; resident in Catskill.

*CALVIN WATERBURY, died Jan. 3, 1874.

*CALVIN WOODBURY, apparently a mistaken spelling of the above.

*FRANCIS CHILDS. See 1834–7.

ERASTUS DICKINSON.
> Born in Plainfield, Mass., April 1, 1807; united with the Cong. Church in Plainfield, March 1, 1826; graduated from Amherst College in 1832; Junior year in Auburn; studied Theology with Rev. Dr. Packard, of Shelburne, Mass.; married to Miss MARIA E. BOWEN, of Woodstock, Conn., Oct. 4, 1835; married to Miss LOIS AMES, of Marshfield, Mass., Nov. 5, 1851.
> Ordained pastor, Canton, Mass., by Council, Sept. 9, 1835; Canton, 1835–7; Chaplin, Conn., 1837–49; Colchester, 1851–5; Sud-

bury, Mass., 1856-69; resident Bricksburg, (now Lakewood) N. J., since 1870.

*ROSWELL DUDLEY.

Came to the Seminary from Austinburgh, O., and the Church in Western Res. Col.; graduated from Western Reserve College, in 1833; Auburn, 1833-4; reported as tea., Ill., in General Catalogue of 1850 and 1853; and as deceased in the W. Res. Catalogue of 1873.

*ASAHEL D. FOOTE. See 1834-7.

*JAMES W. FRASER.

Son of Rev. Alexander Fraser, of Westfield, N. J.; came to Auburn from the Chatham St. Church in N. Y. City; studied at Princeton College; Auburn, 1833-4, and perhaps longer; reported in the General Catalogues of 1850 and 1853 as in Scotland; said to have gone there to claim the title of "Lord Lovatt," of Inverness; said to have become an Episcopalian while in the Seminary; is known to have been in Williamsburgh, L. I., giving music lessons, a few years since; is supposed to have been the Rev. James W. Frazer, pastor of a Baptist Church in that vicinity, who died there a little later.

JOEL S. GRAVES.

Came to Auburn from Church in Fair Haven, Vt.; studied at Middlebury College; Middle year in Auburn.

Ordained (perhaps) at Pittsford, Vt., by Council, Aug. 18, 1836; in Alabama, 1836; Monticello, Fla., agt. and S. S., 1839-47, or longer; Greenfield, Ga., 1850-4; Ocklocknee, 1854-62; supposed to have been brother to Eli Graves, of 1834-7; and to have been still living in 1867.

ROBERT VINCENT HALL.

Born in Stanstead, Canada, Jan. 20, 1810; united with the Cong. Church in Charlotte, Vt., Jan., 1832; studied at Select School and privately; Middle year in Auburn; married to Miss LAURA AUGUSTA NEWTON, of Auburn, N. Y., Aug. 20, 1835; married to Miss ADELIA LOUISA ELLIS, of Lowell, Mass., June 10, 1851.

Ordained at Henrietta, N. Y., by Genesee Consoc., Aug. 18, 1835; Am. Pres. Ch., Laprarie, Can., 1835-37; Cong. Church, Stanstead, 1838-55; Newport, Vt., 12 years from 1855; since resident there, supplying churches.

*ROBINSON SMILEY LOCKWOOD, died Aug. 13, 1876.

ISAAC J. RICE.

Came to the Seminary from Wayne, O.; studied at Hamilton College in Class of 1833; Auburn, Junior, 1833-4; S. S., Vienna, O., 1836; in Canada, according to Gen. Catalogue of 1850, and in Amherstburg, C. W., according to that of 1853.

1834-7.

GAIUS MILLS BLODGETT.

Born in Rochester, Vt., Sept. 15, 1815 ; graduated from Union
College in 1834 ; Princeton, 1834-5 ; Auburn, 1835-7.

Ordained by Presby. of Otsego, Jan. 14, 1846 ; chap. N. Y. State
Lun. Asy., Utica, N. Y., 1844-6 ; Cooperstown, 1846 ; Bethle-
hem to 1851 ; New Scotland, 1852-6 ; Farmington, Ill., 1857-9 ;
Ref. Ch., Stone Arabia, N. Y., 1858-9 ; Palatine Bridge, 1860-2 ;
Hicksville, 1862-3 ; chap. U. S. A., 1863-6 ; U. S Consul,
Frelighsburgh, Canada, 1866-70 ; Cong. Church, Wading River,
N. Y., 1871-6 ; resident N. Y. City.

WILLIAM CURTIS BOYCE.

Born in Homer, N. Y., Feb. 14, 1809 ; united with the Pres. Church,
Cortland, about 1825 ; graduated from Union College in 1830 ;
entered Auburn about 1835, was there about 2 years ; married
to Miss MARIA CYNTHIA HAMILTON, of Fort Plain, N. Y.,
about 1843.

Ordained and installed at Westford, N. Y., by Otsego Presby.,
Sept. 30, 1838 ; Westford 4 years ; supplied at Fredonia, Unadilla, Richfield Springs, Lockport 2nd Ward Ch.; Maine, N.
Y., 1850-6 ; Aurora, N. Y., about 3 years from 1857 ; since resident in Lockport.

THOMAS THAXTER BRADFORD.

Born in Plympton, Mass., June 26, 1809 ; united with the Cong.
Church in Homer, N. Y., Sept. 4, 1831 ; graduated from Hamilton College in 1834 ; married to Miss MARY ELIZA PADDOCK,
of Clinton, May 19, 1846.

Ordained, Gilbertsville, N. Y., by Presby. of Otsego, Jan. 12,
1848 ; tutor, Hamilton College, 8 years, from 1837 ; Pres.
Church, Gilbertsville, N. Y., 1846-50 ; home miss. in Birmingham, (Pittsburgh) Pa., 1851-3 ; Pres. Ch., Waterford, 1853-70 ;
resident in Metuchen, N. J., from 1870.

*HARVEY CHAPIN, died July 27, 1866.

*FRANCIS CHILDS, died Oct. 1, 1841.

*JOHN M. CRABB, died Mar. 17, 1859.

EDWARD HENRY CUMPSTON.

Born in Auburn, N. Y., May 1, 1813 ; united with the First Pres.
Church in Auburn, May 23, 1831 ; graduated from Union Col-
lege in 1833 ; nearly 2 years at Auburn, remainder of course at
Yale ; post grad., Auburn, 1837-8 ; married to Miss CAROLINE
SMELT SKINNER, of New York City, Oct. 9, 1837 ; married to
Miss MARY MITCHELL JAMES, of Lynchburg, Va., June 27,
1844.

Ordained by Assoc. of West Dist. of N. Haven, May 22, 1838 ;
Nantucket, L. I., 1838 ; Village Ch., New York City, 1838-40 ;
home miss. Northampton Co., Va , 6 mos., 1840-1 ; Lynchburg,

Va., 1841-7; Planter, 1847-8; Douglass Ch., 1849; McKemie Ch., and Homes Ch., 1857; Rockville and Bethesda Ch., Md., 1859; Hancock Ch., and Berkeley Springs Ch., 1874; Hancock Ch., 1880; resident Alexandria, Va., supplying Vienna and Lavinsville Chs., 1881.

*ASAHEL D. FOOTE, died June 4, 1837.

*ELI GRAVES, died July 16, 1866.

*SETH PARSONS MERWIN HASTINGS, died Feb. 24, 1876.

*AMOS PAYNE HAWLEY, died Feb. 26, 1866.

GEORGE FABER McEWEN.
Born in Litchfield, N. Y., 1814; came to Auburn from Ann Arbor, Mich.; member of the Church in Sullivan; graduated from Williams College in 1834.
Ordained at Montrose, Pa., by Presby., Sept. 24, 1840; Topsfield, Mass.; in 1871 the Williams College Annals say of him, that he preached for a short time, and is "now somewhere in Wis."

HENRY HORATIO NORTHRUP.
Born in Galway, N. Y., June 13, 1814; united with the 1st Pres. Church in Galway, Autumn of 1833; graduated from Union College in 1834; married to Miss MARYETTE WOOD, of Medina, N. Y., Nov. 16, 1837.
Ordained by Presby. of Washtenaw, Oct., 1838; S. S., Lima and Dexter, 3 years; past. White Pigeon, 4 years; Homer, 4½ years; S. S., Monroe, 2 years; past. Flint, 16 years; S. S., Grand Rapids, 4 years; dist. sec. for Ch. Erec., 2 years; fin. agt. for Kalamazoo Sem., 2 years; Pres. miss., in all, 3 or 4 years; resident at Flint, doing missionary work.

*ROBERT LANGDON PORTER, died early in 1838.

*SOLON G. PUTNAM, died May 19, 1840.

SAMUEL WHITTLESEY RAYMOND, M. D.
Born in New Canaan, Ct., Oct. 2, 1807; united with the Cong. Church in Clinton, N. Y., May, 1830; A. M. from Hamilton College in 1849; married to SARAH MARIA BOWNE, of Brooklyn, N. Y., Oct. 12, 1837.
Ordained at Union Springs, N. Y., by Cayuga Presby., July 1, 1840; Union Springs, Marshall, Kirkland, 15 years in all; for the past 27 years a practicing physician in Clinton.

HENRY STONE REDFIELD.
Born in Watertown, N. Y., Oct. 15, 1811; united with the Pres. Church in Watertown, Aug., 1833; graduated from Hamilton College in 1833; married to Miss MARY EMILINE SHAPLEY, of Oswego, N. Y., 1839; married to Mrs. MARIA C., daughter of Ebenezer HUNTING, of Bellville, N. Y., 1870.
Ordained at Huron, N. Y., by Presby. of Cayuga, Sept. 5, 1839;

Lebanon, N. Y., 1840–5 ; Columbus, 2 years; Oriskany, 1 year ; Phoenix, 1847–52 ; Nat. Bridge, 1853–4; Chester, 1855–60; Woodville, 1862–3 ; enlisted in 185th U. S. Vols., 1864–5 ; Lebanon, 1867–9 ; resident at Westfield since 1870, supplying Churches.

*Ebenezer Weeks Robinson, died April 8, 1869.

*James Maltby Sayre, died May 9, 1874.

James Scott.

Entered Aub. Sen. class, from Newburgh, on dismissal from the Western Theo. Sem. ; the name is omitted from the Gen. Cata logues previous to 1858, and is credited with the record of another man, from that date.

John Frederick Scovill.

Born in Fort Edward, N. Y., May 9, 1812 ; united with the Pres. Church in Chester, N. Y., about 1830; studied at Union College in class of 1836 ; entered Auburn Middle class, Oct. 25, 1835 ; married to Miss Elizabeth Bibier Hasbrouck, at Fort Edward, N. Y., Nov. 14, 1837.

Ordained pastor of Pres. Ch. of Glenn's Falls, N. Y., by Presby. of Troy, Nov., 1837 ; remained there till June, 1842 ; Holland Patent, 1843–9 ; ceased to be a minister of the Pres. Ch. ; on the staff of the N. Y. Evangelist ; engaged in the business of Magazine Publishing, in N. Y. ; resident in Brooklyn, N. Y.

Washington Stickney.

Came to Auburn from Lockport, N. Y. ; graduated from Hamilton College in 1834 ; Auburn the course, and post grad., 1837–8 ; married to Miss Buckingham, of Exeter, N. Y.

Ordained and installed at Verona, N. Y., by Presby., Aug. 3, 1842 ; Exeter, N. Y. ; Verona ; Indep. Ch., Canastota ; Fort Plain ; resident several years in Lockport, N. Y.; went West.

*Thomas Rockwell Townsend, died Sept. 11, 1875.

Robert Edmund Willson.

Born in Amenia, (now Northeast) N. Y., Mar. 28, 1807 ; united with the Cong. Church in Northeast, Spring of 1831 ; graduated from Hamilton College in 1834 ; East Windsor Sem., 1834–5 ; Auburn, 1835–7, and post grad., 1837–8 ; married to Miss Mary Strong, of Phelps, N. Y., Feb. 20, 1838.

Ordained and installed at Hammondsport, N. Y., by Presby. of Bath, Dec., 1838 ; Hammondsport, 14 years ; Corning, 4 years ; Clyde, 14 years ; Havana, 5½ years ; evang., residing in Hudson, N. Y., 1875–8, and since then in Philadelphia, Pa.

Published "A Review of a Farewell Sermon by the Rev. Mr. Russ ;" and sermons, reviews and articles.

*VERNON WOLCOTT, died Oct., 1847.

SAMUEL MILES HOPKINS, D. D.
Born in Geneseo, N. Y., Aug. 8, 1813; united with the Church in
Amherst College, 1832; graduated from Amherst College in
1832; Auburn, 1834-6; Princeton, 1836-7; D. D. from
Amherst College in 1854; married to Miss MARY JANE
HENSON HEACOCK, of Buffalo, May 15, 1838.
Ordained and installed at Corning, N. Y., by Presby. of Chemung,
1839; Corning, 1839-43; Fredonia, 1843-6; professor of Church
History, Auburn Seminary, from 1847.
Published "Manual of Church Polity," 1878; Moderator of Gen-
eral Assembly, at St. Louis, Mo., 1866.

*LEWIS KELLOGG, died Feb. 11, 1882.

DAVID MALIN, D. D.
Born in Philadelphia, Pa., Jan. 21, 1805; graduated from Hamil-
ton College in 1833; Auburn, 1834-6; Princeton, 1836-7;
D. D. from Maryville College.
Ordained and installed at Genoa, N. Y., by Presby. of Cayuga,
Apr. 25, 1838; Genoa, 1838-42; dist. sec. of A. B. C. F. M.,
1842-57; assoc. sec. of Am. Tr. Soc., Phila., Pa., 1857-9;
prin. of Classical School, Phil., 1859-62; Chr. Com., N. Y.
Vols., Phila., 1862-5; U. S. Sub. Treas., N. Y. City, 1865-8;
past. of 15th Ch., Phila., 1870-8; resident in Philadelphia.

ALSTON MYGATT.
Came to Auburn from Church in Clinton, N. Y; born in Clinton,
March 26, 1805; graduated from Hamilton College in 1834;
part of Junior year in Auburn.
Preached and taught in Ga.; reported as there in the Gen. Cata-
logues of 1839, 1850, 1853; said to reside in or near Racine,
Wis.

1835-8.

FENN C. ALVORD.
Came to Auburn from Homer; member of the Church in Homer;
graduated from Union College in 1835; the Gen. Catalogues
report him as in Mich., 1850, 1853, and dead, 1858; the Un. Col.
Gen. Catalogue of 1868 reports him in Mich.

*SILAS HUBBELL ASHMUN, died July 22, 1880.

*WILLIAM BRADFORD, died Apr. 1, 1861.

*BENJAMIN HAYES CADWELL.
Resided in Auburn; entered Aub., Jun. class, Nov., 1832; received
again to Auburn on letter from Union Sem., Va., to Sen. class,
June 10, 1837; according to Gen. Catalogues of 1850, 1853, tea.
in Fulton, N. Y.; starred in 1858, but said to have died in 1859,
act. 46.

*DANIEL GIBBS, died April 27, 1881.

*LEWIS HAMILTON, died Dec. 7, 1881.

HON. JOEL TYLER HEADLEY.
>   Born in Walton, N. Y., Dec. 30, 1814; united with the Church
>   about 1830; graduated from Union College in 1839; Auburn,
>   1836-8; married to Miss ANNA A. RUSSELL, of New York,
>   May, 1850.
>   Ordained pastor, Stockbridge, Mass., by Assoc.; Stockbridge, 2
>   years; abroad, 1842-4; member of N. Y. Legislature, 1854;
>   Secretary of State, 1856-7; resident at Newburgh, N. Y.
>   Published, "A Translation from the German," 1844; "Letters
>   from Italy," 1845; "The Alps and the Rhine," 1845; "The
>   Sacred Mountains," 1846; "Napoleon and his Marshals," 1846;
>   "Washington and his Generals," 1847; "Life of Oliver Crom-
>   well," 1848; "Sacred Scenes and Characters," 1849; "The
>   Adirondack," 1849; "Sketches and Rambles," 1850; "Miscel-
>   lanies," 1850; "The Old Guard of Napoleon," 1851; "Life of
>   Winfield Scott," 1852; "Life of Andrew Jackson," 1852;
>   "History of the Second War with England," 1853; Life of
>   Geo. Washington, 1857; Life of General Havelock, 1859; "The
>   Chaplains and Clergy of the Revolution," 1864; "History of
>   the Rebellion"; "History of the Riots in New York";
>   "Mountain Adventures," 1873; "Explorations in Africa."

*ABEL KNAPP HINSDALE, died Dec. 26, 1842.

PHOTIUS KAVASSALAS.
>   Born in Greece; studied at Yale College; was private secretary
>   in Greece, of President Capodistrias; after whose assassination,
>   he returned to America.
>   Ordained, Halifax, Vt., (Cong.) March 14, 1839; the Auburn
>   General Catalogues speak of him as chaplain, U. S. Navy.

ALFRED CRAFTS LATHROP.
>   Born in Rutland, N. Y., Nov. 12, 1811; united with the Pres.
>   Church in Whitesboro, N. Y., April, 1830; graduated from
>   Oneida Institute in 1836; Middle and Senior years at Auburn;
>   married to Miss STELLA DESIRE HOUGH, of Meriden, Ct., May
>   2, 1839; married to Mrs. MARY J. RAYNARD, April 15, 1875.
>   Ordained at Orville, N. Y., by Onondaga Presby., March 8, 1843;
>   home missionary, (7 years in Collamer Pres. Ch.) 15 years in
>   New York, 15 years in Wis., and 10 years in Minnesota; resi-
>   dent at Glenwood, Minn.
>   Published Memoir of Dr. Asahel Grant, 1846.

*SAMUEL J. McCULLOUGH, died Dec. 20, 1867.

EDWARD REYNOLDS.
>   Born in Grand Isle, Vt., 1809; graduated from Oneida Institute
>   in 1836; Middle and Senior years at Auburn; married to Miss
>   CORNELIA HOUGH, of Meriden, Ct., Oct., 1838.

Ordained pastor by Presby. of Oswego, 1843; Slab City, N. Y., 1 year; Hannibal; Phillipsburg; Sun Prairie, Wis., ; Waterloo He became a Free Will Baptist Elder; has not preached for the past 25 years ; resides in Athens, Ala.

*ELIHU ROWE, died 1840.

*JOHN FINLEY SMITH, died Oct. 4, 1843.

EBENEZER GRANT TOWNSEND.
Born in South Salem, N. Y., Feb. 18, 1813; united with the Church in Lysander, N. Y., 1820; graduated from Oneida Institute, 1836; Auburn, Junior and Middle years; Senior year at Yale ; married to ELIZA EDDY, of Troy, N. Y., 1840.
Ordained and installed at Michigan City, Iowa, by Presby. of Logansport, 1841 ; Michigan City to 1843; Sackett's Harbor, N. Y., 1843–50; Camden, 1850–3; Elbridge, 1853–60; Syracuse, 1860–1; chaplain U. S. A., 1861–5 ; resident Providence Forge, Va., from 1871.

JOHN M. VAN BUREN.
Born in Kinderhook, N. Y., Sept. 20, 1811 ; united with the Ref. Church in Kinderhook, 1831 ; graduated from Union College in 1835; married to Miss FRANCES MARVIN, of Albany, N. Y., 1840; married to Miss MARIA C. HOES, of Kinderhook, 1844.
Ordained pastor, Cohoes, N. Y., by Classis, Apr. 23, 1840; Mt. Morris, 1838–9; Cohoes, 1839–41; Fultonville, 1842–51; New Lots, N. Y., 1852–72; resident in Nyack.
Published "Gospel Temperance," 1877.

*WILLIAM B. WORDEN, M. D., died May 14, 1845.

---

*JAMES HARRIMAN CARRUTH.
Born in Phillipston, Mass., Feb. 10, 1807 ; united with the Cong. Church in Phillipston, about 1826; graduated from Yale College in 1832; two years at Auburn ; third year at New Haven ; married to Miss JANE GRANT, of Steuben-Co., N. Y., Sept. 13, 1841.
Ordained at Cooperstown, N. Y., by Presby. of Otsego, June, 1850; Mexico, N. Y., 1839; Fly Creek, 1850–2 ; Clinton, Kan., 1867; "much of the intervening time was spent in teaching ;" resident Lawrence, Kan.
Published Catalogue of the Plants of Kansas, 1876, (in conjunction with others.)

WILLARD DAVIS.
In Junior class, from Guilford, for 6 months of the year ; named and starred in General Cat. of 1858.

FRANCIS DENISON.
Came to Auburn from Castleton, Vt. ; member of the Church there; in Auburn but a short time ; resident at Kalamazoo, Mich.

JOHN FAIRCHILD.
Entered Seminary from McDonough, as a member of the Baptist Church in Auburn ; Auburn, 1835-7 ; pastor of Baptist Church, Rose, N. Y., about 1850.

*EZRA BENEDICT FANCHER. See 1836-39, died Jan. 7, 1867.

*LEVI M. GRAVES, died Jan. 1, 1881.

*CHARLES LOUIS HEQUEMBOURG. See 1836-9.

*ABEL MOORE HEACOCK, died July 9, 1843.

EDWIN HOYT.
Born in Castleton, Vt., (probably) ; united with the Cong. Church ; graduated from Middlebury College in 1835 ; Aub., Jun. year ; became a Millerite preacher in Western N. Y. This name is *Hoit* in some of the earlier records, and *Holt*, by mistake, in the Catalogue of 1872.

*STANLEY PARMLEE HOUGH, changed to *Hough P. Stanley*, died Sept. 28, 1874.

*DANIEL E. HURLBERT.
Came to Auburn from Madrid ; graduated from Union College in 1837 ; Auburn, 1835-7 : died, according to Un. Col. Gen. Catalogue, in 1849.

JENKIN JENKINS.
Born in England ; came to Auburn from N. Y. City ; Auburn, Junior and Middle years ; Dundaff, Pa., 1840 ; Bethel, 1843 ; Newark, O., 1850, and 1853 ; Walnut Hill, 1860 ; Oneida, Mich., 1861-4 ; Butternut Valley, Minn., 1864-80 ; Courtland, from 1880.

*ROBERT RANSOM KELLOGG, died Sept. 25, 1866.

CHARLES EDWARDS LESTER.
Born in Griswold, Conn., July 15, 1855 : traveled in the South and West ; studied Law 1 year in Miss.; Auburn, 1835-6 ; Liverpool, N. Y., 1837 ; consul at Genoa, 1842-7.
Published " Samuel Houston and his Republic "; " Biographical Sketches of Artists of America "; " The Mountain Wild Flower," 1838 ; " Glory and Shame of England," 1841, and new ed., 1866 ; " Condition and Resources of England," 1842 ; translation of Alfieri's Autobiography, 1845 ; of Massimo d'Azeglio's " Challenge of Barletta," 1845 ; of Machiavelli's, " Florentine Histories," 1845 ; of Ansaldo Ceba's " Citizen of a Republic," 1845 ; " The Artist, Merchant and Statesman," 1845 ; with A. Foster, " Life of Vespucius," 1846 ; " My Cousulship," 1851 ; " The Napoleon Dynasty," 1852 ; " Life of Charles Sumner," 1874 ; " Our First Hundred Years," 1874-5.

ALEXANDER OLYMPUS PELOUBET.
Born in Hudson, N. Y., May 28, 1810 ; united with the Central Pres. Church, Broome St., N. Y., June, 1828 ; graduated from

New York Univ., 1835; Middle year in Auburn; Senior in Union The. Sem., N. Y.; married to Miss HANNAH WARD, of Bloomfield, N. J., Jan. 16, 1839; married to Miss PHEBE WARD, of Bloomfield, 1850; married to Mrs. MARGARET E. KING WHEELER, of Cairo, N. Y., 1861.

Ordained and installed at Mount Hope, N. Y., by Assoc., 1839; Mount Hope, 1½ years; Unionville and West Town Pres. Chs., 4½ years; New Paltz Landing, 1846; Circleville, 1850; Cairo, 1860; Mecklenburgh, 1865-71; Five Corners, 1871-3; Mecklenburgh from 1873.

*LEMUEL STRONG POMEROY, died Feb. 19, 1879.

*JAMES BENJAMIN TOWNSEND, died Jan. 27, 1865.

*THOMAS SYDENHAM WARD, died Feb. 13, 1864.

*CRISPUS WRIGHT, died July 5, 1852.

1836-9.

*EBENEZER CROSS BIRGE, died May 30, 1882.

*SAMUEL WEBSTER BUSH, died March 21, 1877.

NEHEMIAH COBB.

Born in Carver, Mass., Oct. 6, 1808; united with the 1st Cong. Church in Camden, N. Y., July, 1826; studied at Oneida Inst. and Rome and Clinton Academies; married to Miss CAROLINE AUGUSTA HOVEY, of Oberlin, O., June 12, 1840; married to Mrs JANE MELISSA (SKINNER) PARKER, of Omaha, Neb., Mar. 9, 1875.

Ordained at Mt. Morris, Mich., by Presby., Sept. 23, 1840; Mt. Morris, 1839-41; Guilford, N. Y., 1842-7; farmer and Bib. agt., 1847-9; Presbyterial miss., residing at Spring Creek, 1849-54; Elmira, fin. agt. of Fem. Col., 1854-7; So. Bristol, 1857; Strykersville, 1857-9; Cleveland, O., Presb. miss., 1859-60; and Bib. agt., 1861-5; Chicago, Ill., agt. of Union Aid Soc., 1865-8; agt. of Am. Miss. Assoc., 1868-70; Washington, D. C., city Bib. agt., 1871-3, and resident there since.

*EZRA BENEDICT FANCHER, died Jan. 27, 1867.

JOHN M. FRAZER.

Born in Ferrisburgh Vt., 1802; Auburn, Jun., 1837; Sen., 1838-9; post grad., 1839-40.

Ordained and installed at Addison, Vt., (Cong.) Dec. 25, 1840; Addison; Ferrisburgh, 1850; Troy, O., 1853, '58, '61; Nevada, Col., 1866-8; South Windsor, Conn.; Geauga, O.; Clarksfield, 1876-7; Unionville from 1880.

*CHARLES LOUIS HEQUEMBOURG, died Dec. 24, 1875.

*SIMEON JOHNSON, died June 24, 1837.

EPHRAIM WILLIAM KELLOGG.

Born in Sheffield, Mass., May 2, 1811; united with the Cong. Church in Sheffield, 1831; graduated from Williams College in 1836; Auburn, the course, and post graduate, 1839-40; married to Miss LOIS BENNETT, of Auburn, May 3, 1841.

Ordained, Churchville, by Presby. of Rochester, Feb. 18, 1845; Meadville, Pa., 1840-1; Sheffield, Mass., Fairport, N. Y., and Avon, N. Y., each 1 year; Churchville, Millville and Lockport, each 3 years; Tonawanda, 5 years; Oakland and Truxton, each 3 years; Howard, 1877-81; Heuvelton from 1881.

JOHN LORENZO MARVIN.

Came to Auburn from Charlton; graduated from Union College in 1836.

Ordained by Presby. of Oswego, about 1841; supposed to reside in Colon, Mich.

*HANNIBAL SMITH, died June 24, 1837.

*WILLIAM PARKHURST TUTTLE, died June 24, 1837.

*WILLIAM WOODBRIDGE, died June 24, 1837.

---

*HORACE M. CRANE.

Written HIRAM W. CRANE, in the records of the Faculty; entered from Auburn; member of the Church in Williamstown; graduated from Union College in 1836; Auburn, 1836-8; said to have been a teacher, and to have died years ago.

A. GASTON.

Auburn, Jun., 1836-7; the name appears nowhere but in the Annual Cat. for that year.

JONATHAN KNEELAND, M. D.

Born in Spafford, N. Y., 1812; united with the Church in Whitestown about 1835; studied at Oneida Inst.; Auburn, 1836-7; Lane Seminary; married to Miss MIRIAM KNEELAND, of Spafford, 1845.

Practicing physician in Onondaga Co.; now resident in South Onondaga. His son is M. D. KNEELAND, of the Auburn class of 1870-3.

VILLEROY DIBBLE REED, D. D.

Born in Granville, N. Y., Apr. 27, 1815; united with the 1st Pres. Church in Lansingburgh, N. Y., June, 1827; graduated from Union College in 1835; 5 or 6 months at Auburn; about 3 months at Princeton; D. D. from Union College in 1858; married to Miss EMILY WILCOX, Oct. 21, 1845; married to Miss LUCY M. ALLEN, of Buffalo, N. Y., Sept. 5, 1860.

Ordained and installed at 1st Ch. in Stillwater, N. Y., by Presby. of Albany, Dec. 18, 1839; Stillwater, 1838-44; 1st Ch., Lansingburgh, 14 years from 1844; president of Alexander College, Iowa, from 1857; First Ch., Camden, N. J., from 1861.

STEPHEN VORHIS.

Born in Spencer, N. Y., Sept. 15, 1812; united with the First
Cong. Church in Owego, N. Y., Winter of 1830; graduated from
Hamilton College in 1836; Auburn, 1836-8; married to Miss
ELIZABETH SATTERLY LOWE, of Elmira, N. Y., Oct. 28, 1839;
married to Miss ANN LOUISA LORD, of West Almond, N. Y.,
June 18, 1862.

Ordained at Akron, O., by Baptist Council, Apr. 3, 1839; joined
Presby. of Portage a few weeks after; Akron, 1838-40; Cong.
Ch., Danby, N. Y., 1840-53; Phœnix, 1853-7; Pres. Ch., Hammondsport, 1857-65; Newfield, 1876-7; Spencer, 1865-76, and
from 1877.

1837-40.

EDWIN BENEDICT.

Born in Ledyard, (then Scipio) N. Y., Sept. 3, 1813; united with
the Church in May, 1831; graduated from Hamilton College in
1837; married to MARY M. SPENCER, of Sweeden, N. Y., Nov.
2, 1842.

Ordained and installed at Candor, N. Y., by Presby. of Tioga,
Sept. 20, 1842; North Bergen, 1840-1; Candor, 10 years from
1842; Bath, 6 years; Jamesville, 8 years; Moravia, 5 years;
Genoa, 2nd Ch., from 1872.

*JOHN E. CLAGHORN.

Came to Auburn from Castleton, Vt.; member of Church in Castleton; graduated from Middlebury College in 1836; Auburn
the course, and post grad., 1840-1; the Gen. Catalogues report
him as at Castleton, and deceased in 1853.

CHARLES CROCKER.

Came to Auburn from Lockport; member of the Church in
Lockport; studied at Oberlin College in class of 1838; Auburn
Senior class from Oberlin; Friendship, N. Y., to 1849; since
resident at Glenwood, preaching there and elsewhere.

*ORIS FRASER, died July 4, 1877.

HEMINGWAY JACOB GAYLORD.

Born in Otisco, N. Y., Feb. 17, 1813; united with the Cong.
Church in Otisco, June, 1831; graduated from Amherst College
in class of 1837; married to CORDELIA DICKINSON, of Amherst,
Mass., June 22, 1841; married to MARY H. MACK, of Plainfield,
Mass., Nov. 22, 1854.

Ordained and installed at Union, N. Y., by Presby. of Tioga,
May 26, 1842; Union, 1842-7; Plainfield, Mass., 1847;
Makemie Pres. Ch., Va., 1853; Port Penn and Drawyer's,
Del., 1855; Port Penn and Delaware City, 1861; Lincoln,
1866; Eden and Blackwater, 1872; Clyde and Ross, Kan.,
1878; residing in Clyde.

HIRAM WHITNEY GILBERT.
>   Born in Galway, N. Y., Aug. 22, 1809; united with the Pres.
>   Church in Galway, 1830; graduated from Union College in
>   1837; married to Miss CATHERINE ELIZA PEASE, of Auburn,
>   1841.
>   Ordained and installed at Windsor, N. Y., by Presby. of Chenango,
>   Oct. 20, 1841; Windsor, 1840-54; Greene, 1855-60; resident
>   in Binghamton, supplying churches and serving the Bible and
>   Tract Societies, 1860-7; Long Ridge, Conn., 1867-9; Peru,
>   Mass., 1869-74; resident in Binghamton.

*CHARLES ORVILLE HILL, died April 20, 1862.

*WILLIAM MORRIS HOYT, died Dec. 17, 1844.

*RANSOM RICHARD KIRK, died Nov. 16, 1862.

CHARLES MERWIN.
>   Born in Brookfield, Conn., Oct. 1, 1810; united with the Church
>   in Richmond, N. Y., 1827; studied at Univ. of N. Y. City;
>   married to Miss AMELIA OLIPHANT, of Auburn, Aug. 20, 1840;
>   married to Miss SARAH T. RANDALL, of Lewiston, Oct. 21, 1870.
>   Ordained and installed at Sodus, N. Y., by Presby. of Geneva,
>   Feb. 18, 1842; Sodus, 1841-6; Victor, 1847-9; Columbus, Ind.,
>   1850; Lexington, Miss., 1852-3; Panama, N. Y., 1854-5;
>   Georgetown, O., 1855-7; Amesville, 1858-64; Pomeroy,
>   1865-8; Lewiston, N. Y., 1868-70; Dresden, O., 1870-1;
>   Unionville, Ia., 1871-2; Malvern, 1872-5, and still resident
>   there.

ELIOT HALE PAYSON.
>   Born in Winchendon, Mass., Aug. 12, 1808; united with the
>   Cong. Church in Morrisville, 1833; A. M. from Hamilton
>   College in 1847; married to MARY LAW BROBERTSON, of
>   Oswego, 1841; married to ANNE B. CLARK, of Utica, 1858.
>   Ordained and installed at Preble, N. Y., by Cortland Presby.,
>   Oct. 25, 1842; Preble, 1840-5; New Hartford, 1845-61; Ox-
>   ford, 1862-70; Vernon, 1872-8; resident Oneida, N. Y.

*WILLIAM AUGUSTUS SELDEN, died Jan. 12, 1842.

*HARVEY SMITH, died Sept. 21, 1872.

*STEPHEN STANLEY, died Aug. 20, 1854.

*CURTIS THURSTON, died Sept. 22, 1872.

*SAMUEL LAWRENCE TUTTLE, died April 16, 1866.

WILLIAM BLOOMFIELD WALL.
>   Came to Auburn from N. Y. City; mem. of Carmine Street
>   Church; graduated from Union College in 1837.
>   Cumberland, Md., 1843-4; Washington, Ia., 1846; Marion, O.,
>   1851; Mt. Pleasant, Ia., 1852-6; Kossuth, 1856-65; Mt. Pleasant,

1865–8; Princeton, 1869; Animosa, 1870; Salina, 1871–3; Pleasant Plain, 1873–9; Chili, Ill., 1879–81; Macomb, from 1881.

*SAMUEL CORYLUS WILCOX, died March 25, 1854.

HENRY BANNISTER, D. D.
Born in Conway, Mass., Oct. 5, 1812; united with the M. E. Church in Sept., 1828; graduated from Wesleyan Univ. in 1836; Auburn, to Dec. of Middle year; D. D. from Wesleyan Univ. in 1850; married to Miss LUCY KIMBALL, Aug. 12, 1840.
Ordained Deacon, 1842, and Elder, 1844, both in Oneida Conf. of M. E. Church; tea. Cazenovia Sem., 1838–43; prin. of same, 1843–56; prof. of Exegetical Theology, Garrett Biblical Inst., from 1856; resident in Evanston, Ill.
Published a Commentary on Isaiah (in "Whedon's Series,") 1882.

MILTON BRADLEY.
Born in Stockholm, N. Y., Mar. 13, 1812; united with the Pres. Church in Potsdam, N. Y., Autumn of 1829; graduated from Middlebury College in 1835; Auburn, 1837–8; studied privately with Rev. Aaron Foster; married to Miss SARAH JONES, of Fort Covington, N. Y., Sept. 5, 1838.
Ordained at Parishville, N. Y., by Presby. of St. Lawrence, Autumn of 1839; Cong. Ch., Parishville, 1839–43; Pres. Ch., Richland, Mich., 1844–78; still resident there as pastor emeritus.

*ROBERT TAFT CONANT. See 1838–41.

ISAAC PIERSON STRYKER.
Born in Orange, N. J., 1815; united with the Pres. Church in Whitesboro, N. Y., 1830; studied at Oneida Institute; first year at Auburn, second and third at Yale; had previously studied Law; married to ALIDA LIVINGSTON WOOLSEY, of Utica, N. Y., 1848; married to Mrs. ELIZA TURNER, of Whitesboro, N. Y., July 9, 1879.
Ordained at Rock Stream, N. Y., by Presby. of Steuben, Feb. 2, 1843; Watkins, 1842–6; Vernon, 1847–52; Hoboken, N. J., 1852–5; Urbana, Ill., 1856–61; New Milford, Pa., 1863–4; Montrose, 1864; army chaplain, 1864–5; resident in New York City, 1865–80, and Closter, N. J., since 1880.

*ELIAKIM WARE SYLVESTER, M. D., died Mar. 29, 1879.

1838-41.

*DAVID AVERY ABBEY, died Dec. 6, 1865.

*JOHN MILTON BENHAM.
Came to the Seminary from Bridgewater, N. Y.; member of the Church in Cassville; graduated from Hamilton College in 1837;

supply of Church in Worcester, N. Y., 2 years, 1846. It is
said that he ceased to be a minister; went to California, and
soon died.

CHARLES CARROLL CARR.

Born in Romulus, N. Y., March 22, 1812; united with the Pres.
Church in Romulus, May, 1831; graduated from Union Col-
lege in 1838; married to Miss ELEANOR COLWELL, of Romulus,
Aug. 24, 1841.

Ordained and installed at Pres. Ch., Horse Heads, N. Y., by
Presby. of Chemung, June 30, 1841; Painted Post, 1856-9;
Burdett, 1859-63; Horse Heads, 1841-56, and from 1863.

*ROBERT TAFT CONANT, died Jan. 28, 1879.

HORACE FRASER.

Born in Steuben, N. Y., Feb. 9, 1808; united with the Pres. Church
in Phelps, 1830; graduated from N. Y. City Univ., 1837;
Union Theo. Sem., 1836-7; married to SARAH DEY, of Varick,
1837.

Ordained and installed at Branchport by Presby. of Geneva, 1841;
Branchport, 1841-3; Angelica, 1843-4; Branchport again 2
years; Lafayette, 1854-6; Canoga, 1857-60; resident Canoga,
1860-4, Varick, 1864-70, and West Town from 1870.

*GEORGE WILLISTON GRIDLEY, died Sept. 25, 1846.

*HIRAM HARRIS, died Aug. 26, 1872.

PARSONS CLARK HASTINGS, Ph. D.

Born in Clinton, N. Y., Nov. 22, 1813; united with the First
Pres. Church in Auburn, about 1833; graduated from Hamilton
College in 1838; Ph. D. from Hamilton College in 1880;
married to Miss Mary ANN GUERNSEY of Rochester, N. Y.,
May, 1842; married to Miss SARAH SHELDON, of Hartford,
Conn., April 7, 1852.

Ordained and installed at Manlius, N. Y., by Presby. of Onondaga
1845; E. Avon, 1841-2; Cong. Ch., Clinton, 1843-4; Manlius,
1845-51; chap. at Hamilton Col., 1851-4; Cong. Chs. in
Mass., 1855; resident in Brooklyn, N. Y.

WILLIAM HOGARTH, D. D.

Born in Geneva, N. Y., April 3, 1814; united with the First
Pres., Church in Geneva, May 1, 1831; graduated from Union
College in 1840; D. D. from Univ. of N. Y. in 1858; married
to Miss FIDELIA LYMAN HASTINGS, of Geneva, April 26, 1842.

Ordained and installed at Wilmington, Del., by Presby., Dec. 6,
1841; Hanover St. Ch., Wilmington; Geneva, N. Y., First
Pres. Ch., 1846-55; First Pres. Ch., Brooklyn, 1855-8; Jefferson Ave. Pres. Ch., Detroit, Mich., 1858-73; North Pres. Ch.,
Geneva, N. Y., from 1873.

WILLIAM HUNTER.

Born in North of Ireland, Feb. 2, 1813; united with the First

Church of Watertown, N. Y., May 1833; graduated from
Oneida Institute 1838; married to Mary E. Morris, of Auburn,
May 18, 1842.

Ordained and installed at Springwater, N. Y., by Presby. of
Ontario, Sept. 25, 1844; where he yet remains.

*Roderick Lee Hurlburt, died Feb. 14, 1854.

*George Ives King, D. D., died March 12, 1873.

*Charles Gold Lee, died Oct. 9, 1856.

*Foster Lilly, Jr., died Dec. 23, 1855.

Lawrence Mercereau, Jr.

Born in Union, N. Y., July 6, 1811; united with Pres. Ch. there,
1832; graduated from Union College, 1839; studies of Junior
year at Schenectady : Auburn, 1839–41; married to Miss Adelaide Stone, of Rensselaerville, N. Y., Sept. 30, 1846.

Ordained at Candor, N. Y., by Presby. of Tioga, March, 1843;
Deposit, 1841–2; Middleburgh, Ref. Ch., 1842–5; West Troy,
Pres. Ch., 1845 6; Cong. Ch., Groton, 1846–7; Milford, 2
years; Newfield, 1847–50; tea. Ames, 1853–5; tea. Little Falls,
1856–8; tea. Brooklyn, 1869; evang. Brooklyn, from 1874,
supplying at Five Corners, and other places.

*Charles Morgan, died Dec. 18, 1870.

Cyrenius Ransom.

Born in Chazy, N. Y., Oct. 12, 1810; united with the Cong. Church
in Chazy, 1826; studied at Plattsburgh Acad. and Geneva
Lyceum ; married to Miss Mary Esther Scribner, of Plattsburgh, N. Y., Dec. 22, 1841.

Ordained by Presby. of Champlain, Feb., 1842; Union Ch.,
Moriah, N. Y., 18 years ; Pres. Church, Port Henry, 10 years ;
Wadham's Mills, 1866–9; Peru, 1870–2; chaplain of Clinton
State Prison; resident in Dannemora.

*Levi Rose, died June 4, 1852.

*John Tompkins, died Aug. 15, 1866.

Peter Stryker Van Nest, D. D.

Born in Amsterdam, N. Y., Aug. 21, 1813; united with the Ref.
Church in 1830; graduated from Union College in 1838; D. D.
from Centre College in 1876; married to Caroline Barker,
of South Wales, N. Y., Nov. 1, 1842.

Ordained and installed at Flint, Mich., by Detroit Presby., 1842;
Fentonville; Flint; Union Corners; Tuscarora, N. Y., 1851;
Romulus, 1853–5; Iowa City, Ia., 1856–61; Geneva, Wis.,
1861–7; Duquoin, Ill., 1868–70; Elkhorn, Wis., 1871–3;
Centralia, Ill., 1874; Burlington, Wis., 1875; White Hall, Ill.,
1877–9; South Pres. Ch., St. Louis, 1879–81; Genoa Junction,
Wis., 1881.

Published many articles and addresses.

ELIAS OGDEN WARD.

Born in Chatham, N. J., Feb. 5, 1810; united with the Bethany Pres. Church, May 13, 1831; graduated from Hamilton College in 1838; married to AMY EMELINE FARRAR, of Harford, Pa., Oct. 14, 1841.

Ordained and installed at Dundaff, Pa., by Presby. of Montrose, April 13, 1842; Dundaff, 1841–53; Bethany, Pa., from 1853.

SAMUEL WHALEY.

Born in Verona, N. Y., June 16, 1812; united with the Second Cong. Church in Verona, Jan. 1, 1831; graduated from Hamilton College in 1838; married to Miss SOPHIA B. DRESSER, of Goshen, Mass., Sept. 20, 1842.

Ordained at Fulton, N. Y., by Oswego Presby., Nov. 15, 1842; Vernon Centre, N. Y., 1843; Mt. Pleasant, Pa., 1846–57; Providence Ch., Scranton, Pa., 1857–68; evangelist in South and West, 1868–71; Moriches, N. Y., 1872–6; Cutchogue, from 1876.

Published "History of Mt. Pleasant," 1855.

HORACE WINSLOW.

Born in Enfield, Mass., May 18, 1814; united with the First Pres. Church in Rochester, N. Y., 1834; graduated from Hamilton College in class of 1839; Auburn, 1838–40; graduated at Union Theo. Sem., N. Y., in 1841; married to Miss CHARLOTTE H. PETTIBONE, of Simsbury, Ct., May, 1850.

Ordained and installed at New Windsor, N. Y., by North River Presby., May 25, 1842; New Windsor, 1842–3; Lansingburgh, 1843–5; Rockville, Conn., 1845–52; New Britain, 1852–8; Great Barrington, Mass., 1858–62; chaplain U. S. A., 1862; pastor at Binghamton, N. Y., 1863–8; Willimantic, Conn., 1869–81; resident in Simsbury, 1882.

HORACE HILLS, JR.

Born in Auburn, N. Y., Jan 8, 1818; united with the 2nd Pres. Church in Auburn, 1838; graduated from Union College in 1838; Auburn, 1838–40; married to Miss ELIZABETH COOPER ROBERTS, of Middletown, Conn., June 17, 1846; married to Mrs. ABBY LOUISA CRAFTS WILMOT, Nov., 1874.

Ordained Deacon in St. George's Church, N. Y., by Bishop B. T. Onderdonk, April, 1842, and advanced to the Priesthood, about a year later; St. Andrew's Church, Walden, N. Y.; Middletown, Conn.; St. Paul's, Detroit, Mich.; Glenville, Conn.; Newtown; Detroit, again; Rahway, N. J.; Stillwater, Minn.; Wabasha, Minn.; resident there since 1877.

FRANKLIN SHUMWAY HOWE.

Born in Springfield, Vt., Aug. 26, 1809; united with the Pres. Church in Riga, N. Y., 1828; studied at Oxford Acad. and Rochester Inst.; Auburn, 1838–40; studied privately; A. M.

from Marietta College in 1844; married to Miss CLARA PIER-
SON, of New York City, March 13, 1844; married to Miss
MARTHA R. STEWART, of Brooklyn, N. Y., Sept. 4, 1856.
Ordained by Presby. of Transylvania, Nov., 1840; sec. of Am.
S. S. Un., for West and South, 1840–1; Pres. Ch., Louisville,
Ky., 1841; agt., Cincinnati, O., 1844–5; 2d Pres. Church, Chilli-
cothe, 1846–50; organizing Chs., West Hoboken, 6th St., New
York, and 122d St., New York, 1851–4; Phelps, N. Y., 1855–
9; Watkins, 1859–71; Southport, 1871–9; Burdette, from 1879.
Published " Memorial of John Magee," 1870; and occasional dis-
courses.

JOHN WESLEY PRATT.   See 1850–3

WILLARD RICHARDSON.
Born in Harford, Pa., May 23, 1815; united with the Cong.
Church in Harford, 1832; graduated from Hamilton College in
1837; Auburn, Junior and Middle years; Union Sem., N. Y.;
married to Miss HARRIET ANN TYLER, of Honesdale, Pa., May
23, 1840.
Ordained at Mount Pleasant, Pa., by Montrose Presby., 1846;
prin. of Acad. at Harford, Pa., and at Bethany, Pa., 1830–54;
preached, Conklin, N. Y., 1854–64; chap. of 89th N. Y. Vols.,
1863 to close of war; Winnsboro, S. C., 1869; home miss. and
prin of " Fairfield Normal Institute "; supt of Schools, Susquehanna Co., Pa., 1854–7, and Fairfield Co., S. C., 1876–8.

GEORGE WASHINGTON SOUTHWORTH.
Entered Auburn from Prattsburg; member of Church in Amherst
Col.; graduated from Amherst College in 1838; Auburn, 1838–
40; was licentiate of the Presbytery of Bath in 1843; at which
date he suddenly disappeared.

CHARLES CLARK YOUNG.
Born in Whitestown, N. Y., about 1804; united with the Cedar
St. Pres. Church in N. Y. City, in Fall of 1832; graduated from
Union College in 1826; practiced law in N. Y. city; Auburn,
1838–40; married to Miss CHARLOTTE HUNTINGTON, of Rome,
N. Y., Apr., 1833; married to Miss ELISABETH HUNTINGTON, of
Rome, Aug., 1836; married to Mrs. MARY (BROWNELL) MOR-
GAN, of Ledyard, N. Y., May, 1841.
Never was ordained or had a field of labor in the ministry; resi-
dent in Aurora, 1841–58, in Geneva, 1858–68, and since then in
Brooklyn.

1839-42.

JOSEPH DANFORTH BAKER.
Born in Otisco, N. Y., Jan. 5, 1815; united with the Cong. Church
in Otisco, May, 1831; graduated from Amherst College in 1839;
two years at Auburn; married to Miss LUCY DEWEY, of Westfield, Mass., Sept., 1841.

Ordained and installed at Harford, N. Y., by Cortland Presby., June 8, 1842; Scipio, from 1845; Cambridge, Ill., from 1852; Malden, from 1869; Plymouth, from 1873; Danville, Iowa, from 1878.

*CHAUNCEY WALLACE CHERRY, died Oct 15, 1864.

*SPENCER SEARLE CLARKE, died Oct. 12, 1844.

*WILLIAM WELLINGTON COLLINS, died Nov. 21, 1871.

*WILLIAM SHELDON FRANKLIN, died Mar. 6, 1882.

*FRANCIS HAVEN, died Oct. 21, 1842.

*HORACE HENRY HOPKINS, died July 23, 1843.

*MORRISON HUGGINS, died Feb. 15, 1859.

WILLIAM M. LEGGETT.
Came to Auburn from Charlemont, Mass.; mem. of Church there; graduated from Union College in 1839. The Gen. Catalogues report him as tea. in Ky., and the Union Col. Gen. Cat. of 1868, as tea. in Mayfield, Ky.

CHARLES MERRITT MOREHOUSE.
Born in Charlton, N. Y.; united with the Pres. Church in 1838; graduated from Union College in 1839; married to Miss ADELINE A. AVERILLE, of Ontario, Ind., Sept. 25, 1849.
Ordained and installed at Ontario, Ind., by St. Joseph Presby., 1848; Homer, Mich., 1844-5; Maumee, O., 1845-6; Logansport, Ind., 1846-7; Ontario and Greenfield, 1848-51; Allegan, Mich., 1851-4; Baraboo, Wis., 1854-5; Evansville and vicinity, 1855-62; Sun Prairie and vic., 1863-6; Union Grove, 1867-9; resident Evansville, preaching occasionally.

ADDISON MUZZY.
Born in Dublin, N. H., Sept. 20, 1808; united with the Cong. Church in Pulaski, N. Y., 1831; graduated from Hamilton College in 1839; married to Miss LAURA ANN PEASE, of Auburn, 1843.
Ordained pastor, Bristol, O., by Presby. of Trumbull, 1843; Bristol to 1849; agt. of Am. Tr. Soc., Ill., 1850-7; since engaged in fruit and stock farming; resident in Chenoa, Ill., and elder of Church there, till 1882; resident in Ottawa, Kan.

SELDEN E. PECK.
Conditionally admitted to the Aub. Mid. class from Western The. Sem., Oct. 14, 1840.

WILLIAM JAMES SMITH.
Born in Hamburg, N. Y., Aug. 4, 1813; united with the Pres. Church about 1834; studied at Hamilton College; married to Miss HARRIET MARIA LEE, Salisbury, Conn., Aug. 6, 1843.

Ordained and installed at Mill Creek, Pa., by Erie Presby., 1844;
Mill Creek, 1843-8; Delafield, Wis., 1848-53; Sextonville,
1853-8; Osage, Iowa, 1858-66; Waukon, 1866-8; Alden,
1868-73; Prairie City, 1873-4; Newell, Sioux Rapids, &c.,
from 1874; resident Whitehall, Mich.

WILLIAM S. TAYLOR.
Born in Trumansburgh, N. Y., Feb. 14, 1815; united with the
Pres. Church in Trumansburgh, 1832; graduated from Union
College in 1838; married to Miss ELIZABETH L. VAN HORN, of
Manchester, Jan. 14, 1852; married to Miss HARRIET LEWIS,
of Monroe, Sept. 11, 1860.
Ordained at Jonesville, Mich., by Presby. of Marshall, 1844;
Jonesville, 1844-5; Manchester, 1845-8; Lodi, 1848-9; Hills-
dale, 1850-3; agt. of Am. S. S. Un., Detroit, 1854-63; Peters-
burgh, from 1863.

GEORGE NELSON TODD.
Born in Marcellus, N. Y., Apr. 3, 1810; united with the Cong.
Church in Marcellus, 1831; graduated from Hamilton College
in 1839; married to Miss MARY ELLIOTT, of Clinton, Apr. 25,
1842; married to Mrs. ELIZABETH (HURLBUT) HORTON, of
Arkport, Oct. 6, 1875.
Ordained at Phœnix, N. Y., by Presby. of Oswego, 1844; Phœnix;
Ararat and Gibson, Pa., to 1853; Dundaff, 1854-5; Susque-
hanna, 1856-58; Maine and Union Centre, N. Y., 1859-62;
Candor, 1863-8; Bridgeville, Del., 1869-70; Delta, O., 1871-3;
Arkport, N. Y., from 1874.

*TOWNSEND WALKER, died July 31, 1873.

RUFUS A. WHEELOCK.
Came to Auburn from Mannsville; member of the Church there;
graduated from Oneida Inst.; Lysander, N. Y., 1850; Sand
Banks, 1854; Orwell, 1855; Champion, 1856-8; Deer River,
1860-6; Pulaski, 1867; Danby, 1868-9; Mott's Corners,
1870-3; Island Pond, Vt., 1875-8; resident Mannsville, N. Y.

JAMES BALLINTINE.
Born in Lancaster, Pa., Jan. 27, 1810; united with the Pres. Church
in 1828; studied in Geneva, and in Rochester; Auburn, 1839-
41; Princeton, 1841-2; married to Miss SARAH RIPLEY, of
Seneca, N. Y., 1845; married to Miss MARIETTA BRISTOL, of
Gates, N. Y., 1850.
Ordained and installed at Gates, N. Y., by Presby. of Rochester,
1845; Gates, 1842-70; resident in Rochester.

JOHN FLANDERS.
In Auburn Jun. year, from Newburyport, Mass.; graduated from
Oneida Inst.; said to have been a poet, and to have preached
for a time in Northern N. Y.; starred in Gen. Cats. from 1850.

*MOSES SMEDLEY HAWLEY.
    Entered Auburn from Centreville; member of the Church there ;
    graduated from Hamilton College in 1839 ; Auburn, 1839–40;
    preached in St. Joseph's, Mich. ; taught in Adrian and other
    places; starred in Gen. Cat. of 1858; left a widow.

*WILLIAM P. HOTCHKISS.
    Born in Hartford, Conn., 1818; graduated from Oneida Inst.,
    1839; Union Sem., N. Y., 1839–40; Auburn, May, 1840 to
    Oct., 1841.
    Ordained (Cong.) May 11, 1843; Concord, Mich., 1841–3; Cen-
    treville, 1843–4; invalid, 1844–61 ; said to have died at San
    Francisco, Cal. His wife died before him.

ALEXANDER McLEAN.
    Came to Auburn from Brockville, U. C. ; member of Church in
    Brockville; graduated from Middlebury Col. in 1839 ; Auburn,
    1839–40; in 1850 was pastor of a Church in Pictou, C. W.

JOHN WAINWRIGHT RAY.
    Born in Norwich, N. Y., Apr. 13, 1813 ; united with the Pres.
    Church in Binghamton, Apr. 15, 1832 ; graduated from Amherst
    College in 1839 ; Union Sem., 1839–40; Auburn, 1840–1;
    Union, 1841–2 ; married to Miss MARY JANE FENSTERMAKER,
    of Dansville, N. Y., Nov. 28, 1855.
    Ordained in New York City, by 3rd Presby. of N. Y., 1842 ; Pres.
    Church, Glens Falls, 1842–5; Norwich, Conn., 1845–6 ; assist.
    sec. of Am. Ed. Soc., 1846–7 ; Oswego, N. Y., 1847–8 ; Clyde,
    1848–9 ; agt. Am. Tr. Soc., 1849–51 ; Dansville, 1851–2 ; Kala-
    mazoo, Mich., 1852–3 ; Rockville, Conn., 1853–4 ; E. Avon and
    Perry, N. Y., 1855–7 ; editor of *Aurora Beacon*, Ill., 2 years ;
    ed. of *Daily Whig and Rep.*, Quincy, 1860–1 ; Washington, D.
    C., in public service, and newspaper correspondent, 1861–4;
    ord. Deacon, by Bishop Whitehouse, and Priest, by Bishop Mc-
    Coskey, 1865 ; Tecumseh, Mich.; Westfield and Wellsville, N.
    Y. ; gen. agt. of *The Churchman*, 7 years ; in insurance business
    in Rochester.
    Published two Episcopalian Church tracts.

MUNSON S. ROBINSON.
    Born in Brutus, N. Y., May 10, 1812 ; Lane Sem., 1833–4 ; Auburn,
    1839–40; came from Weedsport; member of Church there from
    April 30, 1831 ; now living in California.

*LUCIUS ASCANIUS SWIFT, died Sept., 1849.

*CHARLES EDWIN VAN ANDEN, M. D., died Oct. 19, 1873.

*JEREMIAH WHIPPLE WALCOTT. See 1840–3.

*E. VINE WALES. See 1840–3.

ELIJAH WILSON.
    Born in Philadelphia, Pa., Nov. 19, 1811 ; united with the Ref.
    Ch., 1831 ; graduated from Rutgers College in 1838; Auburn,

1839-41; Princeton, 1841-2; married to Miss Ann Gray, of
Newcastle Co., Del., Nov. 29, 1842; married to Miss Catherine
Wilson, of Wrightsville, Pa., Dec. 15, 1853.
Ordained and installed by Presby. of Newcastle, Oct. 12, 1842;
past. Head of Christiana and Newark, Del., 1842-7; assoc. past.
Mariners' Ch., Phila., 1848-9; past. Wrightsville, Pa., 1849-52;
resident there 1852-5; Media, 1855-61; Camden, N. J., 1861-3;
Wrightsville, Pa., 1863-4; Philadelphia, 1864-6; New Brighton,
1866-75; Oakland, O., 1875-80; resident in Wrightsville, Pa.
Published "The Living Pulpit," 1881.

1840-3.

CHARLES ANDERSON.
Born in Schenectady, N. Y., Aug. 8, 1812; united with the 1st
Pres. Church in Schenectady, May, 1834; graduated from
Union College in 1840; married to Miss Charlotte L. Clary,
of Throopsville, N. Y., Sept. 9, 1844; married to Miss Jerusha
R. Bush, of Spencer, N. Y., May 27, 1874.
Ordained and installed at Sennett, N. Y., by Presby. of Cayuga,
Nov. 14, 1843; Sennett, 1842-64; Union Springs, 1864-8;
Savannah, 1868-70; Sennett again, 1870-7; Castile, 1877-8;
Ref. Ch., Owasco Outlet, from 1879.

*Lewis Benedict, died Jan. 30, 1881.

Peter Hewins Burghardt.
Born in W. Stockbridge, Mass., Sept. 8, 1809; united with the
Brick Church in Rochester, N. Y., 1833; graduated from Union
College in 1840; married to Miss Eliza Jackson Becker, of
Middlebury, N. Y., Apr. 27, 1844.
Ordained at Fentonville, Mich., by Presby. of Detroit, Jan., 1844;
Fentonville, 1 year; Northville, Mich., between 3 and 4 years;
Metuchen, N. J., about 4 years; Greenport, L. I., Cong. Ch., 1
year; at Ref. Ch., West Farms, N. Y., 4 years; Ref. Ch., Glen-
ville, 6 years; chaplain 1st U. S. Chasseurs, 1861, to close of war;
Somers, N. Y., 3 years; Painted Post, 4 years; Silver Creek, 4
years; at Washington, D. C., in Treasury Department, and
supplying Hyattsville Pres. Ch., from 1876.

*Darwin Chichester, died Jan. 11, 1876.

Oliver Perry Conklin.
Born in Genoa, N. Y., Apr., 1814; united with the Cong. Church
in West Aurora, N. Y., 1831; graduated from Hamilton College
in 1840; married to Miss Samantha Ann Knox, of Vernon,
N. Y., Oct., 1843.
Ordained and installed at Brownville, by Presby. of Watertown,
1845; Brownville and Dexter, 1843-8; Berkshire, 1848-56;

Ovid, 1856-61; Berkshire again, 1861-6; Whitney's Point, 1866-9; Charlotte, 1869-73, and still resident there.

JONATHAN COPELAND.

Born in Smithville, N. Y., Feb. 20, 1816; united with the 3rd Pres. Church in Rochester, N. Y., Fall of 1837; graduated from Union College in 1841; married to KEZIAH CLARK, of Nisha-yuna, N. Y., Jan. 30, 1844.

Ordained and installed at Holly, N. Y., by Presby. of Rochester, Nov., 1843; Holly, 1843-59; Champlain, N. Y., 1859-67; Waterbury, Vt., 1867-75; Webster, N. Y., from 1876.

Published occasional sermons.

*RUFUS SPAULDING CUSHMAN, D. D., died May 18, 1877.

JOHN VINSON DOWNS.

Born in Pleasant Valley, N. Y., Oct. 8, 1807; united with the Pres. Church in Seneca Falls, N. Y., Fall of 1832; graduated from Hamilton College in 1840; married to Miss ELIZABETH PERKINS, of Barrington, Ill., Nov. 3, 1848.

Ordained in Chicago, Ill., by Ottawa Presby., Spr. of 1844; Dun-dee, 1844-8; Richmond, 1849-51; Va. Settlement, 1852 and 1859-62; Crystal Lake, 1853-5; Thornton's Station, 1863; resident in Elgin.

ANDREW JACKSON FENNELL, D. D.

Born in Ira, Rutland Co., Vt., June 21, 1815; united with the Cong. Church in W. Rutland, Vt., Jan., 1831; studied at Castle-ton Seminary, several years; A. M. from Middlebury College in 1847; D. D. from same, 1878; married to Miss RACILLIA AU-GUSTA HACKLEY, of Herkimer, N. Y., Oct. 18, 1843.

Ordained by Rutland Association, Sept. 22, 1844; acting pastor of Cong. Ch. in East Groton, N. Y., 1843-6; pastor of Pres. Ch. of Glen's Falls, N. Y., 1846-82.

*GUSTAVUS LEMUEL FOSTER, died Sept. 9, 1876.

CHARLES ROBINSON FRENCH.

Born in Plainfield, Conn., Nov. 1, 1818; united with the Pres. Church in Fredonia, N. Y., 1833; graduated from Oberlin Col-lege in 1840; married to Miss MARTHA IRENE WELLER, of Wilmington, Ill., Dec. 25, 1847; married to Miss SARAH DELIA HYDE, of Lima, Ia., May 18, 1856.

Ordained by Beloit Convention, 1844; home miss. in Ill., 8 years; Monroe, Hadley, Udina; Barton, Wis., 1852-7; Clermont, Ia., 1858-67; Montrose, 1868-9; Grundy, 1870-5; Hopkinton, 1876; Jesup, 1877; Independence, 1878-80; resident in Lewis.

ALBERT HALL GASTON.

Born in Lenox, N. Y., Feb. 1, 1812; united with the 1st Pres. Ch. in Smithfield, N. Y., March, 1825; studied at Whitestown and Cazenovia Seminaries, 4 years; married to Miss MARIA C. PARMELEE, of Cazenovia, Sept. 2, 1843.

Ordained at Three Rivers, Mich., by Kalamazoo Presby., Jan. 17, 1844; Three Rivers, 1843-6; Barre, N. Y., 1846-51; Manlius, 1851-4; Canastota, 1854-6; Hastings, Mich., 1856-63; Princeville, 1863-6; Cassopolis, 1866-71; Burr Oak, 1872-8; Clayton, 1878-82; Marlette, 1882.

JEDIDIAH MILLS GILLETTE.
Born in Rome, N. Y., Apr. 12, 1817; united with the Pres. Church in Rome, N. Y., at age of 14; graduated from Hamilton College in 1838; married to Miss MARY HART ALLEN, of Brockport, N. Y., Aug. 12, 1844.
Ordained and installed at Painsville, O., by Presby. of Geauga, Summer of 1845; Painsville to 1853; Ashtabula, 1854-66; Erie, Pa., 1867-8; Union City, 1869-75; Kane, 1875-8; Ridgway, 1878-81; resident at Kane.

*AMOS DELOS GRIDLEY, D. D., died Oct. 23, 1876.

*LEMUEL WOODRUFF HAMBLIN, died Oct. 12, 1846.

*GROSVENOR WILLIAMS HEACOCK, D. D., died May 6, 1877.

THOMAS MOREY HODGMAN.
Born in Stillwater-on the-Hudson, Jan. 17, 1820; united with the Cong. Church in 1835; graduated from Union College in 1840; married to Miss MARY HURLBUT, of Arkport, N. Y., Sept. 10, 1844.
Ordained and installed at Perry Centre Cong. Ch., N. Y., by Presby. of Genesee, Jan. 10, 1849; Hornellsville, 1843-5; Port Byron, 1845-8; Perry Centre, 10 years from 1848; York, 8 years; Byron, 7 years from 1866; Corfu, (residing at Batavia) a year and a half; Knowlesville, 1874-81; resident in Rochester.
Published a few addresses and sermons.

TIMOTHY DWIGHT HUNT.
Born in Rochester, N. Y., Mar. 10, 1821; united with the 1st Pres. Church in Rochester; graduated from Yale College in 1840; married to Miss MARY HEDGES, of Newark, N. J., Nov. 1, 1843; married to Miss MARY ELIZABETH PRESTON, of Waterville, N. Y., Dec. 4, 1862; married to Miss SARAH NASH, of Marshall, Mich., Aug. 11, 1864.
Ordained at Perry, by Genesee Presby., 1843; mis. Honolulu, Sandw. Is., 1843-8; California, 1848-57; organized, in San Francisco, the first Church in the state; Ithaca, N. Y., 1858-9; Waterville, 1859-65; Niles, Mich., 1865-71; Nunda, N. Y., 1872-6; Sodus, 1876-9; Raisin, Mich., residing in Tecumseh, from 1880.
Published " Past and Present of the Sandwich Islands," 1853; and many addresses and sermons.

WILLIAM EATON KNOX, D. D.
Born in Knoxboro, N. Y., Oct. 16, 1820; united with the Cong. Church in Augusta, N. Y., 1837; graduated from Hamilton

College in 1840; D. D. from Hamilton College in 1865; married to MARY ANN CHANDLER, of Avon, N. Y., June 4, 1844; married to ALICE WOODWARD JENKS, of Toledo, Ohio, Oct. 13, 1846.

Ordained and installed at Watertown, N. Y., by Presby. of Watertown, Feb. 14, 1844; 2nd Pres. Ch., Watertown, 1844-8; Pres. Ch., Rome, 1848-70; First Pres. Ch., Elmira, from 1870.

HENRY MARTIN LANE.

Born in Aurelius, N. Y., Dec. 29, 1819; united with the Pres. Ch. in Westfield, N. Y., about 1833; graduated from Union College in 1839; married to Miss GRACE ABIGAIL SACKETT, of Buffalo, N. Y., Sept. 9, 1864.

Prevented from entering the ministry by loss of hearing; a teacher for many years; resident Jersey City, N. J.

*ALEXANDER McGLASHAN, died Sept. 9, 1867.

SAMUEL ELBERT MINER.

Born in Halifax, Vt., Dec. 13, 1815; united with the Pres. Church in Troy N. Y., 1836; graduated from Oneida Institute; married to Miss MARIA KATHARINE KELLY, of Whitestown, N. Y., Aug., 1843; married to Mrs. LUCY EVANS; married to Miss OLIVE ELECTA HAVEN.

Ordained at Whitewater, Wis., by Beloit Dist. Conv., Feb., 1844; Madison, Wis., 1843; Elkhorn, 1847; Mycena, 1852; Monroe, 1859; in business since 1860; resident in New Hampton, Mo.

SOLOMON R. SCOFIELD.

Born in Dryden, N. Y.. May 30, 1816; united with the Pres. Ch. in Dryden, March, 1831; studied at Hobart College; studied medicine 3 years; married to SARAH ELIZABETH BODLE, (widow), of Hector, N. Y., Apr. 10, 1844; married to Miss ANNA STOUGHTON STODDARD, Oct. 3, 1864.

Ordained and installed at Mecklenburg, N. Y., by Presby., 1844; Aurelius, N. Y., 1842-3; Mecklenburg, 1843-51; farming, 1851 -5; prin. and supt. of Schools, Elmira, 1855-61; Lisle, Cong. Ch., 1861-5; Greenwich, Conn., 1865-7; Pres. Ch., Delaware City, Del., 1867-75; resident Farmington, preaching occasionally from 1875-81; ed., Philadelphia, 1881.

Published "The Christian's Manual," 1850; "Easy Lessons," 1863; School Tablets, Diagrams, &c.; and many editorials on agricultural subjects.

SYLVESTER B. SHEARER.

Born in Stillwater, N. Y., 1813; united with the Pres. Church in Stillwater, about 1836; graduated from Union College in 1840; studied Theology with Rev. E. D. Maltby, 1840-1; Auburn, 1841-3; married to Mrs MARIA DECKER, of Havana, 1851.

Ordained and installed at Jefferson, (now Watkins) by Presby. of Chemung, 1846; Watkins, 10 years; since resident at Havana.

*JEREMIAH WHIPPLE WALCOTT, died Aug. 14, 1880.

*E. Vine Wales, died June 28, 1878.

*Erastus Clark Williams, died Oct. 3, 1878.

---

*Daniel Taylor Bagg.
Came to Auburn from Northampton, Mass.; member of Church in Northampton ; graduated from Union College in 1841 ; Auburn, June to Oct., 1841 ; took charge of a Cong. Church in New York City. The Un. Col. Gen. Cat. dates his death in 1848.

Daniel Clark.
Born in Williamstown, Vt. ; graduated from Dartmouth College in 1839 ; Auburn, 1840-2.
Not ordained ; was a teacher in Richmond and Philadelphia.

Isaac C. Day.
Came to Auburn from the Church in Amherst Col. ; said to have graduated from Amherst College ; perhaps the same with Isaac Day, of Amherst, class of 1841, who is reported in the Triennial of 1878 as a minister, in mercantile business, Providence, R. I.

*William Norris Edwards, died Aug. 3, 1867.

Stephen Decatur Helms.
Born in Bloomingrove, N. Y., March 6, 1815 ; united with the Pres. Church in Seneca Falls, N. Y., 1835 ; studied at Geneva Lyceum and Oberlin College ; in Auburn a few weeks of Senior year, till the death of Prof. Richards. He afterwards studied Theology at Oberlin, and labored for many years in Pres. and Cong. churches, and in editorial work ; resident of Auburn, 1879 -81 ; and in Highland, Iowa, since 1881.

Aaron C. Johnson.
Entered Auburn as mem. of 3rd Church, Newark, N. J. ; Auburn, (apparently) 1840-2 ; starred in Gen Cat. of 1858.

Erastus Martin Kellogg.
Born in Richland, N. Y., Oct. 30, 1815 ; united with the Pres. Church in Prattville, N. Y., 1829 ; graduated from Hamilton College in 1840 ; two years in Auburn ; married to Hannah Read French, of Nashua, N. H., Aug. 25, 1841.
Ordained and installed at New Haven, N. Y., by Oswego Presby., Oct. 26, 1842 ; New Boston, N. H., from 1846 ; Mason Village, from 1852 ; Lyme, from 1871 ; Manchester, N. J., from 1873.

Henry Kendall, D. D. See 1841-4.

Charles Eliphalet Lord, D. D.
Born in Portsmouth, N. H., Feb. 11, 1817 ; united with the Cong. Church in South Berwick, Me., about 1831 ; graduated from Dartmouth College in 1838 ; tea. So. Berwick, 1838-9 ; teacher Kingston, N. C., 1839-40 ; Yale Div. School ; Auburn, 1842-3 ; Union Sem., N. Y., 1843-4 ; D. D. from E. Tenn. Wesleyan

Univ. in 1870; married to Miss Eunice Elizabeth Pike, of
Newburyport, Mass., Jan. 15, 1857.
Ordained, Jonesville, Mich., by Presby., May 8, 1844; Marshall,
Mich., 1844; Niles, 1844-7; Evansville, Ind., 1 year; Cong.
Churches of Stratham, N. H., South New Market, N. H., West-
brook, Me., 2nd Cape Elizabeth, Me., one year each; Mt. Ver-
non, N. H., 1857-61; Easton, Mass., 1863-7; Chester, Vt.,
1867-9; Pres. Church, Beverly, N. J., 1869-70; professor of
Evidences of Nat. and Revealed Theol., Lay College, Brooklyn,
1873-82; also supplying Church at Pelham Manor, 1876-7.

*Cornelius Sanford Mead. See 1841-4.

Lewis Edward Sikes.
Born in Northampton, Mass., Oct. 19, 1810; united with the
Cong. Church in Brattleboro, Vt., Mar., 1834; graduated from
Union College in 1841; Auburn, Junior year; two years at
New Haven; married to Miss Lucretia Smith, of Laporte,
Ind., 1848.
Ordained at Naperville, Ill., by Fox River Union, 1846; home
miss. in Ill., 1846-59, in Mich., 1859-70, and in Kan., from
1870; resident in Vienna, Kan.

Ebenezer Tucker.
Born in Cherry Valley, N. Y., July 29, 1819; united with the
Dutch Ref. Church in Buel, N. Y., about 1839; graduated from
Oneida Inst. in 1840; at Auburn parts of 1841 and 1843; com-
pleted the course at Oberlin; A. M. from Oberlin College, about
1860; married to Lois Patchen, of North Gage, N. Y., Sept.
25, 1844.
Ordained at Oberlin, O., by Lorain Co. Assoc., 1844; at Frede-
ricktown, O., 1844 6; teaching and preaching at Nora, Ill.,
1854-9; president of Liber College, 1859-68; teaching, Union
City, Ind., 1868-9; Straight Univ., New Orleans, 1870-1;
Tougaloo Univ., Miss., 1871-3; prin. of Union Literary Inst.,
Spartansburg, Ind., 1846-54, and from 1873.

Norman Tucker.
Born in Cherry Valley, N. Y., May 1, 1814; united with the Pres.
Church in Cherry Valley, Fall of 1831; graduated from Oneida
Inst. in 1839; at Auburn, Junior and Middle years; married to
Marilla Skiff, of Cicero, N. Y., June 11, 1844.
Ordained at Troy, Mich., by Presby. of Detroit, Feb., 1844;
labored as home miss. in Mich., at Troy and Southfield, at Dear-
born and Nankin, at Wayne, at Webster, at Southfield again, at
Dearborn again, at White Lake and Springfield; health failed
in 1868; resident near Laingsburgh, Mich.

1841 4.

NATHANIEL H. BARNES.
Born in Grafton, Mass., 1816; entered Auburn, Middle class, from Ashville, N. Y.
Ordained and installed at Sinclairville, N. Y., by Council, 1850; Dowagiac, Mich., 1857–62; Kiantone, N. Y., 1862–7; Napoli, 1867–73; Portland, 1873–6; resident at Brooklyn, Mich., and now at Hillsdale, Mich.

JAMES FREDERICK CALKINS
Born in Painted Post, (now Corning) N. Y, Mar. 27, 1816; united with the Pres. Church in Corning, Spring of 1835; graduated from Union College in 1841; married to Miss MARIA LOUISA HANFORD, of Geneva, N. Y., Oct. 8, 1844.
Ordained and installed at Wellsborough, Pa., by Presby. of Pa., Sept., 1844; at Wellsboro, 1844–80; during that time, chap. in U. S. A., and for 5 years, supt. of Schools, Tioga Co., Pa.; East Avon, N. Y., from 1880.

LUTHER CONKLIN.
Born in Aurora, Erie Co., N. Y., Mar. 29, 1817; united with the Cong. Church in Griffin's Falls, 1835; graduated from Hamilton College in 1841; married to Miss ALMIRA HENSHAW, of Leicester, Mass., Nov. 19, 1844.
Ordained at Onondaga Hollow, N. Y., by Presby. of Onondaga, 1845; Liverpool, 1844–6; Moravia, 1846–51; Freeport, Me., 1851–8; East Bloomfield, N. Y., 1858–68; resident near Rochester, preaching as opportunity offers.

*DAVID HENRY HAMILTON, D. D., died July 4, 1879.

JOHN NILES HUBBARD.
Born in Angelica, N. Y., 1815; graduated from Yale College in 1839; Auburn, 1842–4.
Ordained, 1844; Hannibal, N. Y., 1844–53; Dansville, 1854–7; Friendship, 1858–9 and 1861; Belmont, 1860; Hannibal, 1862–6; Lincoln, Cal., 1867–70; Wheatland, 1872; Greyson, 1873–7; Ellis, 1878–80; Tracy, from 1881.

TIMOTHY BLOOMFIELD JERVIS.
Born in Rome, N. Y., Feb. 20, 1809; united with the Church in Rome, March, 1826; civil engineering, 1826–39; Auburn Junior and Senior years; Middle year at Union Sem., N. Y.; married to Miss HELENA M. BOGERT, of New York City, 1837; married to Miss MARY A. HAWES, of Janesville, Wis., 1867.
Ordained and installed at Taberg, N. Y., by Presby. of Oswego, 1842; Taberg; Unadilla; Richfield Spa; Oakfield; Newport, to 1858; Oriskany, 1858–64; Burr Oak, Mich., 1864; invalid for some years; Wells and Columbia, Pa., 1872–5; resident in Elmira, preaching occasionally, from 1875.

HENRY KENDALL, D. D.
Born in Volney, N. Y., Aug. 24, 1815 ; united with the Church in
Volney, about 1831 ; graduated from Hamilton College in 1840 ;
Auburn, 1840-1 and 1842-4 ; D. D. from Hamilton College in
1858 ; maried to Miss SOPHRONIA LUCE, of Buffalo, N. Y., Apr.
25, 1848.
Ordained and installed at Verona, N. Y., by Presby. of Utica, 1846 ;
Verona, 1844-8; Bloomfield, N. Y., 1848-58; Pittsburgh, Pa.,
3rd. Pres. Ch., 1858-61 ; from 1861, sec. of Pres. Bd. of Home
Missions, resident in New York. Trustee of Auburn, 1855-8.
His son was FREDERICK GRIDLEY KENDALL, of 1872-5.

CLAUDIUS BUCHANAN LORD.
Born in Nelson, N. Y., Apr. 6, 1816 ; united with the Pres. Ch.
in Nelson, 1830 ; studied at Hamilton College ; married to Miss
HENRIETTA MILLS, of Auburn, Sept. 17, 1845.
Ordained and installed at Pike, N. Y., by Buffalo Presby., 1844 ;
Pike, 1844-54 ; Springville, 1854-60; Gowanda, 1860-4; Perry
Centre, 1864-7; Athens, Pa., 1867-9 ; Rockford, E. Tenn.,
(resident at Maryville) from 1870.

ADDISON LYMAN.
Born in East Hampton, Mass., Dec. 3, 1813 ; united with the 1st
Cong. Church in East Hampton, March, 1832 ; graduated from
Williams College in 1839 ; married to Miss THERESA LYMAN,
Sept. 9, 1845 ; married to Mrs. CATHERINE A. PITKIN, of Del-
avan, Wis., Dec. 4, 1847.
Ordained by Galena Presby., May, 1847 ; Geneseo, Ill., 1845-7 ;
prin. of Geneseo Acad., 1847-54 ; Sheffield, 1854-68; Kellogg,
Iowa, 1868-70; Valley Church, 1871 ; Mitchelville and Rich-
land, 1872 ; resides in Kellogg.

SABIN McKINNEY.
Born in Binghamton, N. Y., Mar. 7, 1816; united with the 1st
Pres. Church in Binghamton, 1833 ; graduated from Amherst
College in 1841 ; Union Sem., N. Y., 1841-2 ; Auburn, 1842-4 ;
married to Miss ELIZABETH SHELDON CORLISS, of Greenwich,
N. Y., Jan. 27, 1847.
Ordained by Presby. of Tioga, April 16, 1845 ; Bath, N. Y., 1845 ;
Greenwich, 1845-7 ; past. Fredonia, 1847-51 ; Franklin, Pa.,
1851-3 ; Bergen, N. Y., 1854-7 ; health failed ; in business in
Binghamton.

*CORNELIUS SANFORD MEAD, died June 26, 1879.

JOEL WAKEMAN, D. D.
Born in Rhinebeck, N. Y., Oct. 22, 1809; united with the Pres. Ch.
in Prattsburgh, N. Y., 1832 ; studied at Academy in Pratts-
burgh ; D. D. from Alfred Univ. in 1862 ; married to Miss ABI-
GAIL T. JUDSON, of Prattsburgh, Mar. 27, 1838.
Ordained and installed at Almond, N. Y., by Angelica Presby.,
Jan., 1846 ; Almond, 1844-65; Painted Post, 1865-8; Camp-

bell, 1868-72 ; Almond, 1872-4 ; Milburn, 1874-9 ; resident in Painted Post.
Published " Satanic License," 1852 ; " The way to Jesus," 1871 ; " The Fatal Exchange," 1882.

*JAMES BROWN, died July 25, 1851.

*GUSTAVUS F. GOSS, died about Sept. 22, 1846.

*CHARLES JEROME, died May 31, 1873.

WILLIAM W. LORD, Auburn, 1841-3.

JOSIAH LYMAN.
    Born in Easthampton, Mass., Oct. 9, 1811 ; united with the Cong. Church in Easthampton, 1829 ; graduated from Williams College in 1836 ; tea. Canaan and Ithaca, N. Y., and Easthampton, Mass, 1836-41 ; Auburn, 1841-3 ; married to Miss MARY LOUISA BINGHAM, of West Cornwall, Vt., May 22, 1844.
    Never ordained, on account of failure of health ; tea. in Bristol, Conn.; Williston, Vt., and Lenox, Mass.; manufacturer of reflecting telescopes; inventor of the protracting trigonometer ; resident in Lenox, Mass.

JOSEPH RUSLING PAGE, D. D.
    Born in New Bunswick. N. J., Aug. 1, 1817 ; united with the M. E. Church at about 16 years of age ; studied at Friends' School, N. Y. City ; studied with a view to the ministry two years with Rev. Alonzo Welton ; in Seminary, 1841-3 ; D. D. from Hamilton College in 1876; married to Miss LAURA HENDERSON, of Weedsport, Oct. 18, 1843.
    Ordained at Plymouth, N. Y., by Oneida Assoc., Feb. 6, 1839 ; Plymouth, 1838-9; pastor in Perry, 1839-41, 1843-57, 1859-68 ; Cong. Ch., Stratford, Conn., 1857-9 ; fin. agt. of Ingham Univ.; East Avon, N. Y., 5 years ; Brighton, N. Y., from 1875.
    Published several pamphlets; correspondent " Wyoming " of N. Y. Evangelist.

*WILLIAM ROWLATT.
    Born in England; entered Aub. from Park Church, Buffalo ; educated as a sailor ; Auburn, 1841-3 ; married before entering ; said to have gone South; mem. of Presby. of Ottawa ; chap. of Seamen's Beth. Ch., Chicago ; mem. of Presby. of Geneva to 1849.

EBENEZER TUCKER. See 1840-3.

BENJAMIN WELLES. See 1842-5.

1842-5.

HENRY DARLING, D. D., LL. D.
    Born in Reading, Pa., Dec. 27, 1824 ; united with the 1st Pres. Church in Reading, Summer of 1838; graduated from Amherst

College in 1842 ; Union Sem., N. Y., 1842–3; Auburn, 1843–5;
D. D. from Union College in 1860 ; LL. D. from Lafayette
College, 1881 ; LL. D. from Hamilton College, 1881 ; married
to Miss JULIA STRONG, of Fayetteville. N. Y., Sept. 14, 1846 ;
married to Miss OPHELIA WELLS, of Hudson, N. Y., April 29,
1853.

Ordained and installed at Hudson, N. Y., by Presby. of Columbia,
Dec. 30, 1847; Vernon, N. Y., 1846–7; Hudson, 1847–53;
Clinton St. Ch., Phil., 1853–61 ; invalid, 1861–3 ; Fourth Pres.
Ch., Albany, N. Y., 1863–81 ; president of Hamilton College
from 1881.

Published "The Closer Walk," 1863 ; "Christian Unity "; "Doing
Nothing—but Receiving"; "Conformity to the World "; with
many pamphlets, sermons, addresses and articles. Moderator of
Gen. Assembly, 1881.

*WILLIAM RIPLEY DOWNS, died Dec. 21, 1880.

*JOHN J. GARDNER.
Graduated from Middlebury College in 1842; Aub. Sen. class
from The. Dep. of Western Reserve Col.; starred in the Auburn
Gen. Catalogue of 1853; supposed to have died 1850.

NATHANIEL DWIGHT GRAVES.
Born in Belchertown, Mass., Jan. 21, 1814; united with the Pres.
Church in Niagara Falls, Fall of 1832; graduated from Amherst
College in 1842 ; Lane Sem., 1842–3 ; Auburn, 1843–5 ; married
to Miss CORNELIA HANNAH BRADISH, of Floyd, N. Y., Sept.
2, 1845.

Ordained pastor, New York Mills, N. Y., by Presby. of Utica, Jan.,
1846 ; N. Y. Mills, 1846–9; Genoa 1st Ch., 1849–54 ; Cong. Ch.,
Allen's Grove, Wis., 1854–9 ; 2nd Cong. Ch., Beloit, 1859–67 ;
Kewanee, Ill., 1868–71 ; Pres. Ch., Kewanee, past., 1872–5;
Garden Plain from 1875.

*NATHANIEL LASELL, died Feb. 4, 1880.

NATHAN LEIGHTON.
Born in Franklin, (then Lawsville) Pa., Aug. 13, 1813 ; united
with the Pres. Church in Franklin, 1835 ; graduated from Univ.
of the City of N. Y., 1841 ; married to Miss RUTH GARDNER,
of Tunkhannock, Pa., Oct. 17, 1845.

Ordained by Presby. of Montrose, Fall of 1847 ; Moravia, N. Y.,
1845; Cuba, 1846–9; Southport, 1850; Champlain, 1850–4;
Wantage, N. J., 1854–8; Newfoundland, N. J, 1858–67, and
taught there till 1871 ; Jewett, N. Y., 1871–7 ; resident in Tunkhannock.

Published "The Bible and Pulpit for Freedom," 1858.

ALBERT PAINE.
Born in Woodstock, Ct., July 21, 1819 ; united with the Church in
E. Woodstock, 1835 ; graduated from Yale College in 1841 ; Aub.

Sen. class from Yale Div. Sch.; studied also at Andover ; married to SARAH SARGENT, of W. Amesbury, Mass , Nov. 20, 1849.

Ordained pastor, West Amesbury, by Council, 1848 ; West Amesbury to 1856 ; North Adams, 1857–62 ; Chelsea, Mass.; Beloit, Wis.; North Falmouth, Mass.; resident Charleston ; resident Roxbury, 1882.

*JOHN NETTLETON POWELL, died June 27, 1877.

CHARLES RICHARDS.

Born in Darien, Conn., Dec. 9, 1814 ; united with the Cong. Church in Darien, Nov. 6, 1831; graduated from Union College in 1841; Andover, 1841–2 ; taught, 1842–3 ; Union Sem., N. Y., 1843–4 ; Auburn, 1844-5 ; married to Miss CHRISTIANNA BROWN MC-MULDROCK, of Schenectady, N. Y., Sept. 10, 1845.

Ordained and installed at Lakeville, N. Y., by Presby. of Ontario, May 25, 1847 ; Lakeville, 1845–9; Hector, 1849–51 ; Rensselaerville, 1851–5 ; Maumee City, O., 1858–68; Pardeeville, Wis., 1868–73 ; resident South Toledo, O., from 1873.

SAMUEL NEWELL ROBINSON.

Born in North Granville, N. Y., Dec. 19, 1817 ; united with the Church in Pulaski, N. Y., Oct., 1835 ; graduated from Hamilton College in 1841; studied Theology with Rev. Alvan Cobb, 1841–2; married to Miss LUCY SARTWELL JONES, of New York, Aug. 14, 1844.

Ordained in Oswego, N. Y., by Presby. of Oswego, Feb. 12, 1851 ; Williamstown, 1844–5 ; Cabot, Vt., 1846–9 ; Truxton, N. Y., 1849–54; Whitney's Point, 1856–61 ; Guilford Centre, 1861–3 ; Springfield, 1865–8 ; North Walton, 1868–74; Sherman, 1874–6 ; Glenwood, 1879–81 ; East Hamburgh, from 1881.

*LOREN W. RUSS.

In Auburn, Middle year, from W. Bloomfield, N. Y.

Ordained by Bishop De Lancy ; Bath, N. Y.; Jordan ; Hammondsport, 1850 ; Watertown, Wis.; Lafayette, Ind., 1871 ; said to have died at Avon, N. Y.

RICHARD MARSH SANDFORD.

Born in Cheriton, Co. of Kent, England, Dec. 24, 1812 ; united with the Cong. Church in Westmoreland, N. Y., 1831 ; graduated from Hamilton College in 1842 ; married to Miss RUTH HUNGERFORD, of Vernon Centre, N. Y., Oct. 13, 1845.

Ordained at Buffalo, N. Y., by Buffalo Presby., 1846 ; at Griffin's Mills, N. Y., 1845–76 ; also at South Wales, 1862–5 ; and at E. Aurora, 1865 to the present time.

*WILLIAM HENRY SPENCER, died Feb. 17, 1861.

BENJAMIN WELLES.

Born in Wayne, N. Y., Jan. 28, 1818 ; united with the church in Wayne, July 31, 1831 ; graduated from Union College in 1841 ; entered Auburn, June, 1842, but grad. with class of 1842–5 ;

married to MARY EVELINA CROWELL, of Eddytown, N. Y.,
May 17, 1848.
Ordained at Wells and Columbia Ch., Pa., by Presby. of Pa., Nov.
2, 1847; at Wells and Columbia Ch. Pa.; Ulysses, Pa.; Arkport,
N. Y.; Bristol, Ind.; Litchfield, Mich.; Concord, Mich.; West
Creek, Ind.; Rural, Wis.; Farmington, Minn., till 1873; since
then resident at White Bear Lake, Minn.

ERWIN WHEELER ALLEN.
Born in Vernon Centre, N. Y., Nov. 20, 1814; united with the
Cong. Church in Vernon Centre, 1832; graduated from Hamil-
ton College in 1842; Auburn, 1842-3; married to Miss LAURA
HILLS ALLEN, of Northeast, Pa., May 18, 1845.
Ordained at Kirkland, O., by Council, Sept. 22, 1852; Stockbridge,
N. Y., 1843-5; Vernon Centre, 1847-8; farming and preaching,
Kirkland, O., 1849-53; Kirkland and Unionville, 1854-5; Pres.
Ch., Arkport, N. Y., 1855-9; Cong. Ch., Pitcher, N. Y., 1859-
63; Parma Centre, 1866; Stone Church, 1869; Bergen, 1870;
moved to the Pacific coast in 1872; Cong. Ch., Dayton, W. T.,
from 1877.

ARTEMAS DEAN.
Born in Cornwall, N. Y., Feb. 9, 1824; united with the Bethlehem
Pres. Church in Cornwall, March, 1839; graduated from Am-
herst College in 1842; Auburn 1842-3; Andover, 1846-8;
married to Miss EMMA CARLTON, of Chelsea, Vt., Jan., 1849.
Ordained and installed at Johnson, Vt., by Council, Feb., 1849;
Johnson, 1849-51; Newbury, 1851-7; Schenectady, N. Y.,
1859-61; 2nd Ch., Greenfield, Mass., 1861-6; Westborough,
1867-9; Ref. Ch., Owasco Outlet, N. Y., 1873-5; High Bridge,
N. J., from 1875.

*HENRY E. PECK, died July 9, 1867.

NORMAN BARBER SHERWOOD.
Born in Phelps, N. Y., Oct. 6, 1816; united with the Church in
Millville, N. Y., 1830; studied at Oneida Inst. and at Geneva,
N. Y.; Auburn, 1843-4; married to Miss AURILLA FORD, of
New Market, Ont., Aug. 12, 1845.
Ordained, 1845; Kendall, N. Y., 1844-6; Amboy, 1847-9; James-
ville, a few months; then retired, in impaired health, to a farm in
Millville; resident in Saratoga since 1876.

CHARLES WILLIAM TORREY.
Born in Canandaigua, N. Y., 1815; united with Washington St.
Pres. Church in Rochester, N. Y., 1841; graduated from Union
College in 1838; Auburn, 1842-4; studied Theology with Rev.
Luther Halsey, D. D.
Ordained at Cincinnati, O., by Presby. of Cincinnati, Oct., 1845;
agt. of A. B. C. F. M., 1845-7; Delaware, O., 1847-50; E. Cleve-
land, 1850-8; Madison, 1858-67; Collamer, 1867-75; Rich-
wood from 1877.

1843-6.

HENRY HOPKINS DOOLITTLE.

Born in Rutland, N. Y., Sept. 6, 1818; united with Pres. Church in Medina, N. Y., 1834; studied at Ontario Col. Inst., Ind.; married to Miss ROSAMOND COOPER, of Phelps, (now Oaks Corners) N. Y., Aug. 25, 1846.

Ordained at Ontario, Ind., by Presby., 1847; home miss., Leroy, Mich., 1846-7; during the years 1847-50, made several efforts at ministerial labor, but broke down in health, at each effort; entered upon the business of cultivating and improving small fruits; resident at Oaks Corners, N. Y.

Author of a manual on Raspberry Culture, and originator of the " Doolittle " Raspberry, and other varieties.

FREDERICK JOHNSON JACKSON.

Came to Auburn from Rochester; member of Washington St. Ch. there; graduated from Hamilton College in 1843; Cape Vincent, N. Y., 1849-53; Danbury, Conn., 1860-3; said to be in charge of a school in Tarrytown, N. Y.

*JAMES HATCH KASSON, died Nov. 27, 1872.

EDWARD LORD.

Born in Danby, N. Y., March 29, 1821; united with the Cong. Ch. in Danby, Feb., 1839; graduated from Williams College in 1843; married to Miss MARY JANE SANDERS, of Williamstown, Mass., Aug., 1846.

Ordained and installed at Romulus, N. Y., by Presby. of Geneva, Autumn of 1847; Romulus, 1846-52; Fulton, 1852-65, being chap. of 110th N.Y. Regt., 1 year of this time; Adams, 1865-70; Metuchen, N. J., Ref. Ch., 1870-81; resident in Danby, N. Y.

SILAS McKINNEY.

Born in Binghamton, N. Y., Nov. 2, 1818; united with the 1st Pres. Church in Binghamton, about 1831; graduated from Union College in 1842; married to FANNY M. C. NELSON, of Cortland, N. Y., Feb. 27, 1847; married to MARY C. BURT, of Binghamton, N. Y., Feb. 1, 1865.

Ordained at Binghamton, by Presby. of Tioga, 1846; missionary at Natal, S. Africa, 1847-63; Hunter, N. Y., 1867-8; S. Boston, 1869-73; Tuscarora, N. Y., 1875-9; Junius, from 1879, residing at Marengo since 1881.

HENRY ADDISON NELSON, D. D.

Born in Amherst, Mass., Oct. 31, 1820; united with the Cong. Church in Homer, N. Y., May 1, 1831; graduated from Hamilton College in 1840; D. D. from Hamilton College in 1857; married to Miss MARGARET MILLS, of Auburn, Feb. 23, 1847.

Ordained and installed at Auburn, 1st. Pres. Ch., by Presby. of Cayuga, July 29, 1846; Auburn, 1846-56; pastor in St. Louis,

Mo., 1856-68; prof. of Theology in Lane Seminary, 1868-74; pastor of 1st. Ch., Geneva, N. Y., from 1874.
Published "Seeing Jesus," 1869 ; "Sin and Salvation," 1881. Moderator of General Assembly, at Rochester, 1867.

HENRY WEBSTER PARKER.

Born in Danby, N. Y., Sept. 7, 1822 ; united with the 1st Pres. Church in Ithaca, March, 1839; graduated from Amherst College in 1843; married to Miss HELEN E. FITCH, of Auburn, Apr. 20, 1852.
Ordained and installed at Aurora, N.Y., by Presby. of Cayuga, 1847; Aurora to 1850; 1st Pres. Ch., Dansville, N. Y., 1850-2 ; Bedford Cong. Ch., and Central Cong. Ch., Boooklyn, 1852-6; North Cong. Ch., New Bedford, Mass., 1856-63; prof. of Chem. and Nat. Hist., Iowa College, 1864-70; prof. of Ment. and Mor. Sci., Agricultural College, Amherst, Mass., 1870-9; prof. Nat. Hist., Iowa Col., 1879-82 ; resident Grinnell, Iowa.
Published a volume of poems, 1850.

PORTER BROWN PARREY.

Born in Wethersfield Springs, N. Y., 1815 ; united with the Pres. Church in Weth. Spr., July, 1831 ; graduated from Union College in 1842 ; married to Miss NANCY JANE SHELDON, of Fleming, Aug. 25, 1846 ; married to CORNELIA UPSON, of Ontario, Ind., Nov. 4, 1850.
Ordained at Edwardsburg, Mich., by Presby. of St. Joseph, Sept. 29, 1847 ; Middlebury, Ind., 1846-7 ; Buchanan, Mich., 1847-52 ; New Buffalo, 1852-3 ; Ellsworth, Conn., 1853-7 ; Seward, Ill., 1857-65 ; Three Oaks, Mich., 1865-70, and 1872-9 ; Hersey, 1870-2 ; Bridgeman and Coloma, 1879-82.

PARSONS STEWART PRATT.

Born in Sanquoit, N. Y., July 25, 1822 ; united with the Cong. Church in Westmoreland, N. Y., Spring of 1836 ; graduated from Hamilton College in 1842 ; married to Miss MARTHA A. POLLARD, of Clinton, N. Y., July 22, 1846.
Ordained at Edwardsburg, Mich., by Presby. of St. Joseph, Sept. 29, 1847 ; Sumption's Prairie, Ind., 1846-7 ; Niles, Mich., 1847-8 ; Winfield, N. Y., 1848-55 ; Dorset, Vt., from 1856.

*JOHN HARRIS SAGE, died Feb., 1851.

SAMUEL TAYLOR SEELYE, D. D.

Born in Bethel, Conn., Oct. 24, 1822 ; united with the Church in W. R. College, 1838 ; graduated from Western Reserve College in 1843 ; first two years in Theological department of W. R. College ; last year at Auburn ; D. D. from Hamilton College in 1860 ; married to MARIA C. GAYLORD, of Poughkeepsie, N. Y., Apr. 5, 1848.
Ordained and installed at Wolcottville, Conn., by Litchfield North Consoc.,June 17,1846 ; Wolcottville, 1846-55 ; 4th Pres. Church,

Albany, N. Y., 1855–63; Payson Cong. Ch., East Hampton, Mass., from 1863, 13 years ; resident at East Hampton.

ADDISON KELLOGG STRONG, D. D.

Born in Aurora, N. Y., Mar. 27, 1823 ; united with the Church in Clinton, N. Y., 1838 ; graduated from Hamilton College in 1842 ; D. D. from Hamilton College in 1869 ; married to Miss MATILDA E. CLARK, of Spencer, N. Y., Sept. 9, 1846 ; married to Miss MADORAH J. ELDER, of Cortland, N. Y., Oct. 10, 1849.

Ordained and installed at Otisco, N. Y., by Presby. of Onondaga, Dec., 1846 ; Otisco, 1846–55 ; Monroe, Mich., 1855–63 ; for 10 months of that time chaplain of 7th Mich. Vols. ; Galena, Ill., 1863–6 ; Park Ch., Syracuse, 1866–70 ; Pine St. Ch., Harrisburg, Pa., 1870–4 ; 1st Pres. Ch., Kalamazoo, Mich., 1874–6 ; Clyde, N. Y., 1877–9 ; Hoboken, N. J., 1879–82.

EDWARD TAYLOR, D. D.

Born in Lee, Mass., Oct. 6, 1821 ; united with the Church in Williams College, July, 1842 ; graduated from Williams College in 1842 ; D. D. from Olivet College in 1869 ; married to Miss JANE GASTON WOOD, of Aurora, N. Y., Oct. 6, 1847.

Ordained and installed at Hinsdale, Mass., by Council, Feb., 1847 ; Hinsdale, 1847–50 ; John St. Pres. Ch., Lansingburgh, N. Y., 1850–6 ; Kalamazoo, Mich., Cong. Ch., 1856–63 ; South Cong. Ch., Brooklyn, N. Y., 1863–7 ; Binghamton Cong. Ch., 1868–77 ; resident in Binghamton ; acting pastor of Ch. at Norwich, from 1880.

WILLIAM WALLACE WILLIAMS, D. D.

Born in Vernon, N. Y., Oct. 25, 1821 ; united with the Pres. Ch. in Vernon, 1839 ; graduated from Amherst College in 1843 ; D. D. from Hamilton College in 1872 ; married to ANNA E. JEROME, of Camillus, N. Y., Dec. 18, 1849.

Ordained and installed at Camillus, N. Y., by Presby., Feb., 1848 ; Camillus, 1848–53 ; pastor Toledo, O., from 1853.

MORGAN LEROY WOOD.

Born in Amsterdam, N. Y., May 8, 1820 ; united with the Cong. Church in Kingsboro, N. Y., 1839 ; graduated from Union College in 1842 ; Auburn to May 28, 1846 ; married to Miss ELIZABETH WAKEMAN, of Saratoga Co., N. Y., 1847 ; married to Miss MARY WAKEMAN, of Farmersburg, Ia., 1857.

Ordained by Otsego Presby., Apr. 24, 1850 ; Conklin, N. Y., 1848 ; Ludlowville, 1850 ; Tribes Hill, 1853 ; Limestone, Ill., 1859 ; Carrollton, 1862–9 ; Greenfield, 1869–75 ; suffering from loss of voice, 1875–80 ; Belle Plaine, Kan., 1881.

———

ASA ADAMS. See 1844–7.

WILLIAM WEBSTER BELDEN, D. D.

Born in Moscow, N. Y., June 25, 1821 ; united with the 3rd Cong. Church in Hartford, Conn., Mar. 1, 1837 ; graduated from Mun-

son Acad., Mass. ; A. M. from College at Worcester, Mass., 1852 ; D. D. from College of Western Va., 1873 ; Auburn, 1843-5 ; Yale, 1845-7 ; married to Miss ELIZABETH PASSMORE TABOR, of Smithfield, R. I., Aug., 1852.
Ordained pastor, Orange, Conn., by Council, Aug. 23, 1849 ; Orange, 1849-54 ; Palmer, Mass., 1855-6 ; Fitchville, Conn., 1856-60 ; Attleboro, Mass., 1860-5 ; Gardner, 1867-9 ; Bristol, Conn., 1869-73 ; Newburyport, Mass., 1875-7 ; Gloversville, N. Y., Pres. Ch., 1877-8 ; Jordan, 1879-80 ; Guilderland, 1881.

*ASAHEL LYON BROOKS, died Sept. 16, 1879.

GEORGE BUSHNELL, D. D.
Born in Washington, Conn., Dec. 13, 1818 ; united with the Cong. Church in New Preston, Conn., 1832 ; graduated from Yale College in 1842 ; Auburn, 1843-5 ; Yale Div. Sch. ; D. D. from Beloit College in 1879 ; married to Miss MARY ELISABETH BLAKE, of New Haven, Conn., May 21, 1851.
Ordained and installed at Worcester, Mass., by Council, Dec. 3, 1848 ; Worcester, 1848-58 ; Waterbury, 1858-65 ; 1st Cong. Ch., Beloit, Wis., from 1865.

JAMES H. CAPON.
Admitted to Jun. Class, Oct., 1843 ; member of Church in Quality Hill, N. Y. ; not long in the Sem., and never catalogued.

ALEXANDER DICK.
Born in Bathgate, Scotland, July 15, 1818 ; united with the Free Baptist Church in Lanark, Ont., 1836 ; graduated from Hamilton College in 1843 ; at Auburn, 1843-4 ; afterwards in Theo. Dept. of Whitestown Sem. ; married to Miss FRANCES ANNA GLEASON, of Kirkland, N. Y., Sept. 26, 1844.
Ordained and installed at Varysburgh, N. Y., by Com. of Genesee Quar. Meet. of Free Baptists, Dec. 28, 1845 ; seven pastorates in N. Y., Canada W., and O. ; 12 years in educational work ; editor of *Law and Gospel Tribune*, Buffalo, N. Y.

HORACE LYMAN.
Born in East Hampton, Mass., Nov. 15, 1815 ; graduated from Williams College in 1842 ; dismissed from Auburn, Oct. 17, 1845 ; studied at Andover ; married to Miss MARY DENISON, of Castleton, Vt., Oct., 1848.
Ordained at Castleton, (Cong.) Oct., 1848 ; Portland, Or., 1848-54 ; Dallas, 1854-7 ; prof. of Math. in Pacific Univ. from 1857.

*MONTGOMERY MORGAN WAKEMAN, died Sept. 11, 1876.

1844-7.

ASA ADAMS.
Came to Auburn from Franklin, Ia. ; member of Church in W. Res. Col. ; graduated from Union College in 1843 ; Auburn,

1843-4 and 1845-7 ; said to be a lawyer, residing at Bloods,
near Cohocton, N. Y.

HON. JOSIAH BUSHNELL GRINNELL.
  Born in New Haven, Vt., Dec. 22, 1821 ; united with the Church
  in 1841 ; graduated from Oneida Inst. in 1843 ; Auburn, 1845-
  7 ; married to Miss JULIA ANN CHAPIN, of Springfield, Mass.,
  Feb. 5, 1852.
  Ordained and installed at Greenwich, N. Y., (Cong.) 1848 ; Greenwich ; Union Village, 4 years ; Washington, D. C., 1 year ;
  N. Y. City ; voice failed ; founder and president of Grinnell
  Univ., now Iowa College ; State Senator of Iowa, 4 years ;
  author of Iowa Free School law ; member of Congress 4 years ;
  resident, Grinnell, Iowa.

*WM. HOLLISTER GUERNSEY, died April 7, 1850.

WILLIAM GREEN HUBBARD.
  Born in Marshall, N. Y., Sept. 6, 1814 ; united with the Church in
  Panama, N. Y., Dec. 31, 1837 ; graduated from Hamilton
  College in 1844 ; married to L. AMELIA GLEASON, of Clinton,
  N. Y., Oct. 7, 1847.
  Ordained and installed at Summerhill, N. Y., by Cortland Presby.,
  Mar. 13, 1850 ; Meridian, 1847-9 ; Summerhill, 1849-56 ; Dryden,
  1856-60 ; Wilson, 1860-7 ; Schoolcraft, Mich., 1867-9 ; Millville,
  N. Y., 1869-71 ; Barre Centre, 1871-6 ; Mendon, 1876-81 ;
  Parma Centre, 1881.

*ANDREW PHILLIPS, died Oct. 21, 1880.

JOB PIERSON, D. D.
  Born in Schaghticoke, N. Y., Feb. 3, 1824 ; united with the Church
  in Williams College 1842 ; graduated from Williams College in
  1842 ; D. D from Olivet College, 1881 ; married to Miss RACHEL
  W. SMITH, of Geneva, N. Y., Feb. 7, 1849.
  Ordained and installed at Pittsford, N. Y., by Presby. of Rochester,
  Feb. 12, 1851 ; Corning, N. Y., 1847-9 ; Pittsford, 1850-6 ; Victor, 1856-63 ; Kalamazoo, Mich., 1863-8 ; Ionia, Mich., 1868-
  78 ; resident in Ionia, engaged in literary labor.

*WILLIAM WILTSHIRE ROBINSON, died Nov. 14, 1850.

*LYMAN BYLES WALDO, M. D., died July 9, 1879.

*WILLIAM FREDERICK WILLIAMS, D. D., died Feb. 14, 1871.

---

*HENRY BALCH.
  Entered Seminary from the Church in Harwinton, Conn. ; studied
  at Western Reserve ; at Auburn two months ; one year at Lane ;
  was a bookseller at Meadville, Pa., where he died, 1865.

CHARLES LITTLE.

Born in Columbia, Ct., 1818; united with the Church in March, 1841; graduated from Yale College in 1844; two years at Auburn, and third year at Yale; married to CORNELIA MARY NEWTON, of Sherburne, N. Y., Sept. 29, 1847; married to SUSAN ROBBINS of Brockport, N. Y., Sept. 15, 1853.

Ordained at Columbia, Ct., by Council, Sept. 1, 1847; missionary in Madura, India, 1847–59; Manlius, N. Y., about 1 year; Cheshire, Conn., 1862–5; Woodbury, 1865–7; Lincoln, Neb., 1868–70; editor at Crete, Neb., 1872; Corning, Iowa, 1874–5; Lewis, from 1875.

*HENRY VAN VLECK RANKIN, died July 2, 1863.

1845-8.

PHILOS GUNICOS COOK.

Born in Constable, N. Y., Aug. 10, 1807; united with the Am. Pres. Church in Montreal, Can., March, 1827; graduated from Middlebury College in 1833; tea., mostly in Buffalo, N. Y., 1833–45; married to Miss CLARISSA COLUMBIA TOTTINGHAM, of Pittsford, Vt., Oct. 16, 1840.

Ordained and installed at Ludlowville, N. Y., by Presby. of Ithaca, Nov. 15, 1851; chap. of State Pris., Auburn, 1848–51; Pres. Ch., Ludlowville, 1851–6; agt. of Am. S. S. Un., for Western N. Y., 1856–9; city and Beth. miss., Buffalo, 1859–62 and 1865–74; chap. of 94th N. Y. Vet. Vols., 1862–5; Wells St. Pres. Ch., Buffalo, and city miss., 1874–82.

ALBERT H. CORLISS.

Came to Auburn from the Church in Union Village; Auburn, 1846–8.

Ordained and installed at Western, N. Y., by Presby. of Utica, Oct. 3, 1849; Western, to 1852; Marshall, 1852–4; Holland Patent, 1854–70; Lima, 1870–5; Waterville, 1875–82; resident in Utica.

RUSSELL SEARLE EGGLESTON.

Born in Westfield, Mass., Sept. 17, 1816; united with the Cong. Church in W. Springfield, Mass., 1842; married to ELIZABETH TROWBRIDGE, of North East, N. Y., Nov. 6, 1850.

Ordained at Dryden, N. Y., by Council, Oct., 1849; at Dryden, 1848–52; Moravia, N. Y., 1853–5; Madison, O., 1855–9; Greens Farms, Ct., 1859–61; Knowlesville, N. Y., 1861–6; Pompey, 1866–9; Gaines, 1869–76; resident at Gaines.

*GEORGE LYMAN HALL, died Oct. 20, 1857.

*LOREN EATON HAVEN, died July 23, 1849.

JAMES HERVEY JEROME.

Born in Pompey, N. Y., Oct. 23, 1818; united with the Pres.
Church in Pompey, July 6, 1845; studied at Pompey and Homer
Academies; married to Miss MARY ANN CLAPP, of Pompey,
1849; married to Miss LOUISA GREEN, of Cazenovia, 1877.
Preached only a few months; not ordained; resident in Lincoln,
Neb.

CALVIN SPRAGUE SHATTUCK.

Born in Springfield, Mass., Sept. 8, 1822; united with the Olivet
Cong. Church in Springfield, March, 1842; graduated from
Oneida Institute, 1845; Middle year in Lane Seminary; Junior
and Senior years at Auburn; married to Miss ANTOINETTE
BRADSHAW, of Newark, N. Y., Nov. 2, 1859.

Ordained at Center Lisle, N. Y., by Council, Oct. 11, 1849; Groton,
N. Y., 1848-9; Greenwich, 1850-60; Farmington, Pa., 1860-3;
Emerald Grove, Wis., 1863-7 and 1868-70; missionary in
Southwest, 1867-8 and 1870-4; Millville, N. Y., 1874; North
Adams, Mich., to 1882; Litchfield, Mich.

FRANCIS VOLNEY WARREN.

Born in Eden, N. Y., April 18, 1820; united with the Cong.
Church in Eden, April, 1836; studied at Austinburg, O., and
Eden, N. Y.; married to Miss HARRIET NEWEL THOMAS, of
Angelica, June 16, 1849.

Ordained at Bellona, N. Y., by Presby. of Geneva, in 1852;
Angelica, 1848-9; Hopewell, 1849-52; Pulteney, 1852-9;
Wampsville, 1859-64; Wattsburg, Pa., 1864-74; has since
supplied at Fairview, Pa., and Angelica, N. Y., for short
periods; resident at Angelica.

ALANSON THORP WOOD.

Born in Junius, N. Y., Oct. 25, 1816; united with the Pres.
Church in Allen, N. Y., 1834; graduated from Mission Inst.,
Quincy, Ill., 1844; married to Miss CAROLINE SUSAN JUDSON,
of Prattsburgh, N. Y., 1849; married to Mrs. HARRIET PLUMB
HUNTER, of Nevinville, Iowa.

Ordained and installed at West Unity, O., by Maumee Presby.,
1850; West Unity to 1855; Bryan and Farmer; Cohocton, N.
Y., 1857; Branchport, 1858-9; Winslow, Ill., 1860-5; Kendall,
1865-6; Olivet, Iowa; Tecumseh, Falls City, Helena, Neb.;
Beloit, Kan.; resident in Helena, Neb.

DAVID BARR.

Came to Auburn from Niagara, C. W.; member of Church in
Toronto; graduated from Queen's College in 1844; left Jan.
28, 1847; Senior year at Princeton; the Princeton Catalogue
says that he was born in Scotland, and is an Episcopalian.

CHALON BURGESS. See 1846-9.

HIRAM PARKER CROZIER.

Born in Covington, N. Y., Sept. 1, 1823; united with the Cong. Church in Hume, Winter of 1842; studied at Oberlin College 16 months; Auburn, to March, 1846; married to Miss DELIA BETHIAH SMITH, of Pike, Oct. 1, 1847.

Ordained by Whitesboro Assoc.; Dryden Pres. Ch., 1845–7; Peterboro, 1847–8; Huntington, N. Y., 1858–64; resident Brooklyn, N. Y., in business.

*RICHARD SALTER STORRS DICKINSON, died Aug. 28, 1856.

JAMES DOUGLASS. See 1847–50.

PHILANDER GRIFFIN. See 1846–9.

LUTHER CALVIN HALLOCK.

Born in Smithtown, L. Is., May 23, 1816; united with the Christian Church in N. Y. City, 1833; studied at Miller's Place Acad.; Auburn, 1845–6; Union Sem., 1846–8; married to Miss FANNY KATE TUTHILL, of Wading River, L. I., July 30, 1849.

Ordained at Wading River by Consoc. of Long Island, Dec. 8, 1848; Wading River, 1847–52; Charleston, S. C., 1852–3; John's Island, 1854–5; Comac, L. I., 1856–7; health failed; farming, preaching occasionally, and conducting services for the Rocky Point branch of the Mount Sinai Con. Ch.; resident in Rocky Point, L. I.

*ROBERT HUNTER, died March 11, 1872.

SAMUEL LEWIS MERRELL.

Born in Utica, N. Y., Aug. 13, 1822; united with the First Pres. Church in Utica, Aug. 31, 1837; graduated from Williams College in 1845; Auburn, 1845–7; Princeton, 1847–8; married to Miss CORNELIA ELISABETH HALE, of Knoxboro, N. Y., June 1, 1853.

Ordained and installed at Norwich Corners, N. Y., by Oneida Assoc., Jan. 8, 1850; Norwich Corners, 1850; Sangerfield, 1851; Remsen and Alder Creek, 1852–4; Pres. Ch., Martinsburgh, 1854–7; Cape Vincent, 1857–61; chaplain 35th Reg. N. Y. V. 1861–3; Theresa, 1863–7; Lysander, 1867–75; resident at Sacket's Harbor, 1875–81; Camden, Ark., 1881.

EDWARD BROWN WALSWORTH, D. D.

Born in Cleveland, O., 1818; came to Auburn from Church in Palmyra; graduated from Union College in 1844; Auburn, 1845–7; Union Sem., N. Y., 1847–8; D. D. in 1867.

Ordained by Presby., Sept. 27, 1848; E. Avon, N. Y., 1848–52; Marysville, Cal., 1852–61; Oakland, Cal., 1861–4; pres. Pacific Fem. Col., Oakland, Cal., 1864–72; past. Albion, N. Y., from 1872.

GEORGE G. WICKSON, LL. D.

Came to Auburn from Toronto, Can.; member of Church there; dismissed Sept. 16, 1846; said to have been professor in Seminary at Toronto, and to be residing in Lyons, N. Y.

1846-9.

NATHAN BOSWORTH.

Born in Pharsalia, N. Y., Jan. 12, 1819; united with the Cong. Church in Pharsalia, 1836; graduated from Hamilton College in 1846; married to ELIZABETH BURT BODMAN, of Williamsburgh, Mass., 1849.

Ordained and installed at Champion, N. Y. by Black River Assoc., 1851; Verona, 1849-50; Champion, 1850-3; Lowville, 1853-7; Fairport, 1857-64; Pompey Hill, 1864-6; Holley, 1866-8; Hopewell, 1868-70; Williamson, 1870-4; Dundee from 1874.

CHALON BURGESS.

Born in Silver Creek, N. Y., June 24, 1817; united with the Pres. Church in Silver Creek, July, 1838; graduated from Hamilton College in 1844; at Auburn, 1845-6 and 1847-9; married to Miss EMMA J. JOHNSTON, of Ovid, N. Y., June 2, 1853.

Ordained at Dunkirk, N. Y., by Buffalo Presby., 1856; Little Valley, 11 years; Panama, 15 years, preaching also at Ashville, 5 years of this time; Silver Creek, from 1875.

Published many sermons.

SAMUEL MINOR CAMPBELL, D. D.

Born in Campbelltown, N. Y., June 1, 1823; united with the Pres. Church in Campbelltown, April, 1841; studied at Franklin Academy, Prattsburg, and privately; A. M. from Hamilton College, 1855, and D. D. from Hamilton, 1864; married to SOPHIA L. BURTON, of Prattsburgh, N. Y., Sept. 18, 1845; married to Mrs. MARY B. JUDSON, of Prattsburgh, May 1, 1878.

Ordained and installed at Paris Hill, N. Y., by Oneida Assoc., Nov., 1850; Alder Creek, 1849-50; Paris Hill, 1850-7; Dansville, 1857-8; Westminster Ch., Utica, 1858-66; Central Ch., Rochester, 1866-81; First Pres. Ch., Minneapolis, Minn., 1881.

Published "Across the Desert, a life of Moses." 1872; "The Story of Creation," 1877.

*JUSTUS DOOLITTLE, died June 15, 1880.

*SIMEON SARTWELL GOSS, died May 25, 1865.

PHILANDER GRIFFIN.

Born in Warren, N. Y., April 21, 1818; united with the Pres. Church in Little Lakes, Warren, about 1835; graduated from Union College in 1845; entered Aub. 1845, grad. 1849; married to Mrs. MARY MARIA PARKHERST, of Chicago, Ill., April 5, 1851.

Ordained at St. Catherines, Canada, by Buffalo Presby., June 10, 1857; chaplain among sailors and boatmen, Chicago, Ill., 2 years; for Bethel Soc., in Buffalo, N. Y., 11 years; Carlton Pres. Ch., 6 years; Middlefield Centre, 4 years; Otego, 3 years; Guilford Centre, from 1875.

*THOMAS HAZLETT, died Jan 22, 1849.

ISAAC NEWTON HURD.

> Came to Auburn from Aurora; member of Church there ; married to Miss REBECCA L. HUDSON.

> Big Flat, N. Y., to 1851 ; miss., Arcot, India, 1851–7 ; Chintadrepettah, 1857–9 ; Colchester, N. Y., 1860–3 ; Red Bluff, Col., 1864–7 ; San Francisco, Cal., 1867–9; Carson City, Nev., 1870–1 ; Virginia City, 1872–5 ; Oakland, Cal., 1876 ; Menlo Park, 1877–80 ; Tucson, Arizona, 1881 ; Hollister, Cal., 1882.

JEREMIAH PETRIE.

> Born in Herkimer, N. Y., July 16, 1825 ; united with the Pres. Church in Schenectady, 1842 ; graduated from Union College in 1846 ; married to Miss ELIZABETH AGAR, of Penn Yan, June 13, 1852.

> Ordained and installed at Dresden, N. Y., by Presby. of Geneva, Fall of 1849 ; Dresden, 1849–52 ; Volney, 1852–6 and 1868–72 ; Cleveland, 1856–8 ; Westmoreland, 1859–63; Herkimer. Ref. Ch., 1864–8 ; Pompey, from 1872.

*FREDERICK STARR, JR., died Jan. 8, 1867.

---

*NATHANIEL POTTER COLTRIN, died Dec. 26, 1877.

ABIJAH BARNUM DUNLAP.

> Born in Ovid, N. Y., Aug. 29, 1810 ; united with the Church in Yale College, 1831 ; graduated from Yale College in 1833 ; Auburn, 1846–8 ; married to Miss MARY ANN WRIGHT, of LeRoy, N. Y., June 29, 1853.

> Ordained at Lima, Mich., by Council, Oct. 31, 1849 ; Rose Valley, N. Y., 1848 ; Saline, Mich., 1849–50 ; Ovid, N. Y., 1850–3 ; prof. of Languages and Mor. Phil., Ingham Univ., 1853–4; prin., Jonesville, 1854–5 ; prof. of Lang. and Mor. Phil., Elmira College, 1855–8 ; eyes failed; farmer, Traverse City, Mich., from 1863.

*ALBERT MANDELL. See 1849–52.

FREDERICK SCHWARTZ JEWELL, Ph. D.

> Born in Elliott Mission Station, Mo., Jan. 23, 1821 ; united with the Pres. Church in Penville, Tompkins Co. ; studied at Groton and Munro Academies; Auburn from Dec., 1846, to some time in 1849; A. M. from Amherst College in 1851 ; Ph. D. from Lafayette College in 1869 ; married to Miss JULIA ADELAIDE CHAPIN, of Springfield, Mass., Jan. 27, 1854.

> Ordained by Presby. of Ithaca, 1849 ; Cincinnatus, N. Y., 1849–51 ; Morrisville, 1854; tea. Schuylkill Haven, Pa., 1852 ; prof. in Normal Sch., Albany, N. Y., 1854–69 ; preached, Greenbush, 1870–3 ; ord. Dea. by Bishop Doane (Prot. Ep.) March 1, 1874, and Priest., Dec. 20, 1874; St. James Ch., Winsted, Conn., 1875–8 ; Canon in Cathedral, Fond du Lac., Wis., 1878–80; St. Mark's Ch., Evanston, Ill., from 1880.

THOMAS M. McENTEE.
 Auburn, 1846-7; became a lawyer and traveling man; has a family; lives in California.

RICHARD OSBORNE.
 Came to Auburn from Church in Union Village; graduated from Union College in 1846; dismissed Nov. 29, 1847.
 Ordained and installed at Mannsville, N. Y., by Black River Consociation, 1853; Mannsville, 1852-5; Sandy Creek, 1856-61; Colerain, Mass., 1862; Union Village, 1863; Champion, 1864-6; resident Saratoga, from 1877.

1847-50.

*CHARLES LUTHER ADAMS, died Oct. 23, 1852.

*NATHAN ALLEN, died Oct 29, 1864.

SIDNEY HAVENS BARTEAU.
 Born in Windsor, N. Y., Apr. 17, 1822; united with the Pres. Church in Windsor, 1843; studied at Oxford Acad. and De Lancy Inst.; married to Miss JANE LOUISA QUINN, of Clinton, N. Y., July 17, 1850; married to Miss MARY LAMBERT SEWALL, of Milwaukee, Wis., Apr. 15, 1857.
 Ordained and installed at Verona, N. Y., by Presby. of Utica, Feb. 19, 1851; Verona, 1850-2; Oconomowoc, Wis., 1852-6; Synod. miss. of Wisconsin, 1856-9; Pardeeville, 1859-62; Waterford, 1862-4; Burlington and out stations, 1865-70; Zumbrota, Minn., 1870-7; Crookston from 1878.

CHARLES BOYNTON.
 Born in Watertown, N. Y., Jan. 16, 1817; united with the Cong. Church in Watertown, 1839; graduated from Hamilton College in 1847; married to Miss SARAH B. LARNED, of Watertown, Oct. 28, 1851.
 Ordained at Mannsville, N. Y., by Black River Consoc., June, 1851; Union Grove, Wis., 1850-2; Pres. Ch., Mineral Point, 1852-9; Watertown Cong. Ch., 1859-69; Durham, N. Y., 1869-79; Sun Prairie, Wis.

JAMES DOUGLASS.
 Born in Franklin, N. Y., May 7, 1823; united with the Cong. Ch. in Franklin, 1834; graduated from Hamilton College in 1845; Auburn, 1845-6 and 1848-50; married to Miss MARY JANE BURT, of Ithaca, Sept. 13, 1853.
 Ordained and installed at Rutland, N. Y., by Presby. of Watertown, Aug. 14, 1853; Rutland, 1853-64; Pulaski Cong. Ch. from 1864.
 Published addresses, lectures and sermons.

WILLIAM AUGUSTINE FOX.

Born in Williamsburgh, Mass., April 14, 1823; united with the First Pres. Church in Lockport, N. Y., Spring of 1843; graduated from Hamilton College in 1846; married to Miss CHARLOTTE A. CLARK, of Lockport, N. Y., June 20, 1850.

Ordained and installed at Ogden, N. Y., by Presby. of Rochester, Nov. 6, 1851; Ogden, 1851–65; Dunkirk, 1865–9, and still resident there.

PHINEAS CAMP HEADLEY.

Born in Walton, N. Y., June 24, 1819; united with the Church in Litchfield, N. Y., 1831; admitted to practice Law, in Auburn, 1847; took the studies of the Junior year privately and entered Mid. class in Sem.; A. M. from Amherst College in 1860; married to Miss DORA C. BARTLETT, of New Bedford, Mass., May 13, 1851.

Ordained and installed at Adams, N. Y., by Watertown Presby., 1851; Adams, 1850–4; West Sandwich, Mass., 1854–7; Second Cong. Ch., Greenfield, Mass., 1857–61; Plymouth, Mass., 1861; has since supplied Churches, but given much time to writing for publication; resides in Boston, Mass.

Published "Women of the Bible," 1850; "Josephine," 1850; "Louis Kossuth," 1851; "Marquis de Lafayette," 1852; "Mary Queen of Scots," 1853; "Napoleon," 1854; "Court and Camp of David," 1862; "Half Hours in Bible Lands," 1863; "Massachusetts in the Rebellion," 1865; "Secret Service of U. S. in the Civil War," 1866; "Island of Fire," 1874; "Evangelists in the Church," 1877; "Life, Labors and Bible Studies of Rev. Geo. F. Pentecost," 1880; "Boys' Library of American Heroes," (Grant, Ericson, Mitchell, Farragut, Sheridan,) 1863–4; "Public Men of To-day," 1882.

WILLIAM ALLEN NILES, D. D.

Born in Binghamton, N. Y., May 29, 1823; united with the First Pres. Church in Binghamton, 1832; graduated from Williams College in 1847; D. D. from Hamilton College in 1868; married to Miss MARY ELIZABETH WEST, of Binghamton, June 27, 1850.

Ordained at Ithaca, N. Y., by Presby. of Ithaca, June 22, 1850; Beaver Dam, Wis., 1850–3; edited a temperance paper; Watertown, 1853–9; Corning, N. Y., 1859–72; Hornellsville, since 1872. His son Wm. H. graduated in class of 1873–6.

*ALFRED NORTH, died March 3, 1869.

ARMON SPENCER.

Born in Huron, N. Y., Sept. 11, 1818; united with the Pres. Church in Huron, probably in 1832; graduated from Western Reserve College in 1847; Auburn the course, and post grad. in 1855–6; married to Mrs. LYDIA CLARISSA PARTRIDGE, of Newark, N. Y., Nov. 24, 1880.

Ordained at Palmyra, N. Y. by Presby. of Geneva, 1854 ; Cong. Ch.,
Reeds Corners, 1852–4; East Palmyra, 1854–5 ; Bristol, N. Y.,
1857–8; Pres. Ch., Williamson, 1862–70 ; Cambria, Wis., 1870–
1 ; home miss., Mich., 4 years ; Summit, Cong. Ch., 2 years ;
health failed ; resident in Newark, N. Y.
Published " An Opening for a Candidate," 1881.

*ELKANAH WHITNEY, died June 11, 1863.

*WILLIAM BRITTON CHRISTOPHER, died Nov. 7, 1879.

*JOSEPH BUELL WARD, died Sept. 5, 1880.

1848-51.

FRANKLIN DEXTER AUSTIN.
Born in Becket, Mass., Oct. 3, 1819 ; united with the Cong. Ch. in
Worthington, Mass., 1839 ; graduated from Union College in
1845 ; married to CARRIE FLORA SPRAGUE, of Worcester, Mass.,
Jan. 13, 1853 ; married to Miss JULIA M. GODDARD, of Worcester, May 1, 1865.
Ordained and installed at Tolland, Mass., by Council, June 23,
1853 ; East Jaffrey, N. H., from 1857 ; South Royalston, Mass.,
from 1863 ; Dunstable, 1873–80 ; resident in Nashua, N. H.,
supplying at Hudson from 1880.

*HENRY ALLEN AUSTIN, died June 2, 1882.

SERENO EDWARDS BISHOP.
Born in Kaawaloa, Hawaii, Feb. 7, 1827 ; united with the Wash-
ington St. Church in Rochester, N. Y., Apr., 1842 ; graduated
from Amherst College in 1846; married to Miss CORNELIA A.
SESSIONS, of Albany, N. Y., May 31, 1852.
Ordained and installed in N. Y. City, by 3rd Presby. of N. Y.,
June, 1852 ; Seamen's chap. at Lahaina, 1853–62 ; miss. at
Haua, 1862–5 ; prin. of Lahainaluna Sem., 1865–77 ; still resi-
dent there.

*JACOB EDGERTON BLAKELEY, died May 6, 1854.

*THOMAS SCOTT BRADLEY, died June 28, 1863.

*EDWIN HALL CRANE, died Aug. 27, 1854.

CHARLES HENRY DELONG.
Born in Pleasant Valley, N. Y., June 2, 1821 ; united with the
Pres. Ch. in Palmyra, N. Y.; graduated from Union College in
1846 ; married to Miss REBECCA PERRY BROWN, of Delaware,
O., Dec. 27, 1853.

Ordained and installed at Delaware, O., by Franklin Presby., May 5, 1853; Williamson, N. Y., 1851; Delaware, O., 1852–5; Oskaloosa, Iowa, 1855–9; Bath, N. Y., 1860–1; Deposit, 1861–72; Waukegan, Ill., from 1872; Dwight, to 1877; Creston, Iowa, 1878–81; Greenfield, 1877–8 and from 1881.

JAMES EELLS, D. D., LL. D.
Born in Westmoreland, N. Y., Aug. 27, 1822; united with the Pres. Church in Elyria, O., May, 1834; graduated from Hamilton College in 1844; entered Auburn Middle class from Western Reserve The. Sem.; D. D. from New York University in 1861; LL. D. from Marietta Univ., 1881; married to EMMA M. PAIGE, of Auburn, July 1, 1851.
Ordained and installed at Penn Yan, N. Y., by Presby. of Geneva, Aug., 1851; Penn Yan, 1851–4; 2nd Pres. Ch., Cleveland, O., 1855–9 and 1870–4; Brooklyn, N. Y., 1860–70; 1st Pres. Ch., Oakland, Cal., 1874–9; prof. in San Francisco The. Sem., 1877 –9; prof. of Homiletics and Past. The., Lane The. Sem., from 1879.
Published " Memorial of Samuel Eells," 1872.

*ARCHIBALD FERGUSON, died Jan., 1857.

*AUGUSTUS GALESTIN GOULD, died Nov. 7, 1849.

*DAVID F. JUDSON, died Nov. 22, 1867.

RICHARD GOODELL KEYES.
Born in Watertown, N. Y., Jan. 6, 1826; united with the First Pres. Church in Watertown, May 7, 1843; graduated from Hamilton College in 1848; Union Sem., N. Y., 1848–9; Auburn, 1849–51; unmarried.
Ordained at Paris Hill, N. Y., by Oneida Assoc., Sept. 29, 1852; Westford, 1853–4; Painted Post, 1854–6; Watertown, 1857–60; resident Watertown.

JAMES LANDRETH.
Born in Ireland, Oct. 23, 1823; united with the M. E. Church in Lima, N. Y., 1842; graduated from Univ. of Mich. in 1848; married to Miss ADELIA COMSTOCK, of Auburn, 1851; married to Miss SARAH BARKER, of North Hector, N. Y., 1855.
Ordained Deacon, by Bishop Morris, (M. E.) at Penn Yan, N. Y., 1851; ord. Elder by Bishop Janes, at Elmira, 1853; Addison, N. Y.; Starkey; Clifton Springs; Rushville; Naples; prin. of Mansfield Class. Sem., Mansfield, Pa.; Wellsboro, Pa.; Walworth, N. Y.; Sodus; Bellona; Dundee; Dansville; Friendship; Canisteo.

DANIEL BRAYTON LYON.
Born in Edinburgh, N. Y., 1820; graduated from Union College in 1847; Union Sem., N. Y., 1848–9; Auburn, 1849–51.
Ordained in Prot. Ep. Ch.; Saginaw, Mich., 1852–8; Ionia, 1859–63; Ripon, Wis., from 1864; resident Merillon, Wis.

JACOB GERRIT MILLER, D. D.

> Born in Sandlake, N. Y., Sept. 8, 1823; united with the Church in Williams College, Dec., 1843; graduated from Williams College in 1848; D. D. from Maryville College in 1879; married to Miss MARY ABIGAIL HITCHCOCK, of Tomhannock, N. Y., May 5, 1852; married to ANNA WHEELOCK PEAKE, of West Troy, N. Y., Oct. 19, 1858.

> Ordained at Whitehall, N. Y., by Troy Presby., June 14, 1852; Harwinton, Conn., 1854–9; Branford, 1859–64; Montrose, Pa., 1864–81; Marathon, N. Y., from 1881.

> Published several sermons.

*HOMER BARTLETT MORGAN, died Aug. 25, 1865.

*WILLIAM WALLACE PAGE, died Dec. 30, 1871.

JOSIAH ADDISON PRIEST, D. D.

> Born in Albany, N. Y., 1822; united with the Broadway Tab. Church in New York, 1842; graduated from Hamilton College in 1847; Junior year at Union, New York, 1847–8; Mid. and Sen. years at Auburn; D. D. from Hamilton College in 1872; married to FRANCES WALKER, of Cooperstown, N. Y., 1852.

> Ordained and installed at Cooperstown, by Otsego Presby., June 25, 1851; Cooperstown, 1851–5 and 1862–4; Homer, 1855–8; Montclair, N. J., 1858–61; Gloversville, N. Y., 1864–8; Quincy, Ill., 1868–75; Newton, N. J., 1875–80; resident Montclair, 1881.

*MARSHALL DANFORTH SANDERS, died Aug. 29, 1871.

*JOHN DENNIS STRONG, died May 14, 1859.

WILLIAM WAITH.

> Born in London, Eng., Jan. 30, 1824; united with the Cong. Ch. in Ellington, N. Y., 1841; studied privately; married to Miss SARAH ANN POTWINE, of Ellington, Apr. 11, 1848; married to Miss HENRIETTA LOUISA McCONNELL, of Ellington, Aug. 24, 1858.

> Ordained at Westfield, N. Y., by Buffalo Presby., June 15, 1853; Pres. Church, Lancaster, N. Y., from 1851.

SAMUEL JOHN AUSTIN.

> Born in Becket, Mass., Nov. 22, 1824; graduated from Union College in 1847; Auburn, 1848–9; partial course at Hartford, class of 1854–7, and 1 year at Andover; married to Miss JENNIE CLARK, 1858; married to Miss SUSAN M. MILLER, 1863.

> Ordained pastor, Mason Village, N. H., (Cong.) Feb. 25, 1857; Mason Village, 1857–9; Gardner, Mass., 1859–64; Orford, 1864–8; Warren, 1868–77; Chicopee Falls, from 1877.

*DANIEL BOND, died Aug. 20, 1852.

*ARUNAH HALL LILLY, died Aug. 13, 1875.

CHARLES STEBBINS SYLESTER.

Born in Williamstown, Mass., Aug. 12, 1826 ; united with the Cong. Church in Williamstown, July, 1841 ; graduated from Williams College in 1846 ; Auburn, 1849 ; invalid ; grad. Hartford Theo. Sem., 1856 ; married to Miss HARRIET ARMS, of Conway, Mass., May 15, 1857 ; married to Miss JULIA ANN SYKES of Hatfield, Mass., May 11, 1871.

Ordained, Spencertown, N. Y., by Presby. of Columbia, Oct., 1857 ; Spencertown, 1857–62 ; Second Ref. Ch., Coxsackie, 1863–4 ; Cong. Ch., Richmond, Mass., 1865–6 ; Feeding Hills, 1866–81 ; resident Hartford from 1881.

1849-52.

PHILANDER ANDERSON, M. D.

Born in Mercer, Pa., July 15, 1823 ; united with the Pres. Church in Mercer, 1842 ; graduated from Wabash College in 1849 ; Lane Sem., 1849–50 ; Auburn, 1850–2 ; married to Miss EMMA AMANDA DROGAN, of Indianapolis, Ind., Sept. 4, 1851.

Ordained at Huntington, Ind., by Fort Wayne Presby., 1852 ; Hartford City, Ind., 1852–4 ; Zionsville, 1855 ; physician, Zionsville, 10 years, druggist, &c., 7 years, and since 1870, banker ; resident Anthony, Kan.

DAVID EDWARDS BLAINE

Born in Varick, N. Y., March 5, 1824 ; united with the M. E. Church in May, 1842 ; graduated from Hamilton College in 1849 ; married to Miss CATHERINE V. PAINE, of Seneca Falls, N. Y., Aug. 11, 1853.

Ordained at Elmira, N. Y., in E. Genesee M. E. Conference, Aug. 24, 1853 ; Seattle, on Puget Sound, 1853–6 ; Portland, Oregon, 1856 ; Oregon City, 1856–8 ; Corvallis, 1858 ; Santiam Academy, principal, 1858–9 ; Lebanon, 1859–60 ; Lebanon and Albany, 1860–1 ; presiding elder of Upper Willamette district, 1861–2 ; principal of Portland Acad., 1862–3 ; Cazenovia, N. Y., 1863–4 ; resident in Waterloo, 1864–73 ; Barclay, Pa., 1873–4 ; Mainsburg, 1874–6 ; Reading Centre, N. Y., 1876–8 ; Hopewell, 1878–9 ; Richmond from 1879.

ROBERT RUSSELL BOOTH, D. D.

Born in New York, May 16, 1830 ; united with the Rivington St. Church in New York, April, 1847 ; graduated from Williams College in 1849 ; D. D. from Univ. of New York in 1864 ; married to Miss EMMA LOUISE LATHROP, of Auburn, Oct. 26, 1853.

Ordained and installed as colleague pastor of First ch., Troy, N. Y., by Presby. of Troy, Nov., 1853 ; Troy, 1853–8 ; pastor of First Ch., Stamford, Ct., 1858–61 ; of Mercer St. Church, New York, 1861–70; of University Place Church, New York, from 1870.

*JOHN CAMPBELL, died March, 1869.

NATHANIEL GEORGE CLARK, D. D., LL. D.

Born in Calais, Vt., Jan. 18, 1825; united with the Cong. Church in Montpelier, Vt., 1842; graduated from Univ. of Vt., 1845; first two years at Andover and third at Auburn; D. D. from Union College in 1866, and LL. D. from Univ. of Vt., 1875; married to MARY B. REED, of Montpelier, Aug. 16, 1854; married to ELIZABETH S. WORCESTER, of Auburndale, Mass., May 8, 1861.

Ordained at Burlington, Vt., by Council, 1857; prof. of Lat. and Eng. Lit., Univ. of Vt., 1852-62; prof. of Logic, Rhet. and Eng. Lit., Union College, 1862-5; foreign secretary of A. B. C. F. M. from 1865.

Published " Elements of the English Language," 1863; and many articles

THOMAS CONDON.

Born in Ireland; came to Auburn from Camillus; member of Ch. in Camillus.

Home miss., St. Helen's, Or., to 1855; Tualatin, 1855-7; Grand Prairie, 1857-62; Dallas, 1862-74; Forest Grove, 1875-7; prof. in State Univ., Eugene City, from 1877.

S. MILLS DAY.

Born in Richmond, N. Y., Aug. 8, 1827; united with the 1st Pres. Church in Ithaca, N. Y., Jan., 1848; graduated from Union College in 1850; Middle and Senior years at Auburn; married to Miss LUCY E. MAXWELL, of Geneva, N. Y., Nov. 30, 1852.

Ordained and installed at Hammondsport, N. Y., by Presby. of Bath, June 30, 1852; Hammondsport, 1852-7; Havana, 1857 -61; Honeoye Cong. Ch. from 1862.

Published " Pencilings of Light and Shade," 1850.

GEORGE PALMER FOLSOM, D. D.

Born in Buffalo, N. Y., Dec. 16, 1826; united with the Pres. Ch. in Cleveland, O., 1837; graduated from Williams College in 1847; tea. South Bend, 1847-8; in business, 1848-9; D. D. from Williams College in 1881; married to Miss LILLIE GRAHAM FRASER, of Monroe, Mich., Oct. 28, 1852.

Ordained at Batavia, N. Y., by Genesee Presby., 1853; Attica, N. Y., 1852-9; Geneseo, 1859-68; dis. sec. of Church Erec. Bd., at Chicago, Ill., 1869-71; Baraboo, Wis., 1872-8; Chicago, Ill., 1879-80; Iowa City, Ia., from 1880.

Published Sermons and Historical Addresses.

FRANCIS HENDRICKS.

Came to Auburn from Ovid; graduated from Union College in 1846.

Ordained (Pres.) about 1853; New Berlin, Pa., 1853-5, 1857, 1860 -2; Fremont, O., 1856; Northumberland, Pa., 1858; resident in Philadelphia, stated supply of Mantua 2nd Ch. and other Chs., 1862-79; tea., 1880, and chaplain from 1880.

JOHN RUSSELL HERRICK, D. D.
   Born in Milton, Vt., May 12, 1822; united with the Cong. Church
   in Milton, 1831; graduated from Univ. of Vt. in 1847; Andover
   Jun. and Mid. years; Aub., 1851-2; D. D. from Union College
   in 1867, and same from Univ. of Vt.; married to Miss HARRIET
   EMILY BROWNELL, of Sharon, Conn., May 12, 1856.
   Ordained and installed at Malone, N. Y., by Presby. of Champlain,
   June, 1854; Malone, 1854-67; prof. of Theology, Bangor The.
   Sem., 1867-73; South Hadley, Mass., 1874-8; pres. of Pacific
   Univ., Forest Grove, Or., from 1880.
   Published many articles and reviews.

JOEL KENNEDY.
   Born in St. Ann's, Canada, 1816; united with the 1st Pres. Church
   in St. Ann's, 1831; graduated from Western Reserve College in
   1849; married to Miss MARTHA JANE STIMSON, of Allegan,
   Mich., 1864.
   Ordained at Medina, by Presby. of Niagara, 1854; Middleport
   from 1852; Niagara City from 1855; Waterville from 1858; Allegan, Mich., from 1860; Albion, Mich., from 1864; Howell,
   Mich., from 1867; Breckenridge, Hamilton and N. Y. Settlement, Mo., from 1868; Gardner, Ill., from 1875; Joy, 1876-80;
   Avoca, Iowa, from 1880.

*ALBERT MANDELL, died Oct. 7, 1871.

LUTHER PARKER MATTHEWS
   Born in Stockholm, N. Y., March 20, 1824; united with the Cong.
   Church in Berlin, O., 1841; studied at Western Reserve College;
   Auburn Senior class from West. Res.; married to Miss SARAH
   HUBBARD, of Sylvania, O, Feb. 15, 1853.
   Ordained at Sylvania, by Presby. of Monroe, May, 1853; Sylvania,
   1852-4; Garnavillo, Iowa, 1854-61; Colesburg, 1861-75; Post-
   ville, 1875-8; Crete, Neb., from 1878.

FRANCIS SAMUEL McCABE, D. D.
   Born in Terre Haute, Ind., July 8, 1827; united with the Centre
   Pres. Church in Crawfordsville, Ind., 1843; graduated from
   Wabash College in 1849; Lane Sem., 1849-50; Auburn, 1850-2;
   D. D. from Wabash College in 1871; married to Miss ELEANOR
   EMERSON JOHNSON, of Peru, Ind., Sept. 25, 1855.
   Ordained and installed at Peru, by Presby. of Fort Wayne, Oct.,
   1852; Peru, 1852-67; Topeka, Kan., from 1869.

EDWARD DAFYDD MORRIS, D. D.
   Born in Utica, N. Y., Oct. 31, 1825; united with the Ch. in Yale
   College, 1848; graduated from Yale College in 1849; D. D.
   from Hamilton College in 1863; married to FRANCES E. PARM-
   ELEE, of Fair Haven, Ct., 1852; married to MARY BRYANT
   TREAT, of Tallmadge, O., 1867.
   Ordained at Skaneateles, N. Y., by Presby. of Cayuga, 1852; Au-
   burn 2nd Ch., 1852-5; Columbus, O., 1855-68; prof. Eccl. Hist.

Lane The. Sem., 1868–74 ; prof. Theol., Lane The. Sem. from 1874.

Published sermons, articles, &c.; Notes on Theology, 1881.

JOHN CAMPBELL MOSES.
Born in Ticonderoga, N. Y., Feb. 25, 1824 ; united with the Cong. Church in Clymer, N. Y., 1847; graduated from State Nor. Sch., Albany, 1846; married to Miss CATHERINE AURILLA TERRY, of French Creek, N. Y., July 21, 1850.
Ordained and installed at Dundee, N. Y., by Presby. of Geneva, Mar. 15, 1853; Dundee, 1852–6; Lenox, 1856–8; Fowlerville, 1858–62; Dundee, 1862–70; Ellington, Conn., 1870–2; resident in Clinton, Iowa.
Published several sermons.

JOHN NEWBANKS.
Born in Chazy, N. Y., Aug. 30, 1824; united with the Pres. Church about 1841; graduated from Williams College in 1849; Union Sem., 1849–50 ; Auburn, 1850–2; married to Miss MARY TAYLOR WOTKYNS, of Troy, N. Y., May 5, 1845.
Ordained and installed at Chester, N. Y., by Presby. of Troy, Fall of 1853; Troy, 1853–4, and resident there since, in ill health.

*HENRY NORTH PECK, died Mar. 9, 1854.

JAMES PIERPONT.
Born in Pittsford, N. Y., July 28, 1819; united with the Third Pres. Church in Rochester, N. Y., about 1829; graduated from Hamilton College in 1849; married to Miss MARIA CUSHMAN DIBBLE, Oct. 5, 1852.
Ordained at Rochester, N. Y., by Rochester Presby., Oct., 1852 ; went to California in 1853; has served 12 Churches there, of which he organized 6; chaplain of Sailors' Home, San Francisco, from 1879.

HON. JULIUS HAWLEY SEELYE, D. D., LL. D.
Born in Bethel, Ct., Sept. 14, 1824; united with the Cong. Church in Bethel, June, 1843; graduated from Amherst College in 1849 ; one year in Germany in addition to the Auburn course; D. D. from Union College in 1862 ; LL. D. from Columbia College in 1876; married to ELIZABETH TILLMAN JAMES, of Albany, N. Y., Oct. 23, 1854.
Ordained and installed at Schenectady, N. Y., by Classis of Schenectady, Aug. 10, 1853; Schenectady to 1858; prof. of Mor. Phil. and Metaphysics, Amherst College, 1858–75; in Congress, 1875–6; pres. of Amherst Col. from 1877.
Published Translation of Schwegler's History of Philosophy, N. Y., 1856; " Lectures to Educated Hindus," Bombay and Boston, 1873; "Christian Missions," N. Y., 1875 ; sermons, addresses and reviews.

ALFRED MARTIN STOWE.

> Born in Marlborough, Mass., March 9, 1819; united with the Pres. Church in Mexico, N. Y., 1836; graduated from Hamilton College in 1849; married to Miss HARRIET PIERSON TICHENOR, of Canandaigua, June 1, 1854.
>
> Ordained, Waterloo, N. Y., by Geneva Presby., 1852; dist. sec. of Am. Tract. Soc., 1852–60; dist. sec. of Pres. Board of Home Miss. 1860–73; financial sec. of Auburn Theo. Sem. from 1873, residing at Canandaigua, N. Y.

MILTON WALDO, D. D.

> Born in Newark Valley, N. Y., Aug. 28, 1822; united with the Cong. Church in Berkshire, N. Y., July 4, 1840; graduated from Hamilton College in 1848; D. D. from Hamilton College in 1868; married to Miss MARIA L. HARDENBURGH, of Auburn, Sept. 6, 1855.
>
> Ordained at Spencer, N. Y., by Council, Oct., 1852; Spencer, 1852–3; Utica, agt. for Am. Tr. Soc. for Central N. Y., 1853–4; New Orleans, La., agt. for same for five Southwestern States, 1854; Lawrence, Ill., home miss., 1856–8; past. Lacon Pres. Ch., 1858–61; Hornellsville, N. Y., 1861–72; Hudson, 1872–5; Phelps, 1875; Watkins, 1875–82.
>
> Published Historical Sketch of the Thacher family, 1869.

RANSOM BETHUNE WELCH, D. D., LL. D.

> Born in Greenville, N. Y.; united with the Bleecker St. Pres. Church in New York, 1848; graduated from Union College in 1846; Andover, Jun. and Mid. years; Aub., Mid. and Sen.; D. D. from Rutgers College in 1868; also from Univ. of City of New York, 1868; LL. D. from Maryville College, 1872; married to Miss LYDIA B. KENNEDY, of Clifton Park, N. Y., June 5, 1861.
>
> Ordained and installed at Gilboa, N. Y., by Classis of Schoharie, 1854; Gilboa, 1854–6; Catskill, 1856–9; prof. of Log., Rhet. and Eng. Lit., Union College, 1860–76; prof. of Christian Theol., Auburn, from 1876.
>
> Published " Faith and Modern Doubt," 1876; and many articles, addresses, &c.; Notes on Theology, 1881–2.

GEORGE WASHINGTON CONNIT.

> Born in Elyria, O., Sept. 20, 1823; graduated from Williams College in 1849; at Auburn part of Junior year; grad. at Hartford Sem., 1853; married to Miss LUCY I. TYLER, of Williamstown, Mass., Aug. 15, 1853; married to Miss LOUISA HOWE, of Portland, Me., Oct. 30, 1866.
>
> Ordained and installed at Deep River, Conn., (Cong.) Dec. 20, 1854; Deep River, 1854–6; Pres. Ch., Deep River, 1856–62; Ref. Church of Fallsburg, Woodburne, N. Y., 1862–5; New Prospect, 1866–70; became Deacon-Evangelist in Catholic Apostolic Church, July 26, 1876; tea. Fond du Lac, Wis.

*Park Shattuck Donelson, D. D., died May 6, 1882.

Martin Luther Gaylord.
Born in Otisco, N. Y., June 16, 1823; united with the Cong. Church in Otisco, Dec., 1842; graduated from Amherst College in 1848; left Auburn in poor health, at close of 2nd year; married to Miss Elisabeth Edwards, of Southampton, Mass., Nov. 16, 1858.
Never ordained; Fruit Nursery and Farming in Kan., 1855–68, and since in Mass.; resident in Easthampton.

Yates Hickey.
Born in Phelps, N. Y., Oct. 19, 1823; united with the Pres. Ch. in Mishawaka, Ind., May, 1840; graduated from Hamilton College in 1849; Auburn, 1849–51; married to Sarah B. Ingraham, of Geneva, N. Y., March 20, 1851.
Ordained at Palmyra, N. Y., by Presby. of Geneva, 1854; he was engaged for many years in the service of the Am. Tract Soc., and has ever since been in that of the International Sabbath Association. At different times, he has supplied Churches at Greenville, N. Y., at Athens, Pa., and elsewhere; resident Norristown, Pa.

*Henry Lobdell, died Mar. 25, 1855.

John Milton Shaw.
Graduated from Madison Univ. in 1850; Auburn, 1850–1, from Sterling; a minister in the Baptist Church; miss. to Mexico.

David Davis Van Antwerp.
Born in Rensselaer Co., N. Y., Mar. 8, 1822; united with the Reformed Church; graduated from Univ. of Mich. in 1849; at Auburn Junior year; finished his Theological studies at Grand Rapids, Mich.; married to Miss Jane Caroline Faxon, of Albion, Mich., 1851.
Ordained Deacon in 1851, and Priest in 1852, at Grand Rapids, Mich., by Prot. Ep. Bishop of Mich.; St. Stephen's Ch., Terre Haute, Ind.; St. Paul's, Beaufort, N. C.; St. Luke's, Kansas City, Mo.; St. Thomas', Baltimore, Md., where he resides.
Published " Popular History of the Church," 3 vols.

1850-3.

Byron Bosworth.
Born in East Pharsalia, N. Y., Nov. 14, 1823; united with the Pres. Church in Lancaster, N. Y., 1848; graduated from Hamilton College in 1850; entire course at Auburn, and a post graduate year at Princeton; married to Miss Eliza A. Macy, of Hudson, N. Y., Oct. 28, 1855.
Ordained by Presby. of Cayuga, Nov. 5, 1857; Pres. Ch., Champlain, N. Y., 1854–5; Cong. Ch., Morrisville, 1855–6; Homer,

1856-7 ; Kingston, Mass., 1857-9 ; Henrietta, N. Y., 1859-65 ;
Pres. Ch., Victor, 1865-6 ; Phelps, 1866 ; Cong. Ch., Phoenix,
1866-7 ; Pres. Ch., Greenville, 1867-76 ; Hammondsport, from
1876.

*OLIVER BRONSON, died Jan. 10, 1860.

ISAAC EDDY CAREY.
Born in Locke, N. Y., July 29, 1822 ; united with the Cong.
Church in Kiantone, N. Y., 1836 ; graduated from Yale College
in 1849 : married to Miss ELIZA ANN WRIGHT, of Auburn,
Jan. 1, 1851.
Ordained by Presby. of Buffalo, Jan., 1854; Springville, N. Y.,
1853-4 ; First Pres. Ch., Freeport, Ill., 1854-7 and 1862-72 ;
Peoria, Ill., 1857-60 ; Keokuk, Iowa, 1860-2 ; Waterloo, 1873-
5 ; Cong. Ch., Huntsburg, O., 1876-80; resident there.

*LAURENTINE HAMILTON, died April 9, 1882.

*HUBERT PIERRE HERRICK, died Dec. 20, 1857.

CORYDON WEBSTER HIGGINS.
Born in Worthington, Mass., Jan. 18, 1823 ; united with the
Church in Williams College in 1848; graduated from Williams
College in 1849; Middle and Senior years at Auburn; married
to HARRIET WARD CHAPIN, of Rochester. N. Y., June 21, 1853.
Ordained and installed at Spencer, N. Y., by Council, 1855 ;
East Avon, 1853 ; Spencer, 1855 ; Newfield, 1858 ; Big Flats,
1865 ; Cottage Grove, Wis., 1866 ; Osborn, Mo., 1868-80;
Parkville, from 1880.

*EDWARD SILAS LACY, died Aug. 23, 1875.

JOSEPH NELSON McGIFFERT.
Born in New York City, Dec. 8, 1829 ; united with the Pres.
Church in Hudson, N. Y., July 4, 1847 ; married to Miss
HARRIETTE W. PUSHMAN, of Manlius, Nov. 3, 1853.
Ordained at Hillsdale, N. Y., by Columbia Presby, Nov. 15,
1853; Hillsdale, 1853-7 ; Sauquoit, 1857-66 ; Ashtabula, O.,
from 1867.
Published several sermons.

*HENRY NORTON MILLERD, died Sept. 13, 1873.

JACOB KENT WARNER.
Born in Strykersville, N. Y., Sept. 10, 1823 ; united with the
Cong. Church in Strykersville, April, 1842 ; graduated from
Yale College in 1850; married to Miss MARY ANNA PLATT, of
Brooklyn, N. Y., June 30, 1854; married to Miss ELIZABETH
WEBSTER MORON, of Johnstown, Wis., Dec., 1865; married to
Miss MARY LOUISA BROWN, of Burdett, N. Y., Sept. 21, 1871.
Ordained at Waterloo, N. Y., by Presby. of Geneva, 1858 ;
Cong. Ch., Allegany, 1853 ; Pres. Ch., Burdett, 1855 ; Dundee,
1857; Center, Wis., 1859 ; Johnstown, 1862-8 ; resident in
Burdett, N. Y., and Jacksonville, Fla.

WARREN WILLIAM WARNER.
Born in Vernon, N. Y., Nov. 9, 1824; united with the Cong. Church in Oberlin, O., 1841; graduated from Hamilton College in 1850; married to Miss ANNA GATES LEWIS, of Chicago, Ill. Ordained at Mannsville, N. Y., by Black River Consociation, Jan. 20, 1858; New Haven, N. Y., 1854; Belleville, Ill., 1855; Dodgeville, Wis., 1856; Sackets Harbor, N. Y., 1858; Champion, 1859; Paris Hill, 1860; Lebanon, 1862; Lawrenceville, 1864; South Canton, 1866; Norfolk and Raymondville, 1869; Port Leyden, 1871; Volney, 1875–80; Coventryville from 1880.

JOHN ALPHEUS WOODHULL.
Born in Ronconkama, N. Y., Oct. 30, 1825; united with the Cong. Church in Mt. Sinai, L. I., Apr., 1838; graduated from Yale College in 1850; studied at Bangor; admitted to Auburn Middle class, Jan., 1852; graduated at Auburn; studied also at New Haven; married to JOANNA BROWN, of Rocky Point, L. I., July 20, 1853.
Ordained and installed at Wadham's Mills, N. Y., by Essex Co. Consociation, Jan. 1, 1856; New Village and Commack, L. I., 1858–66; Northville, L. I., 1866–9; New Preston, Ct., 1869–72; Groton, Ct., 1872–80; Baiting Hollow, N. Y., from 1880.
Published Review of Cong. Ch. of Groton, Ct., 1877.

JOHN BASCOM, D. D., LL. D.
Born in Genoa, N. Y., May 1, 1827; united with the Pres. Church in Ludlowville, 1843; graduated from Williams College in 1849; Auburn Mid. class, 1851–2; tutor, Williams Col., 1852–3; Andover, 1854–5; LL. D. from Amherst College in 1873; D. D., Iowa College, 1875; married to ABBIE BURT, of Great Barrington, Mass., Dec., 1852; married to EMMA CURTIS, of Sheffield, Mass., Jan., 1856.
Ordained at Pownal, Vt., by Council, Dec., 1859; 19 years prof. of Rhetoric in Williams College; pres. of Univ. of Wis., from 1874.
Published "Political Economy," 1859; "Aesthetics," 1862; "Philosophy of Rhetoric," 1865; "Principles of Psychology," 1869; "Science, Philosophy and Religion," 1871; "Philosophy of English Literature," 1874; "Philosophy of Religion," 1876; "Comparative Psychology," 1878; "Ethics," 1879; "Natural Theology," 1880.

FRANK FIELDS ELLINWOOD, D. D.
Born in Clinton, N. Y., June 20, 1826; united with the Cong. Ch. in Clinton, 1842; graduated from Hamilton College in 1849; Auburn, Mid., 1851–52; Princeton, 1852–3; D. D. from Univ. of N. Y., in 1865; married to Miss ROWANA HURD, of New York, June 26, 1853; married to Miss LAURA HURD, of Fair Haven, Vt., Apr. 15, 1867.

Ordained and installed at Belvidere, N. J., by 4th Presbytery of Phila., June 21, 1853 ; Belvidere, 1853–4 ; Central Ch., Rochester, N. Y., 1854–65 ; sec. of Pres. Com. of Ch.-Erection, 1866–70 ; of the Memorial Fund Committee, 1870–1 ; of the Board of For. Miss., from 1871 ; resident New York.

JOHN DANIEL ENGLISH.
Born in Red Hook, N. Y., Apr. 3, 1827 ; united with St. Peter's Lutheran Church in Rhinebeck, N. Y., at 16 years old ; studied at Hartwick Sem. and Williams College ; in Auburn until the middle of Sen. year ; married to SUSAN ADELINE MILLER, of Hartwick Seminary, Feb. 15, 1853.
Ordained at Rhinebeck, by the New York Synod, Sept. 6, 1853 ; Luth. Ch., Ghent, 1853 ; Middleburgh, 1854–8 ; Fayette, 1858–62 ; 148th N. Y. Vols., 1862–3 ; in the army again, 1864–5 ; tea. Hartwick Sem., 1866–71 ; Pres. Ch., West Fayette, N. Y., 1871 –5 ; farming, near Waterloo.

JOHN WESLEY PRATT.
Born in Pratt's Hollow, N. Y., Dec. 8, 1815 ; united with the M. E. Church in Port Gibson, 1833 ; graduated from Wesleyan Univ. in 1839 ; Auburn, 1838–40, and allowed to attend lectures of Mid. and Sen. classes, Sept., 1851 ; married to Miss CAROLINE STRONG, of Lansing, Dec. 31, 1840.
Ordained at Ithaca, N. Y., in Oneida Conf., by Bishop Janes, 1851 ; Cayuga M. E. Ch., 1840 ; tea. Groton Acad., Farmer, Macedon and Red Creek Acads., 1841–6 ; farming, Lansing, 1847–50 ; M. E. Ch., Port Byron, 1851–2 ; Ludlowville, 1853 ; Ledyard, 1854–5 ; located, 1856 ; farmer, Lansingville, from 1857.

GEORGE W. QUEREAU.
Came to Auburn from Red Creek ; mem. of M. E. Church there ; graduated from Wesleyan Univ. in 1849 ; Aub., Mid., 1851–2 ; said to be a minister of the M. E. Church, in educational work, connected with some Conference in the West.

DANIEL RUSSELL.
Born in Naples, N. Y.; united with the Pres. Church in Watkins, 1843 ; studied at Franklin Acad., Prattsburg ; A. M. from Hamilton College in 1859 ; attended lectures of Mid. and Sen. classes, 1851–2 ; married to Miss MARIA HUNTER, of Wayne, Sept. 22, 1848 ; married to Mrs. MARY JANE WOOD, of Eagle, Oct. 11, 1857.
Ordained and installed at Oramel, by Presby. of Angelica, 1850 ; Oramel, 1849–55 ; Pike, 1855–67 ; Cedar Falls, Ia., 1867–70 ; Manchester, 1870–6 ; West Union, 1877 ; Anamosa, from 1878.

STEWART SHELDON. See 1851–4.

1851-4.

CHARLES FISK BEACH.

Born in Jewett, Greene Co., N. Y., Sept. 5, 1827; united with the
Pres. Church in Hunter, July, 1849; studied at Delaware
Inst. and Prattsville Academy; received the degree of A. M.
from Knox College, Ill., in 1859; married to Miss HARRIETTE
ADELIA LOCKWOOD, of Hempstead, N. Y., June 2, 1851.
Ordained and installed at Springfield, N. Y., by Presby., Jan. 10,
1856; Springfield; missionary work in Iowa; Washington, Ill.,
1859-64; Centralia, 1864-7; Portage City, Wis, 1867-71;
Paris, Ky., 1871-3; editor of " Kentucky Presbyterian," now
" National Presbyterian," from 1873, at Louisville, Ky.
Published " The Christian Worker," 1869, and several sermons
and tracts.

REX RESCUM HART DEXTER.

Born in Fairfield, N. Y., April 2, 1819; united with the First
Pres. Church in Allen, about Nov., 1840; studied at Middle-
bury and Nunda Academies,; Middle and Senior years at
Auburn; married to Miss MARY JANE STAUNTON, of LeRoy,
Nov. 30, 1854.
Ordained at Byron, N. Y., by Presby. of Genesee, April, 1857;
Pike, 1854; Byron, 1856-7; Corfu, 1857-9; Pavilion, 1860-8,
and 1874-6; six years in poor health at Wyoming; Portage-
ville, 1876-80; Bethany Centre, from 1880.

ARCHIBALD McDOUGALL.

Born in Campbeltown, Argyleshire, Scotland, Feb. 22, 1825;
united with the Church in Lockport, N. Y., 1842; graduated
from Union College in 1851; studied with Rev. F. G. Hibbard,
D. D.; Auburn, 1852-4; married to Miss EMILY ELIZABETH
WALKER, of Havana, N. Y., Sept. 23, 1849.
Ordained and installed at Sherburne, N. Y., by Presby. of Chenango,
Feb., 1854; Sherburne, 1854-60; Dryden, 1860-7; Second
Pres. Ch., Bloomington, Ill., 1867-70; resident there; Farm
Ridge, Ill., 1882.

LEVI PARSONS, D. D.

Born in Marcellus, N. Y., Jan. 2, 1829; united with the Pres.
Church in Marcellus, Sept. 1, 1850; graduated from Hamilton
College in 1849; D. D. from Hamilton College in 1874;
married to Miss MARY WADSWORTH, of Richfield Springs, Nov.
21, 1854; married to Miss HARRIETT M. PEASE, of Auburn,
Sept. 14, 1858.
Ordained and installed at Mount Morris, N. Y., by Presby. of
Ontario, July 10, 1856; Otisco, 1854-5; Mount Morris from
1856. Succeeded his father as Trustee of Auburn, 1865.

STEWART SHELDON.

Born in Perry Centre, N. Y., Dec. 20, 1823 ; united with the Cong. Church in Perry Centre, 1841 ; graduated from Hamilton College in 1848 ; Auburn, Mid., 1851-2 ; Sen., 1853-4; married to Miss SARAH WARD, of Perry Centre, July 15, 1852.

Ordained, Warsaw, N. Y., by Council, Aug., 1854 ; York, 1852 ; Silver Creek, 1853 ; Wellsville, 1855-60 ; Pawtucket, R. I., 1860 -6 ; Chilicothe, Mo., 1866-7 ; Lansing, Mich., 1868-9; Yankton, Dakota, general miss., (Cong.) for Southern Dakota, from 1869.

ALLEN TRAVER.

Born in Claverack, N. Y., Dec. 11, 1826 ; united with the Evang. Luth. Church in Ghent, Aug., 1846 ; graduated from Pennsylvania College in 1851 ; admitted to Aub. Mid. class from Union, N. Y, Jan., 1853 ; married to Miss JANE ELIZABETH CLARK, of Hartwick Seminary, N. Y., Nov. 22, 1854.

Ordained at Downsville, N. Y., by Hartwick Synod, Sept., 1854 ; Pres. Ch., Lafayette, 2 years ; Ludlowville, 3 years ; Belmont, 2 years ; Corfu, 2 years ; Wampsville, 2 years ; Dresden, 2 years ; preached temporarily in other places ; resident Rochester, N. Y.

BENJAMIN RUSH CATLIN.

Born in West Winfield, N. Y., Dec. 9, 1829 ; united with the Pres. Church in Clinton, 1851 ; graduated from Hamilton College in 1851 ; Auburn, 1851-2 ; tut. Hamilton Col., 1853-6 ; married to Miss MARY ELIZABETH MORRILL, of Meriden, N. H., July 28, 1856.

Ordained at Meriden, by Council, Jan., 1865 ; chaplain of 115th U. S. C. T. in Va. and in Texas, 1865-6 ; Meriden, N. H., 1866-72 ; examiner of patents, Washington, D. C.

HENRY MARTYN KNOX.

Born in Knoxboro, N. Y., June 10, 1830 ; united with the Cong. Church in Augusta, Aug., 1850 ; graduated from Hamilton College in 1851 ; Auburn, 1851-2 ; married to Miss CHARLOTTE BASS COZZENS, of Vernon, N. Y., Apr. 22, 1857.

Never ordained ; in business in St. Paul, Minn.; for 10 years chairman of the Central Committee of the Minnesota State S. S. Assoc.; "Public Examiner" of State of Minnesota.

HENRY AXTELL LOUNSBURY.

Born in Ovid, N. Y., Oct. 25, 1827 ; united with the Pres. Church in Ovid, July, 1847 ; graduated from Union College in 1849 ; Auburn, 1851-3; Union, N. Y., 1853-4.

Ordained and installed at Hampton Falls, N. H., by Council, Feb. 13, 1856 ; P. Seabrook, N. H., 1856-8 ; S. S. Beverly, Mass., 1858-9; S. S. Wilton, Me., 1860-2 ; S. S. Richmond, Me., 1862 -5 ; Barnstable, (Hyannis) Mass., 1866-9 ; Shirley Village, Mass., from 1870 ; resident Boston; Pres. Ch., Granville, N. Y., 1882.

HON. JOHN THEODORE WENTWORTH.

Born in Greenfield, N. Y.; united with the Cong. Ch. in Plymouth, 1836; graduated from Union College in 1846; Princeton, 1846 -7; studied and practiced Law in Saratoga Springs and Chicago, 1847–53; Auburn, part of 1853–4; married to Miss FRANCES McDONALD, of Saratoga Springs, N. Y., Oct. 4, 1852.

Lawyer, Chicago, Ill., to 1856; since then in Wis., dist. attorney, 4 years, clerk of Circ. Court, 6 years, and Judge of Circ. Court for the past 7 years; resident in Racine.

1852-5.

CHARLES ELIPHALET BAILEY.

Born in Westmoreland, N. Y., July 11, 1822; united with the Cong. Church in Westmoreland about 1837; graduated from Cleveland Univ. in 1851; dismissed from Auburn, May 26, 1853; afterward in Oberlin; married to Miss LAURINDA ADELA CLARK, of Rochester, O., Oct. 1, 1850.

Ordained at Weymouth, O., by Council, May, 1856; Huntington, O., 1854; Weymouth, 1855–6; Ontario, Ill., 1856–7; founder of Grand Traverse College, 1857; Cong. Ch., Benzonia, Mich., 1860–3; sec. and treas., Grand Traverse College, residing in Benzonia, from 1862.

*JOSEPH BRECK.

Hungary; Aub. Sem., 1852–4; Lane Sem., 1854–5; returned to Pesth, Hungary.

*EDWIN OTWAY BURNHAM, died Aug. 1, 1873.

WALTER VARICK COUCH.

Born in Westfield, N. Y., Feb. 18, 1829; united with the First Cong. Church in Clinton, about Feb., 1851; graduated from Hamilton College in 1851; teaching; Aub., 1852–3; Princeton, 1854–6; married to Miss HELEN JANE PAIGE, of LeRoy, N. Y., June 27, 1861.

Ordained and installed at East Pembroke, N. Y., by Presby. of Genesee, Oct., 1857; Moscow, 1856; Cong. Ch., Sherman, 1856–7; E. Pembroke, 1857–60; Ellicottville, 1861–3; dist. sec. of Am. Tr. Soc. from 1864; resident in Rochester.

EDWIN RUTSEN DAVIS. See 1854–7.

*IRA ODELL DeLONG, died May 30, 1868.

*JOHN LEVIS JONES. See 1853–6.

EDWIN DYER NEWBERRY.

Born in Augusta, N. Y., 1827; united with the Church in 1846; graduated from Cleveland Univ. in 1852; at Auburn first half of Junior year; completed the course at Union, New York; married to SARAH F. TAYLOR, of Baltimore, Md., 1857.

Ordained and installed at Philadelphia, Pa., by Third Presby. of Philadelphia, April 14, 1856; Olivet Pres. Ch., Philadelphia, 1856-61; Ionia, Mich., 1861-8; Atco, N. J., 1868-72; First Pres. Ch., Haddonfield, 1872-80; Philadelphia, Pa., (Ev.)from 1880.

ISAAC THOMPSON WHITTEMORE.
Born in Essex, Ct., July 12, 1824; graduated from Madison Univ. in 1852; admitted to Aub., Mid. class, from Theo. Sem. of Madison Univ.; Auburn, 1853-4; married to Miss MARY A. STILLMAN, of Hamilton, N. Y., July 31, 1855.
Ordained at Joliet, Ill., by Presby. of Chicago, Oct., 1856; Ira, N. Y., 1854-6; Pontiac, Ill., 1856-60; Fairbury, 1860-2; Rushville, 1862-4; Plymouth, 1864-9; Solomon City, Kan., 1½ years; Wamego, 2 years; Wathena, 1872-3; Good Hope, Ill., 1873-9; Newton, Iowa, 1879-81; Norwood, Ill.

1853-6.

WILLIAM BURT DADA.
Born in Otisco, N. Y., Oct. 8, 1827; united with the Cong. Church in Homer, 1844; graduated from Hamilton College in 1853; Mid. year at Union, N. Y.; Jun. and Sen. years at Auburn; married to Miss LAURA E. LYON, of Genoa, N. Y., July 3, 1856.
Ordained and installed at Skaneateles, N. Y., by Presby. of Cayuga, July 1, 1856; Skaneateles, 1856-8; Jackson, Mich., 1859-60; Minneapolis and Little Falls, Minn., 1860-1; Cong. Ch., Clear Water, 1861-7; Lake City, 1867-71; East Palmyra, N. Y., Pres. Ch., from 1873.

*DILLIS DYER HAMILTON, died July 22, 1876.

*JOHN LEVIS JONES, died May 3, 1871.

CHARLES S. MARVIN.
Born in Walton, N. Y., 1828; united with the Cong. Church in Walton at about 18 years old; studied at Delaware Lit. Inst.; Jun. and Sen. years at Aub.; Mid. year at Andover; married to Miss MARY EELLS, of Walton, June, 1856.
Ordained at Colchester, N. Y., by Presby. of Delaware, June, 1857; Deansville, 1856-7; past. Harpersfield, 1857-9, and 1864-6; invalid, residing at Walton and supplying Walton 2nd Cong. Ch., E. Pharsalia, Hebron, &c., and serving in the Christian Commission, 1859-64; home miss. in Iowa and Nebraska, 1867-79; Roxbury and Canton, Kan., from 1880.

1854-7.

*JUDSON ASPINWALL, died Oct. 10, 1867.

ALVIN COOPER, M. D.

Born in Jefferson, N. Y., Aug. 3, 1826; united with the Pres. Ch. in Jefferson, Nov., 1851; studied at Delaware Lit. Inst.; graduated from Albany Medical College, with degree of M. D., 1850; took second and third years at Auburn; married to EMMA MANWARING, of Sidney Centre, N. Y., Sept., 1857.

Ordained and installed at Gowanda, N. Y., by Presby. of Buffalo, Jan., 1858; Sidney Centre, 1854–5; Gowanda, 1857–9; Durham, 1859–70; East Palmyra, 1871–2; Junius, 1873–8; Newark, 1878–81; Howard, from 1881.

EDWIN RUTSEN DAVIS.

Born in Lysander, N. Y., Dec. 15, 1823; united with the Pres. Church in Baldwinsville, 1851; graduated from Hamilton College in 1851; Auburn, 1852–3 and 1855–7; married to Mrs. ANNA MARIAH HENRY, of Baldwinsville, Sept. 20, 1854.

Ordained and installed at Onondaga Valley, N. Y., by Presby. of Onondaga, July, 1857; Onondaga Valley, 4 years; Camillus, 5 years; Avon Springs and East Avon, 2 years; Chicago, Ill., acting pastor, 3 years; resident in Chicago, Presbyterial missionary and dist. sec. of Home Missions.

WILLIAM JOHN KNOX.

Born in Augusta, N. Y., May 17, 1828; united with the Cong. Church in Augusta, 1847; graduated from Hamilton College in 1852; tea., 1852–3 and 1854–5; Princeton, 1853–4; Auburn, 1855–7; married to Miss CELIA MARY DAVIS, of Florence, N. Y., Mar. 13, 1861.

Ordained and installed at Bridgewater, N. Y., by Oneida Assoc., June 28, 1862; Cong. Ch., Deansville, 1858–9; Florence, 1859 –61; Bridgewater and Winfield, 1861–3; resident Knoxboro.

ROBERT NORTON.

Born in Goshen, Ct., Feb. 18, 1822; united with the Cong. Church in Goshen, May, 1836; studied at Goshen Academy; took only the Senior year at the Seminary; married to JULIA A. G. HORSFORD, of Moscow, N. Y., Sept. 8, 1849.

Ordained at Rushford, N. Y., by Assoc. of Allegany and Wyoming, July 27, 1858; Second Ward Pres. Ch. of Lockport, 1857–60 and from 1874 to present time; First (American) Pres. Ch., St. Catherine's, Canada, 1860–74.

JACOB POST, D. D.

Born in Amsterdam, Holland, April 20, 1822; united with the French Protestant Church in Amsterdam, 1840; studied in the Netherlands Univ.; Mid. and Sen. years in Auburn; married to LADY HENDRIKA HERMINA COSYN, of Gouda, Holland.

Ordained and installed at Manlius, N. Y., by Onondaga Presby., 1857; Manlius; Oswego; Chicago, Ill., Holland Pres. Ch., 1874–9; Milwaukee, Wis., Perseverance Pres. Ch., 1870–4 and from 1879.

Frank LeBaron Robbins, D. D. See 1855-8.

Hon. Derwin Welton Sharts.
Born in Oxford, N. Y., Aug. 31, 1830; united with the Second Cong. Church in Hamilton, April, 1846; graduated from Madison Univ. in 1854; Hamilton Theo. Sem., 1854-5; Auburn, 1855-7; married to Miss Julia Frances Saxe, of Niagara Falls, June 17, 1861.
Ordained at Greenville, N. Y., by Presby. of Columbia, Sept., 1857; Pres. Ch., Walden, 1857-9; Cong. Ch., Madison, 1859 and 1861-5; Niagara Falls, 1859-61; Chr. Com., 1864-5; Pres. Ch., Solon, O., 1865-8 and Cong. Ch., Chagrin Falls, 1865-6; North Ch., Cleveland, O., 1868-70; Cong. Chs., Aurora and Mantua, 1870-1; Owosso, Mich., 1871-4; and resident there since. Member of Mich. Legislature, 1876 and 1878.

George Van Deurs.
Born in Nakkebœlle, Isle of Fuhnen, Denmark, April 20, 1825; united with the Moravian Church in Christianfeld, Schleswig, April, 1839; graduated from the Moravian Academy in Christianfeld in 1839; at Auburn, Middle and Senior years; married to Selma Rosamunde Suigarde Verbeck, of Utrecht, Holland, April 10, 1854.
Ordained at Pultney, N. Y., by Presby. of Bath, June 23, 1858; Jasper, 1857-8; Philadelphia, Pa., 1858-68; Utica, N. Y., 1872-3; Washington, D. C., 1874-5; Troy, N. Y., Oakwood Av. Ch., 1868-72 and 1875-80; Romeyn Chapel, New York, from 1880.
Published " A Course of Prayer for one Week," 1862

John Franklin Severance.
Member of Church in Amherst College; graduated from Amherst. College in 1848; in Aub. first half of Mid. year.
Tea. in Auburn; preached, Niagara Falls, Wilson, Franklin, N, Y.; chaplain U. S. A.; Sherman, N. Y., 1870; Madison, O. to 1872; not now in the ministry; teaching, Geneva, Ill., 1880.

1855-8.

Lucius E. Barnard.
Born in Waitsfield, Vt., June 14, 1828; graduated from Univ. of Vermont in 1853; Aub. Mid. class, March 23, 1857, from Andover; married to Miss Emma S. Barnard, of Detroit, Mich., May 14, 1861.
Ordained at Amboy, (Belle Isle) N. Y., by Presby., Mar. 8, 1859; Hannibal, 1858-9; Amboy, 1859-60; Waukegan, Ill., 1861-2; Galesburg; Georgia, Vt., 1864; ceased to be a minister; studied Law.

*MILTON A. BROWN, died Summer of 1858.

*ABNER DEWITT, died April 17, 1877.

JOSHUA BEERS HALL.
Born in Madrid, N. Y., July 11, 1826; united with the Cong.
Ch. in Madrid, 1844; graduated from Univ. of Vt., in 1853;
Union, N. Y., 1855-7; Auburn, 1857-8; married to Miss
EUGENIA FRANCES CAMPBELL, of Montpelier, Vt., July 14, 1858.
Ordained and installed at Lysander, N. Y., by Presby., Feb. 8,
1859; Lysander, 1858-64; Tomhannock and Johnsonville, 1864
-7; Olivet Ch., Lansingburgh, 1867-9; Elk Rapids, Mich.,
1870-9; resident in Oviatt from 1879.

EVAN HARRIS.
Born in Wales; studied at Brecon College in class of 1853;
Auburn, 1856-8; reported as supply at Redfield, N. Y., in
Gen. Catalogues of 1858 and 1861; said to have left the
ministry, and returned to Wales.

WILLIAM HENRY McGIFFERT.
Born in New York, N. Y., March 25, 1836; united with the Pres.
Church in Hudson, Jan., 1850; studied privately; married to
Miss FANNIE HELEN HIGBY, of Palmyra, Sept. 6, 1858.
Ordained and installed at Boonville, N. Y., by Presby. of Utica,
Nov. 5, 1858; Boonville, 1858-62; North Adams, Mass., 1862-
5; Pontiac, Mich., 1865-70; 1870-2, in poor health, but preaching as opportunity offered; Calvary Ch., Parkersburgh, W. Va.,
1873-4; First Pres. Ch., Parkersburgh, 1874-5; ill health, 1875
-6; Lonaconing, Md., 1876-8; Orange, Conn., 1879; resident
in New Haven, Conn., 1880; Hudson, N. Y., 1881; Claverack,
1882.

WILSON BARLOW PARMELEE.
Born in Westford, Vt., May 16, 1832; united with the Cong. Ch.
in Tinmouth, Vt., July, 1855; graduated from University of Vt.
in 1853; married to ELIZABETH P. BRAYTON, of Westernville,
N. Y., June 11, 1862.
Ordained and installed at Westernville, N. Y., by Utica Presby.,
Sept. 14, 1859; Westernville to 1869; Little Falls, 1869-72;
since resident at Westernville.

FRANK LEBARON ROBBINS, D. D.
Born in Camillus, N. Y., May 2, 1830; united with the College
Church in Williams College, 1852; graduated from Williams
College in 1854; Aub. Mid. in 1854-7; Sen., 1855-8; D. D.
from Union College in 1878; married to Miss LUCY MORTON
HARTPENCE, Oct. 14, 1874.
Ordained at Columbus, O., by Association; Pres. Ch., Walnut
Hills, O., 1 year; Green Hill Pres. Ch., Philadelphia, Pa., 7
years from 1860; Oxford Pres. Ch., Philadelphia, from 1868.

ALBERT GALLATIN THORNTON.
> Born in Saco, Me., Dec. 31, 1826; member of Church in Scarboro;
> graduated from Bowdoin College in 1848; now living in Ireland.

MATTHEW ALONZO GATES.
> Born in Mendon, N. Y., Nov. 14, 1826; graduated from Mich.
> Univ. in 1855; left Auburn at close of 1857.
>
> Ordained at Salem, N. H., (Cong.) Sept. 2, 1858; Tinmouth, Vt.,
> to 1864; Peru, 1867-8; Warner, 1875-6; resident St. Johnsbury;
> Barnet to 1882.

1856-9.

ISAAC WARREN ATHERTON.
> Born in Milton, Mass., Dec. 27, 1826; united with the Cong.
> Church in Hallowell, Me., about 1842; studied at Beloit
> College; Auburn, 1857-9; married to Miss ADELIA SUSAN
> HIGBEE, of Beloit, Wis., April 9, 1853.
>
> Ordained at Cedar Rapids, Ia., by Iowa City Presby., Sept., 1859;
> Cedar Rapids, 1859-64; Brimfield, Ill., 1866-8; Los Angeles,
> Cal., 1868-71; Riverside, 1871-5; Cloverdale, 1875-7; Kohala,
> Hawaii, 1878-80; Healdsburg, Cal., from 1881.

*ANTHONY DEY AXTELL, died Oct. 17, 1866.

WILLIAM NATHANIEL BACON.
> Born in Orwell, Vt., Oct. 11, 1829; united with the Cong. Church
> in Orwell, March, 1847; graduated from Middlebury College in
> 1853; married to HARRIET EMMELINE CUTTS, of Orwell, July
> 26, 1855.
>
> Ordained and installed at Pomfret, Vt., by Windsor Co. Conference,
> Dec. 28, 1859; Pomfret, 1859-63; Shoreham, Vt., from 1864.

ALPHONSO LOOMIS BENTON.
> Born in Cortland, N. Y., Nov. 9, 1831; united with the Pres.
> Church in Cortland, April, 1849; graduated from Hamilton
> College in 1856; married to Miss EMMA SANDFORD, of Ovid,
> N. Y., Jan. 14, 1860.
>
> Ordained and installed at Lima, N. Y., by Presby. of Ontario,
> Mar. 6, 1861; Lima, 1860-70; associate pastor of Cent. Ch.,
> Buffalo, 1870-2; Fredonia, 1872-82; Montrose, Pa., 1882.

WALTER HALSEY CLARK.
> Born in Milton-on-the-Hudson, N. Y., July 2, 1832; united with
> the College Church in Williamstown, Mass., Spring of 1852;
> graduated from Williams College in 1854; married to Miss
> MARIA M. JACKSON, of Xenia, O., Jan. 1, 1861, at Corisco,
> West Africa.
>
> Ordained at Milton, N. Y., by Presby. of North River, June 30,
> 1859; missionary at Gaboon, Africa, 1859-68; translating and
> printing at home, 1868-70; home miss. in Nebraska, 1870-8;
> principal of Silver Ridge Seminary, Nebraska, from 1878.

FREDERICK WILLSON FLINT.

> Born in Fayetteville, N. Y., May 19, 1833; united with the Pres. Church in Dryden, Aug., 1850; graduated from Union College in 1856; married to Miss EMILY POWERS BEARDSLEY, of Auburn, Oct. 19, 1859.
>
> Ordained and installed at Silver Creek, N. Y., by Presby. of Buffalo, June, 1861; Silver Creek; Cohoes, 1864–6; St. Paul, Minn., supplying House of Hope Pres. Ch. and other Churches, 1866–76; Kingston, Pa., 1876–82; edit., Philadelphia, 1881; Winona, Minn., 1882.

GEORGE WASHINGTON HOOD.

> Graduated from Mich. Univ. in 1856; came to Auburn from Lodi, Mich.; supposed to be farming there.

THOMAS BOYD HUDSON, D. D.

> Born in Auburn, N. Y., July 8, 1826; united with the 1st Pres. Church in Auburn, 1842; graduated from Hamilton College in 1851; D. D. from Hamilton College in 1871; married to Miss MARY MARSHALL CLARK, of Cuyahoga Falls, O., Oct. 5, 1859; married to Miss CLARA BABER, of Cuyahoga Falls, O., June 11, 1863.
>
> Ordained and installed at Union Springs, N. Y., by Presby. of Cayuga; Union Springs, 1859–61; chaplain 75th N. Y. Vols., 1861–2; Fulton, N. Y., 1862–3; North East, Pa., 1864–9; Clinton, N. Y., from 1869.

JOHN FRANCIS KENDALL, D. D.

> Born in Volney, N. Y., March 4, 1832; united with the Cong. Ch. in East Bloomfield, May, 1850; graduated from Hamilton College in 1855; D. D. from Wabash College in 1873; married to JULIA C. BIRDSEYE, of Pompey, N. Y., Sept. 6, 1859.
>
> Ordained and installed at Baldwinsville, N. Y., by Presby. of Onondaga, Aug. 31, 1859; Baldwinsville till 1868; 2nd Ch., Columbus, O., 1868–71; La Porte, Ind., from 1871.
>
> Published "Chart of Scripture Offerings," 1871.

RAPHAEL KESSLER.

> Came to Auburn from Harmony, Pa.; mem. of Church in Susquehanna; graduated from Hedingen Acad., Germany, in 1848.
>
> Ordained, 1859; N. Y. City, 1859–61; Mt. Pleasant, Pa., 1861–5; Webster Groves, Mo., 1865–72; Wilmington, Ill., 1873; Pontiac, 1874–6; Brandt, Pa., from 1880.

ELIZUR NEWELL MANLEY.

> Born in Johnstown, N. Y., Nov. 26, 1826; united with the Cong. Church in Richville, Spring of 1847; graduated from Williams College in 1856; married to Miss CORDELIA MARIA INGERSON, of Evans' Mills, N. Y., May 19, 1858.
>
> Ordained and installed at Oakfield, N. Y., by Presby. of Genesee, June 14, 1859; Oakfield, 1858–63; Boonville, 1863–6; Elba, 1867; Camden, from 1868.

WILLIAM MOORE ROBINSON.

Born in Summit, Pa., Oct. 1, 1827 ; united with the Cong. Church
in Cincinnatus, N. Y., 1850; studied at Hartwick Seminary in
class of 1846; married to CHARITY A. COE, of Paterson, N. Y.,
Sept. 21, 1851.

Ordained and installed at Second Pres. Ch., Genoa, N. Y., by
Presby. of Cayuga, June 22, 1859 ; Genoa, 1858–62; Greene,
1863–4; chaplain 114th N. Y. S. Vols., 1864 to close of war ;
Forestport, N. Y., 1866–9 ; Westernville, 1870–1 ; Rossie,
1872–3 ; Heuvelton, 1874–7 ; Frankville, Iowa, from 1878.

DWIGHT SCOVEL.

Born in Warren, N. Y., May 10, 1834; united with the Cong.
Church in Clinton, 1850; graduated from Hamilton College in
1854; taught in Del. Lit. Inst., 1854–6; married to Miss E. L.
WADSWORTH, at Cherry Valley, June 16, 1859.

Ordained pastor of Oneida Lake and Ridge Chs., by Onondaga
Presby., 1858 ; Oneida Lake and Ridge, 1858–61; Lakeville,
1861–7 ; Mendon, 1867–71; Marcellus, 1871–80; Wilson from
1880.

ARCHIBALD MUIRHEAD SHAW.

Born in Glasgow, Scotland, April 11, 1830 ; united with the Pres.
Church in New York Mills, N. Y., Fall of 1851; graduated
from Hamilton College in 1856 ; married to Miss ALMIRA
FANNY NOWLER, of Oneonta, N. Y., Nov. 24, 1859.

Ordained at Waddington, N. Y., by Presby. of St. Lawrence, 1859 ;
Waddington, 1859–61 ; Lenox, 1861–3 ; Avon, 1863–5 ; Con-
stantia, 1865–7 ; invalid, Benton Harbor, Mich., 1867–8 ; Cong.
Ch., Watervliet, 1868–9 ; Pres. Ch., Concord, 1869–71 ;
Tekonsha, 1871–4; invalid; Glenwood, N. Y., 1876–7 ; resident
Clinton, supplying Williamstown and elsewhere, 1878–82 ;
Lyons Falls, 1882.

CHARLES EDWIN STEBBINS.

Born in Waterloo, N. Y., Feb. 3, 1831; united with the Pres.
Church in Waterloo; graduated from Hamilton College in
1856 ; married to Miss CAROLINE F. STEBBINS, of Waterloo,
Oct. 10, 1859; married to Mrs. LUCY A. BUTTS, of Port
Jervis, N. Y., Dec. 31, 1874.

Ordained and installed at Second Pres. Ch., Galesburg, Ill., by
Presby. of Knox, Dec. 14, 1859 ; Galesburg, 1859–61 ; Phelps,
N. Y., 1861–5 ; Ovid, 1865–70 ; Adams, Mass., 1870–6 ;
Brookfield from 1876.

JOHN TATLOCK, D. D.

Born in Liverpool, Eng., Jan. 29, 1835 ; united with the Church
in Williams College, 1855 ; graduated from Williams College in
1856 ; D. D. from Williams College, 1881 ; married to Miss
LUCY BEMAN WHITMAN, Williamstown, Dec., 1858.

Ordained and installed at South Adams, Mass., by Berkshire North Assoc., Nov. 29, 1859; South Adams, 1859–67; Woodside Pres. Ch., Troy, N. Y., 1867–8; Hoosick Falls from 1868. Published "Bible in Pictures," 1880–2.

GUIDO FRIDOLIN VERBECK, D. D.

Born in Zeist, near Utrecht, Holland, Jan. 23, 1830; graduated from Moravian Acad. in Zeist, 1848; D. D. from Rutgers College in 1875; Japanese order of "the Rising Sun," 1877; married to Miss MARIA MANION, of Philadelphia, 1859.

Ordained by Presby. of Cayuga, Mar. 22, 1859; miss. of the Reformed Ch. to Japan; Nagasaki, 1859–69; Tokio, from 1869; (in Japanese Govt. service, 1863–78; president of Imperial University of Tokio.)

Published in conjunction with other persons, many tracts, public documents, and missionary reports.

BENJAMIN FRANKLIN WILLOUGHBY.

Born in Groton, N. Y., Sept. 10, 1833; united with the First Congregational Church in East Groton, 1847; graduated from Hamilton College in 1856; married to Miss SARAH E. SITTSER, of Auburn, Jan. 25, 1860.

Ordained pastor at Canoga, N. Y., by Presby. of Geneva, 1859; Canoga, 1859–61; Parishville, 1861–2; Verona, 1862–5; Augusta, 1865–9; Sauquoit, from 1869.

CHARLES EUGENE KNOX, D. D.

Born in Knoxboro, N. Y., Dec. 27, 1833; united with the Cong. Church in Augusta, June, 1848; graduated from Hamilton College in 1856; Junior year at Auburn; Middle and Senior years at Union; D. D. from Princeton College in 1874; married to Miss SARAH FAKE, of Clinton, Sept. 27, 1860.

Ordained and installed at Bloomfield, N. J., by Presby. of Newark, June 8, 1864; Newark, 1864–73; president of German Theo. School, Newark, from 1873.

Published "Year with St. Paul," 1863; Course of graded S. S. Text Books, 5 in number, 1864–7; "Love to the End," 1868; "David the King," 1874; Reports for Ger. Theo. School, sermons, &c.

COL. WILLIAM KREUTZER.

Born in Benton, N. Y., Sept. 11, 1828; united with the Pres. Church in Branchport, 1856; graduated from Genesee College in 1854; Auburn, 1857–8; married to Miss EMMA JOSEPHINE WOOD, of Red Creek, April 10, 1866.

Never ordained; teacher; in Vol. service of U. S., 1861–5; in hardware business, Lyons.

Published "98th New York Volunteers," 1878.

1857-60.

JOHN CAMPBELL.

Born in Bangor. Ireland, 1828 ; united with the Pres. Church in
Skaneateles, N. Y., 1850 ; graduated from Hamilton College in
1857 ; nearly completed the course at Auburn ; married to Miss
HANNAH L. VIALL, of Mechanicsville, N. Y., 1863.
Ordained at Peru, N. Y., by Presby. of Champlain, 1860 ; Peru,
1860-1 ; Mechanicsville, 1861-4 ; Taberg, 1864-5 ; Johnson-
ville, O., 1866-7 ; Central Col., O., 1868 ; South Trenton, N.
Y., 1869-71 ; Norwich Corners, 1872 ; Clifton Park, 1873 ; since
then, on a farm, preaching as opportunity offered ; resides at
Clifton Park, N. Y.

JEREMIAH NIXON DIAMENT.

Born in Cedarville, N. J., Oct. 4, 1828 ; united with the Second
Pres. Church in Cedarville, about 1842 ; graduated from Mid-
dlebury College in 1857 ; married to Miss MARY EMMA PET-
TENGILL, of Grafton, Vt., Aug. 9, 1860 ; married to Miss MARY
ELIZABETH HAMILTON, of Belleview, Neb., Apr. 1, 1867.
Ordained and installed at Franklin, Pa., by Presby. of Montrose ;
Franklin, 1860-5 ; Redfield and Osceola, N. Y., 1865-8 ; Stan-
ton, Mich., and other places, 1868-74 ; Cherrytree, Pa., 1875-7 ;
resident, Grant P. O., Pa., 1877-82 ; miss. in Wealaka, Creek
Nation, 1882.

JOHN HENRY DILLINGHAM.

Born in Oneonta, N. Y., Oct. 26, 1830 ; united with the Pres. Ch.
in Oneonta, Apr., 1850 ; graduated from Hamilton College in
1857 ; married to Miss MARY L. WHITE, of Ellington, N. Y.,
Mar. 10, 1861.
Ordained at Barton, Wis., by Presby. of Milwaukee, June 20, 1860 ;
Manitowoc, 1860-3 ; Wenona, Ill., 1863-6 ; Belleville, 1866-9 ;
Fairmount Pres. Ch., St. Louis, Mo., 1869-73 ; Paola, Kan.,
1873-4 ; Rossville, Ill., 1874-80 ; South Saginaw, Mich., from
1880.

WILLIAM HART.

Born in Scotland, 1834 ; united with the Pres. Church in Geneseo,
N. Y., about 1853 ; graduated from Hamilton College in 1855 ;
married to Miss MARY Y. SELOVER, of Auburn, Oct. 30, 1861.
Ordained and installed at Auburn, by Presby. of Cayuga, 1861 ;
chap. 19th N. Y. S. V., 1861-3 ; Pres. Ch., Malden, N. Y., 1863
-8 ; Fifth Pres. Ch., Washington, D. C., 1868-70 ; Bath, Me.,
Cong. Ch., 1870-9 ; Westport, Conn., from 1879.

EDWARD WILLIAM HITCHCOCK, D. D.

Born in Homer, N. Y., May 1, 1833 ; united with the Cong. Ch.
in Homer, May, 1848 ; graduated from Yale College in 1857 ;
D. D. from Hamilton College in 1879 ; married to EVELYN P.
HAWLEY, of Homer, July 19, 1860.

Ordained and installed at Tompkinsville, L. I., by South Classis of New York, Aug 8, 1860; Tompkinsville, 1860–66; New York, 14th St. Pres. Ch., 1866–72; pastor of American Chapel, Paris, since 1872.

GEORGE DINSMORE HORTON.

Born in Lyme, N. Y., Nov. 3, 1829; united with the Pres. Church in Chaumont, N. Y., 1850; graduated from Hamilton College in 1857; married to Miss CARRIE INGERSOLL, of Constantia, Aug. 1, 1860; married to Miss WEALTHY ARCENOE BLAKE, of Coventry, June 25, 1869.

Ordained at Dexter, N. Y., by Presby. of Watertown, July 8, 1862; Dexter and Brownville, 1860–4; Oneida Lake and Ridgeville, 1864–7; Jamesville, 1867–8; Coventryville, 1868–76; resident in Bainbridge.

SMITH HARRIS HYDE.

Born in Youngstown, N. Y., Sept. 28, 1834; united with the Ch. in April, 1848; graduated from Yale College in 1857; married to Miss LUCINDA TAYLOR DAVIS, of Youngstown, Sept. 10, 1862.

Ordained and installed at Rock Hill, by Presby. of St. Louis, Apr. 24, 1861; Rock Hill to 1864; Carrollton, Ill., 1864–80; E. St. Louis, 1880–2; Carthage, 1882.

LEGH RICHMOND JANES.

Born in Chenango Forks, N. Y., Nov. 15, 1833; united with the Pres. Church in Colchester, 1852; graduated from Hamilton College in 1857; married to Miss FLORA W. SMITH, of Syracuse, N. Y., May 16, 1860.

Ordained at Stamford, N. Y., by Delaware Presby., June, 1860; Shortsville, 1860–9, being absent as chaplain 99th Pa. Vet. Vols., from 1864 to close of war; Onondaga Valley, 1869–72; New Market, Tenn., from 1872. Son of Francis Janes, of 1830–3.

DAVID SUMNER JOHNSON, D. D.

Born in Waterford, N. Y., June 4, 1834; united with the Ref. Church in Watervliet, 1852; graduated from Williams College in 1857; Andover, 1857–8; Auburn, 1858–60; D. D. from Blackburn Univ. in 1878; married to Miss HELEN LOUISA WILLARD, of Cayuga, N. Y., June 19, 1860.

Ordained and installed at Waverly, N. Y., by Presby. of Chemung, Sept., 1860; Waverly, 1860–7; Hyde Park, Ill., 1867–81; Second Pres. Ch., Springfield, from 1881.

HERRICK JOHNSON, D. D., LL. D.

Born in Caughnewaga, N. Y., Sept. 22, 1832; united with the First Pres. Church in Buffalo, Fall of 1854; graduated from Hamilton College in 1857; D. D. from Western Reserve College in 1867; LL. D. from Wooster Univ. in 1882; married to Miss CATHERINE SPENCER HARDENBERGH, of Auburn, September 6, 1860.

Ordained and installed at Troy, N. Y., by Presby. of Troy, June 28, 1860; Troy, 1860-2; Third Ch., Pittsburgh, Pa., 1862-8; First Ch., Philadelphia, Pa., 1868-74; prof. of Homiletics and Past. The., Auburn, 1874-80; Fourth Ch., Chicago, Ill., and prof. of Homiletics in Theo. Sem. of the Northwest, from 1880.
Published many sermons, addresses, articles, tracts, Sunday School lessons, &c.; "Christianity's Challenge," 1881.
Moderator of General Assembly, at Springfield, Ill., 1882.

JOHN LEVIS JONES.

Born in Wales, May 1, 1829; united with the Cong. Church in 1845; studied at Whitestown and Cazenovia Seminaries; married to Miss MARGARET LAMSON, of New York Mills, N. Y., Oct. 16, 1861.
Ordained and installed at New Berlin, N. Y., by Chenango Presby., Oct. 8, 1861; New Berlin till 1866; Guilford Centre, 1866-73; Villisca, Iowa, 1873-81; Essex, from 1881.

CHARLES WESLEY MACCARTHY.

Born in Ox Bow, N. Y., March 28, 1830; united with the First Church in Geneseo Village, April, 1849; graduated from Williams College in 1856; married to Miss FLORENCE ELIZA WILCOX, of Oakfield, N. Y., Nov. 22, 1860; married to Mrs. CAROLINE ELISABETH BACHMAN, of Romulus, March 6, 1867.
Ordained by Presby. of Genesee, May 1, 1861; East Pembroke, N. Y., 1860-2; U. S. Army, 1862-5; principal of Rural Seminary, East Pembroke, 1865-6; Portageville, 1866-75; Oneida Valley, Oneida Lake and Ridgeville, 1875-7; Constantia and Cleveland from 1877.

GEORGE W. MACKIE.

Came to Auburn from Rochester; mem. of Brick Church in Rochester.
Ordained about 1860; Lakeville, N. Y., 1861; Adams, 1862-5; Janesville, Wis., 1865-6; Chicago, Ill., 1866-73; Galena, 1873-5; Adams, N. Y., 1876; Chicago, Ill., 1876-8; resident in Adams, N. Y.

AUGUSTUS MARSH.

Born in Aurora, Erie Co., N. Y., June 1, 1834; united with the Pres. Church in Tekonsha, Mich., Aug., 1848; graduated from Univ. of Mich., 1855; married to Miss MARTHA S. HEWITT, of North Sterling, N. Y., Sept. 10, 1863.
Ordained at Blissfield, Mich., by Presby. of Monroe, Nov., 1860; Brooklyn, Mich., 1860-2; Grand Rapids, 1st Pres. Ch., 1862-6; Portland Cong. Ch., 1 year; same place, Pres. Ch., 8 years; Clam Lake, (now Cadillac) since 1875.

MARTIN POWELL ORMSBY.

Born in Underhill, Vt., June 1, 1830; united with the Cong. Church in Greenville, Ill., April, 1848; studied at Greenville

Academy; admitted to practice Law, Sept., 1854 ; married to
Miss M. Catharine Huffman, of Shelbyville, Ill., Dec. 25, 1860.
Ordained at Pisgah, Ill., by Presby. of Illinois, Sept., 1860 ; Shelbyville, Wilmington and Mt. Carroll, Ill., 1860-4 ; Minonk, 1864
-70 ; Winchester, 1871-2 ; Eureka, 1872-80 ; Monticello from
1880

ANDREW PARSONS.
    Born in Sharon Springs, N. Y., Aug. 15, 1830 ; united with the
    First Pres. Church in Elmira, Summer of 1849 ; graduated from
    Williams College in 1857 ; married to Miss Selona White, of
    Auburn, May 22, 1862.
    Ordained at Richfield Springs, N. Y., by Presby. of Otsego, June,
    1860 ; Richfield Springs, 1860-6 ; Ottawa, Kan., 1866-70 ;
    Weyauwega, Fremont and Royalton, Wis., 1870-5 ; Hunter,
    N. Y., from 1875.

GEORGE RANSOM.
    Born in Chazy, N. Y., May 16, 1831; united with the Cong.
    Church in Chazy, March, 1840 ; studied at Champlain and
    Schoharie Academies ; married to Armenia A. Slack, of
    Mexico, N. Y., June 27, 1870.
    Ordained at Redford, N. Y., by Champlain Presby., July 10, 1861 ;
    Redford, 1860-4 ; Muir, Mich., from 1864.

*Thomas W. Roberts, died Sept. 26, 1860.

LEWIS BENJAMIN ROGERS.
    Born in Albion, N. Y., Sept. 10, 1833; united with the First Pres.
    Church in Albion, May, 1848 ; graduated from Union College
    in 1857 ; married to Miss Martha Sophia Goold, of Carlton,
    June 5, 1860.
    Ordained by Niagara Presby., Oct., 1863 ; Honeoye Falls, N. Y.,
    1860-1 ; Marengo, Iowa, 1863-4; Somerset, N. Y., 1867-71 ;
    Millville, 1871-4 ; Pueblo, Col., 1874-5 ; resident in Albion, N. Y.

*Thomas Sherrard, died Aug. 10, 1874.

JOSEPH EMERSON TINKER.
    Born in Honolulu, Sandwich Islands, Jan. 20, 1833; united with
    the Pres. Church in Westfield, N. Y., Oct., 1851 ; graduated
    from Hamilton College in 1857; married to Miss Pamelia J.
    Beard, of Pompey, N. Y., May 14, 1863.
    Ordained and installed at Willoughby, O., by Presby. of Cleveland,
    June, 1860 ; Willoughby, 1860-6 ; Franklinville, N. Y., 1867-
    70 ; Portville, 1870-81 ; Sinclairville, from 1881. Son of Reuben
    Tinker of 1827-30.

EDWIN B. VAN AUKEN.
    Came to Auburn from Rochester, N. Y.; mem. of Wash. St. Pres.
    Church in Rochester ; Honeoye Falls, 1863-5 ; Mendon, 1865-
    7 ; Bergen, 1867-9 ; tea. Rochester, from 1870.

AUGUSTUS FIELD BEARD, D. D.

Born in South Norwalk, Ct., May 11, 1833; united with the First Cong. Church in Norwalk, May, 1851; graduated from Yale College in 1857; one year at Auburn, two years at Union; D. D. from Syracuse University in 1875; married to Miss ELIZA GODDARD, of Cape Elizabeth, Me., Aug. 19, 1861; married to Miss ANNIE D. BARKER, of Calais, Jan. 2, 1865.

Ordained by Fairfield Co. West Assoc., May 24, 1860; Cape Elizabeth, Me., 1860-2; pastor of Central Cong. Ch., Bath, 1862-9; pastor of Plymouth Cong. Ch., Syracuse, N. Y., from 1869.

RICHARD CRITTENDEN.

Aub. Sen. class from Andover; dismissed after one week; finished Theological course in New Haven; Cong. Ch., North Guilford, Conn.; service of Am. S. S. Un.; resident in Bellefonte, Pa.

GEORGE SEAMAN GRAY.

Born in N. Y. City, July 10, 1835; united with the Market St. Ref. Church in N. Y. City, June, 1851; graduated from Yale College in 1857; Auburn, Middle class, 1858-9; Union Sem., N. Y., 1859-60; married to Miss SARAH BROWN, of Cincinnati, O., May 1, 1861.

Never ordained; preached Portland, Me., 1860; Westbrook, 1860-2; Cincinnati, O., 1862-3; tea. Englewood, N. J., 1863-6; since in business in Cincinnati.

MOSES J. LIEBERMAN.

Educated as an Israelitish Rabbi; came from Germany in 1858; Auburn, 1858-9; said to reside in Chicago; engaged in business and lecturing on the Talmud.

DANIEL HENRY ROGAN.

Born in Kingsport, Tenn., June, 1830; united with the Church in Kingsport, 1849; graduated from Amherst College in 1857; dismissed to Maysville Theo. Sem., May 5, 1859; married to HARRIET EATON HUNT, of Amherst, Mass., May 10, 1859.

Ordained and installed at Bristol, Tenn., by Holston Presby., Nov., 1859; Bristol, 1859-61; Bernardston, Mass., 1861-3; First Cong. Ch., Greenfield, 1863; North Amherst to 1866; Pres. Ch., Hudson, Wis., 1870; Cong. Ch., Newton, Iowa, 1871-4; Anoka, Minn., 1875; Univ. Ch., Newton, Ia.; Cedar Rapids, from 1880.

SAMUEL SCOVILLE.

Born in North Cornwall, Ct., Dec. 21, 1834; united with the Cong. Church in North Cornwall, May, 1846; graduated from Yale College in 1857; at Auburn, Feb. 5, 1858 to close of Jun. year; second year at Andover; third year at Union, N. Y.; married to Miss HARRIETT ELIZA BEECHER, of Brooklyn, N. Y., Sept. 25, 1861.

Ordained and installed at Norwich, N. Y., by Susquehanna Assoc., Sept., 1861 ; Norwich, 1861-79 ; Stamford, Ct., from 1879.

DELOS ELIJAH WELLS.

Born in Pompey, N. Y., Jan. 16, 1832 ; united with the First Pres. Church in Pompey, 1853 ; graduated from Williams College in 1854 ; first two years at Auburn ; third year at Lane ; married to Miss ELIZA M. MACY, of Cincinnati, O., Sept. 12, 1860.

Ordained at Pataska, O., by Pataskala Presby., 1860 ; New Philadelphia, O., from 1860 ; Monroeville, from 1864 ; Red Wing, Minn., from 1867 ; Fulton, Ill., from 1873.

JOHN SEYMOUR WHITMAN.

Born in Williamstown, Mass., Nov. 7, 1833 ; united with the Cong. Church in Williamstown, 1846 ; graduated from Williams College in 1854 ; second year at Auburn; first and third at Union ; married to Miss LILLIE ARNE, of Auburn, June 13, 1860.

Ordained at Rochester, Minn., by Council, Sept. 4, 1861 ; Rochester, 1861-2 ; Charlemont, Mass., 1863-5 ; Sprague, Conn., 1865-9 ; Lyndon, Vt., 1871-5 ; Berea, O., 1876-7: Chatham, from 1877.

1858-61.

HORACE HEWS ALLEN.

Born in Honeoye Falls, N. Y., Dec. 27, 1835 ; united with the Church in Honeoye Falls, 1851 ; graduated from University of Rochester, 1857 ; married to SARAH C. HOWARD, of Albion, May 28, 1861 ; married to FRANCES A. FITCH, of Springfield, June 4, 1872.

Ordained at Victor, N. Y., by Rochester Presby., June 11, 1862 ; Cayuga, 1861-9 ; Oneonta, from 1869.

RUFUS APTHORP.

Born in Hinsdale, Mass., Feb. 8, 1828 ; united with the Cong. Church in Hinsdale, Nov., 1847 ; graduated from Williams College in 1857 ; married to H. LOUISA FAY, of Rochester, O., May 14, 1861.

Ordained and installed at Cooper, Mich., by Kalamazoo Assoc., Oct. 16, 1861 ; Cong. Ch., Cooper, 1861-3 ; St. Johns, 1863-7 ; Alpena, 1867-70 ; Allegan, 1870-1 ; DeWitt, Iowa, 1871-5 ; Lanark, Ill., 1876-7 ; Big Rock, Iowa, 1877-80; Rock Falls, Ill., 1880-2 ; Odell, 1882.

HON. CHARLES E. COOTES.

Came to Auburn from Cazenovia, N. Y.; studied at N. Y. Central College; married in Auburn, about 1861 ; resident in Auburn, lawyer, real estate agent, chief of police, police justice.

CHARLES DAVID FLAGLER.

Came to Auburn from Lansingburg, N. Y.; graduated from Union College in 1858.

Chestertown, N. Y., to 1867 ; Au Sable Forks, 1868–9 ; Chateaugay, 1870–8 ; assistant minister, Prot. Ep. Ch., Chester, 1882.

CHESTER WARNER HAWLEY.

Born in Hadley, Mass., Sept. 20, 1834 ; united with the Cong. Ch. in North Hadley, 1850 ; graduated from Amherst College in 1858 ; married to ALZOA A. THOMPSON, of Homer, N. Y., May 7, 1861 ; married to MARTHA JAQUETH, of Liverpool, June 12, 1872.

Ordained and installed at Liverpool, by Presby., May 2, 1861 ; Liverpool, 1861–4 ; chaplain 185th N. Y. S. Vols., 1864–5 ; Waterville, N. Y., 1865–71 ; Batavia, 1871–4 ; Denver, Col., 1874–6 ; Amherst, Mass., 2nd Cong. Ch., 1876–9 ; Atlanta, Ga., 1st Cong. Ch., 1879–81.

HIRAM HILL.

Born in Belleville, N. Y., Aug. 29, 1832 ; united with the Pres. Church in July, 1852 ; graduated from Yellow Springs College in 1857 ; married to Miss LOIS A. BROWN, of Auburn, Oct. 9, 1861.

Ordained at Cape Vincent, N. Y., by Presby. of Watertown, April, 1862 ; Cape Vincent, 1861–5 ; Austin, Nevada, 1865–6 ; Holden, Mass., 1867–72 ; Carthage, 1 year ; Visalia, Cal., 1873–8 ; San Leandro, from 1878.

JOHN LATSHAW LANDIS.

Born in Colebrookdale, Pa., Jan. 9, 1835 ; united with the 1st Pres. Church in Carlisle, 1858 ; studied at Dickinson College ; married to Miss FLORENCE ANNA NILES, of Coudersport, Oct. 17, 1873.

Ordained and installed at Coudersport, by Wellsboro Presby., 1870 ; Abington Ch., Pa., 1861–3 ; service of Chr. Com., 1863–5 ; disabled until 1869 ; Coudersport, 1869–73 ; Presbyterial miss. in Huntingdon, 1873–5 ; Pres. Ch., Franklinville, 1875–6 ; Classical Inst., at Parkersburgh, 1876–9 ; resident in Philadelphia, 1881.

CHARLES CARROLL MCINTIRE.

Born in Springfield, Mass., 1830 ; united with the 1st Pres. Church in June, 1853 ; married to Mrs. JENNIE JOHNSON CRAWFORD, of Albany, N. Y., June 19, 1861.

Ordained at Greene, N. Y., by Council, Sept. 17, 1861 ; Windsor Locks, Conn., 1862–5 ; Lansing, Mich., 1865–8 ; Pontiac, 1868–71 ; Rockport, Mass., 1871–80 ; Pittsford, Vt., from 1880.

CHARLES EDWARD ROBINSON, D. D.

Born in Ludlowville, N. Y., Sept. 5, 1835 ; united with the First Pres. Church in Watertown, May, 1852 ; graduated from Hamil-

ton College in 1857; D. D. from Williams College in 1870; married to Miss CLARA C. VAILL, of Litchfield, Ct., Sept. 9, 1862.
Ordained and installed at Woodbury, Ct., by Litchfield So. Consoc., June 11, 1862; Woodbury, 1861–4; Pres. Ch., Oneida, N. Y., 1864–7; Troy, 1867–78; 1st Pres. Ch., Rochester, from 1878.

WALLACE WALTER THORPE.
Born in Skaneateles, N. Y., Jan. 17, 1833; united with the Pres. Church in Skaneateles, Jan., 1852; graduated from Hamilton College in 1858; married to Miss JULIA MARIA AUSTIN, of Binghamton, May 30, 1861.
Ordained at West Salem, Wis., by the La Crosse Dist. Conv., Feb. 7, 1864; chaplain 3rd N. Y. S. Vols., 1861–2; Cong. Church, Sparta, Wis., 1863–5; Athens, Tenn., Pres. Ch., and prin. of Acad., 1865–9; Waterloo, Ia., 1870–3; Marshalltown, 1874–7; 1st Pres. Ch., East Des Moines, 1877–80; Centreville from 1881.

WILLIAM HENRY WEBB.
Born in Homer, N. Y., June 7, 1833; united with the Cong. Ch. in Homer, 1853; graduated from Hamilton College in 1858; married to Miss H. ELIZABETH PRINCE, of Auburn, May 9, 1861.
Ordained and installed at Suspension Bridge, N. Y., by Ontario Assoc., July 18, 1861; Sus. Bridge, 1861–3; Adrian, Mich., 1865–74; Springfield, O., from 1874.

———

WILLIAM SWAN ADAMSON.
Born in Dundee, Scotland, 1832; united with the Pres. South Ch. in Dundee, 1850; studied at N. Y. Central College and Univ. of Heidelberg; Auburn, 1858–9; Union Sem., N. Y., 1859–61; married, June 20, 1876.
Ordained and installed at Greene, N. Y., by Council, Sept. 17, 1861; Greene, 1861–3; Chr. Com., 1863; Wolcottville, Conn., 1863–6; Ansonia, 1866–71; ord. (Prot. Ep.) Jan. 25, 1874; St. Thomas' Ch., Ravenswood, N. Y., 1874–9; St. Paul's, Phila., Pa., from 1879.

W. L. BEEMER.
At Auburn from Dec., 1858, to Apr., 1859.

JAMES DEANE.
Born in Utica, N. Y., Apr. 21, 1836; united with the Church in Williams College, May, 1855; graduated from Williams College in 1857; Auburn, 1858–60; married to Miss ANNIE MARIA BOSWORTH, of Salisbury, Conn., Oct. 12, 1858.
Ordained at Sandisfield, Mass., by Council, Oct. 31, 1866; home miss. work in Ill., 1860–1; East Canaan, Conn., 1861–2; lieut. and capt. of U. S. Vols., 1862–5; Sandisfield, Mass., 1865–7; Westmoreland, N. Y., 1867–78; Phoenix, 1878–81; Howell's, from 1881.

JAMES BOARDMAN GILBERT.
Born in Pittsford, Vt., Aug. 12, 1826; united with the Cong. Ch.

in Pittsford, 1840 ; graduated from Univ. of Vermont, in 1853 ; Auburn, 1858–60; married to Miss HARRIET BRANNAN EATON, of Dubuque, Ia., Nov. 13, 1862.

Ordained at Dubuque, Ia., by Dubuque Assoc., Oct. 16, 1860 ; Lucas Grove, Lansing, Maquoketa, Mason City, Toledo, Buckingham, Durant, Rockford, all in Iowa, 1860–80; Fontanelle, Neb., from 1880.

MATTHEW LaRUE PERRINE HILL.

Born in East Bloomfield, N. Y., March 11, 1834; united with the 1st Pres. Church in Geneva, 1852; graduated from Williams College in 1858; one year at Auburn and two at Princeton; married to Miss MARCELIA FARNHAM, of Johnstown, Oct. 20, 1870.

Ordained and installed at Little Falls, N. Y., by Albany Presby., Sept. 19, 1861; Little Falls, 1861–8; Gloversville Pres. Ch., 1868–70; Jacksonville, Florida, 1870–2 ; Des Moines, Iowa, 1872–5 ; Corning, N. Y., from 1875.

HENRY RICHARD HOISINGTON. See 1860–3.

ISAIAH BARDSLEY HOPWOOD.

Born in Bredbury, Cheshire, Eng., Nov. 6, 1831; united with the Church in March, 1853; graduated from Univ. of City of New York, 1859 ; Middle year at Auburn ; graduated at Union, N. Y., 1861 ; married to PHEBE L. BERRY, of Dover, N. J., May 9, 1861.

Ordained and installed at Coventry, N. Y., by Presby. of Chenango, July 15, 1861; Coventry, 1861–3; Oxford Furnace, N. J., 1863–5 ; Parkville, L. I., 1865–7 ; Paterson, N. J., 1867–74; Newark, Calvary Ch., from 1874.

WILLIAM LUSK.

Graduated from Union College in 1858; dismissed from Aub., Oct.15, 1858 ; graduated at Princeton ; served several Churches ; rector of P. E. Ch., North Haven, Conn., 1882.

WILLIAM JACKSON STOUTENBURGH.

Born in Macedonia, Pa., Sept. 20, 1833 ; graduated from Williams College in 1858; Auburn, 1858–9 ; Union Sem., N. Y., 1860–1.

Ordained and installed by Presby., Sept. 17, 1861 ; N. Y. City, 1861–4; Cong. Ch., Allen's Grove, Wis., 1864–6 ; Pres. Ch., Manitowoc, 1866–8; Tecumseh, Mich., 1868–74; Birmingham, 1874–6 ; Lapeer, 1876–9 ; South Haven, 1879–80 ; Wilmington, Ill., from 1880.

JOHN COLEMAN TAYLOR.

Born in Benton, N. Y., Feb. 28, 1833 ; united with the Cong. Ch., in Penn Yan, 1849; graduated from Union College in 1858; Jun. year in Auburn, Mid. year in Union, last year in Andover ; married to Miss SARAH J. McCARRICK, of Prattsburgh ; married to Miss SARAH LIFE, of Rye, Feb. 22, 1875.

Ordained and installed at Sweden Center, N. Y., by Rochester
Presby., Feb. 11, 1862; Sweden Center, 1861–5; Corry, Pa.,
1865–7; Groton, N. Y., 1867–71; Hanover St. Cong. Ch., Milwaukee, Wis., 1872–4; Cuba, N. Y., from 1875.

ROBERT C. WALL.
In the Seminary two months; now rector of P. E. Ch., in Carthage, Mo.

1859-62.

JOHN STEBBINS BACON.
Born July 12, 1833; united with the Church in Palmyra, N. Y.,
Oct., 1858; studied at Genesee College; A. M. from Hamilton
College in 1875; married to SARAH H. PRENTISS, of Pultney,
N. Y., May 5, 1858.
Ordained at South Butler, N. Y., by Presby. of Lyons, Sept. 9,
1862; Amboy, 1862–70; Syracuse Fourth Pres. Ch., 1870–6;
Niagara Falls, from 1876.

JAMES BROWN BEAUMONT.
Born in Dresden, N. Y., June 5, 1831; united with the Pres. Ch.
in Penn Yan, 1851; graduated from Amherst College in 1858;
married to Miss ANNA PERSIS GAYLORD, of Naples, N. Y., June,
1862; married to Miss HARRIET NEWELL MORRIS, of Montclair,
N. J., Nov., 1867.
Ordained and installed at Olean, N. Y., by Presby. of Genesee
Valley, May, 1862; Olean, 1862–7; Waverly, 1867–71; Wash-
ingtonville, 1871–82; Chatham, N. J., 1882.
Published several sermons.

IRVING L. BEMAN.
Born in Bethany Center, N. Y., 1834; united with the 1st Pres.
Church in Waterford, Pa., 1852.
Ordained and installed at Cortland, N. Y., by Presby. of Cortland,
1863; Cortland, 1862–5; Philadelphia, Pa., 1865–8; Mechanics-
ville, N. Y., 1869–72; Cong. Ch., Vineland, N. J., 1872–4; Mor-
risania Station, 1877; Crown Point, N. Y., 1878–82; St. John,
N. B., 1882.
Published many popular articles and short stories.

ARCHIBALD CRAWFORD.
Born in Ireland; came to Auburn from Church in Yellow Springs,
Ia.; graduated from Yellow Springs College in 1859.
Cong. Ch., Paris Hill, N. Y., 1863; in Ireland from 1863; minis-
ter of U. P. Church near Newark, N. J., 1871–2; of U. P.
Church in Phila., Pa., 1880.

HORACE FRANKLIN DUDLEY.
Born in Hanover, N. H., Jan. 1, 1832; united with the 1st Cong.

Church in Hanover, 1851 ; graduated from Dartmouth College
in 1859 ; Union, N. Y., 1859–60 ; Auburn, 1860–2 ; married to
Miss JOSEPHINE SAMSON, of Charlestown, Mass., Sept., 1862.
Ordained (Cong.) Sept. 6, 1865 ; Pres. Ch., South Trenton, N. Y.,
1862–5 ; Paris, 1865–7 ; Morrisville, 1867–73 ; Warsaw from 1873.
Published sermons and addresses.

CORLISS BARLOW GARDNER.
Born in Brockport, N. Y., Dec. 1, 1829 ; united with the Pres. Ch.
in Brockport, Feb., 1855 ; graduated from Univ. of Rochester in
1857 ; married to HARRIET FREEMAN, of Rochester, N. Y., Sept.
2, 1862.
Ordained at Clarkson, N. Y., by Presby. of Rochester, Jan. 20,
1863 ; Cuba, 1864–75 ; Westminster Church, Rochester, from
1875.

EDMUND BRIDGES MINER.
Born in Scriba, N. Y., April 26, 1829 ; united with the Pres. Ch. in
Belleville, 1852 ; graduated from Hamilton College in 1859 ;
married to Miss LUCY B. HUNTING, of North Henderson, N. Y.,
Sept. 10, 1862.
Ordained and installed at Baraboo, Wis., by Presby. of Columbus,
Feb., 1863 ; Baraboo, 1862–4 ; Mineral Point, 1864–7 ; Big
Rapids, Mich., 1867–70 ; Camillus, N. Y., 1870–1 ; Westfield,
1871–4 ; Warren, Ill., 1874–6 ; Norwood, 1876–80 ; Paxton,
1880–2 ; Batavia, 1882.

MARCUS NORTH PRESTON.
Born in Lodi, (now Gowanda) N. Y., July 1, 1835 ; united with
the Cong. Church in Berlin, Wis., March, 1853 ; graduated from
Williams College in 1859 ; first year at Union, N. Y.; second
and third at Auburn ; married to Miss REBECCA B. TENNEY, of
Chester, N. H., May 12, 1862.
Ordained and installed at Skaneateles, N. Y., by Cayuga Presby.,
Sept., 1862, where he yet remains.

PHILANDER READ.
Born in Wattsburg, Pa., May 4, 1830 ; united with the Pres. Ch. in
Wattsburg, March, 1850 ; graduated from Amherst College in
1859 ; married to Miss AMELIA LINDIA McNEILL, of Centre
Point, Iowa, Oct. 1, 1868 ; married to Miss MARY JANE MUS-
COTT, of Lewis Co., N. Y., Apr. 29, 1874.
Ordained at Carrollton, La., by Council, Jan. 4, 1863 ; soldier,
1861–3 ; chaplain U. S. A., 1863–5 ; Rolla, Mo., 1866 ; Centre
Point, Iowa, 1867 ; Austin and Harrisonville, Mo., 1869 ; Ellin-
wood, Kan., 1873–80 ; also Atlanta, 1873–7, and Sterling,
1877–80 ; Augusta, from 1880.

JOHN P. ROE.
Came to Auburn from Moodna, N. Y.; mem. of Church there.
Lansingburgh, 1863–4 ; Cornwall, 1865 ; Oshkosh, Wis., from

1866 ; health failed; fruit farmer near Oshkosh for many years ; Pres. Ch., Weyauwega, 1881-2.

*SETH WILLARD SEGUR, died Sept. 24, 1875.

EDWARD PAYSON WILLARD.
Born in Cayuga, N. Y., May 27, 1835 ; united with the Pres. Ch. in Cayuga, 1853 ; graduated from Williams College in 1858; read law one year, before entering Auburn ; married to Miss MARY E. WINNIE, of Carson City, Nevada, May 1, 1867 ; married to Miss FRANCES C. YOUNG, of Philadelphia, Pa., June, 1871.
Ordained at Oakland, Cal., by Presby. of San Francisco, Jan. 8, 1867 ; has labored in Canaan, Ct., Columbia, Cal., Vienna, Mich., Erie, Mich., &c.; Cayuga, N. Y., since 1879.

*WILLIAM AUGUSTUS WOLCOTT, died Nov. 29, 1866.

JOHN CASTLETON LONG. See 1867-70.

NORMAN ALLING MILLERD.
Born in Summer Hill, N. Y., 1827 ; united with the 1st Cong. Ch. in Prairie du Chien, Wis., 1856; graduated from Hamilton College in 1847 ; dismissed to Chicago The. Sem., Aug. 29, 1860; married to Miss CLARA ELIZABETH CHURCH, of Prairie du Chien, 1857.
Ordained at Hartland, Wis., by Pres. and Cong. Conv., Milwaukee Dist., 1861 ; Raymond, Wis., 1860; Quincy, Ill., 1862-4 ; Sheboygan, Wis., 1866-9; Benton Harbor, Mich., 1872-5 ; Chicago, Ill., 1875-7 ; resident there.

1860-3.

WILLIAM RILEY BENHAM.
Born in Fleming, N. Y., Dec. 16, 1838 ; united with the M. E. Ch. in 1850; graduated from Oneida Conf. Seminary in 1860, and from Genesee College in 1866 ; married to Miss MARY AMELIA MATHER, of Livonia, N. Y., Sept. 13, 1865.
Ordained at Waterloo, N. Y., in M E. Church, Sept. 3, 1865 ; Macedon, 1865-6 ; Lima, 1867-9 ; Penn Yan, 1870-1 ; Rochester, 1872; inv., 1873; Victor, 1874-6 ; resident Canandaigua, 1877-81 ; Newark, M. E. Ch., from 1881.

JOHN SHEPARD BINGHAM.
Born in Verona, N. Y., Aug. 8, 1834; united with the Pres. Ch. in Durhamville, Summer of 1852; graduated from Princeton College in 1858; married to Miss MARY WILLIAMSON, of Verona, Aug. 27, 1858.
Ordained at Portageville, N. Y., by Genesee Valley Presby., June, 1864 ; Portageville, 1863-6; Belmont, 1866-70 ; Almond, 1870

−1; tea. Canisteo and afterward Wellsville, 1871–82 ; preaching, Wis., 1882.

FREDERIC AUGUSTUS CHASE.

Born in King's Ferry, N. Y., Jan. 29, 1833 ; united with the Cong. Church in Ann Arbor, Mich., Nov., 1857 ; studied at Mich. University ; A. M. from Milton College, 1872 ; married to Miss JULIA AUGUSTA SPENCE, of Ann Arbor, Mich., Aug. 13, 1863.

Ordained at Parishville, N. Y., by St. Lawrence Consoc., July, 1863 ; Parishville, 1863–5 ; Lyndonville, from 1865 ; took charge of Lyons Female College, Iowa, 1868 ; prof. of Nat. Science in Fisk Univ., Tenn., from 1872.

CHARLES ALBION CONANT.

Born in Temple, Me., July 28, 1833 ; united with the Cong. Church in Temple, 1855 ; graduated from Union College in 1860 ; Bangor Seminary, 1860–2 ; Auburn, 1862–3 ; married to Miss HARRIET LOOMIS BUNN, of Amsterdam, N. Y., 1863.

Ordained at Moravia, N. Y., by Presby. of Cayuga, July, 1864 ; Moravia, 1863–5 ; Five Corners, 1865–71 ; Pike, 1871–2 ; Amherst, Mass., 1872–6 ; Duluth, Minn., 1876–8 ; Cannon Falls, 1878–81 ; St. Paul, 1882.

WILLIAM CONWAY CURTIS.

Born in Norwalk, Conn., May 10, 1837 ; united with the Cong. Church in Norwalk, about 1853 ; graduated from Williams College in 1860 ; married to Miss FANNIE M. NORTON, of East-port, Me., Aug. 26, 1868.

Ordained at Titusville, Pa., by Presby., Sept., 1863 ; Titusville, 1863–5 ; Cong. Ch., Eastport, Me., 1865–6 ; Richmond, from 1868.

WRIGHT CALEB GALPIN.

Born in Candor, N. Y., Dec. 10, 1832 ; united with the First Pres. Ch. in Auburn, Autumn of 1860; graduated from Susquehanna Sem.; 2 years at Yale College, after leaving Auburn ; married to Miss ANN SOPHIA CLARKE, of Binghamton, Sept. 14, 1858 ; married to Miss JULIA ELIZA SMITH, of Dunmore, Pa., 1875.

Ordained at Troy, Pa., by Susquehanna Presby., May, 1873 ; ordination delayed by ill health ; Fremont, Neb., 1868–71 ; Hawley, Pa., 1871–6 ; Unadilla, N. Y., 1876–9 ; resident in Binghamton.

FRANK GILBERT.

Born in Pittsford, Vt., Sept. 28, 1839 ; united with the Pres. Church in Middle Granville, N. Y., 1857 ; graduated from Univ. of Vt. in 1859; married to Miss FRANK BAKER, of Farm-ersville, Cat. Co., N. Y., 1863.

Never ordained ; Scipio, N. Y., 1864–5 ; Peoria, Ill., 1865–6 ; editor of Evening Journal, Chicago.

Published " The World, Historical and Actual," 1882.

HENRY RICHARD HOISINGTON.

Born in Batticotta, Ceylon, Oct. 4, 1836; united with the First Cong. Church in Williamstown, Mass., 1854; graduated from Williams College in 1857; Auburn, 1858-9 and '61-3; married to Miss MARION FENTON, of Mansfield, Conn., Oct. 19, 1865.

Ordained at Warren, O., by Mahoning Presby., May 4, 1864; Warren, 1863-7; Circleville, O., 1867-72; North Pres. Ch., Cleveland, O., 1872-80; Coventry, Conn., from 1881.

Son of Henry Richard Hoisington, of 1828-31.

SENECA MCNEILL KEELER.

Born in Ridgefield, Conn., May 31, 1835; united with the 1st Cong. Church in Ridgefield, Sept., 1852; graduated from Yale College in 1856; married to Miss ALICE B. SMITH, of North Salem, N. Y., Aug. 24, 1857.

Ordained and installed at Guilford Centre, N. Y., by Presby. of Chenango, July 8, 1863; Cong. Ch., Guilford Centre, 1863-6; Smyrna, 1866-70; Madison, 1870-2; 1st Cong. Ch., West Newbury, Mass., 1872-8; Pres. Ch., Newburyport and Cong. Ch., Georgetown, 1878-80; 1st Cong. Ch., Milford, Conn., from 1880.

JOHN REES LEWIS.

Born in Deerfield, N. Y., Jan. 1, 1837; united with the 1st Pres. Church in Utica, Autumn of 1856; graduated from Hamilton College in 1860; married to Miss EMMA JANE MARSH, of Deerfield, Oct. 28, 1863.

Ordained at Morrisville, N. Y., by Oneida Assoc.; Morrisville, 1863-6; Boonville Pres. Ch., 1866-79; Mexico, 1879-81; Middletown from 1881.

WILLIAM WIRT MACOMBER.

Born in Westfield, N. Y., Aug. 7, 1836; united with the Pres. Ch. in Westfield, probably Jan., 1852; graduated from Western Reserve College in 1860; married in Minneapolis, Minn., 1863.

Ordained at 1st Pres. Ch., Buffalo, N. Y., by Presby. of Buffalo, May 20, 1863; Gold Hill and Silver City, Nevada, 1863-5; Marysville, Cal., 1865-8; Kenosha, Wis., 1868-9; Virginia, Nev., 1869-71; 2nd Cong. Ch., San Francisco, 1871-3; Pres. Ch., Jamestown, N. Y., 1873-4; Whitestown, 1875; Evang., Oneonta, N. Y., and Cleveland, O., 1875-9; Pres. Ch., Crestline, O., 1880; Monroe, Mich., 1881-2.

SAMUEL MILLER.

Born in Augusta, N. Y., Nov. 1, 1829; united with the Cong. Ch. in Augusta, Nov., 1850; graduated from Hamilton College in 1860; Aub. Mid. class from Union; married to Miss H. A. HODGES, of Augusta, 1852; married to Miss MARY ABAGAIL BIGELOW, of Auburn, Summer of 1862.

Ordained at Eaton, N. Y., by Oneida Assoc., June, 1864; Eaton from 1862; Sherburne, from 1867; Deansville; Oriskany Falls; Pitcher, from 1878.

*WILLIAM JARVIS GREGG NUTTING, died Oct. 21, 1879.

DAVID HENRY PALMER.

Born in Phelps, N. Y., Oct. 15, 1839; united with the Brick (Pres.) Church in Rochester, 1858; graduated from Univ. of Rochester in 1860; married to Miss JANE ELIZABETH GILMORE, of Aurelius, N. Y., June 25, 1863.

Ordained at Buffalo, N. Y., by Presby. of Buffalo, May 20, 1863; Aurelius, 1862-3; Virginia City, Nev., 1863-4; Columbia, Cal., 1864-6; Prattsburgh, N. Y., 1867-71; Caledonia, 4 months; Brockport, 1872-5; Penn Yan from 1875.

WILLIAM WESLEY PALMER.

Born in Chenango, N. Y., Jan. 4, 1836; united with the Pres. Ch.; studied at Yale College; married to Miss EMMA SOPHIA REDFORD, of Carlton, N. Y., 1863.

Ordained and installed at Owego, N. Y., by Presby.; preached in various Churches; resident in Binghamton, and now in Chenango Bridge.

GEORGE OLCOTT PHELPS.

Born in Gloversville, N. Y., Apr. 25, 1834; united with the 1st Pres. Church in Kingsboro, July 6, 1856; studied at Amherst College; married to Miss SARAH AZUBAH HARRIS, of Newport, N. Y., June 8, 1858.

Ordained and installed at Oneonta, by Presby. of Otsego, June 11, 1863; Oneonta, 1863-9; Valatie, 1869-71; Deposit, 1872-4; Allen St. Ch., N. Y. City, from 1874.

SAMUEL WHEELER PRATT.

Born in Livonia, N. Y., Sept. 9, 1838; united with the Pres. Church in Geneseo, July, 1855; graduated from Williams College in 1860; married to Miss LUCILLA B. FIELD, of Canandaigua, N. Y., Aug. 12, 1863; married to Miss SARA M. McKAY, of Campbell, Feb. 25, 1880.

Ordained pastor, Brasher Falls, N. Y., by Presby. of St. Lawrence, 1863; Brasher Falls, 4 years; Hammonton, N. J., 4 years; Pres. Ch., Prattsburgh, N. Y., 1872-7; Campbell, N. Y., from 1877.

Published "A Summer at Peace Cottage," 1880; correspondent "Steuben" of *N. Y. Evangelist.*

ALBERT CHESTER REED.

Born in Albany, N. Y., Aug. 31, 1832; united with the 14th St. Pres. Church in New York, Nov., 1853; graduated from Williams College in 1860; married to Miss SARAH M. MERRIMAN, of Elbridge, N. Y., March 8, 1865.

Ordained and installed at Elbridge, N. Y., by Cayuga Presby., June 25, 1863; Elbridge, 1863-6; Port Byron, 1866-73; Flushing, L. I., 1873-8; Manchester, Vt., from 1878.

*COMFORT ISRAEL SLACK, died Feb. 24, 1865.

SAMUEL CALISTO VANCAMP.
    Born in Tully, N. Y., June 29, 1837; united with the Cong.
    Church in Truxton, June, 1859; studied at Union College in class
    of 1861; married to Miss LOTTIE A. IDE, of Brooklyn, N. Y.,
    Dec. 24, 1863; married to Miss CLARA S. CRIPPEN, of Worces-
    ter, N. Y., Oct. 7, 1874.
    Ordained at Marathon, by Cortland Presby., July, 1872; Pitcher,
    1869-72; Worcester, 1872-4; Milford, 1874-9; Greene,
    1879-81; resident in Tully.

JOHN EDABDUEL WERTH.
    Born in Malacca, Java, Dec. 7, 1835; united with the Pres.
    Church in Rock Hill, Mo., 1857; graduated from Union
    College in 1859; married to Mrs. L. S. CRAIGUE, Feb. 8, 1882.
    Ordained at Auburn, by Presby. of Cayuga, 1863; chaplain 25th
    N. Y. Vols., 1863-5; chap. 13th Mo. Vet. Cav., 1865-6; St.
    Louis, Mo., 1866-8; Pres. Ch., Warsaw, Ill., 1869; in business,
    Springfield, Mo., 1870-81; Cong. Ch., North Chester, Vt., 1882.

SAMUEL DEWITT WESTFALL.
    Born in Milford, Pa., Dec. 4, 1832; united with the Pres.
    Church, Summer of 1854; graduated from Hamilton College in
    1860; married to Miss HELEN GERTRUDE SMITH, of Ripon,
    Wis., Oct. 15, 1875.
    Ordained at E. Palmyra, N. Y., by Presby. of Lyons, April 10,
    1867; Cong. Ch., Deansville, 1863; tutor, Hamilton Col., 1863-5;
    Arkport, N. Y., 1865-7; Redwood Falls and Beaver Falls,
    Minn., 1869-72; Rushford, 1872-4; Utica, 1874-5, and Fre-
    mont from 1872.

EDWARD PAYSON ADAMS. See 1865-8.

HENRY MARTYN GRANT.
    Born in Oroomiah, Persia, June 3, 1836; united with the 3rd
    Pres. Church in Newark, N. J., Aug., 1840; studied at Hamilton
    College; Junior and Middle years in Auburn; Senior year at
    Union Sem., N. Y.; married to Miss MARY JEANNETTE PUT-
    NAM, of Cortland, N. Y., Aug. 19, 1863.
    Ordained and installed at North Canaan, Conn., by North Litch-
    field Consoc., Nov. 17, 1863; North Canaan, 1863-6; Webster
    Groves, Mo., 1866-70; Smyrna, N. Y., 1870-1; 1st Pres. Ch.,
    Stirling, N. J., 1871-6; New Providence, 1876-8; Middleboro,
    Mass., Cong. Ch., from 1878.

CHARLES WINSLOW HAMLIN.
    Graduated from Hamilton College in 1858; in Aub. from Buffalo,
    N. Y., Sept. and Oct. of Junior year; practicing Law in Buffalo.

ALMON REDFIELD HEWITT. See 1863-6.

BENJAMIN HOWARD, M. D.
Born in England ; studied at Williams College in Class of 1859 ;
Auburn part of Junior year ; M. A. from Williams College in
1869 ; M. D., Coll. of Phys. and Surg., N. Y., 1858 ; surgeon in
U. S. Army from 1861.

J. W. SCOTT KOUGH.
Came to Auburn from Newport, Pa ; graduated from Dickinson
College ; Auburn to March, 1862 ; never ordained ; in forward-
ing business, Newport, Pa.

1861-4.

CLARENCE HALL BEEBE.
Born in Hamilton, N. Y., Jan. 20, 1836 ; united with the M. E.
Church in E. Hamilton, Spring of 1858 ; graduated from
Cazenovia Seminary in 1861 ; married to Miss LUCY A. GRIS-
WOLD, of Vernon Centre, N. Y., Oct. 12, 1864.
Ordained at Winfield, N. Y., by Oneida Assoc., Jan. 10, 1865 ;
Winfield and Bridgewater, 1864–70 ; Clayville Pres. Ch., from
1870.
Published class pamphlet, and occasional lectures.

WILLIS JUDSON BEECHER, D. D.
Born in Hampden, O., April 29, 1838 ; united with the Cong.
Church in Vernon Centre, N. Y., May, 1849 ; graduated from
Hamilton College in 1858 ; D. D. from Hamilton College in
1875 ; married to Miss SARA MARIA BOLTER, of Ovid, N. Y.,
June 14, 1865.
Ordained and installed at Ovid, N. Y., by Presby. of Geneva,
June, 1864 ; Ovid, 1864–5 ; prof. of Moral Science and Belles
Lettres in Knox College, Ill., 1865–9 ; First Church of Christ,
Galesburg, Ill., 1869–71 ; prof. of Hebrew in Auburn, from
1871.
Published " Farmer Tompkins and his Bibles " 1874.

*WILBERFORCE KERR BOGGS, died July 26, 1872.

WILLIAM CAMPBELL.
Born in Yorkshire, England, (at Stubbs, near Pontefract) Oct.
25, 1829 ; united with the 1st Pres. Church in Kossuth, Iowa,
Winter of 1852–3 ; graduated from Yellow Springs College in
1858 ; S. S. missionary, 1858–61 ; married to Miss EMMA CHAR-
LOTTE ATWOOD, of Yellow Springs, Iowa, June 10, 1858.
Ordained and installed at Chaumont, N. Y., by Presby. of Water-
town, Oct., 1864 ; Chaumont, 1864–6 ; Adel, Iowa, 1866–8 ;
Synodical missionary, Iowa, residing at DeSoto, 1868–73 ;
Onarga, Ill., 1873–6 ; Manhattan, Kansas, from 1876.

PHILEMON ROCKWELL DAY.

Born in Elmira, N. Y., Jan. 11, 1838; united with the Cong. Church in West Avon, Conn., 1855; graduated from Williams College in 1861; married to Miss HENRIETTA M. WOODFORD, of West Avon, June 1, 1864.

Ordained at Auburn, by Presby. of Cayuga, May, 1864; chaplain of Y. M. C. A., Troy, N. Y., 1864-9; First Cong. Ch., Saratoga, 1869-73; Burlington, Conn., 1873-8; resident in West Avon, 1878-81; 7th Pres. Ch., N. Y. City, from 1881.

EDWARD DICKINSON.

Born in East Avon, N. Y., Sept. 10, 1832; united with 1st Pres. Ch., Mundy, Mich., 1853; graduated from Univ. of Mich. in 1861; married to Miss ELLEN FRANCES BELL, of Mundy, Aug. 7, 1861.

Ordained at Fentonville, Mich., by Saginaw Presby., Sept., 1864; Fentonville, 1864-8; Winterset, Iowa, 1868-70; Holly, Mich., 1870-4; Evart, 1874-5; Brodhead, Wis., 1875-82; Murphysboro, Ill., 1882.

ALBRO LEANDER GREENE.

Born in Brookfield, N. Y., Feb. 9, 1835; united with the Class of M. E. Church in Brookfield, about 1845; studied at Brookfield and Potsdam Academies; married to Miss AMELIA P. YOUNG, of North Hammond, N. Y., May 26, 1864; married to Miss CLARA N. YOUNG, of North Hammond, May 21, 1873.

Ordained by Presby. of Steuben, Dec. 3, 1865; Poltney, N. Y., 1864-7; Truxton, 1 year; Harrisville, 2 years; Richford, 1870-3; Knowlesville, 1873-4; Riga, 1874-6; Stockholm, 1877-80; DePeyster from 1880.

GAVIN LINDSAY HAMILTON.

Born in Lesmahago, Scotland, Feb. 16, 1831; united with the 1st Cong. Church in Johnsonville, O., Dec. 10, 1854; graduated from Univ. of Rochester in 1861; first and third years at Auburn, Middle year at Rochester; married to Miss CATHERINE ANN SEMPLE, of Rochester, May 10, 1864.

Ordained and installed at Vernon, N. Y., by Presby. of Utica, Jan. 31, 1865; Vernon, 1864-8; Pittsford, 1868-71; Memorial Church, Rochester, 1871-5; Wilson, 1875-9; Parma Centre, 1880-1; Alden from 1881.

JAMES THOMPSON HANNING.

Born in Scotland, Aug. 15, 1840; united with Pres. Church in 1857; studied at Knox Col., Toronto; married to Miss MARIA MANITA TOUSLEY, of Springville, N. Y., July 15, 1865.

Ordained and installed at Gorham, N. Y., by Presby. of Geneva, June 28, 1864; Gorham, 1864-5; Springville, 1865-7; Sandwich, Ill., 1867-8; Marseilles, 1868-71, and in business there since.

ALEXANDER McLEAN HEIZER.
>   Born in Frankfort, O., Oct. 9, 1838; united with the Church, May
>   11, 1850; graduated from Yellow Springs College in 1861; mar-
>   ried to Miss PHAREBY MELVINA TITTERINGTON, May 12, 1864.
>   Ordained at Keokuk, Iowa, by Presby. of Keokuk, June 14, 1864;
>   Black Hawk, Col., 1864; Winterset, Iowa, 1864, for 3 years;
>   Montana, 2 years; Iowa City, preaching at Oxford and other
>   places, 1870-3; Wapello and Toolsboro, Iowa, 1873-9; Medi-
>   apolis, Iowa, 1879-80, and resident there.

HENRY M. HIGLEY.
>   Came to Auburn from Owego; mem. of Cong. Church there; mar-
>   ried before entering the Sem.
>   Ordained at Onondaga Valley, N. Y., by Council, May 31, 1865;
>   Onondaga Valley and Onond. Hill, 1864-5; Gaines, 1865-9;
>   State of Mich., 1869; Addison, N. Y., 1870-2; Otto, 1872-3;
>   Friendship, 1873-8; Salamanca from 1879.

*JOHN W. HOLM, died Sept. 10, 1863.

JOHN KELLAND.
>   Born in Devonshire, Eng., Nov. 21, 1833; came to Auburn from
>   the Church in Flint, Mich.; graduated from Mich. Univ. in 1861;
>   married to Miss FANNY E. SHASLAND, of Finston, Devonshire,
>   Oct. 12, 1861.
>   Ordained and installed at Angola, Mich., by Presby. of St. Joseph,
>   Spring of 1865; Angola and Salem, two years; Omro, Wis., 3
>   years; Lawton, Mich., 2 years; Southfield and Wing Lake;
>   Cass City from 1877.

ALEXANDER LAMBERTON.
>   Born Feb. 28, 1839; came to Auburn from Plattsburgh, N. Y.;
>   graduated from Univ. of Rochester in 1866, after completing the
>   Auburn theological course; married to Mrs. EUNICE B. HUSSEY,
>   of Auburn, May, 1864.
>   Ordained by Presby. of Brooklyn, 1869; Tompkins Ave. Church,
>   Brooklyn, 3 years; since resident in Rochester, N. Y.
>   Published papers on Natural History, &c.

CHARLES MONTGOMERY LIVINGSTON.
>   Born in Gloversville, N. Y., Oct. 18, 1828; united with the Ch. of
>   the Puritans, New York, May, 1847; graduated from Union
>   College in 1851; taught for several years before entering the
>   Seminary; married to Miss MARCIA B. MACDONALD, of Johns-
>   town, N. Y., Sept. 10, 1855.
>   Ordained at Wellsville, N. Y., by Genesee Valley Presby., Aug. 9,
>   1864; Wellsville, 1864-7; Chillicothe, Mo., 1867; Gilbertsville,
>   N. Y., 1868-70; Watertown 2nd Pres. Ch., 1870-7; Cincinnati,
>   O., 25th Ward Pres. Ch., 1877; Cleveland, 1880; Indianapolis,
>   Ind., 1881; Orange Valley, N. J., evang., from 1881.
>   Published Notes on Baptism, 1873.

THEODORE D. MARSH.

Born in Orangeville, N. Y., July 22, 1837 ; came to Auburn from Church in Ann Arbor, Mich.; graduated from Univ. of Mich. in 1857; married to Miss SARAH LAMB, of Branchport, N. Y., May 5, 1864.

Ordained at Tekonsha, Mich., by Presby. of Marshall, Apr., 1864 ; Central City and Black Hawk, Col., 4 years; Hastings, Mich., 1868–74; Paw Paw, 1874–80 ; Grand Rapids from 1880, Synod. miss.

*FREDERICK AUGUSTUS PARMENTER, died Apr. 7, 1865.

CALVIN PERIN QUICK.

Born in Royal Oak, Mich., Oct. 15, 1835 ; united with the Pres. Church in Birmingham, Mich., early in 1847 ; graduated from Univ. of Michigan in 1861; married to Miss SOPHIA WILLCOX LOMBARD, of Pawlet, Vt., May 10, 1864.

Ordained at Fentonville, Mich., by Presby. of Saginaw, Sept. 15, 1864; Flushing, 1864–5 ; Rochester, 1866–9 ; teaching, same place, 1870–1 ; from 1873, Pres. Ch., Concord, Mich.

DAVID MCKIBBEN RANKIN.

Born in Butler Co., Pa., Dec. 16, 1836 ; united with the Pres. Church in Muddy Creek, Pa., Sept., 1858; graduated from the Academy of West Sunbury, Pa., in 1858; married to Miss MARY ELIZABETH RHODES of West Sunbury, Nov. 9, 1859.

Ordained at Cuyahoga Falls, O., by Council, June, 1865 ; Cuyahoga Falls, 2 years ; Spartansburg and Tidioute, Pa., 2 years; Great Bend, 3 years ; Ilion, N. Y., 1871–8; Charlotte, 1878–81 ; Holley, 1881–2 ; Richfield Springs, 1882.

ISAIAH REID.

Born near Salem, Washington Co., Indiana, April 16, 1836 ; united with the Reformed Presb. Church, Sharon, Iowa, Sept., 1856 ; graduated from Yellow Spring College, 1861 ; married to Miss MARY ELLENOR BRADEN, at Northfield, Iowa, June 13, 1860.

Ordained by Keokuk Presby., June 14, 1864 ; Pres. Ch., Nevada, Iowa, 9 years ; Albion, Mich., 16 months; resident Nevada, doing evangelistic work, from 1875 ; mem. of Presby. till 1880; in charge of Indep. Pres. Ch., Centre Grove, 1881–2.

Published " Highway Papers," now " The Highway," monthly from 1875, weekly since 1879 ; tracts, &c.

AUGUSTUS CHESTERMAN SHAW, D. D.

Born in Attica, N. Y., Nov. 13, 1838 ; united with the Brick Ch. in Rochester, N. Y., May 2, 1852; graduated from Univ. of Rochester in 1861; D. D. from Franklin College in 1877; married to Miss UNICY L. FARNHAM of Silver Creek, N. Y., Oct. 10, 1865.

Ordained at Rochester, N. Y., by Presby. of Rochester, Jan. 15, 1865; Clayville, 1864–70; Fulton, 1870–9 ; Wellsboro, Pa., from 1879.

GEORGE GRANTHAM SMITH.

Born in Philadelphia, Pa., Jan. 31, 1833 ; united with the Church in Darby, Pa., 1850 ; graduated from Princeton College in 1861; entire course at Auburn, and a post graduate year, 1873-4 ; married to Miss ANNA MARIA SWIFT, of Auburn, 1866.

Ordained at Philadelphia, Pa., by Phila. 3d Presby., 1864; home missionary in Montana, 2 years ; Savannah, N. Y., 1 year ; Sennett, 1½ years ; Genoa, 2½ years ; Pittsford, 2 years ; Buffalo 6th St. Pres. Church, 1874-8 ; resident in Buffalo, 1878-80 ; Clear Creek, Pres. Ch., 1880-2.

*JOHN BACON STEELE, died Nov. 29, 1863.

WILLIAM WALCOTT WETMORE.

Born in Whitestown, N. Y., Feb. 25, 1842 ; united with the Pres. Church in Whitestown, 1859; graduated from Hamilton College in 1861; married to Miss MARTHA A. McINTYRE, of Ann Arbor, Mich., Oct. 31, 1865.

Ordained at Ann Arbor, Mich., by Presby. of Washtenaw, Oct. 26, 1864 ; Ann Arbor, Pres. Ch., 1864-5 ; DesMoines, Iowa, 1865-6 ; Rock Island, Ill., 1867-8 ; Clinton, Mich., 1868-70 ; Albion, 1871; Wataga, Ill., 1871-4; Cannonsville, N. Y., 1875-81; resident in Ann Arbor, Mich., supplying Church in Plymouth.

*GEORGE WHITE, died Mar. 14, 1870.

JAMES VINCENT BENHAM.

Born in Dryden, N. Y., Feb. 14, 1839; united with the M. E. Church in Skaneateles ; graduated from Cazenovia Sem. in 1861 ; Auburn, 1861-2 ; married to Miss MARY ISABEL HAMILTON, of Lansingville, N. Y., Jan. 1, 1863 ; married to Miss EMMA BAKER, of West Dryden, Sept. 21, 1870.

Ordained at Utica, N. Y., (M. E.) by Bishop Kingsley, Apr. 21, 1867 ; Lansingville, 1862 ; New Hope, 2 years ; Owasco, 3 years ; West Dryden and Asbury, 2 years ; Cincinnatus, 3½ years ; Homer, 2 years ; Newark, 3 years ; Corning, 3 years ; Palmyra, from 1881.

THOMAS CAMPBELL. See 1862-5.

EDGAR J. HUESTON.

Came to Auburn from Petersburgh, Mich. ; Junior year at Auburn ; married to Miss PUTNAM, of Auburn, Aug., 1862 ; enlisted 111th N. Y. Vols., Aug., 1862 ; mustered out as Brevet Major, June, 1865.

*EBENEZER PORTER HYDE, died Aug. 31, 1868.

JOHN GEORGE OSBORNE.
Born in Verona, N. Y.; graduated from Hamilton College in 1861; in the Sem. but a few weeks, leaving by advice of physician; married to Miss HARRIET MACHIN, of Verona, 1861; farming in Joslyn, Ill.

*JAMES EDWARD PIERCE. See 1862–5.

EDWARD PAYSON ROE.
Born in New Windsor, N. Y., 1838; united with the Church in Spring of 1854; studied at Williams College; one year at Auburn; afterward part of a year at Union, New York; married to Miss ANNA PAULINA SANDS, of New York, Nov. 24, 1863.
Ordained at Somers, N. Y., by North River Presby., Summer of 1862; chaplain of Harris Light Cavalry, 1862–4; hospital chaplain at Fortress Monroe, 1864 to close of war; Highland Falls Pres. Ch., 1866–74; resident at Cornwall-on-the-Hudson, from 1874.
Published " Barriers Burnt Away," 1872; " Play and Profit in my Garden," 1873; " What can she do?" 1873; " Opening of a Chestnut Burr," 1874; " Near to Nature's Heart," 1875; " Manual on the Culture of Small Fruits," 1876; " From Jest to Earnest," 1876; "A Knight of the 19th Century," 1877; "A Face Illumined," 1878; " Success with Small Fruits," 1880; " Without a Home," 1881.

EDWIN ALEXANDER SPENCE.
Born in Salem, Mich., Oct. 2, 1837; united with Union Church in Salem, at 11 years old; graduated from Univ. of Mich. in 1860; Auburn, 1861–3; Andover, 1863–4; married to Mrs. SUSANNA M. RICHARDSON, of Ann Arbor, Mich., May 6, 1874.
Ordained at Westford, Mass., by N. Middlesex Assoc., Sept. 27, 1866; 2d Cong. Ch., Dover, N. H., and U. S. Christian Commission, 1864–5; Westford, 1865–8; Wheatland, Iowa, 1872; East Providence, R. I., 1873; but with intervals of ill health, which compelled him to retire; resident in Ann Arbor, Mich.

*GEORGE W. WHITNEY, died 1864.

WILLIAM WILMER.
Born near Cincinnati, O., Oct. 19, 1838; united with the Pres. Church at College Hill, July, 1861; graduated from Farmers' College in 1860; Junior year at Auburn, 2 years at Lane; married to KATE F. WOOD, of Cincinnati, O., May 23, 1865; married to LIZZIE K. PEABODY, of Henniker, N. H., Aug. 18, 1875.
Ordained at Montezuma, Ind., by Crawfordsville Presby., Sept., 1865; Montezuma from 1864; Monticello from 1867; Williamsport and Attica from 1869.

AARON McCRACKEN WOODHULL.
Graduated from Hamilton College in 1861; in Auburn a few weeks; never matriculated.

1862-5.

DAVID IRVING BIGGAR.

Born in Huntingdon, Canada, Jan. 8, 1836; united with the 2nd Pres. Church in Huntingdon, Sept., 1852; graduated from Amherst College in 1862; married to Miss MARY ESTHER WOOD, of Litchfield, N. Y., July 18, 1867.

Ordained and installed, Verona, N. Y.. by Presby. of Utica, June 2. 1865; Litchfield, 1865-7; Verona, 1867-77; Camillus from 1878.

THOMAS CAMPBELL.

Born in England, May 12, 1835; united with the Church in Kossuth, Iowa, April, 1856; graduated from Yellow Spring College in 1860; Auburn, 1861-3 and 1864-5; married to Miss SUSAN HUBBELL, of Auburn, June 15, 1863.

Ordained and installed at Sennett, N. Y., by Presby. of Cayuga, March 22, 1866; Sennett, 1865-7; Shakopee, Minn., 1867-70; Camp Point, Ill., 1870-2; LeSueur, Minn., from 1872.

THOMAS FRANKLIN CHAFER.

Born in Hull, Yorkshire, England, Nov. 11, 1830; united with the Pres. Church in College Hill, O., Nov., 1861; graduated from Farmers' College, in 1861; married to Miss LOIS LOMION SPERRY, of Morgan, O., June 1, 1865.

Ordained at Rising Sun, Ind., by Madison Presby., April 11, 1866; Downer's Grove, Ill., from 1866; Morgan, O., from 1872; E. Smithfield, Pa., 1877-81; Rock Creek, O., from 1881.

THOMAS EDWARD DAVIS.

Born in England, Sept. 21, 1835; united with the Cong. Church in Marcy, N. Y., 1857; studied at Marietta College; A. M. from Marietta, 1876; married to Miss ELLEN ELIZABETH SMITH, of Schroon Lake, N. Y., May 1, 1866.

Ordained at Milwaukee, Wis., by Presby. of Milwaukee, about 1865; Cong. Ch., Racine, 1865-6; Pres. Ch., Mechanicsville, N. Y., 1867-8; Cong. Ch., Unionville, Conn., from 1869.

Published various historical and memorial pamphlets.

HERVEY CROSBY HAZEN.

Born in Ithaca, N. Y., June 26, 1841; united with the Pres. Ch. in Ithaca, Nov. 7, 1852; graduated from Amherst College in 1862; married to Miss IDA JULIA CHAPIN, of Ludlow, Vt., July 2, 1867.

Ordained at Ithaca by Presby. of Ithaca, Aug., 1867; Madura Mission, India, 1867-70; Liverpool, N. Y., 1870-6; Manlius and Jamesville, N. Y., 1876-8; Spencer, N. Y., 1878-9; Manlius, 1879-82; Holley, 1882.

HENRY POST HIGLEY.

Born in Castleton, Vt., Jan. 1, 1839; united with the Cong. Ch. in Castleton, Apr., 1857; graduated from Middlebury College in 1860; married to Miss LILLIE M. CONDIT of Auburn, July 26, 1866.

Ordained at Columbus, Ind., by Madison Presby., Sept. 13, 1865; Vevay, Ind., 1865-6; Cong. Ch., Beloit, Wis., from 1866.

JOHN McLEAN, D. D.

Born in Waterville, N. Y., Sept. 3, 1837; united with the Pres. Church in Vernon Centre, N. Y., 1858; graduated from Hamilton College in 1862; married to Miss CARRIE EVANS, of Beloit, Wis., Oct. 8, 1878.

Ordained and installed at 1st Pres. Ch., Galena, Ill., by Presby., 1866; tutor Hamilton Col., 1865-6; Galena, 1866-72; Beloit, Wis., from 1872.

Published sermons, speeches and essays.

JONATHAN BRADLEY MORSE.

Came to Auburn from Sharon, O.; studied at Oberlin College; married before entering the Seminary.

Ordained and installed at Moravia, N. Y., by Presby. of Cayuga, Sept. 27, 1865; Moravia, 1865-6; Clinton, Ia., 1866-7; tea. Lyons, 1867-8; Pres. Church, Preble, N. Y., 1868-70; Sidney Plains, 1870-4; Whitestown, 1874-6; artist, resident in Utica, from 1876.

JOHN VAN COUGNET NELLIS, PH. D.

Born in Fort Plain, N. Y., July 7, 1833; united with the 1st Pres. Church in Peoria, Ill., April, 1858; studied at Union College; Ph. D. from Union College, 1880; married to Miss M. VIRGINIA METCALFE, of Cherry Valley, N. Y., June, 1865.

Ordained and installed at Jordan, N. Y., by Presby. of Cayuga, June, 1865; Jordan, 1865-8; Dryden, 1868-71; Addison, 1871-3; Gowanda, 1873-8; Gilbertsville from 1878.

EBEN BURT PARSONS, D. D.

Born in Pittsfield, Mass., March 3, 1835; united with the 1st Cong. Ch. in Pittsfield, Jan., 1853; graduated from Williams College in 1859; studied in Harvard Univ. Scientific Department; two years at Union, N. Y., last year at Auburn; D. D. from Maryville College, 1881; married to Miss CLARA BIGELOW, of Baldwinsville, N. Y., June 15, 1869.

Ordained at Madison Square Pres. Ch., N. Y., by Fourth Presby. of N. Y., Apr. 11, 1865; chaplain 116th U. S. Infantry; Turin, N. Y., 1866; Sanquoit, 1867-8; Baldwinsville from 1868.

Necrologist of Williams Col.; published memorial pamphlets.

HENRY THOMAS PERRY.

Born in Ashfield, Mass., May 6, 1838; united with the Cong. Ch. in Ashfield, Sept., 1856; graduated from Williams College in

1862; married to Miss JENNIE H. JONES, of Rolla, Mo., Sept. 19, 1866.
Ordained at North Adams, Mass., by Berkshire N. Assoc., Dec. 20, 1865 ; missionary of A. B. C. F. M., at Marash, and now at Sivas, Turkey.

*JAMES EDWARD PIERCE, died July 13, 1870.

CHANDLER NEWELL THOMAS.
Born in Bangor, N. Y., July 8, 1835; united with the Cong. Ch. in Bangor, June, 1856; graduated from Middlebury College in 1861 ; married to Miss MARION H. MARTIN, of Malone, N. Y., Oct. 17, 1865.
Ordained and installed at Fort Covington, N. Y., by Champlain Presby., July 16, 1865 ; Fort Covington from 1865.

CHESTER COOK THORNE.
Born in Rensselaerville, N. Y., Feb. 27, 1831 ; united with the M. E. Church in Charlotteville, N. Y., 1860; graduated from Union College in 1857 ; first year at Biblical Institute, Concord, N. H.; second and third at Auburn; married to Miss EMELINE MINTHORNE BROWNE, of Owego, N. Y., 1859; married to Miss ELLEN JUDITH DAY, of Deansville, 1868.
Ordained at Jordan, N. Y., by Presby. of Cayuga, June, 1866 ; Deansville, 1865 ; Rensselaerville, 1868-70; Stillwater, 1871-2; Manchester from 1873.
Published several sermons.

*ALBERT TRUE, died Oct. 18, 1871.

HENRY WARD.
Born in Dover, N. Y., Sept. 11, 1835 ; united with the Pres. Ch. in Deposit, N. Y., 1856; graduated from Hamilton College in 1862 ; married to BASHA BARNES, of Buffalo, N. Y., Sept. 28, 1865.
Ordained, Minneapolis, Minn., by Presby. of St. Paul, Jan. 3, 1866; Minneapolis, 1865-7 ; East Church, Buffalo, since 1867.

ABEL SWEET WOOD.
Born in Marcy, N. Y., Nov. 22, 1836 ; united with the 2d Pres. Church in Auburn, 1863 ; graduated from Hamilton College in 1861; Auburn, 1863-5 ; married to Miss SARAH WEEKS, of Verona, N. Y., Dec. 19, 1867.
Ordained and installed at Niagara City, N. Y., by Council, Nov. 13, 1868 ; Verona, N. Y., 1865-7 ; Niagara City, 4 years; Kokomo, Ind., 6 years; St. Joseph, Mich., from 1877.

SOLON COBB.
Born in Carver, Mass., Sept. 12, 1838 ; united with the Cong. Ch. in Carver, 1855 ; Aub. Mid. class from Andover ; one year in

Auburn; married to Miss HANNAH D. ANTHONY, of New Bedford, Mass, June, 1865.

Ordained at Owego, N. Y., by Tioga Presby., Oct. 11, 1864; Owego, 1864-9; Cong. Ch., Medford, Mass., 1869-74; New Bedford, 1874-6; Jacksonville, Fla., 1876-8; Pres. Ch., Erie, Pa., from 1878.

MORTIMER ANDREW HYDE.

Born in Auburn, May 8, 1842; united with the 1st Pres. Church in Auburn, 1854; graduated from Union College in 1862; Auburn, part of 1862-3, and Mid., 1865-6; Gen. Theol. Sem., N. Y., 1867-8; married to Miss ELLA FRANKLIN KLAPP, of Philadelphia, Pa., May 30, 1877.

Ordained Deacon, Trinity Chapel, N. Y., by Bishop Potter; ord. Priest, St. John's Ch., Detroit, Mich., by Bishop McCrosky, May 6, 1869; St. Mark's, Brooklyn, N. Y., 1868-9; Mt. Clemens, Mich., 1869-70; Pekin, Ill., 1871-3; St. Louis, Mo., 1873-6; Mauch Chunk, Pa., 1876-7; Huntington, Conn., 1877-80; Crosswicks and Allentown, N. J., 1880-2.

GEORGE LANSING RAYMOND.

Born in Chicago, Ill., Sept. 3, 1839; united with the Ref. Church in Owasco, N. Y., 1857; graduated from Williams College in 1862; dismissed to Princeton at close of Jun. year; married to Miss MARY ELIZABETH BLAKE of Philadelphia, Pa., July, 1872.

Ordained and installed at Darby, Pa., by Phila. 3d Presby., Apr. 28, 1870; Darby, 1869-74; prof. of Oratory, Williams Col., 1874-81; prof. of Rhetoric, Princeton Col., from 1881.

Published "Colony Ballads," 1876; "Ideals made Real," 1877; "The Orator's Manual," 1879.

1863-6.

GUSTAVUS ROSINBURY ALDEN.

Born in Greene, Me., Feb. 15, 1832; united with the Ref. Church in Richmond, L. I., 1859; married to Miss ISABELLA M. MACDONALD, of Gloversville, N. Y., May 30, 1866.

Ordained and installed at Almond, N. Y., by Genesee Valley Presby., Nov. 14, 1866; Almond, 1866-7; Olean, 1867-9; Nassau, 1869-70; Cooperstown, 1870-3; New Hartford, 1873-6; Greensburg, Ind., 1876-80; Cumminsville, O., 1880-2; Carbondale, Pa., 1882.

Since 1874, Mr. and Mrs. Alden have been associated in the publication of "The Pansy," "The Sabbath School Monthly," &c.

GERMAN HAMMOND CHATTERTON.

Born in Rutland, Vt., July 15, 1832; united with the Cong. Ch. in West Rutland, Summer of 1846; graduated from Middlebury College, 1854; married to Miss ANNA FENTON MAZUZAN,

of Brandon, Vt., Feb., 1857 ; married to Miss ANNA SPEES, of Greenville, N. Y., Nov. 4, 1868.
Ordained in Janesville, Ia., Oct., 1866, by Presby. of Dubuque ; Janesville, 1866–7 ; Ackley, 1867–9 ; Presb. miss., Dubuque, 1869–71 ; resident in Sutherland Falls, Vt., 1871–3 ; preaching Northwood, Ia., 1873–5 : Charles City, 1876 ; Des Moines, 1877 ; resident Sutherland Falls, Vt., from 1878.

T. MADISON DAWSON.
Born in Gloucester Co., N. J., April 10, 1845 ; studied at Crozier College ; A. M. from Wabash College in 1867.
Pres. Ch., Lewisburgh, Pa., 1 year ; Seventh St. Pres. Ch., New York, 3 years ; Monticello, N. Y., 2 years ; East Oakland Pres. Ch., California, 1872–5 ; member of Presby. till 1875 ; writing for the press in Oakland, 1875–8 ; U. S. Consul at Apia, Samoan Islands, 1878.

MERRITT GALLY.
Came to Auburn from Rochester ; graduated from Univ. of Rochester in 1863.
Ordained by Presby. of Lyons, about 1866; Marion, N. Y., 1866–7 ; resident Rochester, 1868–77, and N. Y. City from 1878.

WILLARD PUTNAM GIBSON.
Born in Charleston, Vt., June 24, 1829 ; united with the Pres. Church in Skaneateles, 1853 ; graduated from Oberlin College in 1859 ; married to Miss MARY M. ROOT, of Springville, N. Y., Mar. 21, 1854.
Ordained and installed at Pana City, Ill., by Presby. of Alton, Oct., 1866; Pana, 1866–70; Kingston, Pa., 1871–5 ; New Milford, 1875–6 ; Greenville, N. Y., 1876–81 ; Conklingville, 1882.

ALMON REDFIELD HEWITT.
Born in Greenfield, N. Y., Aug. 12, 1833; united with the Church, Oct. 12, 1851; Auburn, 1860–2; in the Army, 1862–5 ; Auburn, 1865–6 ; married to Miss RACHEL ANN TRAPHAGEN, of Junius, N. Y., Nov. 6, 1866.
Ordained and installed at Weedsport, N. Y., by Presby. of Cayuga, Sept., 1866, where he still remains.

JOEL SPENCER JEWELL.
Born in Elmira, N. Y., Feb. 14, 1832 ; united with the Church in West Newark, Apr., 1851 ; studied at Oberlin College ; married to Miss HARRIET CORTRIGHT, of West Newark, Mar. 19, 1861 ; married to Mrs. SARA JANE KNIGHT, of Auburn, June 5, 1866.
Ordained by Presby. of Cortland, Nov., 1866 ; Preble, N. Y., 1866–8 ; 1st Pres. Ch. of Genoa, (address, Kings Ferry) from 1868.

SOLOMON HORATIO MOON.
Born in Ashford, N. Y., Dec. 5, 1839 ; united with the 1st Cong. Church in Twelve Mile Grove, Ill., June, 1853 ; graduated from

Beloit College in 1863; married to Miss Charlotte Brandt, of Brandt, Pa., Oct. 15, 1868.

Ordained and installed at Susquehanna Depot by Presby. of Montrose, June, 1867; Susquehanna Dep., 1866–71; Gilbertsville, N. Y., 1871–7; Brandt, Pa., 1877–8; Osceola from 1878.

Published historical sermons in 1869 and 1876.

William Noble Page, D. D.

Born in Chelsea, Vt., April 4, 1837; united with the Cong. Church in West Bloomfield, N. Y., Sept. 1, 1863; graduated from Hamilton College in 1863; in the Army, 1862–3; D. D. from Highland Univ. in 1878; married to Miss Jennie N. Peck, of West Bloomfield, Sept. 27, 1862.

Ordained and installed at Trumansburgh, N. Y., by Presby. of Ithaca, June, 1866; Trumansburgh, 1866–9; Jacksonville, Fla., 1869–70; Amenia, N. Y., 1870–3; First Pres. Ch., Leavenworth, Kas., from 1873.

Francis H. Seeley.

Came to Auburn from Middlebury, Vt.; graduated from Middlebury College in 1863.

Pres. Ch., Richfield Springs, N. Y., 1867–82; Delhi, 1882.

Edward Southworth.

Born in Groveland, Mich., Dec. 3, 1834; united with the Free Bapt. Church near Waterford, Pa., 1857; studied at Hamilton College in 1860–1; married to Miss Sarah Huntly Humphrey, of Rochester, N. Y., July 10, 1866.

Ordained and installed at Jefferson, Wis., by Presby. of Milwaukee, Apr. 14, 1867; Jefferson, 1866–7; Palmyra, Cong. Church, 1867–71 and 1874–6; Cresco, Ia., 1871–4; Sheldon from 1878.

Published pamphlets and articles.

Charles Henry Wheeler.

Born in New York, Aug. 18, 1838; united with the Pres. Church in Sag Harbor, N. Y., 1856; graduated from Univ. of Michigan in 1862; married to Mary Louise Young, of Marion, N. Y., 1868.

Ordained at Providence, Pa., by Presby. of Montrose, Apr. 10, 1867; Cong. Ch., New Milford, Pa., 1866–7; Penfield, N. Y., 1867–69; Malta, Ill., (resident in Creston) from 1870.

---

*Emmons Hughitt, died Oct. 28, 1864.

Samuel Swain Mitchell.

Born in Hudson, N. Y., Sept. 8, 1840; united with the 4th Ave. Ch., N. Y. City; graduated from Williams College in 1863; Auburn, 1863–4; Union Sem., N. Y., 1864–6; married to Miss Lucy Myers Wright, of Poughkeepsie, N. Y., Apr., 1867.

Ordained at Morristown, N. J., by Presby. of Newark, Oct. 3, 1866; miss. of A. B. C. F. M., Abeih, Syria, 1866-8; Jefferson, Wis., 1869-70; since resident in various cities in Europe; now in Heidelberg.

JOHN KILBURN WILLIAMS.

Born in Charlotte, Vt., Feb. 21, 1835; united with the Cong. Ch. in Charlotte, May, 1853; graduated from Middlebury College in 1860; Auburn, Jun. year; completed course at Andover; married to Miss ANNA ELIZA DENISON, Sept. 25, 1866.

Ordained and installed at Bradford, Vt., by Council, Nov., 1866; Bradford, 6 years; West Rutland from 1872.

1864-7.

HENRY SAMUEL BARNUM.

Born in Stratford, Conn., Aug. 13, 1837; united with the Pres. Church in Lock Haven, Penn., Dec., 1855; graduated from Yale College in 1862; married to Miss LUCRETIA L. PARKER, of Guilford, Conn., May 22, 1867; married to Miss HELEN RANDLE, of Norwalk, Conn., March 10, 1869.

Ordained at Auburn by Presby. of Cayuga, May 7, 1867; missionary of A. B. C. F. M. at Harpoot, E. Turkey, 1867-72; and at Van since 1872.

GEORGE BAYLESS.

Born in Millburn, N. Y., Jan. 2, 1837; united with the Church in Conklin, 1854; graduated from Hamilton College in 1864; married to Miss CARRIE C. CULVER, of Syracuse, N. Y., May 28, 1867.

Ordained and installed at Phelps, N. Y., by Presby. of Geneva, 1867; Phelps, 2½ years; First Ch., Dubuque, Iowa, 1 year; McGrawville, N. Y., 1871-81; Mexico from 1881.

*WILLIAM B. HENDRYX, died Jan. 1, 1867.

*ISAAC NEWTON LOWRY, died Mar. 16, 1871.

*DARIUS CARTER SACKETT, died Feb. 10, 1871.

JOSEPH EDWIN SCOTT.

Came to Auburn from Buffalo, N. Y.; graduated from Hamilton College in 1859; taught, 1859-64; married to Miss ANNA HIGGINS, of Mecklenburg, N. Y.

Ordained and installed at Millville, N. J., by Presby., 1867; Millville, 1867-70; Indianapolis, Ind., Olivet Pres. Ch., 1870-1; miss. of A. B. C. F. M., Harpoot, and afterward Van, Turkey, from 1872; now at Jonganoxie, Kan.

DARIUS ROVER SHOOP.
>   Born in Freeport, Pa., Jan. 15, 1833; united with the First Cong.
>   Church in Ann Arbor, Mich., June, 1857; graduated from Univ.
>   of Mich. in 1864; married to Miss ANNA E. STANFIELD, of
>   Ann Arbor, June 3, 1867.
>   Ordained at St. Paul's Church, Tenn., by Union Presby., Sept.,
>   1867; Maryville, Tenn., 1867; Bellevue, Mich., 1868-73; supt.
>   of Schools, Eaton Co., 1873-5; Manchester, 1876; St. Louis,
>   1877-8; Hastings, Mich., 1879-80; Bellevue, 1880-2; South
>   Haven, 1882.

SEXTUS EDDY SMITH.
>   Born in Springville, N. Y., Mar. 6, 1842; united with the Pres.
>   Church in Springville, July, 1860; studied at Springville
>   Academy; married to Miss CARRIE MARIAH SQUIRES, of Spring-
>   ville, Aug. 10, 1864.
>   Ordained Barton, Wis., Nov., 1867, by Presby. of Milwaukee;
>   Barton, 1867-9; Gardner, Ill., 1869-71; Union Mills, Ind.,
>   from 1872.

*ALBERT PAYSON WORTHINGTON, died May 6, 1867.

JAMES MCKNIGHT CRAIG.
>   Born near Bristol, England, about 1839; united with the 1st
>   Pres. Church in Utica; graduated from Hamilton College in
>   1864; in Auburn to Dec. 8, 1866; married, about 1868.
>   Ordained, Oct., 1874; teaching, 1867-71; in the ministry of the
>   M. E. Ch., 1871-4; resident in Ripon, Wis., invalid, and
>   afterward past. of an Indep. Ch., 1874-80; Pres. Ch., Manito-
>   woc, from 1880.

WILLIAM HUBBELL FISHER.
>   Came to Auburn from Clinton, N. Y.; graduated from Hamilton
>   College in 1864; Auburn, 1864-5; married to Miss MARY LYON,
>   of Lyon's Falls, N. Y.
>   Never ordained; practicing Law in Cincinnati, O.

MORTIMER ANDREW HYDE.   See 1862-5.

HERMON DUTILH JENKINS, D. D.
>   Born in Columbus, O., Jan. 14, 1842; united with the Pres.
>   Church in Waverly, N. Y., April, 1858; graduated from
>   Hamilton College in 1864; first year in Auburn, last two in
>   Union Sem., New York; D. D. from Beloit College, 1881;
>   married to HARRIET N. BURRILL, of Utica, N. Y., Oct 29,
>   1868.
>   Ordained and installed at Joliet, Ill., by Presby. of Chicago, Sept.,
>   1868; Joliet, 1868-73; Freeport, Ill., 1st Pres. Ch., from 1873.

1865-8.

EDWARD PAYSON ADAMS.
Born in East Bloomfield, N. Y., Dec. 14, 1833; united with the
1st Cong. Church in East Bloomfield, 1849; graduated from
Hamilton College in 1858 ; entered Auburn in 1860 ; re-admitted
to Jun. class, having been in U. S. signal service, 1865 ; married
to Miss CHARLOTTE ADELAIDE STANLEY, of Elmira, N. Y.,
1868.
Ordained and installed at Dunkirk, N. Y., by Presby, of Buffalo,
Dec., 1876; Hannibal, 1868-70; New Berlin, 1870-2; Dunkirk
from 1876; mem. of Presby. to 1881; resident in Dunkirk.

MYRON ADAMS.
Born in East Bloomfield, N. Y., March 12, 1841; united with the
Cong. Church in Butternuts, N. Y., 1858; graduated from
Hamilton College in 1863; married to Miss HESTER ROSE
HOPKINS, of Auburn, N. Y., Sept. 23, 1868.
Ordained and installed at Dunkirk, N. Y., by Presby. of Buffalo, Oct.
19, 1869; Union Springs, 1868-9; Dunkirk, 1869-76; Ply-
mouth Cong. Ch., Rochester, from 1876.

WILLIAM HENRY BATES.
Born in Champion, N. Y., May 20, 1840; united with the M. E.
Church in Champion, probably Mar., 1854; graduated from
Hamilton College in 1865; married to Miss ELLEN JOANNA
PECKHAM, of Pulaski, N. Y., July 8, 1868.
Ordained at McGrawville, N. Y., by Cortland Presby., Jan. 20,
1869; McGrawville, 1868-71; Waverly, 1871-8; Adams, 1878-
80; Clyde from 1880.

DANIEL WEBSTER BEADEL.
Born in Depauville, N. Y., May 17, 1837; united with the M. E.
Church, April, 1857; graduated from Ill. State Normal Univ.;
married to Miss FRANCES HARRIET JOHNSON, of Hannibal, N.
Y., July 13, 1865.
Ordained at Syracuse, in Central N. Y. Conf. of M. E. Ch., by
Bishop Janes, April, 1867; Elbridge, 1868-9; Montezuma,
1869-70; Moravia, 1870-2; presiding Elder; Geddes, 1875-
6; resident there, in ill health; chaplain; Sec'y. of Am. Co-
operative Rel. Assoc.

DANA WILLIAMS BIGELOW.
Born in Waterville, N. Y., Nov. 27, 1843; united with the Church
in Waterville, Mar., 1860; graduated from Hamilton College in
1865; married to Miss KATHERINE HUNTINGTON, of Auburn,
June 24, 1868.
Ordained and installed at Fayetteville, N. Y., by Presby. of
Syracuse, Sept., 1868; Fayetteville, 1868-72; Pitcher, Cong. Ch.,
1872-7; Utica, West Ch., from 1877.

HIRAM WARD CONGDON.
Born in Watertown, N. Y., July 1, 1841; united with the Brick Church in Rochester, N. Y., 1863; graduated from Univ. of Rochester in 1865; married to Miss FLORA A. POTTER, of Camden, N. Y., Sept., 1873.
Ordained at Evans Mills, N. Y., by Presby. of St. Lawrence, Oct., 1875; Coudersport, Pa., 1873-4; Havana, N. Y., 1876-8; Smithville Flats, 1878-81; Wyoming from 1881.

*ALEXANDER DOUGLASS, died Dec. 4, 1875.

STEPHEN GROSVENOR HOPKINS.
Born in Buffalo, N. Y., July 23, 1840; united with the Ref. Ch. of Owasco Outlet, 1857; graduated from Hamilton College in 1863; in the Army; married to Miss MARY COMSTOCK HAIGHT, of Auburn, June 9, 1869.
Ordained and installed at Corry, Pa., by Presby. of Erie, Oct., 1868; Corry, 1868-76; Columbus, O., 1876-9; supplying Churches, 1879-81; Deposit, N. Y., from 1881.
Son of Prof. Samuel Miles Hopkins of 1834-7.

ALBERT FRANKLIN LYLE.
Born in St. Stephens, New Brunswick, April 11, 1839; united with the Howard Pres. Church in San Francisco, Cal., Dec. 6, 1857; graduated from College of California in 1864; married to Miss LOUISA THOMAS, of Union Springs, N. Y., June 22, 1872.
Ordained at 2nd Pres. Ch., Auburn, by Presby. of Cayuga, 1868; home miss. in Colorado, 1868-9; Union Springs, N. Y., 1869-73; West Utica Pres. Ch., 1874-7; Ilion, 1878-81.

GEORGE B. PECK, M. D.
Born in Cincinnati, O., Sept. 14, 1833; united with the Vine St. Cong. Church in Cincinnati, 1847; graduated from Miami Univ. in 1857; graduated from Medical School of Harvard Univ., with degree of M. D., 1863.
Ordained at Venice, O., by Presby. of Cincinnati, Sept. 15, 1875; Beverly, N. J., 1868-9; Bond Hill, O., 1875-6; resident physician and chaplain at Consumptive's Home, near Boston, from 1876.

HENRY MARTYN SIMMONS.
Came to Auburn from Paris Hill, N. Y.; born, 1841; united with the Church after entering Seminary; graduated from Hamilton College in 1864; Auburn, 1866-8.
Licentiate of Presby., to 1870; Unit. Ch., Waukesha, Wis., 1880.

ALFRED SNASHALL.
Born in Kent, England; came to Auburn from the Central Park Church, New York City.
Victor, Iowa, to 1870; Hannibal, N. Y., 1870-2; Wampsville, 1873; resident Binghamton, 1876-7, and Red Creek, 1878; Martville; Portland, Or.

THEODORE TYLER WING, M. D.

Born in Philadelphia, Pa., June 1, 1844; united with the 1st Pres. Church in Carlisle, Pa., 1858; graduated from Dickinson College in 1864; Signal Corps, U. S. Vols.; M. D. from Univ. of Pa., 1873; married to Miss HARRIET SCHLAGER BRANDT, of Brandt, Pa., Oct. 15, 1868.

Not ordained; preached, Onondaga Valley, N. Y., 1868, and Rolla, Mo., 1869; practiced Medicine, Philadelphia, 2 years, and since at Susquehanna Depot.

EDWIN A. BARNES.

Came to Auburn from Church in Kings Ferry, N. Y.; left Dec. 11, 1865.

HOWARD CORNELL.

Born in Milton, N. Y., Sept. 10, 1840; united with the Church, April, 1857; graduated from Union College in 1865; Auburn, 1865-6; Union, N. Y., 1866-8; married to JESSIE KIRBY, of Athens, Pa., Sept. 29, 1880.

Ordained and installed at Constantia, N. Y., by Presby. of Syracuse, March 17, 1874; Constantia, 1871-6; Nichols, 1876-9; Orwell, Pa., from 1879.

BRAINERD TAYLOR DEWITT.

Born in Marietta, O., April 28, 1840; graduated from Marietta College in 1865; Auburn, 1865-6; Lane Sem., 1867-8.

Ordained by Scioto Presby., Apr., 1869; Frankfort, Iowa, to 1871; Van Wert, O., 1871-3; Austin, Minn., 1874; Gilroy, Cal., 1874-6; Columbus, O., 1877; Sturgis, Mich., 1878; Fairview, Pa., from 1878.

*ALEXANDER H. FULLERTON, died about 1875.

RICHARD SILL HOLMES.

Born in Brooklyn, N. Y., July 6, 1842; united with the Cong. Church in Greenwich, Mar., 1857; graduated from Middlebury College in 1862; Auburn, 1865-6; married to Miss FANNIE PARDEE OLMSTED, of Auburn, Oct. 20, 1869; married to Miss ALIDA L. DODGE, of Newburgh, Sept. 7, 1881.

Not ordained; tea. in Auburn to 1878; pres. of Y. M. C. A. of State of N. Y., 1871; general S. S. work, 1878-9; in business in Auburn.

CHARLES MILLS WHITTLESEY.

Born in Ceylon, July 15, 1842; united with the Pres. Church in Dover, N. J., 1853; graduated from Yale College in 1864; two years at Auburn; married to LOUISE A. WAKELEE, of Rochester, N. Y., Oct. 3, 1867.

Ordained at Sidney, N. Y., by Chenango Presby., 1868; New Berlin, 1867-9; Bethany Church, Utica, 1869-70; Chicago, Ill., 1872; Spencerport, N.Y., 1873-9; resident Rochester from 1880.

Published "Gospel Work and Truth," 1878.

1866-9.

CHARLES BOYD.
Came to Seminary from Ottawa, Can.; born 1840; mem. of Gould St. Church in Toronto; graduated from Albert College; Aub. Mid. class, from Nov. 14, 1867; said to have returned to Canada; supposed to be a minister in P. E. Ch.; Lacolle, near Quebec, 1876.

HENRY A. DUBOC.
Born in 1844; came to Aub. from 4th Pres. Church in New Orleans, La.; graduated from Univ. of Rochester in 1875; Ludlow, Vt.; Emporium, Pa., 1873; rect. of P. E. Ch., Tonawanda, N. Y.; prin. of School for ladies, Tonawanda.

ABEL GROSVENOR HOPKINS.
Born in Avon Springs, N. Y., Dec. 5, 1844; united with the Hamilton Col. Church, Winter of 1863-4; graduated from Hamilton College in 1866; married to Miss SOPHIE LOUISA WILLIAMS, of Clinton, N. Y., July 24, 1872.
Ordained at Utica, N. Y., by Presby. of Utica, April 16, 1874; prof. of Latin, Hamilton College, from 1869.
Son of Prof. Samuel Miles Hopkins, of 1834-7.

CHARLES CARRINGTON JOHNSON.
Born in Wampsville, N. Y., July 3, 1837; united with the 1st Cong. Church in Clarkson, N. Y., May, 1853; studied at Kremlin Inst., Buffalo, N. Y., through the College Freshman year; taught, and entered the Army; married to Miss MARY CHARLOTTE GREEN, of Sherburne, N. Y., Aug. 7, 1866.
Ordained and installed at Holley, N. Y., by Presby. of Rochester, Oct. 19, 1869; Holley, 1869-73; Smyrna, Cong. Ch., from 1873.

*JOHN DAVIS JONES, died Oct., 1876.

HIRAM HUNTINGTON KELLOGG, JR.
Born in Galesburg, Ill., Jan. 23, 1842; united with the Pres. Ch. in Washington, Ill., 1863; graduated from Hamilton College in 1866; served in 86th Ill. Vols.; married to Miss MARY E. JACKS, of Batavia, N. Y., Aug. 20, 1874.
Ordained at Central Pres. Ch., Des Moines, Ia., by Presby. of Des Moines, July 14, 1869; organizing and serving Churches in Ia., 1869-71; Pres. Ch., Evans Mills, N. Y., 1871-4; Seneca Castle from 1874. Son of Hiram Huntington Kellogg, D. D., of 1823-6.

HENRY LOOMIS.
Born in Burlington, N. Y., Mar. 4, 1839; came to Aub. from Ch. in Ham. Col.; Capt. of U. S. Vols.; graduated from Hamilton College in 1866; married to Miss JANE HERRING GREENE, of New York City, Mar. 6, 1872.

Ordained at 2d Pres. Church, Auburn, by Presbytery of Cayuga,
Spring of 1869; Jamesville, 1870-1; miss. of Pres. Bd., Yokohama, Japan, 1871-6; resident in San Rafael, Cal., 1876-81;
supt. of work of Am. Bib. Soc., for Japan, residing in Yokohama,
from 1881.

WALLACE BLISS LUCAS.

Born in Cortland, N. Y., Jan. 28, 1843; united with the Presbyterian Church in Cortland, May, 1855; graduated from Hamilton College in 1866; married to Miss MARY J. McQUEEN, of
Morrisville, N. Y., June 30, 1869.
Ordained pastor Meridian, N. Y., by Cayuga Presby., Sept. 29,
1869, and is yet there.

DANIEL CHARLES McCOY.

Born in Clayton, Ill., May 30, 1836; united with the First Pres.
Ch. in Clayton, Jan., 1850; studied at Knox College in class
of 1866; in the Army from 1864; married to Miss AMERICA H.
Pollock, of Burlington, Ia., July 14, 1869.
Ordained at Clayton, Ill., by Presby. of Schuyler, Sept. 1, 1869;
miss. of A. B. C. F. M. to China, from 1869; 1st Pres. Ch. of
Peking, China, from 1872.

EUGENE JOHN RANSLOW.

Born in Georgia, Vt., Oct. 21, 1842; united with the 1st Cong.
Church in Underhill, Vt., July, 1861; graduated from Middle-
bury College in 1866; married to Miss ELLEN ELIZA KINGS-
BURY, of Norwich, Vt., May 11, 1869.
Ordained at Swanton, Vt., by Council, June, 1869; First Church,
Swanton, 1869-75; Wells River, from 1875.

DEVELLO Z. SHEFFIELD.

Born in Gainesville, N. Y., Aug. 13, 1841; united with the Cong.
Church in Castile, May, 1866; studied at Warsaw Academy;
married to Miss ELEANOR WOODHULL SHERRILL, of Pike, N. Y.,
July 27, 1869.
Ordained at Auburn, by Cayuga Presby., Spring of 1869; from
that time missionary near Peking, China.
Published "Digest of Theology," and "Guide to Holiness," both
in Chinese, 1876.

WILLIAM ARMSTRONG SIMKINS.

Born in Moravia, N. Y., Aug. 16, 1839; united with the 1st Pres.
Church in Auburn, Autumn of 1866; graduated from Mich.
Univ. in 1864; married to Miss AMANDA JULIA COBURN, of
Auburn, July 28, 1869.
Ordained and installed at Romulus, N. Y., by Presby. of Geneva,
Feb., 1870; Romulus, 1869-72; Salina, Kan., from 1873.

ERASTUS WILLIAMS TWICHELL.

Born in Springville, N. Y., Aug. 22, 1841; united with the Pres.
Church in Springville, 1860; graduated from Amherst College

in 1866 ; married to Miss SARAH FRANCES GARLOCK, of Auburn,
Oct. 7, 1869.
Ordained at Allegany, N. Y., by Presby. of Genesee, 1869;
Allegany, 1869-70 ; Burdett, 1870-80 ; resident Auburn from
1880, preaching in Ref. Ch., Cato, 1882.

JOSEPH L. WHITING.

Born in Lyndeboro, N. H., Jan. 30, 1835 ; united with the Pres.
Church in Jasper, 1861 ; graduated from Genesee College in
1866 ; married to Miss LUCY E. JACKSON, July 28, 1869.
Ordained at Auburn, by Cayuga Presby., Spring of 1869; mis-
sionary in N. China from 1869.
Published (with others) S. S. Lesson Helps in Chinese, 1878, 1879.

EVARTS KENT.

Born in Benson, Vt., March 12, 1843 ; united with the Cong.
Church in Ripton, Vt., 1863 ; graduated from Middlebury
College in 1865 ; Auburn, 1866-7 ; Andover, 1867-9 ; married
to HELEN M. BECKWITH, of Alstead, N. H., 1872.
Ordained and installed at Michigan City, Ind , by Council, May
23, 1871 ; Mich. City, 1871-80 ; Clinton St. Ch , Chicago, Ill.,
1880-1 ; 1st Ch., Atlanta, Ga., from 1881.

1867-70.

JAMES M. BOYD.

Came to Sem. from Ottawa, Can.; born 1842 ; mem. of Pres.
Church ; studied at Albert College ; Auburn, 1868-70 ; married
July 30, 1873.
Ordained by Presby. of Milwaukee, 1871 ; Barton, Wis., 1870-2 ;
Demorestville, Can., 1872-6, or longer.

DAVID RIDDLE BREED.

Born in Pittsburg, Pa., June 10, 1848 ; united with the Third Pres.
Church in Pittsburgh, 1861 ; graduated from Hamilton College
in 1867 ; married to MARY E. KENDALL, June 16, 1870.
Ordained and installed at St. Paul, Minn., by Presby. of St. Paul,
Sept., 1870, pastor of House of Hope Pres. Church, where he
remains.

JAMES GLENANN BUTLER.

Born in Frampton, Can., Mar. 20, 1837 ; studied at Williams College in class of 1865 ; U. S. military service from 1862 ; married
to MARGARET GRAHAM, of Philadelphia, Pa., May 14, 1864.
Ordained and installed at Grand Tower Ch., Ill., by Presby. of
Cairo, Oct. 29 and 30, 1870, where he remains.

CHARLES PIERPONT COIT.

Born in Hastings, N. Y., May 3, 1839; united with the Baptist
Church in Central Square, N. Y., 1859; graduated from Uni-
versity of Rochester in 1867; married to Miss SUSIE H. WAR-
NER, of Owego, N. Y., Jan. 21, 1874.

Ordained pastor of North Pres. Ch., Binghamton, N. Y., by
Presby. of Binghamton, June, 1870; North Ch., 1870-4; Hamp-
den Pres. Ch., Baltimore, Md., 1874-5; Memorial Pres. Ch.,
Rochester, N. Y., from 1875.

HENRY MARTYN DODD.

Born in Ridgeville, O., Aug. 6, 1839; united with the Cong. Ch.
in Alexander, N. Y., Oct. 2, 1859; graduated from Hamilton
College in 1863; married to Miss ELLA W. ALLEN, of Great
Barrington, Mass., Nov. 30, 1870.

Ordained and installed at Dexter and Brownville, N. Y., by Presby.
of St. Lawrence, Jan. 2, 1873; Pres. Ch., Manlius, 1870-2;
Dexter and Brownville from 1872.

SAMUEL JACKSON FISHER.

Born in 1847; came to Auburn from the Westminster Church in
Utica, N. Y.; graduated from Hamilton College in 1867; married to Miss M. ANNIE SHREVE, of Trenton, N. J., Oct. 20, 1870.

Ordained and installed at Swissvale, Pa., by Presby., Nov., 1870;
yet there.

*WILLIAM RHEEM HALBERT, died Apr. 14, 1881.

OGDEN HENDERSON.

Came to Auburn from Dresden, O.; mem. of Church there; born
1840; graduated from Marietta College in 1865; married to
Miss HELEN FITCH NELSON, of Auburn, Oct. 20, 1870.

Ordained at Auburn 2d Ch., by Presby. of Cayuga, 1872; Scipio,
1871; Newton, Ill., 1872; Nashville, 1873; Centralia, 1874; resident Iowa City, Ia., 1875-80, and Cedar Rapids, 1880; member
of Presby. of Iowa City till 1880.

DAVID JAMES.

Born in Wales, 1836; came to Auburn from Baltimore, Md.; mem.
of Ch. in Carlisle, Pa.; studied at Dickinson College. Wampsville, 1870-1.

ALBERT LEE.

Born in Kirkland, N. Y., Feb. 3, 1841; united with the Pres. Ch.
in Clinton, N. Y., 1863; studied two years at Harvard Univ.;
three years at Auburn, and one at Yale Divinity School; married to Miss H. MARIA DUTTON, June 13, 1876.

Ordained and installed at Rutland, N. Y., by Council, Aug. 10,
1876; Rootstown, O.; Rutland and Burrville, N. Y., 1875-9;
East Watertown, 1880; Dorr, Mich., 1881; Dwight, Ill., 1882.

JOHN CASTLETON LONG.
Born in Manningtree, Eng., 1831; united with the Cong. Church in Griffin's Mills, N. Y., 1848; graduated from Hamilton College in 1857; in Auburn, 1859-60 and 69-70; teacher, 1860-9; married to Miss FRANCES CORNELIA HENSHAW, at Batavia, N. Y., Nov. 29, 1860.
Ordained and installed at Elba by Presby. of Genesee, 1870; Elba, 1870-4; Union Springs, 1874-8; Castile from 1878.

*JOSEPH GROUT LONGLEY, died May 6, 1871.

JOHN MCMASTER.
Born in Spencer, N. Y., Sept. 22, 1839; united with Cong. Church in Spencer, Apr., 1858; studied at Owego Acad.; married to Miss LOUISE REYNOLDS, of Nichols, Oct. 6, 1875.
Ordained at Marathon, N. Y., by Presby. of Binghamton, May, 1872; Copenhagen, 1870-1; Marathon, 1872; Athens, Pa., 1873-81; resident in Spencer.

*GEORGE NORTON, died Oct. 11, 1869.

ALBERT COLE SEWALL.
Born in Blue Hill, Me., March 25, 1845; united with the Pres. Church in N. Granville, N. Y., July, 1858; graduated from Williams College in 1867; married to Miss HELEN S. IVES, of South Easton, N. Y., Jan. 12, 1871.
Ordained and installed at Newark, N. Y., by Presby. of Lyons, Oct. 13, 1871; Newark, 1870-3; Williamstown, Mass., from 1873.
Published " Life of Professor Albert Hopkins," 1879.

GRENVILLE PIERCE SEWALL.
Born in Westbrook, Me., Sept. 18, 1841; united with the Pres. Church in North Granville, N. Y., July, 1858; graduated from Williams College in 1867; married to Miss ROSAMOND E. COLE, of Williamstown, Mass., Sept. 24, 1879.
Ordained and installed at Cayuga, N. Y., by Presby. of Cayuga, Dec. 28, 1870; Cayuga, 1869-79; Troy, Pa., from 1879.

CHARLES H. H. WOLFF.
Born in Holland about 1840; mem. of 1st Pres. Church in Aub.; studied at Amsterdam Gymnasium; married to Miss DUROC, of Auburn, 1870.
Ordained at Auburn by Presby. of Cayuga, 1870; miss. of Ref. Ch. to Japan, in Yokohama, Hirosaki, Nagasaki, 1870-5; Govt. Schools, Japan, 1875-82.

---

*EDWARD GIBBS BICKFORD, died Oct. 19, 1877.

AMORY HOWE BRADFORD.
Born in Granby, N. Y., April 14, 1846; united with the Wesleyan Methodist Church in Penn Yan, about 1860; graduated from

Hamilton College in 1867; one year at Auburn and two at Andover; married to JULIA M. STEVENS, of Little Falls, N. Y., Sept. 22, 1870.

Ordained and installed at Montclair, N. J., by Council, Sept. 28, 1870, where he remains.

HERMAN B. DEAN.

Came to Auburn from Waterloo, N. Y.; mem. of M. E. Church in Dayton, O.; left the Seminary, Apr. 18, 1870; licentiate of Presby. of Geneva, till 1870. His wife died, 1871.

Ordained at Prescott, Wis., (Cong.) May 20, 1873; Ludington, Mich.; St. Clair; Springfield, Ill., 1877; Paris, Texas, 1878.

*ISAAC ANDERSON MARTIN, died Oct. 30, 1875.

MARCY ELLSWORTH NELSON.   See 1868–71.

LUTHER ALLEN OSTRANDER.

Born in Franklinville, N. Y., July 14, 1843; united with the 1st Pres. Church in Chicago, Ill., 1858; graduated from Hamilton College in 1865; 1st year in Chicago; Aub., 1868–9; Union, N. Y., 1869–70; married to Miss ELIZA A. THOMSON, of Constantinople, Turkey, May 25, 1871.

Ordained and installed at Dubuque, Iowa, by Dubuque Presby., Nov. 1, 1871; Dubuque, 1871–6; Owego, N. Y., from 1876.

ELIZUR HULL PRATT.

Born in Durham, N. Y., Aug. 10, 1842; united with the Pres. Ch. in Durham, July, 1862; graduated from Williams College in 1867; Auburn, 1867–9; Union, N. Y., 1869–70; married to Miss KATE E CARTER, of Evans Mills, N. Y., Jan 4, 1871.

Ordained at Adams, N. Y., by St. Lawrence Presby., May, 1871; Cape Vincent, N. Y., 1871–7; ed. Baltimore, Md., 1877–9; asst. ed. of *N. Y. Evangelist* from 1879.

Published "Sketch of Town of Cape Vincent," 1876; Sunday School Catalogue, 1880.

ALEXANDER BROWN RIGGS.

Born in Portsmouth, O., June 21, 1842; united with the 1st Pres. Church in Portsmouth, about March, 1856; graduated from Jefferson College in 1863; 4 years in the study and practice of Law; two years at Auburn, the third at Union N. Y.; married to CHARLOTTE BOWN RICHARDSON, of Brooklyn, N. Y., Oct. 19, 1870.

Ordained and installed at Fort Plain, N. Y., by Montgomery Classis, Dec. 1, 1870; Fort Plain, 1870–6; Pres. Ch., Waterford, from 1876.

EDWARD WILLARD WETMORE.

Born in Detroit, Mich., Sept. 5, 1846; united with the Church in May, 1862; graduated from Univ. of Michigan in 1867; Auburn, 1867–9; married to JULIA RANNEY WELLS, of Howell, Mich., July 27, 1876.

Prof. of Nat. Sci., Robert Col., Constantinople, 3 years; tea. in Greylock Inst., South Williamstown, Mass., 1 year; prof. of Physics and Chem., Detroit High School, Mich., from 1875.

1868-71.

WILLIAM JAMES ARNEY.
Graduated from Vermilion Inst., O.; Aub. Sen class from Western Theo. Sem.
Great Bend, Pa., to 1875; Reading, 1875-8; Blissfield, Mich., from 1878.

HENRY T. COWLEY.
Came to Auburn from Castile, N. Y.; mem. of Church there; born about 1838; graduated from Antioch College in 1867.
Miss. to Dakota Indians, Kamia and Mt. Idaho, Idaho Ter., and Spokane Falls, W. T., 1871-80.

CASSIUS HORATIO DIBBLE.
Born in Stone Church, N. Y., June 21, 1845; united with the Cong. Church in E. Bloomfield, Mar. 2, 1862; graduated from Hamilton College in 1868; married to Miss ALICE MARY CONDIT of Auburn, Sept. 27, 1871.
Ordained at Geneva by Presby. of Geneva, Apr., 1872; asst. past., Pres. Ch., Waterloo, 1871-2; Perry, from 1872.

ALFRED JOHN HUTTON.
Born in Brunswick, N. Y., June 20, 1842; united with the Church in April, 1854; graduated from Williams College in 1866; married to Miss HARRIET WISE HYATT, of New York, Oct. 4, 1871.
Ordained and installed at West Troy, N. Y., by Classis of Saratoga, July, 1871; West Troy, 1871-9; Pres. Church, Cortland, 1879-81; Ref. Ch. on the Heights, Brooklyn, from 1881.

CHARLES FRANCIS JANES.
Born in Downsville, N. Y., Aug. 7, 1847; united with the Cong. Church in Walton, N. Y., 1858; graduated from Hamilton College in 1868; married to Miss MARIA ELIZABETH MCLAURY, of Walton, May 22, 1871.
Ordained and installed at Oxford, N. Y., by Otsego Presby., 1871; Oxford, 1870-3; Corning, Iowa, 1873-7; Verona, N. Y., 1878-82; Onondaga Valley, 1882. Son of Frances Janes, of 1830-3.

HENRY THADDEUS MILLER.
Born in Tuscarora, N. Y., Aug. 17, 1842; united with the Brick (Pres.) Church in Rochester, June 2, 1867; graduated from Univ. of Rochester in 1868; married to Miss JENNIE KENNEDY, of York, N. Y., Oct. 17, 1871.
Ordained and installed at Victor, by Presby. of Rochester, June 1, 1871; Victor, 1871-3; Medina, 1873-5; Chicago, 6th Ch., 1875-82.

MARCY ELLSWORTH NELSON.

Born in Lewis, N. Y., Nov. 17, 1845; united with the Pres. Ch. in Jan., 1867; Auburn, 1867–71; married to Miss FRANCES SOPHIA CONABLE, of Alexander, N. Y., April 16, 1873.

Licentiate of Presby. of Emporia till 1877; Pavilion, N. Y., 1871–2; Branchport, 1872; Hutchinson, Kan., 1874–5; resident Webster, N. Y.

EDWARD ALLEN REED, D. D.

Born in Lansingburgh, N. Y., June 24, 1843; united with the 1st Pres. Church in Lansingburgh, June, 1858; studied at Lansingburgh Acad.; D. D. from Rutgers College in 1881; married to Miss MARY ANNE BLISS, of Lansingburgh, May 30, 1871.

Ordained and installed at Springfield, Mass., by Council, June 14, 1871; 1st Ch. of Christ, Springfield, 1871–8; Madison Ave. Ref. Ch., N. Y. City, from 1878.

CHARLES SPENCER RICHARDSON.

Born in Pittsford, N. Y., Feb. 7, 1845; united with the Pres. Church in Geneva, 1858; graduated from Hobart College in 1865; married to Miss FRANCES M. WEED, of Cambridge, Mass., Feb. 17, 1875.

Ordained at Geneva, N. Y., by Presby. of Geneva, 1871; prof. in Robert College, Constantinople, 1871–4; Pres. Ch., Malone, N. Y., from 1874.

JOHN OGDEN GORDON.

Born in Pittsburgh, Pa., March 10, 1850; united with the 3d Pres. Church in Pittsburgh, 1867; graduated from Western Univ. of Pa., in 1866; 2 years at Auburn; last year at Union, N. Y.; married to EMMA W. BACON of Troy, N. Y., May 31, 1877.

Ordained and installed at Rensselaerville, by Presby. of Columbia, Mar. 26, 1872; Rensselaerville, 1871–80; Lincoln, Neb., from 1880.

CHARLES MARION HOWE.

Born in Girard, Pa., Mar. 21, 1842; united with the 1st Pres. Ch. in Vinton, Iowa, in 1862; graduated from Dartmouth College in 1868, and from Iowa State University in 1867; two years at Auburn, 3d year at Sem. of Northwest; married to Miss MARY O. DENNIS, of Iowa City, Ia., June 15, 1870.

Ordained and installed at Eldora, by Presby. of Waterloo, Nov. 1, 1871; Eldora, 1871–80; Janesville, Iowa, from 1880.

SAMUEL LANTY McAFEE.

Born in Emerson, Mo., May 13, 1841; united with the Pres. Ch. in New Providence, Dec., 1857; graduated from Pardee College in 1869; two years at Auburn, and one at Sem. of the Northwest; married to Miss MARY ESTHER POAGE, of Ashley, Mo., Apr. 19, 1871.

Ordained and installed at Red Oak, Iowa, by Presby. of Mo. River, Dec 17, 1871 ; Red Oak, 1871–82 ; Winnebago City, Minn., 1882.

HENRY NELSON PAYNE.
Born in Horse Heads, N. Y., Nov. 4, 1840; united with the 1st Cong. Church in Janesville, Wis., June 6, 1858 ; graduated from Hamilton College in 1868 ; first year at Chicago The. Sem., second at Auburn, third at Lane ; married to Miss ELIZABETH AMELIA PORTER, of Auburn, Sept. 7, 1871.
Ordained and installed at 1st Pres. Ch., Minneapolis, Minn., by Presby. of St. Paul, Oct. 5, 1871; Minneapolis, 1871–5 ; Onondaga Valley, N. Y., 1876 ; Lima, 1876–8 : Associated Pres. Ch., Oxford, 1879–81 : Boone, Ia., from 1881.

1869-72.

JOHN EVERITT BEECHER.
Born in Ellsworth, Conn., Jan. 22, 1842 ; united with the Pres. Church in Vernon Centre. N. Y., Mar., 1861 ; graduated from Hamilton College in 1869.
Ordained at Cohocton, N. Y., by Presby. of Steuben, Apr. 7, 1875; Pres. Ch., Turin, N. Y., 1872–3 ; Jasper, 1873–5 ; Holt, Mich., 1876–7 ; Bad Axe, 1877–81 ; Chatfield, Minn., 1881–2.

JEREMIAH MEACHAM CHRYSLER.
Born in Theresa, N. Y., Mar. 2, 1841 ; united with the Pres. Ch. in Theresa, Spring of 1859 ; graduated from Hamilton College in 1869 ; married to Miss EMILIE LORD KNOWLES, of Copenhagen, N. Y., June 19, 1872.
Ordained and installed at Collamer, N. Y., by Presby. of Syracuse, May 21, 1872 ; Collamer, 1871–6 ; East Syracuse, 1875–8 ; Stillwater from 1878.

JAMES HUNTER CLARK.
Born in Liberty, O., Dec. 31, 1843; united with Pres. Ch., Liberty, Dec., 1856 ; studied at Washington and Jefferson Colleges ; Aub. Sen. class last half year, from Theo. Sem. of N. W. ; married to Miss AMY H. BELDEN, of Malden, Ill., April 6, 1871.
Ordained and installed at Castile, N. Y., by Presby., 1872 ; Castile, 1872–3 ; Streator, Ill., 1873–5; Atchison, Kan., 1875–8 ; resident Youngstown, O., 1880 ; Millard Ave. Cong. Ch., Chicago, 1882.

HARLAN PAGE DUNNING.
Born in Havana, N. Y., May 22, 1841; united with the Pres. Ch. in Baraboo, Wis , 1864 ; graduated from Beloit College in 1869 ; married to Miss MARY ELIZABETH ALEXANDER, Dec. 25, 1869.
Ordained and installed at Canoga, N. Y., by Presby. of Geneva, May 19, 1872; Canoga, 1872–5; Seattle, W. T., 1875–6; Corvallis, Or., from 1866.

ERWIN COLTON HULL.

Born in Auburn, N. Y., Nov. 1, 1844; united with the Cong. Ch. in Hannibal, N. Y., March 6, 1864; graduated from Hamilton College in 1869; married to Miss ROSANNA STEWART MACK, of Southwest Oswego, N. Y., July 23, 1873.

Ordained and installed at Prairie du Lac, Wis., by Presby. of Wis. River, Oct. 10, 1872; Prairie du Lac, 1872-6; Elba, N. Y., from 1876; Cong. Ch., Ellsworth, Conn., from 1880.

JOHN WILFORD JACKS.

Born in Batavia, N. Y., Sept. 5, 1845; united with the Ham. Col. Church in Nov., 1864; graduated from Hamilton College in 1867; tea. Lowville Acad., 1867-8, and Whitestown Sem., 1868-9. Ordained and installed at Romulus, N. Y., by Presby. of Geneva, Aug. 27, 1872; still there.

DAVID MURRAY.

Born in Ontario, Can., June 26, 1842; graduated from Knox College, Toronto, in 1867; Princeton, 1868-70; Auburn, (on letter from Princeton) 1871-2; married before entering Auburn.

Ordained and installed at Alden, N. Y., by Presby., 1872; Alden, 1872-6; Saline, Mich., 1876-9; mem. of Presby. of Detroit till 1879; said to be practicing Law.

ALBERT BARNES ROBINSON.

Born in Cabot, Vt., Dec. 16, 1846; united with the Cong. Church in Guilford Centre, N. Y., Feb., 1860; graduated from Hamilton College in 1868; married to Miss ELIZA BRONSON COTES, of Springfield, N. Y., May 30, 1872.

Ordained and installed at Unadilla, N. Y., by Otsego Presby., Oct. 30, 1872; Pres. Ch., Unadilla, 1871-6; Tonawanda, 1876-9; Perrysburg, O., from 1879.

THEODORE BAKER WILLIAMS.

Born in Prattsburg, N. Y., Jan. 27, 1845; united with the Cent. Pres. Church in Rochester, Nov., 1866; graduated from University of Rochester in 1869; married to Miss CLARA B. CLARK, of Parma, N. Y., Oct. 3, 1877.

Ordained at Prattsburgh, N. Y., by Presby. of Steuben, Apr., 1873; Campbelltown, 1872-5; Mooers, 1875-6; Unadilla, Stockbridge and Plainfield, Mich., 1876-81; Charlotte, N. Y., from 1881.

———

JOHN LOVELL DOUGLASS.

Born in 1848; came to Auburn from Niles, Mich.; mem. of Ch. in Hamilton Col.; studied at Hamilton College in class of 1869; in Auburn a few weeks of Junior year.

WILLIAM D. DUNCAN.

Born in 1842; came to Aub. from Fulton, Mo.; mem. of M. E. Church in Lima, N. Y.; studied at Genesee College; in service of U. S.; Auburn, 1869-70; said to have married near Rock Stream, N. Y., 1870, and to be resident there.

ISAAC D. FOWLER.
Born in 1846; came to Auburn from York; mem. of Church
there; graduated from Univ. of Rochester in 1869; Auburn,
1869-70; druggist in Lansing, Ia.

JOHN SYLVANUS. See 1870-3.

*CHARLES AUGUSTUS WETMORE, died July 6, 1874.

WILLIAM HENRY WHITING.
Born in Lyndeborough, N. H., Jan. 3, 1842; united with the
Church in Jasper, N. Y., 1858; graduated from Hamilton Col-
lege in 1869; LL. B., 1877; Auburn, 1869; married to Miss
CAROLINE VIRGINIA ANDREWS, of Rochester, Jan. 20, 1874; tea.
House of Refuge, Rochester, 1870-4; practicing Law in Roch-
ester.

1870-3.

LEONARD WILSON CHURCH.
Born in Afton, N. Y., Aug. 25, 1843; united with the Pres
Church in Whitestown, N. Y., 1864; graduated from Whitestown
Seminary, 1870; married to Miss JENNIE PAULINE LAKE, of
Easton, Mass., July 3, 1873.
Ordained at Winfield, N. Y., by Council, Sept. 24, 1873; Winfield
and Bridgwater, 1873-9; New Lebanon from 1879.

SAMUEL LEE CONDE.
Born in Lahaina, Maui, Hawaiian Is., Sept. 20, 1837; united with
the Mission Church in Hawaii, 1850; studied at Oahu, (H. I.)
College; grad. at Normal School, Albany, N. Y., 1858; practiced Law in Madison Co., 1860-70; line and staff officer in
service of U. S.; married to Miss ELISABETH L. COLLIER, of
Chittenango, N. Y., Dec. 30, 1861.
Ordained pastor, Troy, Pa., by Presby. of Lackawanna, May 20,
1873; Troy, 1873-9; evangelist, 1879-80; Pres. Ch., Tunkhannock, from 1880. Son of Dr. Daniel Toll Conde, of 1831-4.

*THOMAS KITCHEL CRANE, died Feb. 20, 1876.

DELOS EDWIN FINKS.
Born in Sherburne, N. Y., Nov. 5, 1842; united with the Church
in Hamilton Col., Nov. 25, 1866; graduated from Hamilton
College in 1870; married to Miss Nettie V. Rogers, of Geneva,
N. Y., May 13, 1873.
Ordained at Auburn, by Cayuga Presby., 1873; home miss. at
Fairplay, Col., 1873-6; Fort Collins, 1876-81; North Denver
from 1881.

*ROSELLE ANDREW FULLER, died Spring of 1880.

CLARK BATEMAN GILLETTE.

Born in Perinton, N. Y., Mar. 25, 1845 ; united with the Pres. Ch. in Victor, N. Y., 1869 ; graduated from Union College in 1871 ; entered Auburn on letter from Union Seminary, middle of Senior year ; post graduate at Lane, 1876-7 ; married to H. ADDIE ANDREWS, Apr. 19, 1875.

Ordained pastor at Emporium, Pa., by Presbytery of Northumberland, Oct. 22, 1873 ; Emporium, 1873-5 ; Milwaukee, Wis., 1875-6 ; Oakfield, N. Y., 1878-80 ; Elba, 1880-1 ; Nelson, Pa., from 1881.

MARTIN ELLIS GRANT.

Born in Henderson, N. Y., June 27, 1843 ; united with the Ham. Col. Church in 1870 ; graduated from Hamilton College in 1870 ; married to Miss DESSIE ELLIS, of Plessis, N. Y., June 6, 1877. Ordained at Fort Dodge, Iowa, by Presby. of Fort Dodge, 1875 ; Moingona, Iowa, 1873-5 ; Plessis, N. Y., 1876-7 ; Cape Vincent, from 1877.

RUFUS SMITH GREEN.

Born in Sidney Plains, N. Y., Apr. 1, 1848 ; united with the Ham. Col. Church in 1863 ; graduated from Hamilton College in 1867 ; married to Miss LUCY ANNA ROBINSON, of Walton, N. Y., July 23, 1873.

Ordained pastor, Westfield, N. Y., by Presby. of Buffalo, Sept. 30, 1874 ; Westfield, 1873-7 ; 1st Pres. Ch., Morristown, N. J., 1877 -81 ; Lafayette St. Ch., Buffalo, N. Y., from 1881.

WILLIAM SYLVESTER HOLT.

Born in Mt. Hawkins, Ill., Aug. 24, 1848 ; united with the 1st Cong. Church in Ripon, Wis., 1866 ; graduated from Ripon College in 1870 ; one year at Seminary of Northwest, 2 years at Auburn ; married to Miss FRANCES ADELLA PRATT, of Webster, N. Y., May 28, 1873.

Ordained at Owatonna, Minn., by Presby. of Winona, Aug., 1873 ; miss. of Pres. Bd. to China, Shanghai, 1873-4 ; Soochow, 1874-6, and in charge of mission press, Shanghai, from 1876.

Published many articles ; editor of *Chinese Recorder*, 1 year ; man. ed. of *The Temperance Union*, Shanghai.

MARTIN DWELLE KNEELAND.

Born in Thorn Hill, N. Y., Sept. 24, 1848 ; united with the Pres. Church in Cazenovia, 1865 ; graduated from Hamilton College in 1869 ; married to Miss SARAH APPLETON LORD, of Montpelier, Vt., Oct. 27, 1875.

Ordained pastor of Pres. Ch. of Waterloo, by Presby. of Geneva, June 1, 1873 ; Waterloo, 1873-82 ; Fredonia, 1882. Son of Doct. Jonathan Kneeland, of 1836-9.

JOHN MCLACHLAN.

Born in Argyleshire, Scotland, Oct. 27, 1843 ; united with the Church in Spring of 1862 ; graduated from Hamilton College, in 1870; married to Miss HARRIET NEWELL ROBINSON, of Walton, N. Y., May 20, 1873.

Ordained pastor, Pleasantville, Pa., by Presby. of Erie, Aug. 19, 1873; Pleasantville, 1873–82; Waterloo, N. Y., 1882.

WILLIAM BARR MINTON.

Born near Gallatin, Tenn., Oct. 21, 1849; united with the Pres. Church in Carlinville, Ill., 1866; graduated from Blackburn University in 1870; Blackburn Theo. Sem., 1870–1; Auburn, 1871–3; married to Miss OLIVIA JEROME HUGHES, of Belleville, Ill., June 7, 1875.

Ordained at Nashville, Ill., by Presby. of Cairo, Spring of 1874; home miss. in Southern Ill., 1873–4; Pres, Ch., Anna, Ill., 1874–7; Fort Wayne, Ind., 1878–81; Litchfield, Ill., from 1881.

WILLIAM AUGUSTUS RICE.

Born in Kingsport, E. Tenn., Nov. 5, 1850; united with the 2nd Pres. Church in Knoxville, Tenn., 1866; studied at Williston Seminary; married to Miss MARY McCLELLAN STEWART, of Vincennes, Ind., Oct. 28, 1869.

Ordained, 2nd Pres. Ch., Auburn, by Presby. of Cayuga, April, 1873; 2nd Pres. Ch., Chattanooga, Tenn., 1873; Westernville, N. Y., 1873–7; Marshall, Mich., 1877–9; Wolcott, N. Y., from 1879.

JAMES ROBERTSON.

Born in Montreal, Sept. 25, 1846; united with the Church in Perry; studied at Alexander and Perry Acads.; married to Miss FRANCES H. ROYCE, of Albion, N. Y., Oct. 9, 1873.

Ordained pastor, Elbridge, N. Y., by Presby. of Syracuse, Nov. 18, 1873; Elbridge, 1873–5; San Diego, Cal., 1876; Sweden, N. Y., 1876–9; Lima, 1879–81; Presb. Hospital, N. Y., 1881; resident in Pike, preaching occasionally.

JAMES SNOW ROOT.

Born in Phelps, N. Y., June 21, 1845; united with the Pres. Ch. in Phelps; graduated from Hamilton College, in 1870; married to Miss EMMA LEILA CLINE, of Phelps, July 27, 1870.

Ordained pastor at Camillus, N. Y., by Syracuse Presby., June, 1873; Camillus, 1873–7; Liverpool, 1877–81; Adams from 1881, Pres. Ch., and prof. of Elocution in Hungerford Col. Inst.

Published Chart of Monthly Concert Work, 1882.

FREDERICK DWIGHT SEWARD.

Born in Laketown, Ind., Dec. 11, 1842; united with the Pres. Ch. in Mankato, Minn., Oct., 1861; graduated from Western Reserve College in 1870; one year at Lane; two years at Auburn; married to Miss EMMA A. HOYT, of Tallmadge, O., June 30, 1871.

Ordained pastor, Hannibal, N. Y., by Presby. of Syracuse, May 14, 1873; Hannibal, 1873–7; Prattsburgh 1877–9; Fowlerville, 1879–81; San Buenaventura, Cal., from 1881.

JOHN SYLVANUS.

Born in Aberystwyth, Wales, 1837; came to Auburn from Church
in Cincinnati, O.; graduated from Marietta College in 1867;
entered Auburn from Lane in 1869, and afterward fell back one
year.

Earlham, Iowa, 1874-5; De Soto, 1876; Palo Pinto, Tex., 1877;
Breckenbridge, 1877-81; Inman, Neb., 1882.

JOSEPH LEONARD WAUGH.

Born in Sauquoit, N. Y., Oct. 21, 1844; united with the Church
in Ham. Col., Feb., 1866; graduated from Hamilton College in
1867; tea. Carthage, N. Y., 1867-8, and Webster Acad., 1869-
70; married to Miss LIBBIE M. CHAPIN, of Russell, N. Y., Sept.
17, 1873; married to Miss BELLE H. TAYLOR, of Brasher Falls,
N. Y., Apr. 19, 1876.

Ordained pastor, Brasher Falls, N. Y., by St. Lawrence Presby.,
July 3, 1873; Brasher Falls, 1873 9; resident St. Albans, Vt.,
from 1879.

MAURICE DWIGHT EDWARDS. See 1871-4.

GEORGE DUFFIELD MEIGS.

Born in Gallipolis, Ohio, Aug. 3, 1844; united with the 1st Pres.
Church in Pottstown, Pa., Jan., 1861; graduated from Lafayette
College in 1865; married to Miss CLARA A. CALKINS, of Wells-
boro, Pa., Jan. 1, 1879.

Ordained at Lawrenceville, Pa., by Wellsboro Presby., Sept. 12,
1876; past. Mansfield, 1876-82; resident Wellsboro, 1882.

HUGH BROWN RICE.

Born in Rogersville, Tenn., 1845; united with the 2nd Pres. Ch.
in Knoxville, Tenn., 1859; graduated from Amherst College in
1870; Auburn, Junior year from Dec. 13, 1870; Christian
Theol. Sem., Eureka, Ill.; married to Miss SADIE EDWARDS, of
Sullivan, Ill., 1872.

Ordained at Webster, Ill., (Christian) 1872; Webster, 1872; Rock
Island, 1873; resident San Francisco, Cal., from 1875.

1871-4.

ROBERT LUCKY BACHMAN.

Born in Kingsport, Tenn., June 14, 1844; united with the Pres.
Church in Jonesboro, Tenn., 1858; graduated from Hamilton
College in 1871; married to Miss MAY ROSE, of East Saginaw,
Mich., Sept. 14, 1876.

Ordained pastor Fayetteville, N. Y., by Presby. of Syracuse, Sept.
29, 1874; Fayetteville, 1874-80; First Church, Utica, from
1880.

HENRY MELVILLE CURTIS.
 Born in Middlebury, (now Akron) O., June 28, 1849; united with
 the 3rd Cong. Church in Sherburne, N. Y., 1864; graduated
 from Western Reserve College in 1871; married to Miss EVA
 CRAMER GOSS, of Auburn, Nov. 12, 1874.
 Ordained by Genesee Valley Presby., Aug., 1875; Olean, N. Y.,
 1874-80; Belvidere, Ill., 1880-1; Flint, Mich., from 1881.

MAURICE DWIGHT EDWARDS.
 Born in Pittsburgh, Pa., Apr. 29, 1847; united with the 3d Pres.
 Church in Pittsburgh, 1863; graduated from Hamilton College
 in 1870; in Auburn 1870-1 and 1872-4; married to Miss
 ANNIE LOUISE DEANE, of St. Paul, Minn., Oct. 3, 1877.
 Ordained pastor of Dayton Ave. Pres. Ch., St. Paul, Minn., by
 Presby. of St. Paul, Oct. 21, 1874, and remains there.

GEORGE FLAVEL HUMPHREYS.
 Born in Athol, Mass., May 4, 1847; united with the Cong.
 Church in Athol, 1865; studied at Williams College in class of
 1871; married to HATTIE BEATRICE HOTCHKISS, of Virgil,
 N. Y., Jan. 23, 1875.
 Ordained and installed at North Church, Amherst, Mass., by
 Council, Jan. 7, 1875; Amherst, 1875-7; Elmwood Cong.
 Ch., Providence, R. I., 1877-82; Milford, N. Y., 1882.

GEORGE CHEEVER JEWELL.
 Born in New York City, May 19, 1844; united with the Pres.
 Church in Hector, N. Y., June, 1858; graduated from Yale
 College in 1871; New Haven Theo. Sem., 1 year; Auburn, 2
 years; married to Miss SUSAN ELIZABETH WILDER, of DeRuyter,
 N. Y., Sept. 17, 1876.
 Ordained pastor, Parma Centre, N. Y., by Rochester Presby., Oct.
 8, 1876; Parma, 1874-7; Cong. Ch., Ellington, 1878-80; Sand
 Bank, 1881-2.

GEORGE WASHINGTON LEONARD.
 Born in Allegan, Mich., Feb. 21, 1840; united with the 1st Pres.
 Church in Auburn, Winter of 1857-8; studied at Auburn Acad-
 emy; married to Miss JANE ANN RATCLIFFE, of Clear Creek,
 Ia., June 9, 1874.
 Ordained at Manchester, Ia., by Dubuque Presby., Oct., 1874;
 Mount Hope Pres. Ch., Union City, 1874-7; Springville, Utah
 Ter., from 1877.

WILLIAM REED.
 Born in Lansingburgh, N. Y., Feb. 24, 1847; united with the 1st
 Pres. Church in Lansingburgh, June, 1863; graduated from
 Hamilton College in 1871; married to Miss LAURA DEXTER
 NORTH, of Clinton, N. Y., July 29, 1874.
 Ordained and installed at Calvary Pres. Ch., Buffalo, by Presby. of
 Buffalo, Dec. 10, 1874; Buffalo, 1874-81; Mt. Ida Memorial
 Ch., Troy, from 1881.

GEORGE RUSSELL SMITH.

> Born in Carlton, N. Y., Oct. 21, 1847; united with the 1st Pres Church in Albion, N. Y., 1861; graduated from Hamilton College in 1870; married to Miss ELIZABETH E. HUTCHINSON, of Gaines, N. Y., June 17, 1874.
>
> Ordained pastor, Dryden, N. Y., by Cayuga Presby., Nov. 18, 1874; Dryden, 1874-6; Elbridge, 1876-80; Marcellus, 1880-2; prin. of Acad., Canandaigua, 1882.

BENJAMIN ALEXANDER WILLIAMSON.

> Born in Washington, D. C., Feb. 3, 1849; united with the 4th Pres. Church in Washington, Aug., 1862; graduated from Columbian College in 1870; married to Miss HATTIE A. PARMELEE of Gouverneur, N. Y., Nov. 9, 1876.
>
> Ordained pastor at Theresa, N. Y., by Presby. of St. Lawrence, Oct. 27, 1874; Theresa, 1874-6; Stillwater, 1876-7; Mirabile, Mo., 1879; Chillicothe, Mo., 1880-1; Hamilton, Ill., from 1881.

*JAMES KINNIER WILSON, died Nov. 26, 1879.

CHARLES ANDERSON, JR.

> Born in Sennett, N. Y., April 4, 1847; united with the Pres. Ch. in Union Springs, N. Y., 1866; graduated from Hamilton College in 1869; instructor in Robert College; Aub. Mid. Class, 1872-3; Senior year at Andover; married to Miss ABBIE FRANCES HAMLIN, of Constantinople, Turkey, June 16, 1873.
>
> Ordained and installed at North Woburn, Mass., by Council, Sept. 2, 1874, where he remains. Son of Charles Anderson of 1840-3.

WILLIAM MCKAY CAMPBELL.

> Born in Embro, Ont., 1846; united with the Knox Church in Embro, 1868; studied at Knox and University Colleges, Toronto; Junior year at Auburn, Mid. & Sen. years at Seminary of N. W. Ordained at Bay City, Mich., by Saginaw Presby., 1877; Idaho Springs, Col., 1875-6; Byron, Mich., 1877-8; Mt. Pleasant, 1879-82; Spring Lake, 1882.

ALLEN FORD DECAMP.

> Born in Charlottburg, N. J., Feb. 9, 1848; united with the 1st Pres. Church in Morristown, N. J., Jan. 6, 1864; graduated from Williams College in 1871; two years at Auburn, third year at Union Theo. Sem., N. Y.; married to Miss ANNA B. WILCOX, of Schenectady, N. Y., Oct. 1, 1874.
>
> Ordained and installed at Shawano, Wis., by Presby. of Winnebago, Jan., 1875; Shawano, 1875-7; South Egremont, Mass., from 1877.

JAMES TOOKER FORD.

> Born in Madura, India, Aug. 3, 1848; united with the Cong. Ch., in Groton, Mass.; graduated from Williams College in 1871; Auburn, 1871-2; Union Sem., N. Y., 1872-4; married to Miss SARAH RUSSELL HOLMES, of Douglas, Wis., Sept. 24, 1877.

Ordained at Madison, Wis., by Wisconsin River Presby., June 6, 1876; Oxford, 1874-7; Black River Falls, 1877-8; Maiden Rock, 1878-81; Oxford from 1881.

CHARLES KIMBALL HOYT.

Born in Sennett, N. Y., July 20, 1846; united with the 1st Pres. Church in Auburn, 1863; graduated from Hamilton College in 1870; Auburn, 1871-3; married to Miss KATE B. STEVENS, of Lee, Mass., July 20, 1881.

Westmoreland, N. H., 1873-4; Knoxboro, N. Y., 1874-5; teaching Waterloo, 1875-7; Oregon, Ill., 1877-8; teaching Saratoga, N. Y., 1879-80; prin. of Aurora Acad., 1882; prof. Eng. Literature, Wells College, 1882.

*FREDERICK GRIDLEY KENDALL. See 1872-5.

EDWARD CHITTENDEN RAY.

Born in Rochester, N. Y., Oct. 12, 1849; united with the Church in Hamilton College, Jan., 1869; graduated from Hamilton College in 1870; Union Sem., N. Y., 1870; Rochester, 1870-2; Auburn, selected studies, 1872-3; married to Miss MARTHA WASHINGTON PRESCOTT, of N. Y. City, Oct. 13, 1874.

Ordained at Vernon Centre, N. Y., by Presby. of Utica, June 19, 1874; Vernon Centre, 1873-5; 3rd Ch., Elizabeth, N. J., 1876-81; Hyde Park, Ill., from 1881.

EDWIN FORREST ROBB. See 1872-5.

JOHN ROSS SUTHERLAND, D. D.,

Born in Kirk Hill, Ont., Nov. 7, 1846; united with the Pres. Church in Cold Springs, Ont., 1869; studied at Knox College, Toronto, in class of 1870; Auburn, 1871-2; Sem. of the Northwest, 1872-4; A.M. from Wooster Univ., 1878; D. D. from Howard University in 1879; married to Miss ADELIA MATTHEWS ATKIN, of New York City, Oct. 7, 1874.

Ordained pastor, 8th Pres. Ch., Indianapolis, Ind., by Presby. of Indianapolis, 1874; Indianapolis, 1874-5; Grand Haven, Mich., 1875-80; Jacksonville, Ill., from 1880.

JAMES URQUHART.

Born in Oxford Co., Ont., about 1842; united with the Pres. Church in Embro, Ont., 1867; studied at Knox College, Toronto; Princeton, Junior year, 1870-1; Auburn, Junior year, 1871-2; engaged in mission work, 1872-3; inmate of Insane Asylum, London, Ont., since 1874.

1872-5.

EUGENE CHEESEMAN.

Born in New Hudson, N. Y., March 11, 1841; united with Cong. Ch., Arcade, N. Y., 1857; 90th N. Y. Vols., 1864-5; graduated

from Hamilton College in 1869; prin. Coxsackie Acad., N. Y.,
1869-70; Marion Col. Inst., 1870-2; Rochester The. Sem.,
1872-3; Auburn, 1873-5; married to Miss M. ELIZA HOLT, of
Webster, N. Y., Dec., 1869.

Ordained at Sidney Plains, N. Y., by Presby. of Otsego, Oct.,
1875; Sidney Plains, 1875-7; Fowlerville, 1878; Rose, 1879-82;
Mt. Pleasant, Mich., 1882.

LYMAN CALVIN GRAY.

Born in Wales, N. Y., Oct. 26, 1843; united with the Church in
Mt. Carroll, Ill., Aut. of 1860; graduated from Knox College,
Ill., in 1871; tea., 1871-2; married to Miss MARY SCRIPPS, of
Astoria, Ill., Aug. 9, 1871.

Ordained pastor at Fort Dodge, Iowa, by Presby. of Fort Dodge,
Oct. 12, 1875; Fort Dodge, 1875-8, and still resident there;
supply at R. R. Chapel, Chicago, Ill., 1879; 2nd Ch., Rolfe,
Ia., from 1881.

EDWARD PAYSON JOHNSON.

Born in Peru, Ind., Jan. 26, 1850; united with the 2nd Pres.
Church in Galesburg, Ill., Dec., 1866; graduated from Wabash
College in 1871; married to Miss CLARA BROWNELL, of Troy,
N. Y., Jan. 23, 1878.

Ordained pastor, Sandy Hill, N. Y., by Presby. of Troy, June 23,
1875; Sandy Hill, 1875-9; Marshall, Mich., from 1879.

*FREDERICK GRIDLEY KENDALL, died Aug. 26, 1881.

LEWIS HALL MOREY.

Born in Medina, N. Y., Oct. 28, 1846; united with the Pres.
Church in Livonia, N. Y., July, 1864; graduated from Univ. of
Rochester in 1872; one year at Rochester Theological Sem-
inary, two years at Auburn; married to Miss MARIA FIDELIA
DAY, of Livonia, Aug. 26, 1874.

Ordained pastor, Pittsford, N. Y., by Rochester Presby., May 25,
1875; Pittsford, 1875-80; Seneca Falls from 1880.

EDWIN FORREST ROBB.

Born in Pittsburgh, Pa., Sept. 7, 1845; united with the U. P.
Church in Aledo, Ill., May 1, 1864; graduated from Cornell
University in 1870; Junior year at Sem. of the Northwest;
Auburn, 1871-3 and 1874-5; married to Miss JULIA A. CHERRY,
of Auburn, June 3, 1873.

Ordained at Auburn, by Cayuga Presby., May, 1873; home miss.
in Colorado, 1873-4; Knoxboro, N. Y., 1875-81; Boonville
from 1881.

ROBERT DILWORTH SCOTT.

Born in Enon Valley, Pa., Dec. 18, 1846; united with the Pres.
Church in Clarkson, O., Dec. 6, 1862; graduated from Western
Reserve College in 1872; married to Miss AMANDA CARPEN-
TER, of Poland, O., May 12, 1875.

Ordained pastor, Youngstown, O., by Presby. of Mahoning, June 8, 1875 ; Youngstown, 2d Pres. Ch., 1875-9 ; 1st Pres. Ch., E. Cleveland, 1879-82 ; Lake 1st Ch., Chicago, Ill., 1882.

CORNELIUS STANTON STOWITS.

Born in Flat Creek, N. Y., Feb. 17, 1846 ; united with the Free Baptist Ch. in Flat Creek, May, 1865 ; graduated from Hamilton College in 1872 ; married to MARIA V. PUTNAM, of Constantine, Mich., May 19, 1875.

Ordained at Bergen, N. Y., by Presby. of Genesee, Sept. 28, 1875 ; Bergen, 1875-7 ; Westfield from 1877.

MORTON FITCH TRIPPE.

Born in Bridgewater, N. Y., Sept. 15, 1847 ; united with the Pres. Church in Rose, N. Y., Jan. 10, 1868 ; graduated from Hamilton College in 1872 ; married to SARAH L. HOLMES, of Bloomsburgh, Pa., May 18, 1875.

Ordained pastor, Augusta, N. Y., by Utica Presby., June 15, 1875 ; Augusta, 1875-9 ; Sodus, 1879-81 ; miss. to Indians at Tonawanda, (resident at Versailles) from 1881.

JAMES ANDERSON. See 1873-6.

GEORGE ROBERT BIRD.

Born in London, Eng., April 23, 1849 ; united with the 1st Pres. Church in St. Catherines, Ont., Nov. 9, 1871 ; graduated from North London Collegiate Institute, Eng., in 1864 ; Junior and Middle years at Auburn ; married to Miss BELLE RATCLIFFE, of Clear Creek, Iowa, Dec. 25, 1874.

Ordained Pastor at Frankville, Iowa, by Presby. of Dubuque, Oct. 14, 1874 ; Frankville, 1874-5 ; home miss. in Utah, 1875-80 ; Seattle, W. T., from 1880.

ROBERT ERVEN CUTLER.

Born in Plymouth, O., March 3, 1846 ; united with the 1st Pres. Church in Plymouth, 1865 ; graduated from Western Reserve College in 1871 ; Junior and Middle years at Auburn ; married to Mrs. LOUISA PLUM, April 2, 1872.

Ordained at Sodus, N. Y., by Presby. of Lyons, Oct., 1874 ; Sodus, 1874-5 ; Cong. Ch., Malden, Ill., 1875-6 ; prin. of Schools, Tiskilwa, Ill., 1876-82, and Harvard, 1882.

LYMAN EDWIN HANNA.

Born in Harrisville, O , July 5, 1847 ; united with the Church in Palmyra, Mich., July, 1867 ; graduated from Western Reserve College in 1872 ; studied at Auburn, 1872-3 ; Union Sem., N. Y., 1873-5 ; married to Miss EMMA HARTMAN, of Medina, O., June 6, 1877.

Ordained at Clayton, Mich., by Presby. of Monroe, Sept. 20, 1875 ; Clayton, 1875-6 ; Bergen, N. Y., 1877-80 ; Corfu from 1880.

BRAINARD GARDNER SMITH.
    Came to Auburn from Canandaigua; mem. of Church there;
    graduated from Hamilton College in 1872; at Auburn a few
    weeks; in business in New York City.

MELANCTHON WOOLSEY STRYKER.   See 1873-6.

*WILLIAM HENRY TALLMADGE, died Feb. 24, 1880.

LEWIS RUSSELL WEBBER.   See 1875-8.

1873-6.

JAMES ANDERSON.
    Born in Sennett, N. Y., May 14, 1850; united with the Pres.
    Church in Union Springs, 1866; graduated from Hamilton
    College in 1872; Auburn, 1872-3 and 1874-6; married to Miss
    SARAH ELIZABETH FOSTER, of Sennett, Sept., 1881.
    Ordained by Presby., 1876; home miss., St. Jo, Texas, from
    1876.   Son of Charles Anderson of 1840-3.

MYRON NEVINS BARTHOLOMEW.
    Born in Augusta, N. Y., September 12, 1846; united with the Pres.
    Church in Augusta, 1859; graduated from Hamilton College in
    1873; in ill health since graduating at Auburn; resident in
    Augusta.   Son of Orlo Bartholomew of 1832-5.

BENJAMIN BONNEY DAYTON.
    Born in Lima, N. Y., April 5, 1854; united with the 1st Pres. Ch.
    in Geneva, March, 1866; graduated from Univ. of Rochester
    in 1873; married to Miss J. ANNA HAY, of Amboy, N. Y., Dec.
    3, 1878.
    Ordained pastor of Pres. Church of Amboy, (Belle Isle) N. Y., by
    Presby. of Syracuse, June 27, 1876; yet there.
    Published series of Church Annuals, &c.

ELIAS BALDWIN FISHER.
    Born in Aurelius, N. Y., Apr. 9, 1841; united with the 1st Pres.
    Church in Auburn, 1866; graduated from Hamilton College in
    1873.
    Ordained and installed, Savannah, N. Y., May 14, 1880; Nichol-
    son, Pa., 1876-7; Savannah, N. Y., from 1879.

FRENCH WILLIAM FISHER.
    Born in Batavia, Genesee Co., N. Y., Nov. 3, 1840; united with
    the 1st Cong. Ch. in Macon City, Mo., Apr., 1870; graduated
    from Genesee College, scientific course, in 1869; Rochester
    The. Sem., Jun. year; Auburn, 1874-6; married to Miss ELISA-
    BETH R. BROWN, of Penfield, N. Y., Dec. 15, 1870.
    Ordained by Ontario Cong. Association, June 7, 1876; Franklin-
    ville, N. Y., 1876-81; Portville from 1881.

CHARLES FREDERIC GOSS.

Born in Meridian, N. Y., June 14, 1852; united with the 2nd
Pres. Church in Auburn, 1865; graduated from Hamilton
College in 1873; married to Miss ROSA E. HOUGHTON, of
Clinton, N. Y., Aug. 30, 1876.

Ordained, Austin, Texas, by Presby. of Austin, 1876; Weatherford, Tex., 1876-8; Limestone, N. Y., 1878-81; Utica, Bethany
Ch., from 1881. Son of Simeon Sartwell Goss, of 1846-9.

ALEXANDER JACKSON.

Born in Glasgow, Scotland, Feb. 13, 1845; united with the Calton U.
P. Ch. in Glasgow, about 1863; studied at Glasgow and Edin-
burgh Universities; studied at U. P. Divinity Hall, Edinburgh;
Mid. and Sen. years at Auburn; married to Miss AGNES MARR
ARMSTRONG, of Townhead, Scotland, Sept. 10, 1872.

Ordained and installed at Pres. Ch., Amenia, N. Y., by Presby.
of North River, 1876; Amenia, 1876-9; Warren, O., from 1879.
Published pamphlets, addresses, &c.

GEORGE MARSH JANES.

Born in Otego, N. Y., Oct. 14, 1843; united with the Cong. Ch.,
Walton, 1855; graduated from Hamilton College in 1866; married to Miss MATTIE VEDDER, at East Pembroke, N. Y., 1868.

Ordained pastor, Colchester Pres. Ch., by Otsego Presby., June
22, 1876; Colchester, (Downsville) 1876-80; Coventry, from
1880. Son of Francis Janes of 1830-3.

*WILLIAM McDUFFEE, died June 2, 1874.

WILLIAM HENRY NILES.

Born in Beaver Dam, Wis., May 6, 1851; united with the 1st Pres.
Church in Corning, N. Y., May, 1866; graduated from Cornell
University, scientific course, in 1872; married to Miss FRANCES
ELIZABETH PRENTISS, of Hornellsville, Oct. 2, 1876.

Ordained by Presby. of Steuben, Sept. 16, 1876; Stephenville,
Texas, 1876-81; Jacksboro from 1881. Son of William Allen
Niles, D. D., of 1847-50.

RANDAL PEASE.

Born in Virgil, N. Y., 1851; united with the Pres. Church in Dryden, Apr., 1865; graduated from Hamilton College in 1871.

Ordained pastor of 2d Pres. Ch. of Oswegatchie by Presby. of St.
Lawrence, June 6, 1876; Oswegatchie, 1875-8; Waddington
from 1879.

WARNER BRADLEY RIGGS.

Born in Macedon, N. Y., Nov. 26, 1849; united with the Western
Pres. Church in Palmyra, June, 1864; graduated from Yale Col-
lege in 1871; married to Miss LILLA GRAHAM, of Austin, Tex.,
May 14, 1878.

Ordained at Austin, Tex., by Presby. of Austin, May 14, 1878;
Brenham from 1878.

MELANCTHON WOOLSEY STRYKER.

> Born in Vernon, N. Y., Jan. 7, 1851; united with the 13th Street
> Church in N. Y. City, 1866; graduated from Hamilton College
> in 1872; Auburn, 1872–3 and 1874–6; married to Miss CLARA
> ELISABETH GOSS, of Auburn, Sept. 27, 1876.
> Ordained pastor, Calvary Ch., Auburn, by Presby. of Cayuga, May,
> 1876; Bergen, N. Y., 1873–4; Auburn, 1876–8; Ithaca, 1st
> Pres. Ch., from 1878.   Son of Isaac Pierson Stryker, of 1837–40.
> Published "The Alleluia," 1879; "Church Praise Book," 1881.

ORMOND WORTHINGTON WRIGHT.

> Born in Acworth, N. H., Sept. 24, 1850; united with the Pres.
> Church in Fredonia, N. Y., 1865; graduated from Hamilton
> College in 1873; married to Miss MINNIE BARKINS STARR, of
> Auburn, Oct. 30, 1877.
> Ordained by Presby. of Emporia, Aug. 4, 1877; Dodge City, Kan-
> sas, 1877–82.

HERMANN CARL GEORGE BRANDT.

> Born in 1851; came to Aub. from Church in Susquehanna Depot,
> Pa.; graduated from Hamilton College in 1872; Auburn, 1873–4;
> married to Miss MARGARET CATLIN, of Clinton, N. Y., Dec.
> 15, 1875.
> Assist. prof. of Mod. Lang., Hamilton College, 1874–6; prof. of
> German, John Hopkins Univ., 1876–82; prof. of German, Ham-
> ilton College, 1882.

FRANK NORTON GREELEY.

> Born in Chicopee Falls, Mass., May 6, 1850; united with the Ch.
> in Aug., 1866; studied at University of Michigan; optional
> studies at Auburn, 1874–6; married to ANNA CHENEY BUCK-
> HOUT, of Oswego, N. Y., May 6, 1873.
> Ordained, Orwell, N. Y., by Council, Nov. 13, 1877; Volney; Or-
> well, 3 years; New Haven to 1881, and still resident there.

FERDINAND KRUG.

> Born in Crumstadt, Germany, Jan. 26, 1849; united with the
> Lutheran Church, 1863; graduated from Western Reserve Col-
> lege in 1873; Auburn, 1873–5; married to Miss MELITTA
> BARNES, of Rock Stream, N. Y., May 24, 1876.
> Ordained pastor, Hanging Rock, O., by Presby. of Portsmouth,
> Nov. 2, 1875; Hanging Rock, 1875–9; Bloomingburgh, from
> 1879.

BENJAMIN FARRINGTON SARGENT.

> Born in Hopkinton, N. H., Mar. 21, 1853; united with the 1st
> Cong. Church in Hopkinton, Mar., 1864; graduated from Ham-
> ilton College in 1873; Junior year, Chicago; Auburn, 1874–5;
> Senior year, Union, N. Y.; married to Miss ELIZA A. PATTER-
> SON, of Whitney's Point, N. Y., May 16, 1878.
> Ordained pastor, Paxton, Ill., by Council, June 22, 1877; Paxton,
> 1877–80; Grand Rapids, Mich., from 1880.

CHRISTOPHER SNYDER VINCENT.
   Born in Coeymans, N. Y., 1845; united with the Christian Ch.,
   1862; graduated from Hamilton College in 1873; at Auburn till
   March, 1874; married to Miss ELLA PALISSA HAMMOND, of Au-
   burn, Apr. 23, 1874.
   Ordained pastor, Turin, N. Y., by Presby. of Utica, Sept. 30, 1874;
   Turin, N. Y., 1874–7; Sinclairville Cong. Ch., 1878–9; Univ.
   Ch., Norwalk, O., 1879–81; 3d Univ. Church, Baltimore, Md.,
   from 1881.

HEZEKIAH WEBSTER.   See 1876–9.

1874-7.

JOHN QUINCY ADAMS.
   Born in Ogden, N. Y., Aug. 8, 1849; united with the Pres. Ch. in
   Ogden, May, 1866; graduated from the Univ. of Rochester in
   1874; married to Miss CLARA SOUTHGATE, of Rochester, N. Y.,
   June 7, 1877.
   Ordained at Hannibal, N. Y., by Presby. of Syracuse, May 28,
   1878; Mexico, 1877–8; Walnut St. Ch., Evansville, Ind., 1878–
   81; Boulder, Col., from 1881.

WILLIAM LUCIAN AUSTIN.
   Born in West Milford, Va., May 30, 1848; united with the 2d Pres.
   Church in Wheeling, W. Va., Oct., 1865; studied at Hampden
   Sidney College; married to Miss MARTHA T. KNIGHT, of Bal-
   timore, Md., June 7, 1877.
   Ordained by Presby. of Steuben, at Naples, N. Y., Oct. 27, 1877;
   Naples, 1877–80; Miles City, Montana, 1880–1; Dunkirk, N.
   Y., from 1881.

CHARLES MARTIN BARTHOLOMEW.
   Born in Augusta, N. Y., July 10, 1849; united with the 1st Pres.
   Ch. in Augusta, March 6, 1870; graduated from Hamilton Col-
   lege in 1874; married to Miss NELLIE MANZER, of Middlefield,
   N. Y., Feb. 5, 1877.
   Ordained at Rushville, N. Y., by Ontario Cong. Conference, June
   27, 1877, where he remains.   Son of Orlo Bartholomew of 1832–5.

JOHN MANLY CHASE.
   Born in Albany, N. Y., March 23, 1849; united with the Congre-
   gational Church in Franklin, N. Y., 1867; graduated from
   Cornell University, scientific course, in 1872; married to Miss
   ELLA ABIGAIL DRAPER, of Westford, N. Y., Aug. 28, 1873.
   Ordained pastor, Worcester, N. Y., by Presby. of Otsego, June 6,
   1877; yet there.

CARLOS TRACY CHESTER.
   Born in Niagara Falls, N. Y., March 17, 1851; united with the
   Pres. Church in Havana, N. Y., Feb., 1867; graduated from

Hamilton College in 1874; married to Miss HELEN HAWLEY,
of Auburn, Sept. 20, 1877.
Ordained pastor, Andrew Pres. Ch., E. Minneapolis, Minn., by
Presby. of St. Paul, Aug. 7, 1877 ; E. Minneapolis, 1877-81 ;
Wilson Ave. Ch., Cleveland, O., from 1881.

EDWARD DILLON.
Born in Philadelphia, Pa., July 25, 1858; united with the Richmond Pres. Church in Philadelphia, June 30, 1867 ; studied
at Univ. of Pennsylvania, 3 years ; 3 years at Auburn, and one
year at the Ref. Pres. Theo. Sem., Philadelphia.
Ordained and installed at Woodbury, N. J., by West Jersey Presby.,
Oct. 4, 1877 ; still there.

CHARLES PAGE EMERSON.
Born in York, Pa., March 28, 1853; united with the Eastburn,
Phila., Church, Winter of 1870-1 ; studied at College of New
Jersey.
Ordained, 1877; Stillwater, Minn., 1877-9 ; Escanaba, Mich.,
1879 ; resident in Philadelphia, Pa., from 1880.

MOSES AARON HOPKINS.
Born in Dublin, Pulaski Co., Va., Dec. 25, 1846 ; united with the
Madison St. Presbyterian Church in Baltimore, Md., Mar., 1874 ;
graduated from Lincoln Univ., 1874; Junior year at Lincoln ;
Auburn, 1875-7 ; married to Miss CARRIE ELIZABETH PAYNE,
of Utica, N. Y., Oct. 14, 1875.
Ordained by Presby., 1877 ; Franklinton, N. C., from 1877.

JOHN KENYON KILBOURN.
Born in Newville, Pa., Jan. 19, 1849 ; united with the Cong. Ch.
in Augusta, N. Y., Sept., 1867 ; graduated from Hamilton Col-
lege in 1874.
Ordained, Clarence, N. Y., by Buffalo Presby., Nov. 11, 1880 ;
Clarence, 1877-81 ; East Mendon, 1882.

GEORGE WILLIAM KNOX.
Born in Rome, N Y., Aug. 11, 1853 ; united with the Pres. Ch. in
Rome, about 1868; graduated from Hamilton College in 1874;
married to Miss ANNA CAROLINE HOLMES, of Auburn, May 11,
1877.
Ordained at Elmira, N. Y., by Presby. of Chemung, June 3, 1877 ;
miss. of Pres. Bd. to Japan from 1877.
Published " Koyeki Mondo," 1st series, 1881, 2d series, 1882. Son
of Dr. Wm. Eaton Knox of 1840-3.

CHARLES MAHLON LOMBARD. See 1875-8.

GEORGE ANGUS McKINLAY.
Born in Pleasant Lake, Ind., Dec. 14, 1847 ; united with the Cong.
Ch. in Ontario, Ind., Nov., 1865 ; studied at La Grange Colle-

giate Institute; Auburn, 1875-7; married to Miss JULIA BRACE PATCH, of Ontario, Ind., Dec. 24, 1869.
Ordained pastor of the Pres. Church of Mirabile, Mo., by Platte Presby., April, 1874; Mirabile, 1872-5; Owasco Outlet Ref. Ch., 1876-7; Carrolton, Mo., 1877-9; Forest City, 1879-81; Gallatin from 1881.

ROBERT McLEAN.
Born in Vernon Centre, N. Y., Feb. 22, 1846; united with the Bap. Church in Vernon, 1863; graduated from Univ. of Rochester, 1874; married to Miss LUCY NORRIS, of Galena, Ill., Aug., 1877.
Ordained at Beloit, Wis., by Presby. of Milwaukee, Sept. 3, 1877; miss. of Pres. Bd., San Felipe, Chili, and Concepcion, Chili, from 1877.
Editor *El Republicano*, weekly paper.

*GEORGE ALVA PENNY, died Sept. 16, 1874.

*GEORGE WOOLSEY RYERSON, died June 7, 1876.

*WILLIAM DAVID SWINTON, died Feb. 10, 1878.

CHARLES HENRY VAN WIE.
Born in Ira, N. Y., Oct. 22, 1851; united with the Pres. Church in Meridian, 1863; graduated from Hamilton College in 1874.
Ordained pastor at Lyon's Falls, N. Y., by Presby. of Utica, Apr., 1878; Lyon's Falls, 1877-80; Williamstown from 1880.

JULIUS EDWARD WERNER.
Born in Wengelsdorf, Prussia, July 17, 1849; united with the Stone St. Pres. Church in Watertown, Apr., 1865; graduated from Williams College in 1874; married to Miss MARY ROBINSON of Canandaigua, N. Y., Oct. 6, 1880.
Ordained pastor, Oaks Corners, N. Y., by Geneva Presby., 1877; Oaks Corners, 1877-81; Haddonfield, N. J., from 1881.

GERARD JOHAN BUSSEMAKER.
Born in Holland, 1845; united with the Mennonite Church in Holland; studied at Almelo Gymnasium, Holland, and at Meadville, Pa.; left the Seminary shortly before the close of Junior year.

JOHN EDWARD CLOSE.
Born in Nailsworth, Glo'shire, Eng., Dec. 12, 1848; united with Cong. Church in Ruscombe, Eng., June, 1864; graduated from Lewisham Congregational School, London, Eng., in 1863; Junior and Middle years at Auburn; married to MARY ELLEN HOOPER, of Stroud, Eng., Oct. 1, 1872.
Ordained pastor, Jordan, N. Y., by Presby. of Syracuse, Feb. 21, 1876; Jordan, 1876-80; Pittsford from 1880.

SETH REED GORDON.

Born in Mercer Co., Pa., Oct. 31, 1852; united with the Unity Pres. Church in Mercer Co., 1865 ; graduated from Westminster College in 1874; Auburn, 1874-5; Western Theol. Sem., 2d and 3d years ; married to Miss FANNIE E. TORRENCE, of Xenia, O., May 8, 1878.

Ordained pastor, Pulaski, Pa., by Shenango Presby., June 19, 1877; Pulaski, 1876-80 ; Sharon (Moon P. O.) from 1880.

EDWARD MARVIN KNOX.

Born in Knoxboro, N. Y., Oct. 16, 1850; united with the Cong. Church in Augusta, N. Y., 1866 ; graduated from Hamilton College in 1874; first two years at Auburn ; Union, New York, 1877-8; married to Miss ELLA ELIZABETH QUA, of New York, Oct. 16, 1878.

Ordained at Aurora, Neb., by Kearney Presby., April 12, 1879; Shavertown, N. Y., 1876-8 ; home miss., Nelson, Neb., 1878-82 ; Malad, Idaho, 1882.

JERMAIN GILDERSLEEVE PORTER. See 1875-8.

THOMAS SMITH SCOTT.

Born in Enon Valley, Pa., Nov. 9, 1849 ; united with the Pres. Church in New Lisbon, O., Mar., 1868; graduated from Western Reserve College in 1874; Auburn, 1874-6 ; Union Sem., N. Y., 1876-7; married to Miss HATTIE ELISABETH OSBORN, of Hudson, O., Nov. 7, 1877.

Ordained, North Benton, O., by Mahoning Presby., Sept. 26, 1877; Collamer, O., 1877-9 ; Westminster Pres. Ch., Rockford, Ill., from 1879.

1875-8.

WILLIAM ALANSON BEECHER.

Born in Vernon Centre, N. Y., Aug. 10, 1852 ; united with the Pres. Church in Vernon Centre, March, 1862 ; graduated from Hamilton College in 1874; Ham. Col. Law School, 1875 ; Yale The. Sem., 1875-7 ; Auburn, 1877-8; married to Miss CARRIE KNIGHT, of Brookdale, Pa., May 24, 1882.

Ordained pastor, DeKalb, N. Y., by Presby. of St. Lawrence, Oct. 10, 1879 ; DeKalb and DeKalb Junction, 1878-81; Conklin from 1881.

HERBERT ERASTUS DAVIS.

Born in Lysander, N. Y., July 11, 1852 ; united with the Pres. Church in Marshall, Mich., Apr., 1875 ; graduated from Univ. of Michigan in 1873; married to Miss M. ETTA HOBART, of Athens, Mich., May 15, 1878.

Ordained at Auburn, by Presby. of Cayuga, May 10, 1878 ; Presbyterial miss. of Lake Superior Presby., 1878-9 ; Negaunee, Mich., from 1879.

SEWARD MANDEVILLE DODGE.
Born in Verona, N. Y., April 13, 1846; united with the Cong.
Church in Rosemond, Ill., Sept., 1860 ; graduated from Hamil-
ton College in 1872; married to Miss ALICE EMILY MILLER, of
Deansville, N. Y., Dec. 5, 1872.
Ordained, Lebanon, N. Y., by Council, Nov. 19, 1878; Lebanon,
1878–80 ; Milford, 1880–1 ; Evansville, Ind., Pres. Ch., from
1881.

GEORGE HENRY FERRIS.
Born in Hillsdale, Mich., Dec. 26, 1853; united with the Pres.
Ch. in Hillsdale, Nov., 1870 ; graduated from Princeton Col-
lege in 1874; tutor in Princeton, 1875–6 ; entered Auburn Mid.
class, on examination ; married to Miss LUCY HALL, of Auburn,
July 2, 1878.
Ordained at Phelps, N. Y., by Presby. of Geneva, Apr. 17, 1878;
miss. of Pres. Bd., Kolapoor, India, from 1878.

AUGUSTUS FREDERICK.
Born in Rupertsberg, Hesse Darmstadt, May 14, 1849; united
with the Church in Port Chester, N. Y., Jan. 12, 1867 ; gradu-
ated from Princeton College in 1875 ; married to Miss SARAH
ELIZABETH TELFORD, of Port Byron, N. Y., June 20, 1878.
Ordained pastor at Swedesboro, N. J., by Presby. of West Jersey,
Oct. 8, 1878 ; Swedesboro, 1878–9 ; Chateaugay, N. Y., from
1879.

*CHARLES HERVEY GASTON, died Feb. 24, 1881.

RICHARD CLEVELAND HASTINGS.
Born in Jaffna, Ceylon, March 27, 1854; united with the 7th St.
Cong. Church in Cincinnati, O., Oct. 7, 1866 ; graduated from
Hamilton College in 1875.
Ordained by Presby. of Utica, Apr. 9, 1878 ; miss. of A. B. C. F.
M. at Jaffna, Ceylon, from 1878.

ARTHUR STEPHEN HOYT.
Born in Meridian, N. Y., Jan. 3, 1851 ; united with the Pres. Ch.
in Meridian, April, 1862 ; graduated from Hamilton College in
1872; instructor in Robert College, 1872–5; married to Miss
MARY EMMA HEWSON, of Auburn, Oct. 9, 1879.
Ordained pastor at Oregon, Ill., by Presby., Dec. 23, 1879 ; Oregon from 1878.

CHARLES MAHLON LOMBARD.
Born in Skaneateles, N. Y., Dec. 25, 1844; united with the 1st
Pres. Church in Schenectady, N. Y., Mar. 26, 1865 ; graduated
from Union College in 1865; in Auburn 1874–5, and 1876–8.
Ordained at Lyons, Iowa, by Presby. of Cedar Rapids, Mar. 9,
1880 ; Lyons from 1879.

WILLIAM JAMES McKEE.

> Born in Harrisville, Butler Co., Pa., Feb. 21, 1851; united with the 2nd Presbyterian Church in Galesburg, Ill., Apr. 7, 1867; graduated from Knox College, Ill., in 1872; married to Miss ABBIE PORTER KETCHUM, of Marshall, Mich., Oct. 22, 1879.
>
> Ordained at Clintonville, Pa., by Butler Presby., June 26, 1878; miss. of Pres. Bd. at Ningpo, China, from 1878.

ENEAS McLEAN.

> Born in Vernon Centre, N. Y., Feb. 19, 1849; united with the Pres. Church in Vernon Centre, Jan., 1863; graduated from Hamilton College in 1875; taught in Robert College; entered the Auburn Middle Class; married to Miss ELLA NORRIS, of Scranton, Pa., June 26, 1878.
>
> Ordained, Cent. Ch., Rochester, N. Y., by Rochester Presby., June 9, 1878; miss. of Pres. Bd. in Valparaiso and Concepcion, Chili, from 1878.
>
> Published some tracts.

JERMAIN GILDERSLEVE PORTER.

> Born in Buffalo, N. Y., Jan. 8, 1852; united with the Union Presbyterian Church in St. Louis, Mo., Spring of 1864; graduated from Hamilton College in 1873; assistant professor of Astronomy, Ham. Col., 1875–7; Auburn, 1874–5 and 1877–8; married to Miss EMILY SNOWDEN, of Washington, D. C., July 3, 1879.
>
> In the service of the U. S. Coast Survey from 1878.

WILLIAM SATTERLEE POTTER, JR.

> Born in State Bridge, N. Y., Dec. 30, 1850; united with the Pres. Church in Hamilton College, Jan., 1875; graduated from Hamilton College in 1875; married to Miss CELIA EMMA CASE, of Verona, N. Y., July 21, 1875.
>
> Ordained at Second Pres. Ch., Auburn, by Cayuga Presby., May 10, 1878; Petoskey, Mich., from 1878.

ARTHUR JOHN WAUGH.

> Born in Sauquoit, N. Y., June 30, 1852; united with the Pres. Church in Carthage, Jan. 1, 1870; graduated from Hamilton College in 1872; married to Miss MARGARET BOYD AGAN, of Saratoga Springs, N. Y., Dec. 17, 1878.
>
> Ordained, Cape Vincent, N. Y., by Presby. of St. Lawrence, Sept. 25, 1878; Plattsburgh, N. Y., 1878–80; Willoughby, O., from 1880.

LEWIS RUSSELL WEBBER.

> Born in Martinsburgh, N. Y., Sept. 18, 1843; united with the Pres. Church in Martinsburgh, July 5, 1857; graduated from Hamilton College in 1872; Instructor at Robert College, 1873–7; Auburn, 1872–3 and 1877–8; married to Miss MARY L. WOOLWORTH, of Copenhagen, N. Y., June 18, 1878.
>
> Ordained, Lyon's Falls, N. Y., by Presby. of Utica, Sept. 10, 1878; Martinsburgh from 1878.

JAMES WILLIAM WHITE.
> Born in Sweden, N. Y., Nov. 4, 1850 ; united with the Pres. Ch. in Sweden, May, 1867 ; graduated from Univ. of Rochester in 1875 ; married to Miss ELLEN MARGARET HILL, of Rochester, N. Y., Sept. 26, 1878.
> Ordained, Rochester, by Rochester Presby., June 11, 1878 ; Cong. Ch., Maine, N. Y., 1878–81 ; Berkshire from 1881.

WARD BATCHELOR.
> Born in Waverly, Pa., Jan. 9, 1850 ; united with the Pres. Church in Waverly ; studied at Cornell Univ.; Chicago Theol. Sem., special course, 2 years, closing 1876 ; Auburn, 2 years elective, 1876–8 ; married to Miss GERTRUDE PEDRICK, of Waverly, Sept. 14, 1873.
> Ordained at Morrisville, N. Y., by Council, Nov. 20, 1879 ; Michigan Centre, Mich., 1874 ; Bristol, Ill., 1874-6 ; Lebanon, N. Y., 1876–8 ; Morrisville, 1878–81 ; miss. Chapel of N. Y. Ave. Pres. Ch., Washington, D. C., from 1881.

ISAAC PRUDENS BIELBY.
> Born in Oriskany, N. Y., March 11, 1847 ; came to Auburn from Pres. Ch., Rome, N. Y.; studied at Whitestown Seminary in 1867–8 ; practiced Law 3½ years ; in Auburn but a short time.

ARCHIBALD HERBERT BILL.
> Born in Morristown, N. J., July 2, 1850 ; united with the Pres. Church in Carlisle, Pa., Sept. 7, 1867 ; studied through Junior year at Dickinson College ; at Auburn partly through the Middle year.

MARCUS DE LAFAYETTE BOOHER.
> Born in Kingsport, E. Tennessee, Feb. 26, 1850 ; united with the Pres. Church in Kingsport, Feb. 14, 1865 ; graduated from Princeton College in 1875 ; Studied Theology Junior year at Princeton, and part of the two following years at Auburn.
> Ordained pastor at Reading, Mich., by Monroe Presby., Aug. 3, 1879 ; Reading from 1879–82 ; Grand Rapids, 1882.

JAMES STEWART CURTIS.
> Born in Jamestown, N. Y., June 7, 1850 ; came to Auburn from the Pres. Church in Hillsdale, Mich.; studied 3 years at Hillsdale College ; left Auburn at close of Junior year, in poor health; resident in Lexington, Ky.

HENRY WESLEY HARVEY.
> Born in Cazenovia, N. Y., Apr. 2, 1847 ; united with the Pres. Church in Richland, Mich., Jan. 1, 1871 ; graduated from Olivet College in 1875 ; Junior year at Yale Divinity School; Middle year at Auburn.

Ordained pastor, Litchfield, Minn., by Presby. of St. Paul, April 17, 1878 ; Wilmar, Minn., 1877–80 ; Paw Paw, Mich., from 1880.

EWEN CAMERON LIVINGSTONE. See 1877–80.

HENRY ELLIOTT MOTT.
Born in Brockport, N. Y., Oct. 17, 1852 ; united with the Church in Hillsdale, Mich., April 10, 1868 ; graduated from Princeton College in 1874 ; 1 year at Auburn ; 2 years in Union, N. Y.; married to Miss EMMA CORNELIA PRATT, of Hillsdale, Mich., Oct. 8, 1878.
Ordained, Hillsdale, by Presby. of Monroe, Nov. 12, 1878 ; Albion, 1878–82 ; Augusta, Me., Cong. Ch., 1882.

HIRAM FOSTER WHITE. See 1876–9.

1876-9.

WILLIAM HERVEY ALLBRIGHT.
Born in Blisworth, Northamptonshire, England, Nov. 25, 1849 ; united with the Baptist Church in Blisworth, 1869 ; graduated from Hamilton College in 1876 ; married to Miss MARY ESTHER MANLEY, of Camden. N. Y., Sept. 16, 1879.
Ordained pastor of Auburn 2nd Ch., by Presby. of Cayuga, June 6, 1879.

CHARLES TAYLOR BURNLEY.
Born in Nottingham, England, Sept. 15, 1846 ; united with the 1st Presbyterian Church in Utica, Nov. 4, 1866 ; graduated from Hamilton College in 1873 ; married to Miss GRACE PHILLIPS, of Pascoag, R. I., July 2, 1873.
Ordained pastor at Sennett, N. Y., by Presby. of Cayuga, June, 1879.

EBENEZER BAKER COBB.
Born in Auburn, Oct. 23, 1855 ; united with the Hamilton College Church in Jan., 1872 ; graduated from Hamilton College in 1875 ; 3 years at Auburn, and post-graduate year at Union.
Ordained pastor, Ramapo, N. Y., by Hudson Presby., April 29, 1880.

CHARLES CARROLL HEMENWAY.
Born in Amber, N. Y., Feb. 17, 1850 ; united with the 1st Church in Marcellus, Sept. 1, 1867 ; graduated from Hamilton College in 1874 ; married to Miss IDA E. SHACKELFORD, of Glasgow, Mo., June 17, 1879.
Ordained pastor of Auburn Central Ch., by Presby. of Cayuga, Apr. 9, 1879.

PALMER S. HULBERT.
Born in Lochaber, Nova Scotia, March 7, 1849 ; united with the Chalmers Church in Lochaber, June, 1869 ; graduated from

Wabash College in 1876 ; married to Miss Rosa M. Stacey, of Auburn, Sept. 16, 1879.

Ordained pastor at Waverly, N. Y., by Presby. of Binghamton, June 19, 1879; Norwich Corners and Litchfield, 1878-9 ; Waverly, 1879-82; Fremont, Neb., 1882.

WILBUR HUTCHINS JOHNSON.

Born in Ovid, N. Y., Feb. 16, 1851 ; united with the Pres. Church in Ovid, July, 1864; graduated from Hamilton College in 1875 ; two years at Union Theo. Sem. ; Senior year at Auburn. Home miss.. Forest River, Dakota, 1881.

*DAVID EDWIN KOHLER, died Dec. 15, 1877.

EDWIN KOONS.

Born in Starkey, Yates Co., N. Y., Feb. 28, 1848; united with the Pres. Church in Rock Stream, N. Y., Mar., 1868 ; studied at Starkey Seminary in 1873-6; married to Miss ABBIE E. WADE, of Malloryville, N. Y., June 10, 1879.

Ordained pastor, Hannibal, N. Y., by Presby. of Syracuse, Oct., 1880 ; Ludlowville, 1879-80; Hannibal from 1880.

WILLARD KING SPENCER.

Born in New Hartford, Conn., Sept. 9, 1853; united with the Re-formed (Dutch) Church in Syracuse, 1870 ; graduated from Hamilton College in 1875 ; married to Miss JENNIE ARRILLA HARRISON, of Palmyra, N. Y., Dec. 24, 1879.

Ordained pastor of 1st Ch., Lansing, Mich., by Presby. of Lansing, Sept. 17, 1879.

GEORGE BLACK STEWART.

Born in Columbus, O., Feb. 28, 1854; united with the 2nd Pres. Church in Columbus, Apr., 1870; graduated from Princeton College, 1876 ; Sem. of North West, 1876-7 ; Auburn, 1877-9; married to Miss MARY ADELINE THOMPSON, of Columbus, O., June 18, 1879.

Ordained pastor of Calvary Ch., Auburn, by Presby. of Cayuga, April 11, 1879.

EDWARD KELLOGG STRONG.

Born in Otisco, N. Y., Sept. 2, 1852 ; united with the 1st Pres. Church in Galena, Ill., May, 1865 ; graduated from Princeton College in 1874.

Ordained pastor, Homer, Mich., by Presby. of Lansing, May 19, 1881; Sharon, Conn., 1879-80 ; Homer from 1880. Son of Dr. Addison Kellogg Strong, of 1843-6.

HEZEKIAH WEBSTER.

Born in Sennett, N. Y., March 31, 1849; united with the Pres. Church in Ham. Col., Nov. 14, 1868; graduated from Hamilton College in class of 1872 ; instructor in Robert College, Turkey ; Auburn, 1873-4 and 1877-9.

Ordained pastor, Belle Valley, Pa., by Erie Presby., Nov. 4, 1879.

PETER ALONZO WESSELS.
Born in Cherry Valley, N. Y., Feb. 12, 1841; united with the Ref. Church in Glenville, N. Y., 1857; studied at Williams College in class of 1876; Drew Theo. Sem., 1876-8; Auburn, 1878-9. Ordained at Humboldt, Neb., by Nebraska City Presby., Sept. 8, 1880; Hansen, Neb., 1879-80; Nemaha City, 1880.

HIRAM FOSTER WHITE.
Born in Palmyra, N. Y., Sept. 11, 1849; united with the Pres. Church in East Palmyra, July, 1869; graduated from Williams College in 1871; Auburn, 1875-7 and 1878-9; married to Miss MARY LOUISA CHAMBERLAIN, of Fond du Lac, Wis., Oct. 15, 1879.
Ordained, Seward, Neb., by Presby. of Nebraska City, April 4, 1880; Beatrice, Neb., 1879-81; Juneau, Wis., from 1881.

ORVILLE COMPTON.
Born in Southport, N. Y., Aug. 30, 1846; united with the Pres. Church in Wells, Pa., early in 1859; studied at Alfred University and Oberlin College, preparatory course; Auburn, special studies, two full years, 1877-9; married to Miss HANNAH JANE MCAFEE, of Athens, Pa., Oct. 16, 1872.
Ordained Deacon, M. E. Church, Autumn of 1872, and Elder, Autumn of 1874; previous to Oct., 1877, had charges at Gaines and New Albany, Pa., and Beaver Dam, New Hope, Borodino, Enfield and North Lansing, N. Y.; Wahoo, (now Bennet) Neb., from 1879.

1877-80.

ALBERT W. ALLEN, JR.
Born in Union Springs, N. Y., Feb. 26, 1854; united with the Pres. Church in Union Springs, Jan., 1866; studied 2 years and 2 terms at Hamilton College in class of 1878; married to Miss AGNES M. HILL, of Auburn, July 7, 1880.
Ordained pastor, Deansville, N. Y., by Council, June 17, 1880.

FREDERICK CAMPBELL.
Born in Paris Hill, N. Y., Jan. 17, 1857; united with the Central Pres. Church in Rochester, N. Y., June, 1867; graduated from Princeton College in 1877; Rochester The. Sem., 1877-8; Auburn, 1878-80; married to Miss MARY B. KNIGHT, of Auburn, Oct. 13, 1880.
Ordained, Painted Post, N. Y., by Presby. of Steuben, Apr. 25, 1882; Painted Post from 1880.

GRAHAM COX CAMPBELL.
Born in Middlestewiacke, Nova Scotia, Nov. 9, 1847; united with

the Pres. Church there, Sept., 1865 ; graduated from Univ. of Minnesota in 1877 ; married to Miss LAURA A. KREIS, of E. Minneapolis., Minn., Aug. 17, 1880.
Ordained at Minneapolis, Minn., by Presby., June 17, 1880 ; miss. of Pres. Bd. in Gaboon, Africa.

FRANK HERBERT COFFRAN.
Born in Springfield, Mass., Apr. 14, 1855 ; united with the 1st Cong. Church in Springfield, Nov., 1870 ; graduated from Amherst College in 1877 ; married to Miss SARAH M. HILL, of Auburn, July 7, 1880.
Ordained pastor, Berkshire, N. Y., by Council, Dec. 8, 1880 ; Berkshire, 1880–1 ; tea. Auburn, 1881–2 ; Pres. Ch., Middlefield Center, 1882.

GEORGE FAIRLEE.
Born in Knox, N. Y., April 9, 1853 ; united with the 1st Pres. Ch., Schenectady, June, 1872 ; graduated from Union College in 1877.
Ordained pastor, Westminster Church, Troy, N. Y., by Presby. of Troy, Sept. 20, 1880.

DEWEY JONES, JR.
Born in Llangranog, South Wales, April 26, 1854 ; united with the Wig Cong. Church in Llangranog, Spring of 1866 ; studied at Carmarthen College and privately ; studied Medicine at Burlington, Vt., after leaving Auburn.
Ordained, Wheatland, Mich., by Council, Mar. 16, 1882 ; resident Fort Wayne, Ind.

EWEN CAMERON LIVINGSTON.
Born in Prince Edward Island, Canada, March 13, 1847 ; graduated from Hamilton College in 1875 : Auburn, 1875–6 and 1878–80.
Mott's Corners, Cong. Ch., 1881.

DWIGHT EDWARDS MARVIN.
Born in Greenwich, N. Y., Feb. 22, 1851 ; united with the Ref. Church in Nyack, N. Y., April 7, 1866 ; studied at Alexander Institute ; studied Theology with Rev. A. B. Riggs, 1 year ; 2d and 3d years at Auburn ; post-graduate year at Union ; married to Miss IDA NORTON WHITMAN, of Troy, N. Y., Oct. 17, 1874.
Ordained pastor, Greenbush, N. Y., by Council, Jan. 17, 1882.

CHARLES MONTERVILLE MCNULTY.
Born in West Middletown, Washington Co., Pa., Aug. 19, 1851 ; united with the Pres. Church in Buffalo, Pa., Spring of 1872 ; studied 2 years at Washington and Jefferson College in class of 1878 ; married to Miss MARY VINTON, of New Philadelphia, O., May 4, 1882.
Ordained pastor, New Philadelphia, by Presby. of Steubenville, Spring of 1881 ; home miss., Col., 1880 ; New Philadelphia ; resident there, 1882.

JAMES STEVENSON RIGGS.
   Born in New York City, July 16, 1853; united with the 2nd St.
   Pres. Church in Troy, N. Y.; graduated from Princeton College
   in 1874; studied abroad before entering Auburn; married, 1881.
   Ordained pastor at Fulton, N. Y., by Presby. of Syracuse, 1880.

FRANCIS EVARTS STOUT.
   Born in Lake Como, Pa., May 31, 1851; united with the Pres. Ch.
   in Lincoln, Del., early in 1870; graduated from Amherst Col-
   lege in 1877; married to Miss MARY ALIDA KEELER, of Auburn,
   June 9, 1880.
   Ordained at Rutland, N. Y., by Council, Aug. 24, 1881; La Crosse,
   Wis., 1880; Rutland from 1881.

JONATHAN SPRAGUE UPTON.
   Born in Tallmadge, O., Dec. 26, 1838; united with the Prot.
   Episc. Church at 21 or 22 years of age; studied at Oberlin College, Freshman and Sophomore years, in class of 1863; married
   to Miss AMORETTE HUTCHINS TREAT, of Tallmadge, Oct. 21,
   1864.
   Ordained pastor, Bridgewater, N. Y., by Council, July 28, 1880.

---

*ALBERT MELVIN COOPER, died Jan. 19, 1881.

WILLIAM WARNER HIBBARD, M. D.
   Born in W. Brookfield, Mass., May 16, 1847; united with the
   Pearl St. Cong. Church in Hartford, Conn., Fall of 1877; grad-
   uated from Worcester High School in 1866; graduated from
   Medical School of Harvard Univ., 1869; Jr. year(irr.)at Hartford
   Sem., Mid. year at Auburn, Sen. year at New Haven; married
   to Miss LIZZIE WOOD DALE, of Springfield, Mass., Apr. 14, 1874.

DAVID ALLEN REED.   See 1878–81.

WILTON MERLE SMITH.   See 1878–81.

1878-81.

CHARLES SUMNER BLODGETT.
   Born in East Windsor, Conn., Sept. 25, 1856; united with the
   Cong. Church in Broad Brook, Spring of 1871; graduated from
   Amherst College in 1878.
   Ordained pastor, Clarence, N. Y., by Presby., April 20, 1882.

D. ALBERT BLOSE.
   Born in Marchand, Pa., May 23, 1854; united with the Pres.
   Church in Mt. Pleasant, Summer of 1871; graduated from Lewis-
   burgh Univ., Pa., in 1878; married to Miss MINNIE CORAY, of
   Canaseraga, N. Y., May 10, 1882.
   Ordained pastor, Dresden, N. Y., by Presby. of Geneva, Jan. 12,
   1881; Ludlowville, 1880; Dresden from 1881.

JOHN BURKHARDT.

Born in Cleveland, O., April 30, 1843; united with the Ass. Ref. Church in Cuylerville, Spring of 1861; studied at Geneseo Academy; married to Miss ELLEN MAGDELENE CASTNER, of Westfield, N. Y., Jan. 2, 1869.

Ordained, St. Edward, Neb., by Presby. of Omaha, Oct. 18, 1881; Oakland, 1881; St. Edward from 1881.

ALFRED HASTINGS BURNELL.

Born in Manipi, Ceylon, Aug. 12, 1852; united with the Cong. Church in Westminster, Vt., early in 1867; studied at Williams College in class of 1878; married to Miss ABBIE J. SNELL, of Rushford, Minn., Aug. 10, 1881.

Ordained, Westminster West, Vt., by Council, June 30, 1881; miss. of A. B. C. F. M., Pasumalai, Madura, India.

HORACE THOMAS CHADSEY.

Born in Schenectady, N. Y., Sept. 27, 1856; united with the 1st Cong. Church in Schenectady, May, 1876; graduated from Union College in 1877; married to Miss ELLA VAN ALSTINE, of Auburn, May 10, 1882.

Ordained and installed at East Pembroke, N. Y., by Presby. of Genesee, Oct. 24, 1882.

PETER LINDSAY.

Born in Roxboroughshire, Scotland, May 30, 1851; united with the United Pres. Church in Wooler, Eng., Fall of 1869; studied at Madison Univ.; Junior year at Madison The. Sem.; Auburn, 1879–81; married to Miss NENE R. PECK, of Oaks Corners, N. Y., May 31, 1882.

Ordained pastor, Seneca Falls, N. Y., by Council, Dec. 13, 1881.

CHARLES GILLETT MATTESON.

Born in Litchfield, N. Y., June 28, 1849; united with the Whitestown Sem. Church in Fall of 1868; graduated from Hamilton College in class of 1876; married to Miss ELLA WALKER, of North Gage, N. Y., Oct. 7, 1875.

Ordained pastor, West Troy, N. Y., by Presby. of Albany, Nov. 1, 1881.

ROYAL CORBIN MOODIE.

Born in Craftsbury, Vt., June 19, 1852; united with the Ref. Pres. Church in E. Craftsbury, June, 1871; graduated from Yale College in 1878; married to Miss CARRIE A. ROOT, of North Craftsbury, May 18, 1881.

Ordained pastor, Los Gatos, Cal., by Presby. of San Jose, Nov. 8, 1881.

WILLIAM LANCASTER OULD.

Born in Baltimore, Md., Nov. 17, 1852; united with the Hampden Sidney College Church in May, 1870; studied at Hampden Sidney College in 1870–2; studied Law 2½ years.

Ordained pastor, Williamsport, Md., by Presby., Jan. 24, 1882.

DAVID ALLEN REED.

Born in Lansingburgh, N. Y., Oct. 3, 1850 ; united with the
Presbyterian Church in Lansingburgh, Spring of 1865 ; graduated
from Hamilton College in class of 1877 ; Auburn, 1877-8 and
1880-1 ; Leipsic and Bonn, Germany, 1878-80; married to Miss
GRACIE CHAPIN, of Springfield, Mass., Aug. 20, 1878.
Ordained pastor of Hope Ch., Springfield, by Council, June 7,
1881.
Published Translation of Christlieb on Christian Missions, 1880.

EDGAR PIERSON SALMON.

Born in Susquehanna Depot, Pa., Aug. 17, 1853 ; united with the
First Ch. of Christ in Galesburg, Ill., May, 1869 ; graduated from
Hamilton College in 1878 ; married to Miss FANNIE EVELYN
HART, of Elmira, Oct. 22, 1881.
Ordained pastor, Oaks Corners, N. Y., by Presby. of Geneva, Sept.
24, 1881.

CHARLES KELSEY SCOON.

Born in Geneva, N. Y., Jan. 23, 1855; united with the U. P. Ch.
in Geneva, when 14 years old ; graduated (B. S.) from Hobart
College in 1876; Junior year in Hartford The. Sem.; Auburn,
1879-81.
Pastor elect at McGrawville, N. Y., 1881 ; compelled to rest, by
ill health ; resident Geneva.

CHARLES HUDSON SMITH.

Born in Elgin, Ill., Nov. 9, 1856; united with the First Cong. Ch.
in Beloit, Wis., Nov., 1872 ; studied three and one-half years at
Amherst College in class of 1877 ; married to Miss HARRIETTE
KNIGHT, of Auburn, Sept. 28, 1881.
Portageville, N. Y., 1881-2.

WILTON MERLE SMITH.

Born in Elmira, N. Y., Apr. 18, 1856; united with the First Pres.
Church in Elmira, Spring of 1868; graduated from Princeton
College in 1877.
Ordained pastor, Cazenovia, N. Y., by Presby. of Syracuse, June
16, 1881.

HALSEY BIDWELL STEVENSON.

Born in Montezuma, N. Y., Feb. 9, 1854 ; united with the Pres.
Church in Cayuga, Feb., 1872; graduated from Williams Col-
lege in 1878 ; Auburn, 1878-9 and 1880-1 ; Union Sem., N. Y.,
1879-80; married to Miss NELLIE M. ROE, of Cornwall-on-the-
Hudson, Oct. 6, 1881.
Ordained pastor, Pottstown, Pa., by Presby., Nov. 7, 1881.

ADRIAN VAN SANTVOORD WALLACE.

Born in Newburgh, N. Y., Sept. 10, 1856; united with the Pres.

Church in Newburgh, Oct., 1868; graduated from Union College in 1878; Auburn, 1879-81.
Lyon's Falls, N. Y., 1881-2.

VERNON NOYES YERGIN.
Born in Wooster, O., Oct. 3, 1850; united with the Pres. Church in La Grange, Ind., Aug., 1869; graduated from Wabash College in 1878.
Ordained pastor, Jordan, N. Y., by Presby. of Syracuse, Oct. 17, 1881.

HOWARD BILLMAN.
Born in West Carlisle, O., Dec. 20, 1854; united with the Pres. Church in W. Carlisle, June, 1870; graduated from Wabash College in 1878; Auburn, 1878-9; Lane Sem.
Ordained pastor, Clifton, O., by Presby. of Cincinnati, 1882.

ROBERT FRANCIS COYLE.
Born in Northumberland Co., Canada, July 28, 1850; united with the Pres. Church in Marquette, Mich., June, 1870; graduated from Wabash College in 1877; Auburn, 1878-9; married to Miss SOPHIA BRANDKAMP, of Crawfordsville, Ind., June 27, 1877.
Ordained at Fort Dodge, Ia., by Presby. of Fort Dodge, Oct. 2, 1879; Fort Dodge from 1879.

MARTIN LUTHER DALTON. In Seminary in class of 1880-3.

EDWARD CHALMERS HAYNES.
Born in Lowell, Mass., Aug. 28, 1854; united with the 1st Cong. Church in Lowell, Jan. 3, 1875; studied at High School, Leominster, Mass.; studied the Classics privately; Auburn, 1878-9; grad. at Bangor Theol. Sem., 1881; married to Miss HESTER R. RAILEY, of Cohoes, N. Y., June 7, 1881.
Ordained at Tomah, Wis., by Council, Apr. 18, 1882; Norfolk and Raymondville, N. Y., Cong. Chs., 1881; Tomah from 1881.

CHARLES SUMNER HOYT.
Born in Meridian, N. Y., May 30, 1856; united with the Second Pres. Church in Auburn, Spring of 1873; graduated from Hamilton College in 1877; Auburn, 1878-80.
Instructor in Robert College, Constantinople.

HENRY PORTER PECK.
Born in Kalamazoo, Mich., Oct. 25, 1853; united with the Cong. Church in Norfolk, Conn., June 5, 1868; graduated from Amherst College in 1878; Auburn, 1878-80; Andover, 1880-2.
Ordained pastor, Plymouth, N. H., by Council, 1882. Son of Henry North Peck, of 1849-52.

CHARLES HOWELL RAY.
Born in Piffard, N. Y., Oct. 12, 1854; united with the Pres. Church in Wyoming, N. Y., Jan. 6, 1867; graduated from

Hamilton College in 1878; in the Sem. but a few weeks; married, and practicing Law in Lyons, N. Y.

JAMES AUGUSTUS WRIGHT.
Born in Paramus, N. J., Aug. 7, 1847; united with the A. M. E. Zion Church in New York, Dec. 20, 1868; selected studies at Auburn, 1878–9 and 1881–2; married to Miss MARY JANE POST, of Paterson, N. J., April 5, 1871.
Ordained Elder, by Bishop Joseph J. Clinton, June 16, 1875; in charge of Zion M. E. Chs. in Auburn and elsewhere, till 1881; miss., Presb., Henderson, N. C., 1882; Pres. Ch., Monroe, 1882.

1879-82.

MALTBIE DAVENPORT BABCOCK.
Born in Syracuse, N. Y., Aug. 3, 1858; united with the Ref. Ch. in Syracuse when 15 years old; graduated from Syracuse Univ. in 1879; married to Miss KATHARINE ELIOT TALLMAN, of Poughkeepsie, N. Y., Oct. 4, 1882.
Ordained pastor, Lockport, N. Y., by Presby. of Niagara, July 13, 1882.

JOHN GILBERT BLUE.
Born in North Gage, N. Y., Sept. 14, 1854; united with the Pres. Church in North Gage, April 11, 1869; graduated from Hamilton College in 1877; married to Miss HELEN MARIETTA GRIDLEY, of Canandaigua. N. Y., Oct. 4, 1882.
Ordained pastor, McGrawville, N. Y., by Presby. of Binghamton, Nov. 14, 1882.

NEWTON WORDSWORTH CADWELL.
Born in Hillsdale, Mich., June 6, 1853; united with the Pres. Ch. in Meridian, Summer of 1865; graduated from Hamilton College in 1876; teaching for 3 years.
Ordained pastor, Westfield, N. J., by Presby. of Elizabeth, July 25, 1882.

JOHN HUGH CAMERON.
Born in Antigonish, Nova Scotia, Sept. 12, 1853; united with the St. John's Church in Halifax, Feb., 1878; graduated from Dalhousie College in 1878; two years of Theology. Pres. College, Halifax; Auburn, 1881–2; married to Miss LOTTIE G. MURRAY, of Lochaber, N. S., June 29, 1882.
Ordained by Presby. of Pictou, July 4, 1882; miss. of Pres. Ch. of Canada, Oak River, Manitoba.

ROBERT AIKMAN CARNAHAN.
Born in Dayton, Ind., Nov. 7, 1857; united with the Pres. Church in Dayton, Jan., 1879; graduated from Wabash College in 1879

Ordained pastor, Hastings, Mich., by Presby. of Lansing, Nov. 1, 1882. Son of James Aikman Carnahan, of 1826–9.

WILLIAM SMITH CARTER.

Born in Albany, N. Y., Jan. 12, 1858 ; united with the Pres. Ch. in Oneida, at 12 or 13 years old ; graduated from Hamilton College in 1879.

Pres. Ch., Mansfield, Pa.

ANDREW SAGENDORPH CARVER.

Born in Union, N. Y., Aug. 5, 1853 ; united with the 1st Pres. Ch. in Binghamton, Fall of 1865 ; graduated from Amherst College in 1879 ; married to Miss ELLA E. ROWE, of Binghamton, May 6, 1882.

Ordained at Binghamton, by Presby. of Binghamton, Apr. 19, 1882 ; home miss., Texas.

PORTER LEE CHESTER.

Born in Geneva, N. Y., Jan. 29, 1857 ; united with the 1st Pres. Church in Geneva, Dec., 1869 ; graduated from Hamilton College in 1879.

Preaching in Ohio.

EDWIN HENRY DICKINSON.

Born in West Springfield, Mass., Oct. 16, 1855 ; united with the North (now Salem St.) Church in Springfield, at 14 years old ; graduated from Amherst College in 1879 ; married to Miss EMMA S. CARTER, of Brooklyn, N. Y., June 29, 1882.

Ordained pastor, Knoxboro, N. Y., by Presby. of Utica, N. Y., July 26, 1882.

WILLIAM EDWIN DODGE.

Born in Ionia, Mich., June 4, 1858 ; united with the 1st Pres. Ch. in Ionia, when 16 or 17 years old ; studied at Mich. Univ. 3 years.

Ordained at 1st Church, Utica, by Presby. of Utica, May 16, 1882 ; miss. of Pres. Bd. to Chili.

GILES HENRY DUNNING.

Born in Mansfield, O., May 7, 1851 ; united with the St. Mark's M. E. Church in Buffalo, N. Y., Feb., 1868 ; studied 2 years at Syracuse Univ. in class of 1878 ; married to Miss MARY E. FOWLER, of Pompey, N. Y., April 20, 1876.

Ordained pastor, Dryden, N Y., by Presby. of Cayuga, Sept. 19, 1882.

JOHN CHRISTIE HENDERSON.

Born in Huntington, Canada, March 5, 1852 ; united with the Wes. Meth. Ch. in Norwich, Ont., when 15 years old ; studied at Wesleyan Theological and McGill Colleges, Montreal.

Ordained, Somerset, N. Y., by Niagara Presby., Oct. 24, 1882.

WILLIAM HAND LESTER.
> Born in West Alexander, Pa., Apr. 5, 1857 ; united with the Cong.
> Church in Amherst Col., Fall of 1876; graduated from Amherst
> College in 1878 ; married to Miss SADIE M. ANDERSON, of Clays-
> ville, Pa., June 15, 1882.
> Ordained, 2d Ch., Auburn, by Presby. of Cayuga, Apr., 1882 ;
> miss. of Pres. Bd. to Chili.

ALEXANDER B. McLEOD.
> Born in Strathalbyn, P. E. Island, Mar. 17, 1853; united with the
> Pres. Church in Summerside, Apr., 1873 ; studied at Dalhousie
> College 3 years; 2 years in Theological College of Halifax;
> Auburn, 1881-2.
> Probationer of Un. Pres. Ch., Canada.

BRADFORD VANVLIET PUTNAM.
> Born in Westfield, N. Y., Dec. 12, 1856 ; united with the Pres.
> Church in Westfield, Spring of 1875 ; graduated from Western
> Reserve College in 1879 ; married to Miss ELLA WHITMAN, of
> Westfield, Oct. 4, 1882.
> Pastor elect, Huntington, L. I.

STANLEY BURROUGHS ROBERTS.
> Born in Phelps, N. Y., Aug. 12, 1855 ; united with the Pres. Ch.
> in Phelps, Fall of 1876 ; studied at Phelps Academy and Centre
> College.
> Ordained pastor, Vernon Centre, N. Y., by Presby. of Utica, June
> 20, 1882.

EDWIN PECK THOMSON.
> Born in Crawfordsville, Ind., Oct. 15, 1858; united with the
> Center Pres. Church in Crawfordsville, March, 1866 ; graduated
> from Wabash College in 1878. In Europe, 1882.

JAMES BUCHANAN UMBERGER.
> Born in Lebanon, Pa., Nov. 17, 1856 ; united with the Grace St.
> Ref. Church in Phila., April, 1873 ; graduated from Ursinus
> College in 1879 ; married to Miss ELLA G. BRUNER, of Norris-
> town, Pa., May 15, 1882.
> Cong. Ch., New Haven, N. Y.

ROBERT ROSCOE WATKINS.
> Born in Deerfield, N. Y., Feb. 14, 1856; united with the Calvinis-
> tic Methodist Church in Steuben, April, 1869 ; graduated from
> Hamilton College in 1879.
> Ordained pastor, Franklinville, N. Y., by Presby., Oct. 25, 1882.

JOSEPH MONROE WRIGHT.
> Born in Russell Co., Va., Nov. 11, 1844 ; united with the United
> Brethren Church near Muscodee, Wis., March, 1857 ; graduated
> from Normal School, Lebanon, O., (B. S.) in 1872; teaching
> public Schools 15 years ; married to Miss MARY ELEANOR
> WOODY, of Thorntown, Ind., Sept. 26, 1867.
> First Pres. Ch., Bloomfield, Ia.

POST GRADUATES.

NOTE. When the date of the death of a post graduate student is given, the full notice of him will be found in the Necrological list, under that date. When only the Seminary class to which he belonged is given, the notice is to be found in its proper place in the list of that class.

1827–28 *LEMUEL BROOKS, class of 1824–7, died Sept. 21, 1881.

ROBERT BOND CAMPFIELD, same class.

*LEWIS DUNHAM HOWELL, same class, died Sept. 25, 1847.

1833–34, *GEORGE GREATHOUSE MCAFEE, class of 1830–3, died early in 1841.

1835–36, *FREDERICK H. BROWN, class of 1832–5, died July 31, 1861.

*RUSSELL SALMON COOK, same class, died Sept. 4, 1864.

ETHAN BARROWS CRANE, same class.

*JONATHAN CRANE, same class, died Dec. 25, 1877.

*DAVID ANDREWS FRAME, same class, died Sept. 24, 1879.

*NORMAN KELLOGG, same class, died Jan. 12, 1879.

*MERIT SIDNEY PLATT, same class, died Dec. 3, 1880.

ABISHAI SCOFIELD, same class.

*CHARLES WILEY, D. D., same class, died Dec. 21, 1878.

1836–37, *JAMES RICHARDS, D. D., LL. D., class of 1833–6, died July 30, 1875.

1837–38, *FRANCIS CHILDS, class of 1834–7, died Oct. 1, 1841.

EDWARD HENRY CUMPSTON, same class.

WASHINGTON STICKNEY, same class.

ROBERT EDMUND WILLSON, same class.

1839–40, JOHN M. FRAZER, class of 1836–9.

EPHRAIM WILLIAM KELLOGG, same class.

1840–41, *JOHN E. CLAGHORN, class of 1837–40.

1842–43, JOHN PORTER, grad. of Yale Theo. Sem.

1847–48, FERDINAND DEWILTON WARD, D. D.
Born in Bergen, N. Y., July 9, 1812; graduated from Union College in 1831; Princeton Theol. Sem., 1831–3; Auburn, post. grad., 1848; D. D. from Washington College in 1861.
Ordained at Rochester, N. Y., by Presby., Aug. 31, 1836; Albion, 1834; 10th Ch., Philadelphia, Pa., 1835–6; miss. of A. B. C. F.

M. in India, (Madura and Madras) 1836–48; 1st Ch., Rochester, N. Y., 1849; 2nd Ch., Geneseo, 1849–58; Central Ch., Geneseo, 1858–61 and 1866–71; chap. U. S. A. 1863–4; Phelps, Groveland, East Avon, N. Y.; dist. sec. Am. Bib. Soc., 1871–5; resident in Geneseo.
Published many volumes and lesser works in Hindu and English.

1856–57, ARMON SPENCER, class of 1847–50.

1858–59, LUCIUS E. BARNARD, class of 1855–8.

1859–60,*ANTHONY DEY AXTELL, class of 1856–9, died Oct. 17, 1866.

1873–74, GEORGE GRANTHAN SMITH, class of 1861–4.

1877–78, SPENCER RANDOLPH BONNELL.
Born in Worcester, Mass., Dec. 29, 1846; united with the Central Cong. Church in Fall River, Mass., Apr., 1862; graduated from Amherst College in 1872; graduated from Andover Seminary in 1877; post-graduate at Auburn, 1878.
Ordained pastor at South Deerfield, Mass., July 2, 1878; South Deerfield, 1878–80; Brighton, Vt., 1880–2; Springwells Church, Detroit, Mich., 1882.

EGBERT CHARLES LAWRENCE.
Born in Borodino, N. Y., June 25, 1845; united with the Pres. Church in Owego, N. Y., May 7, 1865; graduated from Union College in 1869; graduated from Princeton Seminary in 1875; post-graduate at Auburn, 1877–8; married to SARAH JEAN BURTIS, of Buffalo, N. Y., Nov. 27, 1877.
Ordained pastor of Grace Pres. Ch., by Presby. of Brooklyn, Oct. 28, 1875; Owasco Outlet Ref. Ch., 1877–8; Second Ref. Ch., Schenectady, N. Y., from 1878; adj. prof. of History, Union College, from 1880.

1878–79, GEORGE MASON DALLAS SLOCUM.
Born in Schuylerville, N. Y., Jan. 24, 1845; united with the M. E. Church in Schuylerville, 1863; graduated from Union College in 1872; graduated from The. Sem. at New Brunswick, N. J., in 1878; post-graduate, Auburn, 1878–9; married to Miss ELISABETH HART CLAPP, of East Hampton, Mass., May 27, 1879.
Ordained pastor, Knox, N. Y., by Classis of Albany, May 29, 1879; Knox and Berne from 1879.

1882–83, WILSON FLEMING CELLARS
Born in Liberty, O., Dec. 20, 1841; united with the Pres. Church in Liberty, Feb., 1856; graduated from Ohio Wes. Univ. in 1874; grad. from Sem. of the North West in 1872; Auburn, 1882; married to Miss KATE CORLETT, of Chicago, Ill., Sept. 24, 1872.
Ordained pastor, Plymouth, Ill., by Presby. of Schuyler, Feb., 1873; Plymouth, 1872–7; Manitowoc, Wis., 1877–80; Berlin, 1st Ch., O., 1881–2.

NECROLOGICAL LIST.

1822.

JOHN LINCKLAEN, or JAN VON LINCKLAEN, Trustee 1820-1, æt. 54.
Born in Amsterdam, Holland, Dec. 24, 1768 ; united with the
Cong. Church in Cazenovia, N. Y., May 3, 1807 ; educated in
Switzerland ; married to Miss HELEN LEDYARD, of Ledyard, N.
Y., 1797 ; died of paralysis in Cazenovia, Feb. 9, 1822. No
children ; his wife survived till 1845.
Entered the Dutch Navy at the age of 14, where he remained till
he became Lieutenant ; came to America in 1790, as principal
director of the Holland Land Co.; founded Cazenovia in 1793 ;
resided there as agent of the Company, till his death.

1824.

DAVID HYDE, ESQ., Trustee 1820-4, æt. 41.
Born in Sharon, Conn., May 27, 1783 ; never united with the
Church ; studied at Utica ; studied Law with Daniel Kellogg,
Esq., of Skaneateles ; married to Miss OLIVE CAMPBELL, of
Albany, Oct. 16, 1809 ; died of consumption at Auburn, April
12, 1824. He had 2 sons and 2 daughters ; 1 daughter survived
him.
Practised Law in Auburn from 1808; also in mercantile and mill-
ing business from 1810 ; one of the founders of the old Bank
of Auburn.
Treasurer of Sem., 1820-3.

OLIVER PLATT, class of 1823-6.
Graduated from Hamilton College in 1823; came to Auburn as
member of Church in Scipio ; killed by fall from hay mow at
Danby, N. Y., about Sept., 1824.

1825.

GEORGE SEYMOUR, class of 1822-5, æt. 29.
Born at Otsego, N. Y., June 20, 1796 ; united with the Ch. in Hart-
wick, N. Y., Sept. 1, 1816 ; studied at Hamilton College 1 year;
Junior year in Auburn ; left College and Seminary on account

of poor health; preached at Snake Creek, Pa.; never married;
died of consumption at Otsego, June 15, 1825.

1826.

ELISHA COWLES, class of 1823-6, æt. 28.
  Born in Meriden, Conn., June 17, 1798; united with the Cong.
  Church in Otisco, N. Y., Sept., 1817; graduated from Hamilton
  College in 1823; married to Miss EMILY HAYES, of Clinton,
  N. Y., April 20, 1826; died of consumption at Otisco, May 17,
  1826. His wife survived him.

1829.

HENRY AXTELL, D. D., Trustee 1820-9, æt. 56.
  Born in Mendham, N. J., 1773; united with the Pres. Church in
  Mendham; graduated from Princeton College in 1796; taught
  for several years; studied Theology with Rev. Jedediah Chapman; D. D. from Middlebury College in 1823; married to
  HANNAH COOK, of Mendham, 1797; died of hemorrhage of
  lungs at Geneva, Feb. 11, 1829. He had 3 sons and 4 daughters;
  his wife, 3 sons and 2 daughters survived him.
  Ordained co-pastor at Geneva, N. Y., by Presby. of Geneva, July
  12, 1812; Geneva, 1812-29.

COL. SAMUEL BELLAMY, Trustee 1821-9, æt. 73.
  United with the 1st Pres. Church in Auburn, Jan. 27, 1823; died
  Mar. 20, 1829. He was buried in Auburn; his wife, whose
  name was MEHITABEL, survived until 1839; they left no children.
  The "Bellamy and Edwards" Professorship was named from him.

1830.

JOHN LOOMIS HOWARD, class of 1827-30, æt. 27.
  Born in Bolton, Conn., Nov. 20, 1803; united with the Church in
  Bolton, July 4, 1819; graduated from Yale College in 1827; died
  of fever, at Auburn, June 2, 1830.

1831.

JOSIAH JAMES KIRKPATRICK, class of 1825-8.
  (So the name appears in all the records, though he asserted that
  it should be *Kilpatrick*.) Graduated from South Carolina College
  in 1818; entered the Seminary from Rowan, N. C., being a
  member of the 1st Pres. Ch., Columbia, S. C. Licentiate of
  Presby. of Concord, N. C., 1818; died in or before 1831.

HENRY COWLES WILLIAMS, class of 1830-3, æt. 25.
Came to Auburn from Church in Remsen; graduated from Hamilton College in 1827; died of typhus fever at Auburn, Sept. 1, 1831.

HENRY HOTCHKISS, class of 1823-6.
Said to have been born in Clinton, N. Y.; came to Auburn from Church in Paris; graduated from Hamilton College in 1822; Auburn, 2½ years; died of consumption, Strasburg, Va., Oct. 23, 1831.
Probably ordained pastor, Fairfield, N. Y.; Reading, Pa., 1830-1.

1832.

THADDEUS EDWARDS, Trustee 1820-32, æt. 68.
Born in Northampton, Mass., 1764; united with the Pres. Church in Skaneateles, N. Y., Aug., 1805; married to ELECTA SIMONS, of Williamstown, Mass., 1789; died of strangulated hernia at Skaneateles, Apr., 1832. No children; his wife survived him.
He was a farmer by occupation; his name appears in that of the "Bellamy and Edwards" Professorship.

GLEN CUYLER, ESQ., Trustee 1820-2, æt. 57.
Born in Albany, Oct. 16, 1775; married to Miss MARY FORMAN LEDYARD, of Aurora, Dec. 14, 1796; died of debility at Aurora, Sept. 1, 1832. He had 4 sons and 5 daughters; his wife, 2 sons and 3 daughters survived him.
Studied Law five years with Stephen Lush of Albany; admitted as an attorney, Jan. 5, 1796, and practiced Law at Aurora till his death.

1833.

EBENEZER FITCH, D. D., Trustee 1820-7, æt. 77.
Born in Norwich, Conn., Sept. 26, 1756; united with the Church in Yale College, May 6, 1787; graduated from Yale College in 1777; resident graduate, Yale, 1777-9; D. D. from Harvard Univ. in 1800; married to Mrs. MARY BACKUS COGGSWELL, of Windham, Conn., May, 1792; died of asthma at W. Bloomfield, March 21, 1833. He had 10 sons and 1 daughter; his wife, daughter and 5 sons survived him.
Ordained, Williamstown, Mass., by Berkshire Assoc., June 17, 1795; teacher Hanover, N. J., 1779-80; tutor Yale, 1780-3; merchant, 1783-6; tutor and librarian, Yale, 1786-91; preceptor Williamstown Academy, 1791-3; first president Williams College, 1793-1815; pastor West Bloomfield, N. Y., 1815-27; afterward resident at West Bloomfield.
Published "Historical Sketch of Col. Williams and Williams College," 1802.

WILLIAM HEMPHILL, class of 1832-5, æt. 26.

Born in Malta, N. Y., Feb. 1, 1806; united with the Church in Malta Village, 1825; graduated from Union College in 1832; taught in Troy, N. Y., before coming to Auburn, and studied with Drs. Beeman and Kirk; not married; died of fever, at Malta, N. Y., May 15, 1833.

1834.

CHARLES B. WOODBURN, class of 1831-4, æt. 27.

Came to Auburn from Greenville, N. Y.; mem. of Church there; studied at Union College in class of 1832; Auburn, in class of 1830-3, and Mid. 1832-3; died at Spencertown, N. Y., Mar. 14, 1834.

LUCIUS J. CLOSE, class of 1832-5.

Born in King's Ferry, N. Y.; studied at Sharon, Conn.; Auburn, Junior, 1832-3; died of consumption at King's Ferry, June. 1834.

BENJAMIN COTHEN CRESSY, class of 1826-9, æt. 36.

Born in Abington Parish, Pomfret, Conn., Sept. 24, 1798; graduated from Amherst College in 1826; married to Miss EMMA BESTOR, of Simsbury, Conn., Mar. 17, 1829; died of fever at Salem, Ind., July 10, 1834. His wife survived him; they had 2 or 3 children, one of whom died before him.

Ordained at Avon, N. Y., by Presby., Jan. 21, 1829; Salem, Ind., 1829-34; agt. in N. E. for Hanover College and A. H. M. S., 1832-3.

1835.

ABNER P. CLARKE, class of 1824-7, æt. 38.

Came to Auburn from Southampton, Mass.; united with the Cong. Church in Southampton, 1816; graduated from Yale College in 1825; Auburn, Middle and Senior years; died at Augusta, N. Y., Feb. 6, 1835. His wife and 1 daughter (at least) survived him.

Ordained pastor, Preble, N. Y., by Presby. of Cortland, 1827; Preble, 1827-30; Ludlowville, 1831-2; Augusta, 1833-5.

WILLIAM A. RICHARDS, class of 1828-31, æt. 29.

Born in Hanover Neck, N. J.; united with the Church in Hanover; graduated from Princeton College in 1824; never married; died of consumption at Hanover, May 2, 1835.

Member of Presby. of Hanover.

HENRY PIERCE STRONG, Trustee 1829-35, æt. 51.

Born in Salisbury, Conn., Feb. 23, 1785; graduated from Yale College in 1807; Andover Theol. Sem., 1810; married to LAURA CLARK, of Danbury, Conn., Nov. 6, 1810; died of typhus fever at Rushville, N. Y., Aug. 28, 1835. He had 9 sons and 1 daughter ; his wife and 7 sons survived him.

Elizabeth St. Ch., New York City, 1810-13 ; Woodbury, Conn., 1814-16 ; St. Albans, Vt., 1817-21 ; Phelps, N. Y., 1824-33 ; Rushville from 1833.

BENJAMIN FRANKLIN HOXSEY, class of 1827-30, æt. 34.

Born in Williamstown, Mass. ; united with the Cong. Church in Williamstown, May, 1826 ; graduated from Williams College in 1827 ; married to Miss SOPHIA ADALINE BULKLEY, of Williamstown, Sept. 5, 1830 ; died of consumption at Williamstown, Sept. 10, 1835. His 1 son survived him.

Ordained, Henrietta, N. Y., Genesee Consoc., June 2, 1830 ; Fayette, Mo., 1830-2 ; Auxvasse, 1832-4.

PRESTON RICHARDSON, class of 1825-8, æt. 35.

Born in Attleboro, Mass., Jan., 1801 ; united with the Cong. Church in Harford, Pa., 1826 ; graduated from Hamilton College in 1825 ; left the Seminary after 6 mos., in poor health ; taught, founding the Harford Academy ; married to Miss LOIS THAYER, of Harford, 1831 ; died of consumption at Harford, Dec., 1835. He had 1 son and 1 daughter; his wife and daughter survived him.

1836.

MATTHEW LA RUE PERRINE, D. D., Professor, æt. 59.

Born in Freehold, N. J., May 4, 1777 ; graduated from Princeton College in 1797 ; studied Theology with Dr. Woodhull, of Monmouth ; D. D. from Meadville College, Pa., in 1818 ; married to Miss ANNE THOMPSON, of New Brunswick, N. J., about 1800 ; died at Auburn, Feb. 12, 1836. He had no children ; his wife survived him.

Ordained by Presby. of N. Brunswick, June 24, 1800 ; home miss. 4 mos. in 1800 ; pastor, Bottle Hill, N. J., 1802-11 ; Spring St. Pres. Ch., New York, 1811-20 ; prof. of Ch. Hist. and Eccl. Pol. in Auburn, 1821-36 ; gave instruction in Didactic Theology for 2 years.

Published "Letters Concerning the Plan of Salvation," 1816 ; "An Abstract of Biblical Geography," 1835, and sermons, &c.

1837.

ZENAS CLAPP, class of 1822-5, æt. 41.

Born in Deerfield, Mass., Jan. 30, 1796 ; united with the Cong. Ch. in Sunderland, Mass., Sept. 1, 1816 ; graduated from Dartmouth College in 1821 ; in Auburn from Feb. 14, 1825 ; married to PAMELA CLARY in 1822 ; died of consumption in St. Augustine, Florida, Jan. 29, 1837.

Tutor in Amherst College, 1823–4; teacher in Academies in Ashfield, Amherst and Deerfield, Mass., and in Chittenango and Ovid, N. Y.; on a farm in Salina; St. Augustine from 1836.

Hon. Samuel Miles Hopkins, LL. D., Trustee 1832–6, æt. 65.

Born in Salem, Conn., May 9, 1772; united with the Church in Moscow, N. Y., 1815; studied at Yale College; LL. D. from Yale College in 1828; married to Sarah Elisabeth Rogers, of New York, 1800; died of general prostration at Geneva, N. Y., March 9, 1837. He had 3 sons and 4 daughters, all of whom, with his wife, survived him.

Admitted to practice Law, 1793; Oxford, 1793–4; New York from 1794; Albany, 1821–31; Judge of Circuit Court of New York.

Published volume of Chancery Reports, and various treatises on Temperance, State and National Legislatures, Crime, Prison Discipline, &c.

Asahel D. Foote, class of 1833–6.

Came to Auburn from Smyrna, N. Y.; Auburn, 1833–4 and 1835–7; said to have died by drowning at Greene, N. Y., June 4, 1837.

Simeon Johnson, class of 1836–9, æt. 25.

Came to Auburn from Church in Amherst Col.; studied at Amherst College; died by drowning in Owasco Lake, June 24, 1837.

Hannibal Smith, class of 1836–9, æt. 25.

Came to Auburn from Johnson, Vt.; mem. of Church there; died by drowning in Owasco Lake, June 24, 1837.

William Parkhurst Tuttle, class of 1836–9, æt. 22.

Born in Newark, N. J., Dec. 29, 1814; united with the Pres. Ch. in Caldwell, N. J., 1830; graduated from Princeton College in 1836; not married; died by drowning in Owasco Lake, June 24, 1837.

William Woodbridge, class of 1836–9, æt. 23.

Came to Auburn from Stockbridge, Mass.; died by drowning in Owasco Lake, June 24, 1837.

Asa K. Buel, class of 1821–4, æt. 49.

In Auburn 1821–2; married to Miss Benedict, of Genoa, 1823; died of consumption, June 29, 1837; buried in Auburn. He had 1 son and 4 daughters.

Ordained Pastor of Pres. Ch., Aurora, N. Y., by Presby. of Cayuga, July 30, 1823; Aurora, 1823–5; Brutus; Ludlowville, 1828–30; St. Catherines, U. C., 1830–4; Rushville, N. Y., W. C., 1836–7.

Published, as Chn. of Presbyterial Com., "Narrative," of Presby. of Niagara, Canada, 1834.

Elihu Rowe, class of 1835–8, æt. 27.

Born in Sangerfield, N. Y., Sept. 27, 1811; united with the Pres. Church in Manlius, about 1829–30; graduated from Hamilton

College in 1834; Auburn, 1835-6; medical course at Fairfield, N. Y.; not married; died of consumption at Fairfield, Aug. 30, 1837.

Was to have gone as miss. to China.

ASHLEY M. GILBERT, class of 1829-32.

Came to Auburn from Smithfield; mem. of Church in Peterboro; married to Miss ELIZA EASTMAN, of Canada West; died at Colchester, Conn., Sept. 9, 1837. His wife survived him.

Lewiston, N. Y., 1835; Groton, Conn., 1836.

1838.

WILLIAM LEWIS, class of 1827-30, æt. 36.

Born in New Windsor, N., Y.; came to Auburn from Laight St. Church in N. Y. City; graduated from Williams College in 1827; married to Miss POLLY CORNELIUS, of Somers, N. Y., Sept. 15, 1831; died April 4, 1838. He had 2 children; his son survived him.

Rising Sun, Ind., 1833; Darrtown, O., 1834. His monument in the North St. Cemetery, Auburn, says that he devoted himself "to the cause of Education, Temperance and Piety in Canada, New York, Indiana and Ohio."

ROBERT LANGDON PORTER, class of 1834-7, æt. 28.

Born in Prattsburgh, N. Y., Apr. 8, 1810; united with the Church there, Sept. 20, 1829; graduated from Hamilton College in 1833; not married; not ordained; preached at Branchport 5 months; died of consumption at Prattsburgh, May, 1838.

ANSEL BRIDGMAN, class of 1827-30, æt. 34.

Born in Northampton, Mass., 1804; graduated from Williams College in 1827; married to Miss GRAVES, of Hatfield, 1833; married to Miss SAREPTA POOLE, of Troy, O.; died at Huntsburgh, O., Sept., 1838. He had 1 son or more; his wife survived him.

Ordained, Henrietta, N. Y., by Genesee Consoc., June 2, 1830; Farmington and Plymouth, Mich., 1830-3; Huntsburgh, O., (2 years of the time at Batavia also) 1833-8.

MARSHAL LOOK FARNSWORTH, class of 1826-9, æt. 39.

Born in Hawley, Mass., Mar. 11, 1798; united with the Pres. Ch. in Madison, N. Y., about 1818; graduated from Union College in 1825; married to Miss JOANNA BLAKE GOSMAN, of Danby, N. Y., 1830; died of consumption at Danby, Nov. 27, 1838. He had 1 son; his wife and son survived him.

Danby, 1829-30; Candor and Westville, 1831; Elmira, 1831-4; agt. of Am. S. S. Un. for State of Conn.; prin. of School for ladies, Norwich, Conn.; resided in Danby, N. Y., from 1838.

1839.

NATHAN MUNRO, Trustee 1838–9, æt. 48.
Born in Rehoboth, Mass., Mar. 6, 1791 ; united with the Cong. Church in Elbridge, N. Y., Mar. 18, 1821 ; married to Miss CYN-THIA CHAMPLAIN, Mar. 26, 1813 ; died at Elbridge, N. Y., July 5, 1839. He had 4 sons and 2 daughters ; his wife and children survived him.
Resident most of his life in Elbridge, where he was engaged in mercantile pursuits; founded "The Munro Academy of El-bridge," in 1832.

HON. JOHN HARVEY BEACH, Trustee 1822–36, æt. 56
Born in Stratford, Conn., 1783; graduated from Yale College in 1804; married to CHRISTINA CAMPBELL, of Albany, 1811 ; died of affection of duodenum at Auburn, Aug. 8, 1839. He had 5 sons and 2 daughters ; his wife, 3 sons and 2 daughters survived him.
Practiced Law in Whitesboro, N. Y., to 1808, and in Auburn 1808 –20 ; in mercantile business and in banking, milling and manu-facturing in Auburn, Port Byron and Syracuse, from 1820 ; mem. of N. Y. State Legislature.

LORENZO WARRINER PEASE, class of 1830–3, æt. 30.
Born in Hinsdale, Mass., May 20, 1809 ; united with the 1st Pres. Church in Auburn, Mar. 21, 1831 ; graduated from Hamilton College in 1828; entered Auburn late in Junior year, and took part of a post graduate year at Andover ; married to Miss LUCINDA LEONARD, of Auburn, June 25, 1834; died of typhus fever at Larnaca, Cyprus, Aug. 28, 1839. He had 1 son and 2 daughters ; his wife and 1 daughter survived him.
Ordained in Auburn, by Presby. of Cayuga, June 25, 1834 ; Mis-sionary in Cyprus till his death ; donor to the Seminary of the Cypriote collection in the Museum.
Published in Modern Greek, "Franklin's Advice to a Young Tradesman ;" "Muzzy on Tobacco ;" a work on the Sabbath, published after his death, &c.

AARON GARRISON, class of 1824–7, æt. 35.
Born in Shoduc, N. Y., 1804 ; came to Auburn from Church in Nassau ; graduated from Union College in 1825 ; in Auburn part of Jun. and Mid. years; died at East Bloomfield, N. Y., Dec. 11, 1839.
Ordained, Chatham, N. Y., July 3, 1827 ; Moreau to 1829 ; Mount Vernon, 1829–33 ; Waterville, 1833–6 ; Willinck, 1836.

1840.

ALANSON C. HALL, class of 1831–4.
Came to Auburn from Rochester, N. Y.; mem. of 3rd Church there ; studied at Hamilton College ; married to Miss FRANCES

ADELINE WILLARD, of Cayuga, Aug. 21, 1834; married to Miss ALMIRA EDSON, of Hadley, Mass.; died of consumption at Pulaski, Tenn., April 13, 1840. His wife survived him.

Ordained, Rochester, N. Y., by Presby., Sept. 4, 1834; missionary to Ceylon; preached in the Southern States.

SOLON G. PUTNAM, class of 1834–7, æt. 33.

Came to Auburn from Gambier, O.; mem. of Church in Mt. Vernon; graduated from Kenyon College in 1834; died at Granville, O., May 19, 1840.

Past. Guilford, N. Y., 1839–40.

1841.

GEORGE GREATHOUSE MCAFEE, class of 1830–3.

Came to Auburn from New Providence, Ky.; mem. of Church there; graduated from Centre College in 1827; in Auburn the course, and post graduate 1833–4; married near Hopkinsville, Ky.; died of consumption at Hopkinsville, early in 1841. He had one daughter, who, with his wife, survived him.

Ordained at Hopkinsville, Ky., by Presby. of Muhlenburgh, April 15, 1835 : Henderson, Ky., and Evansville, Ind., 1835–7; Elkton, Ky., 1837; Hopkinsville.

JOHN H. REDINGTON, class of 1831–4, æt. 41.

Came to Auburn from Ogdensburgh, N. Y.; mem. of 1st Pres. Church in Troy; Middle and Senior years in Auburn; died at Moscow, N. Y., Sept. 15, 1841.

Moscow, 1835–41.

FRANCIS CHILDS, class of 1834–7, æt. 34.

Came to Auburn from Providence, R. I.; mem. of Richmond St. Church there; Auburn, 1833–4, 1835–7, and post grad., 1837–8; died at Greenfield, O., Oct. 1, 1841.

Ordained pastor, Greenfield, O., by Presby., Nov. 13, 1839; Steuben, O., 1838–9; Greenfield from 1839.

DAVID ROBERTSON DOWNER, class of 1828–31, æt. 33.

Born in Westfield, N. J., August 10, 1808; united with the Pres. Church in Westfield, June 13, 1825; graduated from Yale College in 1828; married to Miss ELIZA SAYRE, of New York, Apr. 18, 1833; died of pneumonia at Westfield, Nov. 28, 1841. He had 3 sons; his wife and sons survived him.

Ordained pastor of West Pres. Church, New York, Mch. 25, 1832, by the Third Presby. of N. Y., and remained there till Oct., 1841.

1842.

WILLIAM AUGUSTUS SELDEN, class of 1837–40, æt. 33.

Born in Haddam, Conn., July 3, 1809; united with the Pres. Ch.; graduated from Union College in 1837; not married; died of consumption at LeRoy, N. Y., Jan. 12, 1842.

Ordained by Presby. of Genesee.

RICHARD MONTGOMERY DAVIS, class of 1828–31, æt. about 46.
Born about 1796 ; in the Army, in war of 1812 ; united with the
Pres. Church in Greenville, N. Y., Sept. 1, 1822 ; graduated from
Union College in 1828 ; married to Miss CATHARINE HUBBELL,
of Berne, N. Y., Feb. 6, 1832 ; died of consumption at Bridge-
water, N. Y., June 13, 1842.
Ordained at Parma, N. Y., by Genesee Consoc., June 8, 1831 ;
Marshall, 1833 ; Springfield, 1835 ; Bridgewater.

DAVID HIGGINS, Trustee 1820–8, æt. 81.
Born in Haddam, Conn., Aug. 6, 1761 ; united with the Church in
Haddam, Autumn of 1779 ; graduated from Yale College in
1785 ; studied Theology with Dr. Smalley, of New Britain, and
Dr. Lyman, of Hatfield, Mass. ; died suddenly at Norwalk, O.,
June 18, 1842. His wife survived him.
Ordained and installed at North Lyme, Conn., Oct. 17, 1787, by
Council ; North Lyme, 1787–1801 ; 1st Church of Aurelius, N.
Y., (now Pres. Ch. of Union Springs) 1801–13 ; 1st Pres. Ch.,
Auburn, 1811–13 ; Bath, 1813–31 ; places in that vicinity, 1831
–5 ; Norwalk, O., supplying various Churches, 1831–42.

GEORGE TAYLOR, class of 1822–5, æt. 45.
Born in Wyalusing, Pa., Nov. 18, 1797 ; studied at Bloomfield, N.
J. ; entered Middle class at Auburn ; married to Miss ABIGAIL
BALDWIN, of Bloomfield, Oct. 18, 1826 ; married to Miss
CAROLINE WARD, Feb. 5, 1835 ; died of malignant erysipelas at
Moravia, June 30, 1842. He had 3 sons and 2 daughters ; his
wife and children survived him.
Ordained, Genoa 2d Ch., by Presby. of Cayuga, Feb. 14, 1826 ;
Pres. Ch., Moravia, 1825–42.

FRANCIS HAVEN, class of 1839–42, æt. 31.
Born in Lebanon, N. Y., Feb. 25, 1812 ; united with the Cong.
Church in Hannibal, 1836 ; graduated from Hamilton College in
1839 ; married to Miss EMELINE POWERS, of Seneca, N. Y.,
Oct. 17, 1839 ; died of consumption at Seneca, Oct. 21, 1842.
He had 1 son ; his wife survived him.

ABEL KNAPP HINSDALE, class of 1835–8, æt. 35.
Born in Torrington, Conn., Oct. 6, 1807 ; united with the Church
in June, 1828 ; graduated from Yale College in 1833 ; married
to Miss SARAH CYNTHIA CLARK, of Derry, N. H., Oct. 1, 1840 ;
died at Mosul, Dec. 26, 1842. His wife survived him.
Ordained, Riverhead, L. I., (Cong.) April 12, 1838 ; miss. of A.
B. C. F. M. among the Nestorians in Persia.

1843.

SAMUEL MANNING, class of 1821–4, æt. 50.
Born in Windham, Conn., April 18, 1793 ; united with the Pres.
Church in Schoharie, N Y., Oct., 1815 ; graduated from Union

College in 1821; Auburn, 1821-2; married to Miss Betsey
Chapman, of Durham, N. Y., July 14, 1823; married to Miss
Eliza Barker, of Durham, Oct. 4. 1841; died of consumption
at Chenango Forks, N. Y., April 16, 1843. He had 4 sons and
3 daughters; his wife, 3 sons and 3 daughters survived him.

Sherburne, N. Y., 1823; Fayetteville; Fly Creek, 1829; Smyrna,
1831; Sidney Plains, 1832; Triangle, 1833; Otselic, 1834;
Masonville, 1833-40; teaching, Montrose, Pa., 2 years.

Abel Moore Heacock, class of 1835-8, æt. 29.
Born in Buffalo, N. Y., Aug. 30, 1814; graduated from Western
Reserve College in 1835; Auburn Middle class from Yale Div.
Sch., Jan. 27, 1837; not married or ordained; died of heart
disease in Buffalo, July 9, 1843.

Horace Henry Hopkins, class of 1839-42, æt. 24.
Born in Sennett, N. Y., May 2, 1819; united with the Church while
in Union College; graduated from Union College in 1839;
not married or ordained; died of consumption at Auburn, July
23, 1843.

James Richards, D. D., Prof. of Christ. The., æt. 76.
Born in New Canaan, Conn., Oct. 29, 1767; united with the Cong.
Church in Stamford, Conn., Sept. 17, 1786; studied Freshman
year at Yale College in 1789-90; honorary degree of A. B. from
Yale, 1794; studied Theology with Drs. Burnett and Dwight;
A. M. from Princeton, 1801; D. D. from Yale in 1815; same
degree from Union, same year; married to Miss Caroline
Cowles, of Farmington, Conn.; died at Auburn, Aug. 2, 1843.
His wife and several sons and daughters survived him.

Ordained pastor, Morristown, N. J., by Presby. of New York, May
1, 1797; Sag Harbor and Shelter Island, L. I., 1793-4; Morristown, 1794-1809; Newark, N. J., 1809-23; professor in Auburn, 1823-43.

Moderator of General Assembly, 1805. A posthumous volume of
Lectures, with biography, published in 1846.

John Finley Smith, class of 1835-8, æt. 28.
Born in Cooperstown, N. Y., July 14, 1815; united with the Pres.
Church in Cooperstown before 1830; graduated from Hamilton
College in 1834; married to Miss Adelaide Gridley, of Clinton, N. Y., April 8, 1840; died at Hammondsport, N. Y., Oct. 4,
1843. He had 1 son and 1 daughter, who, with his wife, died
before him.

Tutor Hamilton College, 1838-9; professor of Latin and Greek,
1839-43.

1844.

Gen. Henry McNiel, Trustee 1820-1 and 1822-31, æt. 81.
Born in Conn., Jan. 11, 1763; united with the Cong. Church in
Paris Hill, N. Y.; married to Mrs. Margaret Simmons Pierce,

of Paris Hill, Nov. 18, 1792; married to Mrs. NANCY STEELE HOPKINS, of Paris Hill, March, 1837 ; died of pneumonia at Clinton, N. Y., May 16, 1844. He had 2 daughters; 1 daughter survived him.

Resided in Paris from about 1790, and in Clinton the last few years of his life ; was school teacher, and surveyor ; member of Legislature for 6 years from 1798 ; town clerk of Paris 18 years, commis. of Com. Schools 4 years, Justice of Peace 4 years.

SPENCER SEARLE CLARKE, class of 1839–42, æt. 29.

Born in South Deerfield, Mass., Oct. 31, 1815 ; came to Auburn from 2d Church, Deerfield ; graduated from Amherst College in 1839 ; not married ; preached a while, near Geneva ; died Oct. 12, 1844.

WILLIAM MORRIS HOYT, class of 1837–40, æt. 30.

Born in New Canaan, Conn., June 3, 1813 ; united with the Pres. Church in Morgan, O. ; graduated from Western Reserve College in 1837 ; married to Miss SUSAN A. EVERETT, May 4, 1841 ; died of pleurisy at Ellsworth, O., Dec. 17, 1844. He had 1 son and 1 daughter, who, with his wife, survived him.

Ordained pastor at Ellsworth, O., by Trumbull Presby., 1842 ; New Haven, N. Y., 1840–1 ; Ellsworth, 1841–4.

1845.

SHELDON DIBBLE, class of 1827–30, æt. 36.

Born in Skaneateles, N. Y., Jan. 26, 1809; graduated from Hamilton College in 1827 ; married to Miss A. TOMLINSON, of Troy, Sept. 5, 1830 ; died of hemorrhage of the lungs at Lahainaluna, Sandwich Islands, June 22, 1845. He had 2 sons and 2 daughters, all of whom, with his wife, survived him.

Ordained at Utica, N. Y., by Oneida Presby., Oct. 6, 1830 ; Hilo, Sandwich Is., 1831–6 ; Theol. Seminary, Lahainaluna, 1836–45.

Published Lectures on Missions, about 1837 ; History of Amer. Missions in Sandwich Islands, 1839 ; "Thoughts from Abroad," 1844.

WILLIAM B. WORDEN, M. D., class of 1835–8.

Came to Auburn from Manlius, N. Y. ; Auburn, 1836–8; married to Miss CHARLOTTE C. PEASE, of Auburn, Oct. 8, 1839 ; died of consumption at Liverpool, N. Y., May 14, 1845. His wife survived him a few months.

Preached at West Dresden, N. Y. ; his health failing, he studied Medicine, and practiced at Liverpool.

1846.

ALFRED ROBERTSON, class of 1831–4, æt. 38.

Born in Lexington, Ky., July 4, 1808 ; studied at Centre College ; Auburn, Junior year; married to Miss JANE TAPPAN, of Harrods-

burg, Ky., 1836; died at Danville, Ky., March 2, 1846. He had
1 son and 3 daughters; his wife survived him.
Teacher in Harrodsburg, 1832-43, and in Danville from 1843.

GUSTAVUS F. Goss, class of 1841-4.
Came to Auburn from Church in Geneva; graduated from Union
College in 1841; Auburn, 1841-2, or longer; taught in Crawfordsville, Ind.; died in battle of Monterey, (another account
says in camp) about Sept. 22, 1846.

GEORGE WILLISTON GRIDLEY, class of 1838-41, æt. 34.
Born in Kirkland, (then Paris) N. Y., Mar. 5, 1814; united with
the Cong. Church in Clinton, N. Y.; graduated from Hamilton
College in 1838; married to Miss HARRIETT NORTHRUP, of
Clinton, N. Y., Jan., 1842; married to Miss SARAH WEED, of
Junius, N. Y., about 1845; died of typhoid fever at Pembroke,
N. Y., Sept. 25, 1846. No children; his wife survived him.
Ordained pastor, Junius, N. Y., by Presby. of Geneva, 1844; Per-
.ry Centre, 1841-4; Junius, 1844-6.

LEMUEL WOODRUFF HAMBLIN, class of 1840-3, æt. 31.
Born in Cayuga Co., N. Y., July 23, 1815; studied at the Geneva
Lyceum; married to Miss JANNETTE CLEMENS, of Geneva, N.
Y., May 25, 1835; died of spinal disease at Elbridge, N. Y.,
Oct. 12, 1846. He had 3 sons and 1 daughter; his wife, 1 son
and 1 daughter survived him.
Ordained pastor, Elbridge, N. Y., by Presby. of Cayuga, and re-
mained there till death.

1847.

CHARLES ROBINSON, class of 1829-32, æt. 45.
Born in Lenox, Mass., Dec. 30, 1801; united with the Cong. Ch.
in Lenox, at 14 years old; studied at Williams College; married
to Miss MARIA CHURCH, of Churchville, N. Y., Apr. 1, 1833;
died at sea, of chronic diarrhea, Mar. 3, 1847. He had 5 sons
and 1 daughter; his wife, daughter and 3 sons survived him.
Ordained at Lenox, Mass., by Assoc., Jan. 16, 1833; miss. of A.
B. C. F. M., Bangkok, Siam.

JOSEPH BELL HYDE, Treasurer 1846-7, æt. 40.
Born in Mystic, Conn., July 27, 1807; united with the Cong.
Church in Bozrah, Conn., July 3, 1823; married to Miss
ELIZABETH BURR, of Hartford, Conn., Oct. 30, 1828; died of
congestion of the brain at Auburn, April 10, 1847. He had 3
sons and 3 daughters; his wife, 1 son and 3 daughters survived
him.
In business in Hartford, Conn., 1824-30; hardware merchant in
Auburn from 1830.

LEWIS DUNHAM HOWELL, class of 1824-7, æt. 43.

Born in Albany, N. Y., Dec. 25, 1803; united with the 1st Pres. Church in Cincinnati, O., about 1822 ; graduated from Cincinnati College in 1822 ; tut. there, 1822-3 ; Auburn, Mid. and Sen. years, and post graduate in 1827-8 ; married to Miss LOIS PHELPS, of Lenox, N. Y., May 6, 1828 ; died of typhoid fever at Geneva, N. Y., Sept. 5, 1846. He had 5 sons and 4 daughters ; his wife, 4 sons and 3 daughters survived him.

Ordained, Cincinnati, O., by Presby., April 26, 1830 ; Springport, N. Y., 1828-9 ; 4th Pres. Ch., Cincinnati, O., 1830-1 ; prof. of Languages, Lane Sem., nearly 2 years ; Maysville, Ky., 1832-3 ; Binghamton, N. Y., 1834; Springport, 1835 ; Cong. Ch., Derby, Ct., 1836-8 ; Onondaga Hollow, N. Y., 1839 ; agt. of Am. Tr. Soc., W. New York, 1839-42; agt. of Ed. Soc., residing in Geneva, from 1842.

VERNON WOLCOTT, class of 1834-7, æt. 39.

Born in Shoreham, Vt., March, 1809; graduated from Union College in 1835; died in New York, Oct., 1847. His wife died Nov. 12, 1844.

Ordained, Vergennes, Vt., (Cong.) Feb. 7, 1838; Ferrisburgh and Monkton, 1837-8; Monkton, 1 year; Whitehall, N. Y., 1 year; Moriah, N. Y., preaching and teaching, 1840-1 ; Brownington, 1842-5.

1848.

BARNABAS PHINNEY, class of 1827-30, æt. 49.

Born in Sheffield, Mass., July 23, 1798 ; graduated from Williams College in 1827 ; Junior and Middle years in Auburn ; married 1829 ; died of yellow fever at Henderson, Miss., Nov. 14, 1848. Ordained pastor, Hanover Soc., Lisbon, Conn., (Cong.) March 3, 1830; Pawtucket, Mass., 1833-6 ; Westborough, 1836; mem. of Assoc. till 1836.

EBENEZER MEAD, class of 1824-7.

Came to Auburn from Greenwich, Conn.; mem. of Greenwich W. Church ; graduated from Yale College in 1823; died of consumption at Greenwich, Dec. 28, 1848. Ordained pastor, Riga, N. Y., by Presby., July 15, 1829 ; Riga to 1833; Knowlesville, N. Y., 1834; Leroy, N. Y., 1837-40.

1849.

ELAM HAVILLA WALKER, class of 1829-32, æt. 50.

Born in Granville, N. Y., Nov. 11, 1798 ; united with the Pres. Church in Warsaw, 1817; studied at Hamilton College from 1824 ; Senior year in Auburn ; married to Miss ALICE P. BACON, of W. Bloomfield, N. Y., Nov. 9, 1832 ; died of bronchocele at Dansville, N. Y., Jan. 11, 1849. No children ; his wife survived him.

Said to have been ordained about 1828; miss. in E. Tenn., 1828–30; Brooks Grove, N. Y., 1830–1; Geneseo, 1832; Fowlerville, 1832–6; Dansville, 1836–49.

THOMAS HAZLETT, class of 1846–9, æt. 27.

Born in 1821; came to Auburn from Church in Fairport; not married; died of consumption at his father's residence in Perinton, Jan. 22, 1849.

SETH SMITH, Trustee 1820–49, æt. 64.

Born in Hadley, Mass., July 4, 1785; united with the 1st. Cong. Church in Hadley, June, 1806; graduated from Yale College in 1803; studied Theology with Dr. Dwight of New Haven, and Dr. Hyde, of Lee, Mass; married to Miss MARGARET PORTER, of Hadley, Oct. 11, 1810; died of neuralgia of the heart, Jan. 30, 1849. He had 1 son and 9 daughters; his wife, son and 4 daughters survived him.

Ordained at Hadley, by Council, Feb., 1808; missionary of Hampshire Miss. Soc., 1808; pastor Genoa, N. Y., 1809–49.

THOMAS COCHRAN, class of 1829–32, æt. 49.

Born near Londonderry, Ireland, in 1800; probably united with the Rev. Philip Hay's Church in Philadelphia, about 1820; graduated from Bloomfield Academy in 1829; married to Miss EMILY BEACH, of Rockaway, N. J., 1832; died of spinal abscess at Newark, N. J., Feb., 1849. He had 5 sons and 5 daughters; his wife, 2 sons and 5 daughters survived him.

Ordained and installed at New Providence, N. J., by Presby. of Elizabeth, July 7, 1835; agt. of Am. Tract Soc., 1832–3; pastor of Pres. Ch., New Providence, 1834–46; agt. of Am. Tract Soc. and Am. Bib. Soc.; 1847–8; organized Church in Newark, N. J., 1848.

DAVID CUSHING, class of 1826–9, æt. 49.

Born in Chesterfield, Mass.; came to Auburn from Church in Williamstown; graduated from Williams College in 1826; Auburn, 1826–8; New Brunswick, 1831; died at Portsmouth, O., June 1, 1849.

Ordained by 1st Classis of Philadelphia, 1831; Walpack, 1831–2; Kinderhook 2d, 1834–5; Pres. Ch., Valatie, N. Y., 1835; Newark, 1838; Portsmouth, O.

LOREN EATON HAVEN, class of 1845–8, æt. 30.

Born in Sangerfield, N. Y., Sept. 11, 1819; united with the 1st Pres. Church in Waterville, Feb. 23, 1837; graduated from Hamilton College in 1844; married to Miss HARRIET ELIZA RICE, of E. Bloomfield, N. Y., July 17, 1849; died at Sangerfield, N. Y., July 22, 1849. His wife survived him.

Ordained, Waterville, N. Y., by Presby. of Utica, 1848; Hector, N. Y., 1848–9; was to have been miss. of A. B. C. F. M. to Fuh Chau, China.

NATHANIEL WILCOX FISHER, class of 1826–9.

Came to Auburn from Newport, N. H., and Church in Amherst Col.; graduated from Amherst College in 1826; married to Miss MARTHA MARIA GRAVES, of Amherst, Mass., July 23, 1829; died of cholera at Sandusky, O., Aug. 1, 1849. His wife and children survived him.

Ordained, Avon, N. Y., by Presby., Feb. 14, 1829; Gallipolis, O., 1829–31; Burlington, O., 1832–5; Marietta, O., agt. of College; Lockport, N. Y., 1839; Palmyra, 1843; Sandusky, O.

LUCIUS ASCANIUS SWIFT, class of 1839–42, æt. 37.

Born in Fairfax, Vt., 1812; came to Auburn from Church in Potsdam, N. Y.; graduated from Middlebury College in 1837. The Middlebury records say that he was unable to complete his Theological course, on account of bleeding at the lungs; that he was engaged in teaching at the South, and died at Fayetteville, N. Y., Sept., 1849.

WILLIAM TOBEY, class of 1827–30, æt. 41.

Born in Ballston, N. Y.; came to Auburn from Ref. Church in Schenectady; graduated from Union College in 1827; died at Scarboro, Me., Sept. 10, 1849. He had 2 children; his wife survived him.

Ordained pastor, Scarboro, 1848; Newfoundland, 1830–1; Hanover, N. J., 1831–4; Genoa 2d Ch., 1835–6; Scarboro, Me., 1848–9.

AUGUSTUS GALESTIN GOULD, class of 1848–51, æt. 28.

Born in Cherry Valley, N. Y., Aug. 31, 1821; united with the M. E. Church, Cherry Valley, at 15 years old; graduated from Hamilton College in 1848; died of typhoid fever at Auburn, Nov. 7, 1849.

1850.

JOHN WATSON ADAMS, D. D., class of 1823–6, æt. 54.

Born in Simsbury, Conn., Dec. 6, 1796; united with the Church in Sullivan, N. Y., 1816; graduated from Hamilton College in 1822: studied privately one year in New York; Auburn Jun. Class, July 16, 1824; D. D. from Columbia College in 1840; married to Miss MARY PHELPS, of Lenox, N. Y., May 3, 1826; died at Syracuse, April 4, 1850. His wife and 2 daughters survived him.

Ordained pastor at Syracuse, N. Y., by Onondaga Presby., June 28, 1826; 1st Pres. Ch., Syracuse, 1825–50.

Published "Sermons on various Subjects," with biographical sketch of the author by Dr. Joel Parker, 1851.

WILLIAM HOLLISTER GUERNSEY, class of 1844–7, æt. 33.

Born in Northfield, Conn., 1817; united with the Church in Northfield, 1831; graduated from Yale College in 1844; married to

Miss SYRENA P. BURWELL, of New Hartford, Conn., 1847; died of cancer in stomach, at Savannah, Ga., April 7, 1850. He had 1 son; his wife and son survived him.

Ordained at Oriskany Falls, N. Y.; Oriskany Falls part of one year.

WASHINGTON THACHER, Trustee 1836–42, æt. 56.

Born in Attleboro, Mass., Feb. 23, 1794; united with the Pres. Ch. in Harford, Pa., 1809; studied at Harford Academy; studied Theology with Rev. John Truair, of Cherry Valley; A. M. from Hamilton College in 1825; married to Miss MARIA M. JOHNSON, of Little Falls, N. Y., 1822; married to Miss SARAH E. MORRILL, of New York, Dec., 1828; died at Utica, N. Y., June 29, 1850. Seven sons and daughters survived him.

Morrisville, 1822–6; Onondaga, 1826–33; Jordan, 1833–42; principal of Academy at Jordan, 1842–3; Eaton, 1843–6; agent of A. H. M. S., 1847–50.

CHARLES JENKINS KNOWLES, class of 1829–32, æt. 47.

Born in Greenville, N. Y., Mar. 14, 1804; united with the Church in Greenville; graduated from Union College in 1828; married to Miss LAVINA SHERRILL, of Greenville, Apr. 30, 1832; died at Riverhead, L. I., Oct. 27, 1850. He had 4 sons and 4 daughters, all of whom, with his wife, survived him.

Ordained, Rodman, N. Y., by Black River Assoc., May 8, 1832; Verona, N. Y., 1835–6; Bellport, L. I., 1836; Riverhead.

ETHAN PRATT, class of 1824–7, æt. 53.

Born in Durham, Greene Co., N. Y., 1797; united with the Ch. in Durham, Mar. 7, 1819; graduated from Union College in 1825; married to Miss ACHSAH GAYLORD, of Greene Co., N. Y.; married to Miss MARGARET SMITH, of Elmira, N. Y.; married to Mrs. OLIVE GRAVES PAINE, of Ashfield, Mass., June 27, 1838; died of typhoid fever at Bainbridge, N. Y., Nov., 1850. He had 3 sons and 1 daughter; his wife and 2 sons survived him.

Missionary in Delaware Co.; Horse Heads; teacher in Elmira; Athens, Pa.; Lowman Hill and Channing, N. Y.; Rock Stream, 1845–50; Bainbridge.

WILLIAM WILLSHIRE ROBINSON, class of 1844–7, æt. 32.

Born in Sherburne, N. Y., Nov. 18, 1818; united with the Pres. Church in Sherburne, at 13 years old; graduated from Yale College in 1844; married to Miss FANNY ROBBINS, of Camillus, N. Y., Sept. 16, 1847; died of typhoid fever at Penn Yan, N. Y., Nov. 14, 1850. He had 2 daughters; his wife and daughters survived him.

Ordained pastor, Penn Yan, N. Y., by Presby., Jan. 18, 1848; Penn Yan, 1847–50.

HERMAN NORTON, class of 1823–6, æt. 51.

Born in New Hartford, N. Y., July 2, 1799; united with the 1st Pres. Church in Auburn, June 10, 1817; graduated from

Hamilton College in 1823; Auburn 1 year, 6 months; said to
have been married to Miss FLINT, of Hartford, Conn.; died of
congestion of the lungs at New York City, Nov. 20, 1850, leaving a widow and children.
Ordained, Utica, N. Y., by Presby. of Oneida, Feb. 9, 1826;
labored as evangelist in revivals, 1826–30; Pres. Ch., cor. of
Prince and Crosby Sts., N. Y., 1830–5; Cincinnati, O., pastor,
1836–8; in poor health, and supply and evangelist, 1838–43;
Sec. of Am. Protestant Soc. and of Am. and For. Christ. Un.,
1843–50, residing in New York City.
Published "The Christian and Deist in Contrast," 1848; "Record
of Facts concerning the Persecutions at Madeira;" "Signs of
Danger and Promise;" "Startling Facts for American Protest-
ants," and some tracts.

SERENO EDWARDS DWIGHT, D. D., Trustee 1834–7, æt. 64.
Born in Greenfield Hill, Conn., May 18, 1786; united with the 1st
Cong. Church in New Haven, Oct., 1815; graduated from Yale
College in 1803; D. D. from Yale College in 1833; married to
Miss SUSAN EDWARDS DAGGETT, of New Haven, Aug. 28,
1811; died of brain disease at Philadelphia, Pa., Nov. 30, 1850.
He had 1 daughter.
Ordained pastor Park St. Ch., Boston, by Council, Sept. 3, 1817;
tutor in Yale, 1806–10; practiced Law in New Haven, 1810–16;
chaplain U. S. Senate, 1816–17; pastor Park St. Church, Bos-
ton, 1817–26; pres. of Hamilton College, 1833–5; resident N.
Haven, 1836–8, and then in New York.
Published "Memoirs of David Brainard," 1822; "An Address on
the Greek Revolution," 1824; "The Death of Christ," 1826;
"The Life of Pres. Edwards," 1830, with edition of Edwards'
Works, 10 vols.; "The Hebrew Wife," 1836; and some sermons.
Some discourses were published with his Memoirs, 1851.

1851.

JOHN HARRIS SAGE, class of 1843–6, æt. 38.
Came to Auburn from Fredonia, N. Y.; mem. of Ch. in Williams
College; graduated from Williams Col. in 1842; not married;
died of malignant fever, at Ashville, N. Y., Feb., 1851.
Cong. Ch., Sinclairville, 1849–50; Ashville, 1851.

JAMES BROWN, class of 1841–4, æt. 32.
Born in Edinburgh, Scotland, 1819; came to Auburn from Church
in Corning; selected studies, Auburn, 1843–4; married to Miss
MARY CORNELIA SKINNER, of Marysville, O., May 24, 1848;
died at Mt. Gilead, O., July 25, 1851. He had 1 son and 1
daughter; his wife and children survived him.
Pastor of Ch. in Mount Gilead.

ISAAC BLISS, class of 1828–31, æt. 47.

Born in Warren, Mass., Aug. 28, 1804 ; united with the Amherst Col. Church in March, 1827 ; graduated from Amherst College in 1828 ; married to Miss ELIZABETH ST. JOHN, of Groton, N. Y., Mar. 21, 1831 ; married to Miss EMILY CURTIS, of Elbridge, August, 1832 ; died at Moline, Ill., August 9, 1851. He had 1 daughter ; his wife and daughter survived him.

Elba, N. Y., 1834 ; Virgil, 1836 ; miss. of A. B. C. F. M., Sandwich Islands, from 1836 ; resident in Ill. from 1846.

HON. NATHANIEL WOODHULL HOWELL, LL. D., Trustee 1821–9, æt. 82.

Born in Blooming Grove, N. Y., Jan. 1, 1770 ; united with the 1st Cong. Church in Canandaigua, Apr. 30, 1815 ; graduated from Princeton College in 1788 ; LL. D. from Hamilton College in 1827 ; married to Miss SALLY CHAPIN, of Canandaigua, Mar. 17, 1798 ; married to Miss FANNY COLEMAN, of Canandaigua, Mar. 10, 1809 ; died at Canandaigua, Oct. 15, 1851. He had 6 sons and 4 daughters ; 4 sons and 1 daughter survived him.

Taught, Montgomery, N. Y., 1789–92 ; practiced Law in New York and in Tioga Co., 1794–6, and in Canandaigua from 1796 ; Attorney General for Western N. Y., 1799–82 ; first Judge of Ontario Co., 13 years from 1819 ; representative in N. Y. State Legislature ; representative in Congress, 1813–14.

1852.

HENRY DAVIS, D. D., Trustee 1820–34, æt. 81.

Born in East Hampton, L. I., Sept. 15, 1771 ; graduated from Yale College in 1796 ; studied Theology with Dr. Charles Backus, then of Somers, Conn.; D. D. from Union College in 1810 ; married to Miss HANNAH PHOENIX TREADWELL, of Plattsburgh, Sept. 22, 1801 ; died of consumption at Clinton, Mar. 8, 1852. He had 4 sons and 1 daughter. His wife, 1 son and 1 daughter survived him.

Ordained 1809 ; tutor in Williams, 1796–8 ; in Yale, 1799–1803 ; prof. of Greek, Union College, 1806–9 ; pres. of Middlebury, 1809–17 ; of Hamilton, 1817–33 ; resided in Clinton, N. Y., until his death.

Published orations, sermons and addresses. President of Trustees of Aub. Sem., 1820–4.

HON. ABNER HOLLISTER, Trustee 1846–52, æt. 69.

Born in Glastenbury, Conn., Sept. 26, 1782 ; united with the Pres. Church in Ira, N. Y.; married to Miss MARY WOODBRIDGE ELWELL, of Manlius, Dec. 3, 1804 ; married to Mrs. NANCY DUNSCOMB KIRKPATRICK, of Syracuse, March 7, 1843 ; died of typhoid fever at Meridian, N. Y., Mar. 13, 1852. He had 6 sons and 4 daughters ; his wife, 5 sons and 1 daughter survived him.

Came to Meridian, 1805 ; farmer, hotel keeper, and county Judge.

LEVI ROSE, class of 1838–41, æt. 49.
> Born in North Branford, Conn., 1803; graduated from Williams College in 1839; entered Auburn Mid. class, Oct., 1839; married to Miss ELIZA STRATTON, of Auburn; died of consumption at Howard, N. Y., June 4, 1852.
>
> Barton, Canada West, 3 years; Burton, O., 1 year; Howard, N. Y., 7 years.

CRISPUS WRIGHT, class of 1835–8, æt. 43.
> Born in Westford, N. Y., 1809; united with Dr. Kirk's Church in Albany; graduated from Oneida Inst.; Auburn, 1836–7; married to Miss BETSEY BURR, of Meredith, N. Y., Feb. 13, 1838; died of apoplexy at Exeter, N. Y., July 5, 1852. He had 2 sons and 4 daughters; his wife, 2 sons and 3 daughters survived him.
>
> Ordained pastor, Coventryville, N. Y., by Presby. of Chenango, June, 1842; Meredith, 1837–9; Windham, 1839–41; Coventryville, 1841–51; resident at Exeter, 1852.

DANIEL BOND, class of 1848–51, æt. 26.
> Born in Adams, N. Y., Sept. 1, 1826; united with the Pres. Ch. in Adams, N. Y., June 27, 1843; graduated from Hamilton College in 1848; Auburn, 1848–50; Union Sem., N. Y., 1850–2; married to Miss MARY SEYMOUR HASTINGS, of New York, 1852; died of typhoid fever at Peekskill, N. Y., Aug. 20, 1852. His wife survived him.
>
> Ordained pastor, Peekskill, N. Y., by Presby., June 29, 1852.

LEVERETT HULL, class of 1824–7, æt. 56.
> Born in Bethlehem, Conn., Dec. 3, 1796; graduated from Hamilton College in 1824; died of cholera, Sandusky, O., Sept. 3, 1852.
>
> Ordained at Utica, N. Y., by Presby., Feb. 4, 1829; Augusta, 1827–30; Deposit; Guilford, 1833; Watertown; Angelica, 1835–8; Dansville, 1843; Sandusky, O., 1846; Sandusky, agt. of A. B. C. F. M., and of Seaman's Friend Soc.

CHARLES LUTHER ADAMS, class of 1847–50, æt. 33.
> Born in Sullivan, N. Y., 1820; united with the Pres. Church in Baldwinsville, N. Y.; graduated from Hamilton College in 1847; Union, N. Y., 1847–8; Auburn, 1848–50; married to Miss AMELIA LEWIS LELAND, of Auburn, Oct. 1, 1850; died of ulceration of the liver at Paris, Wis., Oct. 23, 1852. His wife and son survived him.
>
> Ordained, Baldwinsville, N. Y., by Presby., Oct., 1850; Neenah, Wis., 1850–2.

1853.

ALANSON BALDWIN CHITTENDEN, class of 1824–7, æt. 56.
> Born in Durham, N. Y., Sept. 20, 1797; united with the 1st Pres. Church in Durham, July 7, 1816; graduated from Union College in 1824; Auburn from June 4, 1825 and 1825–6; married to

Miss ANNA C. COTTS, of Saugerties, N. Y., Oct. 12, 1829 ; died of softening of the brain caused by injury, at Schenectady, N. Y., April 12, 1853. He had 1 son ; his wife survived him.

Miss. of Ref. Ch., Montgomery Co., 1827–8 ; Glen, and miss. at Charlestown, 1831–4 ; Amity, 1834–9 ; Westerlo, 1839–40 ; Sharon, 1841–5.

1854.

RODERICK LEE HURLBURT, class of 1838–41, æt. 41.

Born in Castleton, (now Seneca Castle) N. Y., Oct. 3, 1812 ; united with the Pres. Church in Castleton, Jan. 25, 1832 ; graduated from Oberlin College in 1838 ; first two years at Oberlin, Senior year at Auburn ; married to Miss MATILDA HART, of Castleton, Oct. 28, 1841 ; died of typhoid fever at Castile, N. Y., Feb. 14, 1854. He had 1 son and 4 daughters ; his wife and 2 daughters survived him.

Ordained and installed at Youngstown, N. Y., by Presby. ; Littleville ; Youngstown, 1844–52 ; Castile from 1852.

HENRY NORTH PECK, class of 1849–52, æt. 32.

Born in Harwinton, Conn., March 23, 1822 ; graduated from Amherst College in 1849 ; married to Miss ADA PORTER, of New Hartford, N. Y., 1852 ; died of typhus fever at Detroit, Mich., Mar. 9, 1854. He had 1 son, who survived him, Henry Porter Peck, of 1878–81.

Ordained, Paris Hill, N. Y., by Oneida Assoc., Sept. 28, 1852 ; Kalamazoo, Mich., 1852–3 ; Fort St. Cong. Ch., Detroit, 1854.

WILLIAM BROWN, Trustee 1820–35, æt. 84.

Born in Tiverton, R. I., April 30, 1770 ; graduated from Yale College in 1789 ; married to ALICE DEMING, April 9, 1795 ; died of paralysis of the lungs at Brooklyn, N. Y., March 11, 1854. He had 1 son and 1 daughter, both of whom survived him.

Lawyer in Auburn from 1811 ; resident in New York and Brooklyn from 1832. Secretary of Board of Trustees, 1820–34.

SAMUEL CORYLUS WILCOX, class of 1837–40, æt. 44.

Born in Sandisfield, Mass., Dec. 21, 1809 ; graduated from Williams College in 1835 ; married to Miss ANNA BREWSTER, of Rochester, N. Y. ; married to Miss MARY S. DARLING, of Reading, Pa., Dec. 1, 1846 ; died of consumption at Owego, N. Y., March 25, 1854. His wife and 4 children survived him.

Ordained pastor, Owego, N. Y., by Presby. of Tioga, May 25, 1842 ; Berkshire ; Owego, Pres. Ch., 1841–7 ; Williamsburg, Mass., 1847–9 ; Owego, N. Y., Cong. Ch., 1849–53, and resident there till death.

JACOB EDGERTON BLAKELEY, class of 1848–51, æt. 34.

Born in Pawlet, Vt., June 9, 1820 ; graduated from Middlebury College in 1844 ; teaching, 1844–8 ; Union Sem., N. Y., 1848–9 ; Auburn, 1849–51 ; died of consumption at Pawlet, May 6, 1854.

Ordained pastor, East Poultney, Vt., (Cong.) Mar 9, 1853 ; East Poultney, 1851–4.

EDWIN HOLT, class of 1823–6, æt. 49.

Born in New London, Conn., Apr. 17, 1805 ; united with the Ch. of which Dr. Spring was pastor, in New York, April, 1823 ; studied at Columbia College in 1821 ; studied Medicine, nearly completing a course ; married to Miss EMILY TITCOMB, of Newburyport, Mass., July 24, 1828 ; died of Asiatic cholera at Evansville, Ind., July 2, 1854. He had 4 sons and 3 daughters ; his wife, 2 sons and one daughter survived him.

Ordained pastor at Westfield, N. J., by Presby. of Elizabethtown, Nov., 1827 ; Westfield, 1826–30 ; Macon, Ga., 1831–6 ; Portsmouth, N. H., 1836–40 ; Carmine St. Ch., New York, 1843 ; resident Newburyport, Mass., 1846 ; resident Greenland, N. H., 1849–50 ; Madison, Ind., 1851–2 ; resident Evansville, Ind., from 1853.

STEPHEN STANLEY, class of 1837–40.

Born in East Bloomfield, N. Y.; united with the Pres. Church in LeRoy, 1825 ; studied at Hamilton College in class of 1839; married to Miss FIDELIA EMELINE WARNER, of Geneva, N. Y., Sept. 22, 1841 ; died of cholera at Rochester, N. Y., Aug. 20, 1854. He had 3 sons and 1 daughter ; his wife, 1 son and daughter survived him.

Ordained pastor, Fairport, N. Y., by Rochester Presby. ; Fairport, 1 year; practiced Medicine ; sang in public and gave concerts ; resided in Corning.

EDWIN HALL CRANE, class of 1848–51, æt. 29.

Born in Westmoreland, N. Y., May 30, 1825 ; united with the Pres. Church in Clinton, about 1838 ; graduated from Hamilton College in 1844 ; married to Miss ANN ELIZA COWLES, of Otisco, Feb. 22, 1852 ; died of typhus fever, at Gawar, Persia, Aug. 27, 1854. His wife and son survived him.

Ordained, Clinton, N. Y., by Presby., May 28, 1851 ; Cassville, N. Y., 1851–2 ; miss. of A. B. C. F. M. among the Nestorians, 1852–4.

REUBEN TINKER, class of 1827–30, æt. 55.

Born in Chester, Mass., Aug. 6, 1799 ; united with the 1st Cong. Church in Hartford, Conn., Aug. 6, 1820 ; graduated from Amherst College in 1827 ; married to MARY T. WOOD, of Chester, Mass., Nov. 14, 1830 ; died of malignant tumor at Westfield, N. Y., Oct. 26, 1854. He had 3 sons and 4 daughters, all of whom, with his wife, survived him. One son is Joseph Emerson Tinker, of 1857–60.

Ordained at Chester by Mountain Assoc., Nov. 3, 1830; miss. of A. B. C. F. M., to Sandwich Islands, 1831–40 ; Madison, O., 1841–5 ; Westfield, N. Y., 1845–54.

1855.

HIRAM HICKOK SEELVE, Trustee 1848–55, æt. 52.
  Born in Lansingburgh, N. Y., April 30, 1803; united with the Ch.
  in Lansingburgh at about 18 years of age; studied at Academy
  in Lansingburgh; married to Miss MARY TAYLOR, of Lansingburgh; died at Geneva, N. Y., Jan. 1, 1855. His wife died
  Sept., 1856; no children.
  Relinquished preparation for the Ministry on account of failing
  eyesight; merchant in Burlington, Vt., till 1828; merchant in
  Geneva from 1828.

NATHAN BENJAMIN, class of 1831–4, æt. 43.
  Born in Catskill, N. Y., Dec. 14, 1811; united with the Williams-
  town Church while Sen. in College; graduated from Williams
  College in 1831; Junior and Middle years in Auburn; grad.
  at Andover; married to Miss MARY G. WHEELER, of N. Y.
  City, April 26, 1836; died of typhus fever at Constantinople,
  Jan. 27, 1855. He left a widow and children.
  Ordained Williamstown, Mass., (Cong.) Apr. 21, 1836; agt. A. B.
  C. F. M., and attending Medical lectures in New Haven,
  1834–6; missionary at Athens, Smyrna, and Constantinople,
  1836–55.

FRANCIS JANES, class of 1830–33, æt. 52.
  Born in East Hampton, Mass., May 18, 1803; united with the
  Cong. Church in East Hampton, May 5, 1823: graduated from
  Williams College in 1828; Junior and Middle years at Auburn;
  married to Miss EMILY A. MARSH, of Lisle, N. Y., Oct. 21,
  1832; died of typhoid fever at Dansville, N. Y., Jan. 20, 1855.
  He had 4 sons; his wife and 3 sons survived him. Sons in the
  classes of 1857–60, 1868–71 and 1873–6.
  Ordained, Chenango Forks, N. Y., by Assoc., 1832; Chenango
  Forks; Walton, 1837; Union, 1839–41; Otsego, 1842; Madison:
  Sauquoit; Colchester (Downsville) from 1846.

STEPHEN PEET, class of 1822–5, æt. 58.
  Born in Sandgate, Vt., 1797; united with the Cong. Church in
  Lee, Mass., at 16 years of age; graduated from Yale College in
  1823; Princeton, 1823–4; Auburn, Senior year; studied also
  at New Haven; married to Mrs. MARTHA DENISON SHERMAN,
  May 1, 1826; died of inflammation of lungs at Chicago, Ill.,
  March 21, 1855. He had 3 sons and 2 daughters, all of whom,
  with his wife, survived him.
  Ordained and installed at Euclid, O., Feb. 22, 1826; Euclid,
  1826–33; agt. Am. Bethel Soc., residing at Cleveland, O., and
  Buffalo, N. Y., 1833–7; Green Bay, Wis., 2 years, from 1837;
  1st. Pres. Ch., Milwaukee, 1839–41; gen. agt. of A. H. M. S.
  1841–2; founder and general agent of Beloit College; Cong.
  Ch., Batavia, Ill.; one of the founders of Chicago Theological
  Seminary; in 1836, editor of the *Buffalo Spectator*.

HENRY LOBDELL, M. D., class of 1849–52, æt. 28.
> Born in Danbury, Conn., Jan. 25, 1827; united with the Amherst College Church, Nov. 9, 1845; graduated from Amherst College in 1849; entered Auburn Junior class, Jan., 1850, from Yale Divinity School; received the degree of M. D., in New Haven, Jan., 1850; teacher Danbury, Conn., 1850–1; Andover, and Union Sem., N. Y., each a few weeks, in 1851; married to Miss Lucy Williams, of Ridgefield, Conn., April 9, 1850; died of fever at Mosul, March 25, 1855. His wife, 1 son and 1 daughter survived him.
> Ordained at Pilgrim Church, Brooklyn, (Cong.) Oct. 12, 1851; miss. of A. B. C. F. M. at Mosul, 1851–5.

HARVEY REXFORD HITCHCOCK, class of 1828–31, æt. 55.
> Born in Great Barrington, Mass., March 13, 1800; united with the Cong. Church in Great Barrington, 1817; graduated from Williams College in 1828; married to Miss Rebecca Howard, of Owasco, N. Y., Aug. 26, 1831; died of dysentery at Kaluoaha, Sandw. Is., Aug. 29, 1855. He had 3 sons and 1 daughter; his wife and sons survived him.
> Ordained, Auburn, by Presby. of Cayuga, Sept. 20, 1831; missionary at Kaluoaha, Molokai, sailing for the field, Nov., 1831.

JACOB CATLIN, class of 1821–4, æt. 56.
> Born in New Marlboro, Mass., 1799; united with the 1st Cong. Ch. in New Marlboro, Mar. 3, 1816; graduated from Williams College in 1820; preached for a while, but was not ordained; druggist in Patterson, N. J, in New York, and in Brattleboro, Vt., where he died Aug. 31, 1855.

GEORGE HORNELL, class of 1825–8, æt. 65.
> Born in Hornellsville, N. Y.; united with the Pres. Church in Almond, N. Y., about 1821; studied at Canandaigua and Aurora Academies; admitted to the bar in 1813; Auburn Middle class, 1825–6, and Senior, 1827–8; married to Miss Sarah Thacher, of Hornellsville, March, 1813; died of hemorrhage from lungs at Commerce, Mich., Sept. 9, 1855. He had 4 sons and 2 daughters; his wife, 1 son and 2 daughters survived him.
> Ordained by Presby. of Bath, about 1827; preached in Hornellsville, N. Y.; miss. of A. B. C. F. M. among the Indians of the N. W., 1828; Auburn, Mich.; Adrian; White Lake, 1837–49; service of Am. S. S. Un. and of Am. Tr. Soc.

FOSTER LILLY, JR., class of 1838–41, æt. 44.
> Born in Hawley, Mass., June 6, 1812; united with the Pres. Ch. in Binghamton; graduated from Williams College in 1838; married to Miss Caroline Bentley, 1848; died of brain disease at Andover, N. Y., Dec. 23, 1855. He had 1 son; his wife survived him.
> Ordained, Spencer, N. Y., by Presby., Sept. 11, 1849; Chenango Forks; Gainsboro, Can. West, 1842; Deposit, N. Y., 1842–5;

Hornellsville, 1845–9 ; Kennedyville, 1849–52 ; home miss. in Wheeler, Spencer, Hume.

WARD CHILDS, class of 1825–8, æt. 55.
　　Born in Thetford, Vt., 1800; studied at Phillips Academy ; died at Chagrin Falls, O., Dec. 27, 1855.
　　Morgan and Rome, O., 1829–35 ; Warsaw, N. Y., 1836 ; Perry Village, 1836 ; 2d Ch., Sheldon, 1837–51 ; Mesopotamia, O., from 1854.

1856.

ROBERT WILLIAM HILL, class of 1823–6, æt. 54.
　　Born in Berkshire, Mass., 1803 ; united with the Pres. Church in Riga, N. Y.; graduated from Hamilton College in 1823 ; married to Miss ELIZABETH A. TENEYCK, of Owasco Lake, Fall of 1826 ; died of heart disease at Rochester, Jan. 16, 1856.　He had 3 sons and 2 daughters ; his wife, 2 sons and 1 daughter survived him.
　　Ordained pastor, Ira, N. Y., by Presby. of Cayuga, July 12, 1826; Ira, 1826–9; East Bloomfield, 1829–48 ; Mendon, 1848–53 ; editor of *Genesee Evangelist* from 1851 ; resided in Rochester from 1853.
　　Published " Protestant Churches Defended ;" " Civil Liberty."

RICHARD SALTER STORRS DICKINSON, class of 1845–8, æt. 32.
　　Born in Longmeadow, Mass., April 3, 1824; united with 1st Pres. Church in Auburn, N. Y., 1840 ; graduated from Amherst College in 1844; Auburn, 1845–7; Union, N. Y., 1848–9 ; married to Miss MARGARET SHIPPEN MCILVAINE, of Philadelphia, Sept. 8, 1855 ; died of rupture of the aorta at Edinburgh, Scotland, Aug. 28, 1856.　Eldest son of Professor Baxter Dickinson ; no children ; his wife survived him.
　　Ordained pastor of Houston St. Pres. Ch., N. Y., by 3d Presby. of N. Y., Mar. 28, 1849 ; N. Y., 1849–53 ; associate pastor with Rev. Albert Barnes of 1st Pres. Ch., Philadelphia, 1853–5; in 1856, he started on a tour of Europe, preparatory to taking charge of the American Chapel in Paris, which had recently been established by Dr. Kirk, acting for the American and Foreign Christian Union.

ELEAZAR HILLS, Trustee 1824–50, æt. 70.
　　Born in Conn. ; married to Miss SARAH WOLCOTT BISSELL, of Pittsfield, Mass. ; died of heart disease at New York City, Sept. 25, 1856.　He had 3 sons and 2 daughters ; his wife, 2 sons and 1 daughter survived him.
　　Merchant in Auburn from 1815.

SAMUEL NICHOLAS SHEPARD, class of 1822–5, æt. 57.
　　Born in Lenox, Mass., Sept. 25, 1799 ; united with the Cong. Church in Lenox, Oct. 20, 1822 ; graduated from Williams

College in 1821 ; Auburn 2 years, 1822–4 ; married to MARTHA
BRACE, of Newington, Conn., Aug. 28, 1832 ; died of apoplexy
at Madison, Conn., Sept. 30, 1856. He had 2 sons and 3
daughters ; his wife, 1 son and 3 daughters survived him.

Ordained pastor at East Guilford, (now Madison) Conn., by West
Consoc. of New Haven Co., Nov. 2, 1825, where he remained
till his death.

CHARLES GOLD LEE, class of 1838–41.

Came to Auburn from Rochester, N. Y. ; united with the 1st
Church in Rochester; A. M. from Hamilton College in 1846 ;
died at Rochester, N. Y., Oct. 9, 1856.

First minister of Park Church, Syracuse ; resided in Syracuse and
in Rochester.

JAIRUS BURT, class of 1824–7, æt. 62.

Born in Southampton, Mass., Mar. 16, 1795 ; united with the
Cong. Church in Southampton, at 21 years old ; graduated
from Amherst College in 1824 ; Auburn a year and a half ;
finished the course with Rev. Sylvester Burt ; died at Canton,
Conn., Jan 15, 1857. He had 1 son, who went before him ; his
wife survived him.

Ordained pastor at Canton Centre, by Hartford North Assoc.,
Dec. 20, 1826, and remained there till death.

ARCHIBALD FERGUSON, class of 1848–51.

Came to Auburn from Ogdensburgh, N. Y. ; died at Charlotte, N.
Y., Jan., 1857.

Pittsford, N. Y., 1852 ; Charlotte, 1853–7.

JAMES ADAMS, class of 1826–9.

Born in North Carolina, 1800 ; united with the Pres. Ch., Bloomfield, N. J., before 1820 ; came to Auburn from Bath, N. C. ;
graduated from Princeton College in 1824 ; Auburn, catalogued
Jun. and Mid. in class of 1824–7, Mid. in 1825–8, Sen. in
1826–9 ; married to Miss FANNY MARIA THOMPSON, of Schenectady, Oct. 17, 1833 ; died of consumption at Union Church,
Miss., Feb. 7, 1857.   He had 3 sons, who, with his wife, survived him.

Ordained, 1830 ; prin. of Acad., Bloomfield, N. J ; Pres. Ch., Dundaff, Pa., 1830–3 ; Monticello, N. Y., 1833–53 ; taught at Covington, Miss., Buffalo, N. Y., and Union Church, Miss.

MORRIS BARTON, class of 1823–6, æt. 57.

Born in Scipio, N. Y., Aug. 14, 1799 ; united with the 1st Pres.
Church in Auburn, Oct. 24, 1817 ; graduated from Hamilton
College in 1823 ; married to Miss ANN P. THOMPSON, of Broad-
alban, N. Y., Aug. 18, 1827 ; died of apoplexy at Romulus, Feb.
13, 1857. He had 5 sons and 5 daughters ; his wife, 5 sons and
4 daughters survived him.

Ordained pastor at Romulus, N. Y., by Presby., Nov. 21, 1825 ;
Romulus till 1846, and resident there till his death.

DIRCK CORNELIUS LANSING, D. D., Professor, æt. 72.

Born in Lansingburgh, N. Y., Mar. 3, 1785; united with the Ch. in Yale Col. in 1802; graduated from Yale Col. in 1804; D. D. from Williams Col. in 1826; married to Miss ELIZABETH VANDERHEYDEN, of Lansingburgh, Feb. 14, 1805; married to Miss LAURA ALEXANDER, of Onondaga, Feb. 11, 1813; married to Miss Susan FRANCES VAN RAUST, of New York, Nov. 28, 1831; married to Mrs. LAURA CAMP DICKINSON, of Hanover, N. H., April 15, 1852; died of inflammation of stomach at Walnut Hills, O., Mar. 19, 1857. He had 6 sons and 7 daughters; his wife, 3 sons and 5 daughters survived him.

Ordained pastor at Onondaga, N. Y., by Presby., Dec., 1807; Onondaga 8 years from 1806; Stillwater, 1814-16; Park St. Church, Boston, Mass., 1816; Auburn 1st Ch., 1817-29; Utica 2nd Ch., 1829-33; Houston St. Pres. Ch., New York, 1833-5; resided at Auburn, 1835-8; Ill., 1838-9; Utica, Syracuse and Auburn, 1839-46; Chrystie St. Church, N. Y., 1846-8; Clinton Ave. Church, Brooklyn, 1848-55; trustee of Auburn, 1820-30 and 1835-57; vice pres. of Trustees, 1820-4; prof. of Sac. Rhet. and Past. The., 1821-6; he served without salary, and, as financial agt., raised large sums for the Seminary.

Published "Sermons on Important Subjects," 1825.

LEONARD ELIJAH LATHROP, D. D., Trustee, æt. 61.

Born in Hebron, Conn., Aug. 26, 1796; graduated from Middlebury College in 1815; studied Theology with Dr. Matthews of N. Y. City, and with Rev. John M. Mason, D. D.; teaching in Kinderhook, N. Y., and in New York City, and afterward in Wilmington, N. C.; D. D. from Hobart College in 1840; married to Miss MARIA LUDLOW, of Kinderhook, June, 1819; died of heart disease at Sharon, Conn., Aug. 17, 1857. He had 6 sons and 6 daughters; his wife, 5 sons and 4 daughters survived him.

Ordained pastor, Wilmington, by Presby., Jan. 10, 1823; Wilmington, 1819-24; Salisbury, Conn., 1824-36; 2d Pres. Ch., Auburn, 1836-51; Sharon, Conn., 1853-7. Trustee of Aub., 1837-43 and 1846-53.

HENRY DWIGHT, Trustee 1827-55, æt. 74.

Born in Springfield, Mass., June 25, 1783; united with the 1st Church of Christ in Springfield, Nov. 7, 1808; graduated from Yale College in 1801; in business for several years; studied Theology with President Dwight at New Haven, and with some one at Princeton, N. J.; married to Mrs. SUSAN MILES SILL, of Utica, May 17, 1814; died of general prostration at Geneva, N. Y., Sept. 7, 1857. He had 2 sons and 1 daughter, who, with his wife, survived him.

Ordained pastor at Utica, N. Y., by Presby., Feb. 3, 1813; Utica, 1st Ch., 1813-17; his voice failing, he engaged in banking, Geneva, N. Y., where he remained from 1817; director of A. H. M. S. from its organization, and president of the same, 1837-57; vice pres. of Trustees of Aub. Sem., 1830-55.

GEORGE LYMAN HALL, class of 1845–8, æt. 42.
Born in Augusta, N. Y., Oct. 28, 1815; united with the Cong.
Church in Augusta; studied at Augusta Acad.; taught the same
7 years; A. M. from Hamilton College in 1854; married to
Miss ELLEN MARY CLEAVER, of Marcy, N. Y., Oct. 23, 1850;
died of fever at Mecklenburgh, N. Y., Oct. 20, 1857. He had 2
sons and 1 daughter; his wife, 1 son and daughter survived
him.
Burdett, N. Y., 1847–50; Phillipsville, 1850–1; supplying at
Trenton and other places, 1852–5; Mecklenburgh, 1855–7.

JOHN DUNBAR, class of 1832–5, æt. 53.
Born in Ware, Mass., Mar. 7, 1804; united with the Cong. Church
in Ware, Feb. 4, 1827; graduated from Williams College in 1832;
Auburn, Junior and part of Middle year; married to Miss Es-
THER SMITH, of Hadley, Mass., Jan. 12, 1837; died of intermit-
tent fever, at Robinson, Kan., Nov. 1, 1857. He had 3 sons and
4 daughters, all of whom survived him.
Ordained at Ithaca by Cayuga Presby., May, 1833; missionary
among the Pawnee Indians, 1834–47; preaching, farming, and
State Superintendent of Schools, Oregon, Mo., 1848–55; moved
to Kansas.
Published "The Pawnee's Book," 1836.

HUBERT PIERRE HERRICK, class of 1850–3, æt. 31.
Came to Auburn from McDonough; graduated from Amherst
College in 1849; married to JULIA   , of Granville, O.,
1853; died of African fever, at Nengenenge, W. Africa, Dec. 20,
1857.
Ordained 1853; Gaboon mission of A. B. C. F. M., 1853–7.

1858.

HON. ELIJAH RHOADES, Trustee 1848–54, æt. 67.
Born in Chesterfield, Mass., Mar. 7, 1791; united with the Pres.
Church in Manlius, N. Y., July 22, 1831; studied at Williams
College in class of 1813; married to Miss ANNA LUCIA GARDI-
NER, of Manlius, Mar. 4, 1818; died at Pittsfield, Mass., Feb.
9, 1858. His wife and adopted daughter survived him.
He was a merchant by occupation. He was County Clerk, and in
1841, State Senator.

HENRY RICHARD HOISINGTON, class of 1828–31, æt. 57.
Born in Vergennes, Vt., Aug. 23, 1801; united with the Pres. Ch.
in Buffalo, N. Y., about 1822; graduated from Williams College
in 1828; married to Miss NANCY LYMAN, of Chester, Mass.,
Sept. 21, 1831; died of heart disease at Centre Brook, Conn.,
May 16, 1858, on the Sabbath, while preaching from the words,

"To-day if ye will hear his voice, harden not your hearts." He had 3 sons and 3 daughters ; his wife, 1 son and 3 daughters survived him. His son, H. R. H., Jr., grad. in class of 1860-3.

Ordained pastor, Aurora, N. Y., by Presby., Aug. 30, 1831 ; Aurora, 1831-3 ; miss. in Ceylon, principal of Batticotta Seminary, 1833-50 ; Cong. Church, Williamstown, Mass., 1853-6 ; Centre Brook, Conn., 1857-8.

Published "The Oriental Astronomer," 1848.

MILTON A. BROWN, class of 1855-8.

Came to Auburn from Palmyra, N. Y.; graduated from Univ. of Rochester in 1855 ; married before entering Sem. ; died Summer of 1858. His wife and 2 sons survived him.

Appointed chap. of Auburn Prison.

JOHN HARVEY RICE, class of 1831-4, æt. 58.

Born in Sharon, N. Y., March 9, 1800 ; catalogued Senior in 1833-4 ; not elsewhere mentioned in the Auburn records : married to Miss PHŒBE C. EASTMAN ; married to Miss LOUISA N. DOTY, Nov. 6, 1849 ; died of heart disease at Greene, Pa., June 21, 1858. His wife, 2 sons and 1 daughter survived him.

Ordained, Rodman, N. Y., by Black River Assoc., May 8, 1832 ; Cambria, N. Y. ; Beamensville, and Grimsby. C. W.; Rutland, N. Y.; Barton, C. W.; Grand Haven, Mich.; Gowanda, and Sheridan, N. Y.; Wattsburgh, and Wayne, Pa ; Clymer, N. Y.; Middlebrook and Greene, Pa., 1856-8.

1859.

MORRISON HUGGINS, class of 1839-42, æt. 42.

Born in Marion, N. Y., Aug. 3, 1817 ; graduated from Union College in 1837 ; married to Miss ABIGAIL FLEMING ; married to Miss ISABELLA G. SIMPSON ; died of pneumonia at Rockford, Ill., Feb. 15, 1859. His wife and 3 children survived him.

Ordained pastor, Havana, N. Y., by Presby. of Chemung, 1842 ; Havana, 1842-56 ; Rockford, Ill., 1856-9.

JOHN M. CRABB, class of 1834-7, æt. 55.

Born in Garrard Co., Ky., 1804 ; graduated from Miami Univ. in 1834 ; Western The. Sem. ; Auburn, Dec., 1834 to 1836 ; married to Miss AMANDA R. ROOT, May 17, 1838 ; married to Miss MAHITABLE FORD, May 31, 1849 ; married to Miss CATHERINE REECE, Mar. 20, 1855 ; died of dropsy at Bryan, O., Mar. 17, 1859. His wife and 4 children survived him.

Ordained, May 15, 1838 ; New Lexington, O., 1839-41 ; Lima, 1842-7 ; Montpelier, 1851-2 ; Williams Centre, 1853-5 ; Bryan from 1856.

JOHN DENNIS STRONG, class of 1848-51, æt. 38.

Born in Rockaway, N. J., Jan. 26, 1821 ; graduated from Williams College in 1848 ; married to Miss JULIA C. CHASE, of Auburn ;

died at Lowville, Wis., May 14, 1859, of inflammation of liver. His wife and only son survived him.

Fort Madison, Iowa, 1851 ; Iowa City, 1851–5 ; Springfield, 1855–6 ; Fairplay, Jamestown, Lowville, and Leeds, Wis., 1856–9.

ABSALOM K. BARR, class of 1829–32, æt. 53.

Born in Rowan Co., N. C., Oct. 4, 1806; united with the Church while in College ; graduated from Univ. of N. Carolina in 1826 ; taught 2 years ; Union The. Sem., Va.; Aub., 1831–2 ; married to Miss MARIETTA LOCKWOOD, of Sennett, N. Y., Sept. 17, 1833 ; married a second time ; died of heart disease at Springfield, O., June 5, 1859. He had 5 or more children ; his wife and 3 children survived him.

Ordained by Concord Presby., Nov. 5, 1834 ; Mecklenburgh Co., N. C., 1832–5 ; Onondaga and Yates Counties, N. Y., 1835–43 ; Richland Co., O., 1843–54 ; resident Springfield, O., from 1854.

NATHANIEL MARCUS CRANE, class of 1833–6, æt. 54.

Born in West Bloomfield, N. J., Dec. 12, 1805 ; graduated from Washington College in 1832 ; Auburn Senior class on dism. from Western Theol. Sem. ; married to Miss JULIA A. OSTRANDER, about 1836 ; died of typhoid fever at Indian Town, Iowa, Sept. 21, 1859. His wife, 2 sons and 4 daughters survived him.

Ordained by Presby. of Cayuga, Autumn of 1836 ; miss. among the Tamul people in Southern Hindustan, 1836–44 ; resided 2 years in N. J., and 2 in Warren Co., Pa. ; Sugar Grove and Irvine, 6 years ; Bethesda, New Bethlehem and Middle Creek, 1854–7 ; Indian Town, Iowa, from 1858.

FRANKLIN PUTNAM, class of 1822–5, æt. 58.

Born in Marietta, O., July 22, 1801 ; united with the Church in 1823 ; graduated from Ohio Univ. in 1823 ; married to Miss ANNIE G. BRICE, of Athens, O., 1826 ; died of congestion of lungs at Thorntown, Ind., Oct. 11, 1859 ; his wife and 3 sons survived him.

Ordained and installed at Springfield, O., by Presby. of Dayton ; Springfield, 1827–8 ; Dayton, 1829–36; Circleville, 1837–42 ; 2nd Pres. Ch., Delaware, O., 1843 ; resident in Tiffin, supplying Churches from 1846 ; Greenville to 1855, and 1857 ; Republic, 1856 ; Thorntown, Ind., from 1858.

Published a volume on the Division of the Presbyterian Church in 1837.

1860.

OLIVER BRONSON, class of 1850–3, æt. 34.

Born in Utica, N. Y., Jan. 9, 1826 ; united with the 2d Pres. Ch. in Albany about 1842 ; graduated from Union College in 1845 ; practiced Law in Utica ; Middle and Senior years in Auburn ; married to Miss ANNIE LIGHTBODY, of Utica, 1853 ; died of hemorrhage from lungs, Jan 10, 1860. His wife and 1 child survived him.

Ordained pastor, Kinderhook, N. Y., by Classis of Rensselaer, May, 1854; Sherburne, N. Y., 1853-4; Kinderhook, 1854-7; invalid; Janesville, Wis., Pres. Ch., 1857-60.

ABRAHAM D. BRINKERHOFF, class of 1830-3, æt. 65.

Born in Fishkill, N. Y., June 5, 1795; studied at Columbia College; part of Middle year in Auburn; married to Miss MATILDA L. MOORE, of Champlain, N. Y.; died of a spinal affection at Champlain, Mar. 2, 1860. His wife survived him.

Ordained and installed at Chazy, N. Y., by Champlain Presby., Sept., 1833; Chazy; Plattsburgh; Keesville; Champlain, 1839-50; Chazy, 1852-7.

HENRY ROOT, class of 1831-4, æt. 47.

Born in Canaan, N. Y., July 17, 1813; studied at Williams College in class of 1833; married to Miss LAVINIA NORTON; died of bilious pneumonia at Feltz, Mich., Apr. 5, 1860. His wife and 1 child survived him.

Ordained pastor, by Washtenaw Presby., 1835; Ashtabula, O., 2d Ch., 1834-5; Dexter, Mich., 1835-6; Sylvan, Mich., 1836-9; Howell, 1839-42; Addison, 1843; Granville; Raisin and Dover; Bunker Hill; Portland, 1854-8; Feltz, 1858.

THOMAS W. ROBERTS, class of 1857-60, æt. 30.

Born in North Wales, (Montgomeryshire) Oct. 10, 1830; studied at Whitestown Sem.; died from railroad accident, at Cayuga, N. Y., Sept. 26, 1860.

Ordained, New York Mills, N. Y., by Assoc. of Welsh Congregationalists, Nov. 14, 1856; Cayuga, Pres. Ch., 1860.

TIMOTHY STOW, class of 1824-7, æt. 62.

Graduated from Hamilton College in 1823; Auh. Senior class from Bolton; licentiate of the Northern Associate Presbytery; died at Lawrence, Mich., Oct. 13, 1860.

Ordained, Greene Co., N. Y, by Presby., Nov., 1827; Elbridge, 1827-32; Montrose, Pa., 1834-8; resident in Montrose, and in New Bedford, Mass., from 1854.

ALFRED COBB, Trustee 1854-7, æt. 63.

Born in Stonington, Conn., 1797; united with the 2d Pres. Church in Phila., Pa., at about 20 years of age; studied at Stonington Acad.; married to Miss MARY BICKFORD, of Syracuse, N. Y., 1852; died of prostration at Canandaigua, N. Y., Dec. 17, 1860. No children; his wife went before him.

In wholesale grocery business, Philadelphia, to 1822; Valparaiso, S. America, mining and shipping, 1822-40; for a time U. S. consul; resident in Chittenango, N. Y., 1840-5, and in Syracuse, from 1845, in mercantile pursuits and manufacturing. Vice pres. of Auburn Trustees, 1855-7.

BENJAMIN BREARLEY STOCKTON, Trustee 1820–22, æt. 71.

> Born in Hackettstown, N. J., Jan. 31, 1790; graduated from Middlebury College in 1809; graduated at Andover Seminary; died of decay of vital powers at Williamsburg, L. I., Jan. 10, 1861.
>
> Ordained by Utica Presby., 1812; labored in Skaneateles; Palmyra; Pompey from 1829; Camillus; LeRoy, 1833–5; Montgomery from 1835; Brockport; Geneseo; Phelps; resident in Williamsburg from 1858.

WILLIAM HENRY SPENCER, class of 1842–5, æt. 47.

> Born in Madison, Conn., Oct. 13, 1813; came to Auburn from the Church in Mt. Morris; graduated from University of N. Y.; married to Miss ALMIRA HOPKINS, of Williamstown, Mass.; died of gangrene of the liver at Chicago, Feb. 17, 1861. He had 1 son and 2 daughters; his wife, son and 1 daughter survived him.
>
> Ordained pastor, Utica, N. Y., by Presby. of Utica, 1845; 1st Pres. Ch., Utica, 1844–50; 1st Pres. Ch., Milwaukee, Wis., 1850–4; Sec. of Ass., Com. of Pub., Philadelphia, 1855–6; pastor, Rock Island, Ill., 1857–8; Westminster Ch., Chicago, Ill., 1859–61. Trustee of Auburn, 1849–51.

WILLIAM H. BRADFORD, class of 1835–8, æt. 47.

> Born in Cooperstown, N. Y., Aug. 5, 1814; united with the Church in Homer, N. Y.; graduated from Hamilton College in 1833; studied Law 2 years; married to Miss SARAH COBB, of Chicopee Falls, Mass.; died of heart disease at Homer, N. Y., Apr. 1, 1861. One son survived him.
>
> Ordained pastor, Berkshire, N. Y., by Tioga Presby., 1838; Berkshire, 2 years; assistant editor, and at times sole editor of the New York *Evangelist*, for 17 years; wrote also for other periodicals, and edited school books published by Ivison & Phinney; resident at Homer, N. Y., from 1858.

SOLOMON STEVENS, class of 1821–4, æt. 66.

> Born in Cavendish, Vt., Sept. 5, 1795; united with the Cong. Ch. in Brandon, Vt., Nov. 1, 1818; graduated from Middlebury College in 1821; married to Miss BETSEY HICKOK, of Venice, N. Y., Mar. 7, 1825; died of heart disease at Cleveland, O., June 7, 1861. No children; his wife survived him.
>
> Ordained at East Groton by Cayuga Presby., July 8, 1828; Aurora; Danby, N. Y., 1829–32; Castle Creek; China, 1835; Orangeville, N. Y., 1839; Peru, O., 1840; Dover, 1843; Newton Falls, 1843 and 1860–1; Avon, 1851; Somerset, Mich., 1854–8.

FREDERICK H. BROWN, class of 1832–5, æt. 55.

> Born in Stockbridge, Mass., Nov. 1, 1806; united with the 1st Church in Auburn, Nov. 5, 1826; Auburn, 3 years and post graduate 1835–6; married to Miss SAMANTHA CHANDLER, of

Auburn ; died of paralysis at Sandusky, O., July 31, 1861. No children ; his wife survived him.

Ordained pastor, Ludlowville, N. Y., by Presby. of Cayuga, Aug. 30, 1836 ; Ludlowville ; Brownhelm, O., 6 years ; Medina, 7 years to 1852 ; chap. of Beth. Soc., Cleveland, 1853-4 ; Youngstown, 1854-7 ; agt. Beth. Soc., 1857-8.

CLEMENT LONG, D. D., LL. D., Professor, æt. 55.

Born in Hopkinton, N. H., Dec. 1, 1806 ; graduated from Dartmouth College in 1828 ; Andover Seminary ; D. D. from Dartmouth College in 1849 ; LL. D. from Western Reserve in 1860 ; died at Hanover, N. H., Oct. 14, 1861.

Ordained April 6, 1836 ; prof. of Philosophy, Western Reserve College, 1834-44 ; prof. of Theology, Western Reserve, 1844-52 ; prof. of Christ. Theol., Auburn, 1852-4 ; prof. of Int. Phil. and Pol. Econ., Dartmouth, 1854-61.

BENJAMIN COLEMAN SMITH, class of 1825-8, æt. 61.

Born in Windsor, Vt., May, 1800 ; mem. of 1st Pres. Church in Auburn ; studied privately ; married to Miss SUSAN J. AMMERMAN, of Auburn ; died of heart disease at Prattsburgh, N. Y., Oct. 17, 1861. He had 7 children ; his wife and 2 children survived him.

Ordained at Windsor, Vt., by Assoc., June 22, 1836 ; chaplain Auburn Prison 12 years ; agt. West. Ed. Soc. 2 years ; Pres. Ch., Aurelius, 1843 ; Prattsburgh, 1844-59.

1862.

CHARLES CHURCHILL, class of 1830-3, æt. 54.

Born in New Lebanon, N. Y., Sept. 2, 1808 ; united with the Church in New Lebanon, Feb. 4, 1827 ; graduated from Williams College in 1830 ; married to Miss ANN BOWMAN, Dec. 2, 1844 ; died of pneumonia at New Lebanon, March 21, 1862. He had 1 son and 1 daughter ; his wife and children survived him.

Never ordained ; preached, as licentiate of Columbia Presby., in New York and Mass.

CHARLES ORVILLE HILL, class of 1837-40, æt. 59.

Born in Sunderland, Vt., July 11, 1803 ; labored in preaching and teaching, was never settled in the ministry ; died Geneseo, N. Y., April 20, 1862.

JAMES FITCH COGGSWELL, class of 1822-5, æt. 73.

Born in Williamstown, Mass., 1789 ; united with the Cong. Ch. in West Bloomfield, N. Y., July 8, 1821 ; graduated from Williams College in 1808 ; 1 year in Auburn from Oct., 1822 ; never married ; died of consumption at Rising Sun, Ind., May, 1862.

Had charge of Academies in West Bloomfield, Penn Yan, Millville, Cherry Valley, Middleport and Ithaca, N. Y., and South Bend, Ind.

JOSIAH HOPKINS, D. D., Trustee 1831–46, æt. 76.

Born in Pittsford, Vt., Apr. 18, 1786 ; united with the Cong. Ch. in Pittsford, Jan. 13, 1803 ; A. M. in 1813, and D. D. in 1843, from Middlebury College ; married to Miss ORRIL DIKE, of Pittsford, Oct. 13, 1808 ; married to LOVINIA FENTON, of Rutland, Vt. ; died of asthma at the Water Cure, Geneva, N. Y., June 21, 1862. He had 1 daughter ; his wife survived him.
Ordained pastor, New Haven, Vt., June 14, 1809 ; New Haven, 1809–30 ; Auburn 1st Ch., 1830–46 ; afterward preached temporarily in various places ; Seneca Falls, 1851–5.
Published "The Christian Instructor," 1847.

RANSOM RICHARD KIRK, class of 1837–40, æt. 47.

Born in Shoreham, Vt., 1815 ; came to Auburn from the Church in Crown Point ; studied at Middlebury College ; married to Miss MARY DOXTATER, of Adams, N. Y. ; died suddenly, on Broadway, N. Y. City, Nov. 15, 1862. His wife survived him.
Ordained by Presby., 1840 ; Adams ; Camden to 1848 ; N. Y. Mills, 1849–57 ; Potsdam, 1857–60 ; resident in Adams from 1860.

ASA HIXON, class of 1825–8.

Born in Medway, Mass. ; united with the Church in Medway ; graduated from Brown Univ. in 1825 ; died at West Medway, Mass., Nov. 16, 1862.
Ordained colleague pastor, Cong. Ch., Oakham, Mass., Oct. 7, 1829 ; Oakham, 1829–31 ; Ira, N. Y., 1831–3 ; Locke, 1834 ; Medway, Mass., in poor health ; Franklin, 1857–8 ; West Medway.

1863.

RICHARD WOODRUFF, class of 1829–32, æt. 62.

Born Oct. 19, 1800 ; came to Auburn from W. Hartford, Conn. ; mem. of Church there ; graduated from Union College in 1829 ; Auburn, 1829–31 ; died at Richford, N. Y., Mar. 9, 1863.
Ordained colleague pastor, South Brookfield, Mass., Feb. 5, 1834 ; South Farms, Conn., 1839 ; Unionville, 1842–6 ; Danby, N. Y., 1855–6 ; Deposit, 1857 ; Richford, 1858–63.

WARREN ISHAM, class of 1824–7, æt. 53.

Born in Mass., 1800 ; graduated from Union College in 1821 ; catalogued in Aub. Mid. class, 1825–6 ; twice married ; died of bilious pneumonia at Marquette, Mich., May 18, 1863. His wife and 3 children survived him.

Ordained by Detroit Presby., 1839 ; preached but seldom, owing
to throat difficulty ; editor of *The Ohio Observer*, Hudson,
O. ; editor of a paper devoted to religion and anti-slavery, and
afterward of an agricultural paper, Detroit, Mich., to 1856 ;
resident Wyandotte, 1857 ; Marquette, editor, from 1859.
Published "The Mud Cabin ;" " Travels in the East."

ELKANAH WHITNEY, class of 1847–50, æt. 43.
　Born in Yonge, Dist. of Johnson, N. C., Feb. 1, 1820 ; united with
the Church at 20 years of age ; studied at Whitestown Sem. ;
entered Auburn Senior class ; married to Miss PHEBE C. STILES,
of Newark, N. J., Aug. 3, 1853 ; died, June 11, 1863, at Oxford,
Mich. He had 3 children, one of whom survived him.
　Ordained at Madrid, N. Y., April 15, 1851 ; 1 year each at
Batavia, Ill., Dundee and Crystal Lake, and Parishville, N. Y. ;
Paw Paw, Mich. ; New Baltimore ; in Kansas, 1859–61 ; Oak-
wood, Mich., from 1861.

TERTIUS REYNOLDS, class of 1826–9, æt. 63.
　Born in Warren, Conn., March 29, 1800 ; came to Auburn from
Church in Warren ; graduated from Amherst College in 1827 ;
Auburn, Mid., 1827–8 ; married to Miss ELIZA TALBOT, of
Athol, Mass., June 1, 1829 ; died of typhoid fever, at Pine
Island, Minn., June 25, 1863. He had 1 son and 3 daughters ;
his wife and daughters survived him.
　Parishville and Pierpont, N. Y., 1830–1 ; Constable, 1833 ; Keene,
1836–7 ; Fairfax and Fairfield, Vt., 1837–42 ; Fairfax, 1842–4,
and resident there till 1855 ; resident Pine Island, Minn.,
1855–63.

THOMAS SCOTT BRADLEY, class of 1848–51, æt. 38.
　Born in Lee, Mass., Apr. 15, 1825 ; graduated from Williams College in 1848 ; Aub. Sen. class from East Windsor The. Sem. ;
studied with Dr. Todd of Pittsfield, 1851 ; married to Miss
HARRIET L. REED, of Milan, O., Oct. 26, 1853 ; died of typhoid
fever at Philadelphia, June 28, 1863. His wife survived him.
　Ordained and installed at Wilton, Conn., (Cong.) July, 1853 ;
Lanesboro, Mass., 1851–2 ; Cornwall, Conn., 1852 ; Wilton,
1853–8 ; tea. Norwalk, Conn. ; past. New Lebanon, N. Y. ; Capt.
9th Co., N. Y. Sharpshooters, 1862–3.

HENRY VAN VLECK RANKIN, class of 1844–7, æt. 38.
　Born in N. J., Sept. 11, 1825 ; graduated from Princeton College
in 1843 ; teacher ; Auburn, 1844–5 ; Princeton Theol. Sem.,
1845–7 ; died of chronic diarrhea at Tung Chow, China, July 2,
1863. He had 2 sons and 2 daughters ; his wife and children
survived him.
　Ordained by Presby. of Elizabeth, July 18, 1848 ; First Pres. Ch.,
Rochester, 1848 ; miss. of Pres. Bd. in Ningpo, China, 1848–63.

JOHN WILLIAM HOLM, class of 1861-4, æt. 26.
> Born in St. Thomas, West Indies, 1837; united with the Dutch Ref. Ch. in St. Thomas, Mar. 27, 1853; studied two years at Ashmun Institute; died of typhoid fever in New York City, Sept. 10, 1863.

JONATHAN PARSONS HOVEY, D. D., class of 1833-6, æt. 53.
> Born in Weybridge, Vt., Oct. 10, 1810; came to Aub. from Gouverneur, N. Y.; studied at Indiana College; married to Miss CATHERINE M. WEED, of Auburn; died of inflammation of lungs in New York City, Dec. 16, 1863.
>
> Ordained pastor, Gaines, N. Y., by Presby. of Niagara, March, 1837; Gaines; Burdett; Richmond, Va.; Eleventh Pres. Ch., N. Y. City, 1850-63; chap. 71st Regt., N. Y. Vols., 1862.

1864.

THOMAS SYDENHAM WARD, class of 1835-8, æt. 52.
> Born in Bloomfield, N. J., Oct. 23, 1811; came to Aub. from Ch. in Bloomfield; graduated from Univ. of N. Y. City in 1835; Auburn, 1835-7; Union Sem., N. Y., 1837-8; died at Carbondale, Pa., Feb. 13, 1864.
>
> Ordained by Presby., 1839; p. Hanover, N. J., 1839-42; Sparta, 1844-6; resident Bloomfield, 1842-3 and 1847-50; Carbondale, Pa., 1851-64.

ORLO BARTHOLOMEW, class of 1832-5, æt. 63.
> Born in Goshen, Conn., Oct. 20, 1801; united with the Cong. Ch. in Goshen, 1822; graduated from Union College in 1832; married to Miss JULIA A. PECK, of Skaneateles, Nov. 15, 1836; died of kidney complaint at Augusta, May 7, 1864. He had 5 sons and 1 daughter; his wife, 4 sons and daughter survived him. His son Myron in 1873-6, Charles, in 1874-7.
>
> Ordained pastor, Augusta, N. Y., by Presbytery of Utica, Aug. 24, 1836; Henrietta, 6 mos.; Augusta till death, his burial occurring on the 28th anniversary of the beginning of his labors.

RUSSELL SALMON COOK, class of 1832-5, æt. 53.
> Born in New Marlborough, Mass., March 6, 1811; came to Aub. from Church in Syracuse; studied Law; Auburn Middle and Senior years, and post graduate 1835-56; married to Miss ANN MARIA MILLS, of Auburn, Nov. 1, 1837; married to HARRIET NEWELL RAND, of Pompey Hill, N. Y.; married to HARRIET ELLESWORTH, of Hartford, Ct.; married to Miss MALAN, of Geneva, Switzerland; died at Pleasant Valley, N. Y., Sept. 4, 1864. He had 2 sons and several daughters; his wife survived him.
>
> Ordained pastor, Lanesboro, Mass, Cong., Jan. 18, 1837; Lanesboro, 1836-9; sec'y Am. Tract Soc., 1839-56; sec'y of Am. Sab. Com., N. Y., from 1857.

CHAUNCY WALLACE CHERRY, class of 1839-42, æt. 52.
Born in New Haven, N. Y., Jan. 16, 1813; graduated from
Oneida Institute in 1838; married to Miss LOUISA MARIA
HOPKINS, of Auburn, July 23, 1842; died of congestive chills at
Helena, Arkansas, Oct. 15, 1864. He had 6 daughters; his
wife and 5 daughters survived him.
Ordained pastor at Canoga, N. Y., by Geneva Presby., 1842;
Canoga, 1842-50.

EMMONS HUGHITT, class of 1863-6, æt. 24.
Born in Genoa, N. Y., July 28, 1840; united with the 2nd Church
in Genoa, Dec. 10, 1860; graduated from Amherst College in
1863; dismissed to Union, N. Y., at opening of Mid. year;
died of small pox in New York, Oct. 28, 1864.

NATHAN ALLEN, class of 1847-50, æt. 45.
Born in Lansing, N. Y., Mar. 9, 1820; united with the Church in
1842; graduated from Hamilton College in 1848; Aub. Mid.
class, 1848-9; grad. 1850; died of typhoid fever, at Utica, N.
Y., Oct 29, 1864.
Ordained by Presby. of Angelica, 1850; Cong. Ch., Castile, N.
Y., 2 years; Cuba, Pres. Ch., 1853-9; Springville from 1859.

LEVI PARSONS, Trustee 1820-64, æt. 85.
Born in Northampton, Mass., August 20, 1779; united with the
Cong. Church in West Hampton, Mass., 1803; graduated from
Williams College in 1801; studied Theology with Dr. Alvan
Hyde, of Lee, Mass.; married to Miss ALMIRA RICE, of Mar-
cellus, N. Y., Oct. 9, 1809; died of cholera morbus at Marcel-
lus, Nov. 20, 1864. He had 4 sons and 4 daughters; 3 sons
and 3 daughters survived him.
Ordained pastor at Marcellus, N. Y., by Council, Sept. 16, 1807;
preached at Marcellus 32 years, and resided there till his death.
President of Trustees of Auburn, 1830-64.

DANIEL VAN VALKENBERG, class of 1824-7, æt. 60.
Born in Manheim, N. Y., Jan. 8, 1805; united with the 1st Pres.
Church in Auburn, Oct. 21, 1824; graduated from Union College in 1824; married to Miss MARY WEBER, of Richfield;
married to Miss JULIA F. TRACY, of Norwich, Conn.; died of
inflammation of bowels at Springfield, N. Y., Nov. 24, 1864.
His wife and 6 children survived him.
Ordained at Vernon Centre, N. Y., by Presby. of Oneida, July
13, 1831; Richfield Springs, 1830-45; Mexico; Taberg, 1848-
52; Exeter, 1852-7; Springfield from 1858; one account says
Springfield 36 years in all.

CHARLES YALE, class of 1821-4, æt. 68.
Born in Lenox, Mass., Aug. 21, 1796; at Auburn, 1822, 6 mos.;
married to SALLY JONES, of Johnstown, N. Y., May 25, 1820;
died of stoppage of lower orifice of stomach, at Ripon, Wis.,
Nov. 28, 1864. He had 2 sons and 2 daughters; 1 son and 2
daughters survived him.

Ordained pastor, Pultney, N. Y., by Presby. ; Pultney, 1825 ; Centreville, Ala., 1843 ; resident Gloversville, N. Y., 1847, Brownsville, 1850, and Ripon, Wis., 1852.

FREDERICK WILLIAM GRAVES, class of 1829–32, æt. 59.

Born in Leverett, Mass , Mar. 9, 1806; united with the Church in his 14th year; graduated from Amherst College in 1825 ; taught ; married to Miss SUSAN ELIZABETH HAYT, of Corning, N. Y., Apr. 25, 1834; died of consumption at Canandaigua, Dec. 8, 1864. He had 2 sons and 2 daughters; his wife and children survived him.

Ordained pastor, Alton, Ill., by Presby., Nov. 18, 1835 ; First Free Ch., Lockport, N. Y.; Alton, Ill., 1835–8; Edwardsville, 1838–9 ; in N. Y. City and State, supplying Chs., and laboring for Temperance and in revivals.

GEORGE W. WHITNEY, class of 1861–4.

United with the Pres. Church in Owego ; was a lawyer before entering the Seminary; left Auburn, March 4, 1862 ; not married ; died at Binghamton, N. Y., 1864.

Ordained at Center Lisle, N. Y., by Council, Mar. 30, 1863.

1865.

AMBROSE EGGLESTON, class of 1821–4, æt. 72.

Born in Northeast, N. Y., May 16, 1793 ; came to Auburn from Ch. in Windsor, N. Y.; graduated from Yale College in 1813 ; taught; studied Law 1815–18 ; practiced at Unadilla, N. Y.; Auburn, 1821–2; married to Miss ELIZABETH B. HARPER, of Windsor, Aug. 18, 1819; died of paralysis at Coldwater, Mich., Jan. 23, 1865. His wife and one or more sons survived him.

Ordained pastor, Coventry, N. Y., by Presby. of Chenango, 1825 ; Palmyra, 1 year ; Coventry, 1824–30 ; resident Windsor, 1831–4 ; Cong. Ch., Egremont, Mass., 2 years ; Fallsburg, N. Y., Ref. Ch., 1836–7 ; resident Windsor, 1837–42 ; Fulton, and Ref. Ch., Breakabin, 1843–5 ; since 1846, resident in Albany, Windsor, Deposit, Binghamton, N. Y., Great Bend, Pa., and Coldwater, Mich.

JAMES BENJAMIN TOWNSEND, class of 1835–8, æt. 54.

Born in Hebron, N. Y., Aug. 8, 1810 ; came to Auburn from Church in Hebron ; graduated from Union College in 1835 ; Auburn, 1835–7 ; Union, 1837–8 ; married to Miss CORDELIA DUNNING, of Fairfield, N. Y., Sept. 6, 1839 ; died of consumption, at Bloomington, Ill., Jan. 27, 1865. His wife survived him ; no children.

Ordained by Presby. of Buffalo, 1840 ; Knoxville, Tenn., in charge of a Ladies' Seminary ; Goochland Co., Va., 1842–3 ; Paris and

Florida, Mo., 1843-4 ; Free Ch., St. Louis, 1844-50 ; 3rd Ch., Cincinnati, O., 1850-2 ; in business in St. Louis, Mo., 5 years ; farming near Bloomington, Ill.

COMFORT ISRAEL SLACK, class of 1860-3, æt. 30.
Born in Mexico, N. Y., Aug. 12, 1835 ; graduated from Hamilton College in 1860 ; married to Miss S. RANSOM ; died of scarlet fever in Newton, Ia., Feb. 24, 1865. His wife survived him.
Ordained pastor of Westminster Ch., Newton, Ia., by Presby. of Des Moines, 1863.

FREDERICK AUGUSTUS PARMENTER, class of 1861-4, æt. 24.
Born in Owego, N. Y., June 6, 1841 ; united with the Cong. Church in Owego, 1863 ; studied privately ; not married ; died by accident on R. R., at Elizabeth, N. J., April 7, 1865.
Ordained and installed at Elizabeth, by Council, June 8, 1864, remaining there till his death.
Published many fugitive pieces and one sermon.

SIMEON SARTWELL GOSS, class of 1846-9, æt. 42.
Born in Claremont, N. H., June 23, 1823 ; united with the Church at 9 years old ; graduated from Union College in 1846 ; married to Miss MARY CATHERINE WEAVER, of Penfield, N. Y., July 23, 1849 ; died by overturning of a coach, at Rochester, N. Y., May 25, 1865. He had 2 sons and 1 daughter, who with his wife, survived him. His son Charles Frederic grad. in class of 1873-6.
Ordained pastor, Meridian, N. Y., by Presby. of Cayuga, 1849 ; Meridian, 1849-62 ; agt. of Aub. Sem., 1862 ; chaplain 75th Reg. N. Y. Vols., 1862-3.

MOODY HARRINGTON, class of 1830-3, æt. 68.
Came to Auburn from Cornish, N. H. ; mem. of Church in Amherst Col. ; graduated from Amherst College in 1831 ; middle and Senior years in Auburn ; married to Miss JULIA MACK, of Amherst, Dec. 16, 1835 ; died at Albany, N. Y., Aug. 5, 1865.
Camillus, N. Y., to 1840 ; Morrisville, 1840 ; Preble, 1849-51 ; Lafayette, 1851 ; Morrisville, 1853-4 ; Middlefield, Mass., 1855 -9 ; Agawan, 1860 ; Montgomery, 1861 and 1863 ; W. Springfield, 1862 and 1864-5.

HOMER BARTLETT MORGAN, class of 1848-51, æt. 38.
Born in Watertown, N. Y., May 31, 1827 ; graduated from Hamilton College in 1847 ; Union, N. Y., 1847-8 ; tea., 1848-9 ; Auburn, 1849-51 ; married to Miss HARRIET GERTRUDE BUTTRICK, of Clinton, Sept., 1851 ; married to Mrs. SUSAN HUNTINGTON (KELLOGG) SUTPHEN, of Marsovan, Nov. 9, 1853 ; died of typhoid fever at Smyrna, Aug. 25, 1865. He had 2 sons and 4 daughters ; his wife, 2 sons and 1 daughter survived him.

Ordained by Presby. of Watertown, July 9, 1851 ; miss. of A. B. C. F. M., Salonica, 1852–3 ; Smyrna, 1853–6 ; Antioch, Syria, from 1856.

MILTON KIMBALL, class of 1826–9, æt. 66.

Born in Boscawen, N. H., Feb. 20, 1799 ; united with the Church at the age of 20 ; graduated from Amherst College in 1826 ; one year at Andover, Middle and Senior years at Auburn ; married to Miss LOUISA WILCOX, of Ogden, July 23, 1829 ; died at Augusta, Ill., Oct. 10, 1865.

Ordained at Auburn, by Presby., July 21, 1829 ; Chester, O., 1829–33 ; agt for A. B. C. F. M. in Ill. and Mo., 1834–6 ; Pres. Ch., Augusta, Ill., 1836–46 ; then resident in Augusta.

ALFRED WRIGHT, class of 1827–30, æt. 63.

Born in Chicopee, Mass., March 17, 1803 ; probably united with the Cong. Church in Springfield ; graduated from Amherst College in 1827 ; married to Miss LOUISA CAROLINE BARBOUR, of Auburn, 1830 ; died of congestion of the lungs at Durango, Iowa, Nov. 18, 1865. He had 2 sons and 2 daughters ; his wife, 1 son and 1 daughter survived him.

Ordained, Henrietta, N. Y., by Genesee Consoc., June 2, 1830 ; home miss. in Missouri, in Belmont, Mount Prairie, Pleasant Hill, Paris, Florida, 1830–46 ; Anamosa, Iowa, 1846–53 ; Quasqueton, 1853–5 ; resident there, supplying Churches, 1855–9 ; Green Mountain, 1859–60 ; Durango and Cottage Hill, 1863–5.

DAVID AVERY ABBEY, class of 1838–41, æt. 53.

Born in Olive, N. Y., (Shokan P. O.) Apr. 6, 1813 ; united with the Ref. Church in Shokan about 1830 ; graduated from Yale College in 1838 ; married to Miss BLANDINA M. BROADHEAD, Shokan, 1842 ; died of typhoid fever at Apalachin, N. Y., Dec. 6, 1865. His wife and 1 daughter survived him.

Ordained pastor, St. Catherines, Can. ; St. Catherines ; Lundy's Lane ; Orange, N. Y. ; Mead's Creek to 1852 ; Rondout, 1853–4 ; West Dresden, 1854–7 ; New Milford, Pa., 1857–62 ; Apalachin from 1862.

SIMEON SHURTLEFF, M. D., class of 1832–5, æt. 58.

Born in Montgomery, Mass., July 9, 1808 ; united with the Cong. Church in Blandford, March 5, 1826 ; graduated from Amherst College in 1832 ; Auburn, 1832–3 ; M. D. from Berkshire Med. Col. in 1835 ; married to Miss MARY ANN PHELPS, of Simsbury, Conn., Jan. 12, 1837 ; died of typhoid pneumonia at Simsbury, Dec. 23, 1865. No children ; his wife survived him.

Physician at Simsbury, 1835–41 ; at Westfield, Mass., 1841–65. Made special studies and collections in Conchology, and in New Eng. Nat. History.

1866.

SAMUEL LEE, class of 1832-5, æt. 60.

Born in Jericho, Vt., July 20, 1805 ; united with the Church at 19 years old ; graduated from Vermont Univ. in 1831 ; Auburn, 1832-3 ; married to Miss SUSAN HYDE ; died of consumption at Hudson, O., Jan. 28, 1866. His wife and 5 children survived him.

Ordained by Oneida Assoc., Sept. 23, 1834 ; Cazenovia, N. Y., 1 year ; Medina, O. ; Claridon ; Pres. Chs., Mantua and Streetsborough ; Mantua to 1855, and resident there, 1856-8 ; resident Hudson, 1859-62, and Mantua Centre from 1863.

ISAAC CRABB, class of 1825-8, æt. 69.

Came to Auburn from Lansingburgh ; mem. of Church in Ballston ; graduated from Union College in 1826 ; married to Mrs. ELIZABETH (NELSON) CHOATE, of Auburn, about 1834 ; died at Madison, Mich., Mar. 29, 1866. No children ; his wife survived him.

Ordained pastor Groveland, N. Y., by Presby. of Ontario, Mar. 10, 1831 ; Groveland, 1831-2 ; Phelps, 1836 ; Chapinville, 1837 ; Mecklenburgh, 1839-43 ; Dover, Mich., 1846 ; Madison, 19 years.

SAMUEL LAWRENCE TUTTLE, class of 1837-40, æt. 51.

Born in Bloomfield, N. J., Aug. 25, 1815 ; united with the Pres. Church, Bloomfield, 1830 ; graduated from Princeton College in 1836 ; married to Miss AMELIA CAMP, of Newark, N. J., June 8, 1841 ; married to Miss MARGARETTA THOMPSON, of Madison, N. J., Jan. 15, 1861 ; died of inflammatory rheumatism, at Madison, April 16, 1866. He had 3 sons ; 2 sons survived him.

Ordained pastor, Caldwell, N. J., by Newark Presby., Mar. 9, 1841 ; Caldwell, 1840-9 ; Am. Bib. Soc., 1849-54 ; Madison Ch., N. J., 1854-62 ; Am. Bib. Soc., 1862-6.

Published "Hist. of the Pres. Church, Madison, N. J.," 1855 ; "Madison, N. J., in the Revolution ;" and important documents on Bible cause.

MILES POWELL SQUIER, D. D., Trustee 1838-45, æt. 74.

Born in Cornwall, Vt., May 4, 1792 ; graduated from Middlebury College in 1811 ; Andover Sem., 1811-14 ; D. D. from Middlebury College in 1852 ; married to Miss CATHERINE SEYMOUR, of Rome, N. Y., Feb. 22, 1820 ; resident in Geneva from 1826 ; died of exhaustion at Geneva, June 22, 1866. His wife survived him.

Ordained pastor, Buffalo, N. Y., by Presby. of Geneva, May 3, 1816 ; Vergennes, Vt., 1814-15 ; miss., Western, N. Y., 1815-16 ; Buffalo 8 years ; financial ag't of Auburn Sem., 1 year ;

Geneva, ag't A. H. M. S., 1826-33; founded the Geneva Lyceum, 1831; managed Lyceum and supplied various Churches,
1833-45; working for Beloit College, Wis., 1845-9; prof. of Int.
and Mor. Phil., Beloit, 1849-63, and emeritus prof. till his death.
Published "The Problem Solved," 1855; "Reason and the Bible,"
1860; Tracts of Am. Tr. Soc., Nos. 446, 464, 481, 483; and
posthumously, "Autobiography and Miscellaneous Writings,"
1867; "The Being of God," 1868.

ELI GRAVES, class of 1834-7, æt. 63.
> Born in Rupert, Vt., Feb. 18, 1803; came to Aub. from Church
> in Fairhaven, Vt.; studied privately; married to Miss NAOMI
> WHEDON, of Hebron, N. Y., 1829; died of typhoid fever at
> Quitman, Ga., July 16, 1866. His wife, 1 son and 1 daughter
> survived him.
> Ordained by Council, Aug. 27, 1837; Boston, (Bethany Ch.) Ga.,
> and many other Churches in Georgia and Florida.

HARVEY CHAPIN, class of 1834-7, æt. 68.
> Born in N. Y., 1798; came to Aub. from Warsaw, and Church in
> W. Res. Col.; studied at Western Reserve College; Auburn,
> 1835-7; died in burning house at Tipton, Mo., July 27, 1866.
> Ordained, Perry Village, by Presby., Oct, 1839; Owatonna, Minn.,
> 1855-65; Tipton, Mo., from 1865.

JOHN McDONALD, class of 1824-7, æt. 70.
> Born in Brooke Co., Va., (now W. Va.) July 25, 1794; studied at
> Ohio Univ.; Auburn, 9 mos., entering June 13, 1825; married
> to Miss NANCY N. MEANS; died of congestion of bowels at
> Charlestown, Ill., Aug. 15, 1866. His wife and 9 children sur-
> vived him.
> Ordained pastor, Burlington, O., by Athens Presby., 1827; Bur-
> lington, O., till 1828; Bethesda Ch., Ky., 1828; Shippingsport,
> Ill., 1830; Union Grove, Ill., 1831-2; Manchester, O., 1834;
> Pleasant Prairie and Charlestown, Ill., from 1836.
> NOTE.—The Aub. Catalogues star this name from 1836. The
> identity is doubtful.

JOHN TOMPKINS, class of 1838-41, æt. 56.
> Born in Vernon, N. Y., April 30, 1810; united with the Pres. Ch.
> in Vernon, 1828; graduated from Hamilton College in 1838;
> married to CORNELIA KILBOURNE, of Marshall, N. Y., Sept. 29,
> 1841; died of neuralgia of the stomach at Marcellus, N. Y.,
> Aug. 15, 1866. He had 3 sons and 1 daughter, who, with his
> wife, survived him.
> Ordained pastor, Marcellus, N. Y., by Presby. of Cayuga, Feb. 22,
> 1842, where he remained till death.

OREN JOHNSON, class of 1829-32, æt. 66.
> Born in Coleraine, Mass., Feb. 22, 1801; united with the Cong.
> Church there, Sept. 28, 1828; graduated from Williams College

in 1829; married to Miss SARAH F. BROWN, of Newark, N. J., Jan. 3, 1855; died of internal tumor at Beaver Dam, Wis., Sept. 20, 1866. No children; his wife survived him.

Ordained by Bath Presby., Sept. 17, 1833; Woodhull, Jasper, Kennedyville, Avoca, N. Y., and Elkland, Pa., 11 years; home miss., Beaver Dam, 1844, and resident there till his death.

ROBERT RANSOM KELLOGG, class of 1835–8, æt. 53.

Born in Hudson, N. Y., May 18, 1813; united with the Cedar St. Pres. Church in N. Y., 1828; graduated from Univ. of N. Y. City in 1835; Auburn, 1835–7; Union Sem., N. Y., 1837–8; married to Miss MARY ELIZABETH MORSE; died of congestion of brain at Milford, Pa., Sept. 25, 1866. His wife and 3 children survived him.

Ordained pastor, Dover, N. J., by Newark Presby., Dec. 5, 1838; Dover, 1838–9; Brooklyn, N. Y., 4th Ch., 1839–40; Cong. Ch., Romeo, Mich., 8 years; 2nd Pres. Ch., Detroit, 8 years; dist. sec. of Am. and For. Chr. Un., 2 years, LeRoy, N. Y., past. and chan. of Ingham Univ., 2 years; Lima, 2 years; Milford, Pa., from 1861.

ANTHONY DEY AXTELL, class of 1856–9, æt. 32.

Born in Auburn, N. Y., March 5, 1834; united with the 1st Ch. in Geneva, November 30, 1860; graduated from Williams College in 1854; married to Miss ALMENA BRADLEY, of Olean, N. Y., 1862; died of consumption at Olean, Oct. 17, 1866. No children; his wife survived him.

Ordained by Presby. of Troy, Feb., 1866; Olean, N. Y.; Olivet Ch., Lansingburgh, 1865.

SAMUEL DUNTON, class of 1826–9, æt. 69.

Born in Cambridge, N. Y., Mar. 23, 1798; came to Aub. from Church in Amherst College; graduated from Amherst College in 1826; married to Miss SARAH MARIA CARPENTER; died of consumption, Oct. 29, 1866. His wife, 1 son and 1 daughter survived him.

Ordained Winfield, N. Y., by Council, Sept. 16, 1830; Norwalk and Peru, O., 1830–1; Florence, 1832; Fitchville, 1832–5; Eden from 1836; Huron from 1843; Malta, N. Y., 1845–8; resident Saratoga Springs from 1850.

WILLIAM AUGUSTUS WOLCOTT, class of 1859–62, æt. 35.

Born in Aurora, Erie Co., N. Y., Dec. 8, 1831; came to Auburn from Church in Griffin's Mills; graduated from Hamilton College in 1859; married to Miss AMANDA S. HOTCHKIN, Aug. 20, 1862; died of consumption at Pultney, N. Y., Nov. 29, 1866. He had 1 son; his wife and son survived him.

Ordained pastor, Campbelltown, N. Y., by Chemung Presby., 1863; Campbelltown, 1862–3, when his health failed.

WILLIAM BEARDSLEY, class of 1823–6, æt. 69.

Born in New Fairfield, Conn., Dec. 11, 1797; united with the Ch. in ampton Village, N. Y., 1816; graduated from Hamilton

College in 1823; Auburn, 1 year and 6 mos., 1823-4 and 1828-9; married to Miss BETHIAH VAN VALKENBURGH, of Auburn, Oct. 19, 1825; died of inflammation of bowels, at Wheaton, Ill., Dec. 13, 1866. He had 1 son and 2 daughters; his wife, 1 son and 1 daughter survived him.

Ordained at Hampton Village, N. Y., Sept. 9, 1829, by Oneida Assoc.; Evans and Eden, 1829-31; Jefferson, O., 1831; Andover, 1831-3; Freedom, 1833-4; Atwater, 1833-7; West Bloomfield, N. Y., 1838; tea. Mission Inst., Quincy, Ill., 1839-47; tea. Griggsville, 1 year; Bristol, 1848-52; Victoria, 1852-7; Farm Ridge, 1857-9; prof. Wheaton College, 1859-66.

1867.

FREDERICK STARR, class of 1846-9, æt. 41.

Born in Rochester, N. Y., Jan. 23, 1826; united with the 1st Pres. Church in Rochester, 1836; graduated from Yale College in 1846; married to Miss HELEN S. MILLS, of Auburn, July 23, 1850; died of typhoid fever, at St. Louis, Mo., Jan. 8, 1867. He had 2 sons and 5 daughters; his wife, 1 son and 3 daughters survived him.

Ordained pastor, Weston, Mo., by Lexington Presby., 1850; Weston, Mo., 1850-5; sec. Wes. Ed. Soc., and agt. Aub. Sem., 1855-61; Pres. Ch., Penn Yan., 1861-4; St. Louis, Mo., 1864-7.

EZRA BENEDICT FANCHER, class of 1835-8, æt. 57.

Born in Patterson, N. Y., Nov. 9, 1810; united with the Pres. Ch. in Richfield Springs, N. Y., 1830; graduated from Union College in 1835; at Auburn, 1835-6 and 1837-9; married to Miss LUCETTA McGRAW, of McGrawville, N. Y., 1842; died of inflammation of bowels, at McGrawville, Jan. 27, 1867. He had 4 sons and 3 daughters; his wife, 4 sons and 2 daughters survived him.

Ordained at McGrawville, by Cortland Presby., July, 1841; labored there 27 years, until his death.

HARPER BOIES, class of 1826-9, æt. 70.

Born in Blandford, Mass., April 21, 1797; came to Aub. from Ch. there; graduated from Williams College in 1826; Auburn Jun. and Mid. years; married to Miss LETITIA SHEPARD, of Blandford, June 8, 1820; married to Miss MARGARET HOTCHKISS, of Harpersfield, June 26, 1850; died of inflammation of the lungs, at Harpersfield, Mar. 7, 1867. He had 3 sons and 1 daughter; his wife survived him.

Ordained pastor, Harpersfield, N. Y., by Presby., July 28, 1830; Tolland, Mass., 1829-30; Harpersfield, 1830-5; Dalton., 1835-41; tea. Granville; Harpersfield, 1850-7, and resident there till death.

ARTHUR BURTIS, D. D., class of 1830–3, æt. 59.

Born in New York City, Oct. 25, 1807 ; united with the Rutgers St. Pres. Ch in N. Y., June, 1829; grad. from Union College in 1827 ; 2 years in Princeton, and Senior year in Auburn ; D. D. from Union College in 1850; married to Miss GRACE E. PHILLIPS MORSE, of Cherry Valley, 1833 ; died of inflammation of bowels at Oxford, O., Mar. 23, 1867. His wife, 3 sons and 3 daughters survived him.

Ordained pastor, Fort Plain, N. Y., by Montgomery Classis, 1835 ; Fort Plain ; Little Falls, Pres. Ch.; Cherry Valley, agt. of Am. Tr. Soc.; Binghamton, 1 year; Oxford, 7 years; Vernon, 1 year; Buffalo, 1st Ch , 1847 ; South Pres. Ch., Buffalo, 3 years, and Tabernacle Ch., 4 years, and 2 years agt. of Am. and For. Christ. Un.; preparing young men for College ; prof. elect of Greek, Miami Univ , 1866–7.

CHARLES DANFORTH, class of 1826–9, æt. 67.

Born in Rupert, Vt., Aug. 23, 1800 ; united with the Pres. Church ; graduated from Williams College in 1826; married to Miss COR-NELIA FLOWERS SADD, of Austinburg, O., Apr., 1830; died of typhoid fever at Oberlin, O., Apr. 29, 1867. He had 2 sons and 3 daughters ; his wife, and 1 daughter survived him.

Ordained at Auburn by Presby., July 21, 1829 ; home miss., Ind. and O. ; Mantua, 1832–3 ; Brookfield and Hubbard, 1833–4 ; Orwell, 1834–42 ; Brush Creek and Sinking Spring, 1843–50 ; Guilford, 1850–3 ; resident Oberlin, from 1853.

ALBERT PAYSON WORTHINGTON, class of 1864–7, æt. 25.

Born in Milford, Mich., July 5, 1842 ; graduated from Hamilton College in 1864 ; died at West Durham, N. Y., May 6, 1867. His wife survived him.

HENRY MILLS, D. D., Professor of Biblical Criticism, æt. 81.

Born in Morristown, N. J., March 12, 1786 ; united with the Pres. Church in Morristown ; graduated from Princeton College in 1802 ; teaching for several years ; tutor in Princeton, 1810–11; studied Theology with Dr. Jas. Richards, at Morristown; D. D. from Amherst College, 1833; married to Miss MARIA MOORE BARKINS, April 30, 1816; died of nervous prostration at Auburn, June 10, 1867. He had 2 sons and 5 daughters; his wife and 3 daughters survived him.

Ordained pastor, Woodbridge, N. J., by Presby. of New Jersey, 1816; Woodbridge, 1816–21 ; professor in Auburn, 1821–54, and emeritus professor till his death.

Published " Hymns from the German," 1845 ; " Hymns of Hildebert ;" and many articles.

WILLIAM B. HENDRYX, class of 1864–7, æt. 29.

Born in Ovid, N. Y., May 28, 1838 ; united with the Pres. Church in Tecumseh, Mich, July, 1858; graduated from Michigan University in 1864 ; married to Miss DELIA ELIZA CONKLING, of Tecumseh, Aug. 14, 1862 ; died of typhoid fever at Tecumseh, June 21, 1867. He had 1 daughter ; his wife and daughter survived him.

Not ordained ; preached at Reedsburg, Wis.

HENRY E. PECK, class of 1842–5, æt. 46.

Born in Rochester, N. Y., 1821 ; graduated from Bowdoin College in 1841 ; at Lane, 1842–3 ; at Oberlin, 1843 ; Auburn Mid. Class from Jan., 1844 ; died in Hayti, July 9, 1867.

The Aub. Gen. Catalogues place him at Rochester, N. Y., 1850, and prof., Oberlin, O., 1861 ; the Year Books place him in Ohio, 1854, Wellington, 1857 ; Oberlin, 1858–60 and 1862–7 ; Wakeman, 1861.

WILLIAM NORRIS EDWARDS, class of 1840–3, æt. 55.

Born in Richmond, July 4, 1812 ; came to Auburn from Church in Williams College ; grad. from Williams College in 1838 ; Auburn, 1840–2 ; married to Miss MARY KELLEY, of Troy, O., July 10, 1856 ; died suddenly at Troy, Aug. 3, 1867. No children ; his wife survived him.

Teacher Nunda, N. Y., 1838–40 ; invalid, 1843–5 ; tea. of Acad., Lebanon, O., 1845–7 ; tea. Vincennes, Ind. ; tea. Dayton, O., 4 years ; supt. of Union Sch., Troy, O., 1852–67.

ALEXANDER McGLASHAN, class of 1840–3, æt. 61.

Born in Queenstown, Canada, Feb. 23, 1812 ; united with the Church at about 20 years old ; studied at Geneva Lyceum and Hobart College ; married to Miss ELLEN BUELL, of East Bloomfield, N. Y., Dec. 16, 1857 ; died of chronic diarrhea at St. Catherines, Can., Sept. 9, 1867. His wife and 2 sons survived him.

Ordained by Presby. of Cayuga, 1843 ; service of Am. Tract Soc., and afterward, of Am. Sea. Fr. Soc., Mobile, Ala., 1843–59 ; past. Pelham, Can., 1859–63 ; New York City, 1863–6 ; established " Church of the Sea and Land ;" Bethel work, St. Catherines, 1866–7.

VINAL SMITH, class of 1829–32, æt. 66.

Came to Auburn from Otisco ; graduated from Union College in 1829 ; Auburn Middle Class, June, 1831, from Union Theological Seminary, Va. ; married to Miss EMILY F. BASSETT ; died of bowel disease, at Shortsville, N. Y., Sept. 28, 1867. He had 1 daughter ; his wife and daughter survived him.

Ordained, Champion, by Black River Assoc., Sept. 4, 1832 ; most of his life a teacher in Liberty, Va.

JUDSON ASPINWALL, class of 1854–7, æt. 34.

Born in Genoa, N. Y., Feb. 24, 1823 ; united with the Pres. Ch. in Elmira, N. Y. ; graduated from Williams College in 1854 ; Aub. Mid. and Sen., 1855–7 ; married to Miss HARRIET ANN McWILLIAMS, of Elmira, June 29, 1857 ; died Oct. 10, 1867, of

intermittent bilious fever, at Baxter Springs, Kan. He had 3
sons and 2 daughters, all of whom, with his wife, survived him.
Ordained and installed at Keokuk, Iowa, by Presby., Dec. 30,
1858 ; Jordan, N. Y., 1857-8 ; Keokuk, 1858-9 ; Warsaw, Ill.,
1859-61 ; Olathe, Prairie City and Black Jack, Kan., 1861-4.

ALFRED WHITE, class of 1827-30, æt. 68.
Born in Hebron, Conn., Dec. 13, 1799 ; united with the Church in
Williamstown, Mass., July 20, 1812; graduated from Williams Col.
in 1827 ; married to Miss PAMELIA JUDD, of Williamstown, Aut.
of 1830; married to Miss R. C. BIRGE, Dec., 1840 ; died of
tumor on neck at South Williamstown, Oct. 19, 1867. He had
1 son and 4 daughters; the son, at least, survived him.
Ordained by Genesee Consoc., 1832 ; Mexicoville, N. Y.; Candor ;
Fairport ; Constantia ; Frankfort ; Granby, Conn., 1847-8 ; Onondaga Hill, N. Y., 1850 ; Jamesville, 1851-2 ; Otsego ; Cooperstown ; Hartland, Conn , 1859-60 ; U. S. Sanitary Commission,
1865 ; Westford, Conn., 1865-7 ; resided at South Williamstown,
Mass.

DAVID FAIRMAN JUDSON, class of 1848-51, æt. 45.
Born in Prattsburgh, N. Y., Feb. 1, 1823 ; united with the Church
there, Jan. 7, 1838 ; studied at Prattsburgh Acad. ; married to
Miss MARY BEACH LAWRENCE, of Prattsburgh, 1844 ; died of
pneumonia at Seneca, Kan., Nov. 21, 1867. He had 2 sons and
4 daughters, all of whom, with his wife, survived him.
Ordained at Naples, N. Y., by Presby. of Bath, 1852 ; Gaines, N.
Y., 1851-3 ; Smyrna, 1853-7 ; Addison, 1857-62 and 1865-7 ;
resident Prattsburgh, 1862-5.

NICOLL HAVENS DERING, M. D., Trustee 1857-63, æt 74.
Born in Shelter Island, Jan. 1, 1794 ; united with the Brick Ch.
in New York ; graduated from Yale College in 1813; M. D.
from the College of Physicians and Surgeons, N. Y., in 1817 ;
married to Miss FRANCES HUNTINGTON, of Rome, June 6, 1826;
married to Miss SARAH HUGGINS STRONG, of New York, Oct.
1, 1844 ; died of nervous prostration at Utica, N. Y., Dec. 19,
1867. He had 1 son and 6 daughters ; his wife, son and 4
daughters survived him.
Practiced Medicine in New York City, 1817-42 ; Rome, 1842-7;
Utica from 1847.

SAMUEL J. McCULLOUGH, class of 1835-8, æt. 58.
Born in Dickinson, Pa., 1809 ; came to Aub. from Church in
Ithaca, N. Y.; graduated from Union College in 1835 ; died at
Tioga, Pa., Dec. 20, 1867.
Ordained pastor, Honeoye Falls, by Presby., Oct. 30, 1839 ;
Honeoye Falls ; Lawrenceville ; Farmington, Richmond, Sulli-
van, 1849-51 ; Tioga, Pa., from 1851.

1868.

EBENEZER C. BEACH, class of 1826-9, æt. 66.
Born in Kingsboro, N. Y.; united with the Church there; graduated from Middlebury College in 1826; died at Lysander, N. Y., April 26, 1868.
Ordained by Presby. of Albany, 1831; Baldwinsville, N. Y., 1829–30; Lysander, 1830–58, and resident there till death.

IRA ODELL DELONG, class of 1852–5, æt. 44.
Born in Pleasant Valley, N. Y., Sept. 2, 1824; united with the Pres. Church in Palmyra; Lane Sem., Junior year; Auburn, 1853–4; Union Sem., N. Y., 1854–5, and post grad. 1858–9; married to Miss SUSAN ELIZABETH UPHAM, of Brunswick, Me., June 24, 1863; died in Macedon, N. Y., of consumption, May 30, 1868. He had one daughter; his wife survived him.
Ordained by Presby. of Ontario, June 23, 1863; Keokuk, Iowa, 1 year; Hornellsville, N. Y., 1859–61; Nunda, 1861–3; Macedon, 1863–4; Honeoye Falls, 1864–8.

HON. HIRAM FOOTE MATHER, Trustee 1829–45, æt. 72.
Born in Colchester, Conn., Feb. 13, 1796; united with the Church in Yale College, July 4, 1813; graduated from Yale College in 1813; studied Theology two years at Andover; studied Law with Wm. Brown, Esq., of Auburn; married to Miss SALLY ANN HYDE, of Auburn, April 8, 1821; married to Miss MARY PARSONS COLE, of Auburn, Nov. 26, 1831; married to Mrs. ANNA TALLMAN (SMITH) NORTON, of Chicago, Oct. 15, 1857; died of pneumonia at Chicago, Ill., July 11, 1868. He had 5 sons and 5 daughters; his wife, 4 sons, and 2 daughters survived him.
Practiced Law in Elbridge till 1844; State Senator, 1828–32; practiced Law in Niles, Mich., 1844–53, and was Circuit Court Commissioner; practiced Law and was Master in Chancery in Chicago, from 1853.

JEREMIAH WOODRUFF, class of 1828–31, æt. 68.
Born in Litchfield, Conn., 1800; Auburn 6 months from Dec., 1829, from Lisle, N. Y.; died of dropsy, at Lansing, Iowa, July 25, 1868. His wife and 1 child preceded him; he left children.
Ordained (probably) by Chenango Presby., 1831; Preston, N. Y., 1831; Triangle, 1832–5; Chenango Forks, 1836–49; Baker, 1849; Triangle, 1849–51; Richford, 1851–6; So. Bristol, 1857; Cohocton, 1858–60; Penfield, 1860–6; Lansing, Ia., 1867.

EBENEZER PORTER HYDE, class of 1861–4, æt. 31.
Born in Youngstown, N. Y., Oct. 28, 1837; united with the Ch. in Youngstown, at about 16 years of age; studied at Yale College in class of 1863; Aub. Jun. class from New Haven The. Sem.,

Feb. 14, 1862; returned to New Haven at close of Mid. year; married to Miss CARRIE W. HIGBY, of New Haven, July 15, 1863; died of consumption at New Haven, Conn., Aug. 31, 1868. He had 1 son, who, with his wife, survived him.

Served one year as Army chaplain; So. Coventry, Conn., 1865-7.

SIMEON BENJAMIN, Trustee 1841-68, æt. 76.

Born in Upper Aquabogue, L. I., May 29, 1792; united with the Church in Aquabogue, at 14 years of age; married to Miss SARAH WICKHAM GOLDSMITH, of Mattituck, L. I., March 20, 1816; died of inflammation of the lungs at Elmira, Sept. 1, 1868. He had 3 sons and 4 daughters; one daughter survived him.

In business in New York, 1810-12; in Aquabogue, 1812; after a few years, wholesale dry goods merchant in New York; from 1835, in Elmira, N. Y., banking and railroad business.

ENOCH KINGSBURY, class of 1826-9, æt. 68.

Born in Langdon, N. H., Apr. 21, 1800; united with the Church before 1826; graduated from Amherst College in 1827; Auburn Middle year; Union The. Sem. of Va., 1828-9; married to Miss FANNY ROSANNA GOODWIN, of Simsbury, Conn.. Nov. 1, 1830; died of consumption at Danville, Ill., Oct. 26, 1868. He had 5 sons and 3 daughters; his wife, 2 sons and 1 daughter survived him.

Ordained at South Hadley, Mass., by Assoc., Nov. 3, 1830; home miss., Va., 1828-9; Danville, Ill., preaching also in other fields, 26 years from 1830; afterward resident in Danville, preaching there and elsewhere.

WILLIAM WEED MARVIN, class of 1824-7, æt. 75.

Born in Argyle, N. Y., Sept. 26, 1793; united with the Church in Walton, N. Y., before 1824; married to FANNY CORNWELL, of Walton, Nov. 23, 1839; died of old age at Unadilla, N. Y., Oct. 28, 1868. He had 3 daughters; his wife and daughters survived him.

Resided in Walton, N. Y.; was in the Seminary a year or more, from June, 1825; left in poor health and became deranged. After his recovery, he lived on a farm.

1869.

JOHN CAMPBELL, class of 1849-52.

Came to Auburn from Perth, C. W.; graduated from Hamilton College in 1849; Spencer, N. Y., 1854-8; Melbourne, Canada E., 1867; died in Canada, Mar., 1869. His wife, 3 sons, and 6 daughters survived him.

ALFRED NORTH, class of 1847–50, æt. 62.

> Born in Exeter, N. H., about 1807 ; learned the printing business ; studied Hebrew, Latin and Greek privately, 1830–2, and earlier ; printer, N. Y., 1832–4 ; for A. B. C. F. M., Singapore, Ind., 1834–43, and Madura, 1843–7 ; married to Miss BRYAN ; married to Miss MARTHA BRYAN ; died of pneumonia at Chilton, Wis., Mar. 3, 1869. He had 2 sons and 2 or more daughters.

> Ordained about 1851 ; Middlefield Centre, N. Y., 1852–6 ; Pittsford, 1856–60 ; Attica, 1860–4 ; resident in LeRoy, 1864–5 ; farming in Kan., 1866 ; home miss., Tipton, Mo., 1867–8 ; Chilton, Wis., 1868–9.

EBENEZER WEEKS ROBINSON, class of 1834–7, æt. 57.

> Born in Granville, N. Y., May 1, 1812 ; united with the Church in Pulaski, 1831 ; graduated from Hamilton College in 1834 ; married to Miss SARAH BACON ADAMS, of Franklin, Mass., 1838 ; died of pneumonia at Washington, D. C., April 8, 1869. He had 3 sons and 3 daughters ; his wife, 1 son and 3 daughters survived him.

> Ordained pastor, Assonett, Mass , by Council, May 2, 1838 ; Assonett, 12 years ; Sprague, Conn., 6 years ; Bethany, 12 years ; secretary and treasurer of Howard University, 1868–9.

> Published " Ecclesiastical History of Connecticut," 1861.

GEORGE NORTON, class of 1867–70, æt. 26.

> Born in Sangerfield, N. Y., Sept. 21, 1843 ; came to Aub. from Ch. in Hamilton Col. ; graduated from Hamilton College in 1866 ; tea. Lookout Mountain, Tenn., 1866–7 ; died in St. Paul, Minn., Oct. 11, 1869.

HON. FREDERICK STARR, Trustee 1855–69, æt. 71.

> Born in Warren, Conn., May 1, 1799 ; united with the 1st Pres. Church in Rochester, 1822 ; married to Miss LUCY ANN HILLS, of Rochester, Nov. 23, 1831 ; twice married ; died in Rochester Nov. 27, 1869. He had 5 sons and 2 daughters ; his wife, 3 sons and 2 daughters survived him.

> Resident in Rochester, N. Y., from 1822 ; cabinet maker ; piano manufacturer, 1850–64 ; member of State Legislature, 1839 ; proprietor of the *Genesee Evangelist*.

> President of Trustees of Auburn, 1865–9.

JOHN BERRIEN FISH, class of 1823–6, æt. 75.

> Born in Connecticut Farms, N. J., July 23, 1794 ; united with the Church in Gallipolis, O., Fall of 1821 ; Middle and Senior years at Auburn ; married to LUCIA HULL, of Bridgewater, N. Y., 1826 ; married to NANCY STEVENS, of Patterson, N. Y., Aug. 23, 1837 ; died of diabetes at Catskill, N. Y., Dec. 22, 1869. He had 9 children, 8 of whom, with his wife, survived him.

> Ordained 1828 ; preached at Canterbury, Liberty, Monticello, Sidney Plains, Hartwick, Sangerfield ; Sidney Plains again, to 1852 ; Hunter, 1853–4 ; Big Hollow, 1854–60 ; resident Hughsonville, 1861–2, and then at Catskill.

1870.

JOHN KEEP, Trustee 1832-4, æt. 89.

Born in Longmeadow, Mass., Apr. 20, 1781 ; graduated from Yale College in 1802; studied Theology with Rev. Asahel Hooker, of Goshen, Conn.; married to Miss LYDIA HALE, of Goshen, 1805 ; died of old age at Oberlin, O , Feb. 12, 1870. He had 1 son, who survived him.

Ordained pastor, Blandford, Mass., 1805 ; Blandford, 1805-21 ; Homer, N. Y., 1821-33 ; Cleveland, O., 1st Pres. Ch., 1833-6 ; financial agent, Oberlin College, 1837-9 and from 1850; Wooster, O.; Lockport, and Albion, N. Y.; Mansfield, O., Hartford, O., Arcade, N. Y., Litchfield, O., 1840-50.

BLACKLEACH BURRITT GRAY, class of 1827-30, æt. 72.

Born in Sherburne, N. Y., Mar. 31, 1797 ; studied at Hamilton College; Auburn, 1827-9 ; married to Miss MARY NASH AR-NETT, of Auburn, Sept. 25, 1829 ; died of pneumonia at Canandaigua, Feb. 18, 1870. He had 4 sons and 2 daughters ; his wife, 3 sons and 1 daughter survived him.

Ordained pastor, Sheridan, N. Y., by Presby., May 12, 1830 ; Sheridan, 1829-33; Byron, 1833-7; Jamestown, 1837-9; Brighton, 1840-50 ; Seneca Castle, 1850-68 ; resident Canandaigua from 1868.

GEORGE WHITE, class of 1861-4, æt. 36.

Born in Huntingdon, Canada, Jan. 29, 1834 ; united with the Pres. Church in Huntingdon, about 1854; graduated from Williams College in 1861 ; married to Miss HARRIET A. BEALE, of Spencertown, N. Y., June 15, 1864 ; died of consumption at Schaghticoke Point, Mar. 14, 1870. No children ; his wife survived him.

Ordained pastor at Old Schaghticoke, N. Y., by classis of Saratoga, Oct. 14, 1864; where he remained 5 years.

GARDNER K. CLARK, class of 1823-6, æt. 74.

Came to Auburn from Church in Bradford, Vt. ; graduated from Union College in 1823; Auburn, 1824-5 ; died at Saratoga, Minn., Mar. 19, 1870.

Ordained at Danby, N. Y., by Presby., June 21, 1831; Spencer, 1828-32 and from 1838 ; Preble, 1832-8 and 1850-5 ; Saratoga, Minn., from 1855.

BARUCH BUTLER BECKWITH, class of 1827-30, æt. 65.

Born in Lyme, Conn., March 29, 1805 ; united with the Williams Col. Church in 1823; graduated from Williams College in 1827 ; 2 years at Auburn and 1 at Yale Div. Sch. ; grad. 1831 ; married to Miss MARIA ELY STERLING, of Lyme, Conn., May 23, 1832 ; died of nervous prostration at Gouverneur, N. Y., July 4, 1870. He had no children ; his wife survived him.

Ordained pastor at Athol, Mass., by Council, June 1, 1831; Athol,
1831–4; Walpole, N. H., 1835–6; Castine, Me., 5 years from
1837; Hill, N. H., 1 year; Perry, N. Y.; Gouverneur, N. Y.,
1844–66.

JAMES EDWARD PIERCE, class of 1862–5, æt. 31.
Born in West Townshend, Wyndham Co., Vt., Aug. 12, 1839;
united with the Cong. Church in West Townshend, 1853; grad·
uated from Middlebury College in 1861; Auburn, 1861–3 and
1864–5; tutor in Middlebury, 1863–4; married to Miss FRANCES
HALL, Auburn, July 11, 1866; died of heart disease at Auburn,
July 13, 1870. He had 1 son; his wife and son survived him.
Ordained by Cayuga Presbytery, March 22, 1866; professor of
Hebrew Language and Literature in Auburn, 1865–70.

CHARLES MORGAN, class of 1838–41, æt. 58.
Born in Columbus, N. Y., Jan. 15, 1813; united with the Cong.
Church in Columbus, about 1829; graduated from Union Col-
lege in 1838; married to Miss SUSAN CLARK, of Schenectady,
N. Y., Aug. 23, 1841; died of pneumonia at East Troy, Wis.,
Dec. 18, 1870. He had 3 daughters; his wife and daughters
survived him.
Ordained at Auburn, by Presby. of Cayuga, 1841; Geneseo, N.
Y., 2 years from 1841; Granada, Miss., 1844–7; Attica, N. Y.,
1847–50; Geneva, Wis., 1858–9; East Troy, 1850–8 and 1859–70.

1 8 7 1 .

WILLIAM WISNER, D. D., Trustee, æt. 89.
Born in Warrick, N. Y., April 18, 1772; admitted to practice Law,
1805; studied Theology with Rev. Simeon R. Jones; A. M.
from Williams College in 1820; D. D. from Delaware College in
1842; married to Miss JULIA CARPENTER; died in Ithaca, Jan.
7, 1871.
Preached in Athens, Pa., 4 years from 1811; Ithaca, N. Y., 1816–
31; Brick Ch., Rochester, 1831–5; First Pres. Ch., St. Louis,
Mo., 2 years; Ithaca again, 1838–49; afterward resident in
Ithaca.
Trustee 1820–34 and 1846–63. Moderator of Gen. Assembly, 1840.
Published "Incidents in a Pastor's Life," 1852.

DARIUS CARTER SACKETT. class of 1864–7, æt. 31.
Born in Canandaigua, N. Y., Dec. 7, 1839; united with the Church
at the age of 17; graduated from Hamilton College in 1864;
married to Miss MITTIE C. SMITH, of Canada, Dec. 19, 1866;
died of consumption, at Canandaigua, Feb. 10, 1871.
Ordained pastor at Rock Stream, N. Y., by Presby. of Chemung,
June 12, 1867; Rock Stream, 1866–71.

ROBERT WOODRUFF CONDIT, D. D., Trustee 1852–8, æt. 75.

Born in Stillwater, N. Y., Sept. 17, 1795 ; united with the Church in Hanover, N. J. ; graduated from Princeton College in 1814 ; D. D. from Hamilton College in 1847 ; married to HARRIETTE WHITTLESEY, of Danbury, Conn., 1818 ; died of paralysis at Oswego, N. Y., Feb. 11, 1871. He had 1 son and 6 daughters ; his son and 5 daughters survived him.

Ordained pastor, Montgomery, N. Y., by Presby., Dec. 13, 1820 ; preaching in the South, 1818–20 ; Montgomery, 1820–30 ; 1st Pres. Ch., Oswego, 1831–71.

WILLIAM FREDERICK WILLIAMS, D. D., class of 1844–7, æt. 53.

Born in Utica, N. Y., Jan. 7, 1818 ; united with the 1st Pres. Ch. in Utica, 1831 ; studied at Yale College ; married to Miss SARAH POND, of Rome, N. Y.; married to Miss HATTIE HARD-ING, of Auburndale, Mass ; married to Miss CARRIE BARBOUR, of Philadelphia ; married to Miss CATHERINE POND, Verona Centre ; died of dysentery at Mardin, E. Turkey, Feb. 14, 1871. He had 3 sons and 1 daughter ; his wife, 2 sons and daughter survived him.

Miss. of A. B. C. F. M. at Beirut, Mosul, and Mardin.

ISAAC NEWTON LOWRY, class of 1864–7, æt. 29.

Born in Mecca, Ind., Nov. 30, 1842 ; united with the Church in Wabash College, early in 1861 ; graduated from Genesee College in 1864 ; married to Miss MARY E. SMITH, of Auburn, July 23, 1867 ; died of consumption at Minneapolis, Minn., Mar. 16, 1871. He had 1 daughter ; his wife survived him for a short time.

Ordained at Lima, N. Y., by Presby., July 16, 1867 ; miss. of A. B. C. F. M. in Syria, 1867–70 ; East Avon, N. Y., 1870–1.

JOHN LEVIS JONES, class of 1853–6, æt. 45.

Born in Ireland, Dec. 11, 1825 ; united with the Pres. Church in Schaghticoke, N. Y., 1842 ; studied at Acad., Salem, N. Y.; Auburn, Mid., 1853–4 ; Sen., 1855–6 ; married to Miss RUTH ANN LOCKE, of Chester, N. Y., June 25, 1854 ; died of cancer of stomach at Solomon City, Kan., May 3, 1871. He had 1 son and 5 daughters ; his wife, son and 4 daughters survived him.

Ordained and installed at Whitney's Point, N. Y., 1854 ; Sweden and Riga, to 1860 ; home miss., Emerson, Mo., 1860–1, and Camp Point, Rushville, Brooklyn, Ill., 1861–5 ; Mattoon, 1865–8 ; Salina, Solomon City and vicinity, Kan., from 1868.

JOSEPH GROUT LONGLEY, class of 1867–70, æt. 48.

Born in Hawley, Mass., May 26, 1823 ; came to Auburn from Church in Hawley ; studied at Amherst College ; engaged in teaching ; in the Army ; agt. for Freedmen ; after graduating preached occasionally ; A. M. from Amherst, 1869 ; not married ; died of consumption at Greenville, Ill., May 6, 1871.

HUGH CARLISLE, class of 1826-9, æt. 71.

Came to Auburn from Philadelphia; mem. of 5th Pres. Church there; graduated from Amherst College in 1826; died at Rootstown, O., June 22, 1871.

N. C., from 1829; Rough Creek, Va., from 1832; West Hanover, Ind., 1836; Cape Vincent, N. Y., from 1846; resident Catasauqua, Pa.; Birmingham, O., 1854-6; Hartford, 1856-8; resident Croton, 1858-70, and Rootstown, 1871.

MARSHALL DANFORTH SANDERS, class of 1848-51, æt. 48.

Born in Williamstown, Mass., July 3, 1823; graduated from Williams College in 1846; taught in Social Circle and Athens, Ga., 2 years; married to Miss GEORGIANA KNIGHT, of Peru, Mass., Sept. 4, 1851; married to Miss CARRIE E. WEBB, of Adams, N. Y., April 6, 1870; died suddenly in Ceylon, Aug. 29, 1871. His wife and 6 sons survived him.

Ordained in Peru, Mass., (Cong.) 1851; miss. of A. B. C. F. M. in Ceylon from 1851 to his death; prin. of Batticotta Sem.

ARISTARCHUS CHAMPION, Trustee 1842-8, æt. 87.

Born in Westchester Parish, Colchester, Conn., Oct. 23, 1784; united with the Cong. Church in Westchester, May 21, 1809; graduated from Yale College in 1807; never married; died of old age at Rochester, N. Y., Sept. 18, 1871.

He resided in Rochester most of his life, and was occupied in the care of his father's and his own property.

CHARLES GRANDISON CLARK, class of 1826-9, æt. 75.

Born in Preston, Conn., April 8, 1796; came to Aub. from Church there; graduated from Amherst College in 1827; married to Miss ELIZABETH PLATT, of Ann Arbor, Mich., Aug. 30, 1830; married to Miss MARY E. CHADWICK, of York, N. Y., Aug. 31, 1859; died of paralysis at Ann Arbor, Mich., Oct. 2, 1871. He had 3 sons and 1 daughter; his wife and 1 son survived him.

Ordained at Madison, N. Y., by Oneida Assoc., Sept. 9, 1829; Webster, Mich., 1829-48; Kensington and New Hudson, 2 years; Lodi, 2 years; Webster again, 1852-8; afterward resident at Ann Arbor.

ALBERT MANDELL, class of 1849-52, æt. 45.

Born in Aurora, N. Y., Jan. 6, 1827; united with the Pres. Church in Aurora, Spr. of 1843; studied at Cayuga Lake Acad.; Auburn, 1846-7, 1848-9, 1851-2; post grad. year in Union Sem., N. Y.; married to Miss ELIZABETH MARIA JOY, of Ludlowville, N. Y., Jan. 4, 1853; died of congestion of lungs at Penn Yan, Oct. 7, 1871. He had 3 sons; his wife and 1 son survived him.

Ordained pastor, Westernville, by Presby. of Utica, Aut. of 1855; Ludlowville, 1850; Westernville, 1855-8; Skaneateles, 1858-60; Newark, N. J., 1862; Madison, 1862-9; resident Aurora from 1870.

ALBERT TRUE, class of 1862-5, æt. 32.

Born in Owego, N. Y., Oct. 30, 1839; came to Aub. from Cong. Church there; graduated from Williams College in 1862; married to Miss MARIA PITCHER, of Warren, Pa., May 16, 1865; died of nervous exhaustion at Saratoga, N. Y., Oct. 18, 1871. His wife and adopted daughter survived him.

Ordained 1865; Cedar Falls, Iowa, 1865-6; Elbridge, N. Y., from 1866.

WILLIAM WELLINGTON COLLINS, class of 1839-42, æt. 55.

Born in Smyrna, N. Y., Jan. 6, 1816; united with the Cong. Ch. in Smyrna, 1831; graduated from Hamilton College in 1839; married to SARAH ELEANOR LACEY, of Preble, Aug. 2, 1846; died of typhoid fever at Parma, Mich., Nov. 21, 1871. He had 3 daughters; his wife and daughters survived him.

Summer Hill, N. Y., from 1841; Preble from 1843; Pres. Church, Onondaga Valley, from 1846; Sodus from 1849; E. Palmyra from 1854; Dundee from 1858; Eddytown from 1859; Maine from 1860; Penfield from 1864; Quincy, Tekonsha and Parma, Mich., 1866-71.

JOEL TALCOTT, class of 1825-8, æt. 72.

Born in Vernon, Conn., 1799; united with the Church in Vernon, 1818; graduated from Yale College in 1825; died in Wakeman, O., Dec. 25, 1871.

Ordained at Hartford, Conn., by North Assoc., July 1, 1828; Wellington, O., 1828-39; Sullivan, 1839-45; Brighton, O., 1846; Charleston, 1849; Wakeman, 1850; resident in Wakeman till death.

WILLIAM WALLACE PAGE, class of 1848-51, æt. 54.

Born in Albany, N. Y., July, 1818; came to Auburn from 4th Ch. there; graduated from Union College in 1842; Union, N. Y., 1842-3; Auburn, 1849-51; died at Troy, N. Y., Dec. 30, 1871.

Ordained pastor, Kent, Conn., by Litchfield North Consoc., Dec. 7, 1853; Scipio, N. Y., 1851-2; Union Springs, 1852-3; Kent, 1853-5; Ridgebury, 1856-7; 2nd Ch., Danbury, 1857; Rough Creek, Va., 1858-9; Guilderland, N. Y., 1862-5; Troy, 1865-7, and resident there till death.

1872.

JOHN KELLEY, M. D., class of 1827-30, æt. 74.

Born in Hampstead, N. H., Jan 1, 1798; united with the Cong. Church in Hampstead, June 13, 1819; graduated from Williams College in 1825; in Seminary part of Junior year; M. D. from Fairfield Med. College; married to CATHARINE MARIA SWEETMAN, of Carlisle, N. Y., 1834; died Jan. 16, 1872, in Esperance, N. Y. He had 2 sons and 3 daughters.

Practiced Medicine in Fultonville, in Carlisle 14 years, and in Esperance the remainder of his life.

GEORGE WASHINGTON THOMSON, class of 1833–6, æt. 60.
    Born in Clark's Mills, N. Y., Sept. 3, 1811 ; united with the Ch. in Clinton, N. Y., Sept. 4, 1831 ; graduated from Hamilton College in 1833 ; married to Miss ELIZABETH BRAINARD, of Verona, N. Y., 1839 ; died of mesenteric rupture at Buffalo, N. Y., Feb. 6, 1872.   His wife, 2 sons and 2 daughters survived him.
    Ordained pastor, Munnsville, N. Y., by Oneida Presby., June 11, 1838 ; Munnsville, about 2 years ; in charge of the "Polytechny" School, Chittenango, 1840–5 ; Onondaga Academy, 1845–7 ; Riga Academy, 1847–9 ; in business ; teaching a School for boys Syracuse ; in business ; supplied Churches as opportunity offered ; resided in Syracuse and afterward in Buffalo.

ROBERT HUNTER, class of 1845–8, æt. 52.
    Born in New Lebanon, N. Y., 1820 ; came to Aub. from Church in Miss. Inst. ; graduated from Mission Institute, Ill., 1845 ; Auburn, 1845–7 ; died March 11, 1872.
    Charlestown, O.,·1848–52 ; Clay, Iowa, 1858–61 ; Columbus City, 1861–8 ; Nevinville from 1868.

MOSES ASHLEY CURTIS, D. D., class of 1827–30, æt. 64.
    Born in Stockbridge, Mass., 1808 ; united with the Church in Williamstown, 1826 ; graduated from Williams College in 1827 ; in Auburn 3 months of Junior year ; D. D. from the Univ. of N. Carolina in 1852 ; married in N. C., 1834 ; died in Hillsborough, N. C., Apr. 10, 1872.
    Ordained Priest in P. E. Church, at Richmond, Va., May 31, 1835 ; officiated in North and South Carolina.
    Published reviews, sermons, and papers on botanical subjects.

JOSEPH STEELE, class of 1824–7, æt. 71.
    Born in Kingsboro, N. Y. ; June 8, 1801 ; joined the Church at Kingsboro, July 20, 1817 ; graduated from Union College in 1824 ; married to Miss JULIA A. BACON, in 1830 ; married to Miss HARRIET B. HOPKINS, of Great Barrington, Mass., Feb. 12,'1835 ; died of heart disease at Mobile, Ala., April 25, 1872.   His wife, with 1 daughter and 2 of their 3 sons, survived him ; one son was John Bacon Steele of 1861–4.
    Ordained at Albany, N. Y., by Presby., Jan. 10, 1828 ; Saratoga Springs, 1828–9 ; Cong. Church in Castleton, Vt., 1828–54 ; teacher in Burr Seminary, 1854–6 ; lived in Middlebury, Vt., preaching, &c., from 1856.

JOEL CAMPBELL, class of 1824–7, æt. 76.
    Came to Auburn from Woodbridge, N. J. ; mem. of Church there ; graduated from Amherst College in class of 1825 ; died of congestion of lungs at La Fayette, N. J., May 15, 1872.   He had 1 son and 1 daughter ; his wife, son and daughter survived him.

Honesdale, Pa., 1829–35; Utica, N. Y., S. S. agt., 1836–7; Hamburgh, N. J., 1838–56; La Fayette, N. J., 1856–69, and resident there till death.

WILBERFORCE KERR BOGGS, class of 1861–4, æt. 33.

Born in Bucyrus, O., April 17, 1839; united with the United Brethren Church in Westerville, O., 1858; graduated from Otterbein University in 1861; Aub. Mid. class from Western The. Sem., Jan., 1863; married to Miss ELLEN THOMPSON, of Ticonderoga, N. Y., April 18, 1865; died of fever at Oxford, Kansas, July 26, 1872. He had 3 sons and 1 daughter; his wife, sons and daughter survived him.

Ordained by Iowa City Presbytery, at Marengo, Iowa, April 23, 1865; Wellsboro, Pa.; Ottumway and Marengo, Iowa, 1864–6; miss. work in Emporia, Wichita, Oxford, Belle Plaine, and Willington, Kansas, 1868–72.

HIRAM HARRIS, class of 1838–41, æt. 60.

Born in Gorham, N. Y., July 29, 1812; came to Auburn from Ch. there; married to Miss LUCINDA BARTLETTE, in Auburn, Jan. 28, 1841; died at Reed's Corners, N. Y., Aug. 26, 1872; Mrs. Harris survived him; 1 son died young.

Ordained at Scott, by Presby. of Cortland, Oct. 18, 1843; Bristol; Scott; Junius; Borodino; Reed's Corners; Webster.

JOSEPH MERRILL SADD, class of 1827–30, æt. 70.

Born in East Hartford, Conn., Nov. 6, 1801; united with the Church there, July, 1821; graduated from Williams College in 1827; married to Miss CORINNA G. SADD, of Austinburg, O., July, 1830; died at Louisville, Ky., Sept. 6, (or Sept. 12) 1872. His wife survived him.

Ordained, Henrietta, N. Y., by Genesee Consoc., June 2, 1830; Missouri, 1830–5, home missionary and principal of School in Farmington; Castile, N. Y., 1836–42; Northern Indiana, preaching, teaching and distributing Bibles; agt. A & F. C. Union, 1854–63; City miss., Louisville, Ky., from 1863.

HARVEY SMITH, class of 1837–40, æt. 61.

Born in Coventry, N. Y., Oct. 14, 1811; united with the Pres. Church in Coventry, about 1817; studied at Oneida Institute; married to Miss ANNA DRESSER, of Mt. Morris, Mar. 13, 1841; died of dysentery at Phelps, Mo., Sept. 21, 1872. He had 2 sons and 1 daughter; his wife, daughter and 1 son survived him.

Ordained and installed at Triangle, N. Y., (Cong.) June 2, 1842; Triangle, 1842–5; Masonville, 1845–53; teaching at Deposit, 1853–6; preaching in Chenango Forks, 1853–7; Maine Village, 1857–9; South Amenia, 1859–72.

CURTIS THURSTON, class of 1837–40, æt. 63.

Born in New Lisbon, N. Y., Sept. 10, 1809; united with the Church in New Lisbon, at the age of 21; graduated from Union

College in 1837 ; married to Miss JULIA ANN SPAULDING,
of Athens, Pa., April 15, 1846 ; died of heart disease, instantly, at
Athens, Sept. 22, 1872. He had 3 sons ; his wife and sons
survived him.

Ordained pastor, Athens, Pa., by Presby., Feb. 24, 1841 ; Athens
and Factoryville, Pa., 7½ years, from Oct. 10, 1840 ; resided at
Athens and "supplied vacant Churches and destitute places,"
1848–72.

JAMES HATCH KASSON, class of 1843–6, æt. 54.
Born in Sherburne, N. Y., Feb. 16, 1817 ; united with the Church
in Lenox, before 1839 ; studied at Hamilton College in class of
1843 ; married to Miss MARY SHERWOOD ROBBINS, of Camillus,
N. Y., Sept. 3, 1846 ; died of chronic diarrhea at Grinnell, Ia.,
Nov. 27, 1872. He had 3 sons and 1 daughter ; his wife and
sons survived him.

Ordained at Waupun, Wis., by Madison Dist. Conv., Autumn of
1847 ; pioneer miss. in Marquette Co., Wis., 1846–51 ; Baraboo,
1851–5 ; disabled by partial paralysis, residing in Delaware,
Co., Iowa, 1855–67, and in Grinnell from 1867.

NATHANIEL CATLIN CLARK, class of 1829–32, æt. 71.
Born in Benson, Vt., Aug. 12, 1801 ; united with the Church at
18 or 19 years old ; graduated from Middlebury College in 1828 ;
married to Miss JULIA BARROWS, Oct. 22, 1832 ; died of pneumonia, Dec. 3, 1872, at Elgin, Ill. His wife survived him ; 4
children died before him.

Ordained May 4, 1833 ; Napierville, Ill., and other Churches, 1833
–6 ; St. Charles and Elgin, 1837–9 ; Elgin from 1839 ; ministered,
at times, to other Churches.

1873.

GEORGE IVES KING, D. D., class of 1838–41, æt. 58.
Born in Adams, N. Y., June 1, 1815 ; came to Auburn from
Church in Hudson ; graduated from Union College in 1837 ;
D. D. from Union College in 1865 ; married to Miss EMILY B.
SPRAGUE, of Belleville, N. Y., Oct. 12, 1840 ; died in New Or-
leans, La., March 12, 1873. His wife survived him.

Prin. of Union Academy, Belleville, 1840–3 ; past. of Pres. Church
in Westernville, from 1843 ; Hanover, N. J., from 1849 ; 1st Pres.
Ch. in Quincy, Ill., 1855–67 ; Pres. Ch. in Jerseyville, 1868–73.

JOEL PARKER, D. D., class of 1824–7, æt. 74.
Born in Bethel, Vt., Aug. 27, 1799 ; united with the Pres. Church
in Livonia, N. Y., May 11, 1817 ; graduated from Hamilton
College in 1824 ; D. D. from Princeton College in 1839 ; married
to Miss HARRIET PHELPS, of Lenox, N. Y., May 9, 1826 ; died

of apoplexy in New York, May 2, 1873. He had 2 sons and 8
daughters ; his wife, 1 son and 4 daughters survived him.
Ordained pastor of 3rd Pres. Ch., Rochester, N. Y., by Presby.,
Feb., 1827 ; Rochester, 1826–30 ; Dey Street Pres. Church in
New York, 1830–33 ; 1st Ch., New Orleans, 1833–8 ; Broadway
Tabernacle in New York, 1838–40 ; president and prof. of Sac.
Rhet. in Union Theological Seminary, 1840–2 ; Clinton St. Pres.
Church in Philadelphia, 1842–52 ; Bleecker Street Church, New
York, 1852–62 ; Park Street Church in Newark, 1862–68.

CHARLES JEROME, class of 1841–4, æt. 58.
Born in Pompey, N. Y., Jan. 2, 1815 ; united with the Church in
Pompey, March 7, 1831 ; graduated from Hamilton College in
1839 ; Auburn, 1841–3 ; New Haven, 1844–5 ; married to
Miss ELIZABETH REED, of Baldwinsville, N. Y., Dec. 23, 1846 ;
married to Miss HARRIET SWEETLAND, of Cazenovia, N. Y.,
Oct., 1859 ; died of Bright's disease in Clinton, May 31, 1873.
His wife, 4 sons and 1 daughter survived him ; 1 son preceded
him.
Ordained and installed at Oxford, N. Y., by Presby., Feb. 1, 1848 ;
Collamer, 1845–6 ; Oxford, 1847–50 ; Bergen, 1850–3 ; Ellicot-
ville, 1855–60 ; South Trenton, 1860–2 ; then moved to Clinton,
N. Y., and supplied Churches.

TOWNSEND WALKER, class of 1839–42, æt 62.
Born in Monterey, Mass., Nov. 10, 1811 ; united with the Cong.
Church in Monterey, May 4, 1834 ; graduated from Williams
College in 1839 ; married to ANN ANDERSON, of Fulton, N. Y.,
Sept. 30, 1842 ; died of consumption at Goshen, Mass., July 31,
1873. His wife died July 31, 1874 ; he had 1 son and 1
daughter ; both survived him.
Ordained pastor of Pres. Ch. in Baldwinsville, N. Y., by Onondaga
Presbytery, Mar. 12, 1844 ; Baldwinsville, 1842–52 ; 2nd Cong.
Church, Huntington, Mass., 1853–65 ; Cong. Church, Goshen,
1868–73.

EDWIN OTWAY BURNHAM, class of 1852–5, æt. 49.
Born in Ghent, Ky., Sept. 24, 1824 ; united with the Cong. Ch.
in Madison, N. Y., March 6, 1842 ; graduated from Hamilton
College in 1852 ; dismissed from Auburn, Dec. 21, 1852, and
completed the course at Union Theo. Sem., N. Y. ; married to
Miss REBECCA ELIZABETH RUSSELL, of Sterling, Minn., July
3, 1860 ; died of consumption at Los Angeles, Cal., Aug. 1,
1873. He had 3 sons and 1 daughter ; his wife and 2 sons
survived him.
Teacher in Pennington, N. J., 1855–6 ; preached at Columbus
City, Iowa, 1856–7 ; Wilton, Minn., from 1857 ; also preaching
and teaching at Tivoli, for a few years, when failing health compelled him to give up the work of the ministry.

HENRY NORTON MILLERD, class of 1850–3, æt. 43.

> Born in Summer Hill, N. Y., Aug. 5, 1830; united with the 1st Pres. Church in Auburn, 1846; graduated from Hamilton College in 1850; married to Miss ELIZABETH JANE STORRS, of Eaton, N. Y., Oct. 3, 1855; died of paralysis of brain and throat, Auburn, Sept. 13, 1873. He had 2 daughters; his wife and daughters survived him.
>
> Ordained pastor in Aurelius, N. Y., by Presby. of Cayuga, July 10, 1855; Aurelius to Dec. 13, 1859; Truxton, N. Y., 6 years and 5 months; Williamstown, N. Y., 5 years; Holland Patent, N. Y., 1871–3.

HORACE HILLS, Trustee 1828–40, æt. 86.

> Born in East Hartford, Conn., Oct. 31, 1787; united with the Church in Hadley, Mass.; married to ALMIRA WILCOX, of Middletown, Conn., July 17, 1811; died at Buffalo, N. Y., Sept. 18, 1873. He had 2 sons and 4 daughters; his sons and 2 daughters survived him; one son in 1838–41.
>
> In mercantile business in Auburn for about 30 years; resident in Buffalo since 1847.

CHARLES EDWIN VAN ANDEN, M. D., class of 1839–42, æt. 55.

> Born in Auburn, Jan. 4, 1819; united with St. Peter's Church in Auburn, Feb., 1838; graduated from Union College in 1839; Auburn, 1839–40; unmarried; died from accident in Auburn, Oct. 19, 1873.
>
> Practicing physician in New York City and Auburn.

JOHN BACON STEELE, class of 1861–4, æt. 35.

> Born in Castleton, Vt., son of Joseph Steele of 1821–4, June 17, 1838; came to Aub. from Ch. in Middlebury; graduated from Middlebury College in 1860; taught, Malden, N. Y., 1860–1; married to Miss SARAH LOUNSBURY RANDLE, of Norwalk, Conn., Aug., 1865; died of typhoid fever at Middlebury, Vt., Nov. 29, 1873. He had 1 son and 2 daughters; his wife, son and daughters survived him.
>
> Ordained by Council, Middlebury, Aug. 16, 1865; Pres. Ch., Castile, N. Y., 1864–67; Glenwood, 1867–9; health failed; in business in Middlebury, till his death.

1874.

CALVIN WATERBURY, class of 1833–6, æt. 65.

> Born in Middletown, N. Y., April 21, 1809; 1 year at Lane Seminary, 2 at Auburn; married to Miss PRISCILLA BETTS, of N. Y., Jan. 8, 1836; married to Mrs. ANN P. BACHMAN PHIPPS, Sept. 19, 1867; died at Rotherwood, Tenn., Jan. 3, 1874, leaving wife, 4 sons and 1 daughter.

Pastor at Gilbertsville, N. Y., for 8 years ; First Pres. Church at
Freeport, Ill., 1842–7 ; Victor, and Bergen, N. Y., Knoxville,
Ill., Cedar Falls, Iowa, and Jonesboro and Kingsport, Tenn.

SAMUEL WARE FISHER, D. D., LL. D., Trustee 1860–71, æt. 60.
> Born in Morristown, N. J., Apr. 5, 1814 ; united with the 1st Pres.
> Church in Paterson, N. J., July 3, 1831 ; graduated from Yale
> College in 1835 ; Middletown, Conn., 1 year, Princeton, 2 years,
> Union, 1 year ; D. D. from Miami Univ. in 1852 ; LL. D. from
> Univ. of the City of N. Y. in 1859 ; married to ANNA CAROLINE
> JOHNSON, of Morristown, Oct. 22, 1839 ; married to JANE JACK-
> SON, of Newark, N. J., May 18, 1842 ; died of congestion of the
> brain at College Hill, O., Jan. 18, 1874. He had 5 sons and 3
> daughters ; his wife, 3 sons and 1 daughter survived him ; sons
> in 1864–9, and 1867–70.
> Ordained pastor, West Bloomfield, N. J., by Presby. of Newark,
> Apr., 1839 ; West Bloomfield, 1839–43 ; 4th Pres. Ch., Albany,
> N. Y., 1843–6 ; 2d Pres. Ch., Cincinnati, O., 1846–58 ; pres. of
> Hamilton College, 1858–67 ; Westminster Church, Utica, N. Y.,
> 1867–71 ; resident, paralyzed, at College Hill, O., 1871–4.
> Moderator of General Assembly, 1857 ; published "The Three
> Great Temptations," 1852 ; "Occasional Sermons and Ad-
> dresses," 1860 ; "Life of Christ," posthumously.

GEORGE RANDALL HOWE SHUMWAY, class of 1831–4, æt. 66.
> Born in Oxford, N. Y., Jan. 28, 1808 ; united with the Pres. Ch.
> in Oxford in 1820 ; obtained his literary and classical education
> at Oxford Academy ; married to Miss EMILY CHARLOTTE FORD,
> of Lawrenceville, Pa., Feb. 17, 1835 ; died of congestion of the
> lungs at Lawrenceville, Jan. 28, 1874. He had 1 son and 3
> daughters ; his wife, 1 son and 1 daughter survived him.
> Ordained pastor, Palmyra, N. Y., by Geneva Presby., Jan. 1, 1835 ;
> Palmyra, 1834–42 ; Newark, 1844–70 ; Fall Brook and Tioga,
> Pa., and Peach Orchard and Painted Post, N. Y.

HON. JOHN PORTER, Trustee 1834–73, æt. 83.
> Born in Hadley, Mass., Oct. 24, 1790 ; united with the 2d Pres.
> Church in Auburn, Dec. 1, 1853 ; graduated from Williams Col-
> lege in 1810 ; married to Miss ABIGAIL MARTHA PHILLIPS, of
> Middletown, Conn., Feb. 17, 1825 ; died of paralysis at Auburn,
> Feb. 3, 1874. He had 3 sons and 2 daughters ; his wife, 1 son
> and 1 daughter survived him.
> Resident in Auburn from 1812 ; practicing Law from 1815 ; Sur-
> rogate from 1828, 8 years ; State Senator, 1843–7 ; secretary of
> Trustees of Aub. Sem., 1834–44.

JAMES MALTBY SAYRE, class of 1834–7, æt. 60.
> Born in Catskill, N. Y., March 4, 1814 ; united with the Pres. Ch.
> in Catskill, June 5, 1831 ; graduated from Williams College in
> 1834 ; entered the Middle class at Auburn, on dismission from
> Princeton, June, 1836 ; he never married ; died of pneumonia at
> Catskill, May 9, 1874.

Ordained pastor, Rondout, N. Y., by Presby. of North River, Sept. 18, 1839; Rondout to 1842; from this time his health did not allow him to do professional work; resided in Catskill, engaged in business.

WILLIAM McDUFFEE, class of 1873–6, æt. 27.
Born in Philadelphia, May 29, 1847; united with the Olivet Pres. Church in Philadelphia, June 8, 1866; studied at Hamilton College in class of 1873; unmarried; died of consumption in Philadelphia, June 2, 1874.

CHARLES AUGUSTUS WETMORE, class of 1869–72, æt. 31.
Born in Norwich, N. Y., Nov. 8, 1843; united with the Cong. Ch. in Norwich, Jan., 1862; graduated from Hamilton College in 1869; left the Seminary on account of ill health in the Fall of 1870; married to Miss SARAH A. POLLARD, of Seneca Falls, Mar. 21, 1871; prin. of Leicester Academy, Mass., from the Spring of 1871; died of heart disease at Waumtek Hotel, Jefferson, N. H., July 6, 1874. His wife and 1 daughter survived him.

TERTIUS DUNNING SOUTHWORTH, class of 1826–9, æt. 73.
Born in Rome, N. Y., July 25, 1801; united with the Cong. Ch. in Bridgewater; graduated from Hamilton College in class of 1827; Andover, 1826–7 and 1828–9; Auburn, 1827–8; married to Miss MARTHA WARREN, of Weathersfield, Vt., June 17, 1839; died at Bridgewater, N. Y., Aug. 2, 1874. No children; his wife survived him.
Ordained at Utica, N. Y., by Oneida Presby., Oct. 7, 1832; Bridgewater; Sauquoit, 1830–2; Claremont, N. H., 1833–8; Franklin, Mass., 1838–50; Lyndon, Vt., 1852; White Creek, N. Y., and Bennington and Pownal, Vt., 1852–7; Kenosha, Wis., 1859–68; resident Bridgewater from 1869.

WILLIAM TODD, class of 1821–4, æt. 73.
Born in Marcellus, N. Y., March 8, 1801; united with the Pres. Church in Marcellus, Oct. 5, 1817; graduated from Hamilton College in 1821; married to Miss LUCY BROWNELL, of Penn Yan, N. Y., Dec. 12, 1828; married to Mrs. CLARISSA ANNETTE FROST WOODWARD, in India, Dec., 1836; married to Miss RUTH SOUTHWICK, of Poughkeepsie, Oct., 1840; died of paralysis at Madura, Kan., Aug. 10, 1874. No children; his wife survived him.
Ordained at Ira, N. Y., by Presby. of Cayuga, July 12, 1826; Benton, 1828–30; West Dresden, 1830–3; miss. at Jaffna, Ceylon, and at Madura, India, 1833–9; Perryville, Md.; Warren, Pa.; Sugar Grove; Ellington, N. Y., 1849–51; Grand Detour, Ill., 1854–8; Junction City, Kan.; Madura; farmer at Madura, 1872–4.

THOMAS SHERRARD, class of 1857–60, æt. 45.
Born in Co. of Antrim, Ireland, December, 1829; united with the Church at Tecumseh, Mich., Oct., 1851; graduated from Univ.

of Michigan in 1857; Auburn Junior class, on dismission from
Princeton, Feb. 5, 1858; married to Miss VALERIA DIANTHA
GRAY, of Milwaukee, June, 1860; died at Brooklyn, Mich., of
brain disease, Aug. 10, 1874. He had 2 sons and 6 daughters;
his wife, 2 sons and 4 daughters survived him.

Ordained at New Duquoin, Ill., by Presby. of Alton, Apr. 14, 1861;
Centralia, 1860–64; Pres. Church, Brooklyn, Mich., 1865–75.

OBADIAH COTTGRAVE BEARDSLEY, class of 1826–9, æt. 76.

Born in Harpersfield, Delaware Co., N. Y., June 3, 1798; united
with the Pres. Church in Eden, N. Y., 1820; graduated from
Union College in 1826; married to Miss CLARISSA POMEROY
RUST, of Skaneateles, Oct. 24, 1830; died of palsy, at Albion,
Aug. 23, 1874. He had 2 sons and 1 daughter; his wife and
daughter survived him.

Ordained by the Buffalo Presby., at Sheridan, May 12, 1830;
home miss. in Stockton, Charlotte and Gerry, 2 years; Pres.
Church of Silver Creek, from April 1, 1832, 13½ years; Pres.
Church of Honeoye Falls, from Oct., 1846, 11 years; Middleport from Nov., 1858, 3 years.

DAVID DOWNS GREGORY, class of 1827–30, æt. 72.

Born at Sand Lake, N. Y., Aug. 27, 1802; came to Aub. from
Church in Deposit; graduated from Williams College in 1827;
Auburn, 1827–9; Andover, 1829–30; married to Miss SARAH
SALOME RHOADES, of Skaneateles, N. Y., Nov. 29, 1830; married to Miss ELIZABETH BURY, of Grosse Ile, Mich., Jan. 29,
1852; died at Binghamton, Sept. 16, 1874. His wife and daughter survived him.

Ordained at Fredonia, N. Y., by Buffalo Presby., Nov. 10, 1831;
Ripley, 1830–1; Fredonia, 1831–3; Westfield, 1833–8; Binghamton, 1838–47; Tabernacle Church, Cincinnati, O., 1847–52 and
1858–9; North East, N. Y., 1852–8; Prattsburgh, 1859–66; supplied Chs. in vicinity of Binghamton.

GEORGE ALVA PENNY, class of 1874–7, æt. 26.

Born in Unadilla Forks, N. Y., May 21, 1848; united with the
Church in Hamilton College, April, 1871; graduated from Hamilton College in 1874; not married; died in Auburn, Sept. 16,
1874.

STANLEY PARMLEE HOUGH, class of 1835–8, æt. 61.

His name was afterwards changed to HOUGH P. STANLEY; born
in Bristol, Conn., Jan. 15, 1814; united with the 1st Pres. Ch.
in Brooklyn, N. Y., 1828; graduated from Oneida Institute in
1836; studied at Yale College; Mid. year at Auburn; Princeton The. Sem., 1837; married to Miss ANN PARKER GREEN, of
Whitesboro, N. Y., Oct. 18, 1841; married to Miss CAROLINE
ELIZABETH WILCOX, of Whitesboro, Dee. 1, 1847; died of dropsy
at Chicago, Ill., Sept. 28, 1874. He had 2 sons and 4 daughters,
who, with his wife, survived him; 1 child went before him.

Ordained, Marshall, N. Y., by Whitesboro Assoc., Apr. 8, 1840; Oriskany, N. Y.; his health failed; edited *Friend of Man*, at Utica, N. Y.; in commission business in Chicago, Ill.

HON. JARED FORDHAM OSTRANDER, class of 1832–5, æt. 69.

Born in Plattekill, Ulster Co., N. Y., Sept. 13, 1805; united with the 1st Cong. Church in Pompey, 1826; graduated from Oneida Institute in 1832; Auburn, Jun. and part of Mid. years; married to Miss ROWENA WELLS, of Pompey Hill, July 23, 1834; died of cancerous disease of stomach at Mantorville, Wis., Nov. 19, 1874. His wife, 1 son and 2 daughters survived him.

Ordained, Oswego, N. Y., by Assoc., Sept. 3, 1834; Oswego, 1834–5; South Onondaga, 1835–6; Milwaukee, Wis., 1836–8; Jefferson Co., Wis., on a farm, but preaching much, and doing miss. work, 1838–66; resident Mantorville, from 1866; Judge of Probate of Dodge Co.

HON. GERRIT SMITH, LL. D., Trustee 1834–7, æt. 78.

Born in Utica, N. Y., March 6, 1797; united with the Pres. Ch. in Peterboro, N. Y., Mar. 17, 1826; graduated from Hamilton College in 1818; LL. D. from Adrian College; married to Miss WEALTHY ANN BACKUS, of Clinton, N. Y., Jan. 11, 1819; married to Miss ANN CARROLL FITZHUGH, of Geneseo, Jan. 3, 1822; died of dropsy of the brain in New York, Dec. 2, 1874. He had 7 children; his wife, 1 son and 1 daughter survived him.

Admitted to practice Law, 1853; member of Congress, 1853; active and noted as a public man, an orator, and an opponent of slavery.

Published, besides pamphlets and articles, "Gerrit Smith in Congress," 1855; "Sermons and Speeches," 1861; "The Religion of Reason," 1864; "Speeches and Letters"; "The Theologies," 1866; "Nature the Base of a Free Theology," 1867; "Correspondence with Albert Barnes," 1868.

SIDNEY HOLMAN, class of 1830–3, æt. 75.

Born in Royalston, Mass., Jan. 5, 1800; came to Aub. from Ch. there; graduated from Williams College in 1830; Auburn from June, 1831, through the Middle year; married to Miss MYRA FISHER, of Templeton, Mass., Jan. 8, 1833; married to Miss L. C. GRISWOLD, of Brandon, Vt., after 1852; died at Goshen, Mass., Dec. 31, 1874. He had 1 son and 3 daughters, and left a widow and 2 daughters.

Ordained and installed at Saugus, Mass., (Cong.) Jan. 16, 1833; Saugus, 1832–4; Killingly, Conn., 1836–8; Webster, Mass., 1838–40; Millbury, minister and resident, 1840–56; Holyoke, 1856–62; Goshen, 1862–5; Windsor, 1865–9; Gohsen, 1870; East Weathersfield, Vt., from 1871.

JOSEPH AYER PEPOON, class of 1823–6, æt. 78.

Born in Hebron, Conn., March 5, 1797; united with the 1st Church, Painesville, O., May 10, 1818; entered the Auburn Mid.

class, April 20, 1825, and studied part of a year; married to
Miss SARAH EUNICE STARKE, of Mecca, O., March 5, 1833;
married to Mrs. JANE KING SMITH, of Claridon, O., Oct. 28,
1852; died of pneumonia at Kingston, Mich., Dec. 31, 1874.
He had 1 son and 3 daughters; his wife, son and 2 daughters
survived him.

Ordained by Grand River Presby., Feb. 6, 1828; Mantua, O.,
1826–7; Thompson, 1829; Parkman, 1829–30; Bloomfield,
and Bristol, 1830; Greene, 1830–2; Mecca and Bazetta, 1831–
2; Batavia, Orwell and Southington, 1833; Bricksville, 1833–4;
Munson, 1835–40; afterward resident in Munson; resident
Kingston, Mich., from 1872.

1875.

ALEXANDER H. FULLERTON, class of 1865–8.
Born in Philadelphia, Pa.; united with the Chambers Pres. Ch.
in Phila.; before entering Sem., chaplain in U. S. A.; Auburn,
from Dec., 1865 and 1866–7; probably not married; died in
Philadelphia, about 1875.
Ordained before going to Beverly; Beverly, N. J., 1870–2.

BENNETT FAIRCHILD NORTHROP, class of 1824–7, æt. 73.
Born in Brookfield, Conn., Oct. 16, 1801; united with the Cong.
Church in Bethel, Sept., 1817; graduated from Yale College in
1824; admitted to the Auburn Jun. class, April 20, 1825;
married to Miss MARTHA STILLMAN, of Wethersfield, Conn.,
May 5, 1827; married to Miss ELIZABETH COTTON BULL, of
Hartford, June 24, 1845; died of softening of the brain at
Griswold, March 4, 1875. He had 5 sons and 3 daughters;
his wife and 3 daughters survived him.
Acting pastor, Tolland, Mass., 1827–8; ordained pastor of First
Cong. Church, Manchester, Conn., Feb. 4, 1829; dismissed,
Oct. 29, 1850; agt. of Am. S. S. Union, 1850–2; pastor at
Griswold, Conn., 1853–70.

JOSIAH BACON, class of 1821–4, æt. 78.
Born in Egremont, Mass., Oct. 29, 1796; united with the Cong.
Church in Egremont, Nov. 22, 1816; graduated from Williams
College in 1820; nearly finished Auburn course, but stopped by
ill health; never married; died at Egremont, of congestion of
the lungs, April 14, 1875.
Licensed by Berkshire Assoc., 1825, but never ordained; preached
1 year at Freedom, O.; taught in Va.; engaged in farming in
Egremont.

TERTIUS STRONG CLARKE, D. D., class of 1824–7, æt. 76.
Born in Westhampton, Mass., Dec. 17, 1798; united with the
Cong. Church in Westhampton; graduated from Yale College

in 1824; D. D. from Hamilton College in 1856; married to AL-
MIRA ABIGAIL MARSHALL, of Granville, Mass., Sept., 1827;
died at Neath, Pa., April 14, 1875. He had 1 son and 4 daughters; 2 daughters survived him.

Ordained pastor of Cong. Church, South Deerfield, Mass., Oct. 3,
1827; S. Deerfield, 1827–34; Haddam, Conn., 1834–7; Stockbridge, Mass., from 1837, 12 years; Penn Yan, N. Y., from 1850;
Pres. Church, Franklin, N. Y., from 1852; Cuyahoga Falls, O.,
from 1858; Pres. Church, Weedsport, N. Y., 1864–5; afterwards
resided at Cuyahoga Falls, and preached occasionally.

CALVIN MORRILL, class of 1830–3, æt. 69.

Born in Boscawen, N. H., Dec. 6, 1805; united with the Boscawen Church, Jan. 16, 1820; graduated from Dartmouth College
in 1829; Auburn, 1830–2; Andover, 1837; married to Miss
MARY CLARK, of Boscawen, Feb. 28, 1846; died of brain paralysis at Webster, May 14, 1875. His wife survived him; no
children.

Never ordained; farmer in Webster, N. H.; active as a citizen
and Church member.

JAMES RICHARDS, JR., D. D., LL. D., class of 1833–6, æt. 62.

Born in Newark, N. J., July 21, 1813; son of Prof. James
Richards, D. D.; joined 2d. Pres. Church, Auburn, Jan. 20,
1834; student of Union and Hamilton Colleges, in class of
1834; Auburn the course and post grad., 1836–7; A. M. from
Hamilton College, 1839; D. D. from Lafayette College, 1850;
LL. D. from Planters' College; married to Miss ELIZABETH
BEALS, of Canandaigua, N. Y., Aug. 25, 1836; married to Miss
SARAH WISNER, of Penn Yan, Nov. 16, 1847; married to Mrs.
HELEN S. FRANKLIN, of N. Y. City, July 26, 1857; died
suddenly at Edinburgh, Scotland, July 30, 1875. His wife, 2
sons and 3 daughters survived him; 1 daughter went before
him.

Ordained pastor at Aurora, N. Y., by Presby. of Cayuga, July 18,
1837; Penn Yan, from 1841; Morristown, N. J., from 1847;
prof. of Mor. Phil. and Belles Lettres, Planters' College, Miss.,
from 1853; minister in New Orleans; teacher and minister in
Litchfield, Conn.; pastor in East Boston, Mass., from 1870, in
Charlestown, W. Va., from 1872.

Published "The Safe Side," 1875.

ROYAL MANN, class of 1829–32, æt. 70.

Born in Orford, N. H., Nov. 6, 1805; graduated from Dartmouth
College in 1829; Aub. Sen. class from " the Union Seminary ;"
married to Miss SARAH P. LEE, of Rochester, Oct. 13, 1839;
married to Mrs. MARY A. RICH RAYMOND, of Penfield, Jan. 31,
1861; married to Mrs. LAURA DURFEE, of Marion, Oct. 16,
1866; died of inflammation of kidneys at Marion, Aug. 10, 1875.
His wife survived him; his one son died in the Army in 1863.

Ordained, Marion, Mar. 10, 1839; teaching in N. Y. City, 1834-8; Marion from 1839, and teacher of Greek and Latin in the Marion Institute for 3 years; Chili; Webster; Marion again; Hector; Penfield, 1859; resident in Marion.

ARUNAH HALL LILLY, class of 1848-51, æt. 56.

Born at Castle Creek, N. Y., March 18, 1819; united with the 1st Pres. Ch. of Binghamton, about 1834; graduated from Williams College in 1848; 2 years at Union Seminary, N. Y.; Mid. year at Auburn; married to Miss SOPHIA M. CLARK MARSH, of Milton, N. Y., Jan. 22, 1852; died of paralysis of the bladder at Troy, Kansas, Aug. 13, 1875. His wife, 2 sons and 3 daughters survived him.

Ordained in N. Y. City by 3rd Presby. of N. Y., Oct. 10, 1851; Cranesville, (now Cranford) N. J., 1851-3; Centreville, N. Y., 1853-5; Sherman, Cong. Ch., 1 year; Silver Creek, 1856-9; East Palmyra, 1859-70; Troy, Kan., from 1871.

EDWARD SILAS LACY, class of 1850-53, æt. 49.

Born at Galway, N. Y., Nov. 27, 1826; united with the Cong. Ch. in Clinton, Nov. 5, 1848; graduated from Hamilton College in 1850; married to Miss ISABELLA HILL BORLAND, of Montgomery, N. Y., Dec. 6, 1859; died at St. Helena, Cal., Aug. 23, 1875. His wife, 1 son and 2 daughters survived him.

Ordained, 1st Ch., Syracuse, by Presby. of Onondaga, Apr. 12, 1854; home miss. in Crescent City, Cal., 1 year; 1st Cong. Church in San Francisco, to 1864; invalid in Europe, 2 years; farming near Martinsburgh, W. Va., 3 years; Cong. Church in Brooklyn, Cal., 1871-74.

THOMAS ROCKWELL TOWNSEND, class of 1834-7, æt. 70.

Born at South Salem, N. Y., July 6, 1805; united with the Church in Lysander, about 1830; married to Miss JANE HOLMES, of Genoa, Oct. 1, 1828; married to Miss ANGERLINE BARTLETT SHAPLEY, of Oswego, Oct. 18, 1834; died at Meridian, Sept, 11, 1875. He had 2 daughters; his wife and 2 grand children survived him.

Ordained pastor at Cayuga by Cayuga Presby., Oct. 30, 1838; chap. of Aub. State Prison from 1840; pastor at Fulton, from 1843; Burdett from 1851; Dinsmore and Hyde Park, Pa., from 1855; lived at Meridian, N. Y., and supplied Churches from 1866.

CALEB PERKINS SEYMOUR, class of 1832-5, æt. 67.

Born in Granby, Conn., June 8, 1808; united with the Cong. Ch. in Otis, Mass., 1826; graduated from Williams College in 1832; never married; found dead in a deserted house, at Sedalia, Mo., Sept. 20, 1875.

Licensed by Cayuga Presby. in 1835; never ordained or settled over a Church; he engaged in business in Ravenna, O., and afterward taught in Illinois, Iowa, Arkansas, Missouri, Texas, Montana and Kansas.

SETH WILLARD SEGUR, class of 1859–62, æt. 44.

　　Born in Chittenden, Vt., Dec. 24, 1831 ; united with the Church in Pittsfield, at the age of 14 ; graduated from Middlebury College in 1859 ; married to Miss ELLEN L. BLOSSOM, of Pittsfield, Sept. 13, 1859 ; died of typhoid fever, while visiting at Tallmadge, Ohio, Sept. 24, 1875. His wife and son survived him.

　　Ordained by Council, in Pittsfield, May 28, 1862 ; pastor of Cong. Church in Tallmadge, Ohio, for 9 years ; Gloucester, Mass., 2 years ; West Medway, 2 years.

WILLIAM URIAH BENEDICT, class of 1829–32, æt. 67.

　　Born in Stamford, Conn., Sept. 25, 1808 ; joined the Pres. Church of Scipio, N. Y., at 10 years of age ; graduated from Williams College in 1829 ; married to Miss ALMIRA ANN BENNETT, of Owasco Lake, Jan. 18, 1834 ; died in Vermontville, Mich., Oct. 18, 1875. His wife, 2 sons and 2 daughters survived him ; two children died before him.

　　Ordained and installed at Ira, by Presbytery of Cayuga, June 10, 1834 ; Ira, 5 years ; Sweden, 2 years ; Richmond, 1½ years ; Vermontville, Mich., teaching and preaching since 1842 ; sec'y and treas. of Olivet College 5 years of that time.

ISAAC ANDERSON MARTIN, class of 1867–70, æt. 35.

　　Born in Jefferson County, Tenn., 1841 ; united with the Pres. Church in Strawberry Plains, 1852 ; studied 2 years in Maryville College in class of 1860 ; Auburn, 1867–9 ; Lane, 1869–70 ; married to MARGARET AULT, of Knox Co., Tenn., in 1873 ; died of typhoid fever at Strawberry Plains, Tenn., Oct. 30, 1875. He had 2 sons ; his wife and sons survived him.

　　Ordained, 1871 or 1872, by Presby. of Union ; resident at Strawberry Plains and stated supply of Mount Horeb, St. Paul's, and Hebron, E. Tennessee, from 1871.

JAMES SKINNER SEYMOUR, Trustee 1829–45, æt. 85.

　　Born in West Hartford, Conn., Apr. 15, 1791 ; united with the 1st Pres. Church in Auburn, Apr. 27, 1821 ; never married ; died of old age at Auburn, Dec. 3, 1875.

　　Clerk in Bank of Hartford ; cashier in the Bank of Auburn, 1817–49 ; president of same, 1849–75 ; by bequest founder of Seymour Library and Seymour Hospital in Auburn.

ALEXANDER DOUGLASS, class of 1865–8, æt. 37.

　　Born in Cavan, Ontario Co., Canada, Aug., 1838 ; united with the Millbrook Church in Cavan, at the age of 15 ; studied 3 years in Genesee College and Michigan University ; married to Miss ALICE MARVIN, of Lima, N. Y., March, 1861 ; died at Lima, N. Y., Dec. 4, 1875. One daughter preceded him ; his wife, 2 sons and 2 daughters survived him.

　　Ordained at Mendon, N. Y., by Presbytery of Rochester in 1871 ; Seneca Castle, and Evans Mills, 1868–71 ; Mendon, 1871–2 ; Menasha, Wis., 1872–3, when health failed.

BAXTER DICKINSON, D. D., Professor, æt. 81.

> Born in Amherst, Mass., April 14, 1795; united with the Cong. Church in Amherst, 1811; graduated from Yale College in 1817; graduated from Andover The. Sem. in 1821; D. D. from Amherst College in 1838; married to Miss MARTHA BUSH, of Boylston, Mass., June 4, 1823; died of debility of old age at Brooklyn, N. Y., Dec. 7, 1875. He had 3 sons and 6 daughters; his wife, 1 son and 3 daughters survived him; one son was R. S. S. Dickinson, of the class of 1845–8.
>
> Ordained pastor of Cong. Church, Longmeadow, Mass., March 5, 1823; Longmeadow, 1823–9; 3d Pres. Church, Newark, N. J., 1829–35; prof. of Sac. Rhet. and Past. Theol., Lane Seminary, 1835–9; prof. of Sac. Rhet. and Past. Theol. in Auburn, 1839–47; acting prof. at Andover Sem. in same chair, 1848; agt. and sec. of Am. and For. Chr. Un., at Boston, Mass., 1850–9; resided at Lake Forest, Ill., 1859–68; afterward in Brooklyn.
>
> Wrote the "Auburn Declaration," in 1837; Moderator of General Assembly at Philadelphia in 1839.

CYRUS HUDSON, class of 1825–8, æt. 75.

> Born in Dorset, Remington Co., Vt., June 30, 1800; united with the Cong. Church of Dorset in 1817; graduated from Middlebury College in 1825; married to Miss ELIZA MARSH, of Vt., Jan. 23, 1829; died in Springfield, Ill., Dec. 11, 1875. He had 2 sons and 5 daughters; his wife, 1 son and 2 daughters survived him.
>
> Ordained by Presby. of Cayuga, at Scipio, N. Y., Feb. 3, 1830; home miss. at Milan, and W. Groton, to 1831; pastor at Canaan Four Corners, 4 years; Curtisville, Mass., 3 years; agt. of Am. Tract Soc., 1837–49; pastor at Mount Morris, N. Y., 1840–7; Dorset, Vt., 1847–54; afterward engaged in various labors; resident in Belvidere, and in Springfield, Ill., from 1868.

CHARLES LOUIS HEQUEMBOURG, class of 1836–9, æt. 64.

> Born at New Haven, Conn., July 15, 1811; graduated at Yale College in 1835; Auburn, from Yale Col. Ch., 1835–9; married to Miss EMILIA SOPHIA WILLIAMS, Oct. 25, 1842; died at McPherson, Neb., Dec. 24, 1875. He had 4 sons and 3 daughters; his wife, 3 sons and 2 daughters survived him.
>
> Ordained and installed at Dunkirk, N. Y., Oct. 24, 1841; Fredonia, 1 year; Dunkirk, 4 years; Jamestown, 3 years; Dansville, 7 years; Warren, Pa., 7 years; appointed Army chaplain at Fort Kearney, in 1868; transferred to Fort McPherson, Neb., in 1874.

1876.

JONATHAN BAILEY CONDIT, D. D., Professor, æt. 67.

> Born in Hanover, N. J., Dec. 16, 1808; united with the Pres. Ch. in Woodbridge, Aug. 5, 1825; graduated from Princeton College in 1827; graduated from Princeton Theol. Sem. in 1830;

D. D. from Princeton College in 1847; married to Miss ELIZA KETURAH WOODHULL, of Lawrenceville, N. J., July 14, 1831; married to Miss SARA STRONG WOODHULL, of Longmeadow, Mass., in 1836; died of prostatic hypertrophy, at Auburn, Jan. 1, 1876. He had 1 son and 5 daughters; his wife and 2 daughters survived him.

Ordained pastor of Cong. Church, Longmeadow, Mass., by Council, July 14, 1831; prof. of Rhetoric in Amherst College, 1835–8; past. of Cong. Church, Portland, Me., 1838–45; 2d Pres. Ch., Newark, N. J., 1845–50; prof. of Sac. Rhet. and Past. Theol., Lane Seminary, 1851–5; prof. of Sac. Rhet. and Past. Theol., Auburn, 1854, and emeritus prof. till death. Moderator of General Assembly at Syracuse in 1861.

DARWIN CHICHESTER, class of 1840–3, æt. 59.

Born in Fishkill, N. Y., April 2, 1817; united with the Brick Pres. Church in Rochester, April 28, 1833; graduated from Union College in 1839; married to Miss AMANDA BARRIS, of Chagrin Falls, O., 1843; married to Miss CAROLINE ELIZABETH CHAPIN, of Rochester, Feb., 1850; died of apoplexy, Hammondsport, N. Y., Jan. 11, 1876. He had 2 sons and 5 daughters, all of whom, with his wife, survived him.

Ordained at Jackson, Mich., by Jackson Assoc., Aug 22, 1843; 1st. Cong. Church of Jackson, 1843–4; Attica and Pembroke, N. Y., 1844–9; North East, Pa., 1850; Mount Morris, N. Y., 1851–5; Corning, 1856–9; Wolcott, 1859–63; Burdett, 1863–9; Hammondsport, till his death.

Published "Hannah's Vow, or Hallowed Motherhood," 1873.

ISAAC JONES, class of 1824–7, æt. 89.

Born in Norwich, Vt., 1789; united with the Pres. Church while young; entered Sem. from Church in Stafford; married to Miss WALTERS, of Western N. Y., 1829; married to Miss MARIA W. FINLEY, of Bethel, Va., 1837; married to Miss ELLENA M. BOUCHELLE, of Morganton, N. C., Aug. 10, 1842; died of old age at Columbia, Mo., Jan. 27, 1876. He had 1 child; his wife survived him.

Ordained by Presby. of Genesee, Feb. 2, 1829; resident in Middlebury Village, N. Y., preaching in revivals; supply at Mayville, 1830–2; evang. in Va., 1832–4; Hebron, Va., 1835–9; Columbia, Mo., 1840–6; resident at Columbia.

THOMAS KITCHEL CRANE, class of 1870–3, æt. 46.

Born in Middletown, N. Y., April 26, 1830; united with the Cong. Ch. in New Milford, Pa.; studied in Select School there; married to Miss PHEBE LOUISA CRANE, of New Milford, Aug. 24, 1854; married to Miss ROSETTA M. ROUNDS, Sept. 2, 1873; died of blood poisoning at Presb. Hospital, N. Y., Feb. 20, 1876. He had 2 sons and 2 daughters; 1 daughter survived him. He became an invalid soon after graduating.

SETH PARSONS MERWIN HASTINGS, class of 1834–7, æt. 63.
 Born in Clinton, N. Y., April 13, 1813 ; united with the Cong.
 Church in Clinton, May 1, 1831; graduated from Hamilton
 College in 1833 ; admitted to the Auburn Mid. class from
 Andover, Oct. 15, 1835 ; married to Miss ELIZABETH BARNARD
 BUTTRICK, of Clinton, Oct. 1, 1838 ; died of paralysis, at Ac-
 cord, N. Y., Feb. 24, 1876. He had 3 sons and 1 daughter ;
 2 sons and the daughter survived him.
 Ordained at Clinton, by Presby. of Utica, Feb. 21, 1838; Pres.
 Church at Vernon Centre, 1839–41 ; Moravia, 1842–5 ; Summer
 Hill, 1845–8 ; Pompey Hill, 1848–55 ; Ref. Church at Chitte-
 nango, 1855–9 ; Coxsackie, 1860–70 ; Accord, 1870–6.

AMOS PAYNE HAWLEY, class of 1834–7, æt. 62.
 Born in Moreau, N. Y., May, 1813 ; united with the Pres. Church
 in Warren, Pa., 1831 ; graduated from Western Reserve College
 in 1834 ; Auburn Mid. class from Lane Sem., Oct. 14, 1835 ;
 married to Miss SARAH ARTIMICIA HARVEY, of Poughkeepsie,
 N. Y., in 1838 ; died of paralysis of the heart at Jersey City, N.
 J., Feb. 26, 1876. He had 2 sons ; his wife survived him.
 Ordained pastor at Springville, N. Y., by Buffalo Presby., Jan. 30,
 1839 ; Springville from March, 1838; soon after his ordination,
 he was injured by the fall of a tree, and was never able to preach
 afterward ; resided in Jersey City, N. J.

ORSON PARKER, class of 1830–3, æt. 75.
 Born in Methuen, Mass., Oct. 9, 1800 ; united with the Pres. Ch.
 in Adams, N. Y., 1831 ; practiced Law at Adams, 1826–31 ; entered the Mid. class at Auburn, Oct. 13, 1831, and remained 1
 year ; married to Miss CELESTINE GRIDLEY, of Adams, 1826;
 married to Miss DIANA ELEANOR ATHERTON, of Henderson,
 Sept. 3, 1832 ; died of paralysis at Havana, March 14, 1876. He
 had 4 sons and 5 daughters ; his wife, 2 sons and 2 daughters
 survived him.
 Ordained at Rodman, N. Y., by the Black River Assoc., May 9,
 1832 ; labored as an evangelist, every year, without intermission,
 till his death, assisting in more than 400 revivals; was engaged
 in a revival meeting at Havana, when stricken with the paralysis which terminated his life.
 His book on revivals, "The Fire and the Hammer," with biographical sketch, published in 1877.

JONATHAN BANCROFT PARLIN, class of 1833–6, æt. 69.
 Born in Middlesex Co., Mass., Feb. 24, 1807 ; united with the
 Cong. Church in Stockholm, N. Y. ; studied at Potsdam Acad.
 and Western Reserve College ; married to Miss ESTHER MOR-
 GAN, of Potsdam, N. Y. ; married to Miss SARAH ALMA LAW-
 RENCE, of Norwalk, O., Apr. 10, 1855 ; died of bilious colic at
 Stacyville, Ia., Apr. 29, 1876. He had 2 sons and 3 daughters ;
 his wife, 2 sons and 2 daughters survived him.

Ordained by Black River Assoc., 1838; Monroeville, O., Cong.
Ch., 10 years to 1849; Birmingham, O., 1850–2; Vermillion,
1853–4; Colesburg, Iowa, 1855–61; Republic, Pres. Ch., 1861–4;
Stacyville, Cong. Ch., 1866–9, and resident there till death.

GEORGE WOOLSEY RYERSON, class of 1874–7, æt. 28.
　Born in New York City, Jan. 2, 1848; united with the State St.
Cong. (afterward Pres.) Church, Autumn of 1866; studied at
Rutgers College in class of 1870; in business in Buffalo, 1871–4;
married to Miss ELLEN I. GAZLAY, of Buffalo, Feb. 5, 1874;
died of typhus fever at Auburn, June 7, 1876. His wife survived him.

SILAS CLARK BROWN, class of 1825–8, æt. 79.
　Born in Easthampton, Mass., Sept. 2, 1797; united with the Ch.
in Prattsburgh, N. Y., Feb. 21, 1819; graduated from Union
College in 1826; entered Aub. Jun. class, June, 1826, and re-
mained through Mid. year; married to Miss MARY CLEVELAND,
of Brooklyn, Conn., Aug. 16, 1830; died of brain disease at
West Bloomfield, June 14, 1876. He had 2 sons and 2 daugh-
ters, all of whom, with his wife, survived him.
　Ordained and installed at West Bloomfield, N Y., by Presby. of
Ontario, April 23, 1828; West Bloomfield, 1828–37; Batavia,
1835–6; York, 1837–42; Pembroke, 1842–6; resident at West
Bloomfield from 1847, supplying at Centerfield, 1847–9, West
Bloomfield, new Church, 1849–54, Bristol, 1854–60, and other
Churches for a few years longer.
　Published several sermons.

DILLIS DYER HAMILTON, class of 1853–6, æt. 53.
　Born in Sharon, Vt., Jan. 14, 1824; united with the Cong.
Church in Royalton, 1842; graduated from Univ. of Roch-
ester in 1853; entered the Auburn Sen. class from Rochester The. Sem., Jan. 21, 1856; married to Miss ELIZA SAUN-
DERS, at West Gaines, N. Y., Jan. 3, 1854; died of stomatitis at
Pompeii, Mich., July 22, 1876. He had 3 sons and 5 daughters;
3 sons and 4 daughters survived him.
　Ordained at Cambria Center, N. Y., by Council, Oct. 13, 1858;
Akron, 1857–9; Cambria, 1859–63; Clarence, 1863–6; Somerset, 1 year; Pompeii, Mich., 1868–76. During the eight years
of this last pastorate, he also preached in Ithaca, Mich., and
other neighboring places.

ROBINSON SMILEY LOCKWOOD, class of 1833–6, æt. 70.
　Born in Springfield, Vt., Aug. 10, 1806; united with the Pres. Ch.
in Potsdam, N. Y., 1822; graduated from Middlebury College
in 1832; Auburn, 1 or 2 years from 1833; married to Miss
SARAH ANN NOBLE, of Canton, N. Y., Oct., 1835; married to
Miss AGNES RADLE, of Meadville, Pa., Nov., 1843; married to
Mrs. NANCY BATES, of Piqua, O.; died of heart disease at

Mount Vernon, O., Aug. 13, 1876. He had 2 sons and 3 daughters; 1 son and 3 daughters survived him.

Ordained pastor of Pres. Ch., Girard, Pa., by Presby. of Erie, Jan. 11, 1837; Girard, 1837–41; Meadville, Pa., 2d Pres. Ch., 1841–3; practiced Law, Erie, 1846–7; preached, Piqua, O., 1849–50; Berlin Heights, 1858; Steuben, Cong. Ch., 1859–60; resident in Chicago, Ill., 1864–70, in Ludlow, Ill., 1871–3, in Texas, 1873–6.

GUSTAVUS LEMUEL FOSTER, class of 1840–3, æt. 58.

Born in Royalton, N. Y., May 5, 1818; united with the Cong. Ch. in Gasport, 1833; graduated from the Oneida Institute in 1840; Auburn from March 10, 1841; after graduating at Auburn, 1 year at Yale Div. School; married to Miss CAROLINE RASH, of Ann Arbor, Mich., Dec. 31, 1844; married to Miss H. ELIZABETH PETTENGILL, of Grantville, Mass., May 13, 1852; died of dysentery at Lapeer, Mich., Sept. 9, 1876. He had 13 children; his wife, 3 sons and 7 daughters survived him.

Ordained pastor of Cong. Church, Dexter, Mich., by Jackson Assoc., Dec. 25, 1844; Jackson, 1846–52; Union Church, Clinton, 1846–54; Pres. Church, Ypsilanti, 1854–62; Coldwater, 1862–5; Cong. Church, Bethel, Conn., 1865–7; Pres. Church, Howell, Mich., 1867–72; Lapeer, Mich., from 1873.

MONTGOMERY MORGAN WAKEMAN, class of 1843–6, æt. 56.

Born in Ballston, N. Y., June 14, 1820; united with the First Pres. Church in Ballston in 1832; sustained examination in College studies at entering Seminary; A. M. from Union College in 1846; Auburn to middle of Sen. year; married to Miss ALIDA A. CONDE, of Charlton, N. Y., in 1840; died of nervous prostration, at Otho, Iowa, Sept. 11, 1876. He had 2 sons and 2 daughters; his wife and 1 son survived him.

Ordained by Presby. of Cayuga, 1849; preached at Union, N. Y., to 1853; Warren Co., 1853–7; Lafayette, N. Y., 1858–63; National; Farmersburg, Iowa, 1863–73: afterward at Maywood and Des Plaines, Ill.

JONATHAN ALDEN WOODRUFF, class of 1831–4, æt. 68.

Born in Coventry, Conn., April 18, 1808; united with the Pres. Church in Wayne, O., in 1825; graduated from Hamilton College in 1831; Junior year in Auburn; married to Miss SUSAN OSBORNE, of Candor, N. Y., 1831; married to Miss AURELIA TALCOTT, of Hartford, Conn.; married to Miss EMILY S. GRIFFITH, of Phelps, N. Y., Dec. 25, 1872; died of dropsy at Imlay City, Mich., Sept. 29, 1876. He had 6 sons and 7 daughters; his wife, 1 son and 3 daughters survived him.

Ordained pastor, 2nd Ch., Madison, O., 1834; Warren, 1832–4; Unionville and Madison, 1834–5; Monroe, 1836–7 and 1839–40; Wooster, 1838; Stephenson, Ill., 1841; chan. of Rock Island Univ. from 1842; Newton Falls, O., 1849; Conneautville, Pa., 2 years; teacher, Olean, N. Y., 1853–5; Conneaut, O., 1856–7;

Allison, Lapeer and Goodland, Mich., 1859–62; Pres. Ch.,
Allison, Mich., 1863–7; resident at Burnside and afterward at
Imlay, 1868–76.

JOHN DAVIS JONES, class of 1866–9, æt. 37.
Born in Pembrokeshire, South Wales, Aug. 14, 1839; graduated
from Hamilton College in 1866; married to Miss MARY L.
FISHER, of Pella, Iowa, March, 1872; died of consumption at
Pella, Oct., 1876. He had 1 son and 2 daughters; his wife and
2 children survived him.
Ordained by Utica Presbytery, Dec., 1869; Unionville, Ia., 1869–
70; English Settlement, 1870–2; Monroe, O., 1873–4; then
resident at Pella, an invalid, till his death.

AMOS DELOS GRIDLEY, D. D., class of 1840–3, æt. 57.
Born in Clinton, N. Y., Nov. 3, 1819; united with the Cong. Ch.
in Clinton in 1838; graduated from Hamilton College in 1839;
studied at Andover after leaving Aub.; D. D. from Olivet Col-
lege in 1876; married to Miss ELLEN M. BRISTOL, of Clinton,
April 17, 1843; married to Miss MARY TWINING, of New Haven,
Conn., Sept. 25, 1872; died of pleuro-pneumonia at Clinton,
Oct. 23, 1876. He had 2 daughters; his wife and daughters
survived him.
Ordained, probably by Oneida Assoc., June 11, 1846; Pres. Ch.,
Waterville, N. Y., 1847–51; then resident in Clinton till death.
Published "Thoughts for the Afflicted," 1854, and "History of
Kirkland," 1874.

SAMUEL WOODBURY, class of 1826–9, æt. 82.
Born in Groton, N. H., May 29, 1794; entered Auburn Jun. class
from the Bowery Pres. Church, N. Y., "on satisfactory testimonials of his classical attainments," Nov. 13, 1826; licentiate of
Newark Presby.; never married; died of old age at Natick,
Mass., Nov. 17, 1876.
Ordained to labor in Cairo, N. Y., by Presby. of Columbia, April
21, 1841; left Cairo about July 24, 1842; resided in New York
and preached occasionally; New Lebanon; Freetown, Mass.,
1848–52; Chiltonville, Mass., 1859–65; resident at Chiltonville,
1865–9, at Freetown, 1869–72, at Natick, 1872–6.

ISAAC FOOTE ADAMS, class of 1825–8, æt. 75.
Born in Hamilton, N. Y., Dec. 4, 1801; united with the Pres. Ch.
in Sherburne Hill, 1816; graduated from Hamilton College in
1825; married to Miss LAURA AUSTIN, of Skaneateles, Nov. 9,
1831; died of heart disease at Norwich, Nov. 23, 1876. He
had 4 sons and 2 daughters; his 2 daughters survived him.
Ordained by Chenango Presby., Sept. 10, 1828; 1 year at Mt.
Pleasant, Pa.; Pitcher, N. Y., 1830–4 and 1840–5; Columbus,
1834–40; Triangle, 1845–9; then called home to Sherburne, to
assist in the care of his father; Seeley Creek, Pa., 1855–61;
Summer Hill, N. Y., 1861–70; then resident in Auburn till shortly before his death.

RICHARD KAY, class of 1829–32, æt. 78.

Born in Dublin, Ireland, Jan. 16, 1799 ; united with the English Ep. Church, in childhood ; removed to Canada West in 1819 ; some years later studied at Hadley, Mass.; studied Theology with Rev. Mr. Woodbridge, of Hadley, Mass.; Auburn, 1830–2 ; married to Miss MARY ANNE FLYNN, of Auburn, June 6, 1832 ; died of apoplexy at Lansing, Mich., Jan. 2, 1877. He had 5 sons and 5 daughters ; his wife and 3 sons survived him.

Ordained pastor, Victor, N. Y., by Council, Jan. 23, 1833 ; Victor, 1832–5 ; Holley, 1838–40 ; Warsaw, 1840–7 ; Groveland, 1847–9 ; Oakland, 1849–52 ; Bennington, Mich., 1852–77.

JOHN CHASE LORD, D. D., class of 1830–3, æt. 71.

Born in Washington, N. H., Aug. 9, 1805 ; united with the 1st Pres. Church in Buffalo, N. Y., Spring of 1830 ; studied at Madison Univ. and Hamilton College in 1820–4 ; lived in Buffalo, 1825–31 ; admitted to practice Law, Feb. 19, 1828 ; Auburn, 1831–3 ; D. D. from Hamilton College in 1841 ; married to Miss MARY ELIZABETH JOHNSON, of Buffalo, Dec. 9, 1828 ; died of brain disease, at Buffalo, Jan. 21, 1877. He had 1 adopted daughter ; his wife and daughter survived him.

Ordained by Buffalo Presby, Sept. 4, 1833 ; 2nd Pres. Church, Geneseo, N. Y., 1833–5 ; Central Pres. Church, Buffalo, from its organization, 1835–73.

Moderator of General Assembly at Charleston, S. C., 1852 ; published "Lectures to Young Men," 1838 ; "Lectures on Civilization, &c.," 1851, and many sermons and pamphlets.

JOHN GRAY, class of 1826–9, æt. 77.

Born in Dorset, Vt., Sept. 21, 1799 ; united with the Pres. Church in Cherry Valley, N. Y., in 1820 ; studied at Cherry Valley Academy ; married to Miss MARY KEELER HOYT, of Cherry Valley, Sept. 15, 1830 ; she died Dec. 3, 1863 ; died of general prostration, at Moreland, Jan. 31, 1877. He had 2 sons and 3 daughters, all of whom survived him.

Ordained at Root, N. Y., by Classis of Schoharie, July 6, 1831 ; Root, 1829–32 ; Worcester, 1832–4 ; Southport, 1834–6 ; Moreland, 1836–8 ; Mead's Creek, Campbell, Hornby, &c., 1838–64 ; Livingstonville, Smithville, Cherry Valley and Monterey, are also named without date, as fields where he labored.

BEAUFORT LADD, class of 1824–7, æt. 79.

Born in Franklin, Conn., Sept. 19, 1798 ; united with the Cong. Church in Franklin, July 1, 1821 ; graduated from Amherst College in 1824 ; Auburn, 1825–7 ; married to Miss MARY LORD ; married to Mrs. CLARISSA H. WOOD, May 4, 1849 ; died of consumption at Victory, March 19, 1877. He had no children ; his wife survived him.

Ordained at Oriskany Falls, N. Y., by Oneida Assoc., Sept. 10, 1834 ; preached at Burlington, Columbus, Sangerfield, Clarence, Parma Centre, Fowlerville, Rose Valley, Collamer, Victory.

In 1860 he retired from pastoral work to a farm in Victory, N. Y.

SAMUEL WEBSTER BUSH, class of 1836-9, æt. 71.

Born in Virginia, July 10, 1806 ; united with the Cong. Church in Lenox, Mass., 1834 ; read Law ; edited the *Pittsfield Argus*, and the *Journal and Argus*, 1829-33 ; married to Miss BETSEY WEED, of Binghamton, Feb. 12, 1840 ; died of fever at Binghamton, March 21, 1877. He had 1 son and 3 daughters ; his wife and children survived him.

Ordained pastor at Binghamton by Presbytery of Tioga, Nov. 20, 1839 ; Binghamton, 5 years ; Skaneateles, 7 years ; Norwich, 4 years ; Cooperstown, 7 years ; resident of Binghamton from 1862 ; chaplain of State Inebriate Asylum, 1866-77.

ABNER DEWITT, class of 1855-8, æt. 51.

Born in South Hadley, Mass., Aug. 7, 1826 ; united with the Plymouth Church in Cleveland, O., 1853 ; graduated from Williams College in 1851 ; practiced Law in N. Y. and Ohio, 1852-5 ; married to Miss MARY E. HASTINGS, of South Hadley, Mass., Nov. 4, 1858 ; died of consumption at Troy, N. Y., April 17, 1877. He had 2 sons and 3 daughters ; his wife, 1 son and 2 daughters survived him.

Ordained pastor in Hoosic Falls, N. Y., by Presby. of Troy, in 1859 ; Salina, N. Y. ; Hoosic Falls to 1866 ; pastor of Park Church, Troy, N. Y., 1866-71 ; of Third Pres. Church, Troy, N. Y., 1871-7.

JOHN REID MOSER, class of 1825-8, æt. 78.

Born in Brooklyn, L. I., July 26, 1799 ; united with the Pres. Ch. in Chester, N. Y., Oct. 5, 1820 ; graduated from Williams College in 1825 ; entered Auburn, May 31, 1826 ; entered Princeton June 27, 1828 ; Aub. Mid., 1827-8 ; married to Miss LUCY PORTER RHOADES, of Skaneateles, N. Y., May 23, 1831 ; died of Bright's disease at Syracuse, Apr. 18, 1877. He had 1 son and 2 daughters ; his wife and son survived him.

Ordained at Sag Harbor, L. I., by Presby. of Long Island, April 17, 1833 ; Westhampton, L. I., 1830-4 ; Riverhead, 1834-6 ; Carbondale, Pa., 1836-40 ; Oaks Corners, N. Y., 1841-8 ; afterward agt. of Am. Bib. Soc., and preaching occasionally ; living at Sodus, Geneva, Phelps and Syracuse.

GROSVENOR WILLIAMS HEACOCK, D. D., class of 1841-3, æt. 55.

Born in Buffalo, N. Y., Aug. 3, 1822 ; united with the Central Pres. Church in Buffalo in 1834 ; graduated from Western Reserve College in 1840 ; D. D. from Hamilton College in 1856 ; married to Miss NANCY RICE STONE, of Buffalo, June 13, 1848 ; died of heart disease at Buffalo, May 6, 1877. He had 4 sons and 2 daughters ; his wife, 2 sons and 2 daughters survived him.

Ordained pastor of the Lafayette Street Pres. Church, Buffalo, Oct. 20, 1845, and retained that pastorate till his death.

RUFUS SPAULDING CUSHMAN, D. D., class of 1840–3, æt. 62.

Born in Fair Haven, Vt., Aug. 31, 1815 ; united with the Cong. Church in Fair Haven, Sept. 4, 1831 ; graduated from Middlebury College, 1837 ; at Lane, 1840–1, at Auburn, 1841–3 ; D. D. from Middlebury College in 1872 ; married to Miss SARAH FOX GIBSON, of Sandy Hill, N. Y., Aug., 1846 ; died of prostatic hypertrophy at Manchester, May 18, 1877. He had 1 son and 2 daughters, all of whom survived him ; Mrs. Cushman died June 13, 1877.

Ordained pastor of Cong. Church of Orwell, Vt., Dec., 1843 ; Orwell till 1862 ; Cong. Church of Manchester, 1862–77.

THOMAS REED RAWSON, class of 1831–4, æt. 74.

Born in Townshend, Vt., July 10, 1803 ; united with the Cong. Church in Townshend, Oct. 5, 1823 ; graduated from Amherst College in 1830 ; married to Miss LOUISA WARNER DAWES, of Cummington, Mass., Oct. 17, 1834 ; married to Miss SARAH ANN THOMAS, of Vernon, N. Y., Oct. 20, 1856 ; died of cancer of the stomach at Albany, May 20, 1877. He had 3 sons and 3 daughters ; his wife, 3 sons and 2 daughters survived him.

Ordained pastor of Cong. Ch., Peru, Mass., July 10, 1834 ; Peru, 1834–6 ; Malta, N. Y., 1841–2 ; he lived at Albany, 1836–41, and 1842–77 ; superintendent of the Albany Tract and Miss. Soc. ; chaplain at the old Albany Bethel, at the Penitentiary, and at the U. S. Hospital during the war.

Published "Dominic and Patrick ; or, The Bible vs. The Papacy."

CALVIN CLARK, class of 1832–5, æt. 72.

Born in Westhampton, Mass., March 27, 1805 ; united with the Cong. Church in Westhampton Nov 5, 1826 ; graduated from Williams College in 1832 ; married to Miss EVELINA PORTER GREVES, of Skaneateles, N. Y., Oct. 5, 1835 ; died of heart disease, at Marshall, Mich., June 4, 1877. No children ; his wife survived him.

Ordained at South Bend, Ind., by Presby. of St. Joseph, April, 1836 ; preached in Mich., at Homer, Marshall, &c., 1835–7 ; Richland, 1837–43 ; miss. for Western Mich., 1843–5 ; home mission agt. for Mich., 1845–54 ; Hillsdale, 1854–8 ; district sec. of A. B. C. F. M., for Northern Ill., 1858–63 ; dist. sec. of Home Missions for Mich., 1863–69 ; supplied Churches, and was agent for Mich. Female Seminary, 1869–72 ; Synodical miss., 1872–7.

JOHN NETTLETON POWELL, class of 1842–5, æt. 59.

Born in Clinton, N. Y., Oct. 21, 1818 ; united with the Cong. Church in Clinton in 1835 ; graduated from Hamilton College in 1840 ; taught two years ; Auburn Sen. class from Yale, Oct. 21, 1844 ; married August 24, 1845, to Miss MARY E. WALRATH, of Chittenango ; died of typhoid pneumonia at Medford, Minn., June 27, 1877. He had 2 sons and 3 daughters ; his wife, sons and 1 daughter survived him.

Ordained at Chelsea, Ill., by Presby., Feb. 18, 1846; Chelsea, 1846–50; Winslow, 1850–9; Peterboro, N. Y., 1860–62; principal Yates Polytechnic Institute, Chittenango, N. Y., 1862–3; Rosendale, Wis., 1863–70; Plymouth, 1871–75; Medford, Minn., 1875–77.

ORIS FRASER, class of 1837–40, æt. 69.

Born in Steuben, N. Y., Feb. 9, 1808; united with the Pres. Ch in Phelps, 1830; graduated from Univ. of N. Y. City in 1837; studied at Union The. Sem.; entered Auburn, Junior, Dec. 9, 1837; married to Miss JANE A. FINN, of Florida, N. Y., 1840; died of apoplexy caused by sunstroke, at Florida, July 4, 1877. He had 1 son and 2 daughters; his wife and daughters survived him.

Ordained pastor of Pres. Ch., Bath, N. Y., by Presbytery, Feb., 1841; Bath, 1840–43; Springfield and Brooklyn, Pa., 1844–7; Rock Stream and Eddytown, N. Y., 1848–62; afterward resident at Florida, N. Y.

FRYE BAILEY REED, class of 1824–7, æt. 84.

Born in Brookfield, Vt., July 14, 1793; came to Aub. from Church there; graduated from Middlebury College in 1824; married to ASENATH SMITH, of Brookfield, 1828; died of old age at Prescott, Wis., Aug. 24, 1877. He had 4 sons and 1 daughter; his wife and 2 sons survived him.

Ordained, Clintonville, N.Y., by Presby, April 29, 1830; Charlotte, Waitsfield, Barnard, Vt.; Clintonville to 1840 or longer; Westville, 1843; Moira, 1846; resident Moira, 1849–53; resident Omro, Wis., 1854–75, and Prescott, from 1876.

EDWIN HALL, D. D., Professor, æt. 76.

Born in Granville, N. Y., Jan. 11, 1802; united with the Cong. Church in Granville, Sept., 1821; graduated from Middlebury College in 1826; studied Theology privately; was tutor in Middlebury, and afterward had charge of Middlebury Academy; D. D. from Middlebury College in 1846; married to Miss FANNY HOLLISTER, of Granville, Sept. 2, 1828; died of congestion of the lungs at Auburn, Sept. 8, 1877. He had 5 sons and 3 daughters; his wife, 4 sons and 2 daughters survived him.

Ordained at Hebron, N. Y., by Presby. of Troy, Aug. 27, 1830; Glen's Falls and Sandy Hill, 1830–31; had charge of Academy at Bloomfield, N. J., 1831–2; First Cong. Church of Norwalk, Conn., 1832–54; prof. of Christian Theology at Auburn, 1854–76; emeritus professor, 1876–7.

Published "Law of Baptism," 1840; "Refutation of Baptist Errors," 1840; "Law of Baptism," enlarged edition, 1846; "The Puritans and their Principles," 1846; "Historical Records of Norwalk," 1847; "Shorter Catechism, with Analysis and Proofs," 1859; with many articles, tracts, etc.

JOHN BOWER PRESTON, class of 1827–30, æt. 75.

    Born in Rupert, Vt., Dec. 29, 1802 ; united with the Cong. Church in Rupert, 1820; graduated from Middlebury College in 1826 ; married to MARY WHEATON, of Hebron, N. Y., July 4, 1831 ; married to CLARISA NORTH, of Farmington, Conn., 1833 ; died of heart disease at Chicago, Oct. 17, 1877. He had 5 sons and 1 daughter ; his wife, 4 sons and 1 daughter survived him. One son is Marcus North Preston, of 1859–62.

    Ordained at Henrietta, N. Y., by Genesee Consoc., June 2, 1830 ; Fredonia, 1830–5 ; Gowanda, 1835–41 ; Attica, 1841–8 ; Byron, 1848–50 ; Berlin, Wis., 1850–60 ; Omro, 1860–5 ; Cape Vincent, 1865–71 ; Woodville, 1871–4 ; Manlius, 1874–6.

EDWARD GIBBS BICKFORD, class of 1867–70, æt. 33.

    Born in Honeoye Falls, N. Y., July 27, 1844 ; united with the Pres. Church in Lima, Jan. 3, 1864 ; graduated from Genesee College in 1867 ; 2 years at Auburn ; 1 year at Union The. Sem., where he graduated ; married to Miss HARRIET STORRS WILLIAMS, of Columbus, N. Y., 1870 ; died of small pox at Marash, Turkey, Oct. 19, 1877 He had 3 sons ; his wife and 2 sons survived him.

    Ordained pastor at Chaumont, N. Y., by Presby. of St. Lawrence, Mar. 5, 1872 ; Chaumont, 1871–4 ; missionary professor at Marash, Turkey, 1874–7.

LUKE DE WITT, class of 1825–8, æt. 80.

    Born in Salisbury, N. Y., March 12, 1797 ; united with the Church in Salisbury ; studied at Fairfield Academy ; married to Miss EUNICE MARIETTA SERVIS, of Putnam, O., Apr. 28, 1831 ; died of pneumonia at Latta's, O., Oct. 31, 1877. He had 3 sons and 1 daughter, who with his wife, survived him.

    Ordained at Litchfield, N. Y., by Oneida Presby., Aug. 6, 1828 ; Litchfield, N. Y., 1828–30; Salem, O, 1830–2 ; Logan, 1835 ; Albany, 1852 ; Marietta, miss., 1836–7 ; Big Bottom, 1839 ; Marietta, 1840; Chester, 1844; Amestown, 1846–8 ; Lee, 1849 ; Albany, 1852.

EDWARDS MARSH, class of 1828–31, æt. 73.

    Born in Malta, N. Y., Oct. 5, 1804 ; united with the Cong. Church of Bennington Centre, Vt., Aug. 13, 1820; graduated from Hamilton College in 1827 ; married to Miss HANNAH G. THOMPSON, of Sparta, N. Y., Feb. 7, 1832 ; she died at Nunda, 1844; married to Miss CATHERINE A. CHILDS, of York, July 17, 1845 ; died of paralysis at Freeport, Ill., Nov. 5, 1877. He had 3 sons and 2 daughters ; his wife, 2 sons and 1 daughter survived him.

    Ordained by Presby. of Onondaga, Sept. 7, 1831 ; pastor of Hamilton and Barton, Canada, 7 or 8 years ; Avon, N. Y. ; Nunda, 1842–9 ; Ypsilanti, Mich., 1849–51 ; Canton, Ill., 1852–68 ; afterward at Washington, Mt. Carrol, and Freeport, Ill.

RICHARD DE FORREST, class of 1830–3, æt. 75.

Born in N. Y. City, May 24, 1802 ; united with the Cong. Church in Chili, N. Y., 1820 ; studied at Rochester Classical School ; Jun. and Mid. years in Auburn; married to Miss CHARLOTTE MCKEE, of Adams, N. Y., 1823; married to Mrs. SARAH DART HUMPHREY, of Vernon, Conn., Sept. 27, 1852 ; died suddenly of heart disease, Chicago, Ill., Nov. 20, 1877. He had 1 daughter, and 4 step-children, all of whom survived him.

Ordained at Champion, N. Y., by Black River Assoc., Sept. 4, 1832 ; in charge of Churches in Western N. Y., to 1840 ; preached as evangelist 7 years ; resident in Rochester.

JOEL GOODELL, class of 1827–30, æt. 78.

Born in Templeton, Mass., July 22, 1799 ; studied at Hamilton College, and came to Aub. from Church there; married to Miss LUCY CHILDS, of Niagara Falls, N. Y., Aug. 30, 1830; married to ELMIRA BRIGHAM, of Dunkirk, N. Y., 1833; married to Miss CLARISSA PLATT, of Oberlin, O., 1844 ; died in Tabor, Iowa, Nov. 24, 1877. He had 10 children; his wife and 5 children survived him.

Ordained at Henrietta, N. Y., by Genesee Consoc., June 2, 1830 ; home miss. in Missouri, 1830–2; Chester, O., 1832–3 ; Franklin, 1833–4; Harrisville and Westfield, 1834–5 ; Chatham, 1835 ; on a farm at Harrisville, supplying Churches as health permitted, till 1854; Clinton, 1854–6 ; Graham, Iowa, 1857–63 ; Percival, 1863–4 ; Tabor from 1864.

DAVID EDWIN KOHLER, class of 1876–9, æt. 27.

Born in Royalton, N. Y., Oct. 7, 1850 ; united with the Central Pres. Church in Auburn, Jan. 7, 1877; graduated from Cornell University in 1873; died of consumption at West Shelby, N. Y., Dec. 15, 1877.

JONATHAN CRANE, class of 1832–5, æt. 64.

Born in Schenectady, N. Y., March 27, 1814; united with the 1st Pres. Church in Schenectady, 1830 or 1831; graduated from Union College in 1832; Auburn the course, and post grad., 1835–6; married to Miss ANNA H. WHITING, of Brooklyn, N. Y., June 11, 1837; died of apoplexy at Middletown, N. Y., Dec. 25, 1877. He had 3 sons and 3 daughters ; his wife, 3 sons and 1 daughter survived him.

Ordained pastor, Attleboro, Mass., Oct. 20, 1836; Attleboro, 1836–54 and 1858–9 ; 20th St. Cong. Church, New York, from 1854; Waltham, Mass., and Patchogue, L. I., 1859–60; Middletown, N. Y., 1860–8 and 1875–7 ; St. Joseph, Mo., and Kalamazoo, Marshall, Mattawan and Plainville, Mich., 1868–75.

Published " Memorial of Mrs. Hannah Sandford " and " Memorial of Jonathan Crane," his father.

NATHANIEL POTTER COLTRIN, class of 1846–9, æt. 58.

Born in Steubenville, O., Feb. 17, 1820 ; united with the Centre Church in Crawfordsville, Ind., Apr. 3, 1843 ; graduated from

Wabash College in 1845; Auburn Mid. Class from Lane, Nov. 17, 1847; remained one year, and then took a year of private study; married to Miss ELECTA M. HOLLAND, of Belchertown, Mass., Apr. 3, 1851; died of typhoid pneumonia at Centralia, Ill., Dec. 26, 1877. He had 7 sons and 1 daughter; his wife, 3 sons and 1 daughter survived him.

Ordained at Mendon, Ill, by Illinois (now Quincy) Assoc., Oct. 13, 1850; Jacksonville, Chandlerville, Plymouth, 1850-7; Griggsville, 1857-61; chap. in the Army, and supply at Litchfield and Wythe, 1861-5; Sandoval and Clement, 1867-77.

1878.

WILLIAM DAVID SWINTON, class of 1874-7, æt. 26.

Born in St. Louis, Beauharnois Co., Canada, April 18, 1852; united with the Pres. Church in Beloit, Wis, Spring of 1873; graduated from Beloit College in 1874; died of consumption at Milwaukee, Feb. 10, 1878.

ELIAS RIGGS FAIRCHILD, D. D., class of 1824-7, æt. 77.

Born in Morristown, N. J, Aug. 17, 1801; united with the 1st Pres. Church, Mendham, Oct. 1, 1820; studied at Amherst College in 1821-2; Auburn, 1825-7; D. D. from College of Miss. in 1846; married to Miss HANNAH HUDSON, Jan. 14, 1824; she died April 7, 1825; married to Miss MATILDA McGOWEN, March 17, 1829; died of disease of kidneys at Morristown, April 22, 1878. His wife survived him; no children.

Ordained by Newark Presby., 1829; a few months at Lexington Heights, N. Y., and Bainbridge, N. Y.; agt. of Am. Bib. Soc., 1827-9; pastor at Hardyston, N. J., 1829-38; Montgomery, N. Y., 1838-9, 1847-9 and 1860-1; sec. of the Phila. branch of the A. H. M. S., 1839-47; agt. and sec. of the A. and F. Chr. Un., 1849-60; minister at Port Jervis, N. Y., 1862-6; Mt. Freedom, N. J., 1866-70; New Providence, N. J., 1871-5.

LUMAN COGGSWELL GILBERT, class of 1833-6, æt. 73.

Born in Augusta, N. Y., June 8, 1805; united with the Church in Peterboro, about 1820; graduated from Western Reserve College in 1833; married to Miss CAROLINE RIPLEY, of Marlboro, Conn., Oct. 5, 1841; died of typhoid fever at Lone Tree Lake, Minn., June 4, 1878. He had 1 son and 4 daughters; his wife and son survived him.

Ordained, Bristol, Ill., by Ottawa Presbytery, July 16, 1840; Aquabogue, L. I., 1836-8; Bristol, Ill., 1839-41; Sterling and Buffalo, 1841-7; Crete, Cong. Ch., 1847-59; Princeton, Minn., 1859-65; East Prairieville, 1866-74; then resident at Lone Tree Lake.

E. VINE WALES, class of 1840–3, æt. 62.

Born in Plymouth, N. Y., Oct. 29, 1816; united with the Cong. Church in Plymouth, 1831; graduated from Oneida Inst. in 1839; entered Auburn Mid. class, Dec., 1840, but graduated 1843; married to Miss HELEN MARIA COMSTOCK, of Laurens, N. Y., 1849; died of paralysis of the throat at Oneonta, N. Y., June 28, 1878. He had 1 son and 1 daughter; his wife and daughter survived him.

Ordained pastor, Laurens, N. Y., by Otsego Presby., 1844; Laurens, 1844–55 and 1861–5; York, 1855–8; Sprakers, Ref. Ch., 1858–61; resident Oneonta from 1865; retired 1872.

ERASTUS CLARK WILLIAMS, class of 1840–3, æt. 62.

Born in Utica, N. Y., Sept. 6, 1816; united with the Pres. Church in Dunkirk, 1832; graduated from Hamilton College in 1840; Auburn Mid. class, Oct. 18, 1841; married to Miss CORINNA N. WEBSTER, Kingsville, O., Oct., 1846, who died in Feb., 1860; married to Miss HELEN M. O'BRIEN, of Cleveland, O., March, 1864; died of bronchial consumption at Dunkirk, Oct. 3, 1878. He had 2 sons and 1 daughter; his wife, 1 son and daughter survived him.

Ordained pastor at Kingsville, O., by Grand River Presby., 1843; Kingsville, 1843–53; resigned on account of failing health; resident in Dunkirk.

COMFORT HAMILTON, M. D., class of 1827–30, æt. 72.

Born in Vermont, Jan. 9, 1807; united with 1st Pres. Church in Schenectady, May 1, 1825; graduated from Union College in 1826; Auburn, Jun. year; M. D. from Buffalo Med. College in 1853; married to Miss AMORETTA WARRINER, of Gainesville, N. Y., Dec. 2, 1832; died of ulceration of stomach at Central Road Station, Pa., Oct. 9, 1878. He had 2 sons and 1 daughter; his wife, 1 son and daughter survived him.

Practiced Medicine from about 1829, principally in Portage and Buffalo, N. Y., and in Conneautville, Sharon and Erie, Pa.

CHARLES WILEY, D D., class of 1832–5, æt. 68.

Born in Halburt, L. I., 1810; united with Dr. Joel Parker's Ch. in N. Y. City in 1828 or 1829; studied at Columbia and Princeton Colleges in 1825, '30, '31; entered Jun. Class in 1832, "on testimonials of his literary acquirements;" Auburn, the course, and post grad., 1835–6; studied also at New Haven; D. D. from Hamilton College in 1846; married to Miss ELIZA P. LYMAN, of Boston, Mass., May 1, 1839; died of paralysis at Orange, N. J., Dec. 21, 1878. He had 3 sons and 2 daughters; his wife, 2 sons and 1 daughter survived him.

Ordained pastor at Northampton, Mass., by Council, Nov. 8, 1837; Northampton, 1837–45; Ref. Ch., Utica, N. Y., 1845–55; pres. of Milwaukee Univ., Wis, 1855–7; Pres. Ch., Lafayette, Ind., 1858–9; Cong. Ch., Birmingham, Conn., 1859; Ref. Ch., Geneva, N. Y., 1859–65; in charge of a private school at Hackensack, N. J., 1866–71; from that time resident at Orange.

He edited the "Ordo Series of the Classics," published by Henry
Holt & Co., Cæsar's Commentaries, 1873, Cicero's Orations,
1873, Virgil's Æneid, 1874 ; he also published "Principles of
Love to God," about 1850, and "Ten Reasons Why I am not a
Churchman," about 1864.

1879.

GEORGE CLINTON WOOD, class of 1827-30, æt. 74.
  Born in New York City, May 20, 1805 ; united with the Cong. Ch.
  in Williamstown, 1825 ; grad. from Williams College in 1827 ;
  married to Miss FRANCES EMELINE BULKLEY, of Williamstown,
  August 3, 1830 ; died of cerebro spinal meningitis at Jacksonville, Ill., Jan. 5, 1879. He had 2 sons and 1 daughter ; his
  wife, 1 son and daughter survived him.
  Ordained at Henrietta, N. Y., by Genesee Assoc., June 2, 1830 ;
  St. Charles, Mo., 1830-2 ; Salem, 1833-7 ; Pleasant Hill, 1838-9 ;
  prof. in Marion College ; Illinois from 1839 ; Jerseyville to
  1850 ; Homer, Mich., 1851-2 ; Greenville, Ill., 1853-7 ; Jacksonville, Presb. miss. from 1858.

NORMAN KELLOGG, class of 1832-5, æt. 78.
  Born in Sheffield, Mass., Mar. 4, 1801 ; united with the 1st Cong.
  Church in Sheffield in 1822 ; studied privately ; entire course
  at Auburn, and 6 months as post graduate ; married to Miss
  MARY CAROLINE MASON, of Sheffield, Oct. 17, 1827 ; died of
  paralysis at Sheffield, Jan. 12, 1879. His wife survived him ; no
  children.
  Ordained pastor in Mishawaka, Ind., by St. Joseph Presby., 1836 ;
  Mishawaka, 1836-59 ; Paw Paw, 4½ years ; Stony Creek, 6 years ;
  resident at Sheffield, 1871-9.

JAMES AIKMAN CARNAHAN, class of 1826-9, æt. 76.
  Born in Nicholas Co., Ky., Dec. 2, 1802 ; united with the Pres.
  Church in Concord, Ky., Sept., 1817 ; studied with William W.
  Martin, Livonia, Ind., and privately at Louisville, Ky. ; entered
  the Sem. Jun. class on examination ; married to Miss ISABELLA
  LYNN, of Livonia, Ind., Jan. 30, 1830; married to MARTHA A.
  DAWSON, of Ross, Ind., Feb. 12, 1839 ; married to Mrs.
  CATHERINE B. JUDSON, of Milan, O., Sept., 1853; died of
  softening of the brain at Dayton, Jan. 19, 1879. He had 4 sons
  and 8 daughters ; his wife, 3 sons and 5 daughters survived
  him. His youngest son is Robert Aikman Carnahan, of 1879-
  82.
  Ordained at E. Genoa, N. Y., by Presby. of Cayuga, July 8, 1829 ;
  Lafayette, Ind., 1830-4; Dayton, Ind., 1834-52 and 1856-79 ;
  Delhi, 1852-6 ; trustee of Wabash College, from its foundation
  in 1832 to his death.

ROBERT TAFT CONANT, class of 1838–41, æt. 69.

Born in Barre, Mass., Sept. 1, 1810; united with the Cong. Ch. in Barre, 1826; graduated from Amherst College in 1836; entered Auburn, Apr. 5, 1838; Middler, 1838–39 and 1839–40; married to Miss CAROLINE EMILY WESTON, of Peru, N. Y., Oct. 13, 1841; died of nervous prostration at Ogdensburgh, N. Y., Jan. 28, 1879. He had 3 sons and 2 daughters; his wife, 1 son and 1 daughter survived him.

Ordained pastor, Clintonville, N. Y., by Presby. of Champlain, Nov. 4, 1841; Clintonville, 1840; Moira, 1844–6; West Oswegatchie, 1846–8; Morristown, 1848–54; Evans Mills, 1854–7; Antwerp, 1857–62; Heuvelton, 1862; resident in Ogdensburgh, N. Y., from 1865, teaching and supplying pulpits, as his health permitted.

Published sermons and articles.

LEMUEL STRONG POMEROY, class of 1835–8, æt. 67.

Born in Otisco, N. Y., Feb. 1, 1812; graduated from Hamilton College in 1835; Auburn, Junior and Middle years; married to Miss MARETT ABIGAIL ELDER, of Cortlandville, N. Y., May 20, 1837; married to Miss SARAH HALE, of Cortlandville, Feb. 8, 1853; married to Miss MARY ARMSTRONG, of Bricksburg, N. J., Dec. 16, 1868; died of paralysis at Junius, Feb. 19, 1879. He had 3 sons and 4 daughters; his wife, 1 son and 2 daughters survived him.

Prin. of Acad. at Elbridge, 1837; taught in Homer, Elbridge and Cortland, 7 years, also supplying Churches; in business in Cortland to 1850; farming at Otisco, 1850–68; minister, Truxton, and Pompey Hill, 1868–71; Savannah, 1871–8; Junius from 1878.

ELIAKIM WARE SYLVESTER, M. D., class of 1837–40, æt. 64.

Born in Cazenovia, N. Y., April 28, 1814; united with the Cong. Church in Williamstown, Mass., 1831; graduated from Union College in 1836; left Auburn on account of ill health, 1839; married to FANNY ARMS, of Conway, Mass., Oct., 1842; married to ELLETTA WHITLOCK, of Lyons, N. Y., Jan. 21, 1874; died of Bright's disease in N. Y. City, March 29, 1879. He had 2 sons and 1 daughter, who, with his wife, survived him.

Practiced Dentistry for many years, and at length became fruit grower, resident at Lyons, N. Y.

Published many papers on Horticulture and Pomology.

JAMES BLAKE WILSON, class of 1827–30, æt. 80.

Born in Whitesboro, N. Y., Aug. 20, 1799; graduated from Hamilton College in 1827; married to Miss MARY L. DUTTON, of Vernon, Spring of 1832; married to Miss ELISABETH BUSHNELL, of Ararat, Pa., 1860; died at Stockton, N. Y., Apr. 25, 1879. One daughter survived him.

Ordained by Presby. of Grand River, 1831 ; Huntsburg, O., 1830–2 ; Thomson, 1832–3 ; Sherman, N. Y., Wattsburgh, Pa., Stockton, Sheridan, Colden, Chapinsville, Sand Banks and Orwell, N. Y., 1833–49 ; Elysium, Ill., 2 years ; miss. of Presby. of Belvidere ; then laid aside by ill health for 3 years ; Waltham, Ill., 1857 ; Shabbony Grove, Ill., 2 years ; Ararat, Pa., 1859–63 ; resident at Great Bend, 1863–71.

EBENEZER SEYMOUR, class of 1824–7, æt. 78.

Born in Stillwater, N. Y., Sept. 15, 1801 ; united with the Cong. Church in Stillwater, about 1814 ; graduated from Union College in 1824 ; taught for a few months, and entered Sem. in Jan., 1825 ; married to MARY HOE, of New York City, Aug. 9, 1831 ; died of inflammation of bladder at Bloomfield, N. J., June 21, 1879. He had 4 sons and 2 daughters ; his wife, 3 sons and 2 daughters survived him.

Ordained by Albany Presby. in 1828 ; pastor, Albia, N. Y., 1831–2 ; Bloomfield, N. J., pastor, 1834–47 ; then established Bloomfield Institute for Classical and English education, over which he presided until 1860.

CORNELIUS SANFORD MEAD, class of 1841–4, æt. 61.

Born in West Charlton, N. Y., 1818 ; came to Aub. from Church in Glenville ; graduated from Union College in 1841 ; entered Auburn, 1840, but grad. in 1844 ; twice married ; his wife MARIA LOUISA, died Aug. 18, 1860, leaving 3 children ; he died June 26, 1879 ; a widow, 3 sons and 3 daughters survived him. Rotterdam, 1st Ref. Ch., 1844–9 ; Herkimer Village, 1849–59 ; resident Chatham 1859–70 ; prin. of Spencertown Acad., 1 year ; supplied Churches at Ghent, Stuyvesant Falls, New Concord, &c.

DAVID HENRY HAMILTON, D. D., class of 1841–4, æt. 66.

Born in Canajoharie, N. Y., Oct. 29, 1813 ; came to Aub. from M. E. Church in Amsterdam ; graduated from Union College in 1839 ; studied Law in Amsterdam, and practiced ; D. D. from Union College in 1862 ; married to Miss MARTHA S. WOOD, of Amsterdam, 1843 ; died of white softening of the brain at Kingsboro, N. Y., July 4, 1879. He had no children ; his wife survived him.

Ordained pastor in Trumansburgh, N. Y., by Presby., Sept. 1, 1844 ; Trumansburgh, 1844–55 ; New Haven, Ct., 1855–8 ; studying at Univ. of Berlin, 2 years ; Jacksonville, Ill., 1860–72 ; Ripley, O., 1872–9.

Published "Autology," 1873 ; and articles and addresses

LYMAN BYLES WALDO, M. D., class of 1844–7, æt. 64.

Born in Edmeston, N. Y., Apr. 9, 1815 ; united with the Pres. Ch. in Newark Valley, Apr., 1831 ; graduated from Hamilton College in 1844 ; M. D. from Cleveland Homœopathic Med. College in 1863 ; married to MARY S. McENTEE, of Whitestown, N. Y., July 8, 1847 ; died of bilious fever, at West Troy, N. Y., July 9, 1879. He had 3 sons and 1 daughter ; his wife, 2 sons and daughter survived him.

Ordained by Presby. of Buffalo, Dec. 26, 1849 ; Huron, N. Y., 1847 ; Centreville, 1849–53 ; invalid and agt. of Am. Bib. Soc., 1853–6; Cong. Ch., Eaton, N. Y., 1856 ; practiced Medicine in Adams, N. Y., 1863–9, in Oswego 4 years, in Lansingburgh 5 years ; resident at West Troy from 1878.

ASAHEL LYON BROOKS, class of 1843–6, æt. 61.

Born in Nelson, N. Y., June 18, 1818 ; united with the Pres. Church in Mayville, N. Y., May, 1835 ; studied two years at Hamilton College ; in Seminary Jun. and Mid. years ; married to Miss SARAH T. WARNER, of LeRoy, N. Y., Dec. 17, 1845 ; died of bilious fever, at Wernersville, Pa., Sept. 16, 1879. He had 3 sons and 1 daughter ; his wife and children survived him.

Ordained pastor of 4th Ch., Troy, N. Y., by Troy Presby., Sept., 1847 ; Hamilton, 1845–7 ; Troy from 1847 ; Corning from 1849 ; Albion from 1851; Bridgeport, Conn., from 1854 ; Chicago, Ill., from 1856 ; Indianapolis, Ind., from 1859 ; Chicago from 1862 ; Peoria from 1865 ; Decatur from 1868 ; Danville, 1870–9.

DAVID ANDREWS FRAME, class of 1832–5, æt. 74.

Born in Bloomfield, N. J., 1805 ; united with the Church about 1828 ; graduated from Princeton College in 1832 ; at Auburn 4 years, then at East Windsor fifteen months, and afterward at New Haven ; died at Montclair, N. J., Sept. 24, 1879. He had 1 son and 1 daughter ; the daughter survived him.

Preached in Binghamton, and in Conn. and N. J. ; in charge of Bloomfield Academy, 1841 ; of Ashland Hall School, Montclair, N. J., from 1845.

WILLIAM JARVIS GREGG NUTTING, class of 1860–3, æt. 43.

Born in Hudson, O., July 14, 1836 ; united with the Pres. Church of Lodi Plains, Mich., at 9 years of age ; graduated from Illinois College in 1856 ; Aub. Mid. class from private study ; married to Miss LUCY GALE, of Peoria, Ill., Oct., 1863 ; married to Miss EMILY BABCOCK, of Unadilla, Mich., May, 1865 ; died of typhoid fever, at St. Clair, Mo., Oct. 21, 1879. He had 4 sons and 3 daughters ; his wife, 2 sons and 2 daughters survived him.

Ordained and installed at Unadilla, Mich., by Presby. of Washtenaw, Spring of 1863 ; Unadilla, 1863–5; health failed ; Winchester, Ill., 1869 ; resident at St. Clair, Mo.

WILLIAM BRITTON CHRISTOPHER, class of 1847–50, æt. 62.

Born in Binghamton, N. Y., Aug. 15, 1817 ; united with the Pres. Church in Marion, N. Y., 15 years of age ; graduated from Union College in 1847 ; entered Auburn from Princeton, Jan., 1848 ; married to Miss LUCINDA PINE, of Union Centre, N. Y., Sept. 1, 1848 ; died of nervous prostration at Union Centre, Nov. 7, 1879. He had 2 sons and 1 daughter ; his wife and children survived him.

Ordained at Center Lisle, by Susquehanna Assoc., Oct. 16, 1849 ; Union Centre, 1849–50 ; Hancock, 1850–2 ; Oneonta and Otego,

1852-4 ; Lacon, Ill., 1854-9 ; Second Ch., Galena, Ill., 1859-60 ; Galena Cong. Ch., 1860-1 ; Mendota, 1862-7 ; on a farm in Iowa, 1867-71 ; also, editing *National Prohibitionist*, of Chicago, 1866-70 ; leader of colony at Cheever, Kansas, 1871 ; Cong. Ch., Wabaunsee, 1874-5 ; Pres. Ch., Wamego, 1875-7 ; resident in Binghamton, N. Y., 1878 ; Union Centre, 1879.
Published "The Prophetic Antichrist found in the System of American Slavery," 1862 ; two funeral sermons, 1863.

JAMES KINNIER WILSON, class of 1871-4.
Born in Scotland ; came to Aub. from Fullerton Ave. Church in Chicago ; studied at Princeton College ; First two years in Sem. of N. W. ; part of Sen. year in Auburn ; died Nov. 26, 1879. His wife, AGNES L. H., and 1 or more children survived him.
Cedarville, N. J., 1875-7; Wakeeney, Kan., 1877-9.

PHILEMON HALSTED FOWLER, D. D., Trustee 1851-76, æt. 66.
Born in Albany, N. Y., Feb. 9, 1814; graduated from Hobart College in 1832 ; tutor in Hobart one year ; Theological course at Princeton ; D. D. from Williams College in 1863 ; married to Miss JEANNETTE HOPKINS, of Geneva, N. Y., 1837; died, Utica, Dec. 19, 1879. He left 1 son and 2 daughters ; his wife and 1 son died before him.
Ordained by Presby. of Albany, Sept., 1836 ; Second Pres. Ch., Washington, D. C., 1835-9 ; First Pres. Ch., Elmira, N. Y., 1839-50 ; First Pres. Ch., Utica, 1851-65 ; afterward resident at Utica and San Matteo, Fla. Moderator of Gen. Assembly, 1869, in New York.
Published "Presbyterianism in Central N. Y.," 1877; also a volume on the relations of Labor and Capital, a Memoir of Maj. Wm. Fowler, and many articles, addresses, &c.

1880.

GEORGE PIERSON, class of 1825-8, æt. 74.
Born in Orange, N. J., Oct. 16, 1805 ; united with the 1st Pres. Church in Orange, Oct. 1, 1821 ; graduated from Princeton College in 1824 ; Middle year at Auburn ; Studied with Dr. Wilson in Va.; married to Miss ELIZA LINDSLEY DAY, of Orange, N. J., Oct. 29, 1828 ; married to Miss CAROLINE STULL, of Port Jervis, Jan. 16, 1860; died of Bright's disease, at Florida, N. Y., Feb. 2, 1880. He had 3 sons and 5 daughters ; his wife, 2 sons and 3 daughters survived him.
Ordained at Orange, June 22, 1829, by Presby. of Newark ; ass't pastor of Orange First Ch., 1829-31 ; Orange 2nd Ch., 1831-4 ; Wantage, N. J., 1835-9 ; Florida, N. Y., 1839-78.

NATHANIEL LASELL, class of 1842-5, æt. 66.
Born in Schoharie, N. Y., Feb. 4, 1814 ; united with the Lutheran Church in Schoharie at age of 14 ; graduated from Williams

College, 1839 ; Auburn Mid. class from Union, N. Y.; married to Mrs. Susan Shaw Todd Winkley, of Amesbury, Mass., June 25, 1856; died of disease of the heart, at Amesbury, Feb. 4, 1880. No children ; his wife survived him.

Ordained and installed, Cong. Ch. of West Stockbridge, Mass., by Council, May 15, 1850; West Stockbridge, 1850-3 ; Amesbury, 1853-56 ; Exeter, N. H., 1856-60 ; Union Church, Salisbury, Mass., 1860-4 ; Brentwood, N. H., 1866-9 ; West Newbury, Mass., 1869-73 ; Mattapoisett, Mass., 1875-8.

WILLIAM HENRY TALLMADGE, class of 1872-5, æt. 35.

Born in Pultney, N. Y., June 13, 1845 ; united with the 1st Pres. Church in Ithaca, N. Y., about 1864 ; graduated from Cornell University in 1871 ; Jun. year at Auburn, Mid. year at Union Seminary, N. Y., Sen. year at San Francisco ; married to ALICE E. GRANT, of Union, N. Y., April 26, 1870; died of consumption at Elk Grove, Cal., Feb. 24, 1880. He had 1 son and 1 daughter, who, with his wife, survived him.

Ordained at Sacramento, Cal., by Sacramento Presby., October 3, 1876 ; Woodbridge and Elk Grove from 1875.

LEWIS REMA LOCKWOOD, class of 1827-30.

Aub. Middle class, 1828-9, from Harpersfield ; married to MARY KIZE, of Vt.; married to CLARISSA TUTTLE, of Windham, N. Y.; married a third time ; married to SABRINA ROBINSON, of Cameron, N. Y.; died Spring of 1880, leaving 6 or more children.

Windham, N. Y., 1836-7 ; Cameron, N. Y., and Elkland, Pa., about 1841-3 ; resident Cameron, preaching part of the time, 1852-9 ; Fredericksburg, Ia., 1860-1, and afterward resident there and at Fairbanks ; mem. of Presby. to 1862.

ROSELLE ANDREW FULLER, class of 1870-3, æt. 37.

Born in Philadelphia, N. Y., July 16, 1843; united with the Central Cong. Church in Bangor, Me., July 10, 1870 ; graduated from Amherst College in 1869; Bangor Theo. Sem., 1869-70 ; Auburn, 1871-3 ; married to Miss FLORA LOUISA BOOTH, of Westfield, Wis., Oct. 15, 1875 ; died of consumption at Santa Barbara, Cal., (another account says El Paso, Col.) Spring of 1880. His wife died the following Winter ; one daughter survived them.

Shawano, Wis., 1873-4 ; Colby and Dorchester, 1874-7 ; then in California till his death.

JOHN EASTMAN, class of 1831-4, æt. 77.

Born in Amherst, Mass., July 19, 1803 ; studied at Amherst and Williams Colleges ; studied Theology with Rev. T Packard, D. D., of Shelburne ; in Auburn part of Senior year ; A. M. from Amherst in 1851 ; married to Miss PRUDENCE DOLE, of Charlemont, Mass., July 28, 1834; died of brain disease at Wellesley,

May 19, 1880.   He had 2 sons and 2 daughters ; his daughters survived him.

Ordained at Charlemont, Aug. 13, 1834 ; Fulton, N. Y., 1834-7 ; Mexico, 1838-40 ; Evans' Mills (Le Roy) 1841-3 ; Hawley, Mass., 1843-7 ; West Hawley, 1847-55 and 1871-7 ; Danville, Vt., 1857-67 ; in Ohio and Indiana 1868-71 ; resident at Amherst, 1877-8, and afterward at Wellesley.

Published two funeral sermons.

CHARLES EDWIN FURMAN, D. D,, class of 1825-8, æt. 79.

Born in Clinton, Dutchess Co., N. Y., Dec. 13, 1801 ; united with the Church in Ballston Centre, Summer of 1821 ; graduated from Union College in 1826 ; Mid. and Sen. years at Auburn ; D. D. from Hamilton College in 1878 ; married to Miss HARRIET EMELINE JOHNSON, of Rochester, N. Y., Jan. 19, 1831 ; died of kidney disease at Rochester, June 10, 1880.   He had 2 sons and 3 daughters, all of whom survived him.

Ordained at Skaneateles, N. Y., by Presby. of Cayuga, June 17, 1830 ; agt. of Am. Tr. Soc. in Ohio, 1828-9 ; Fort Wayne, Ind., Winter of 1829-30 ; Clarkson, N. Y., 5½ years ; Hamilton, Canada, 2 years ; Brick Church, Rochester, Winter of 1837-8 ; Victor, 1838-46 ; Medina, 1846-54 ; afterward resident in Rochester till death ; service of Am. Bib. Soc., 5 years ; supply at Chili, 2 years, Brighton 1 year, Gates 2½ years, Clarkson 2½ years, and elsewhere for short periods.

Published " Home Scenes," 1874 ; " Valley of the Genesee," 1879 ; and several occasional poems.

JUSTUS DOOLITTLE, class of 1846-9, æt. 56.

Born in Rutland, N. Y., June 23, 1824 ; united with the Pres. Ch. in Medina, 1834 ; graduated from Hamilton College in 1846 ; married to Miss SOPHIA A. HAMILTON, of Auburn, June 20, 1849 ; married to Miss LUCY E. MILLS, of Shanghai, China, Jan. 11, 1859 ; married to Miss LOUISA JUDSON, of Galesburg, Ill., Feb. 1, 1866 ; died of softening of the brain at Clinton, N. Y., June 15, 1880.   He had 4 sons and 2 daughters ; his wife, 3 sons and 1 daughter survived him.

Ordained at Auburn by Presby of Cayuga, June 20, 1849 ; miss. to China, in Foochow, Tientsin and Shanghai, 1849-69 and 1872-3 ; resident in Clinton since 1873.

Published " Social Life of the Chinese," 2 volumes, 1865 ; " Vocabulary and Handbook of Chinese Language," 2 volumes, 1873.

WILLIAM CARPENTER WISNER, D. D., Trustee 1863-76, æt. 72.

Born in Elmira, N. Y., Dec. 7, 1808, son of Dr. William Wisner, Trustee 1820-76; united with the Pres. Church in Ithaca, April 27, 1821 ; graduated from Union College in 1830 ; studied Law ; studied Theology privately; D. D. from Union College in 1851 ; married to Miss JANE E. HANFORD, of Scottsville, Nov. 11, 1834 ; died of progressive paralysis at Lockport, July 14, 1880. He had no children ; his wife and adopted daughter survived him.

Ordained pastor of 3d Church, Rochester, N. Y., by Presby., Oct. 24, 1832 ; Rochester, 1831-2 ; Athens, Pa. ; East Avon, N. Y., 18 months; 2d Church, St. Louis, Mo., 1836 ; Lower Church, Lockport, N. Y., 1837-42 ; 1st Church, Lockport, 1842-76.

Moderator of General Assembly in St. Louis, 1855 ; published "Prelacy and Parity," 1844, and many sermons and articles.

SILAS HUBBELL ASHMUN, class of 1835-8, æt. 71.

Born in Champlain, N. Y., July 31, 1809 ; united with the Church in Champlain, Sept. 4, 1831 ; graduated from Union College in 1835 ; married to Miss MARY VAN SANTVOORD, of Schenectady, N. Y., Aug. 22, 1838; died of inflammatory rheumatism at Falls City, Neb., July 22, 1880. He had 4 sons and 2 daughters ; his wife, 2 sons and 2 daughters survived him.

Ordained pastor, Henrietta, N. Y., by Presby , 1841 ; Henrietta, 5 years; Riga, 5 or 6 years ; Adams Basin, 1 year; Waupun, Wis., 6 years ; Rural, 1858-67 ; resident at Rural to 1876, at Humboldt, Neb., 1877-8, at Falls City from 1879.

JEREMIAH WHIPPLE WALCOTT, class of 1840-3, æt. 68.

Born in Cumberland, R. I., Nov. 27, 1812 ; graduated from Dartmouth College in 1839 ; Auburn, 1839-40 and 1841-3 ; teaching, 1840-1 ; married to Miss HANNAH BURTON CHURCH, of Bristol, R. I., May 21, 1844 ; married to Miss CAROLINE COOPER, of Auburn, June 27, 1853 ; died of cancer in throat at Green Lake, Wis., Aug. 14, 1880. He had 3 sons and 1 daughter ; his wife and 2 sons survived him.

Ordained at Stockbridge, Wis., by Winnebago Dist. Conv., June 30, 1852 ; Virgil, N. Y., 1843-6 ; had charge of Munro Acad., Elbridge, 1846-48 ; Auburn Female Seminary, 1848-50 ; preaching Menasha, Wis., 1850-3 ; Ripon, founder of Ripon College, and instructor and financial agent of same, 1853-8 ; resident in Ripon, preaching as opportunity offered, 1858-73 ; in Green Lake, preaching, &c., from 1873.

JOSEPH BUELL WARD, class of 1847-50, æt. 53.

Born in Rochester, N. Y., Sept. 20, 1827 ; united with the Cong. Church in Marietta, O., 1845 ; graduated from Marietta College, 1846 ; Jun. year at Lane, Mid. year at Auburn; married to Miss ELIZA A. CARTER, of Marietta, 1853; died of malarious fever in Rochester, N. Y., Sept. 5, 1880. He had 1 son and 1 daughter; his wife and daughter survived him.

Never ordained; in business in Rochester. Very active and effective in Presbyterian Christian work.

SAMUEL HANSON COX, D. D., LL. D., Professor, æt. 87.

Born in Rahway, N. J., Aug. 25, 1793 ; united with the First Pres. Church in Newark, 1814; studied at Bloomfield Acad. ; studied Law; studied Theology with Dr. James Richards and Dr. James P. Wilson; A. M. from Princeton College in 1818; D. D. from Williams College in 1823; LL. D. from Marietta

College in 1855 ; married to Miss ABIAH HYDE CLEVELAND, of Norwich, Conn., April 7, 1817 ; married to Miss ANNA BACON, of Hartford, Conn., in 1870 ; died of old age at Bronxville, N. Y., Oct. 2, 1880. He had 6 sons and 9 daughters ; his wife, 4 sons and 5 daughters survived him.

Ordained pastor, Mendham, N. J., by Presby., July 1, 1817 ; Mendham, 1817–20 ; Spring St. Church, New York, 1820–25 ; Laight St. Church, New York, 1825–35 ; one of the founders of Union Theological Seminary ; prof. of Sacred Rhetoric and Pastoral Theology, Auburn, 1835–7 ; 1st Pres. Church, Brooklyn, 1837–54 ; resident at Owego, 1854–6 ; president of Ingham Univ., 1856–63 ; resident in New York, 1863–70, in Bronxville from 1870.

Moderator of General Assembly, 1846. Published " Quakerism not Christianity," 1833 ; " The Ministry we Need," 1835 ; " Memoirs of Evarts," Cornelius Wisner—Introduction, 1835 ; " Theopneuston," 1842 ; " Bower's History of the Popes, with Continuation," 1847 ; " Interviews, Memorable and Useful," 1853 ; with many sermons and contributions to papers and reviews.

ANDREW PHILLIPS, class of 1844–7, æt. 58.

Born in Hyde Park, N. Y., Aug. 11, 1822; united with the Ref. Church in Hyde Park, 1841 ; studied at Acad. in Hyde Park ; studied Law and was admitted to practice ; Studied Theology 2 years with Dr. Ludlow, of Poughkeepsie ; Senior year at Auburn ; never married ; died of consumption at Hyde Park, N. Y., Oct. 21, 1880.

Ordained at Amenia, N. Y., by Hudson River Presby., Spring of 1847 ; Stamford, 1847–8 ; Cannonsville, 1848–53 ; Waddington, 1853–6 ; Morristown, 1856–67 ; Kingston, Tenn., 1867–70 ; North Newburg, N. Y., 1870–75 ; resident at Hyde Park from 1875.

LUTHER HALSEY, D. D., LL. D., Professor, æt. 87.

Born in Schenectady, N. Y., Jan. 1, 1794; united with the Pres. Church in Newburg, N. Y., May 1, 1814 ; graduated from Union College in 1812 ; studied Medicine ; studied Theology with Rev. John Johnson, D. D., of Newburg ; D. D. from Washington College in 1831 ; LL. D. from same, 1871 ; married to Mrs. ANNA GARDNER SMITH, of Newburg, Jan. 1, 1818 ; died of old age at Norristown, Pa., Oct. 29, 1880. His wife died Feb. 22, 1874 ; no children.

Ordained pastor, Blooming Grove, N. Y., by Presby., Aug. 7, 1816 ; Blooming Grove, 1816 ; prof. of Nat. Phil., Princeton College, to 1829 ; prof. of Theol. in Allegheny, 1829–36 ; prof. of Ecc. Hist. and Ch. Pol., Auburn, 1837–44 ; again at Blooming Grove ; instructor in Ch. Hist., Union Sem., N. Y., 1847–50 ; resident in Hammonton, N. J. ; lecturer extraordinary in Practical Theol., Allegheny, 1872–7 ; prof. emeritus, Allegheny, from 1877.

Published a pamphlet on Baptism about 1820 ; Introduction to "The Memoirs of John Frederick Oberlin," 1830 ; and sermons and articles.

ERASMUS DARWIN WILLIS, class of 1829–32, æt. 77.

Born in Franklin, N. Y., Aug. 6, 1803 ; united with the Church at 17 years of age ; graduated from Williams College in 1829 ; married to Miss ELIZA (another account says, CORNELIA) TOWNSEND, of Walton, N. Y., April 30, 1833 ; died at Baraboo, Wis., Nov. 12, 1880. He had 1 son and 1 daughter ; the son survived him.

Ordained by Columbia Presby., 1832 ; Morrisville, N. Y., 1832–3 ; Eaton, 1834–43 ; Walton, N. Y., and Carbondale, Pa., 1843–51 ; resident at Rockford, Ill., 1851–5 ; act. past. Pecatonica, 1855– 61 ; resident Rockford, sometimes supplying Chs., 1861–79, and then at Baraboo.

MERIT SIDNEY PLATT, class of 1832–5, æt. 76,

Born in New Milford, Conn., March 15, 1805 ; united with the Cong. Church in New Milford, Sept., 1832 ; studied at Sharon Acad., Conn. ; two years at Auburn ; third year at New Haven ; fourth year at Auburn ; married to Miss ORINDA GAYLORD, of New Milford, Sept. 20, 1832 ; died at Glassboro, N. J., of paralysis, Dec. 3, 1880. He had 2 sons and 1 daughter ; his wife and 1 son survived him.

Ordained and installed at Madison, N. Y., by Oneida Assoc., Oct. 5, 1838 ; New Preston, Conn., 1836–7 ; Madison, N. Y., 1837–54 ; Hamilton, 1854–65 ; Franklinville, N. J., from 1865 ; for 10 years of that time supplied also at Newfield and North Vineland, residing at Glassboro.

WILLIAM RIPLEY DOWNS, class of 1842–5, æt. 70.

Born in Pleasant Valley, N. Y., July 6, 1810 ; united with the Central Pres. Church, in New York City, July 18, 1830 ; graduated from Hamilton College in 1842 ; married to Miss SARAH HOLLEY, of Auburn, Sept. 22, 1845 ; died in Chicago, of internal hemorrhage, Dec. 21, 1880. He had 3 sons and 3 daughters ; 2 daughters survived him.

Ordained at Flagg Creek, Ill., by Ottawa Presby., May 26, 1847 ; home miss. in Marengo, Cass, Dupage, Ill., 1845–51 ; prin. of Greenwood Acad., Ill., 1851–2 ; Hornby, Orange, Howard, N. Y., 1852–62 ; resident in Chicago, Ill., from 1862.

1881.

LEVI M. GRAVES, class of 1835–8, æt. 71.

Born in Canaan, N. Y., May 12, 1810 ; united with the Cong. Ch. in Canaan ; graduated from Union College in 1835 ; Auburn, 1835–6 ; graduated at Allegheny ; married to Miss SARAH

SMITH, of Philadelphia, Pa., June 25, 1844; died of jaundice at Rosston, Pa., Jan. 1, 1881. His wife and 2 daughters died before him.

Ordained and installed at Boiling Spring, Pa., by Presby. of Blairsville, May, 1840; Warren (now Apollo) Boiling Spring, to 1841; Crooked Creek and Appleby Manor, 1841–6 and 1850–2; Rosston, Pa., 1862–73, and resident there till death.   .

HIRAM HUNTINGTON KELLOGG, class of 1823–6, æt. 78.

Born in Clinton, Oneida Co., N. Y., Feb. 26, 1803; united with the Cong. Church in Clinton, May, 1820; graduated from Hamilton College in 1822 ; married to Miss MARY GLEASON CHANDLER, of Augusta, N. Y., Oct. 13, 1829; died of pneumonia, at Mount Forest, Ill., Jan. 1, 1881. He had 6 sons and 5 daughters ; 3 sons and 4 daughters survived him ; one son in class of 1866–9.

Ordained by Presby. of Oneida, Feb., 1827 ; preached in Camden, Bridgewater, and Salina, N. Y.; founder of Female Seminary, Clinton, and principal, 1833–9 and 1847–61; first president of Knox College, Ill., 1839–45; pastor of First Church of Christ, Galesburg, 1845–7 ; Washington, 1861–2 ; home mission secretary, residing in Chicago, 1862–5 ; Marshalltown, Iowa, 1866–7 ; teaching Des Moines, 1868–9 ; Pres. Chs., Guthrie and Dexter, 1870–5 ; since resident at Mount Forest, supplying Churches.

Published occasional sermons and addresses.

HON. JEREMIAH POMEROY, class of 1829–32, æt. 77.

Born in Southampton, Mass., May 4, 1804 ; united with the Cong. Church in Southampton at 18 years of age; graduated from Amherst College in 1829; married to Miss ALMIRA MORTON, of Hatfield, Oct. 28, 1832 ; died of old age at South Deerfield, Jan. 5, 1881. His wife and 4 children survived him.

Ordained at Painted Post, N. Y., by Presby. of Bath, Oct. 7, 1833 ; Jasper, 1832–4 ; Cohocton, 1834–6 ; Troy, N. H., 1836–44; Harrisville, 1845–50; Rowe, Mass., 1853–6 ; West Hawley, 1856–8 ; West Cummington, 1858–61 ; Readsboro, Vt., 1861–4; resident South Deerfield, Mass., from 1865 ; member of New Hampshire Legislature, 1844, and of Massachusetts Constitutional Convention, 1853.

NATHANIEL SHEFFIELD SMITH, class of 1822–5, æt 91.

Born in Eaton, N. Y., Feb. 2, 1790 ; united with the Cong. Church in Sherburne ; entered Auburn Middle class ; married to Miss SARAH BRYANT LORD, of Morrisville, April, 1832; died of old age, at Buffalo, Jan. 10, 1881. His wife and adopted son survived him.

Ordained by Oneida Presby., June 25, 1825 ; Vernon, N. Y., 1828–9 ; Western, 1831 ; Warren, 1833 ; Philadelphia, Pa.; Sheridan, N. Y., 1842 ; Buffalo, 1845 ; resident in Buffalo till his death.

ALBERT MELVIN COOPER, class of 1877–80, æt. 30.
> Born in Saline, Mich., June 2, 1851 ; united with the Pres. Church
> in Saline, March, 1864 ; graduated from Michigan University
> in 1876 ; in Norcross, Ga., and Highlands, N. C., since 1878 ;
> licentiate of Southern Presbyterian Church ; died of consump-
> tion, at Highlands, January 19, 1881 ; unmarried.

LEWIS BENEDICT, Jr., class of 1840–3, æt. 66.
> Born in Madison, N. Y., Jan. 14, 1815 ; united with the Pres. Ch.
> in Vernon, Apr., 1831 ; graduated from Hamilton College in
> 1839 ; married to Miss MARTHA D. TYLER, of Holland Patent,
> July, 1847 ; married to Miss FRANCES BEATTIE WHEAT, of
> Rome, Sept. 3, 1850 ; died at Aurora, Ill., Jan. 30, 1881, of heart
> disease. He had 1 son and 5 daughters, all of whom, with his
> wife, survived him.
> Ordained at Whitewater, Wis., by Beloit Conv., Feb., 1844 ; Rock-
> ton, Ill., Cong. Ch., 1843–52 ; Aurora, 1852–8 ; Geneva, 1858–9 ;
> Brimfield, 1859–63 ; Lawn Ridge, 1863–70 ; resident at Aurora.

GEORGE ROBERT RUDD, class of 1823–6, æt. 80.
> Born in Vergennes, Vt., July 16, 1801 ; united with the Pres. Ch.
> in Nov., 1817 ; graduated from Hamilton College in 1823 ; mar-
> ried to Miss FANNIE BEARDSLEE, of Auburn, Oct. 2, 1827 ; died
> of paralysis in Lyons, N. Y., Feb. 1, 1881. He had 5 sons and
> 2 daughters ; his wife, 2 sons and 1 daughter survived him.
> Ordained and installed at Scipio, N. Y., by Presby. of Cayuga, Feb.
> 21, 1827 ; Scipio to 1829 ; Prattsburgh, 5 years from 1830 ; la-
> bored in Buffalo, Fredonia and Dunkirk ; agt. Western Ed. Soc.
> from 1839 ; financial agt. Auburn Sem. ; prin. of Auburn Female
> Seminary, 4 or 5 years ; in his 50th year retired to business, at
> Lyons.
> Published sermon on "The Bible in our Public Schools," 1870.

CHARLES HERVEY GASTON, class of 1875–8, æt. 31.
> Born in Munnsville, N. Y., Oct. 6, 1849 ; united with the Cong.
> Church in Munnsville, Jan. 1, 1860 ; graduated from Hamilton
> College in 1875 ; married to Miss CLARA J. STERRETT, of Phil-
> adelphia, Oct. 2, 1878 ; died at Evans Mills, N. Y., Feb. 24,
> 1881. His wife survived him.
> Ordained pastor at Heuvelton, N. Y., by Presby. of St. Lawrence,
> Sept. 25, 1878 ; Heuvelton, 1878–80 ; Evans Mills, 1880.

JARED LEIGH ELLIOTT, D. D., class of 1831–4, æt. 74.
> Born in Washington, D. C., June 24, 1807 ; graduated from Prince-
> ton College in 1831 ; Auburn, Jun. and Mid. years ; Princeton,
> Sen. year ; died at Washington, D. C., April 16, 1881.
> Ordained pastor, Mariner's Church, Philadelphia, by Presby. of
> Phila., Sept., 1835 ; Poughkeepsie, N. Y., 1834–5 ; Philadelphia,
> 1835–6 ; Washington, D. C., and Frederick, Md., 1836–7 ; chap.
> U. S. Navy, 1838–42 ; agt. Am. Sea. Fr. Soc., 1843 ; chap. U.
> S. A., 1844–9 ; act. mast. U. S. N., 1861 ; chap. U. S. A., 1863–81.

WILLIAM RHEEM HALBERT, class of 1867–70, æt. 37.

Born in Carlisle, Pa., July 4, 1844; united with the 1st Pres. Ch. in Carlisle, March 14, 1858; studied at Dickinson College 3 years; married to Miss CATHERINE HANNAH LINE, of Carlisle, Dec. 6, 1866; died of paralysis at Carlisle, April 24, 1881. His wife and 3 children survived him.

Ordained and installed at Apalachin, N. Y., by Presby. of Binghamton, Nov. 15, 1870; Apalachin, 1870–2; Atglen, Pa., (supplying also in Christiana) 1872–8; since 1878 at Carlisle, in poor health.

DANIEL GIBBS, class of 1835–8, æt. 73.

Born in Hartford, Vt., Nov. 12, 1807; united with the North Ch. in Hartford, Sept., 1828; graduated from Middlebury College in 1835; married to Miss ELMIRA BALDWIN, of Bristol, Conn., Nov. 6, 1838; died at Hartford, Conn., April 27, 1881. He had 2 sons and 1 daughter, all of whom, with his wife, died before him.

Ordained and installed at West Bloomfield, N. Y., by Ontario Presby., Sept., 1839; miss. agent, Willoughby, O., 1847–52; Hartford, O., 1853; resident Ripley, N. Y., 1855–7; Norwich Corners, 1858–9; afterward resident in the following places, laboring more or less actively: Pitcher, Oneida, Apalachin; Gilead, Conn., 1866–7; East Hartford, 1868–73; resident in Hartford, 1874–81.

EDWARDS ABBOTT BEACH, class of 1824–7, æt. 85.

Born in Tinmouth, Vt., Sept. 6, 1796; united with the Church in New Lebanon, N. Y., July 2, 1818; graduated from Amherst College in 1824; entered Auburn near the close of Junior year; married to Miss RHODA C. CHURCHILL, of New Lebanon, N. Y., Aug. 11, 1829; died at Champaign, Ill., May 23, 1881. He had 4 sons and 3 daughters, all of whom, with his wife, survived him.

Ordained and installed at Stephentown, N. Y., by Presby. of Troy, June 11, 1828; Stephentown to 1835; Groton, 1835–40; Homer, O., 1843–50; resident Johnstown, O., Beloit, Wis., Granville, O., and Champaign, Ill., from 1850.

MARVIN ROOT, class of 1829–32, æt. 79.

Born in Coventry, Conn., Oct. 7, 1802; united with the 1st Cong. Church in North Coventry; graduated from Williams College in 1829; six months of Junior year in Auburn; two years in Yale Sem.; married to Miss LOXEA BUSHNELL, of Westbrook, Conn., Sept. 24, 1834; died of consumption at Rock Creek, Ill., June 6, 1881. He had 5 sons and 1 daughter; his wife, 4 sons and daughter survived him.

Ordained at Robbinston, Me., (Cong.) Sept. 25, 1833; in Maine 2 years; Wapping, Conn.; East Windsor, 1836–40; Colporteur and miss. in Conn., 1840–55; Mendon, Ill., 1855; Udina, 1856 –8; Elk Horn Grove, 1858–60; Byron, 1860–2; Eagle Point,

1862–3; resident in Rock Creek, near Lanark, 1864–76 and from 1880, and in Racine, 1876–80.

FREDERICK GRIDLEY KENDALL, class of 1872–5, æt. 33.
  Born in Bloomfield, N. Y., Feb. 1, 1849; united with the Church in Hamilton College, Mar. 27, 1869; graduated from Hamilton College in 1871; at Auburn 1871–2 and 1873–5; married to Miss ELIZABETH TEN EYCK BURR, of Auburn, June 23, 1875; died of apoplexy at sea, Aug. 26, 1881; his wife survived him.
  Ordained pastor, Grand Rapids, Mich., by Presby., 1875; Grand Rapids, 1875–80; then visited Europe and died while on his return. Son of Dr. Henry Kendall of 1841–4.

LEMUEL BROOKS, class of 1824–7, æt. 84.
  Born in Brookfield, Conn., Nov. 27, 1797; united with the 1st Cong. Church in Washington, Conn., 1815; studied at Phillips Academy; in Auburn the course, and resident graduate 1827–8 · married to Miss MARION BROWN, of Ogden, N. Y., 1827; died at Churchville, N. Y., Sept. 21, 1881. His wife and 4 daughters survived him.
  Ordained pastor at Penfield, N. Y., by Rochester Presby., Mar. 18, 1829; Penfield from 1828; Attica; Bethany; Covington, 1 year; Chili, 4 years; Churchville, 4 years; Webster, 1841–7; lost his voice; resident at Churchville.

HON. EDWIN BARBER MORGAN, Trustee 1870–81, æt. 75.
  Born in Aurora, N. Y., May 2, 1806; studied at Cayuga Lake Academy, Aurora; married to Miss CHARLOTTE FIDELIA WOOD, of Aurora, Sept. 23, 1829; died of paralysis at Aurora, Oct. 13, 1881. He had 3 sons and 3 daughters; 1 son and 1 daughter survived him; his son is Henry A. Morgan, Trustee from 1882.
  He always lived in Aurora and did business there; one of the original proprietors of the *New York Times*; one of the founders of the Wells & Fargo Express Co., and one of the original shareholders of the U. S. Express Co.; for many years president of the two former of these corporations, and director of the latter; active in other large enterprises, and in public trusts; member of Congress, 1853–9.
  The Dodge-Morgan Library building is named for him, and Morgan Hall for his son Alonzo.

HENRY PHILIP TAPPAN, D. D., LL. D., class of 1824–7, æt. 77.
  Born in Rhinebeck, N. Y., April 18, 1805; united with the Ref. Ch. in New Paltz, 1821; graduated from Union College in 1825; entered Mid. class at Auburn, and graduated; D. D. from Union College in 1845; LL. D. from Columbia College in 1853; made Cor. Member of Inst. of France, 1856; married to Miss JULIA LIVINGSTON, of New York City, April 17, 1828; died of paralysis of the heart at Vevey, Switzerland, Nov. 15, 1881. He had 1 son and 4 daughters; his wife and 1 daughter survived him.

Ordained and installed at Pittsfield, Mass., by Berkshire Assoc., Sept., 1828; assist. pastor Ref. Ch., Schenectady, 1827-8; Pittsfield, 1828-32; prof. of Int. and Mor. Phil. in the Univ. of the City of N. Y., 1832-8; in New York and Brooklyn, preaching, teaching and publishing; president of University of Michigan, 1852-63; resident at Berlin, Paris, Nice; at Basle, Switz., 1874-80, and at Vevey from 1880.

Published (according to Allibone) "Review of Edwards' Inquiry into the Freedom of the Will," N. Y., 1839; "The Doctrine of the Will Determined by an Appeal to Consciousness," 1840; "The Doctrine of the Will applied to Moral Agency and Responsibility," 1841; these three republished, with additions, Glasgow, 1857; "Elements of Logic," N. Y., 1844; revised, 1856; Int. to "Illustrious Personages of the 19th Century," 1853; Treatise on University Education, 1851; "A Step from the New World to the Old and Back Again," 1852; with many addresses, articles, tracts, &c.

ADAM MILLER, class of 1824-7, æt. 75.

Born in Canajoharie. N. Y., Jan. 13, 1807; united with the 1st Pres. Church in Auburn, Oct. 21, 1824; graduated from Union College in 1824; married to Miss ANNA BACON CURTIS, of Auburn, Apr. 30, 1828; died of softening of the brain at Harford, Dec. 1, 1881. He had 8 sons and 6 daughters; 6 sons and 3 daughters survived him.

Ordained at Harford, Pa., by Susquehanna Presby., Sept. 17, 1829; Oswego Falls, N. Y., 1827-8; Harford from 1828, being installed there Apr. 28, 1830.

Published prize essay on the Traffic in Ardent Spirits, 1855; History of the Presbytery of Montrose, 1872; Historical Discourses, Harford, Pa., 1844, 1878; sermon at funeral of Rev. Edward Allen, 1877.

LEWIS HAMILTON, class of 1835-8, æt. 71.

Born in Rockaway, N. J., July 10, 1810; united with the Pres. Church in Rockaway, 1825; studied at Bloomfield Academy, and at Williams and Union Colleges; married to Miss RUEY HOYT BACON, of Branchport, N. Y., 1840; married to Miss MARY ELIZA BALCOM, of Campbell, Feb., 1843; died, struck by locomotive, at Pueblo, Col., Dec. 7, 1881. He had 1 son and 1 daughter; the daughter survived him.

Ordained pastor, Addison, by Presby. of Chemung, July 2, 1840; Branchport, 1 year; Addison, 2½ years; Campbell, 4 years; Hunt's Hollow, 2 years; Dunkirk, 4 years; Clarence, 2 years; Lima, Ind., 2½ years; Muscatine City, Kan., 1859; Pike's Peak, Col., 1860-3; U. S. Army, 1863-8; Central City, Col., 1869; Denver, 1870-7; Poncha Springs, 1878-80; Irwin, 1881; for many years marked H. R., though actively at work.

1882.

RALPH CLAPP, class of 1824–7, æt. 86.

 Born in Southampton, Mass., Jan. 19, 1796 ; united with the Cong. Church in Southampton, July, 1816 ; graduated from Amherst College in 1825 ; Auburn, Senior, a short time. from Dec. 2, 1826, having previously studied Theology with Dr. John Woodbridge, of Hadley, Mass. ; married to Miss MARY DEXTER, of Amherst, Mass., May 22, 1828 ; married to Miss SOPHIA MARSH, of Bethany, N. Y., Feb. 28, 1841 ; married to Miss SARAH SOBRINA BROWN, of Canadice, Jan. 15, 1854 ; married to Mrs. MARGARET BALLARD, of Pekin, Sept. 28, 1858 ; married to Miss CATHERINE COMBS, of Phelps, Sept. 8, 1869 ; died of congestion of the lungs at Phelps, Jan. 19, 1882. His wife and 2 sons survived him.

 Ordained pastor, Bergen, N. Y., by Presby., Feb. 19, 1829, over Church of Byron, Bergen and Clarendon ; Parma and Greece, 1827–8 and 1832–44 ; Bergen, 1828–32 ; in the ministry of the M. E. Church, in 13 charges in Western, N. Y., 1845–67 ; then resident in Phelps, in superannuated relation.

LEWIS KELLOGG, class of 1834–7, æt. 76.

 Born in Mexico, N. Y., Nov. 20, 1805 ; united with the Pres. Ch. in Mexico, June, 1821 ; graduated from Oneida Institute in 1834 ; Auburn, 1834–5 ; A. M. from Middlebury College in 1846 ; married to ABBY HALSEY LINDSLEY, of Troy, N. Y., Nov. 24, 1836 ; died of paralysis, at Whitehall, N. Y., Feb. 11, 1882. He had 6 sons and 2 daughters ; his wife, 2 sons and 1 daughter survived him.

 Ordained and installed at Whitehall, N. Y., by Presby. of Troy, Nov. 1, 1837 ; Whitehall, 1837–54 and 1862–8 ; Oswego, 2d Church, 1854–6 ; Trumansburgh, 1856–62 ; North Granville, 1870–9 ; resident at Whitehall from 1879.

 Published 4 sermons.

ERASTUS NOBLE NICHOLS, class of 1824–7, æt. 84.

 Born in Amherst, Mass., Oct. 21, 1797 ; united with the Pres. Ch. in Munnsville, N. Y., Dec., 1818 ; studied at Hamilton College in class of 1824 ; Middle year in Auburn ; A. M. from Hamilton College in 1874 ; married to Miss MARGARET LUDLUM LITTELL, of Auburn, Nov. 1, 1827 ; died in Tecumseh, Mich., Feb. 17, 1882. His wife survived him ; they had no children.

 Ordained and installed at Hector, N. Y., by Presby. of Geneva, Nov., 1827 ; Hector, 1 year ; Aurora, 3 years ; Vernon Centre, 2 years ; Clinton, Mich., preaching 9 years, and agent of A. B. C. F. M. 3 years, from 1835 ; afterward preached occasionally till 80 years of age ; resident in Tecumseh, Mich.

WILLIAM SHELDON FRANKLIN, class of 1839–42, æt. 70.

 Born in Aurora, N. Y., Oct. 22, 1811 ; united with the Pres. Ch. in Genoa, N. Y., 1828 ; studied at Cayuga and Cortland Academies,

and Cazenovia Seminary; A. M. from Madison Univ. in 1855;
married to Miss HARRIET NEWELL PUTNAM, of New Woodstock,
N. Y., Aug. 23, 1842; married to Miss MARY CLARINDA PUT-
NAM, of Eaton, Feb. 6, 1850; died of nervous prostration, at
Danforth, (in Syracuse) March 6, 1882. His wife and son sur-
vived him.

Ordained pastor, Five Corners, N. Y., by Cayuga Presby., Jan. 9,
1844; Five Corners, 1842–64; Camden, 1864–7; Marcellus,
1867–70; Ludlowville, 2 years; Jamesville, 2 years; Ridgeville
and Oneida Lake, 2 years; general sec. of Y. M. C. A., Syracuse, 2 years; resident in Syracuse from 1870.

Published several sermons.

HON. JOHN FISHER, Trustee 1863–70, æt. 76.

Born in Londonderry, N. H., Mar. 13, 1806; united with the Pres.
Church in LeRoy, N. Y.; married to Miss CATHERINE WYMAN
BLANCHARD, of Wethersfield Springs, N. Y., Sept. 18, 1833;
died of general debility, at Batavia, Mar. 28, 1882; he had 7
sons and 2 daughters; his wife and 1 son survived him.

Came early to LeRoy, N. Y.; in dry goods business in La Grange;
Warsaw; Hamilton, Canada, 1835–55; Batavia, N. Y., from
1855; Mayor of Hamilton; member of Congress, 1868–70.

LAURENTINE HAMILTON, class of 1850–3, æt. 55.

Born in Catlin, (now Dix) N. Y.; united with the Baptist Church
in Townsend, N. Y., Feb., 1842; graduated from Hamilton College in 1850; married to Miss ISABELLA MEAD, of Gorham, Me.,
May 3, 1855; married to Mrs. CLARA FERSON BATCHELDER, of
Berkeley, Cal., July 27, 1875; died of apoplexy at Oakland, in
the pulpit, Apr. 9, 1882. He had 2 sons and 2 daughters; his
wife, 2 sons and 1 daughter survived him.

Ordained pastor, Ovid, N. Y., by Presby. of Geneva, Jan., 1854;
Ovid, 1853–5; home miss. Columbia, Cal., 1855–9; San Jose,
1859–64; 1st Pres. Church, Oakland, 1864–9; Independent
Church of Oakland from 1869.

Published "The Future State and Free Discussion," 1869; "A
Reasonable Christianity," 1880; sermons weekly in the *Oakland Daily News*, for several years.

PARK SHATTUCK DONELSON, D. D., class of 1849–62, æt. 57.

Born in Colerain, Mass., Apr. 17, 1825; united with the M. E.
Church in 1835; graduated from Univ. of Mich., 1849; at Auburn, 1849–51; D. D. from Asbury Univ. in 1858; married to
Miss KATHARINE H. DEXTER, of Dexter, Mich., Sept., 1851;
died of enlargement of the heart, at Dexter, Mich., May 6,
1882. He had 1 son and 2 daughters; his wife, 1 son and 1
daughter survived him.

Ordained at Kalamazoo, Mich., by Bishop Janes, (M. E.) 1853;
prof. of Anc. Lang., Albion Col., Mich., 1851–4; Lansing,
Mich., M. E. Ch., 1854–6; pres. of Ohio Wes. Fem. Col., 1856

–73 ; St. Paul's Ch., Toledo, O., 1873–5 ; presid. Eld., Toledo
Dist., 1875–9 ; Trinity Ch., Lima, 1879–81 ; Kenton, 1881–2.

EBENEZER CROSS BIRGE, class of 1836–9, æt. 72.
> Born in Underhill, Vt., June 5, 1810; united with the 1st Cong.
> Church in Underhill ; studied at Jericho Acad. and Jackson
> (So. Hanover) College ; Princeton, 1836–7 ; Auburn, 1837–9 ;
> married to Miss LYDIA BACON STEBBINGS, of Burlington, Vt.,
> Sept. 26, 1839 ; died of Bright's disease at Chicago, Ill., May 30,
> 1882. He had 1 son and 6 daughters ; his wife, son and 5
> daughters survived him.
> Ordained pastor, E. Berkshire, Vt., by Northwestern Assoc., Aug.
> 27, 1840 ; E. Berkshire, 1840–2 ; Stockholm, N. Y. ; after 4
> years, went West as home miss. ; Wilmington, O. ; Momence,
> Ill., 1850–5 ; Algonquin, 1856–61 ; Hambden, O., 1862 ; Jericho,
> Vt., 1863–5 ; Underhill, 1867–74 ; Londonderry, 1874–81 ;
> resident in Chicago from 1881.

HENRY ALLEN AUSTIN, class of 1848–51, æt. 61.
> Born in Becket, Mass., Nov. 22, 1821 ; united with the Cong. Ch.
> in Worthington, Mass., 1840 ; graduated from Union College in
> 1847 ; married to Miss MARY WRIGHT JOHNSON, of Becket,
> Sept. 28, 1851 ; married to Miss CARRIE FRANCES MAXIM, of
> Paris, Me., Nov. 30, 1871 ; died of disease of the liver at Pleas-
> anton, Mich., June 2, 1882, leaving a widow, 1 son and 2
> daughters.
> Ordained and installed at Otis, Mass., by Council, 1852 ; Otis,
> 1851–4 ; West Hartland, Conn., 1854–5 ; Huntington, 1856–9 ;
> farming in Ohio, 1860–4 ; resident in Pleasanton, Mich., preach-
> ing part of the time, from 1864.

CHARLES FREDERICK HALSEY, class of 1832–5, æt. 79.
> To the statistics on page 42 add : Died of senile debility at Fos-
> terburg, Ill., Aug. 17, 1882. He had 4 sons and 7 daughters ;
> his wife, 1 son and 5 daughters survived him.

WILLIAM MASON RICHARDS, class of 1832–5, æt. 77.
> To the statistics on page 42 add : Died of inflammation of the
> bladder at Berlin, Wis., Aug. 29, 1882. He had 1 son and 1
> daughter ; his wife and daughter survived him.

ERASTUS JUDD GILLETT, M. D., D. D., class of 1826–9, æt. 82.
> To the statistics on page 27 add : Died of heart disease at Coun-
> cil Bluffs, Iowa, Nov. 7, 1882. He had 2 sons and 3 daughters ;
> 1 son and 2 daughters survived him.
> He was born May 13, 1800, made M. D. in 1864, and pres. of
> Fac. at Keokuk, 1865.

TITUS COAN, D. D., class of 1830–3, æt. 81.
> To the statistics on page 37 add : Died at Hilo, Hawaii, Dec. 1,
> 1882.

CORRECTIONS AND ADDITIONS.

The evidence shows the existence of the relation of father and son in the following instances not mentioned in the Catalogue : WILLIAM WISNER, Trustee 1820–63, fath. of WILLIAM CARPENTER W., Trustee 1863–76 ; LEVI PARSONS, Trustee 1820–64, son in 1851–4 ; SAMUEL MILES HOPKINS, Trustee 1832–8, fath. of SAMUEL MILES H. of 1834 –7 ; JOHN KEEP, Trustee 1832–4, fath. of THEODORE JOHN K. of 1832–5 ; JOHN J. KNOX, Trustee elect, 1845, fath. of WILLIAM EATON K. of 1840–3, of HENRY MARTYN K. of 1851–4, and of CHARLES EUGENE K. of 1856–9 ; FREDERICK STARR, Trustee 1855–69, fath. of FREDERICK S. of 1846–9 ; JOHN JERMAIN PORTER, Trustee from 1876, fath. of JERMAIN GILDERSLEEVE P. of 1874–7 ; HENRY AUGUSTUS MORGAN, Trustee 1882, son of EDWIN BARBER M., Trustee 1870–81 ; JAMES BOYLAN SHAW of 1829–32, fath. of AUGUSTUS CHESTERMAN S. of 1861–4 ; DANIEL TOLL CONDE of 1831–4, son in 1870–3 ; SAMUEL MILES HOPKINS of 1834–7, sons in 1865–8 and 1866–9 ; ISAAC PIERSON STRYKER of 1837–40, son in 1873 –6 ; HORACE HILLS, JR., of 1838–41, son of HORACE H., Trustee 1828–40 ; CHARLES ANDERSON of 1840–3, sons in 1871–4 and 1873–6 ; WILLIAM EATON KNOX of 1840–3, son in 1874–7 ; SAMUEL NEWELL ROBINSON of 1842–5, fath. of ALBERT BARNES R. of 1869–72 ; ADDISON KELLOGG STRONG of 1843–6, son in 1876–9 ; SAMUEL MINOR CAMPBELL of 1846–9, fath. of FREDERICK CAMPBELL of 1877–80 ; MATTHEW LARUE PERRINE HILL of 1858–61, son of ROBERT WILLIAM H. of 1823–6 ; MARCUS NORTH PRESTON of 1859–62, son of JOHN BOWER P. of 1827–30 ; WILLIAM HUBBELL FISHER of 1864–7, and SAMUEL JACKSON F. of 1867–70, sons of SAMUEL WARE F., Trustee 1860–71 ; EDWARD PAYSON JOHNSON of 1872–5, son of ASA J. of 1827–30.

Page 12, HENRY KENDALL should be credited to 1841–4.

Page 17, the names of Profs. RICHARDS and LONG should be starred.

Page 46, insert dash after CALVIN WOODBURY ; and for the first article substitute :

EDWARD COPE.
>   Born in New Lisbon, N. Y., May 25, 1806 ; united with the Pres. Church in Cooperstown, 1827 ; studied 2 years at Centre College in class of 1837 ; Sen. year at Auburn, from Western Theo. Sem., 1835–6 ; married to EMILY KILBOURN, of Paris, N. Y., Sept. 29, 1836.
>   Ordained at Clinton, N. Y., by Presby., 1836 ; miss. of A. B. C. F. M. at Madura, and afterward in Batticotta, Ceylon, 1836–48 ;

since his return, preaching steadily at Noblesville, Mt. Upton, E. Guilford, and Guilford and Norwich, N. Y., residing in Gilbertsville from 1854.

Page 52, substitute: EDWARD REYNOLDS.

Born in South Hero, Vt., June 28, 1808 ; united with the Cong. Church in Burlington, about 1829 ; graduated from Oneida Institute in 1836 ; Mid. and Sen. years at Auburn, 1836–8 ; married to Miss CORNELIA HOUGH, of Meriden. Conn., Nov. 19, 1838.

Ordained at Hannibal, N. Y., by Oswego Presby. ; Georgetown, 1838–9 ; Hannibal, 1839–41 ; Phillipsville, 1841–5 ; York and Medina, Wis., 1845–9 ; Winnebago Co. and vicinity till within a few years ; most of his ministry was in the Free Will Baptist connection ; resident in Athens, Ala.

Page 54, substitute: JENKIN JENKINS.

Born near Swansea, So. Wales, July 29, 1803 ; united with the Indep. Church near Swansea, 1819 ; studied at Carmarthen Acad., and privately ; Auburn, 1836–7, from May 1836 ; married to Miss SARAH DAVIES, of Berth Swyd, So. Wales, Sept. 10, 1830 ; married to Miss ANNE JENKINS, of Bradford Co., Pa., Oct. 10, 1836.

Ordained pastor of a Welsh Cong. Ch., N. Y., Nov., 1832 ; New York, 1832–6 ; Dundaff, Pa., Pres. and Welsh Cong. Chs., 1837–47 ; Newark and Granville, O., 1848 ; Cambria, Wis., organizing Chs. &c., 1848–55 ; Big Rock, Ill., 1855–6 ; Cambria and South Bend, Minn., from 1856 : P. O. address Courtland.

Published a vol. of Autobiography in 1872.

Page 57, substitute: CHARLES CROCKER.

Born in Buxton, Me., Nov. 5, 1810 ; united with the 1st Pres. Church in Lockport ; studied at Oberlin College, in class of 1838 ; Lane Sem. ; Oberlin ; Auburn Sen. year, 1839–40 ; married to Miss ALMEDA SCOTT, of Cambria, N. Y., Sept. 9, 1839.

Ordained pastor, Friendship, N. Y., by Angelica Presby., Oct. 1841 ; Friendship, 1841–7 ; Glenwood, preaching there and elsewhere, 1847–70, and resident there to 1882 ; Arkansas City, Kan.

Page 66, substitute: MOSES SMEDLEY HAWLEY.

Born in Canandaigua, N. Y., Jan. 29, 1812 ; united with the Cong. Church there, about 1830 ; graduated from Hamilton College in 1839 ; Auburn, Jun., 1839–40 ; married to Miss MARIA JANE RIPLEY, of Livonia, N. Y., Oct. 31, 1845.

Never ordained ; licensed by Ontario Presby., Aug., 1843 ; taught in Lyons, 1840–1, and in Livonia, 1841–2 ; preaching and teaching, St. Joseph, Mich., 1843–5 ; Pres. Ch., Albion, 1845–6 ; tea. Albion, 1846–9 ; Ypsilanti, 1849–52 ; Adrian, 1852–5, and other places a few years ; preaching much, from 1843 ; resident Hartford, Mich.

MUNSON S. ROBINSON.
Born near Weedsport, N. Y., May 16, 1812 ; united with the
Pres. Church in Weedsport, April 30, 1831 ; graduated from
Oberlin College after leaving Auburn ; Lane Sem., 1833–4;
Auburn, Jun.,1839–40 ; married to Miss CLARA WHITNEY, Cleve-
land, O., March 16, 1858.
Ordained by Assoc. ; mining in Cal., 1850–3, and farming there
since ; resident Eldorado.

Page 71, substitute : DANIEL CLARK.
Born in Williamstown, Vt., Nov. 1, 1812 ; united with the Cong.
Church 1831 ; graduated from Dartmouth College in 1839 ;
Auburn, 1840–2 ; married to Miss NANCY POMEROY BROWN, of
Templeton, Mass., 1844.
Ordained at Cazenovia, N. Y., by Assoc. of Central N. Y., 1842 ;
Warren, Vt., 1844–7 ; tea. in Richmond and in Philadelphia ;
address Lindley Post C., Phila.

Page 73, to the notice of NATHANIEL HARRISON BARNES, add :
Born Nov. 10, 1816; united with Pres. Ch., Panama, N. Y., about
1838 ; studied at Jamestown ; studied Theol. 1 year with Rev.
L. H. Parker, of Wayne, Pa. ; married to Miss ANN BENNIE, of
Olean, N. Y., Oct. 28, 1847; married to Miss SARAH E. LADD,
of Brooklyn, Mich., Jan. 16, 1856. Portland, N. Y., from 1844 ;
Olean ; Versailles.

To the notice of JOHN NILES HUBBARD, add :
Born Aug. 27 ; united with 1st Pres. Ch., of Dansville, Winter of
1831 ; studied Theol. with Rev. Leverett Hull, before entering
Auburn ; married to Miss MARGARET McDOUGAL, of North
Sterling, Feb. 18, 1845.
Ordained pastor, by Presby. of Oswego, Summer of 1844 ; Friend-
ship and Belmont, 1858–61.

Page 82, make the date of marriage of HORACE LYMAN, Nov. 1, 1848.

To the notice of GEORGE C. WICKSON, add :
Completed Theo. course at the Cong. Acad., Toronto ; preached
a year or two ; never ordained ; for nearly 30 years elder of
Pres. Ch., Lyons; resident in San Francisco, Cal.

Page 89, substitute : RICHARD OSBORNE.
Born in Fonda's Bush, N. Y., Dec. 25, 1821 ; united with the Cong.
Church, Jan., 1840 ; graduated from Union College in 1846 ;
Auburn, 1846–7 ; Andover, 1847–9 ; married to Miss DIANTHA
LORINDA GUNN, of Greenwich, N. Y., Oct., 1856 ; married to
Mrs. CHARLOTTE ELIZA (LINDSAY) BAKER, of Northumberland
N. Y., Oct. 17, 1867.
Ordained at Champion, N. Y., by Black River Assoc., Jan., 1853 ;
Sandy Creek, 1852–9; Mannsville, 1852–5 ; Colerain, Mass.,
1860–2 ; Champion, N. Y., 1863–5 ; Green Island, 1865–8 ; res-
ident Saratoga from 1877.

Page 95, add to notice of FRANCIS HENDRICKS:
Born in Fayette, N. Y., Dec. 20, 1820; tea. in Ovid and Elmira, 1846–50; Aub. from Apr., 1850; called to Dryden, 1852; Fremont, O., 1855–6; Northumberland, Pa., from 1857; Drawyer's Pres. Ch., Del., from 1861; pastoral work, Philadelphia, 1863–74; chap. of Pres. Hospital.

Page 102, substitute: GEORGE WORTHY QUEREAU, D. D.
Born in Bangall, N. Y., June 9, 1827; united with the M. E. Ch. in Red Creek, 1840; graduated from Wesleyan Univ. in 1849; Auburn, 1851–3; D. D. from Northwestern Univ. in 1866; married to Miss SUSAN HIGGINS SMITH, of Fall River, Mass., Apr., 1855.
Ordained (M. E.) 1857; in charge of Providence Conference Sem., E. Greenwich, R. I., 1853–9; Jennings Sem., Aurora, Ill., 1859–73; resident in Aurora, in poor health.

Page 111, substitute: RAPHAEL KESSLER.
Born in Trillfingen, (Hohenzollern) Germany, Oct. 27, 1828; united with the Rom. Cath. Church in 1841; graduated from Hedingen Gymnasium, 1848; Auburn, 1857–9; married to Miss NANCY HANNAH BRANDT, of Brandt, Pa., May 5, 1859.
Ordained by 3d Presby. of N. Y., 1860; Rivington St. Ger. Pres. Ch., 1859–62; Mt. Pleasant and Uniondale, Pa., 1862–7; Webster Groves, Mo., 1867–72; Wilmington, Ill., 1872–3; Pontiac, 1873–5; Brandt, Pa., 1880; resident Holland Patent, N. Y.

Page 128, Mrs. W. W. PALMER's name was REXFORD.

Page 134, make the date of death of JOHN BACON STEELE, 1873.

Page 140, add to notice of MERRITT GALLY:
Born at Perry, N. Y., Aug. 15, 1838; first joined "Brick" Ch., Rochester; married to Miss MARY ALLEN CARPENTER, of Rye, N. Y., Aug. 15, 1866; ordained pastor, Marion, Mar. 11, 1867; Marion, 3 years.

Page 142, make the date of death of WILLIAM B. HENDRYX, June 21.

To notice of JOSEPH EDWIN SCOTT, add:
Born in Johnston, Vt., Sept. 28, 1836; joined Pres. Ch. in Delaware City, Del., Apr., 1863; married to Miss ANNIE ELMA JANE HIGGINS, Aug. 13, 1862; ordained by West Jersey Presby., Oct., 1867; resident Tonganoxie, Kan.

Page 152, to notice of HERMAN B. DEAN, add:
Married again; Weatherford, Tex.; rect. of P. E. Ch., Concordville, Pa., 1882; Havre de Grace, Md.

Page 156, make WILLIAM D. DUNCAN resident in Elmira, N. Y.

Page 168, to notice of HERMANN CARL GEORGE BRANDT, add:
Born in Germany, Dec. 15, 1850; united with Ch. at Susquehanna Depot, 1868. Published edition of Lessing's "Nathan der

Weise," 1880 ; Rules for writing German with Latin letters ; and many Philological articles.

Page 176, erase the final E from the name of LIVINGSTON.

Page 180, to notice of JAMES STEVENSON RIGGS, add :
Joined Ch., July, 1865 or 1866 ; married to Miss L. A. BURROUGHS, of Medina, N. Y., Oct. 20, 1880 ; ordained Aug. 2, 1880.

Page 199, to notice of JAMES RICHARDS, add :
It is said that he had 7 children ; 2 sons and 2 daughters survived him.

Page 200, to notice of SHELDON DIBBLE, add :
Joined Pres. Ch., Skaneateles, Oct. 3, 1819.

Page 213, to notice of ELEAZAR HILLS, add :
Born in East Hartford, Conn. ; came to Auburn 1806.

Page 233, to notice of ALBERT PAYSON WORTHINGTON, add :
Joined the Ch. in Panama, N. Y. ; married to Miss ADDIE E. HUMPHREY, of Durham, Oct. 19, 1866 ; his son, born after his death, died April, 1869.

Page 236, to notice of JEREMIAH WOODRUFF, add :
Converted, 1825 ; before going to Auburn, studied with Rev, Samuel Orton ; married to Miss NANCY SPENCER, of Hartford. Conn., 1821 ; married to Miss CLARISSA THOMSON, of Chenango Forks, N. Y., 1851 ; he had 6 sons and 3 daughters ; his wife, 4 sons and 2 daughters survived him ; ordained, (Cong.) 1832.

INDEX.

www.ingramcontent.com/pod-product-compliance
Lightning Source LLC
Chambersburg PA
CBHW060551030726
47498CB00005B/1345